SHERLOCK BONES

AND THE
NATURAL HISTORY MYSTERY

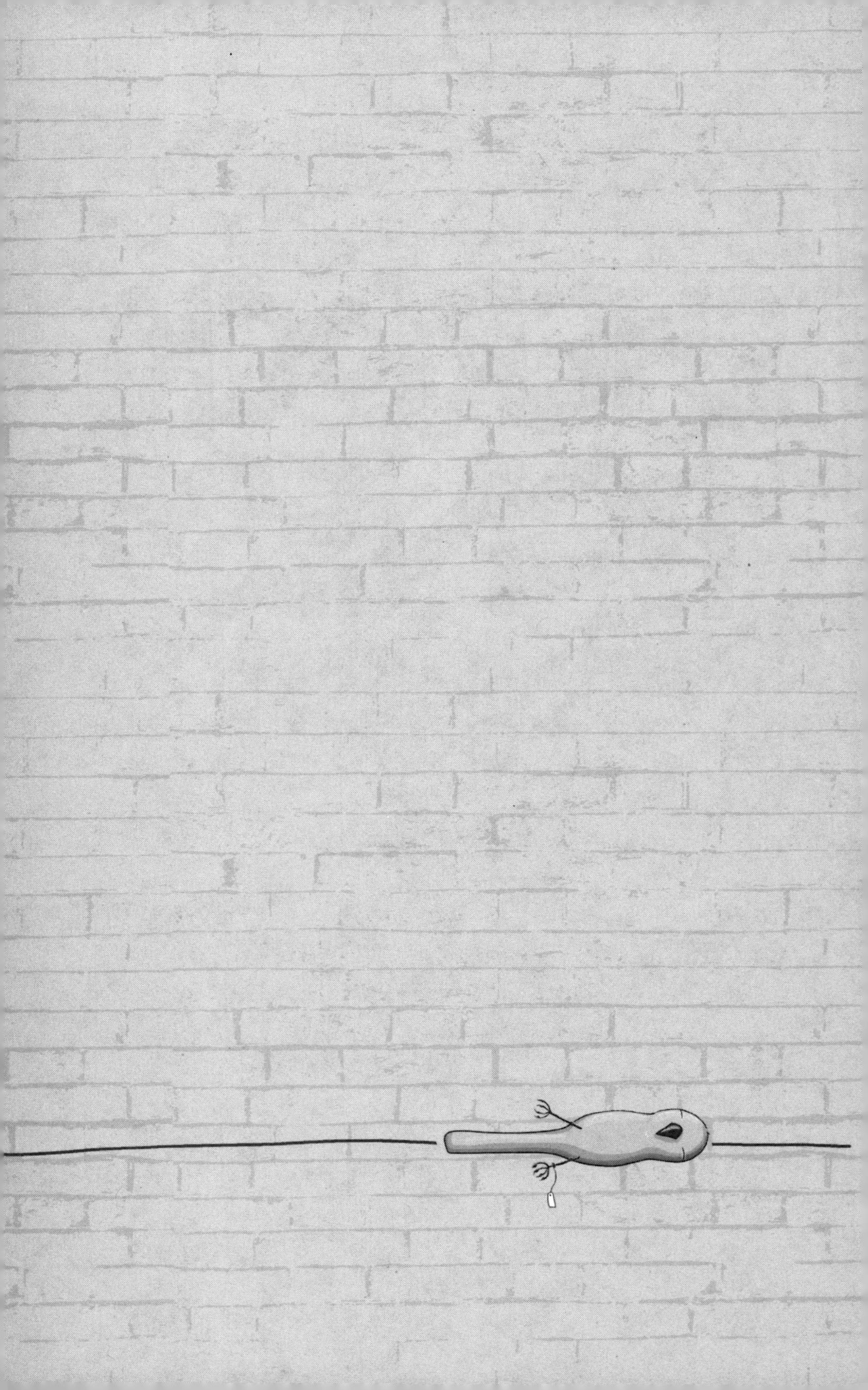

SHERLOCK BONES

BONES

AND THE
NATURAL HISTORY
MYSTERY

RENÉE TREML

ETCH
HOUGHTON MIFFLIN HARCOURT
Boston   New York

STATE NATURAL

ROAR

Find your Culture

SEE THE WORLD'S LARGEST GEMSTONE

THE ROYAL BLUE DIAMOND

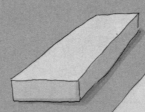

Dedicated to my writing partner in crime,
Amanda, who has been on Sherlock Bones's
journey almost as long as I have.

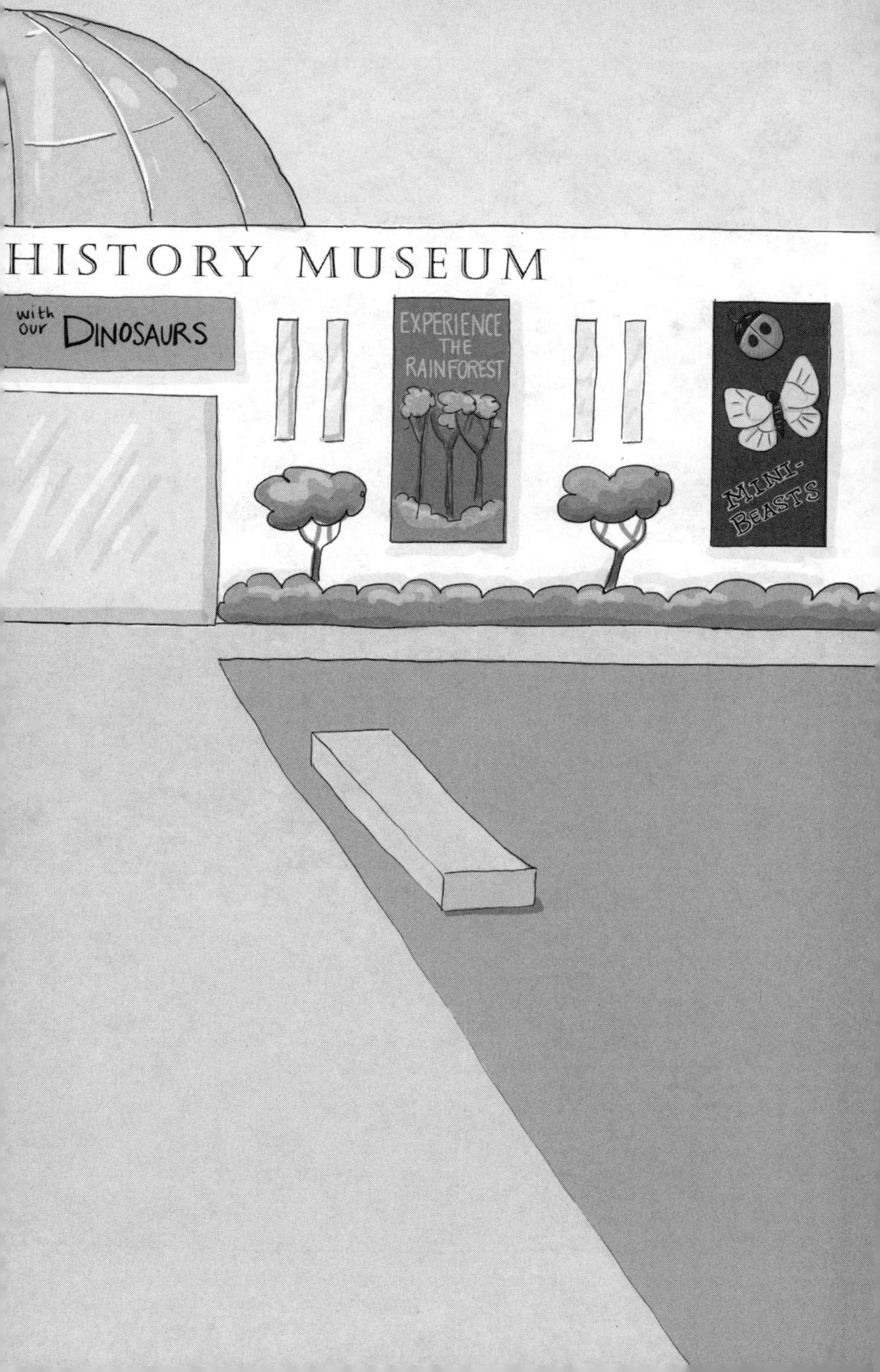
HISTORY MUSEUM
with our DINOSAURS
EXPERIENCE THE RAINFOREST
MINI-BEASTS

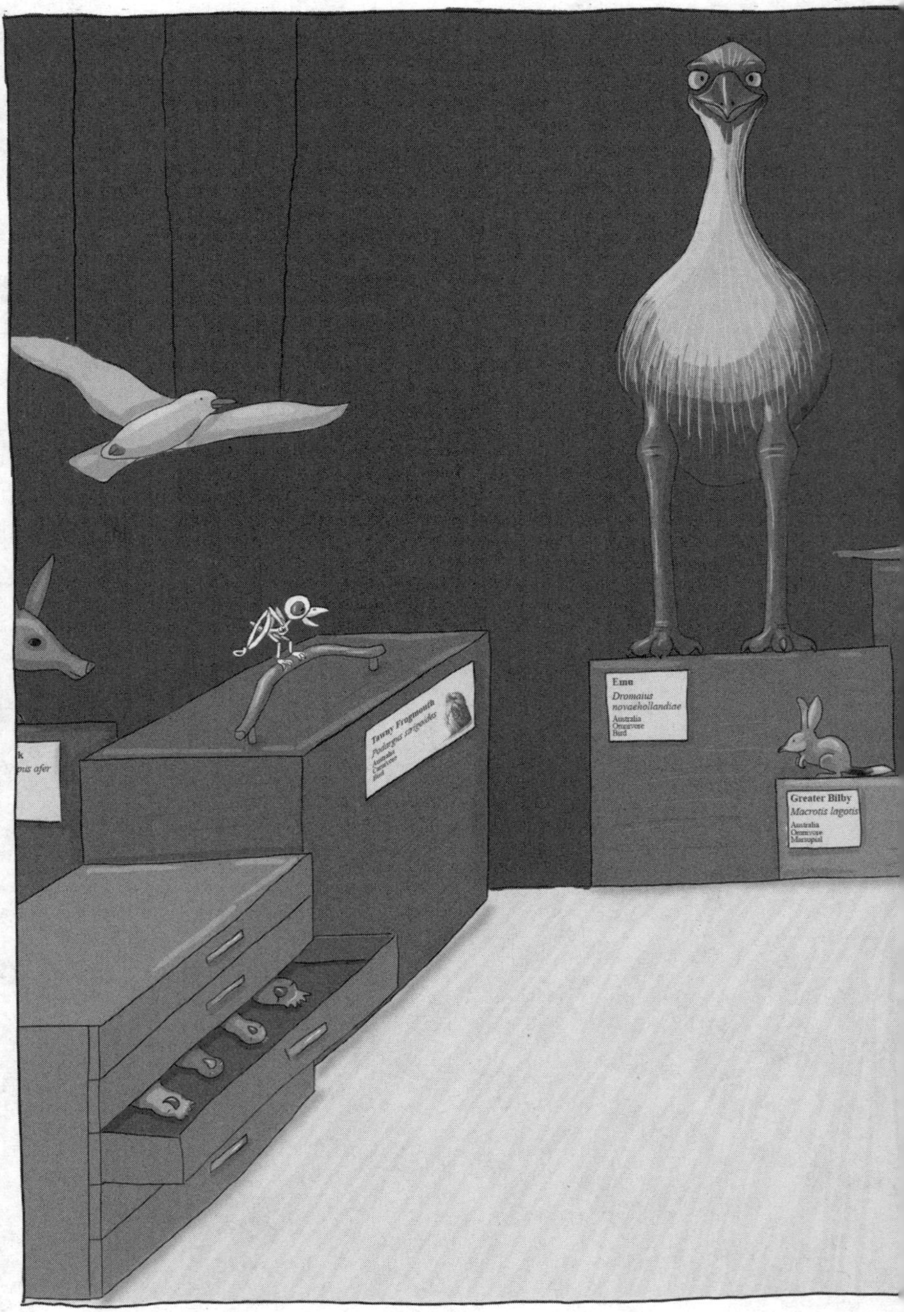
Tawny Frogmouth
Podargus strigoides
Emu
Dromaius novaehollandiae
Australia
Omnivore
Bird
Greater Bilby
Macrotis lagotis
Australia
Omnivore
Marsupial

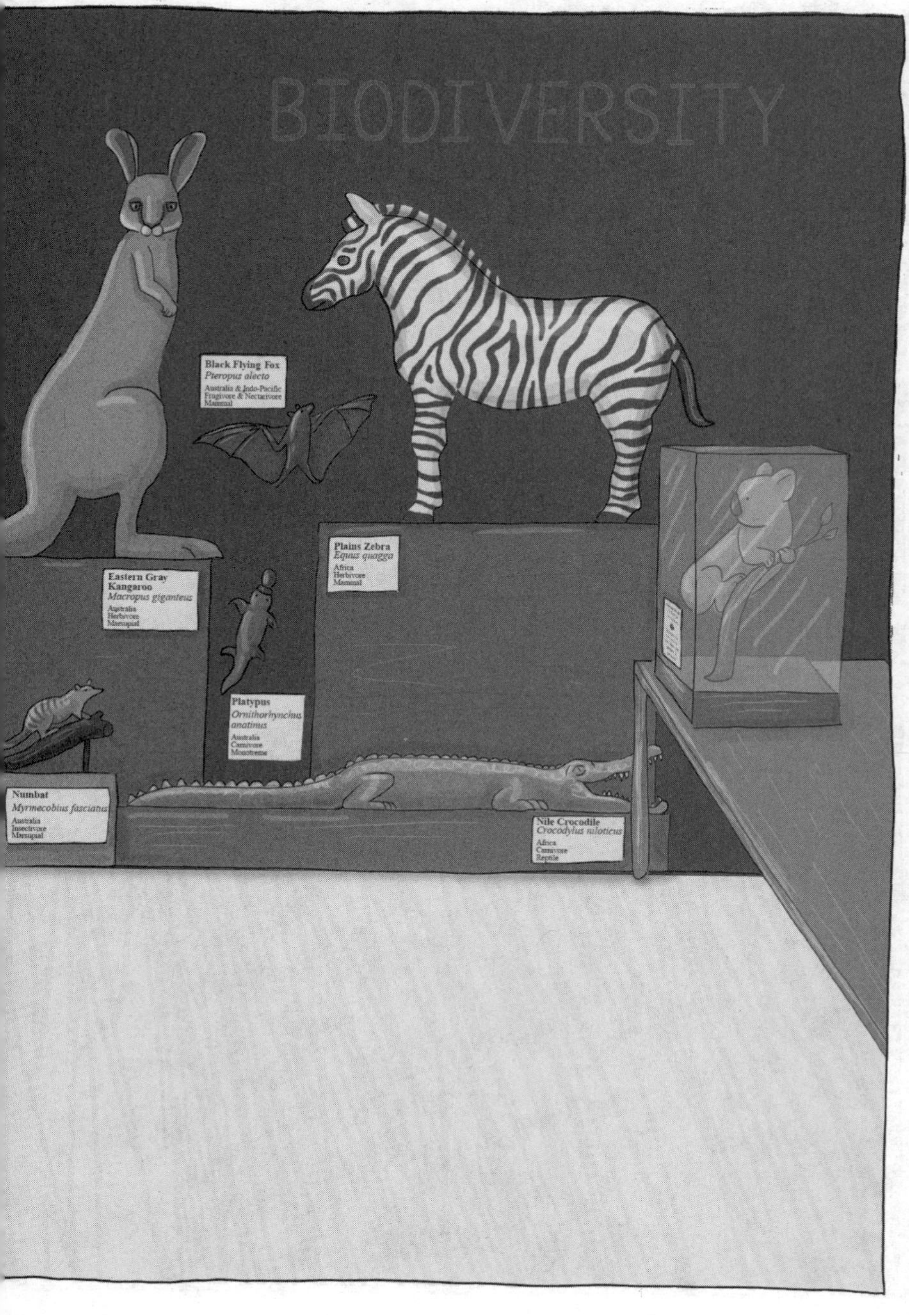
BIODIVERSITY
Black Flying Fox
Pteropus alecto
Australia & Indo-Pacific
Frugivore & Nectarivore
Mammal
Plains Zebra
Equus quagga
Africa
Herbivore
Mammal
Eastern Gray Kangaroo
Macropus giganteus
Australia
Herbivore
Marsupial
Platypus
Ornithorhynchus anatinus
Australia
Carnivore
Monotreme
Numbat
Myrmecobius fasciatus
Australia
Insectivore
Marsupial
Nile Crocodile
Crocodylus niloticus
Africa
Carnivore
Reptile

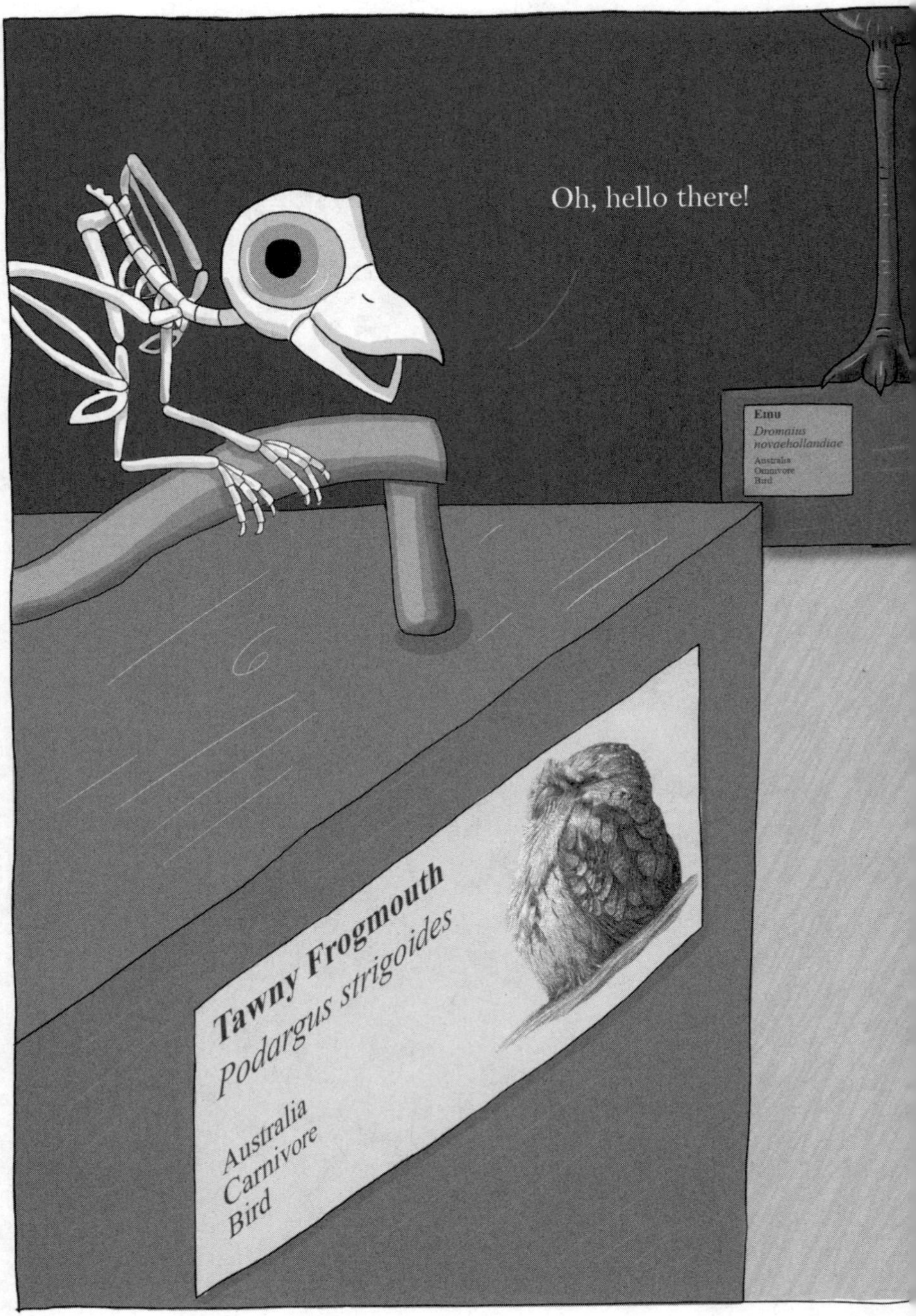
Oh, hello there!
Emu
Dromaius novaehollandiae
Australia
Omnivore
Bird
Tawny Frogmouth
Podargus strigoides
Australia
Carnivore
Bird

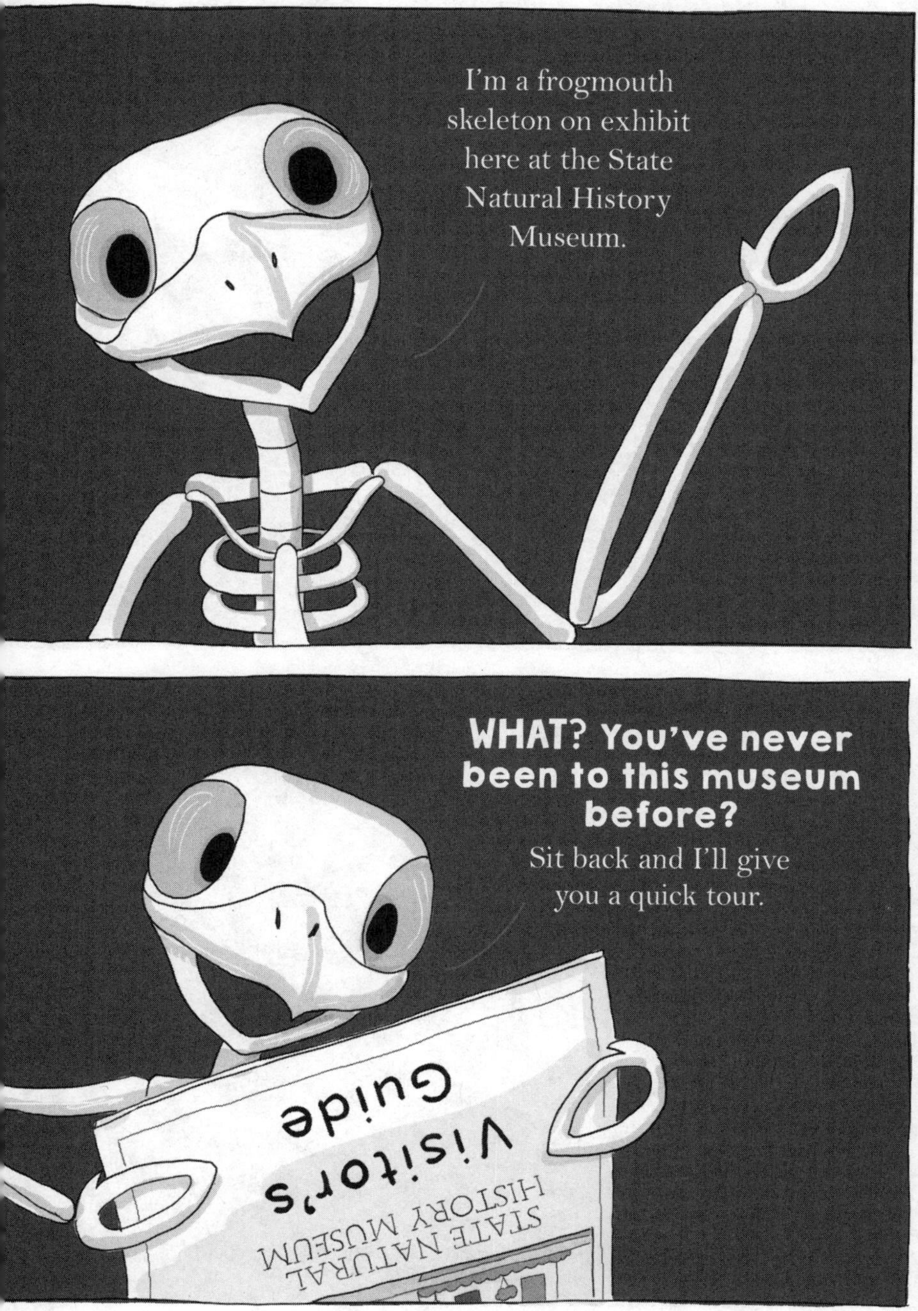
I'm a frogmouth skeleton on exhibit here at the State Natural History Museum.
WHAT? You've never been to this museum before?
Sit back and I'll give you a quick tour.
Visitor's Guide
STATE NATURAL HISTORY MUSEUM

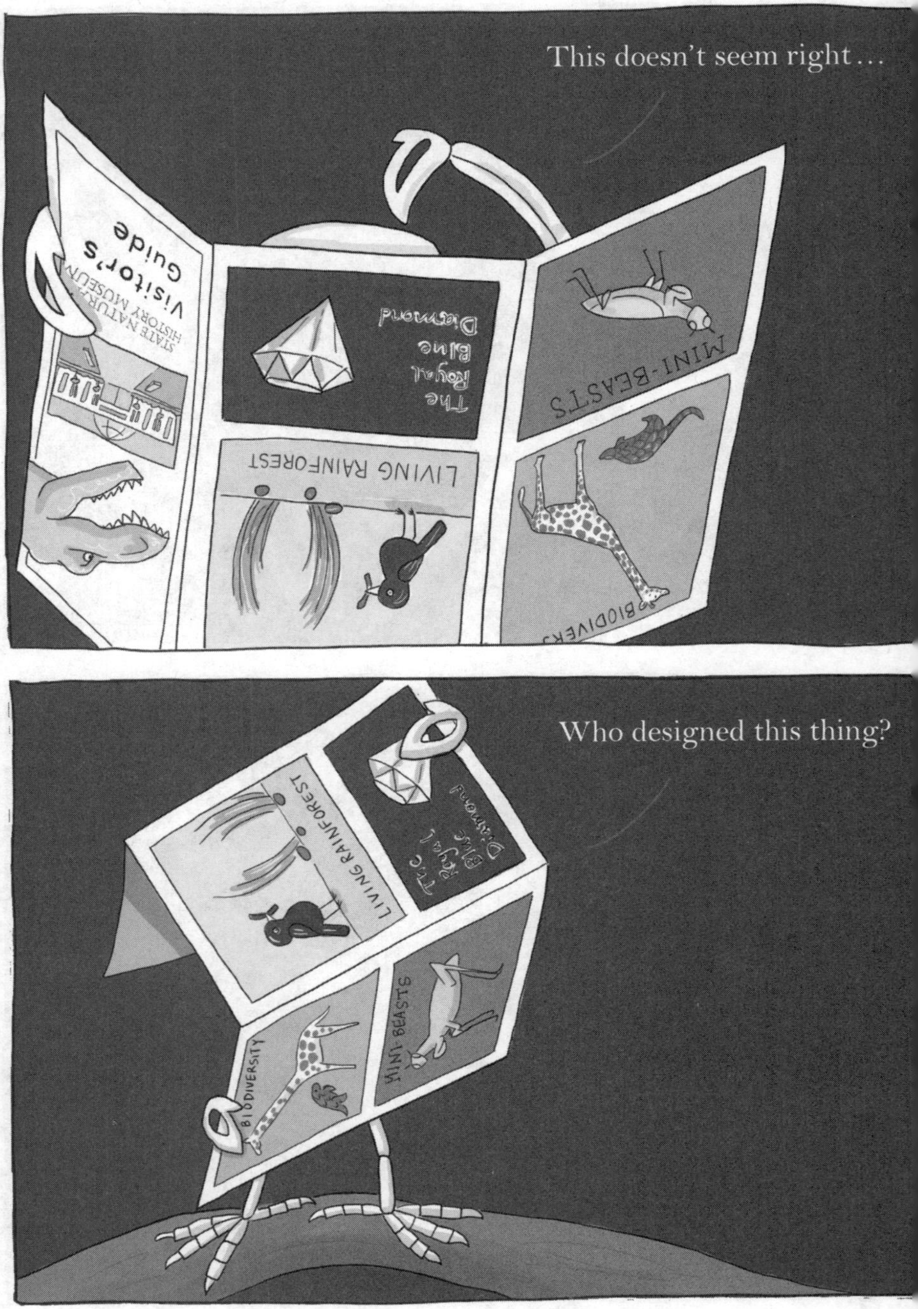
This doesn't seem right…
STATE NATURAL HISTORY MUSEUM
Visitor's Guide
The Royal Blue Diamond
LIVING RAINFOREST
MINI-BEASTS
Who designed this thing?
LIVING RAINFOREST
MINI-BEASTS
BIODIVERSITY

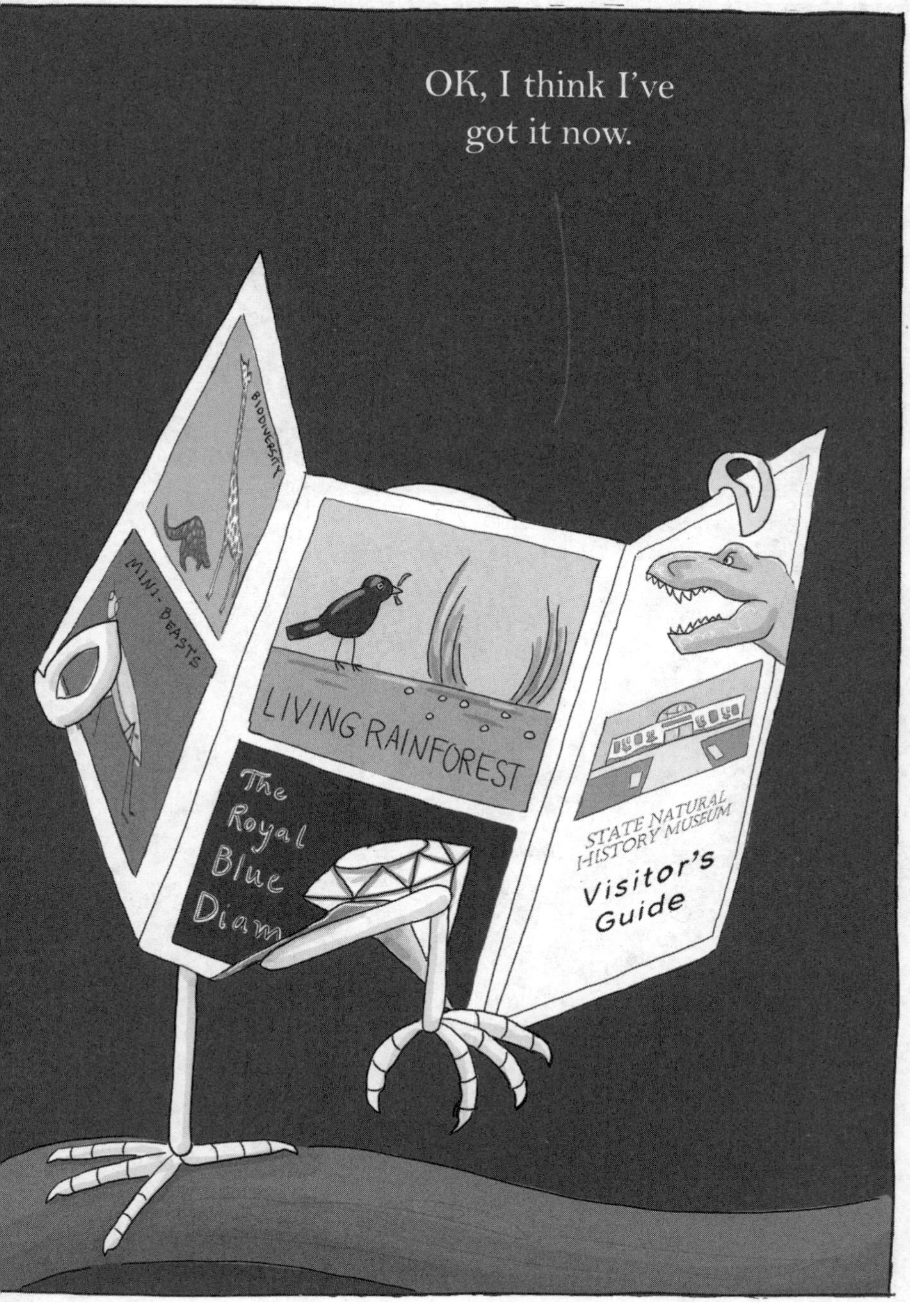
OK, I think I've got it now.
BIODIVERSITY
MINI-BEASTS
LIVING RAINFOREST
The Royal Blue Diam
STATE NATURAL HISTORY MUSEUM
Visitor's Guide

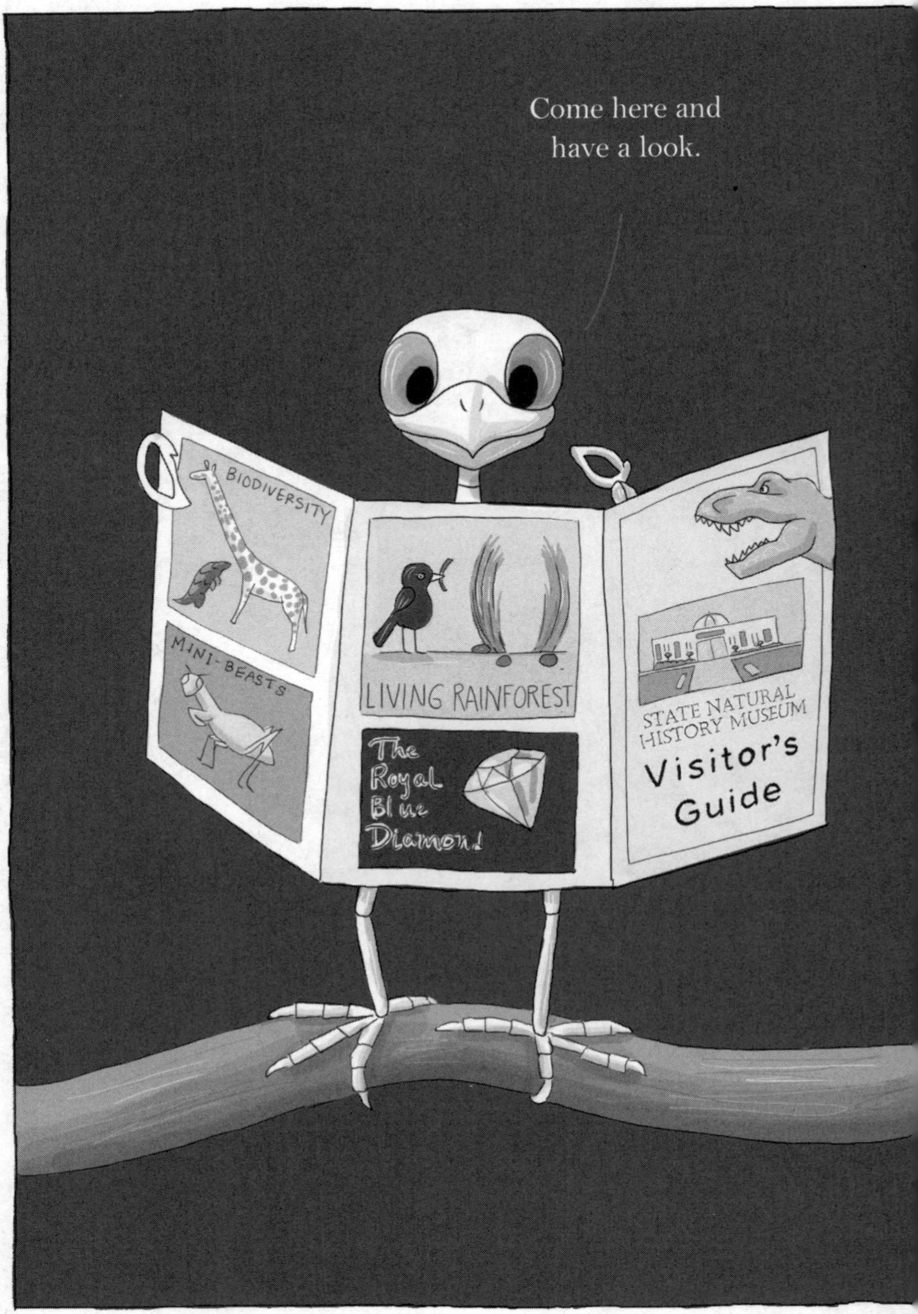
Come here and
have a look.
BIODIVERSITY
MINI-BEASTS
LIVING RAINFOREST
The Royal Blue Diamond
STATE NATURAL HISTORY MUSEUM
Visitor's Guide

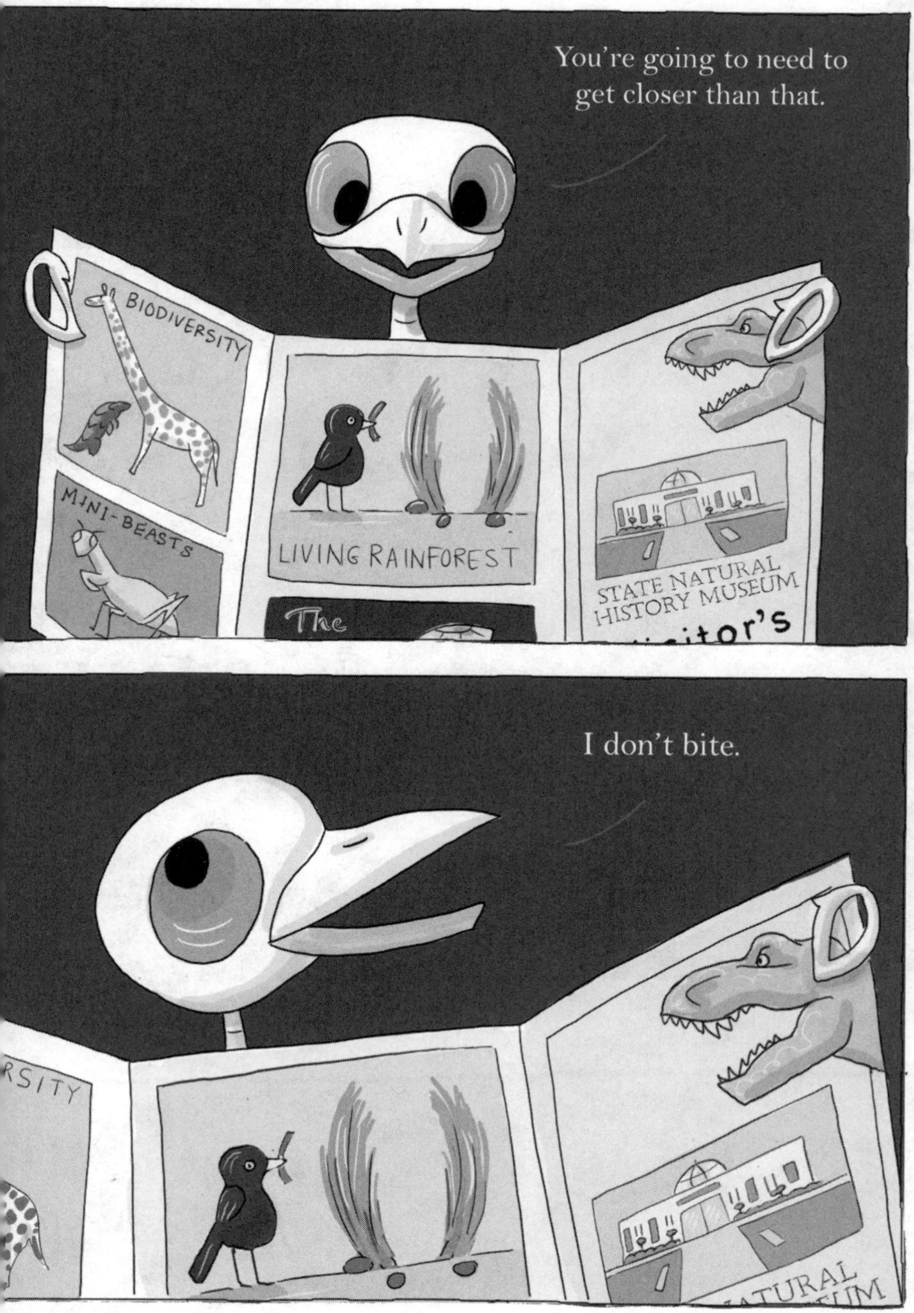
You're going to need to get closer than that.
BIODIVERSITY
MINI-BEASTS
LIVING RAINFOREST
The
STATE NATURAL HISTORY MUSEUM
I don't bite.
RSITY

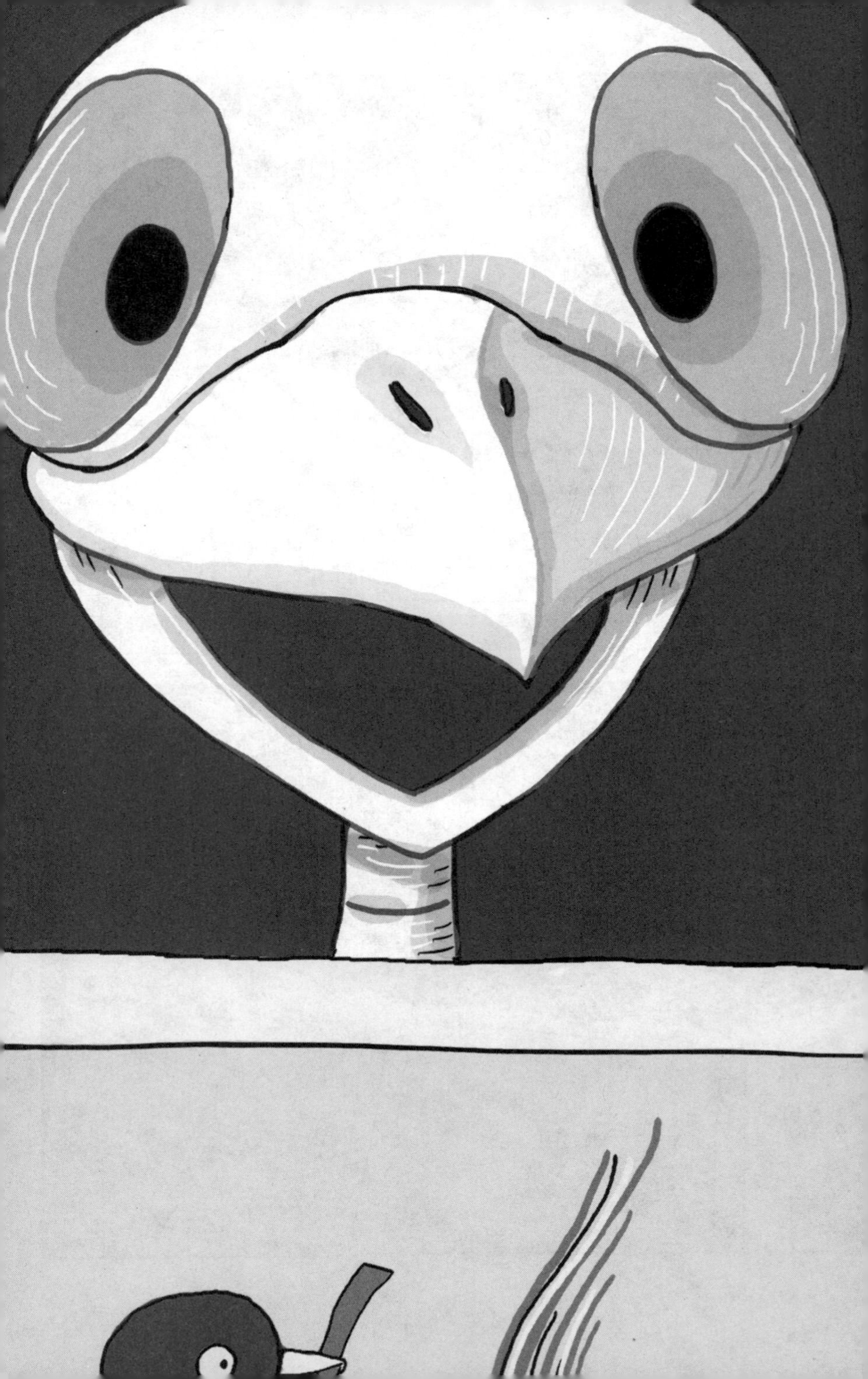

WHOA.
That's close enough!

Ever heard of personal space?

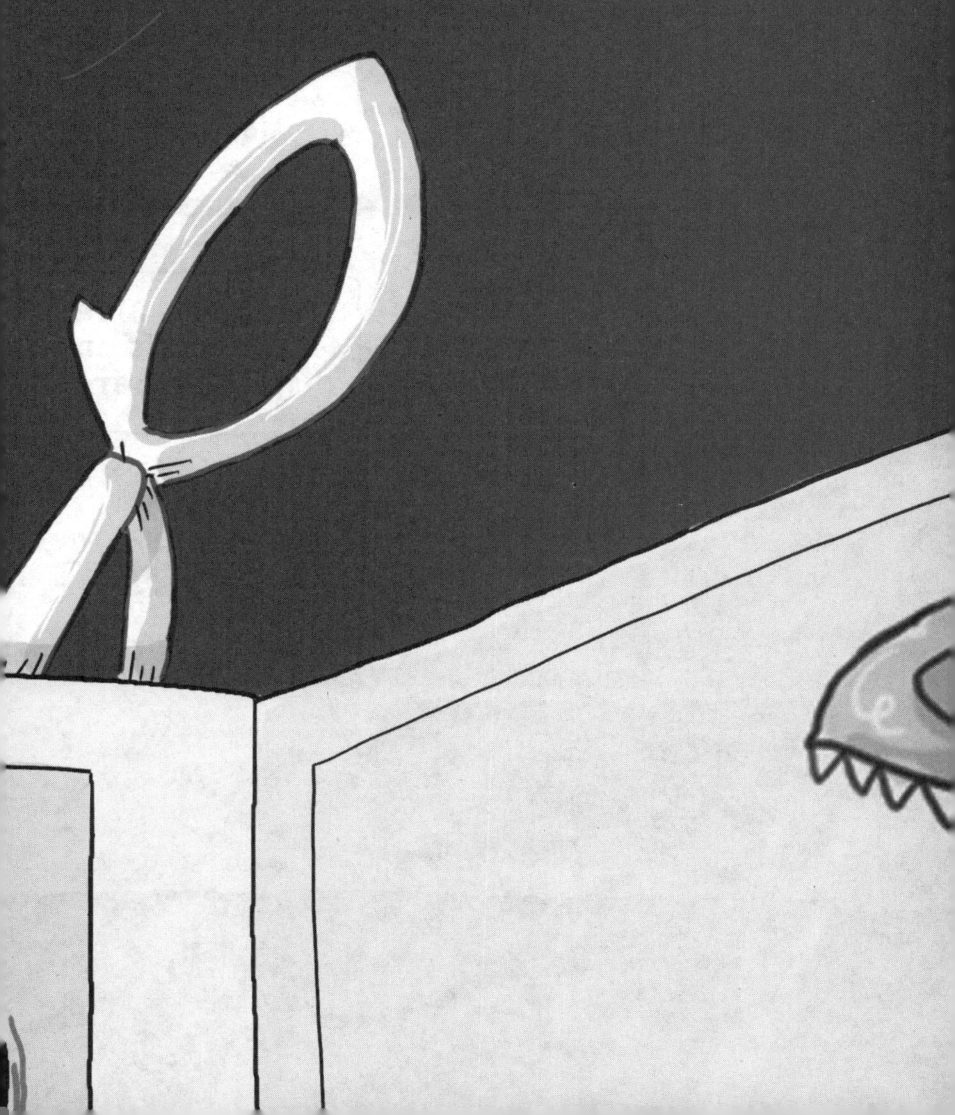

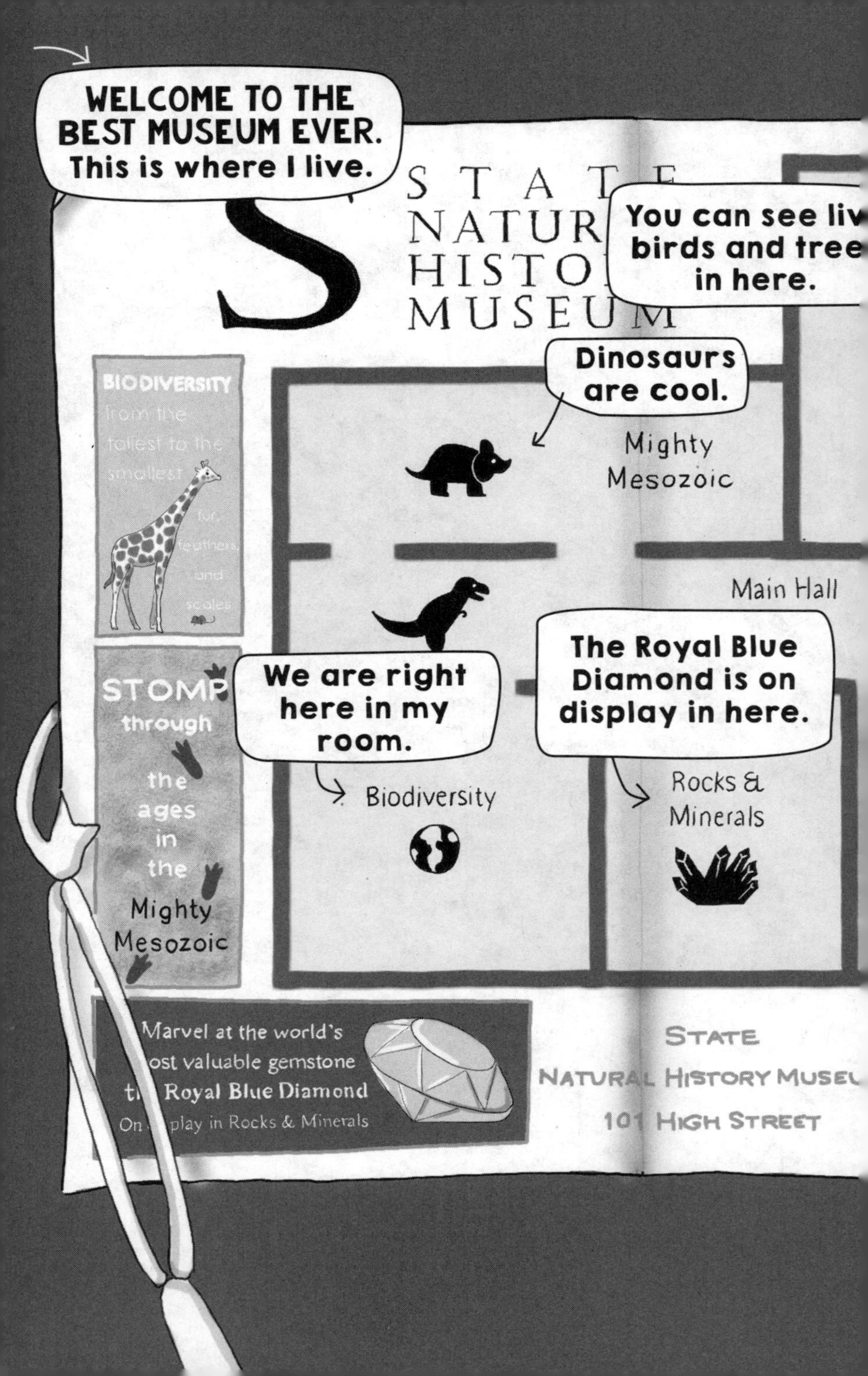
WELCOME TO THE BEST MUSEUM EVER. This is where I live.
STATE NATURAL HISTORY MUSEUM
You can see liv birds and tree in here.
Dinosaurs are cool.
Mighty Mesozoic
BIODIVERSITY from the tallest to the smallest fur, feathers, and scales
Main Hall
STOMP through the ages in the Mighty Mesozoic
We are right here in my room.
The Royal Blue Diamond is on display in here.
Biodiversity
Rocks & Minerals
Marvel at the world's most valuable gemstone the Royal Blue Diamond
On display in Rocks & Minerals
STATE NATURAL HISTORY MUSEU
101 HIGH STREET

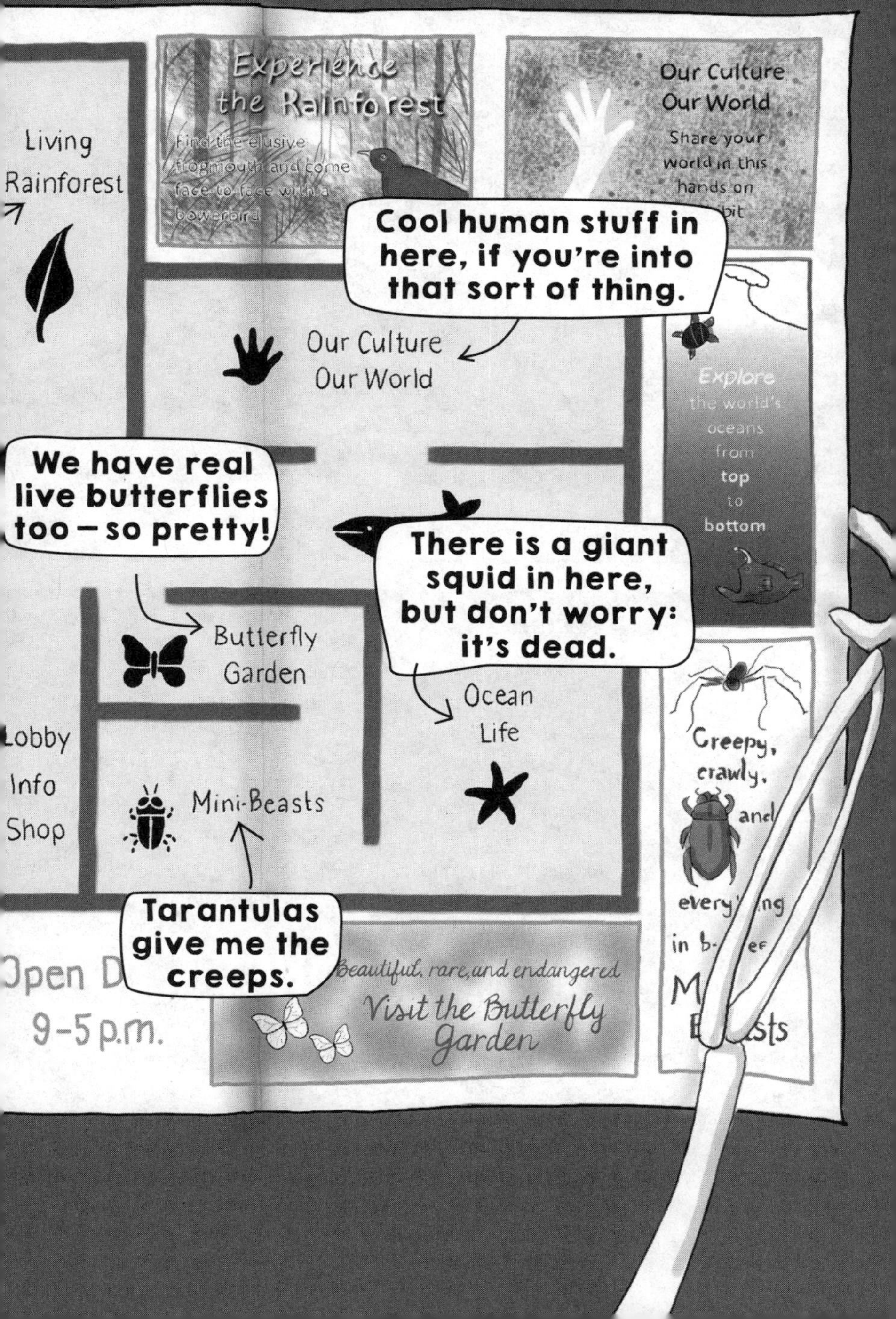

Experience the Rainforest
Find the elusive frogmouth and come face-to-face with a bowerbird
Our Culture Our World
Share your world in this hands on
Living Rainforest
Cool human stuff in here, if you're into that sort of thing.
Our Culture Our World
Explore the world's oceans from top to bottom
We have real live butterflies too — so pretty!
There is a giant squid in here, but don't worry: it's dead.
Butterfly Garden
Ocean Life
Creepy, crawly, and
Lobby
Info
Shop
Mini-Beasts
Tarantulas give me the creeps.
9–5 p.m.
Beautiful, rare, and endangered
Visit the Butterfly Garden

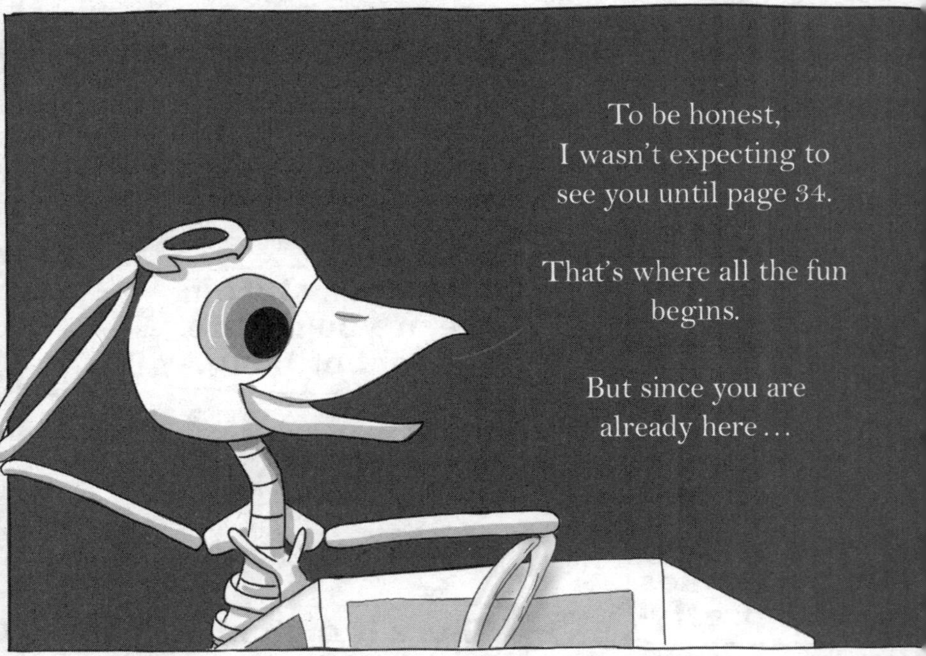
To be honest, I wasn't expecting to see you until page 34.
That's where all the fun begins.
But since you are already here . . .

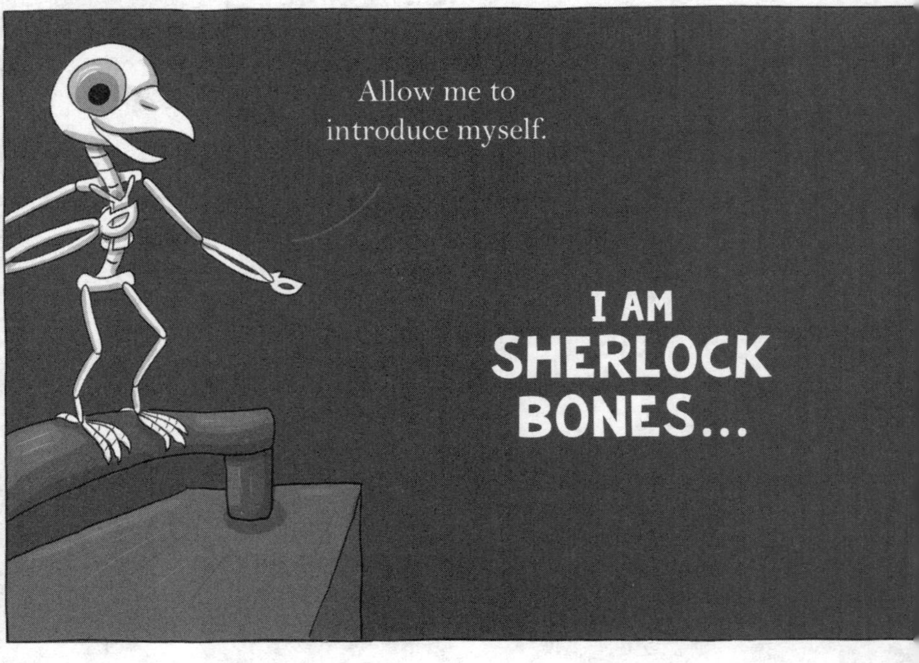
Allow me to introduce myself.
I AM SHERLOCK BONES...

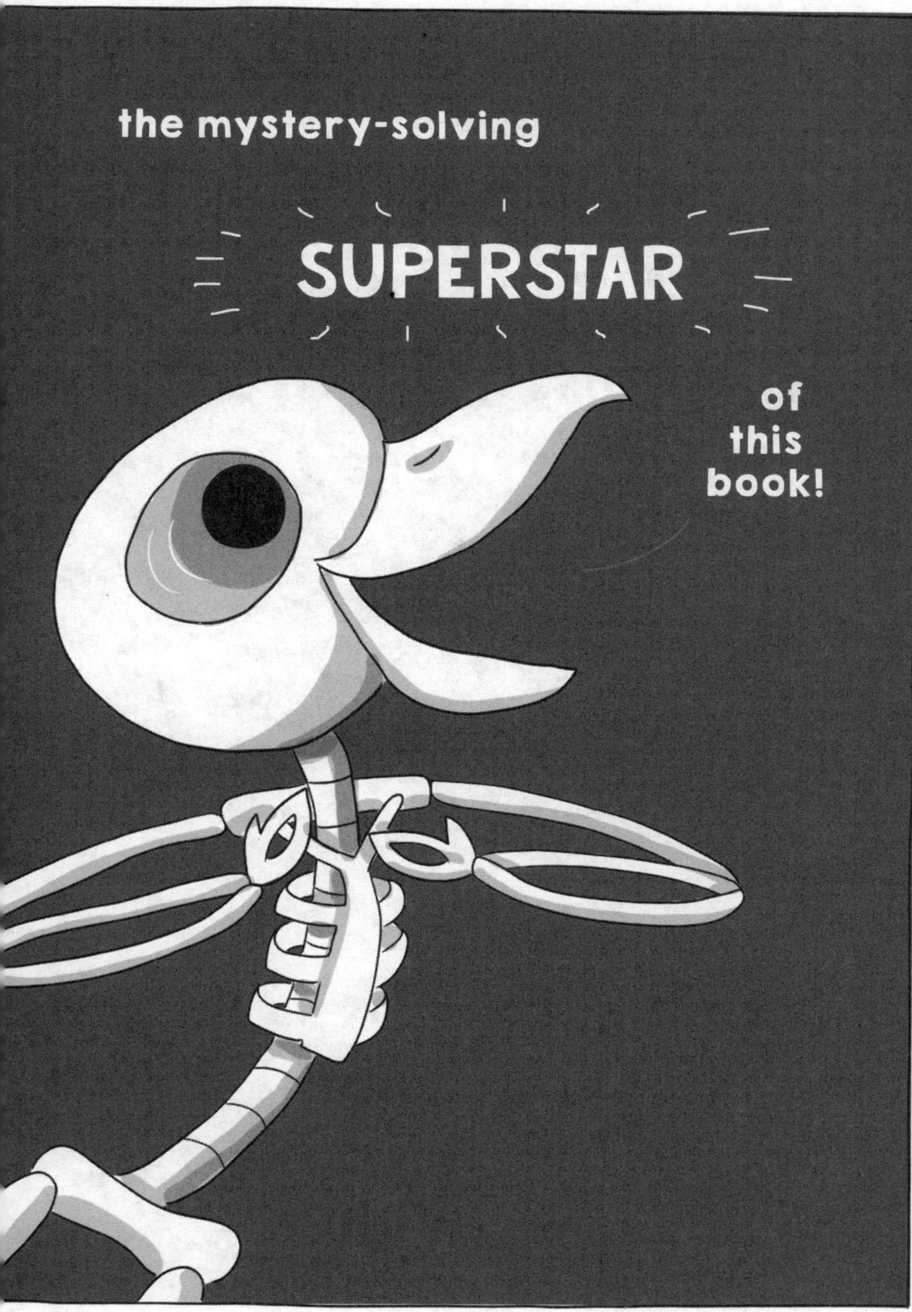
the mystery-solving
SUPERSTAR
of this book!

Oh, right.
SORRY, WATTS.

I *totally* meant to
say "WE."

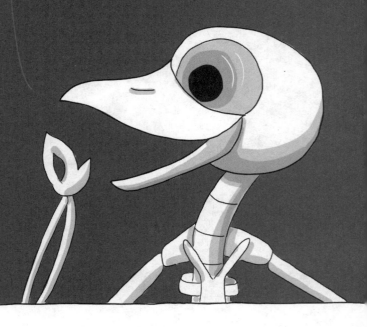

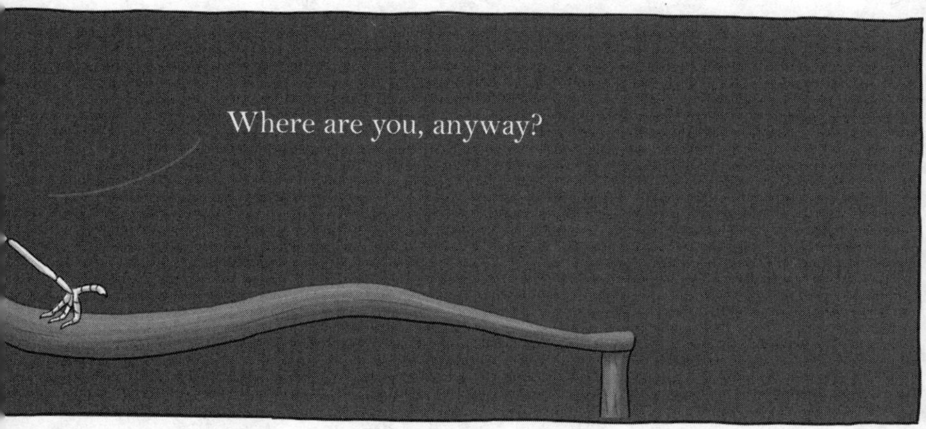
Where are you, anyway?

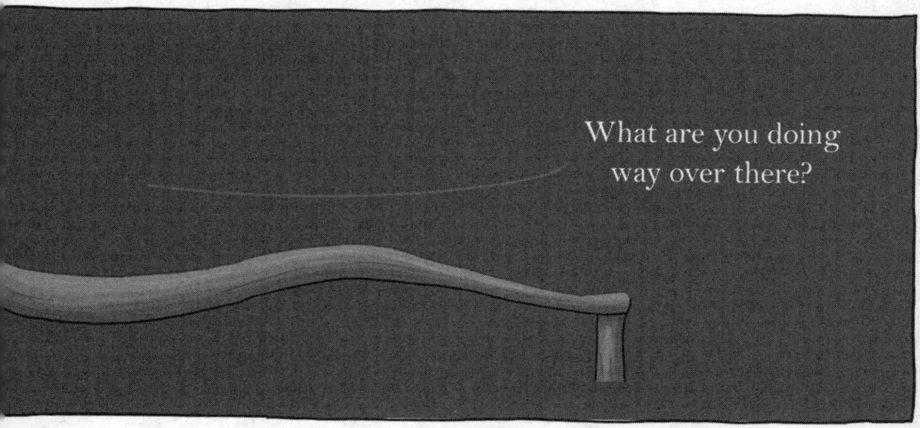
What are you doing way over there?

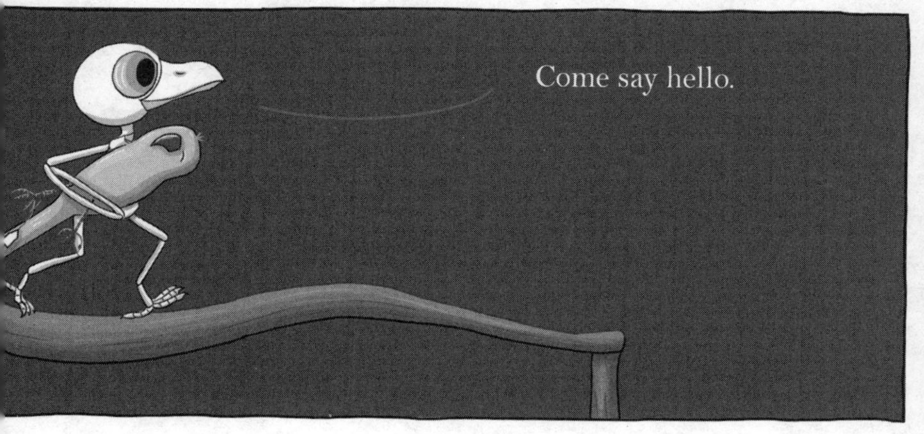
Come say hello.

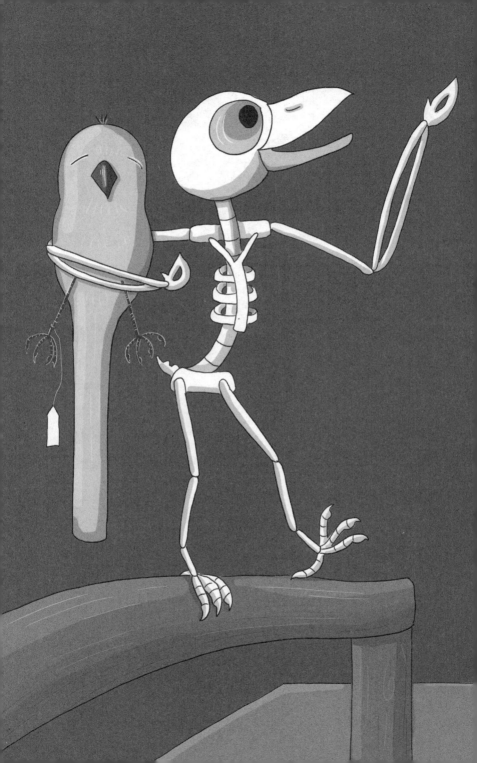

This is my trusty partner, Watts,

and together

WE are...

mystery-solving

SUPERSTARS!

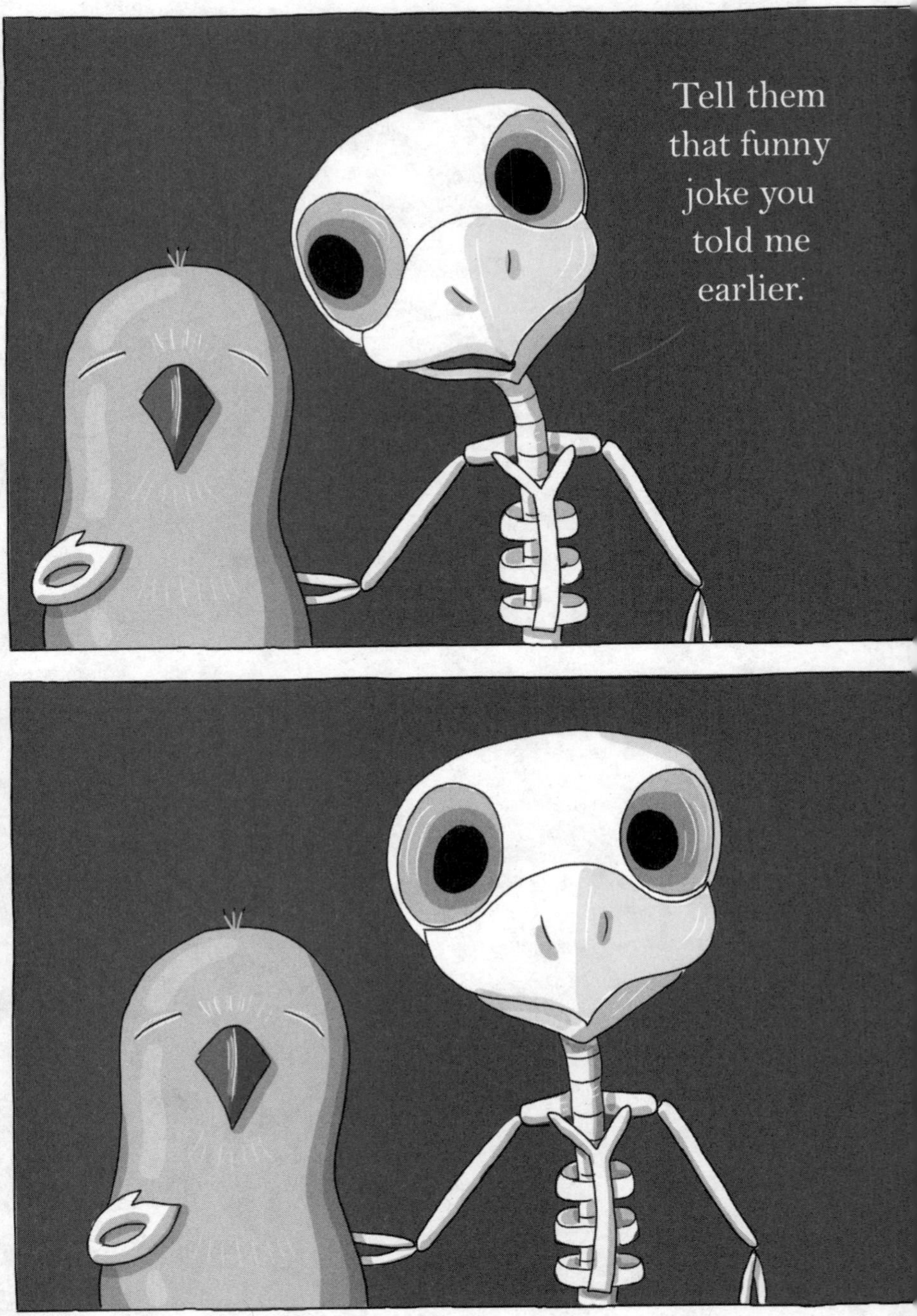
Tell them that funny joke you told me earlier.

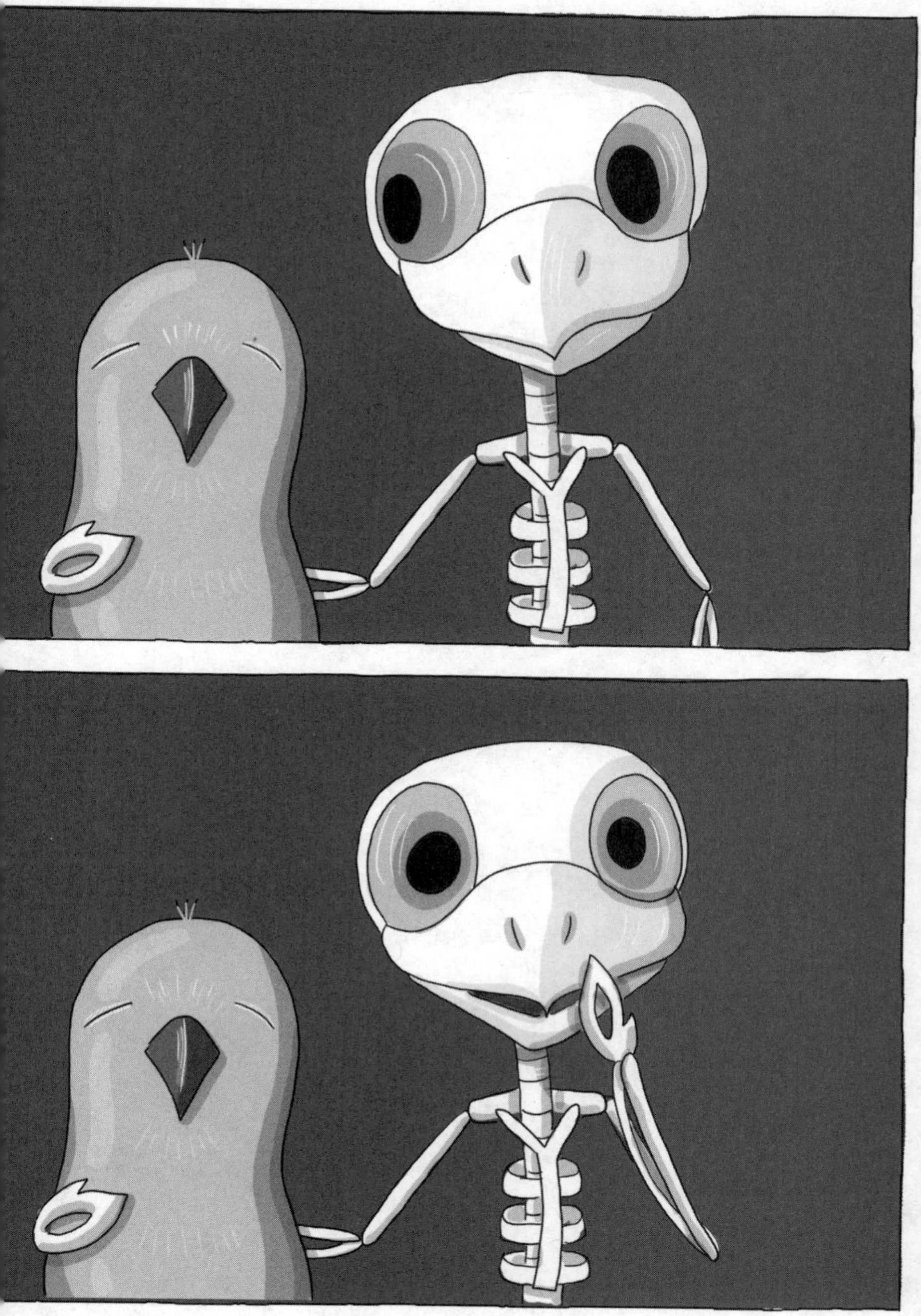

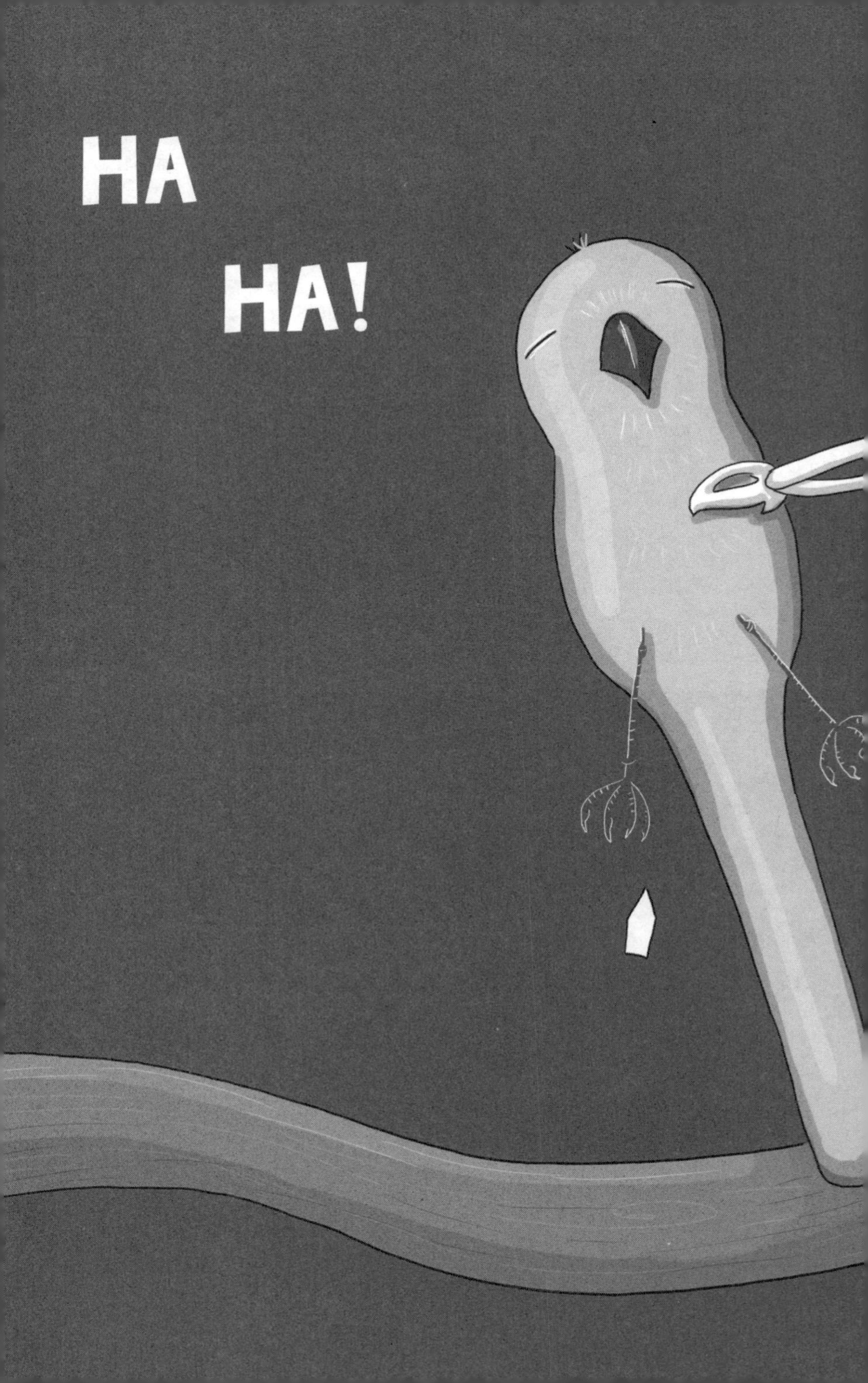
HA
HA!

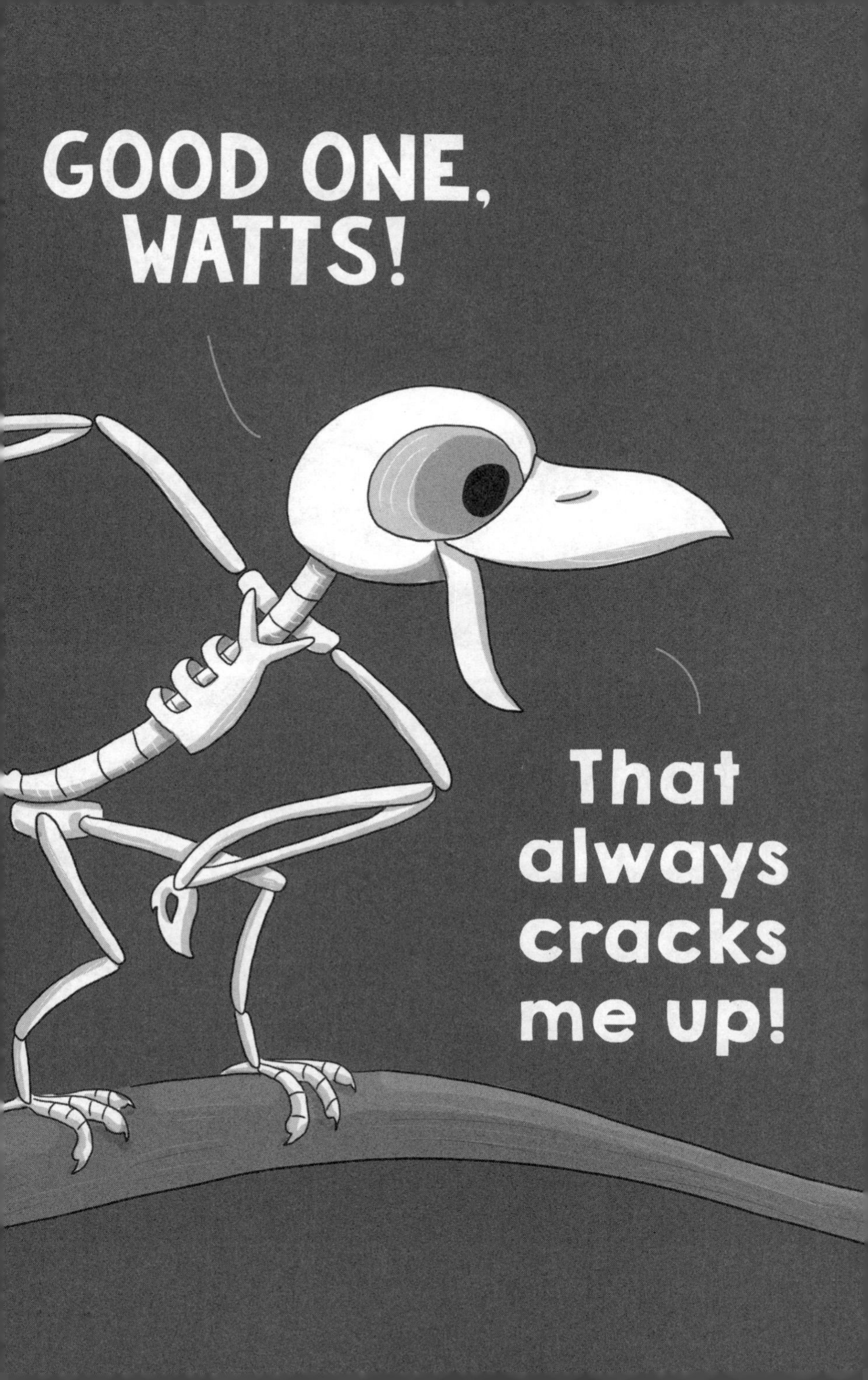
GOOD ONE, WATTS!
That always cracks me up!

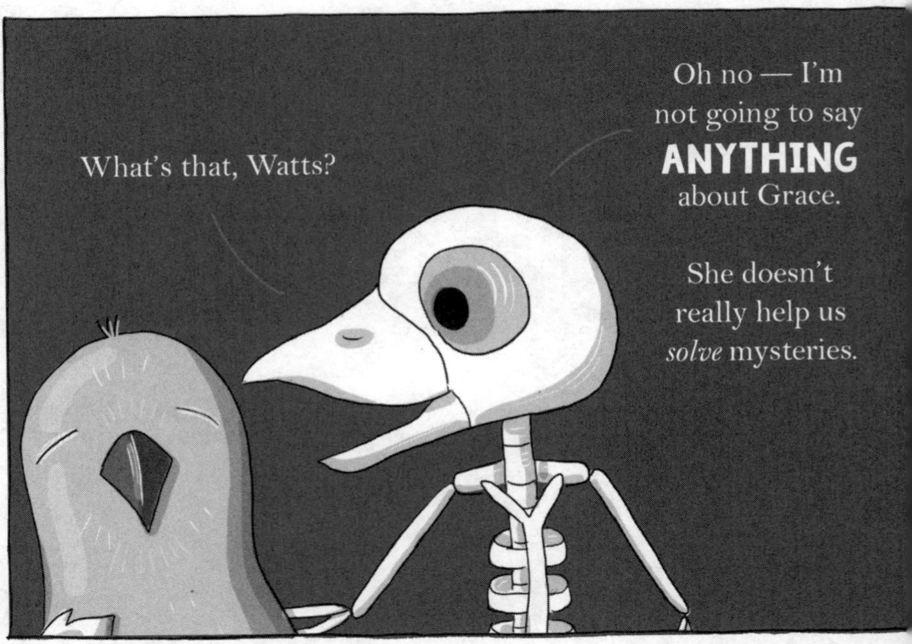
What's that, Watts?
Oh no — I'm not going to say **ANYTHING** about Grace.
She doesn't really help us *solve* mysteries.

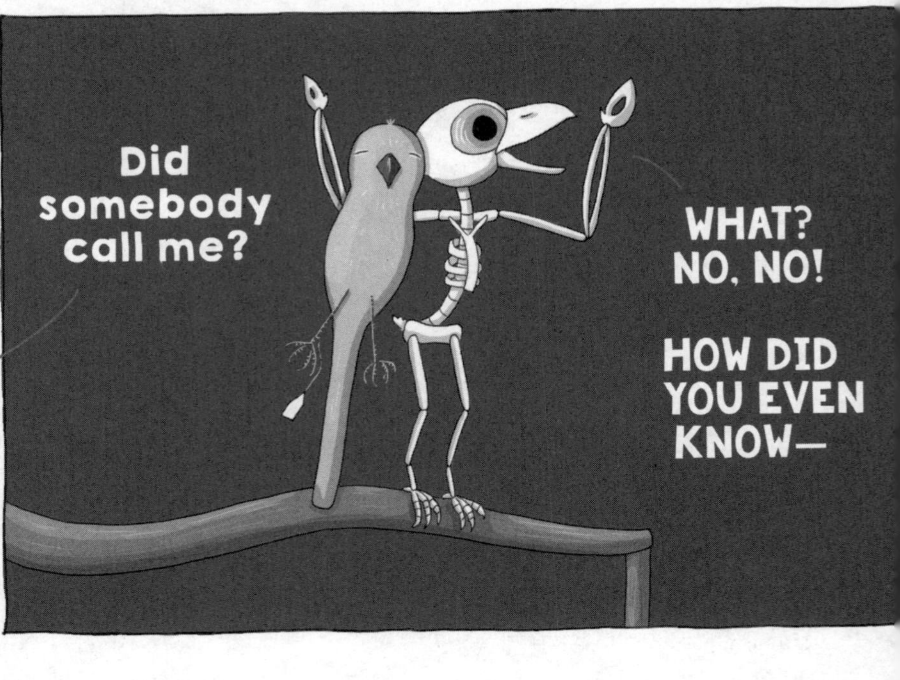
Did somebody call me?
WHAT? NO, NO!
HOW DID YOU EVEN KNOW—

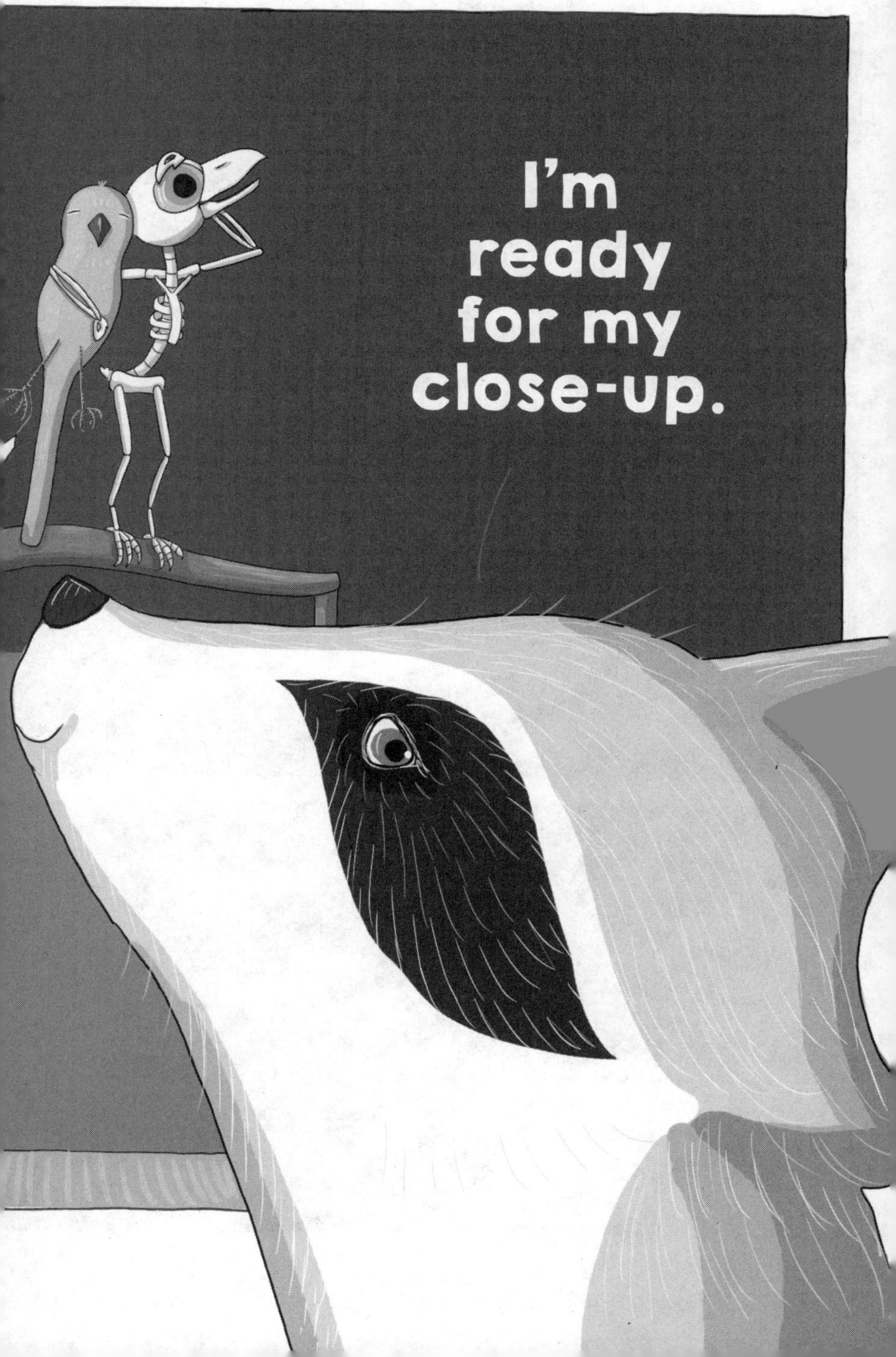
I'm
ready
for my
close-up.

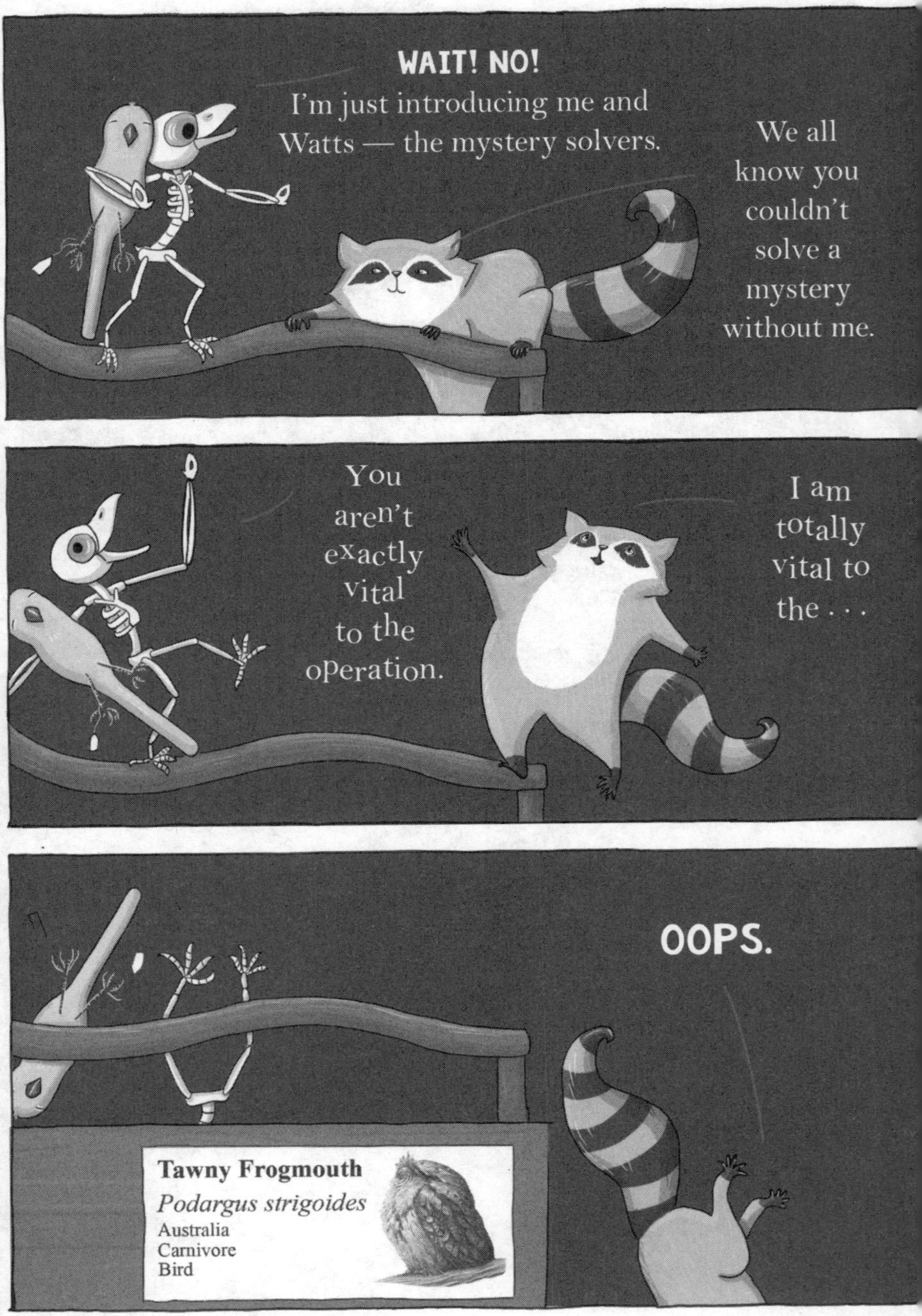
WAIT! NO!
I'm just introducing me and Watts — the mystery solvers.
We all know you couldn't solve a mystery without me.
You aren't exactly vital to the operation.
I am totally vital to the . . .
OOPS.
Tawny Frogmouth
Podargus strigoides
Australia
Carnivore
Bird

Maybe it's best if you flip ahead to page 34 now.

That's where the story starts.

Just skip the next page.

Don't look down.

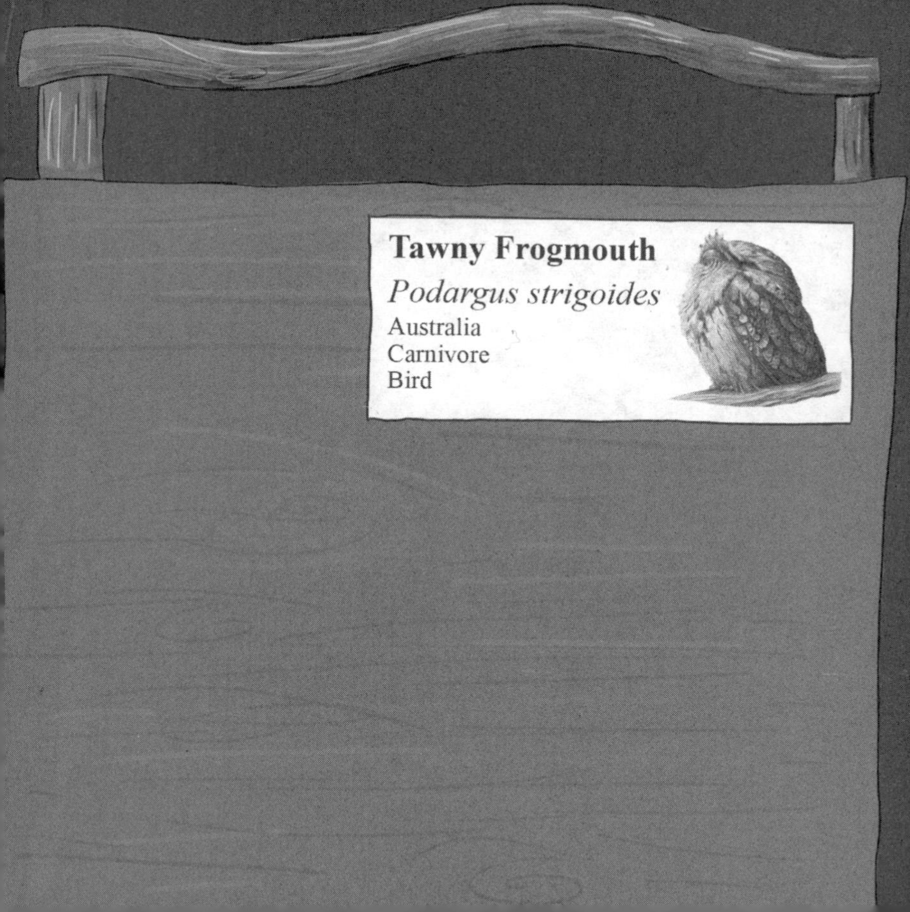

Tawny Frogmouth
Podargus strigoides
Australia
Carnivore
Bird

Ahh . . . this is better than that

BEAD-MASSAGE THINGIE

on the museum director's chair.
You really should try it, Bones.
It's very relaxing.

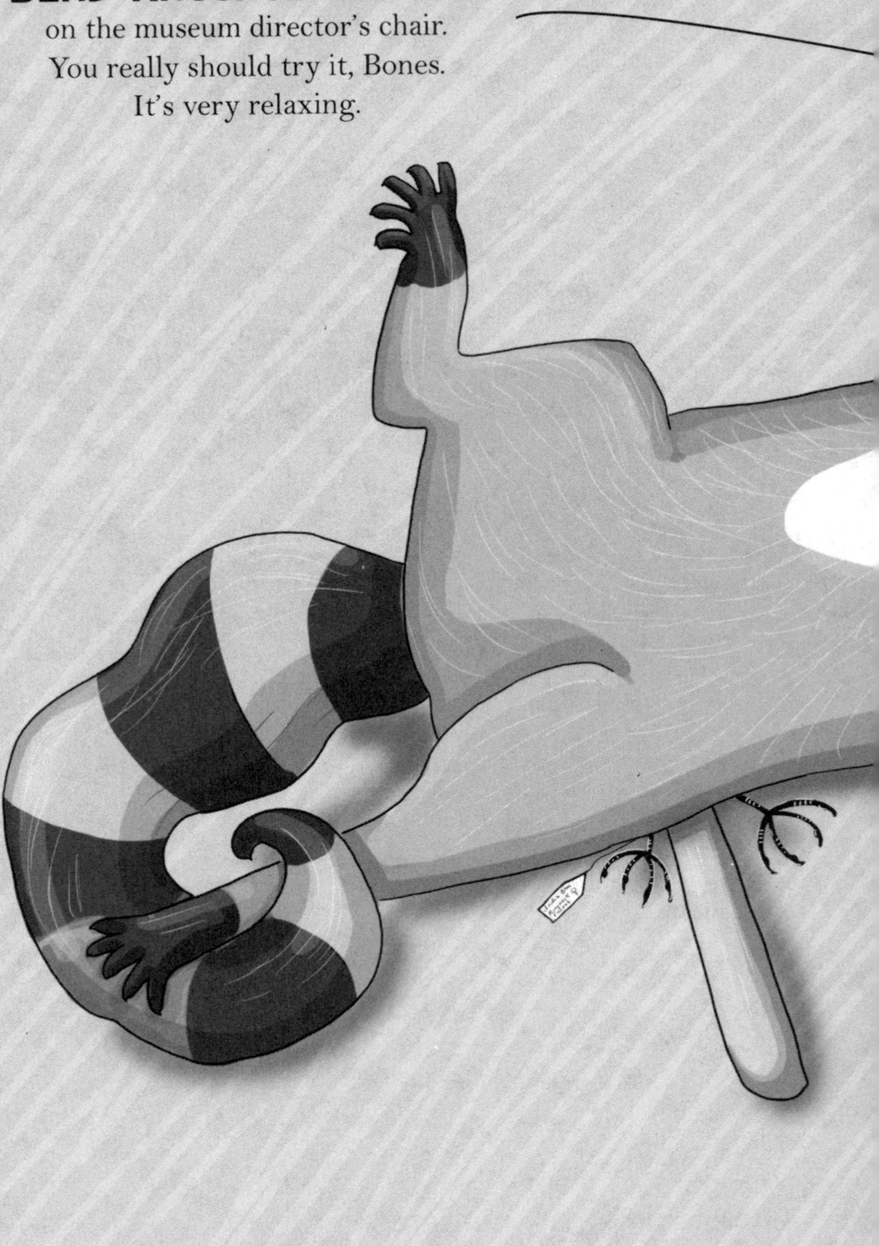

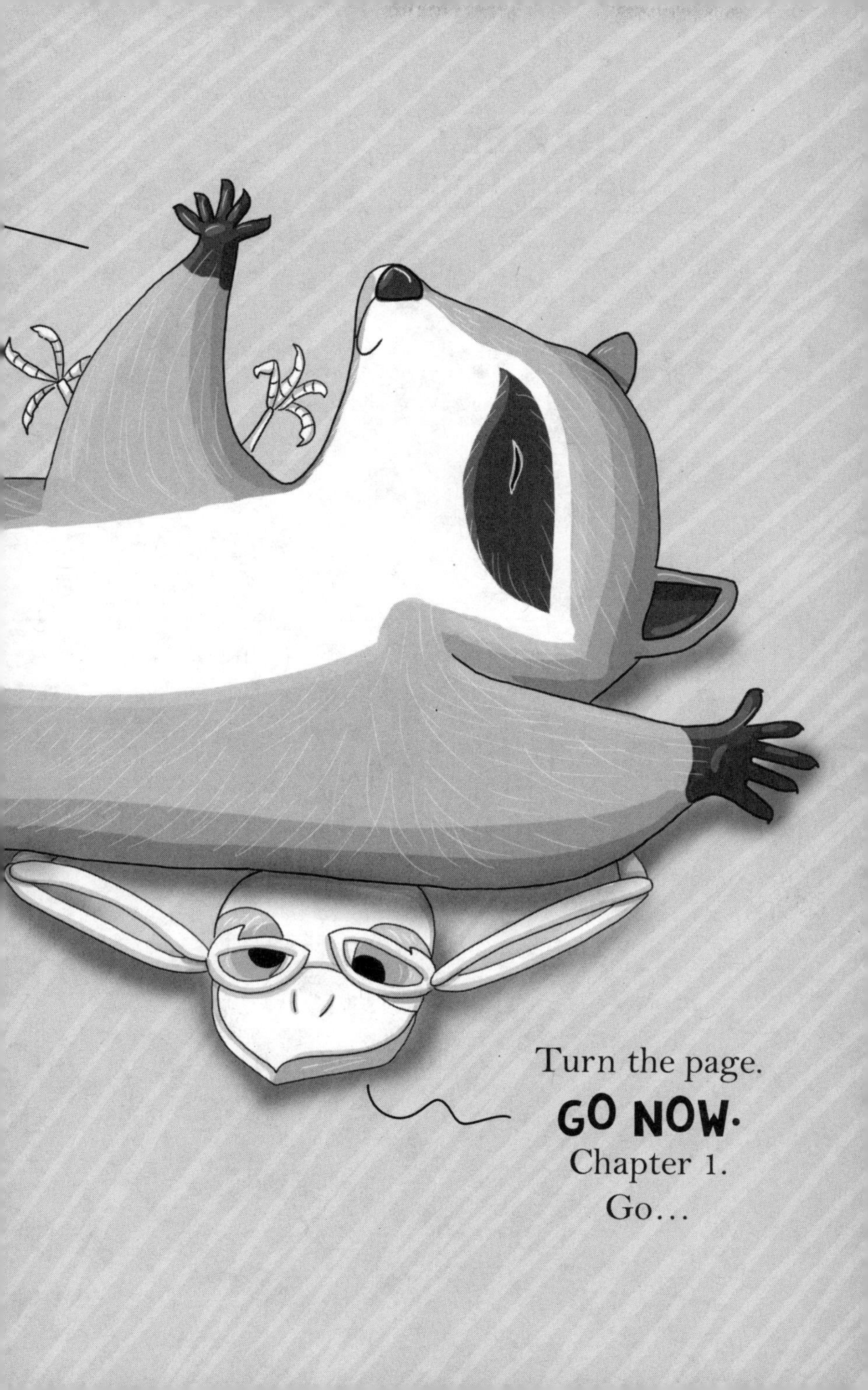
Turn the page.
GO NOW.
Chapter 1.
Go…

CHAPTER I
Closing Time

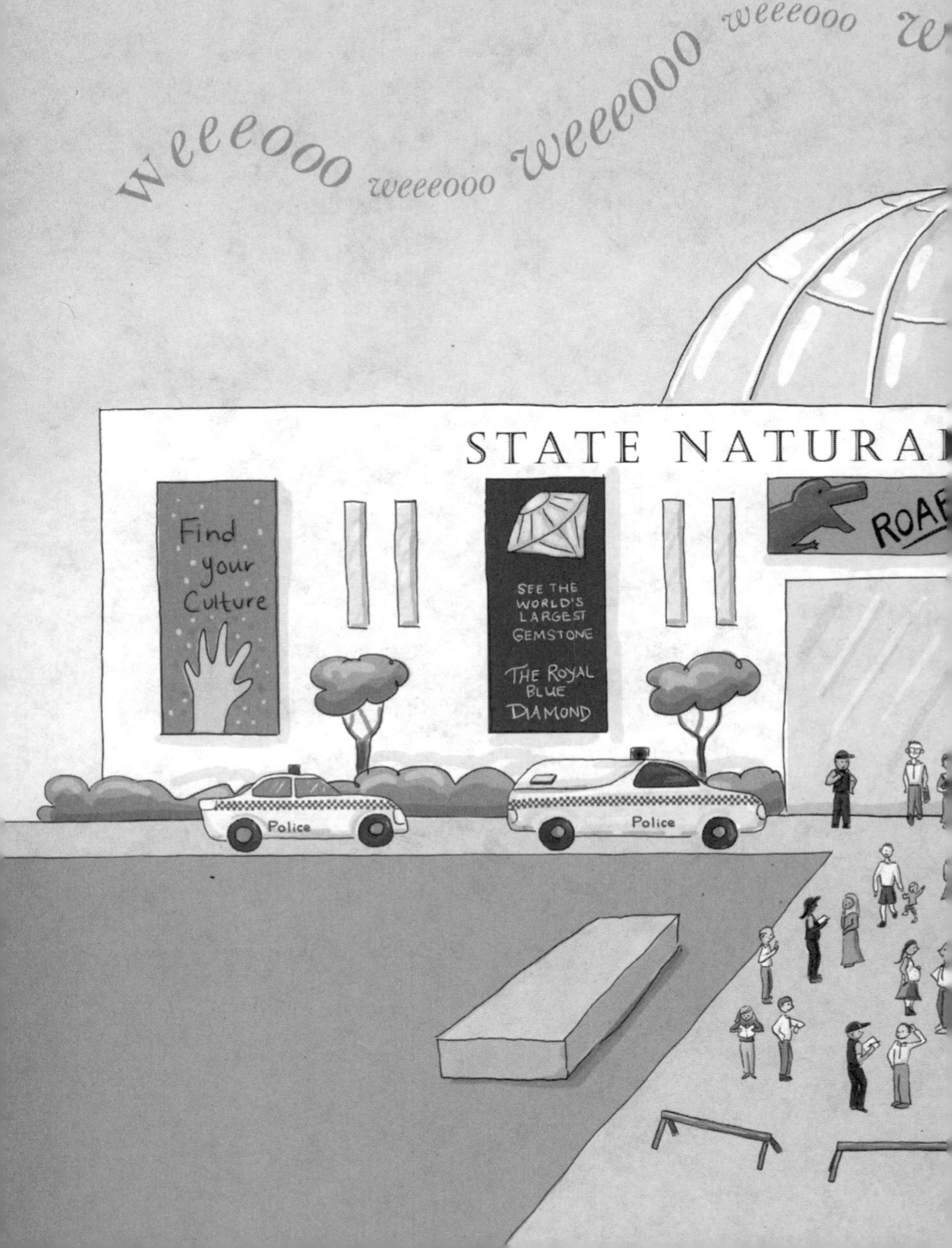
weeeooo weeeooo weeeooo weeeooo
STATE NATURA
Find your Culture
SEE THE WORLD'S LARGEST GEMSTONE
THE ROYAL BLUE DIAMOND
ROA
Police
Police

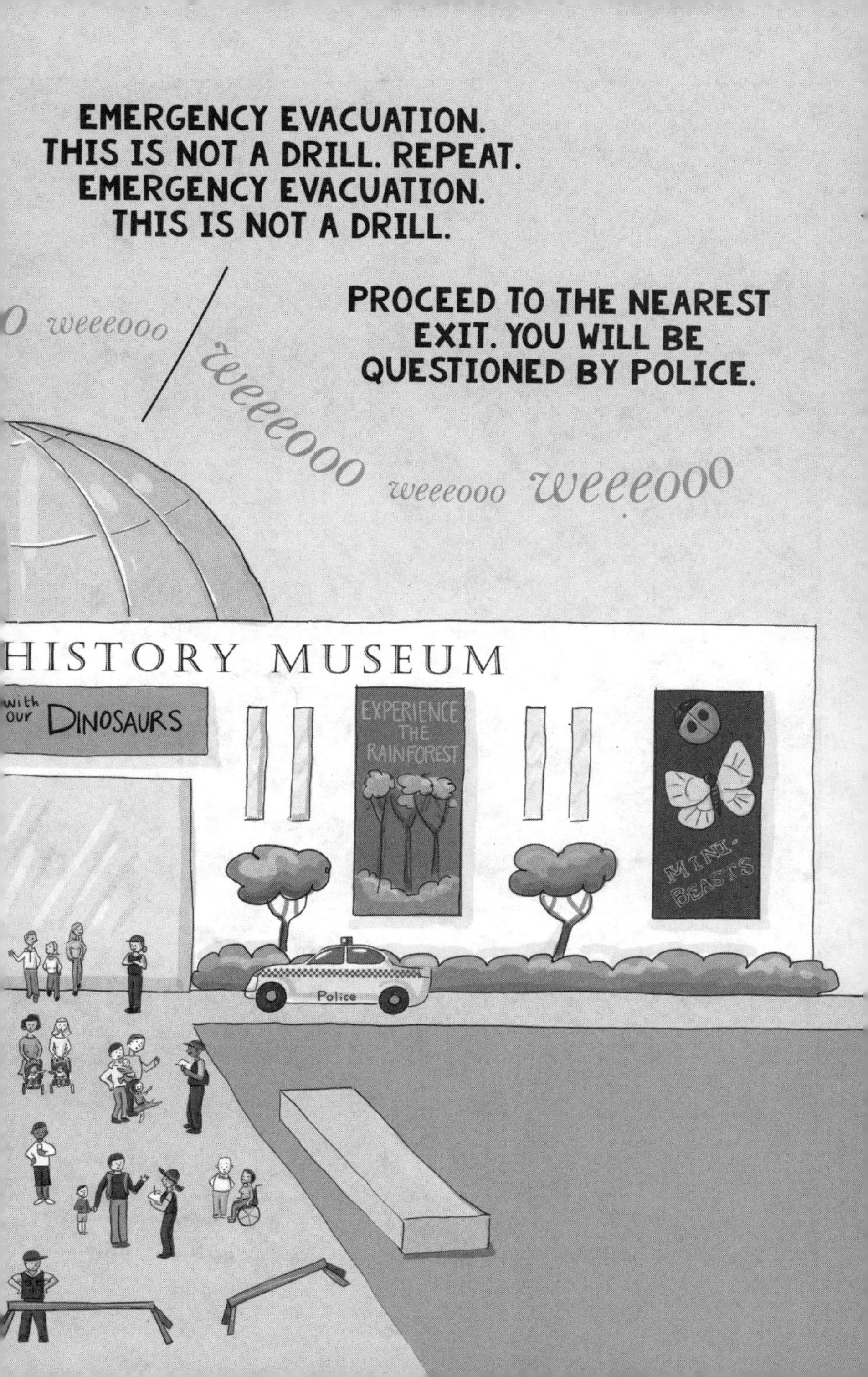
EMERGENCY EVACUATION.
THIS IS NOT A DRILL. REPEAT.
EMERGENCY EVACUATION.
THIS IS NOT A DRILL.
PROCEED TO THE NEAREST EXIT. YOU WILL BE QUESTIONED BY POLICE.
weeeooo
weeeooo
weeeooo
weeeooo
HISTORY MUSEUM
with our DINOSAURS
EXPERIENCE THE RAINFOREST
MINI-BEASTS
Police

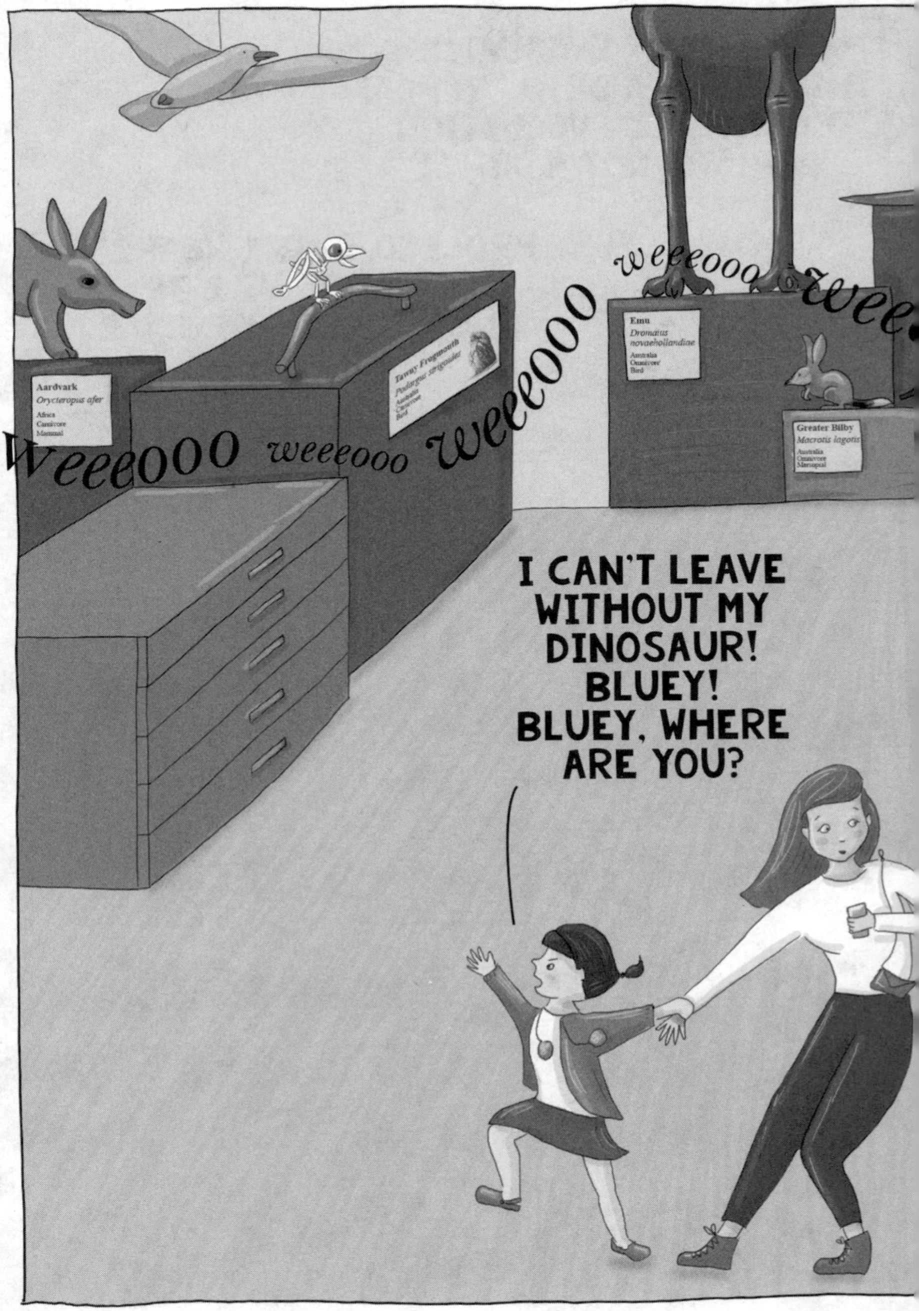
Aardvark
Orycteropus afer
Africa
Carnivore
Mammal
Tawny Frogmouth
Podargus strigoides
Emu
Dromaius novaehollandiae
Australia
Omnivore
Bird
Greater Bilby
Macrotis lagotis
Australia
Omnivore
Marsupial
Weeeooo weeeooo weeeooo weeeooo
I CAN'T LEAVE WITHOUT MY DINOSAUR! BLUEY! BLUEY, WHERE ARE YOU?

weeeooo *weeeooo* *weeeooo* *weeeooo* *weeeooo*

Black Flying-fox
Pteropus alecto
Australia & Indo-Pacific
Frugivore & Nectarivore
Minimal

Eastern Gray
Kangaroo
Macropus giganteus
Australia
Herbivore
Marsupial

Platypus
Ornithorhynchus anatinus
Australia
Carnivore
Monotreme

Plains Zebra
Equus quagga
Africa
Herbivore
Minimal

Nile Crocodile
Crocodylus niloticus
Africa
Carnivore
Reptile

Are you sure
we can't have
another look
around?

It's her
favorite toy.
She can't do
anything
without it.

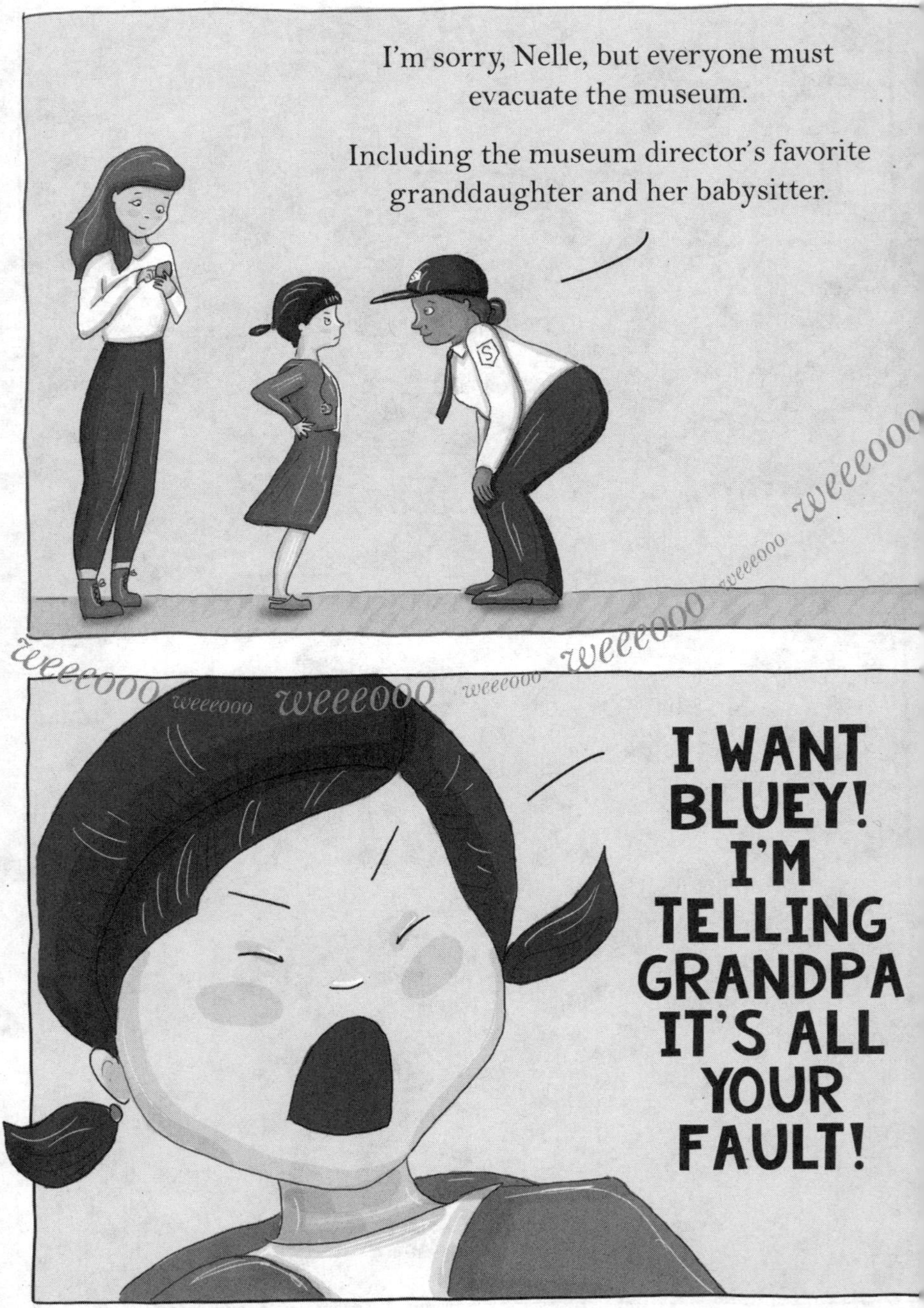
I'm sorry, Nelle, but everyone must evacuate the museum.
Including the museum director's favorite granddaughter and her babysitter.
weeeooo
weeeooo
weeeooo
weeeooo
weeeooo
weeeooo
weeeooo
weeeooo
weeeooo
I WANT BLUEY! I'M TELLING GRANDPA IT'S ALL YOUR FAULT!

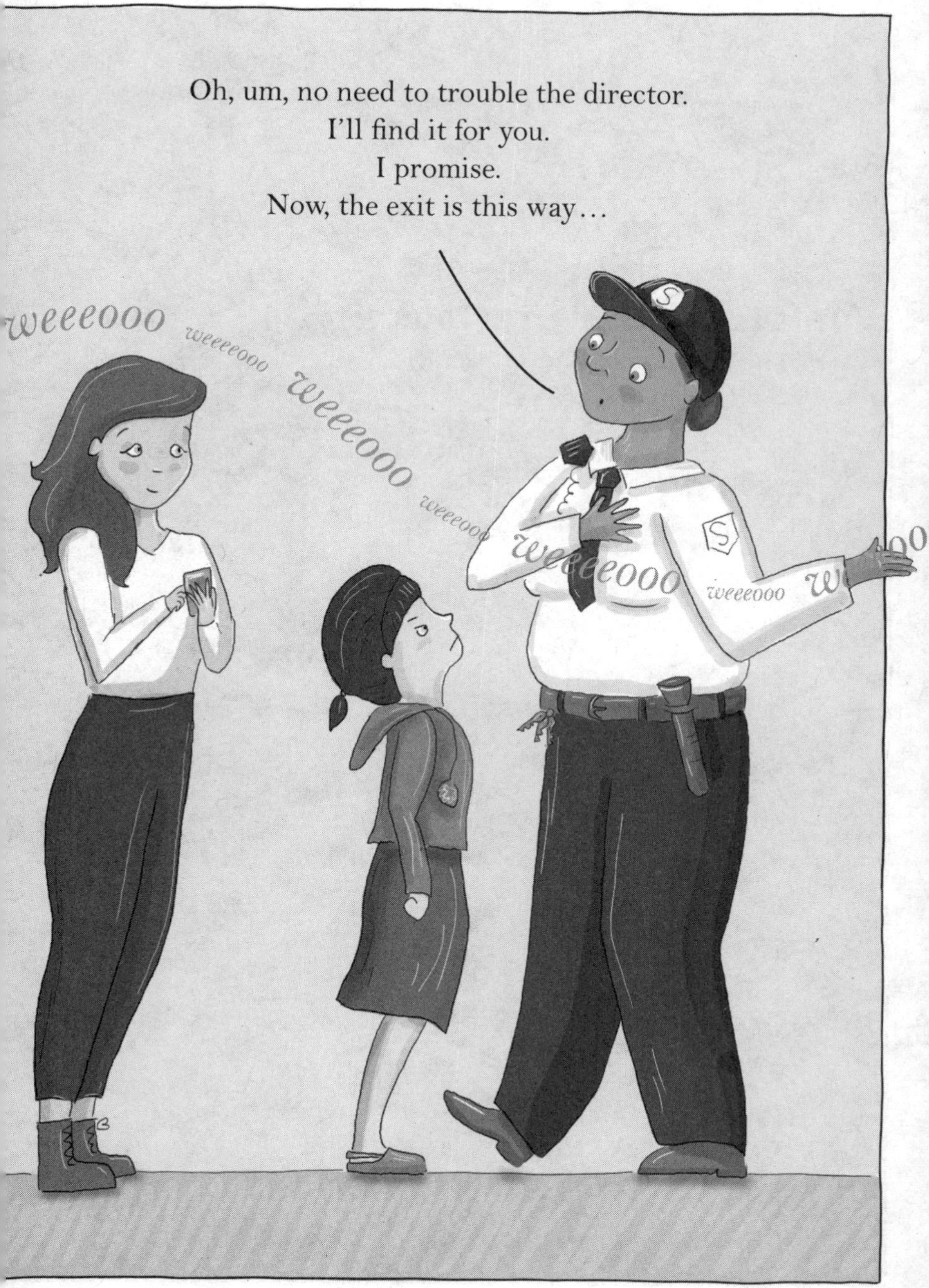
Oh, um, no need to trouble the director.
I'll find it for you.
I promise.
Now, the exit is this way…
weeeooo
weeeeooo
weeeooo
weeeooo
weeeeooo
weeeooo

weeeooo weeeooo weeeooo weeeooo weeeoo

WOW!
This is seriously serious.
The museum has never been
evacuated before.

Emu
*Dromaius
novaehollandiae*
Australia
Omnivore
Bird

Greater Bilby
Macrotis lagotis
Australia
Omnivore
Marsupial

Short-b
Tachygla
Australia
Insectivore
Monotreme

Tawny Frogmouth
Podargus strigoides
Australia
Carnivore
Bird

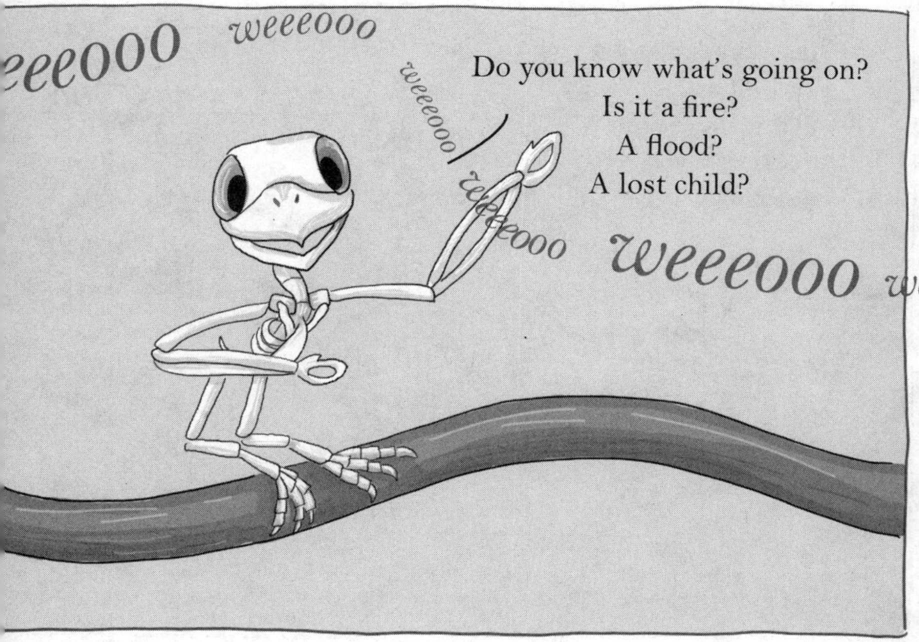

eeeooo
weeeooo
weeeooo
Do you know what's going on?
Is it a fire?
A flood?
A lost child?
weeeooo
weeeooo
wee

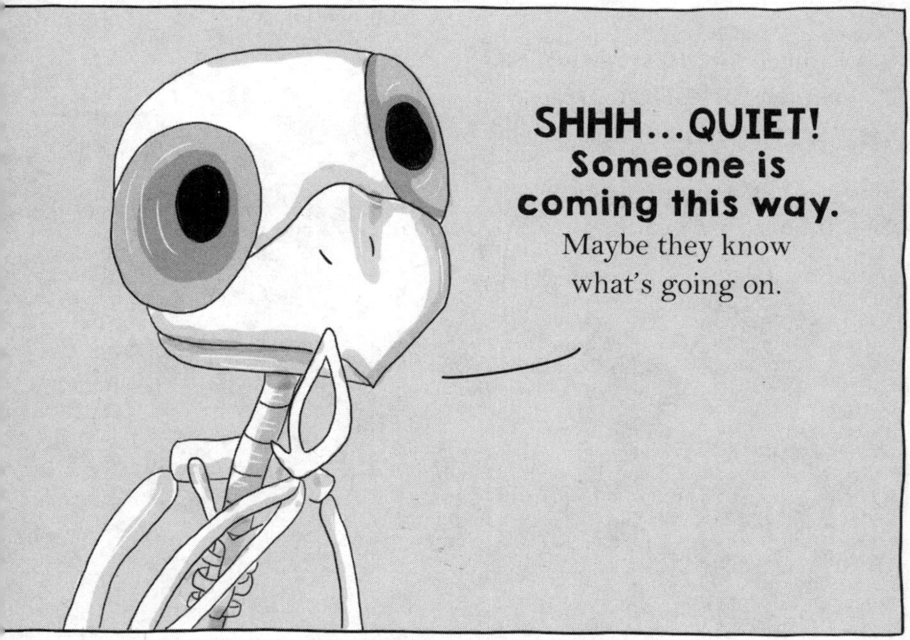

SHHH...QUIET!
Someone is
coming this way.
Maybe they know
what's going on.

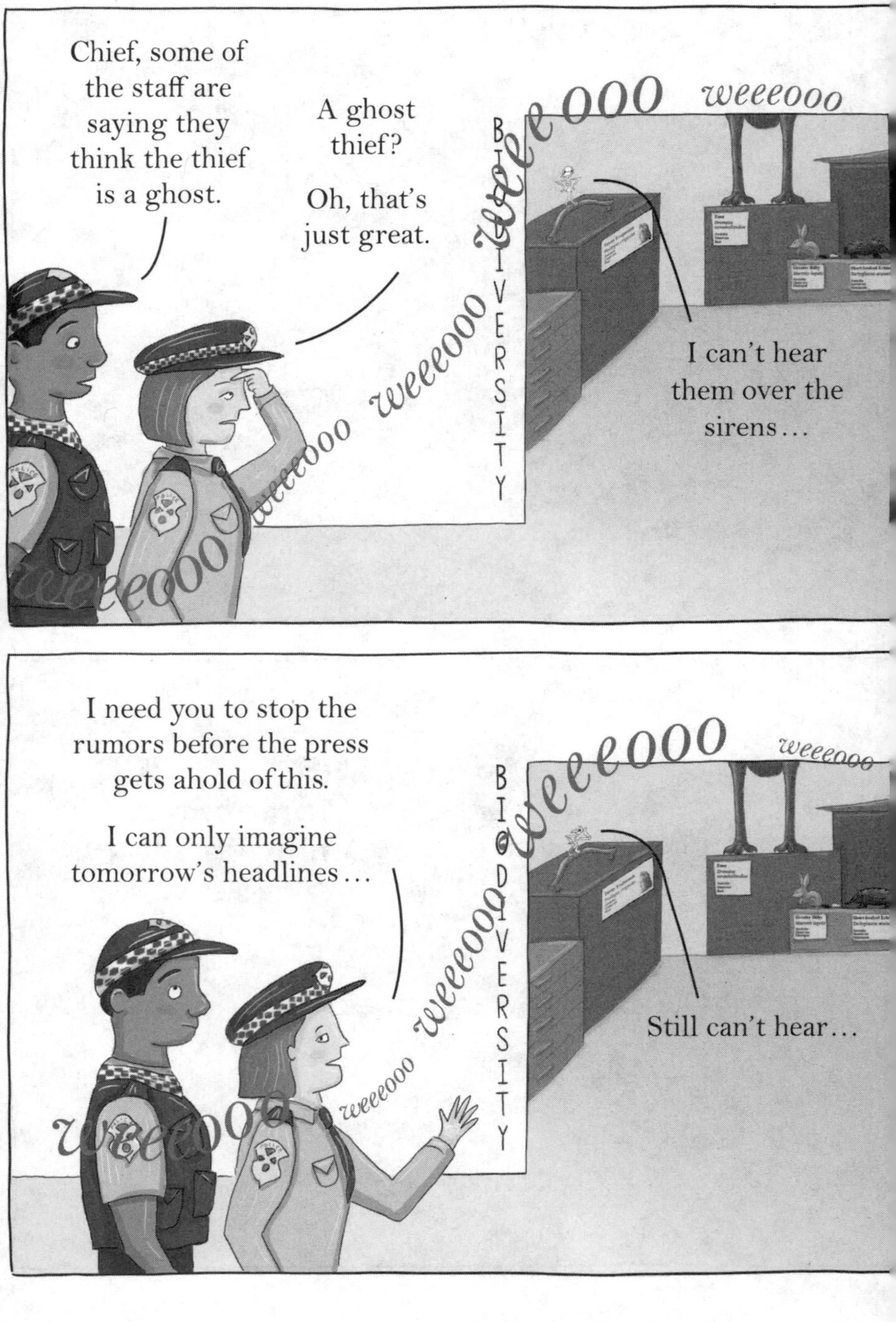
Chief, some of the staff are saying they think the thief is a ghost.
A ghost thief?
Oh, that's just great.
weeeooo
weeeooo
weeeooo
weeeooo
weeeooo
weeeooo
BIODIVERSITY
I can't hear them over the sirens…
I need you to stop the rumors before the press gets ahold of this.
I can only imagine tomorrow's headlines…
weeeooo
weeeooo
weeeooo
weeeooo
weeeooo
BIODIVERSITY
Still can't hear…

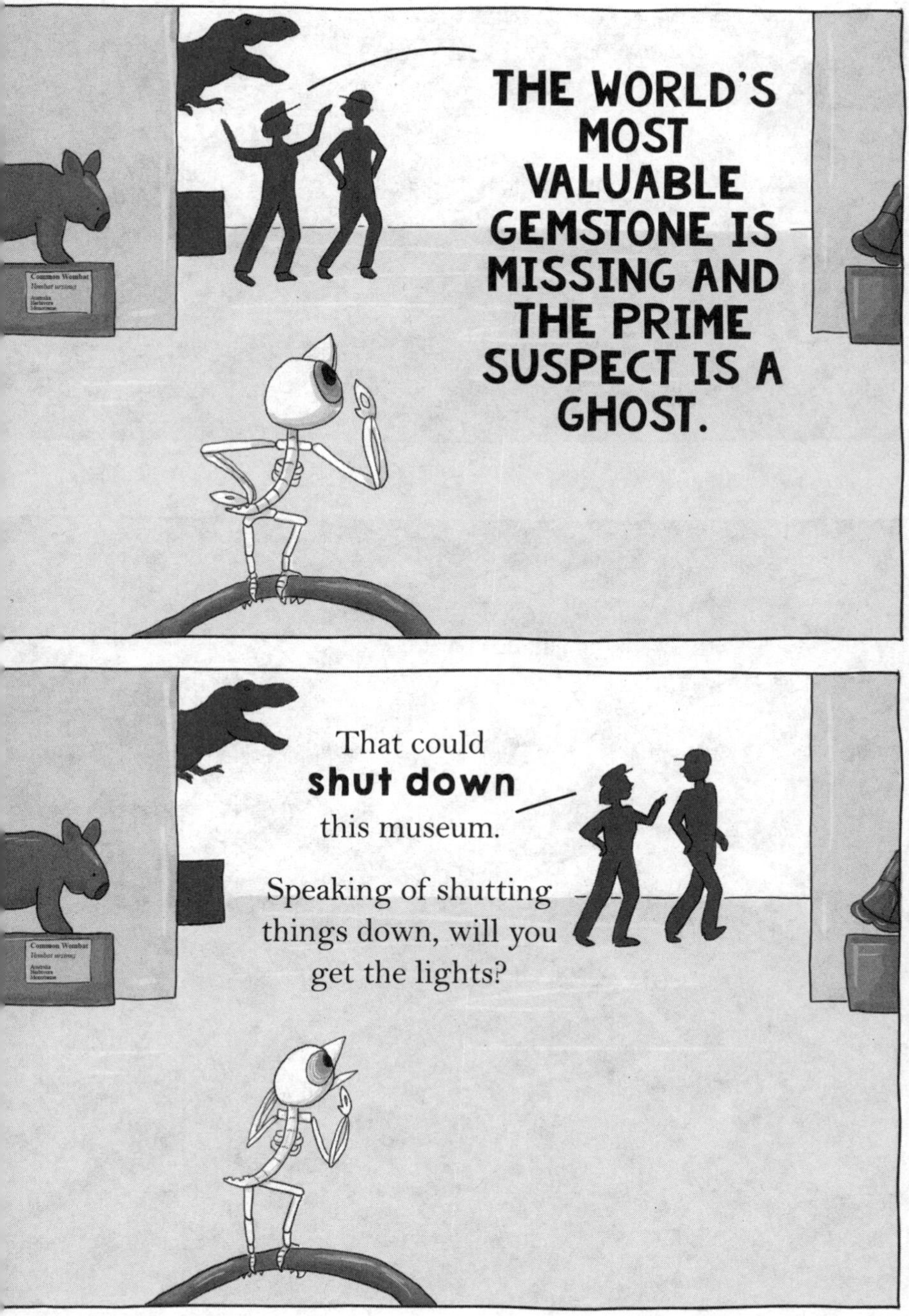
THE WORLD'S MOST VALUABLE GEMSTONE IS MISSING AND THE PRIME SUSPECT IS A GHOST.
That could **shut down** this museum.
Speaking of shutting things down, will you get the lights?

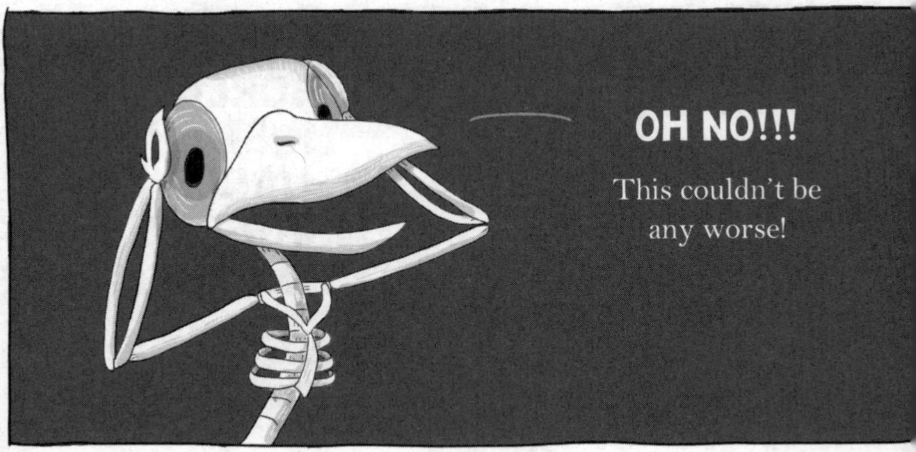
OH NO!!!
This couldn't be any worse!

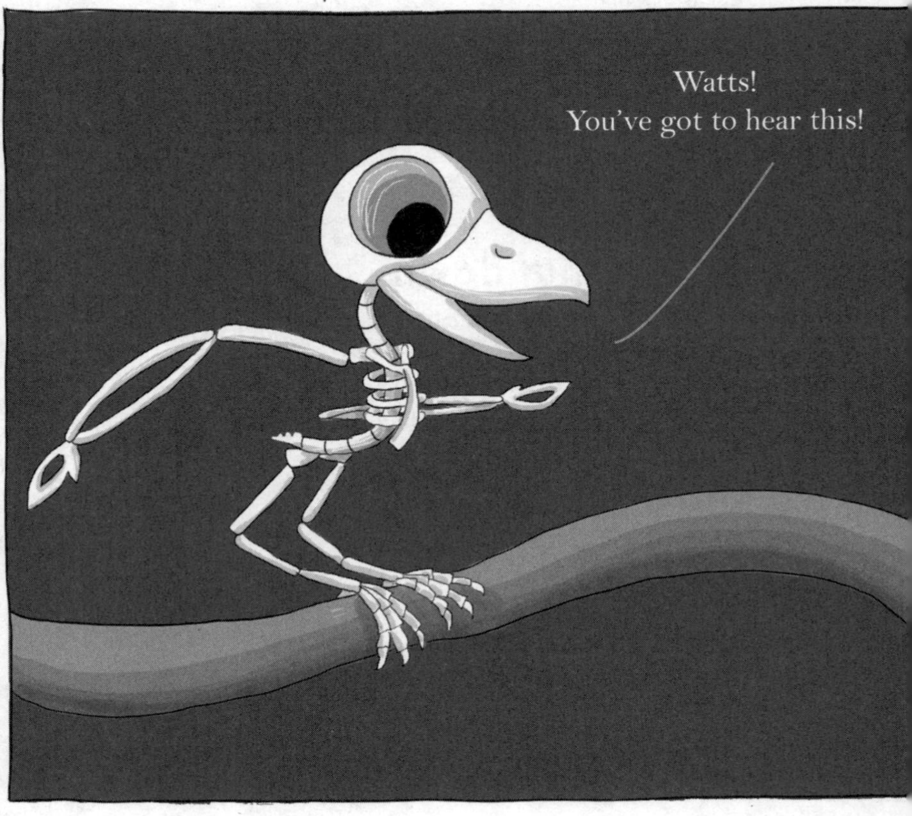
Watts!
You've got to hear this!

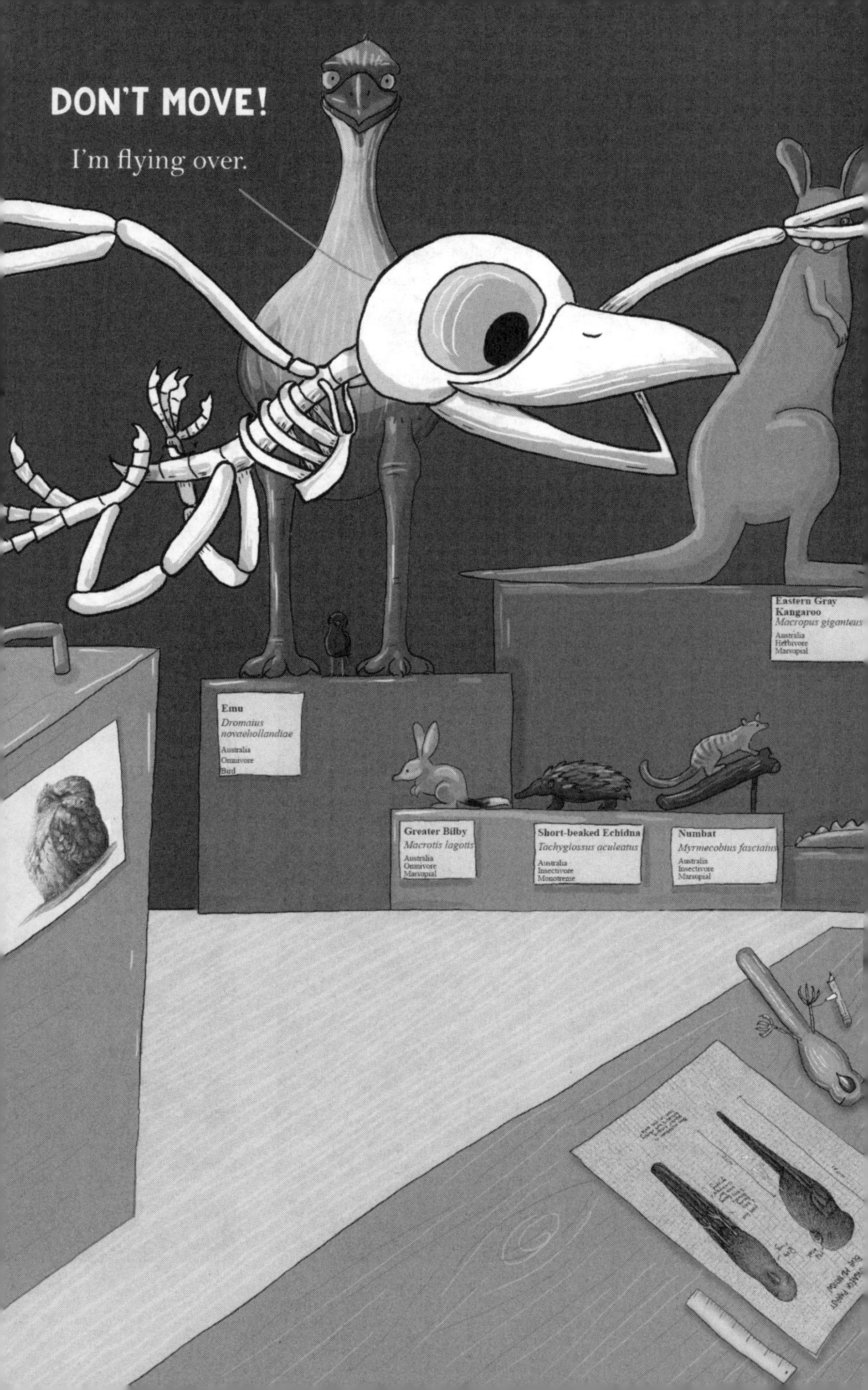
DON'T MOVE!
I'm flying over.
Eastern Gray Kangaroo
Macropus giganteus
Australia
Herbivore
Marsupial
Emu
Dromaius novaehollandiae
Australia
Omnivore
Bird
Greater Bilby
Macrotis lagotis
Australia
Omnivore
Marsupial
Short-beaked Echidna
Tachyglossus aculeatus
Australia
Insectivore
Monotreme
Numbat
Myrmecobius fasciatus
Australia
Insectivore
Marsupial

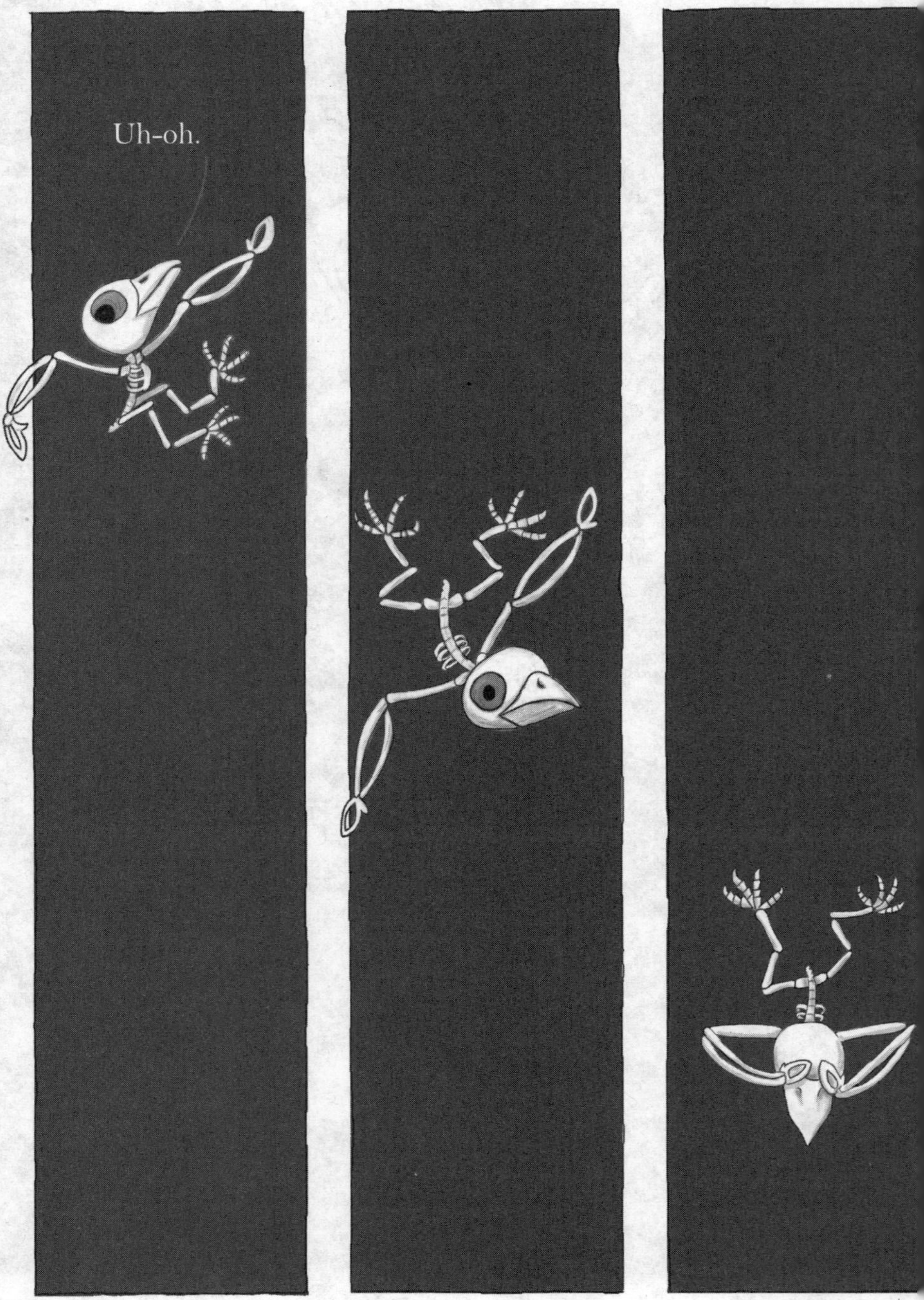
Uh-oh.

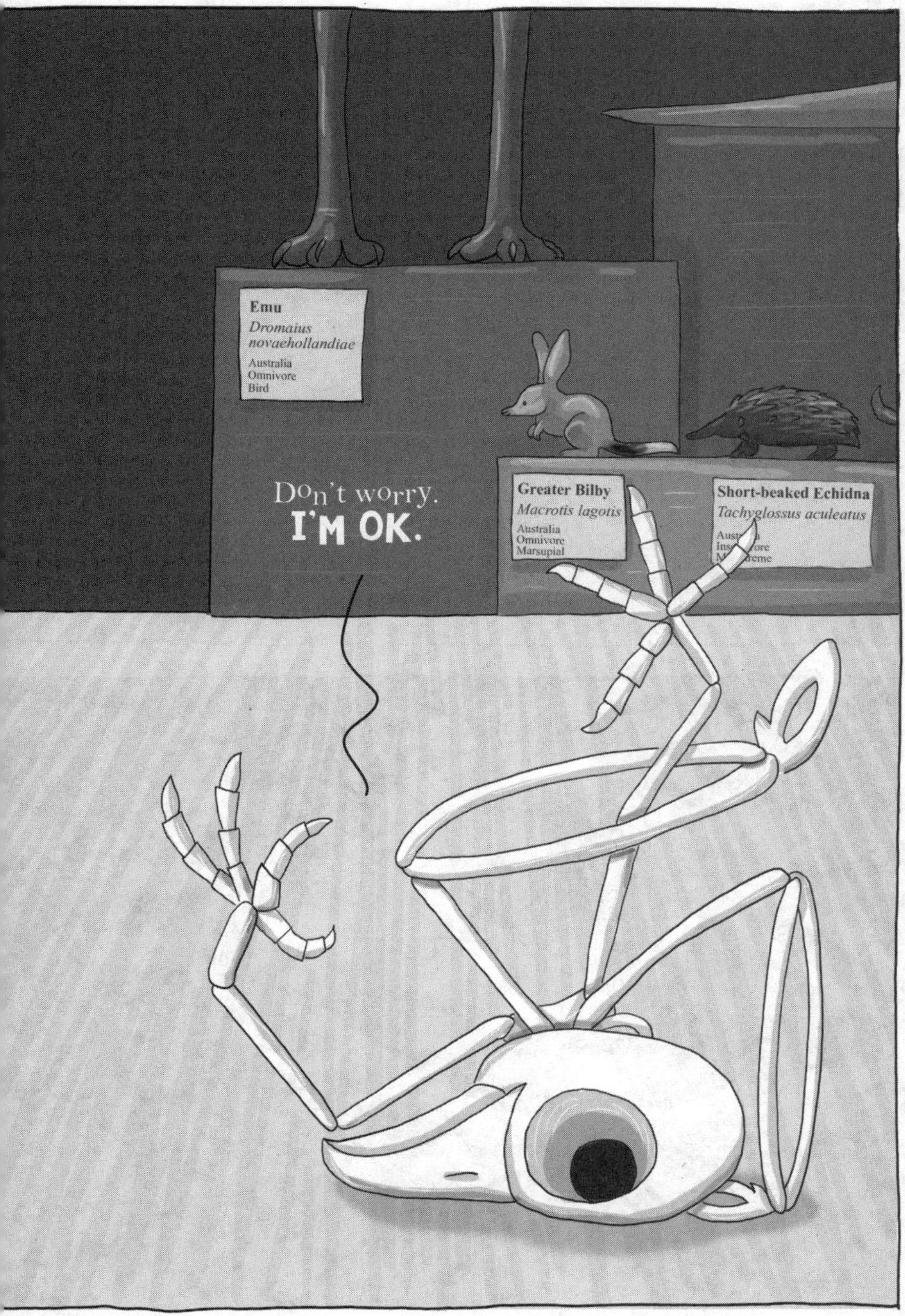
Emu
Dromaius novaehollandiae
Australia
Omnivore
Bird
Greater Bilby
Macrotis lagotis
Australia
Omnivore
Marsupial
Short-beaked Echidna
Tachyglossus aculeatus
Don't worry.
I'M OK.

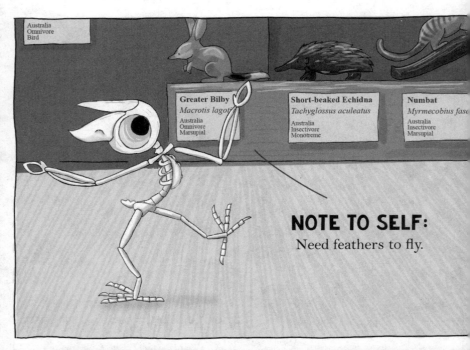

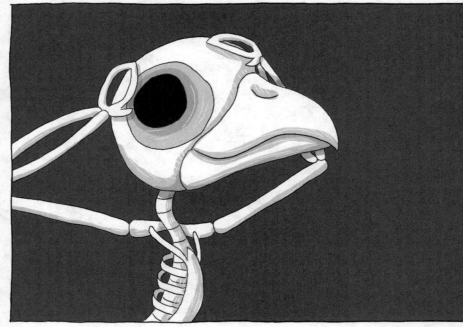

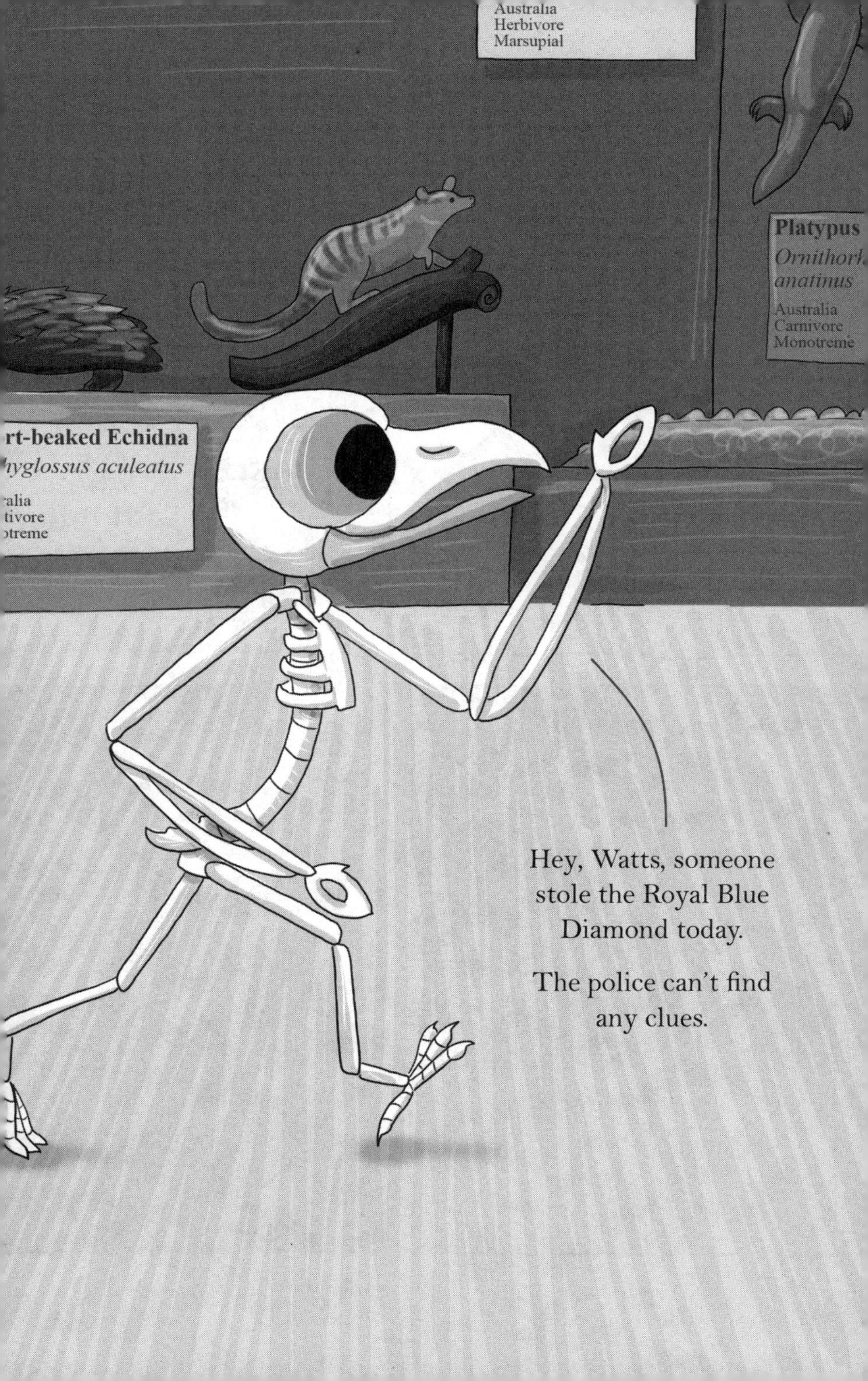
Australia
Herbivore
Marsupial
Platypus
Ornithorh
anatinus
Australia
Carnivore
Monotreme
rt-beaked Echidna
hyglossus aculeatus
Hey, Watts, someone stole the Royal Blue Diamond today.
The police can't find any clues.

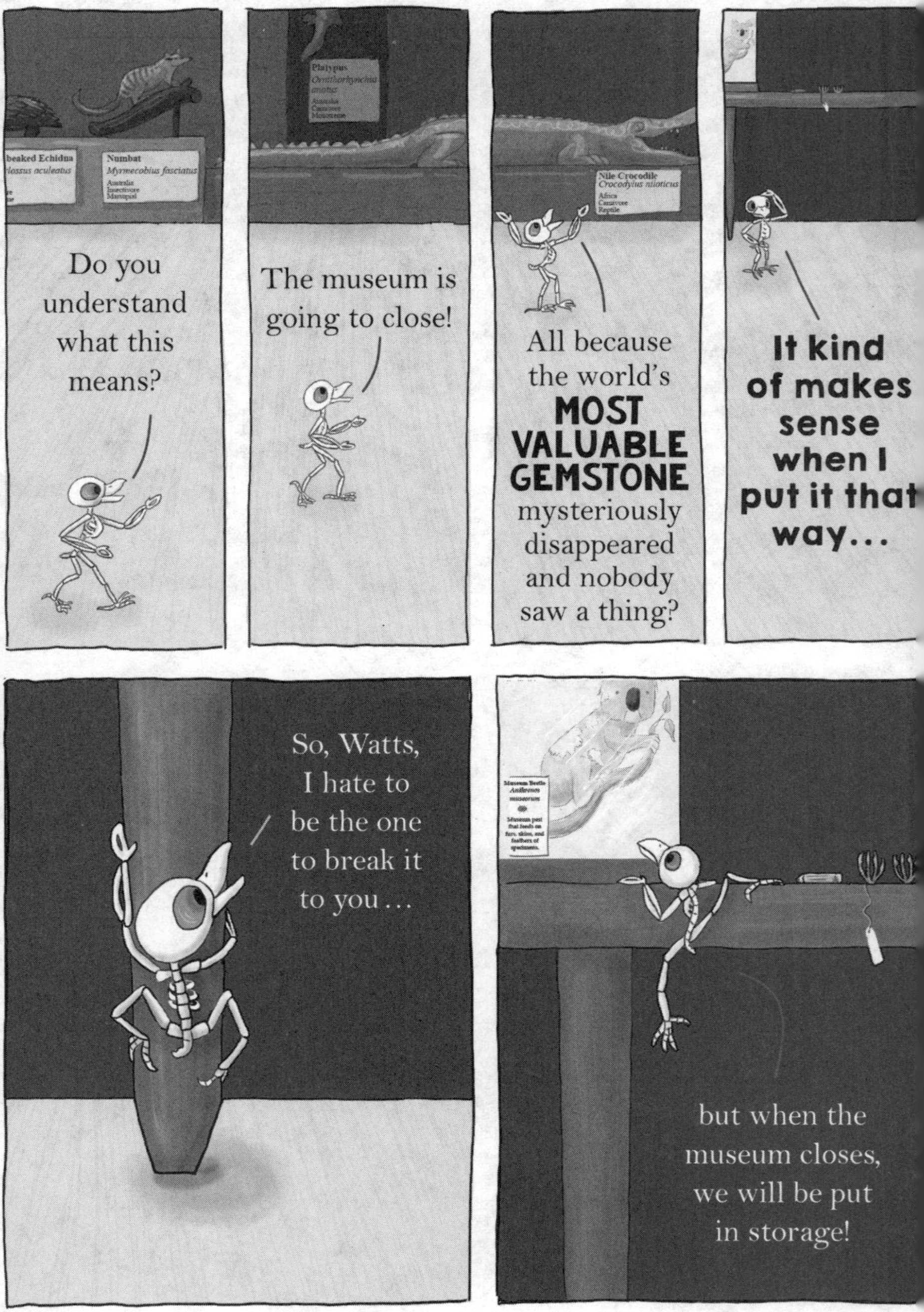
Numbat
Myrmecobius fasciatus
Do you understand what this means?
Platypus
The museum is going to close!
Nile Crocodile
Crocodylus niloticus
All because the world's **MOST VALUABLE GEMSTONE** mysteriously disappeared and nobody saw a thing?
It kind of makes sense when I put it that way...
So, Watts, I hate to be the one to break it to you...
but when the museum closes, we will be put in storage!

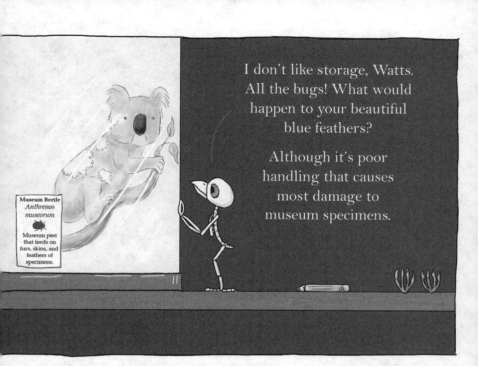

Museum Beetle
*Anthrenos
museorum*

Museum pest
that feeds on
furs, skins, and
feathers of
specimens.

I don't like storage, Watts. All the bugs! What would happen to your beautiful blue feathers?

Although it's poor handling that causes most damage to museum specimens.

I hope we get a really good packer.

But regardless, we would still be together, right, Watts?

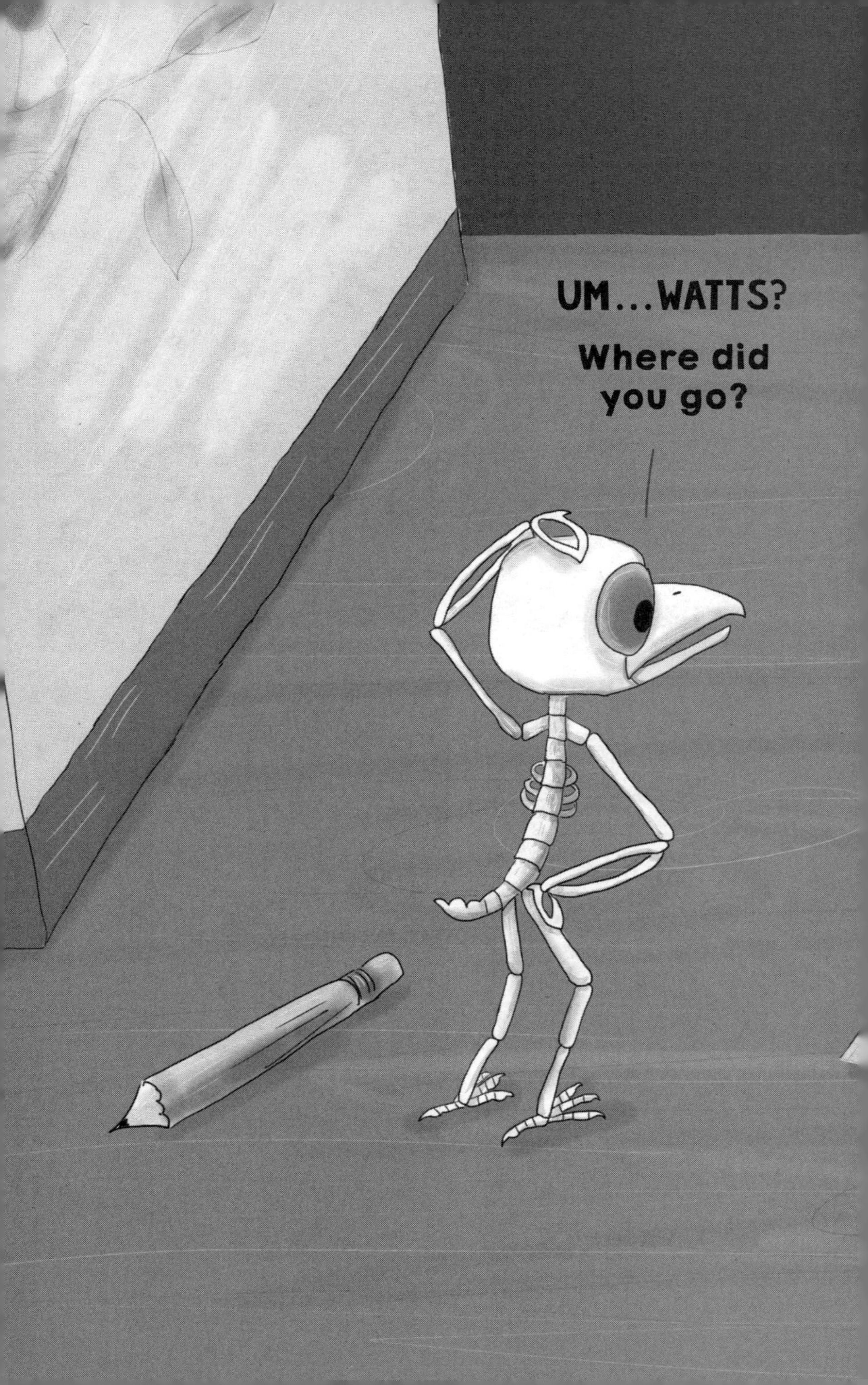
UM...WATTS?
Where did you go?

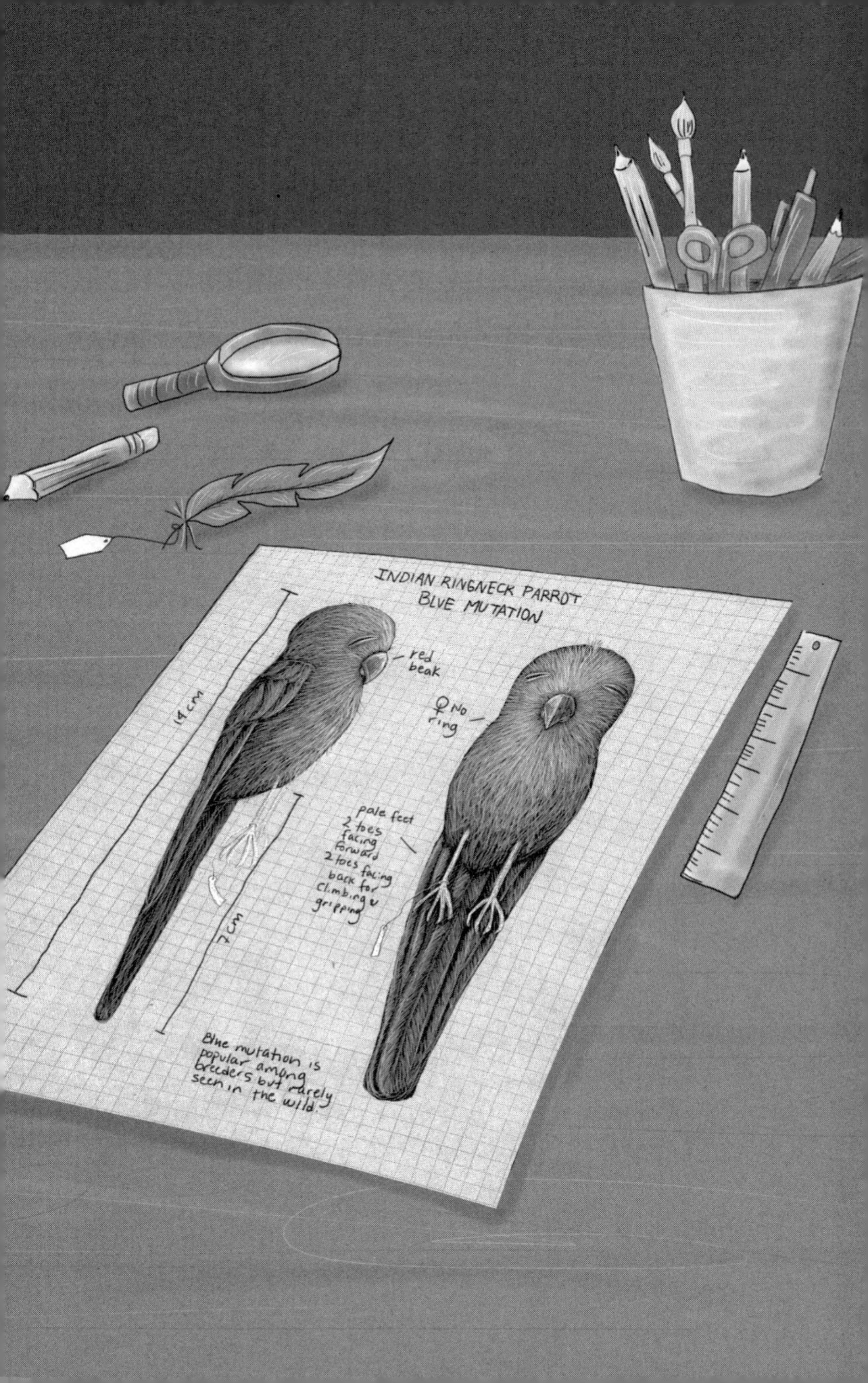
INDIAN RINGNECK PARROT
BLUE MUTATION
red beak
14cm
♀ No ring
pale feet
2 toes facing forward
2 toes facing back for climbing & gripping
7cm
Blue mutation is popular among breeders but rarely seen in the wild.

CHAPTER 2
A Bit of Fluff

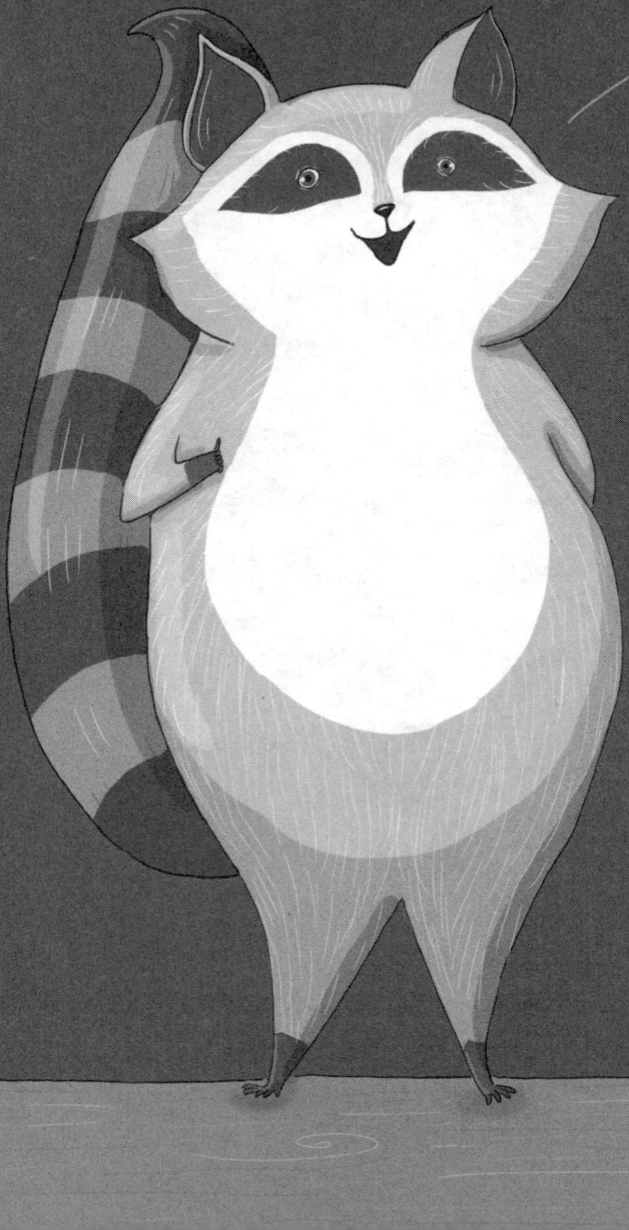

Well, how-dee-do and nice to meet you.

I'm Grace.

I'm not from around here.

In fact, I don't even know where I am, but it is so great to have somebody to talk to.

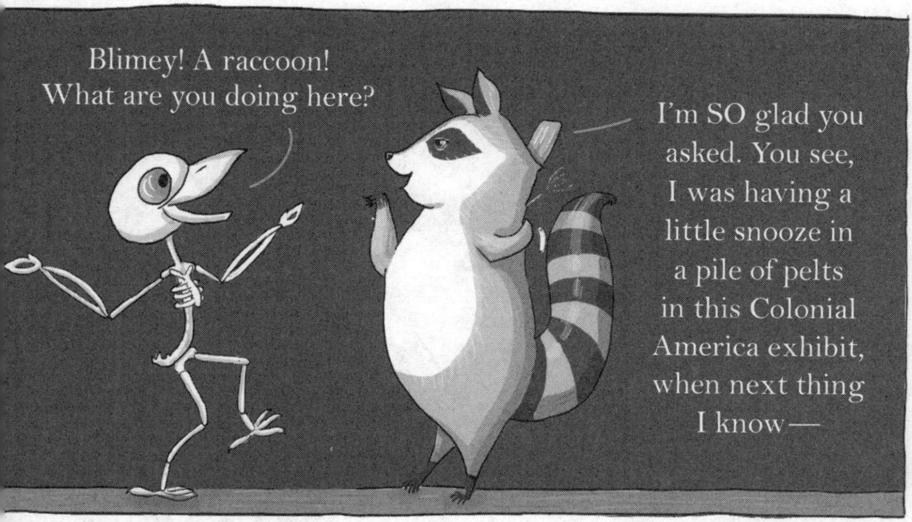
Blimey! A raccoon!
What are you doing here?
I'm SO glad you asked. You see, I was having a little snooze in a pile of pelts in this Colonial America exhibit, when next thing I know—

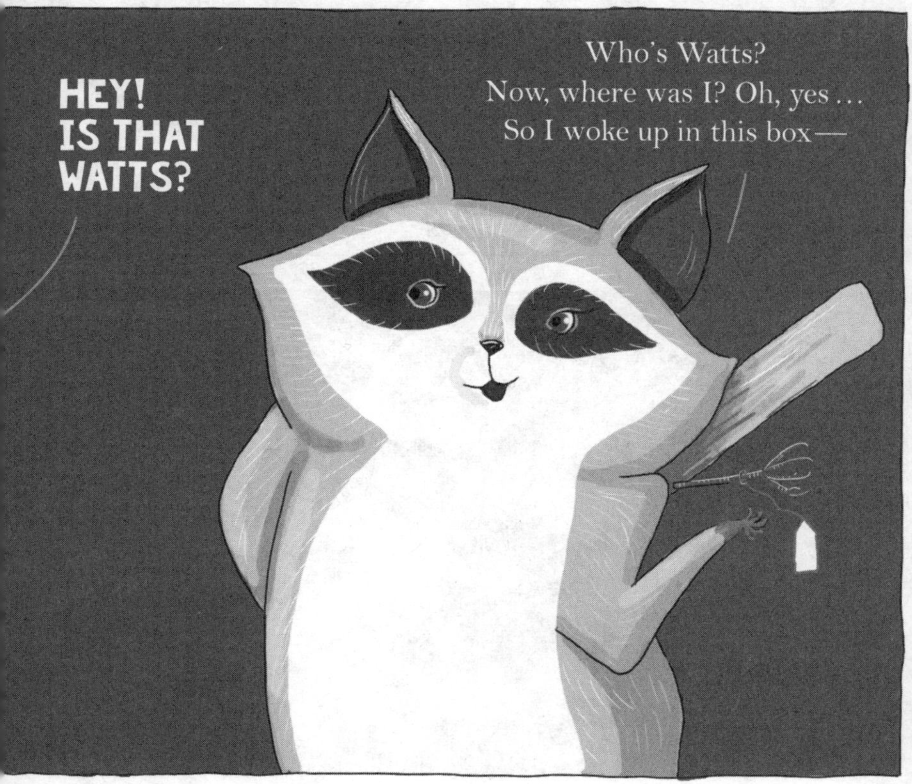
HEY! IS THAT WATTS?
Who's Watts?
Now, where was I? Oh, yes . . .
So I woke up in this box—

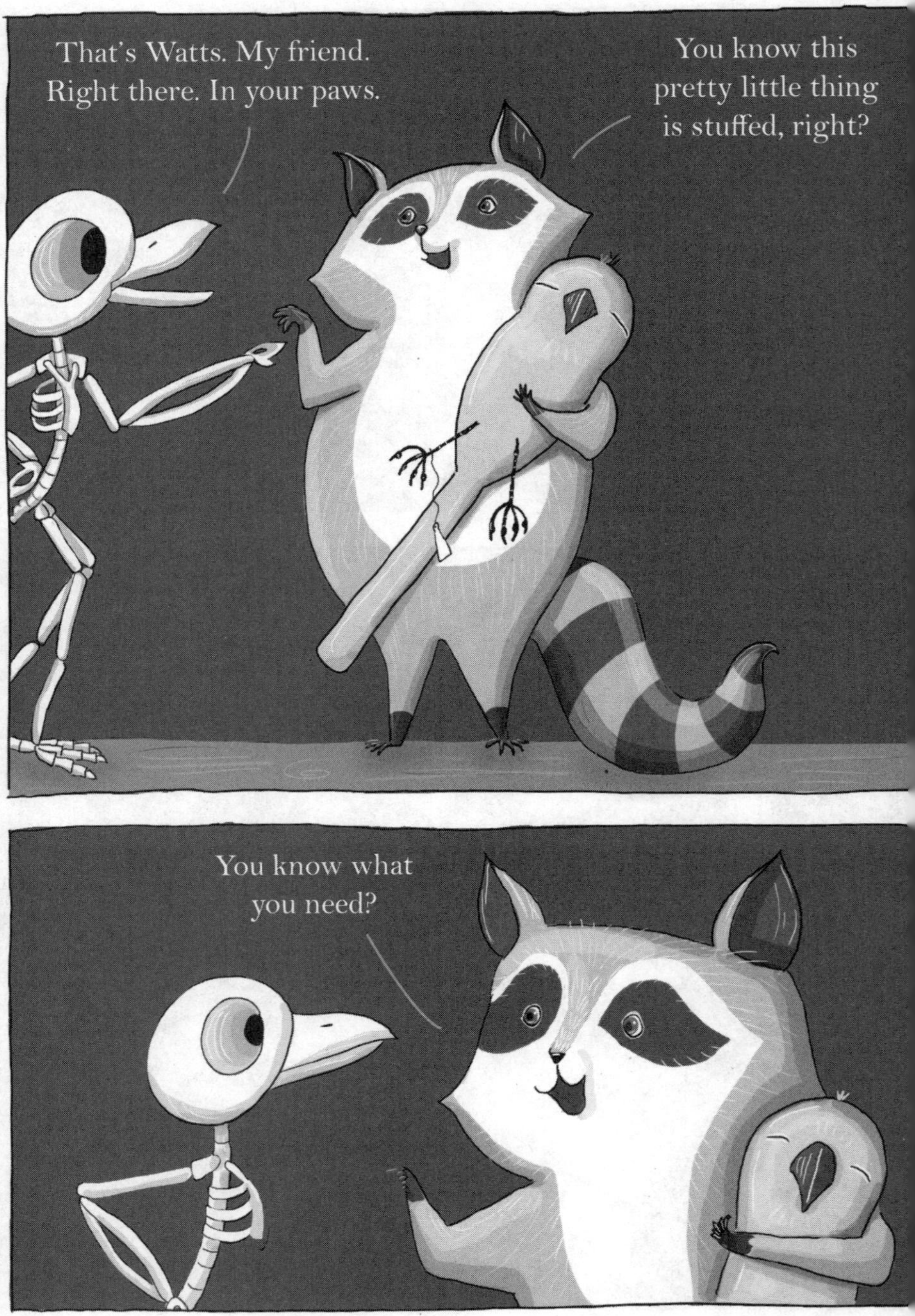
That's Watts. My friend.
Right there. In your paws.
You know this pretty little thing is stuffed, right?
You know what you need?

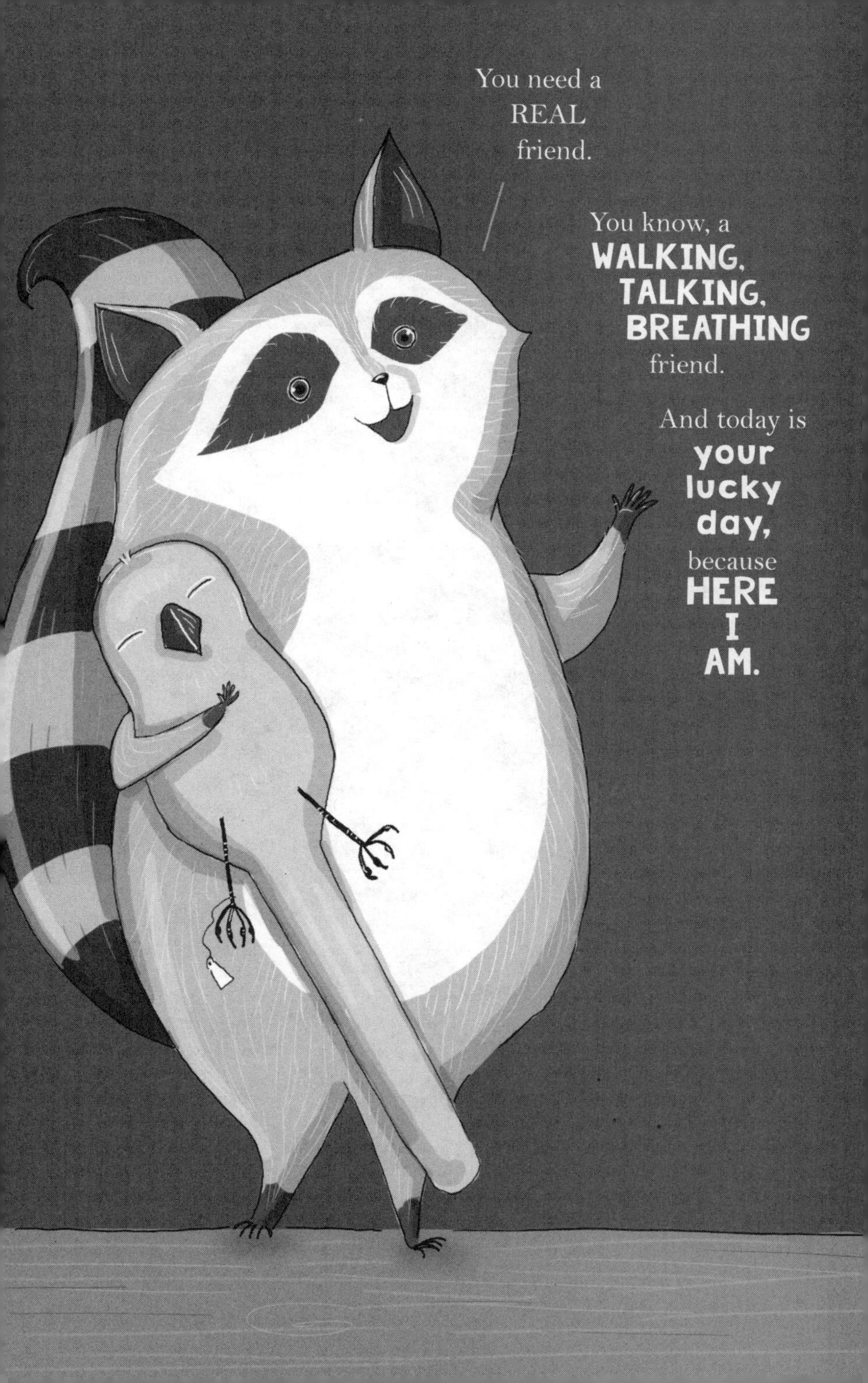
You need a REAL friend.
You know, a **WALKING, TALKING, BREATHING** friend.
And today is **your lucky day,** because **HERE I AM.**

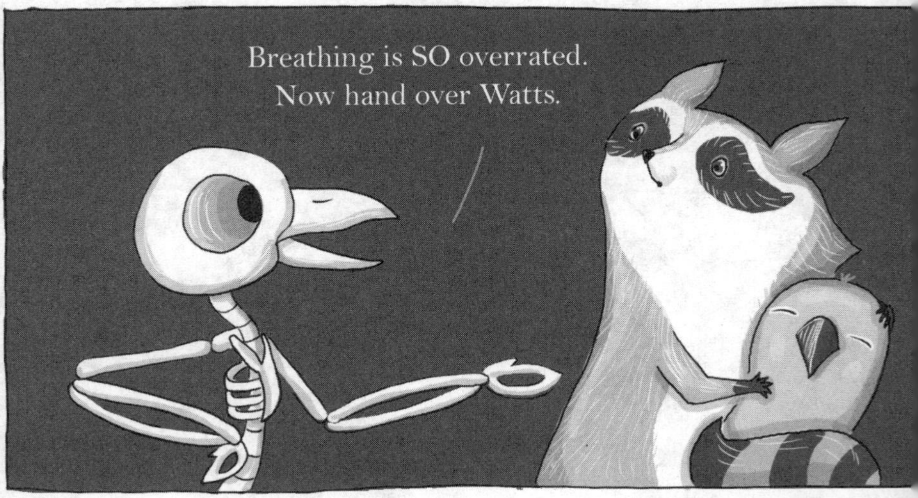
Breathing is SO overrated.
Now hand over Watts.

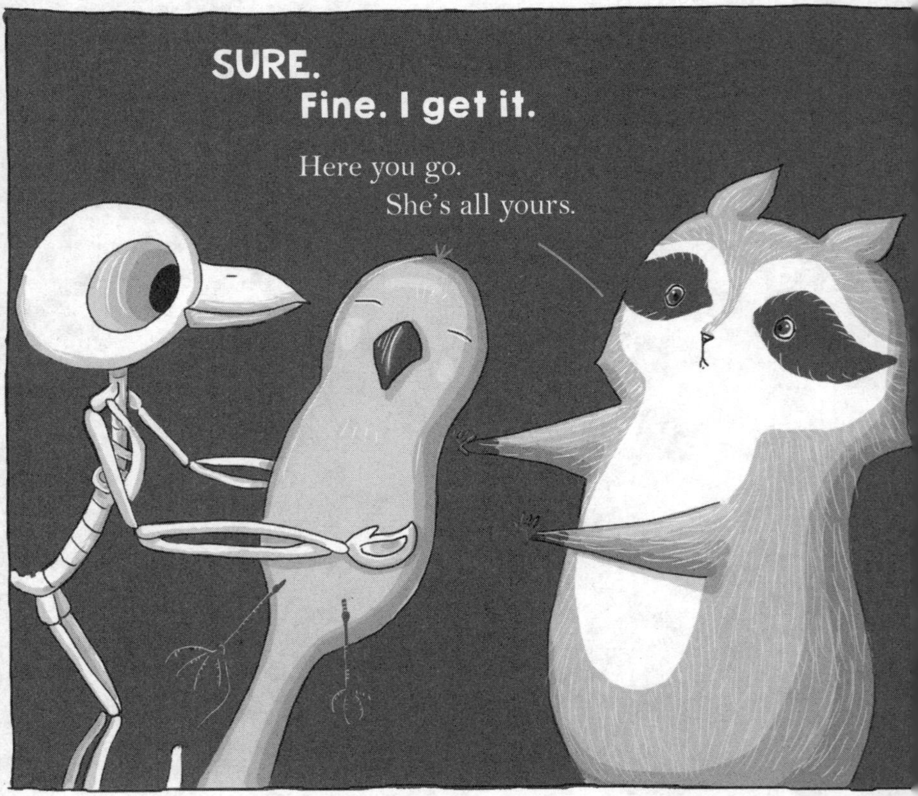
SURE.
Fine. I get it.
Here you go.
She's all yours.

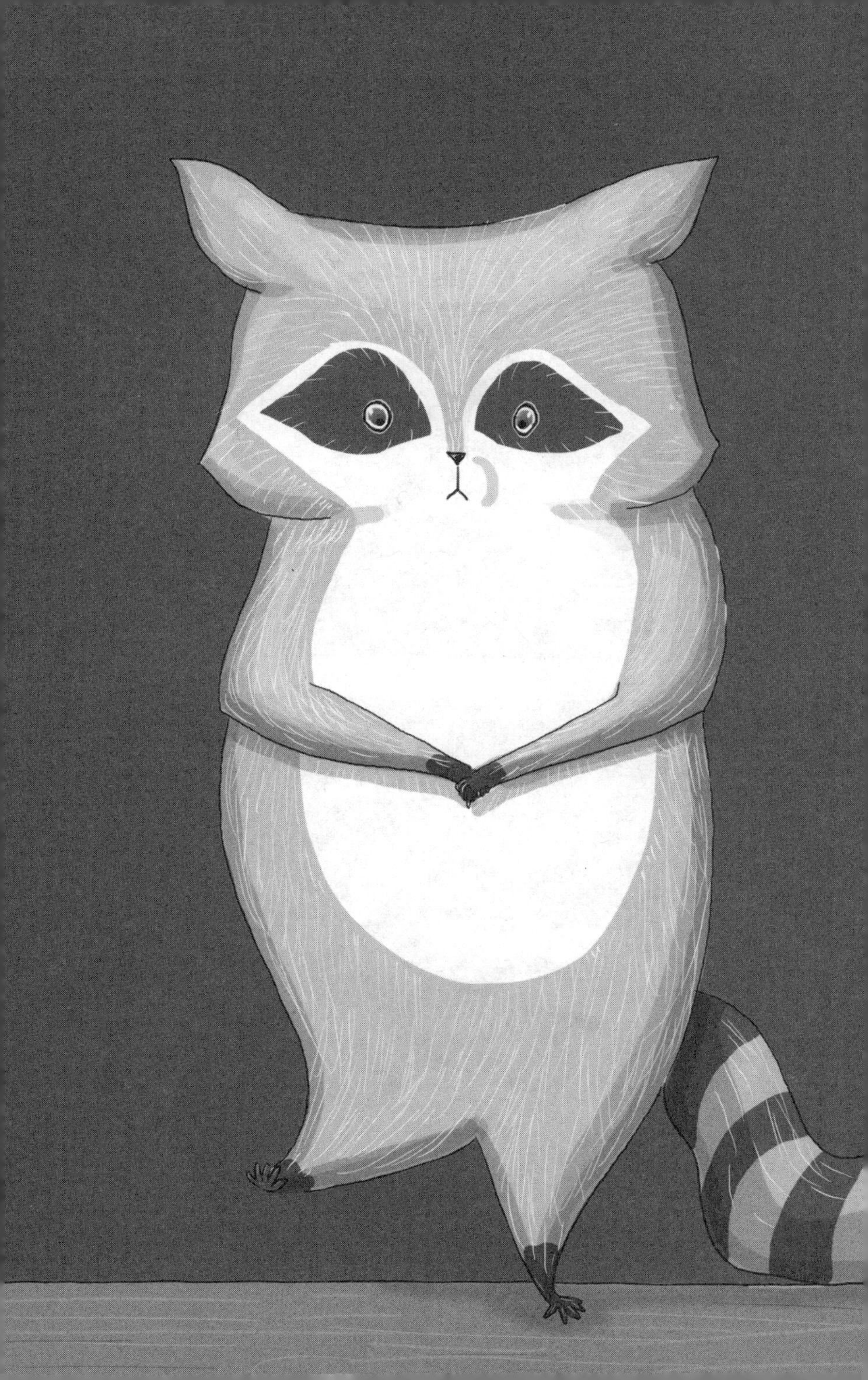

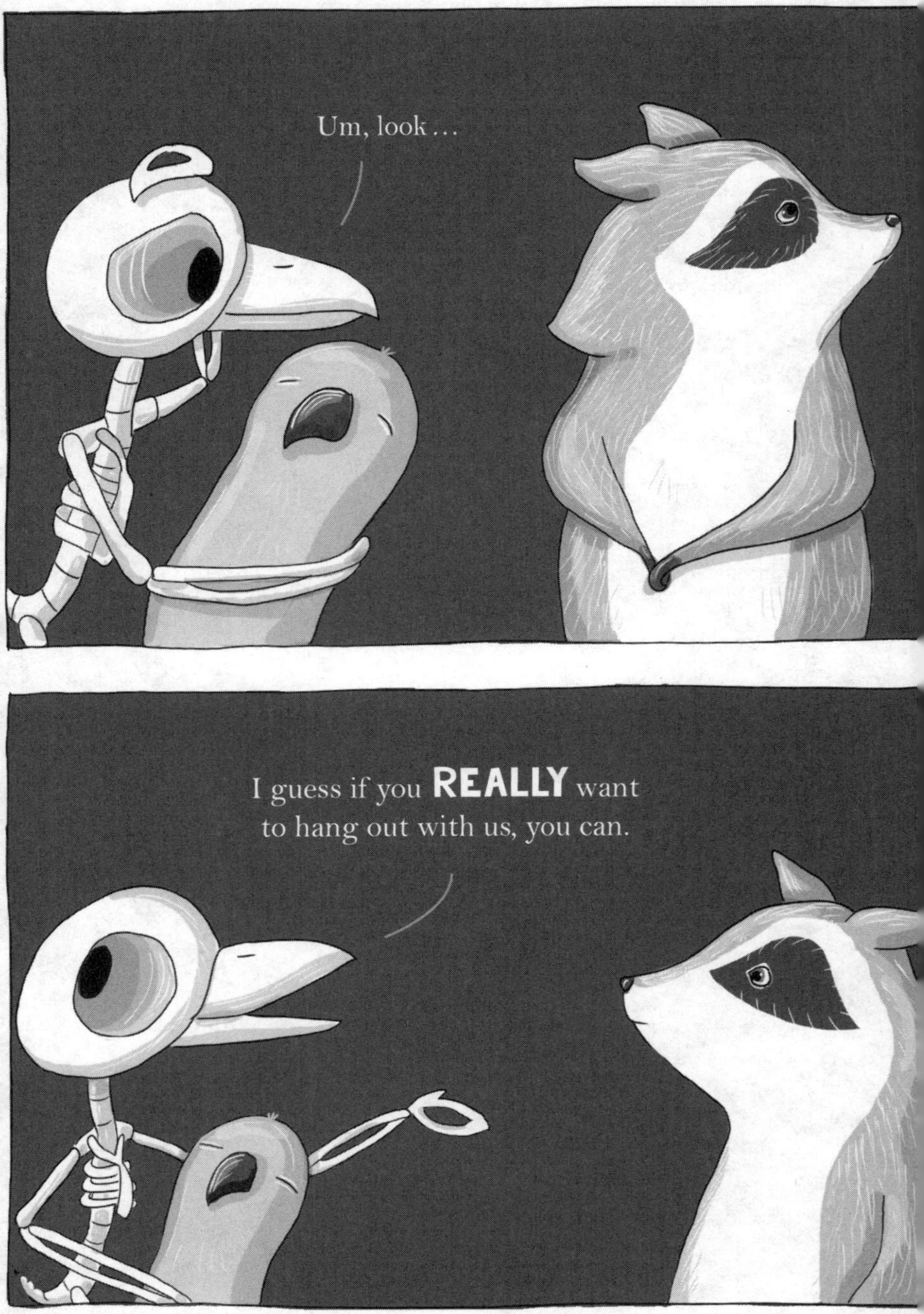
Um, look . . .
I guess if you **REALLY** want to hang out with us, you can.

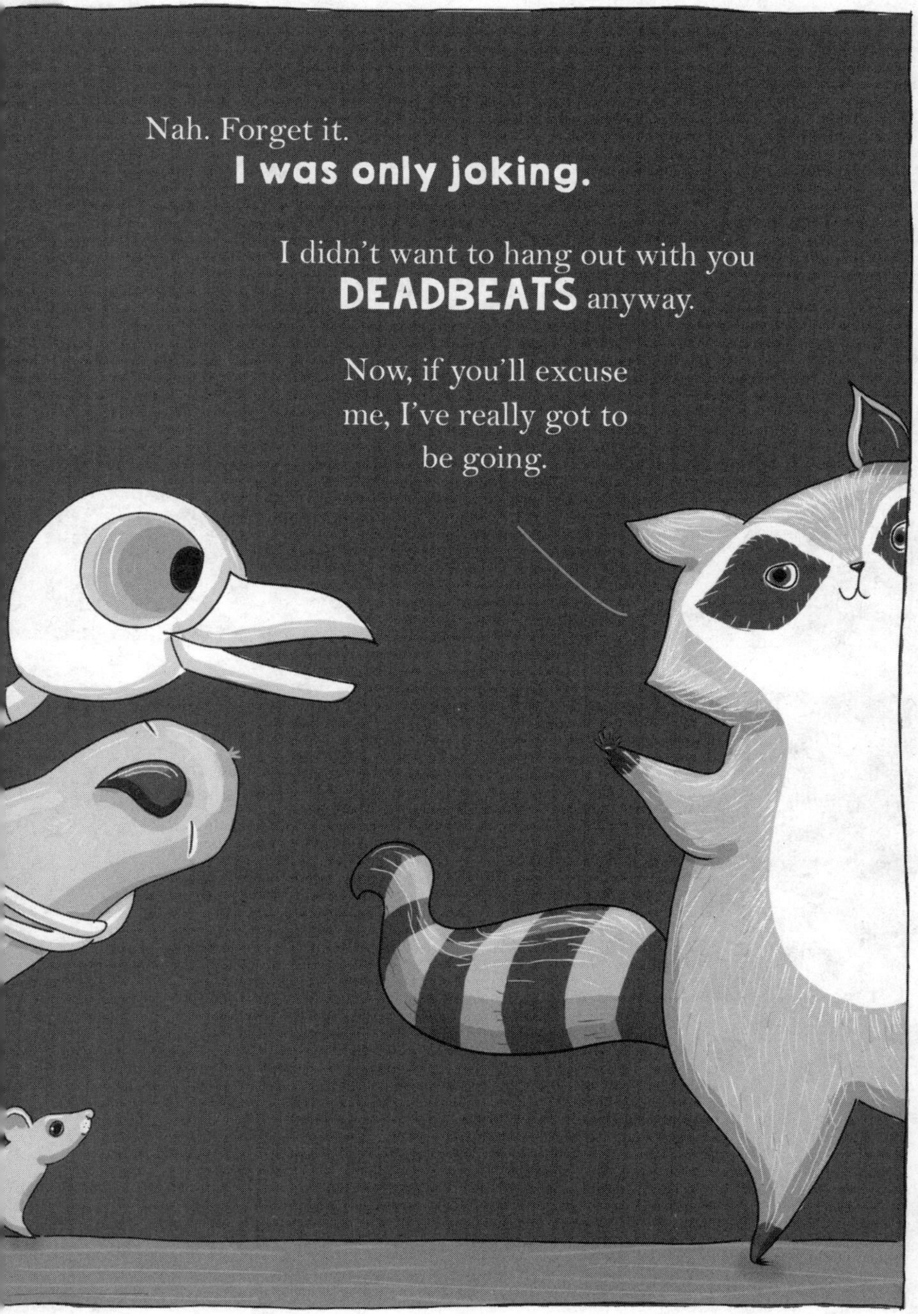
Nah. Forget it.
I was only joking.
I didn't want to hang out with you DEADBEATS anyway.
Now, if you'll excuse me, I've really got to be going.

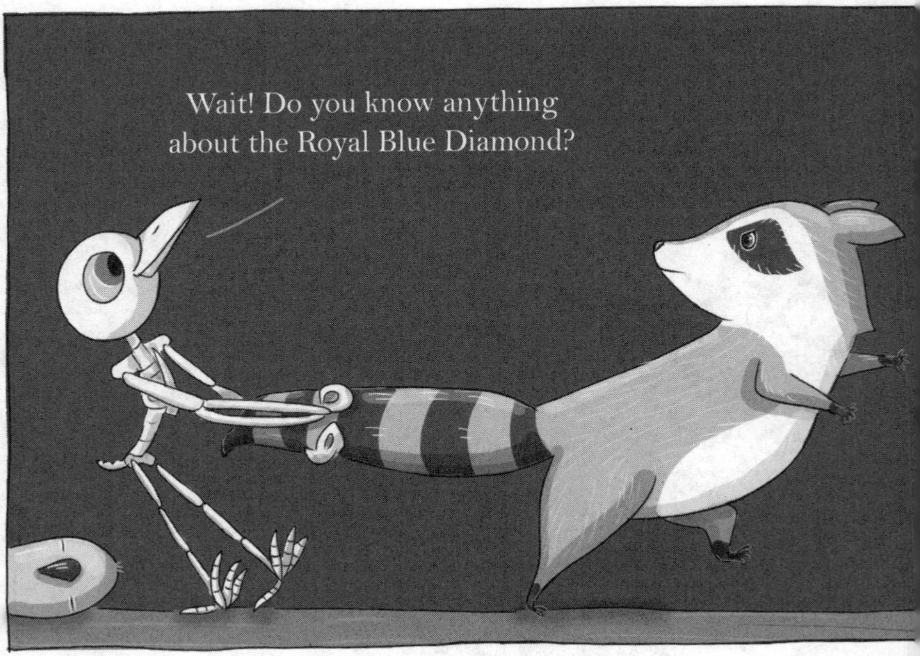
Wait! Do you know anything about the Royal Blue Diamond?

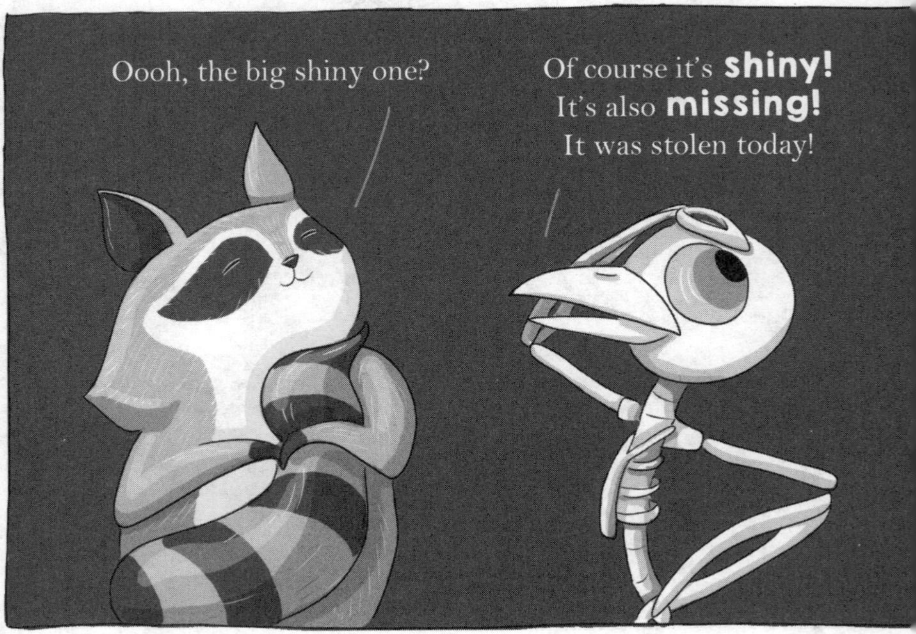
Oooh, the big shiny one?
Of course it's **shiny!** It's also **missing!** It was stolen today!

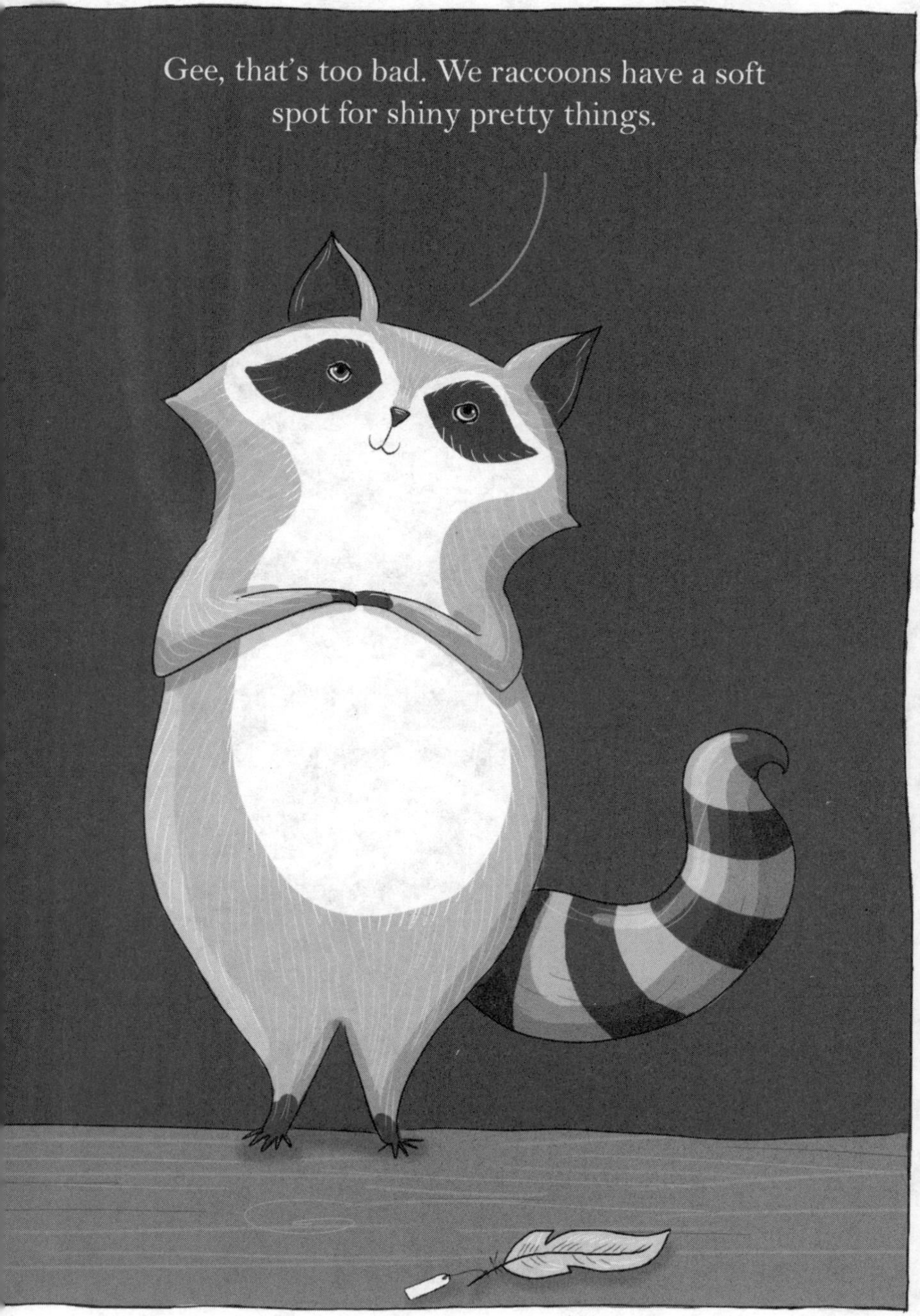
Gee, that's too bad. We raccoons have a soft spot for shiny pretty things.

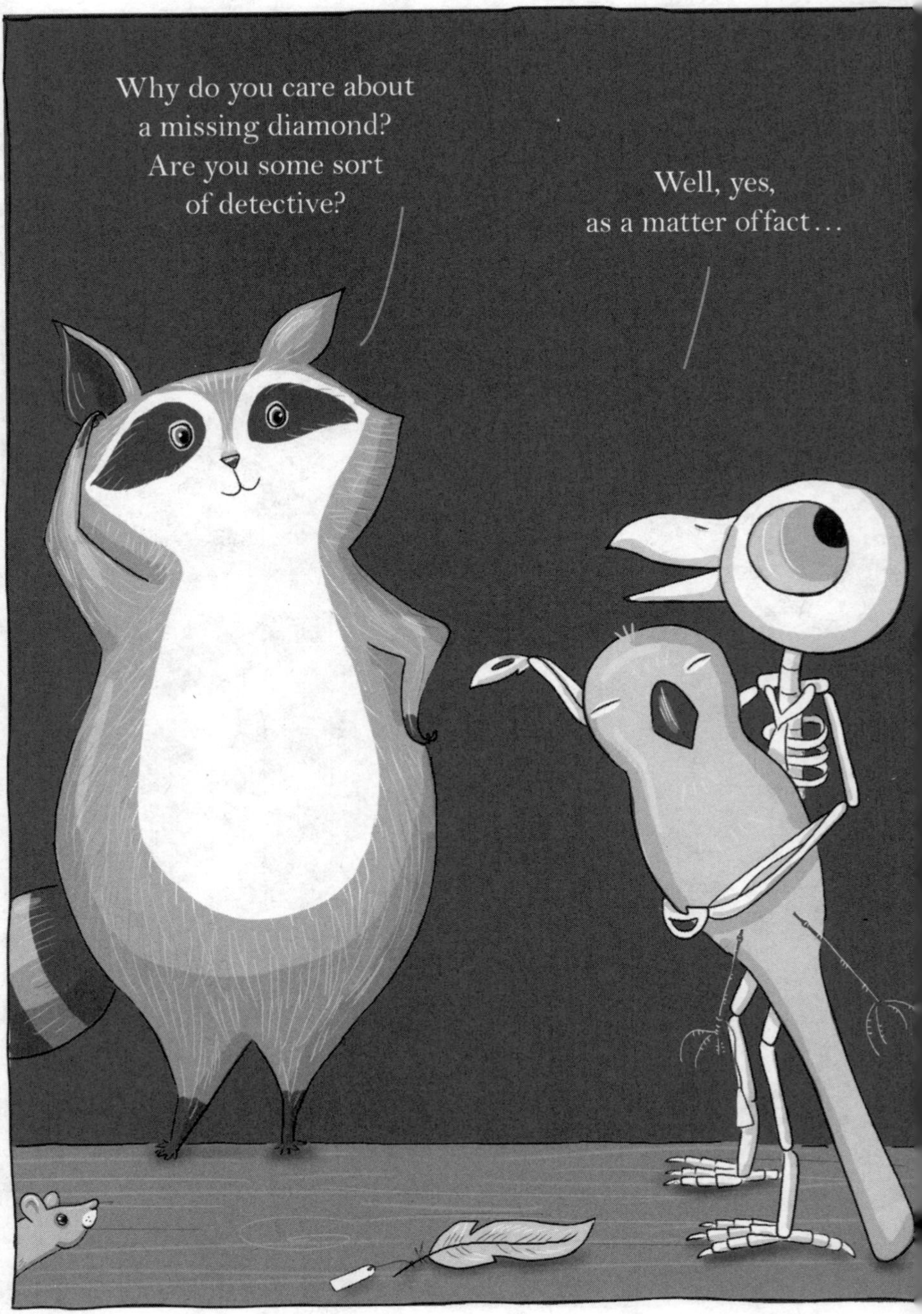
Why do you care about a missing diamond? Are you some sort of detective?
Well, yes, as a matter offact…

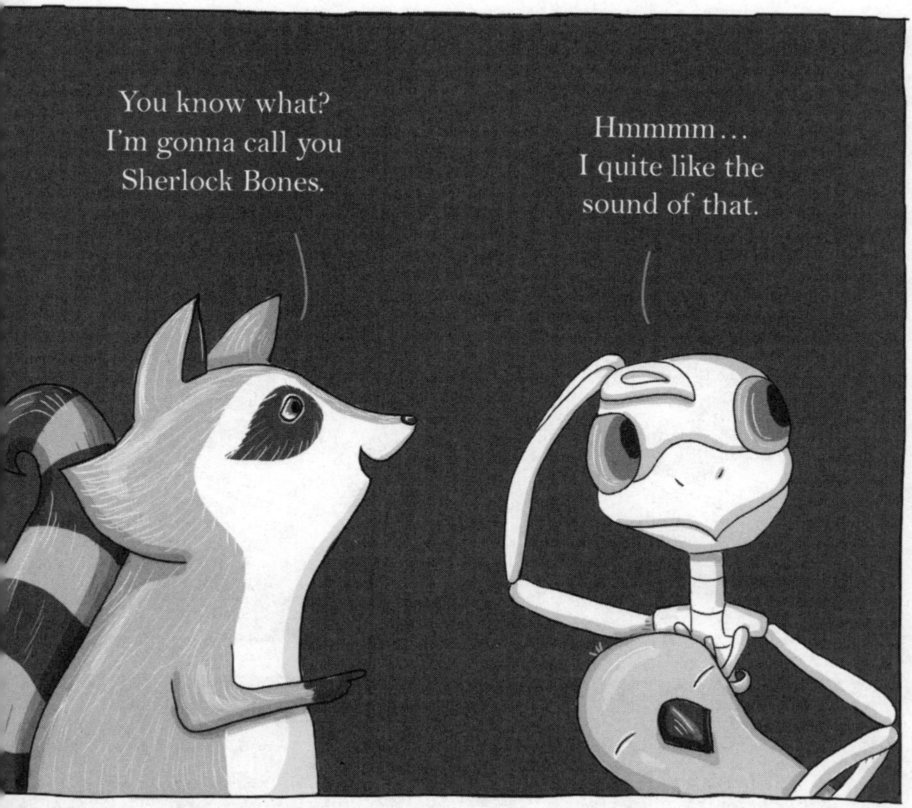
You know what?
I'm gonna call you
Sherlock Bones.
Hmmmm…
I quite like the
sound of that.

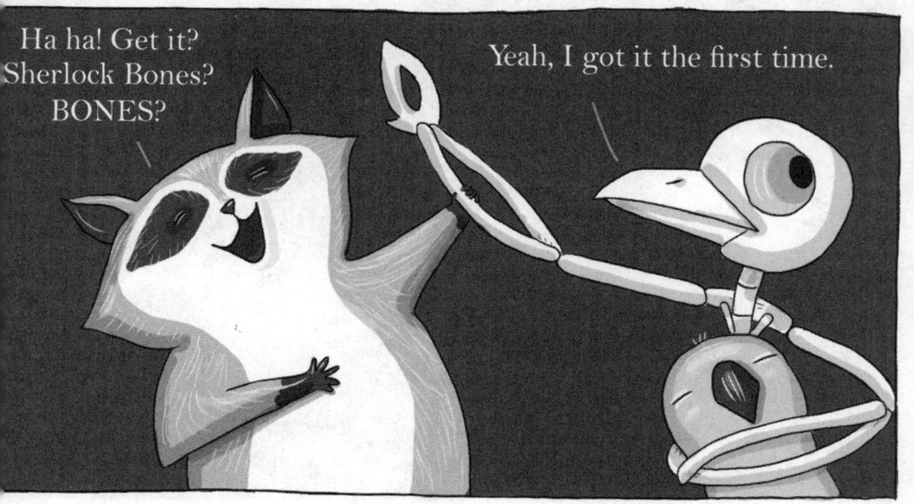
Ha ha! Get it?
Sherlock Bones?
BONES?
Yeah, I got it the first time.

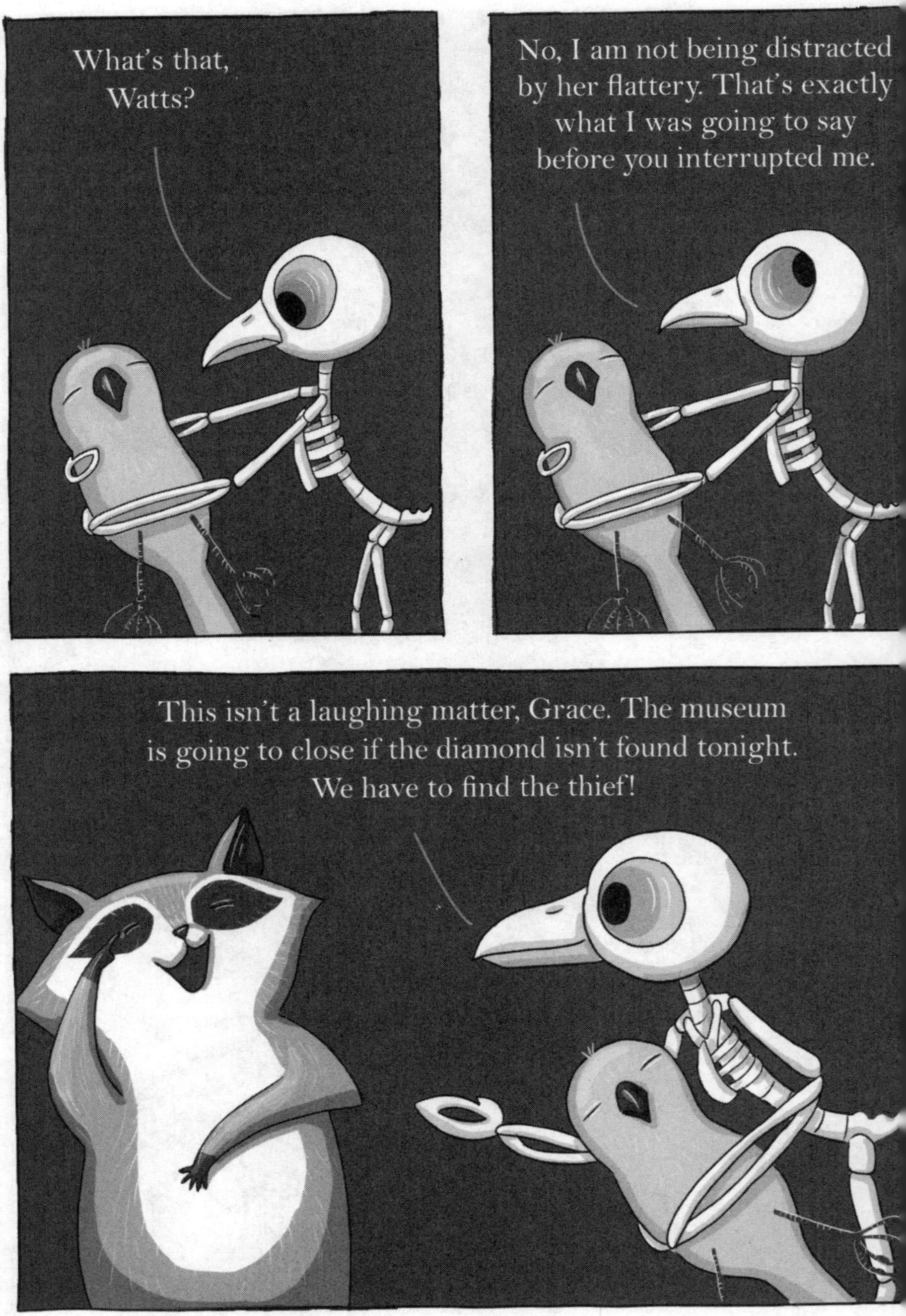
What's that, Watts?
No, I am not being distracted by her flattery. That's exactly what I was going to say before you interrupted me.
This isn't a laughing matter, Grace. The museum is going to close if the diamond isn't found tonight. We have to find the thief!

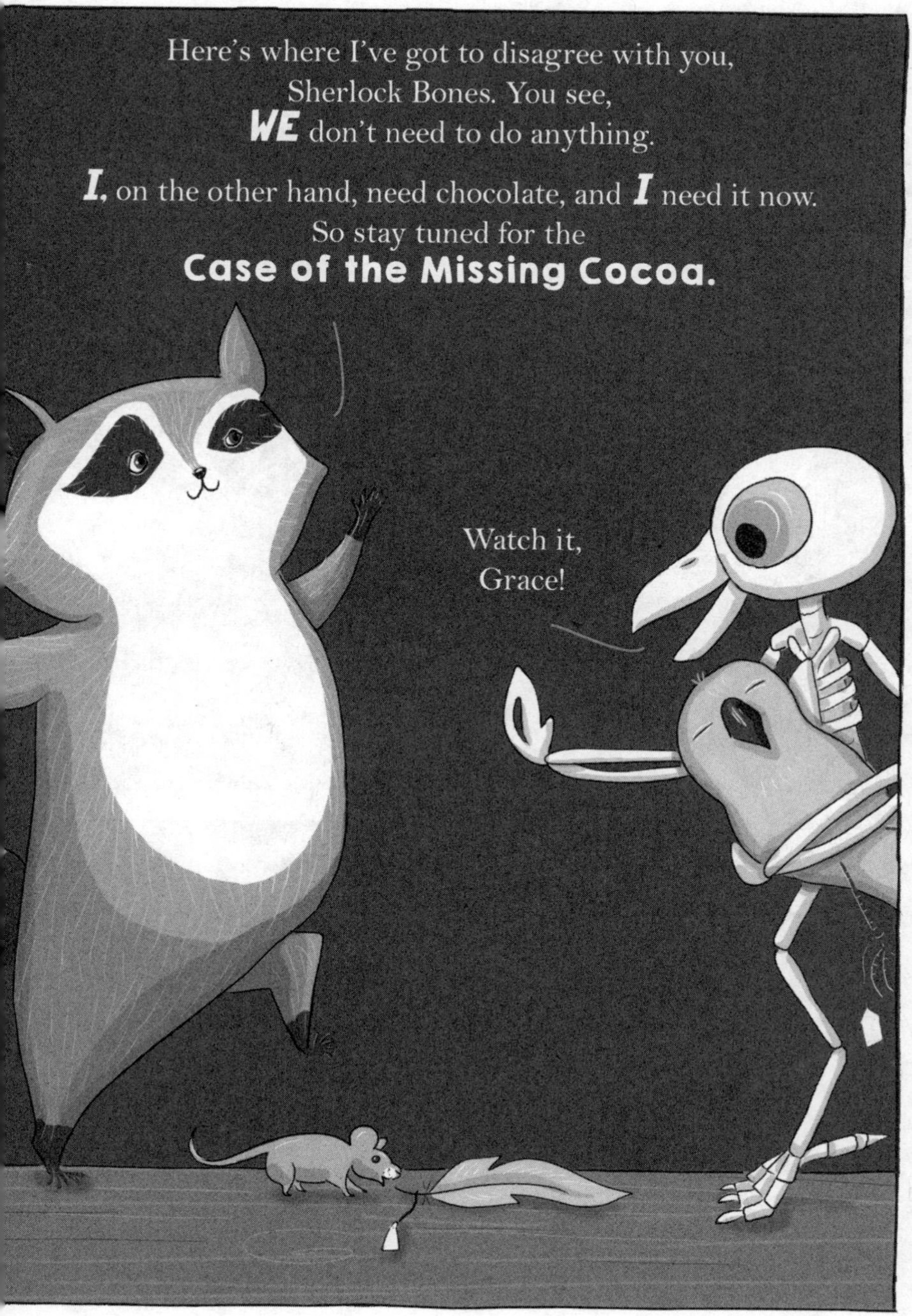
Here's where I've got to disagree with you, Sherlock Bones. You see, WE don't need to do anything.
I, on the other hand, need chocolate, and I need it now. So stay tuned for the
Case of the Missing Cocoa.
Watch it, Grace!

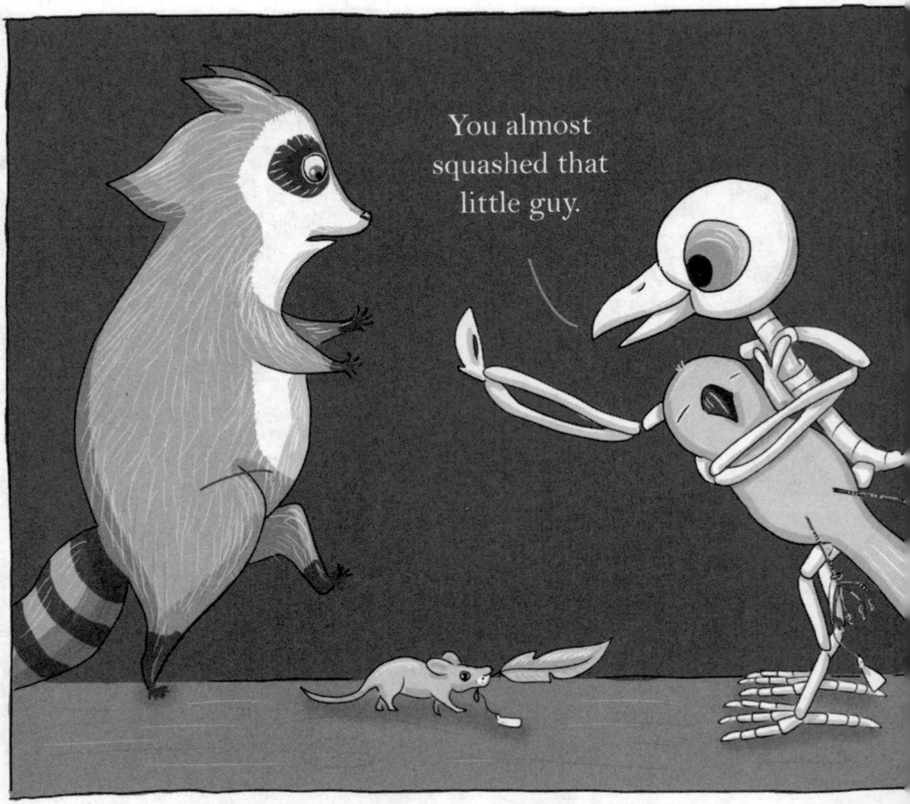
You almost squashed that little guy.

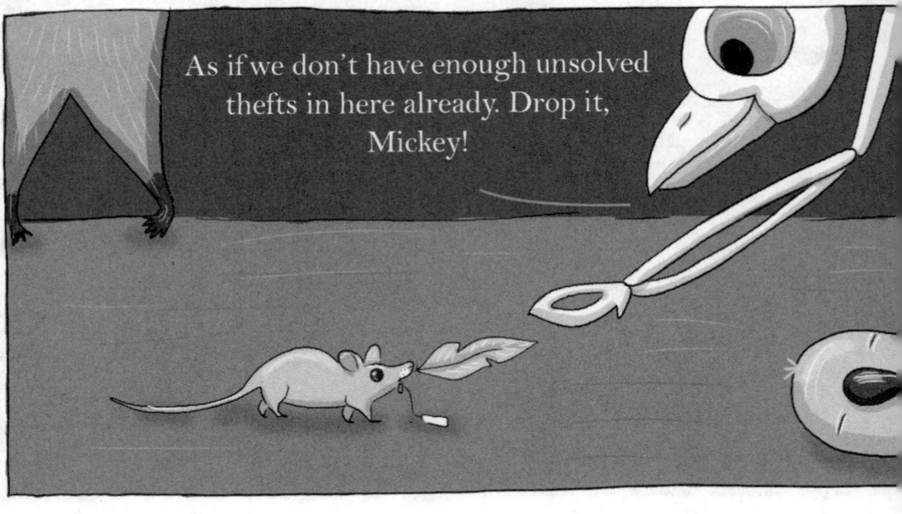
As if we don't have enough unsolved thefts in here already. Drop it, Mickey!

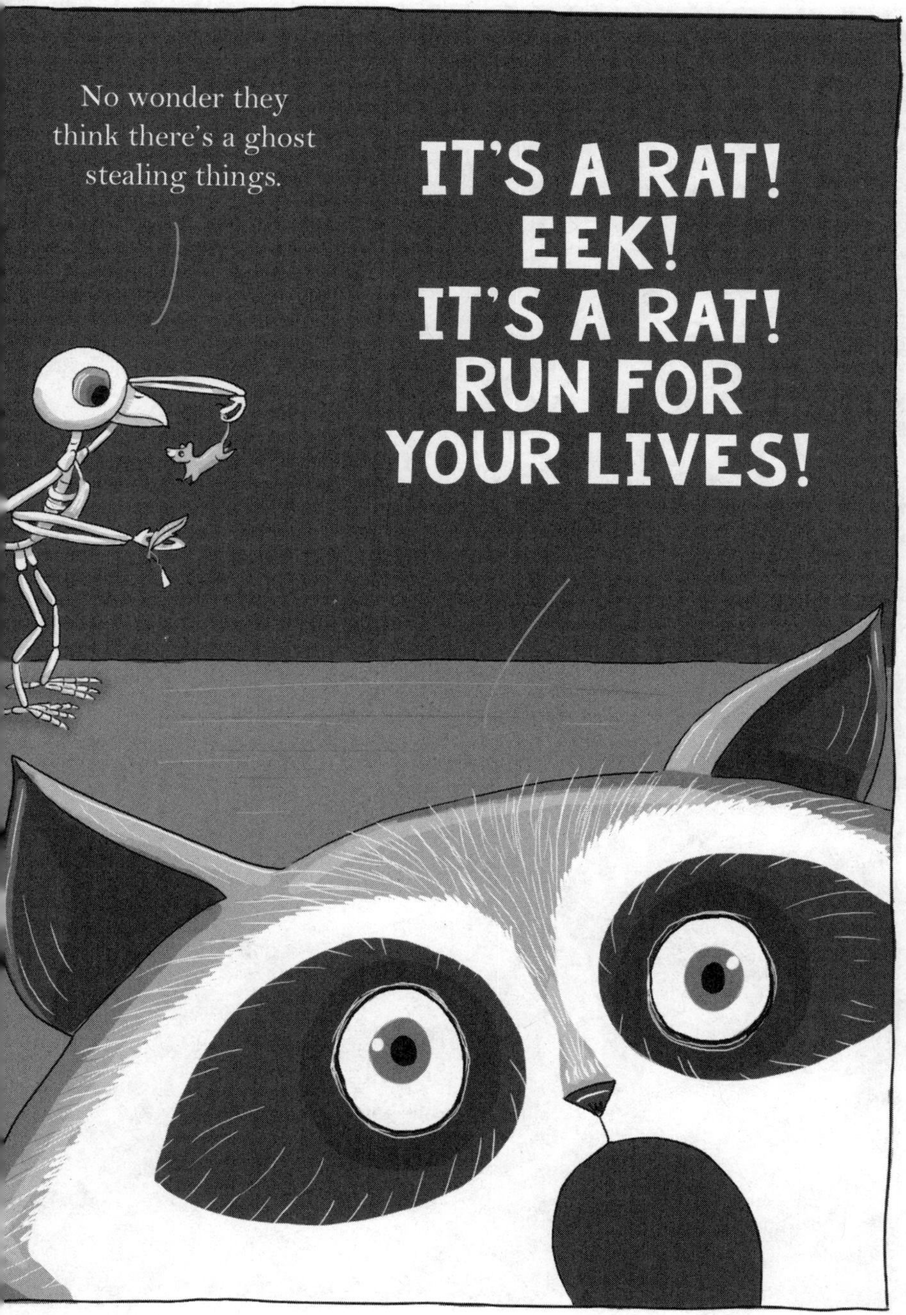
No wonder they think there's a ghost stealing things.
IT'S A RAT! EEK! IT'S A RAT! RUN FOR YOUR LIVES!

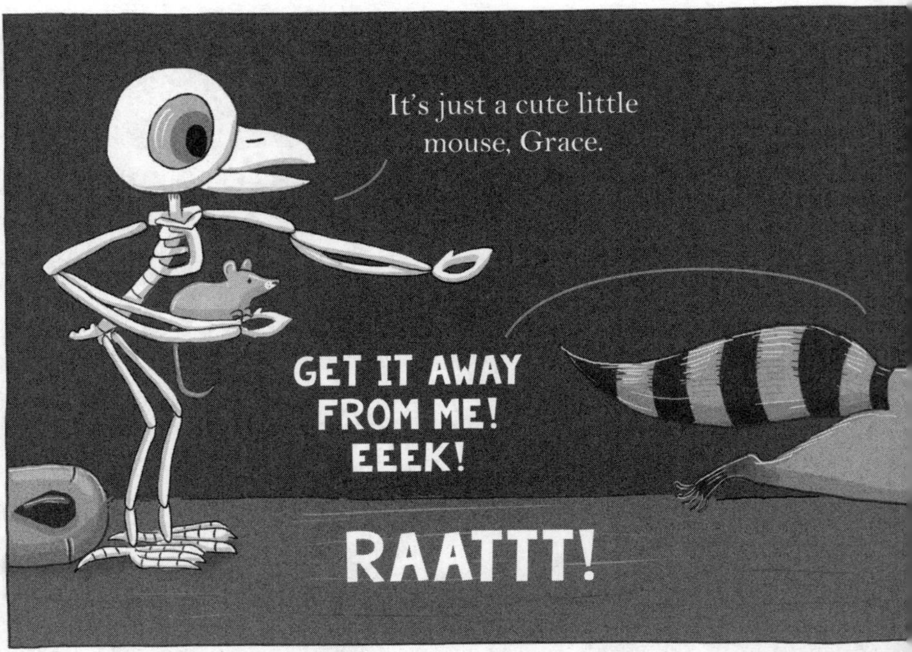
It's just a cute little mouse, Grace.
GET IT AWAY FROM ME! EEEK!
RAATTT!

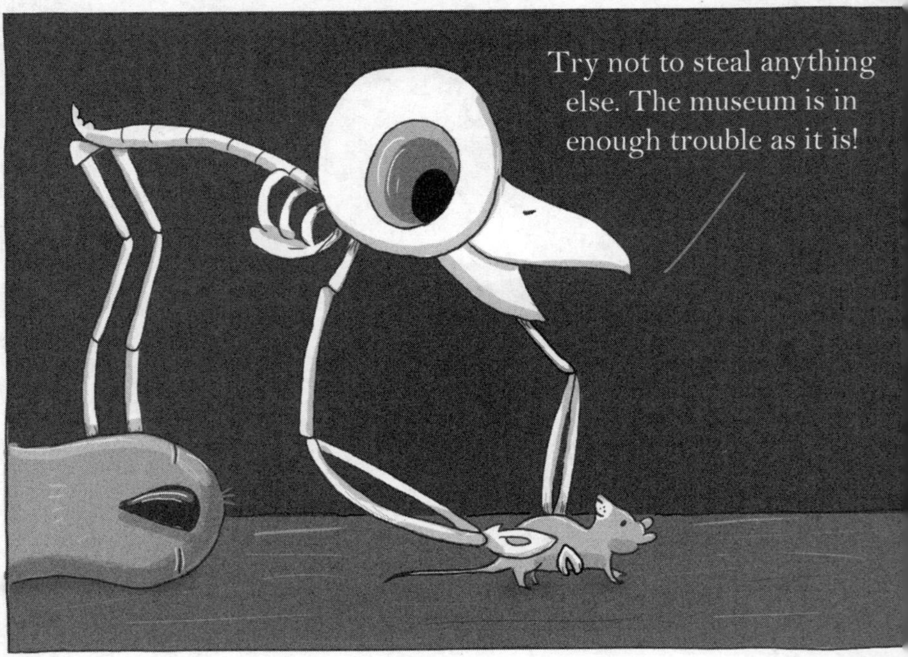
Try not to steal anything else. The museum is in enough trouble as it is!

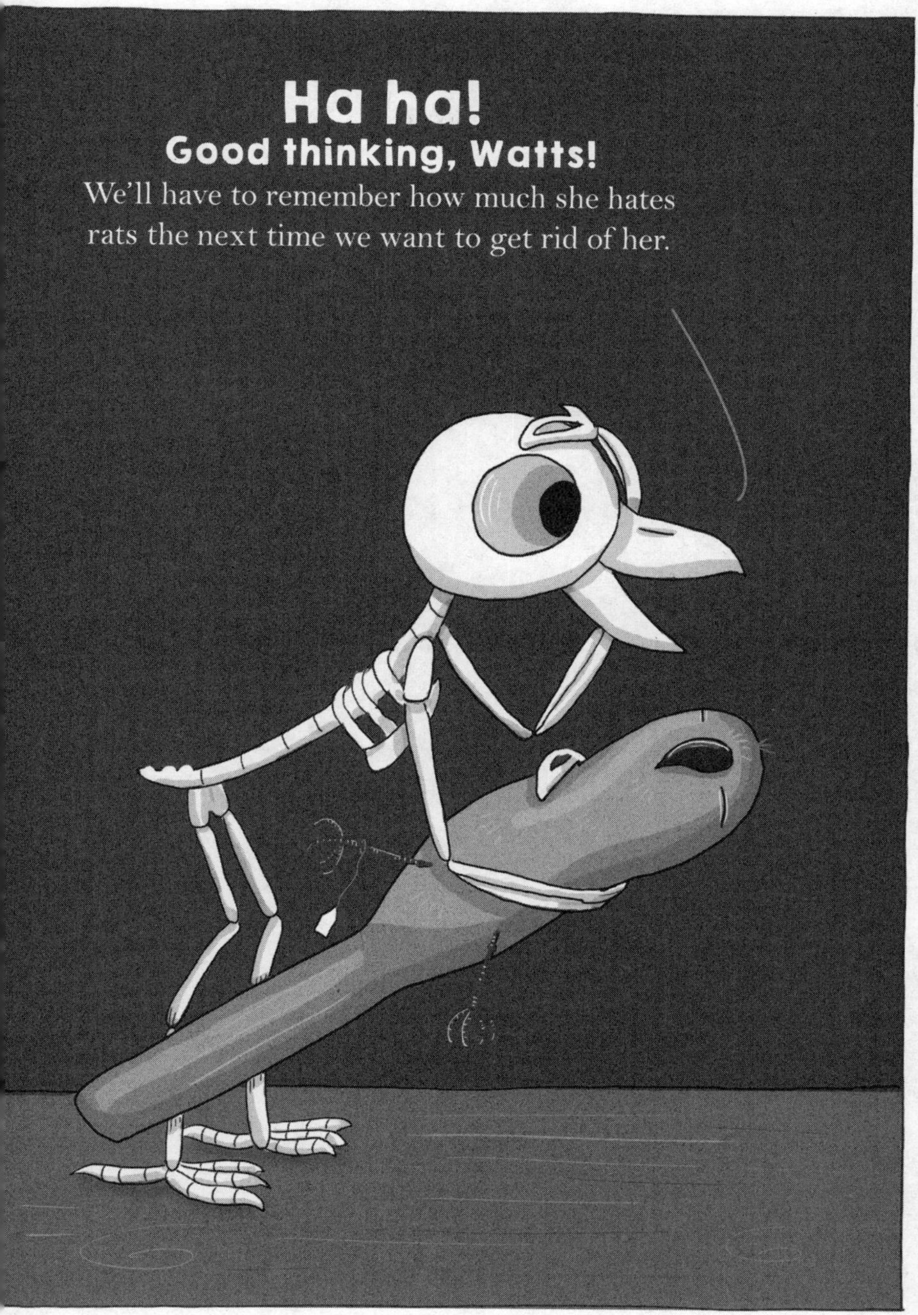
Ha ha!
Good thinking, Watts!
We'll have to remember how much she hates rats the next time we want to get rid of her.

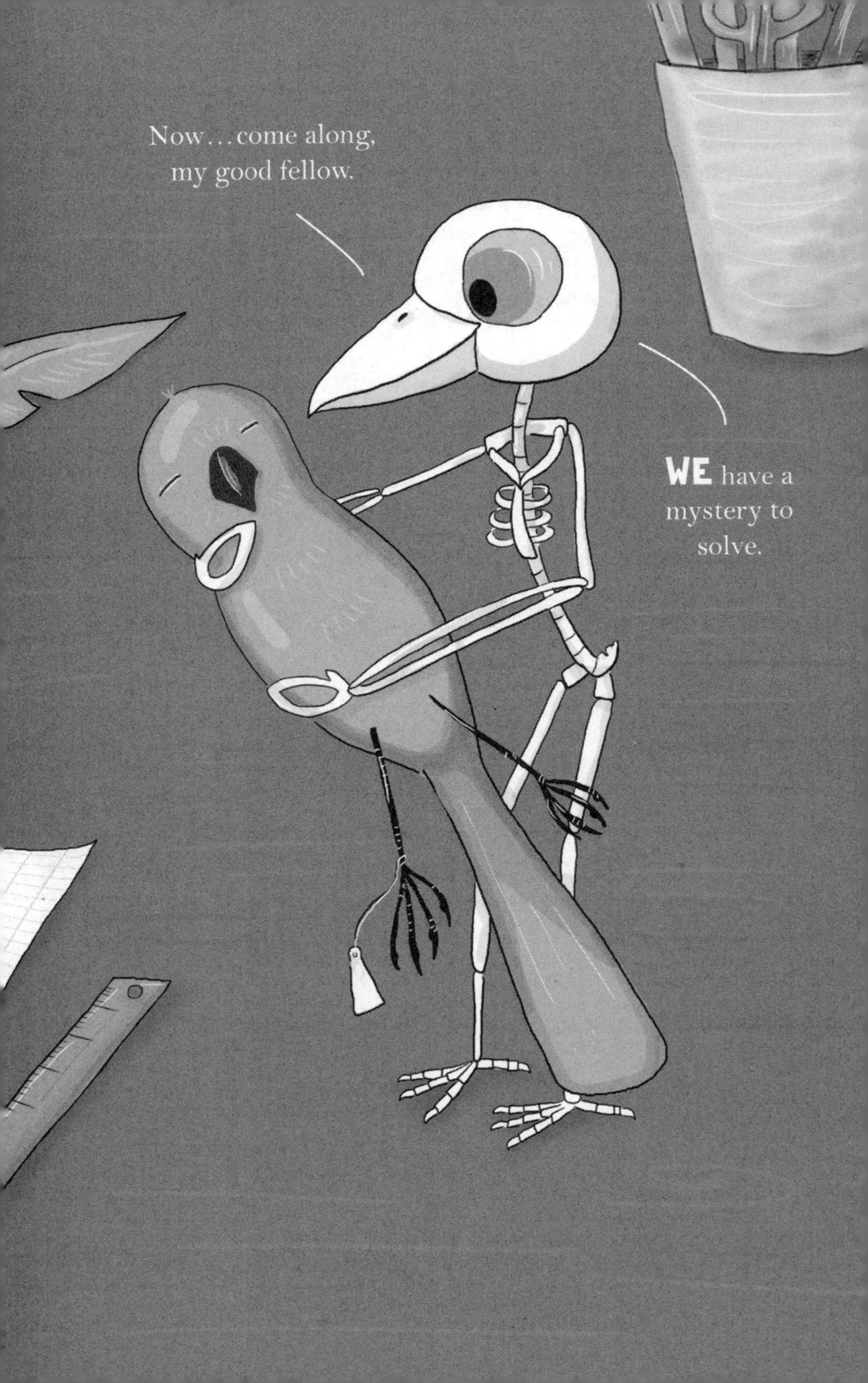
Now…come along, my good fellow.
WE have a mystery to solve.

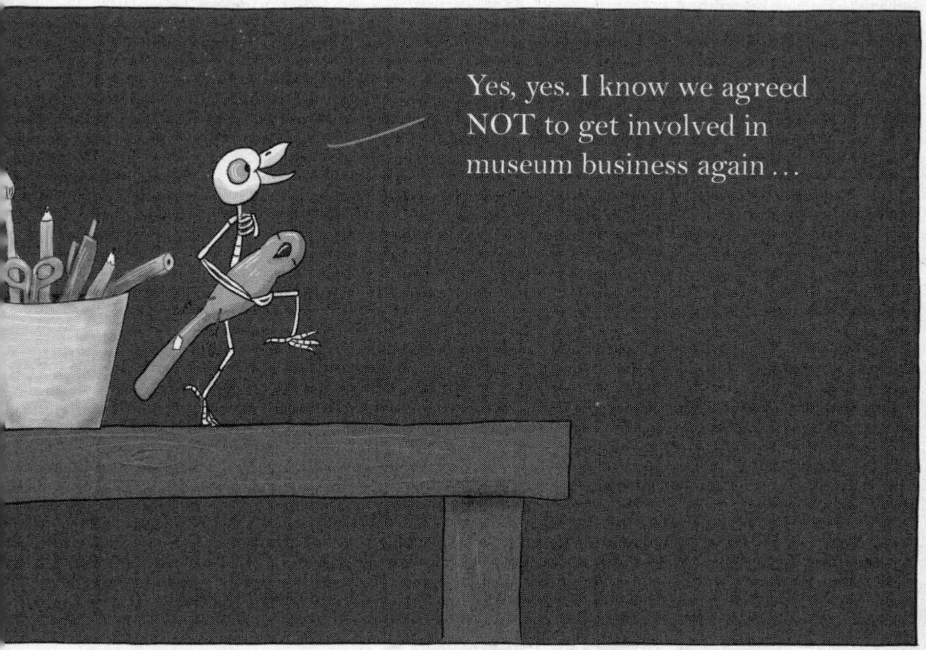
Yes, yes. I know we agreed NOT to get involved in museum business again . . .

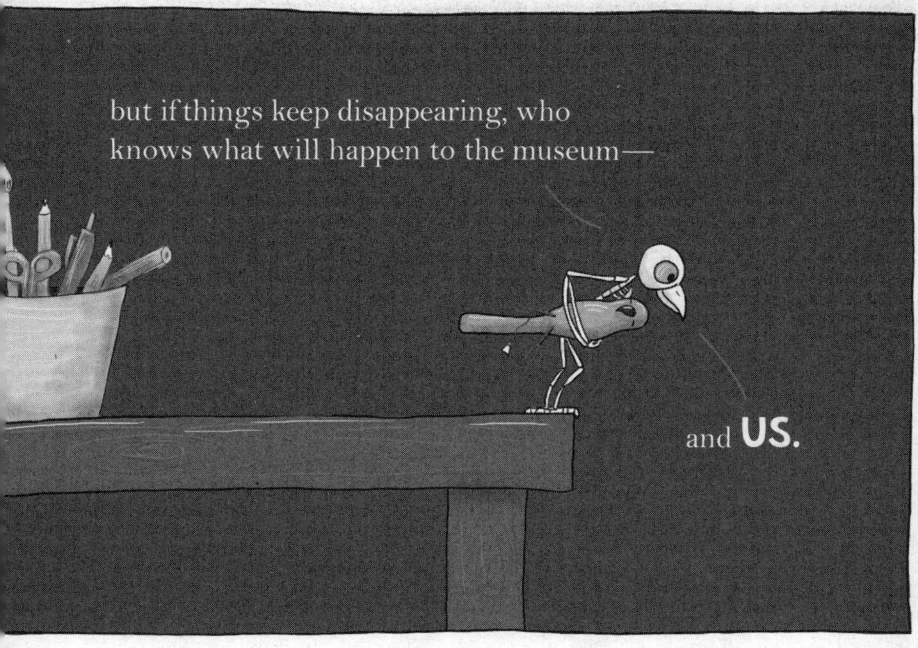
but if things keep disappearing, who knows what will happen to the museum—
and US.

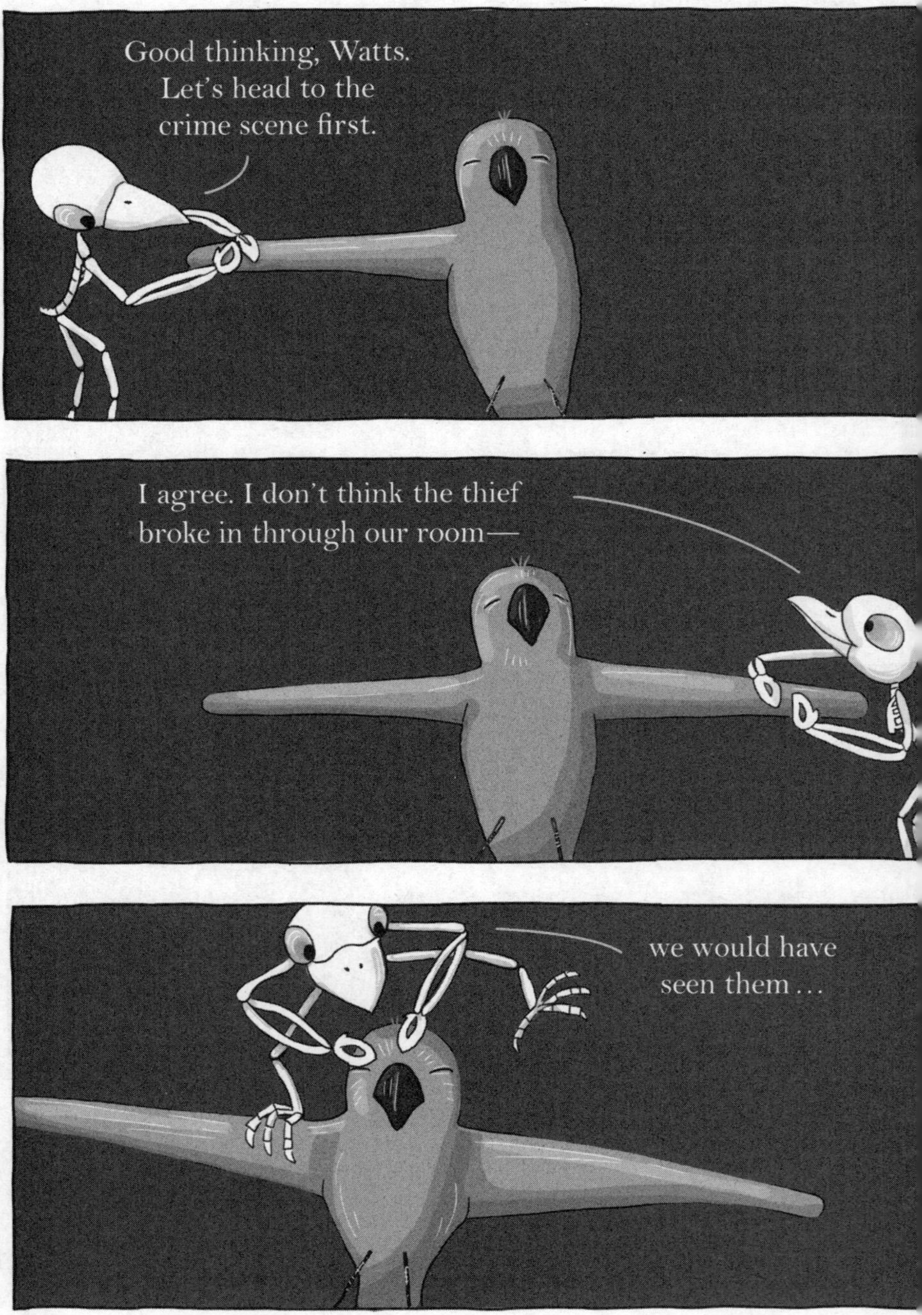
Good thinking, Watts. Let's head to the crime scene first.
I agree. I don't think the thief broke in through our room—
we would have seen them . . .

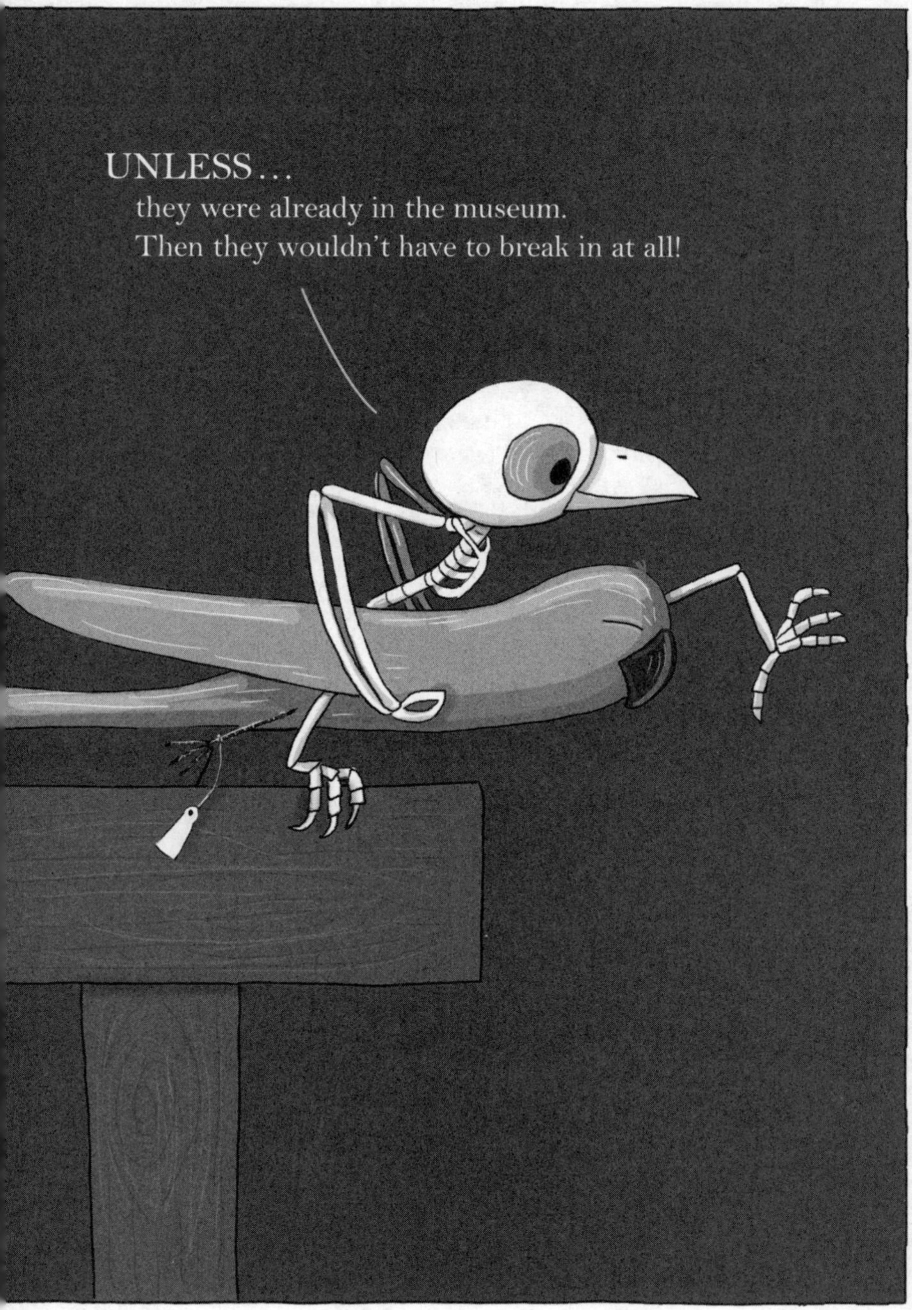
UNLESS...
they were already in the museum.
Then they wouldn't have to break in at all!

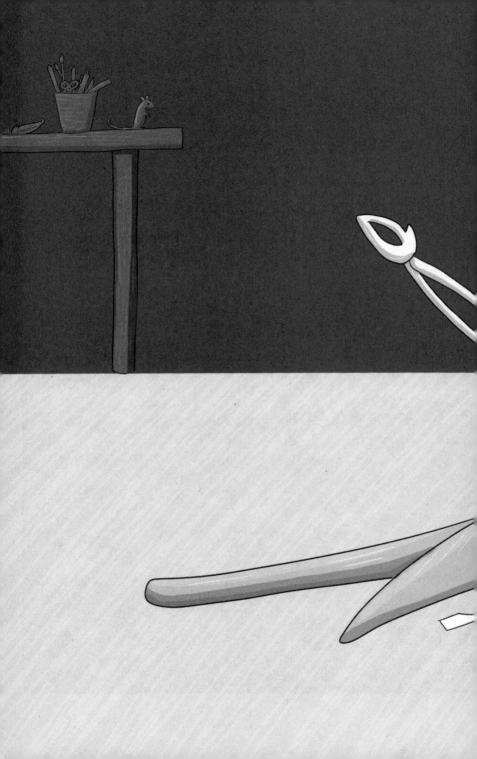

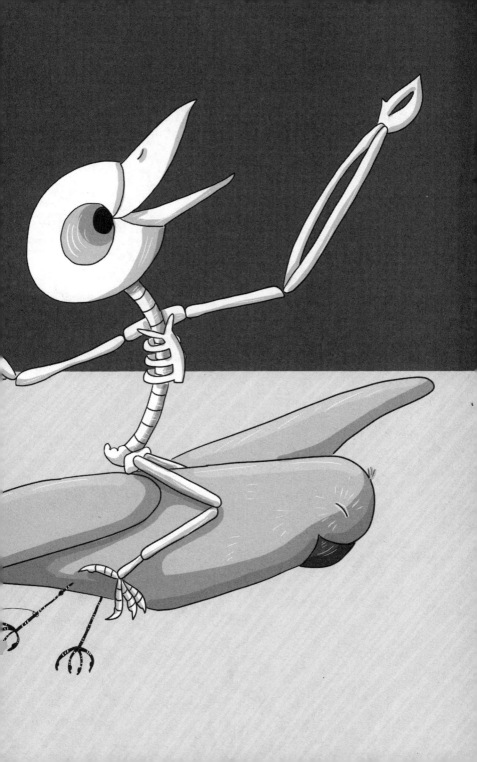

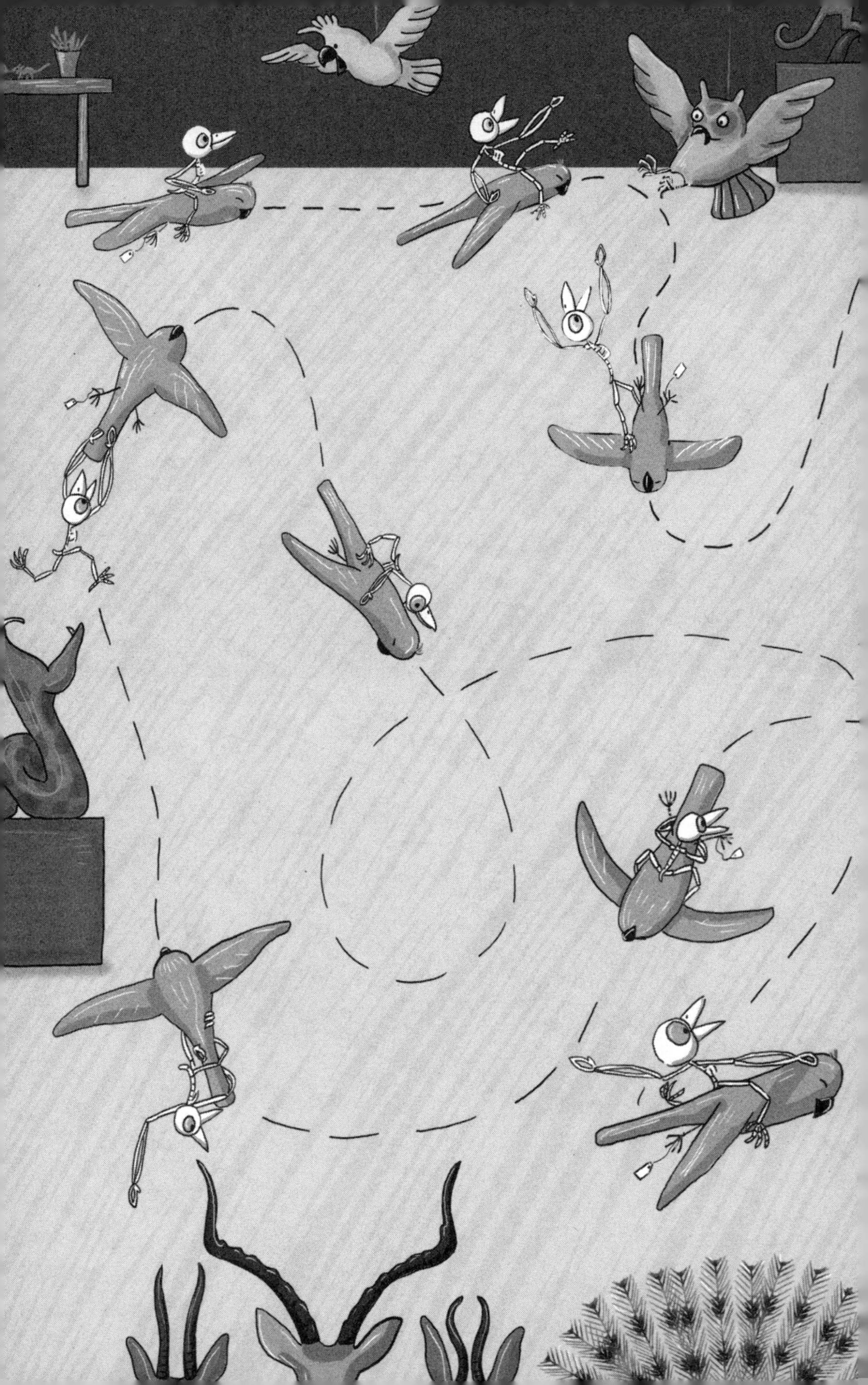

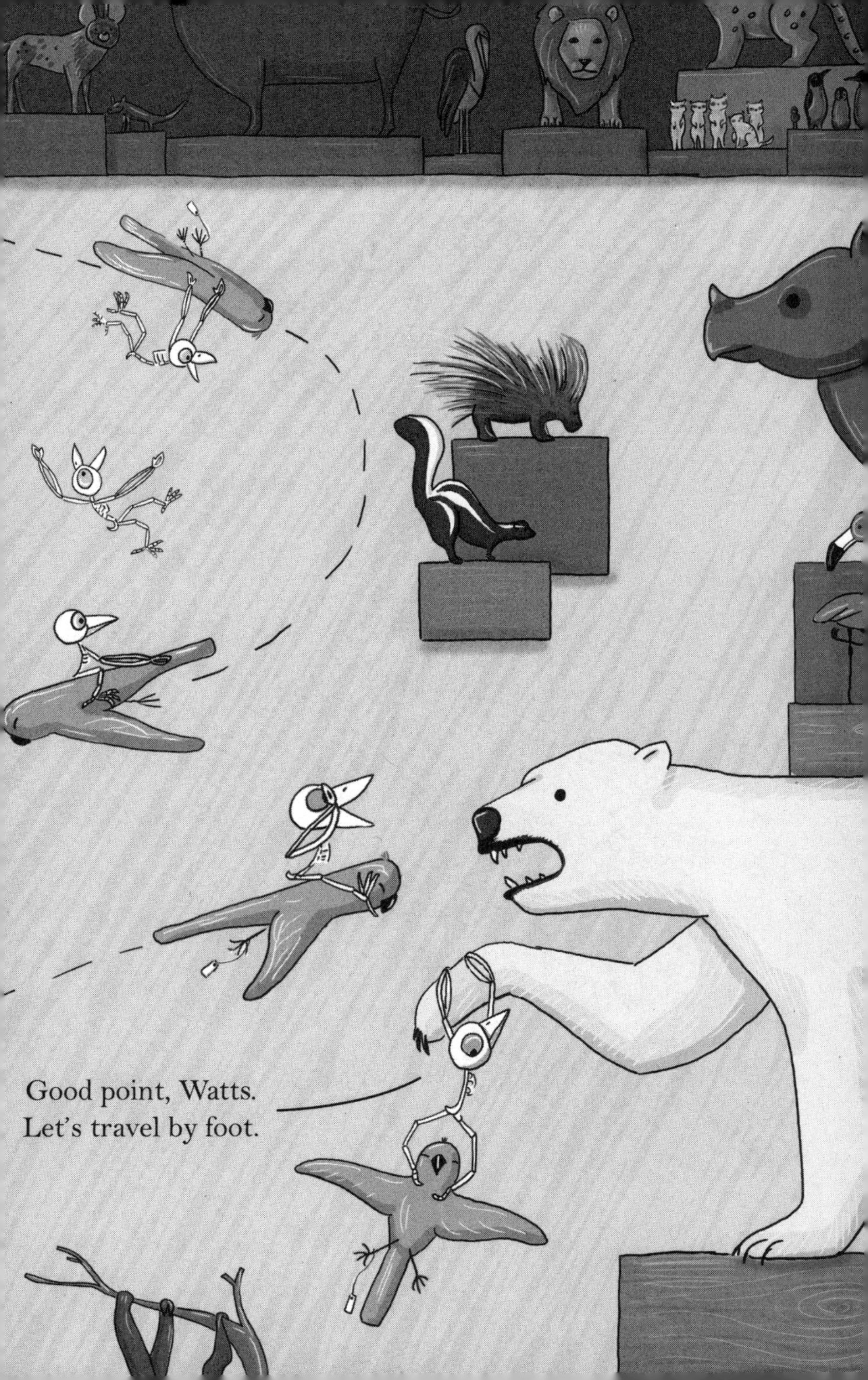
Good point, Watts.
Let's travel by foot.

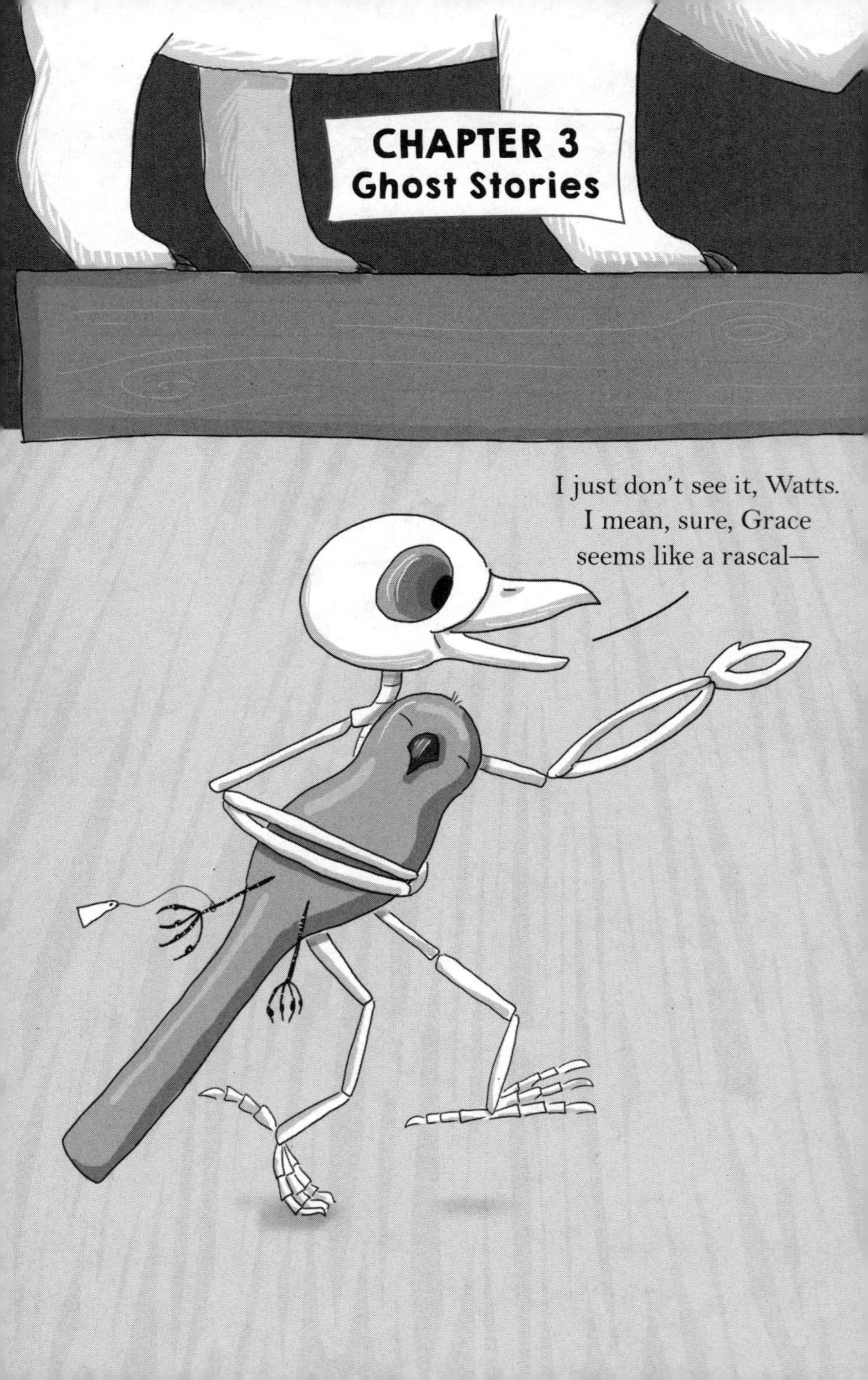
CHAPTER 3
Ghost Stories
I just don't see it, Watts.
I mean, sure, Grace
seems like a rascal—

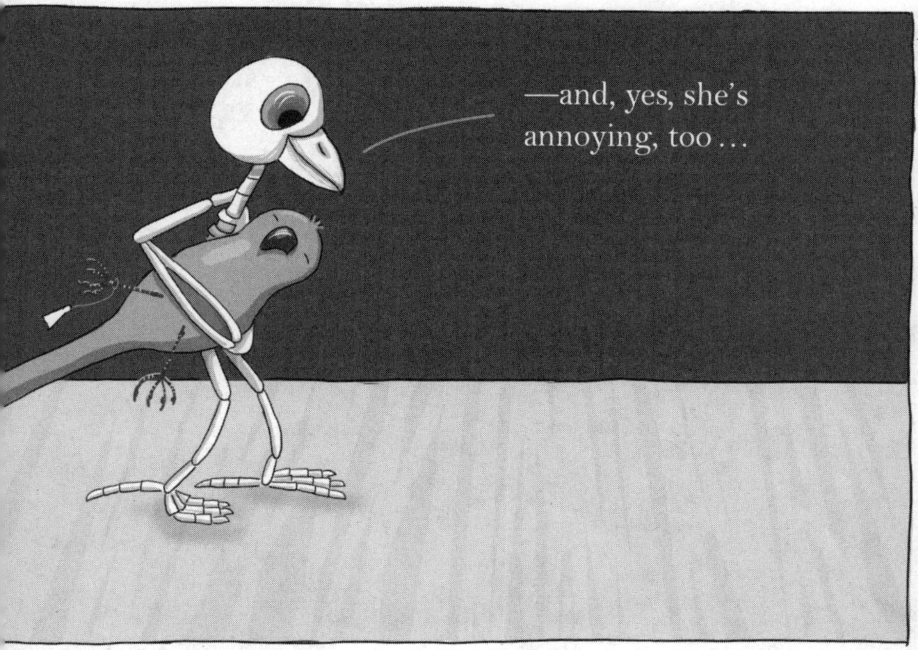
—and, yes, she's
annoying, too…

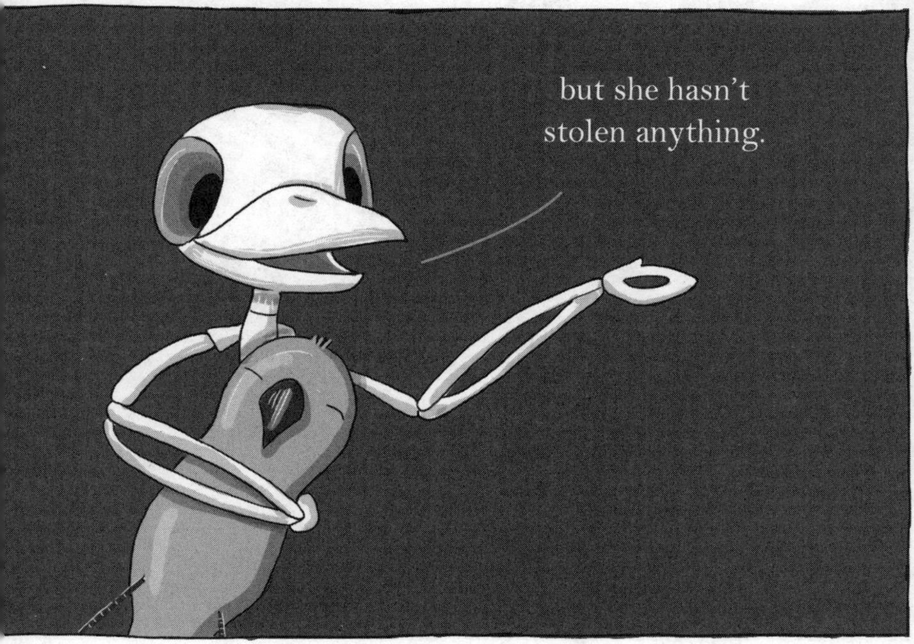
but she hasn't
stolen anything.

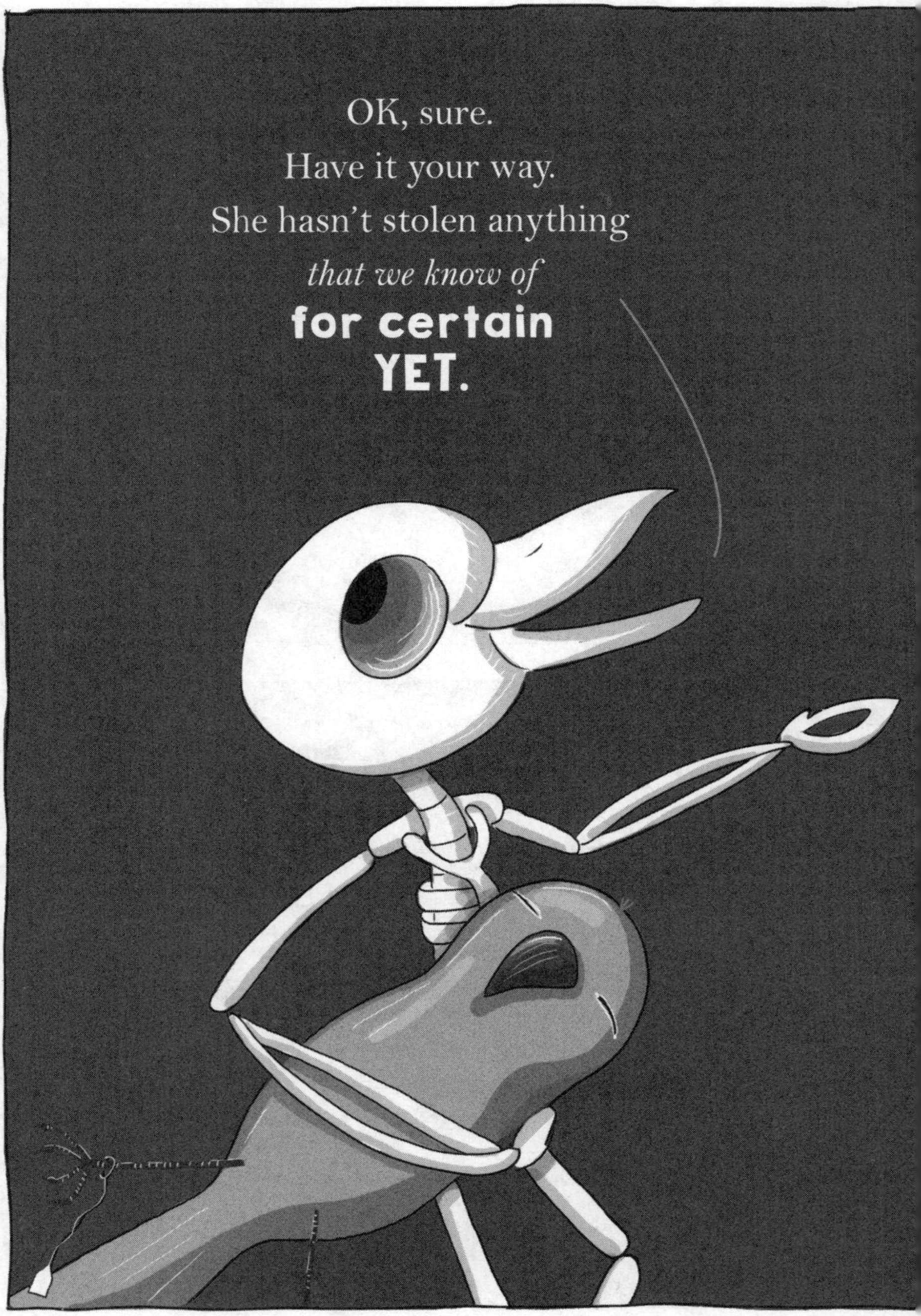
OK, sure.
Have it your way.
She hasn't stolen anything
that we know of
for certain
YET.

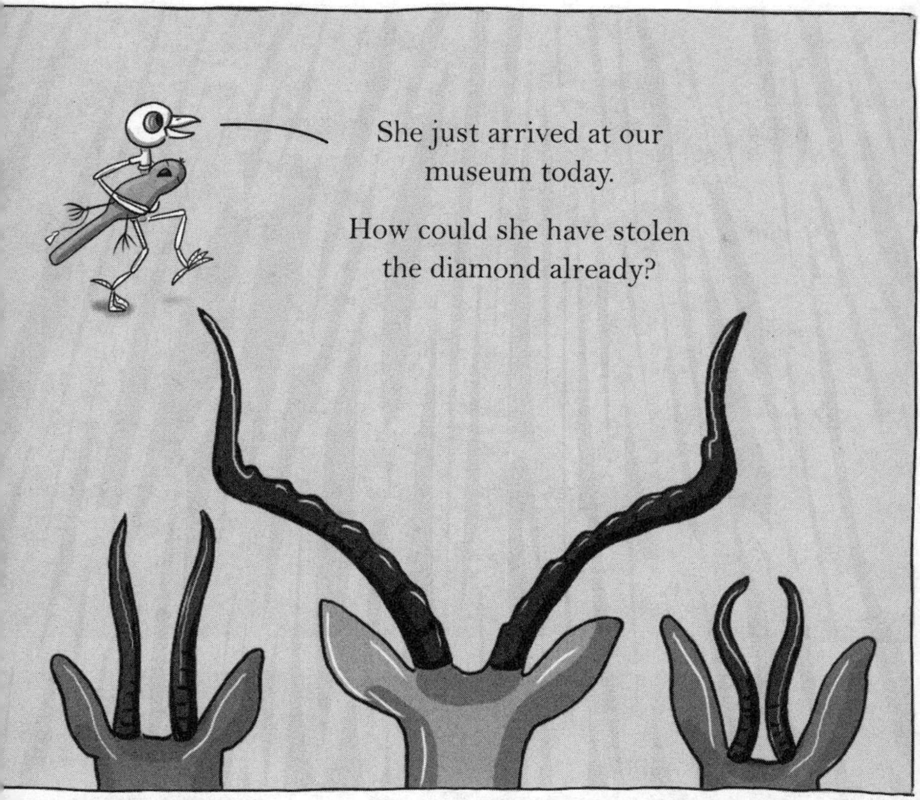
She just arrived at our museum today.
How could she have stolen the diamond already?

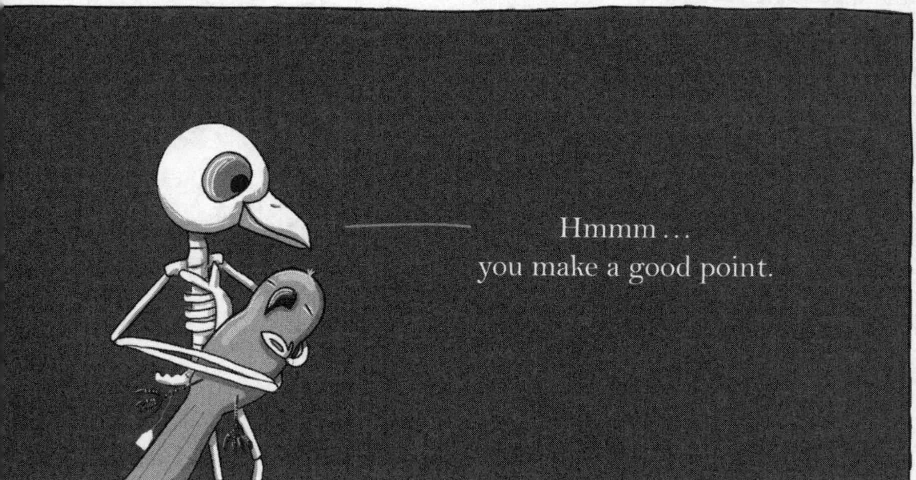
Hmmm . . . you make a good point.

It is awfully suspicious that she showed up on the *exact same day* the diamond was stolen.

OK, I agree. We can keep an eye on her…

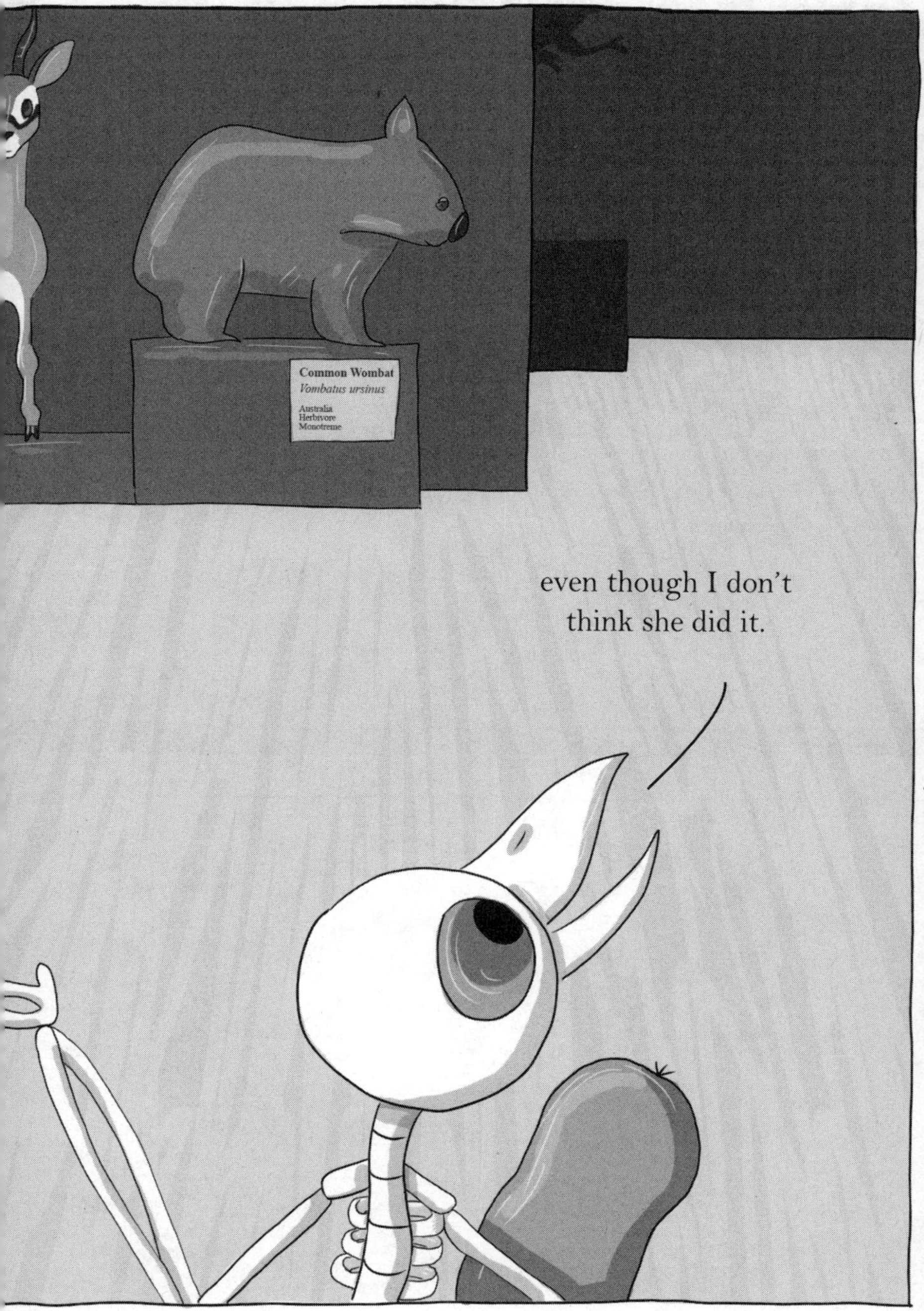
Common Wombat
Vombatus ursinus
Australia
Herbivore
Monotreme
even though I don't
think she did it.

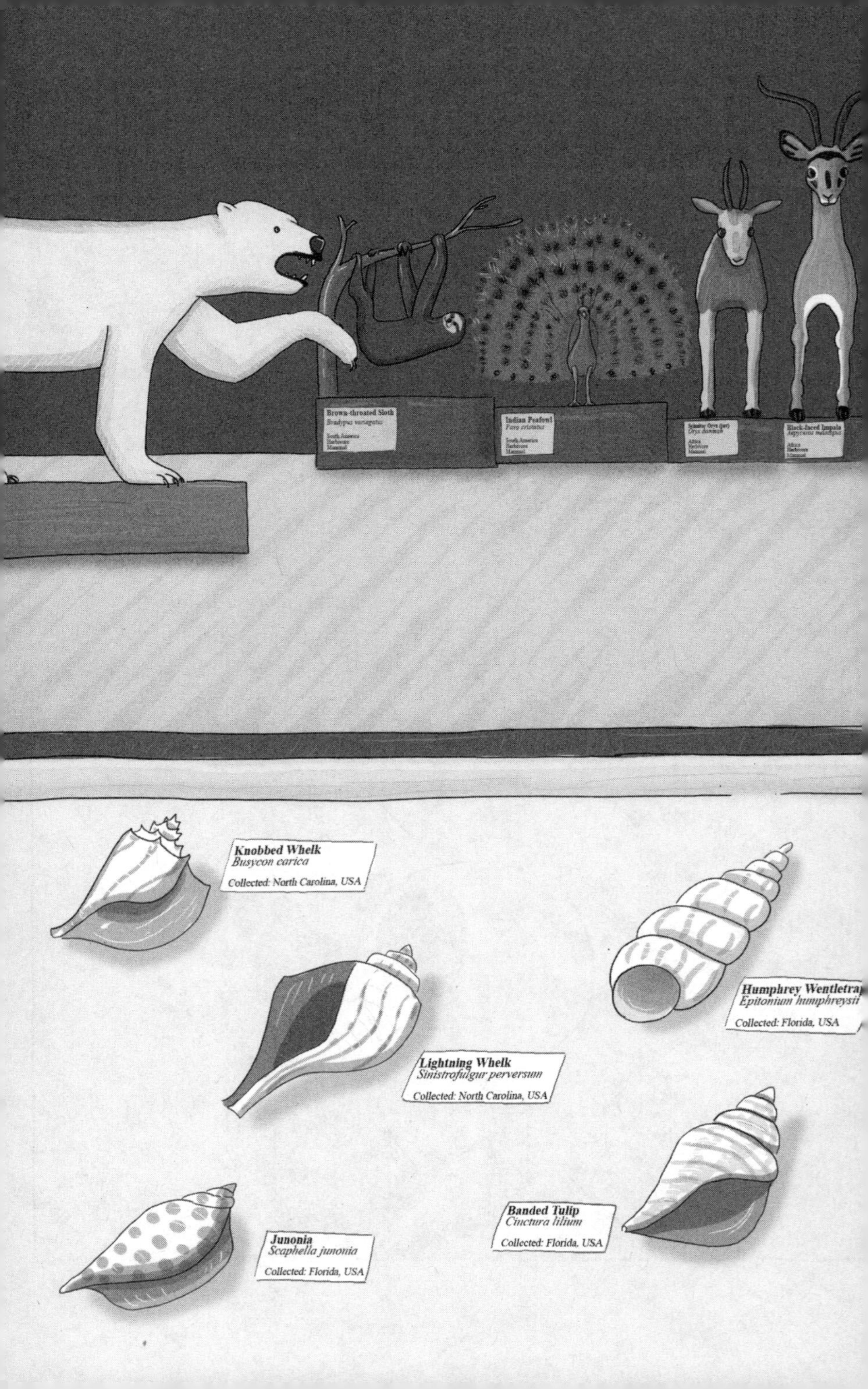

Brown-throated Sloth
Bradypus variegatus
South America
Herbivore
Mammal
Indian Peafowl
Pavo cristatus
South America
Herbivore
Mammal
Africa
Herbivore
Mammal
Black-faced Impala
Africa
Herbivore
Mammal
Knobbed Whelk
Busycon carica
Collected: North Carolina, USA
Humphrey Wentletra
Epitonium humphreysii
Collected: Florida, USA
Lightning Whelk
Sinistrofulgur perversum
Collected: North Carolina, USA
Banded Tulip
Cinctura lilium
Collected: Florida, USA
Junonia
Scaphella junonia
Collected: Florida, USA

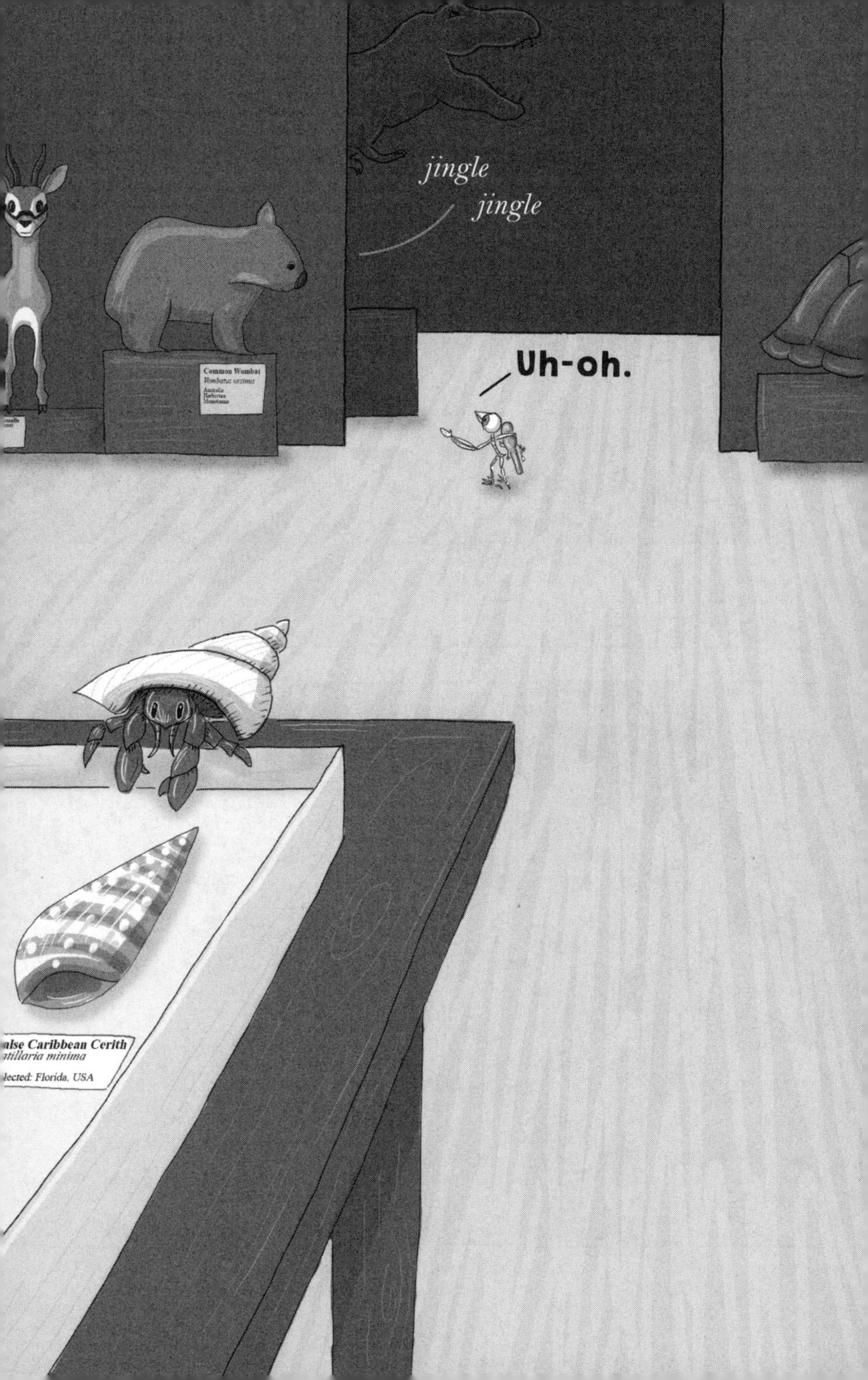
jingle
jingle
Uh-oh.
Common Wombat
Vombatus ursinus
alse Caribbean Cerith
atillaria minima
lected: Florida, USA

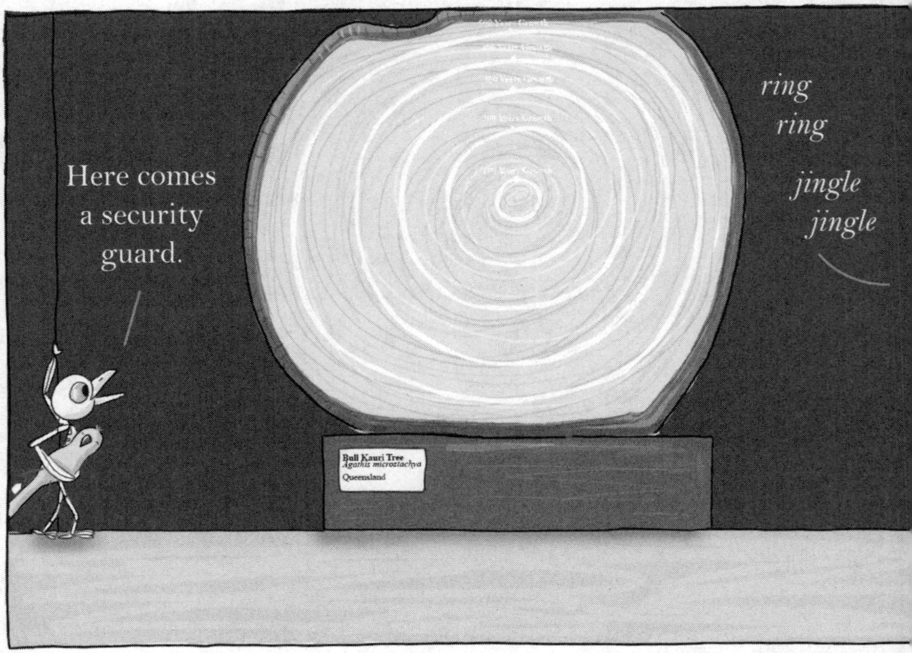
Here comes a security guard.
ring
ring
jingle
jingle
Bull Kauri Tree
Agathis microstachya
Queensland

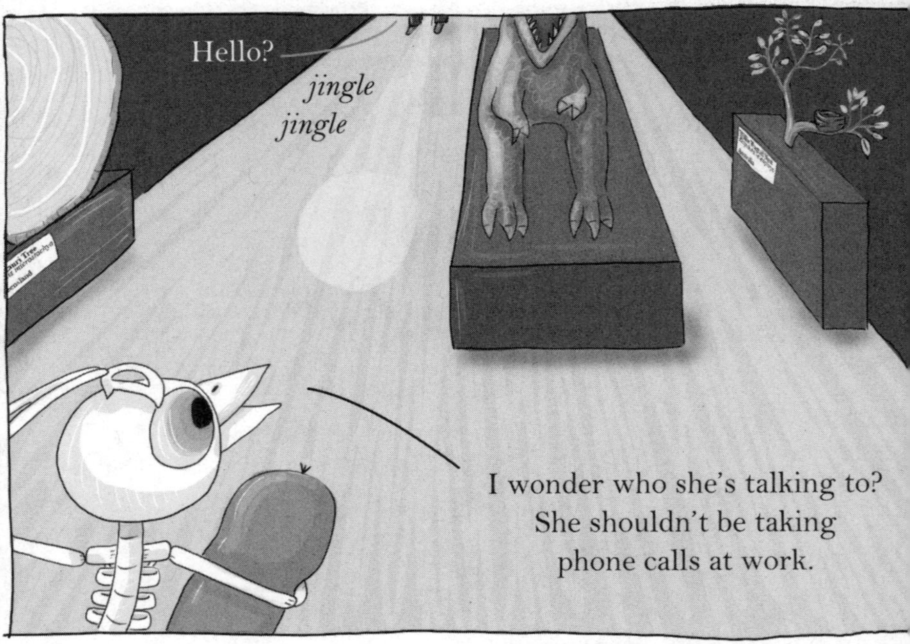
Hello?
jingle
jingle
I wonder who she's talking to? She shouldn't be taking phone calls at work.

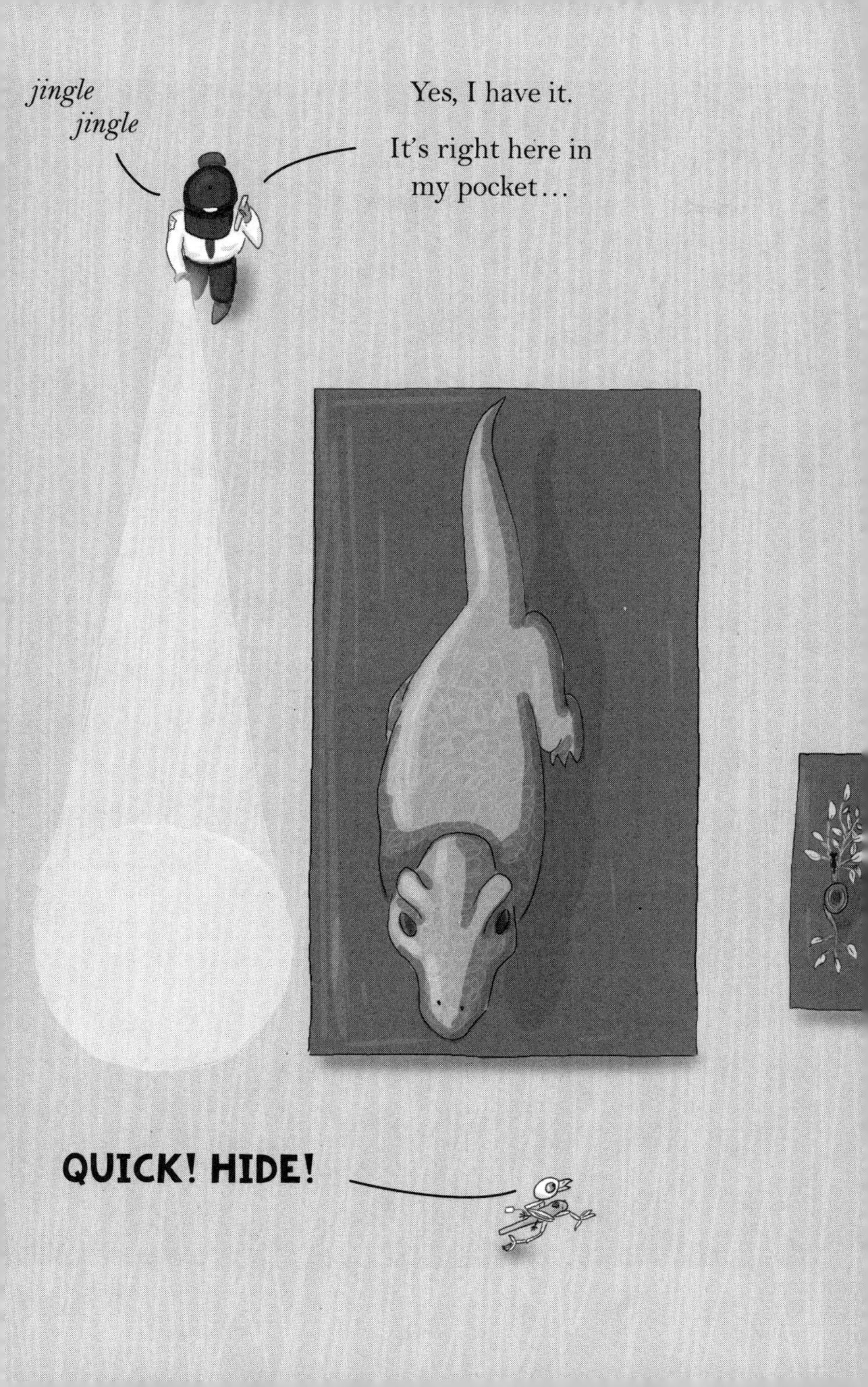
jingle
jingle
Yes, I have it.
It's right here in my pocket…
QUICK! HIDE!

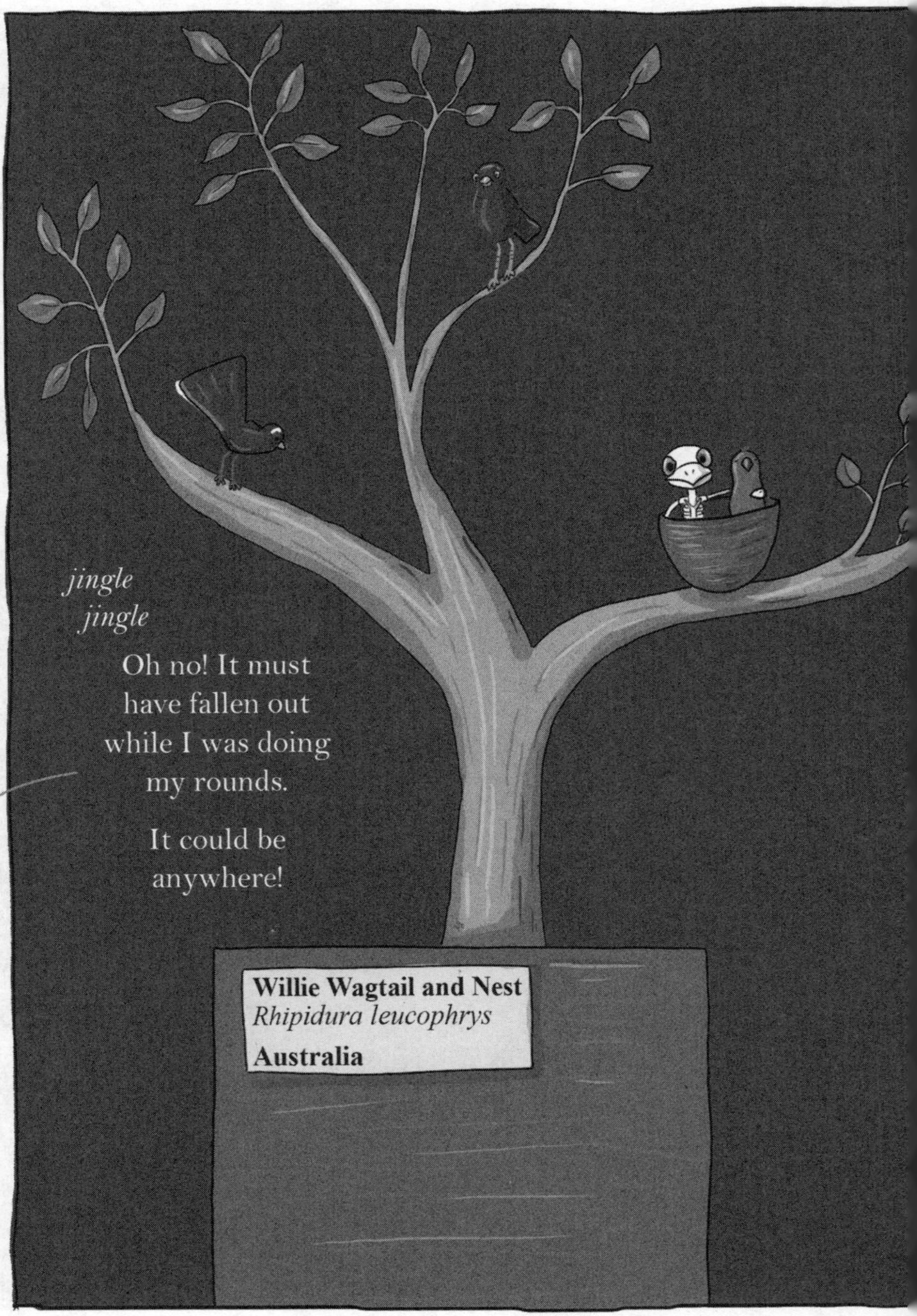
jingle
jingle
Oh no! It must have fallen out while I was doing my rounds.
It could be anywhere!
Willie Wagtail and Nest
Rhipidura leucophrys
Australia

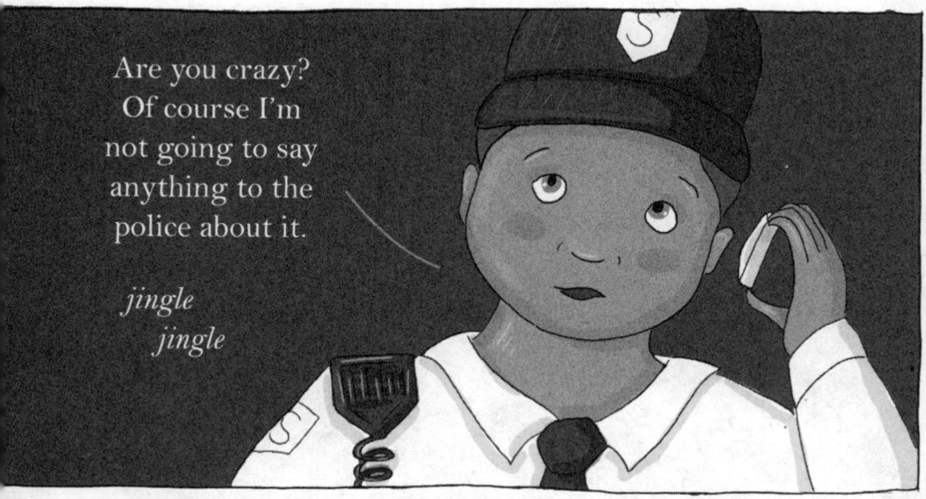
Are you crazy? Of course I'm not going to say anything to the police about it.
jingle
jingle

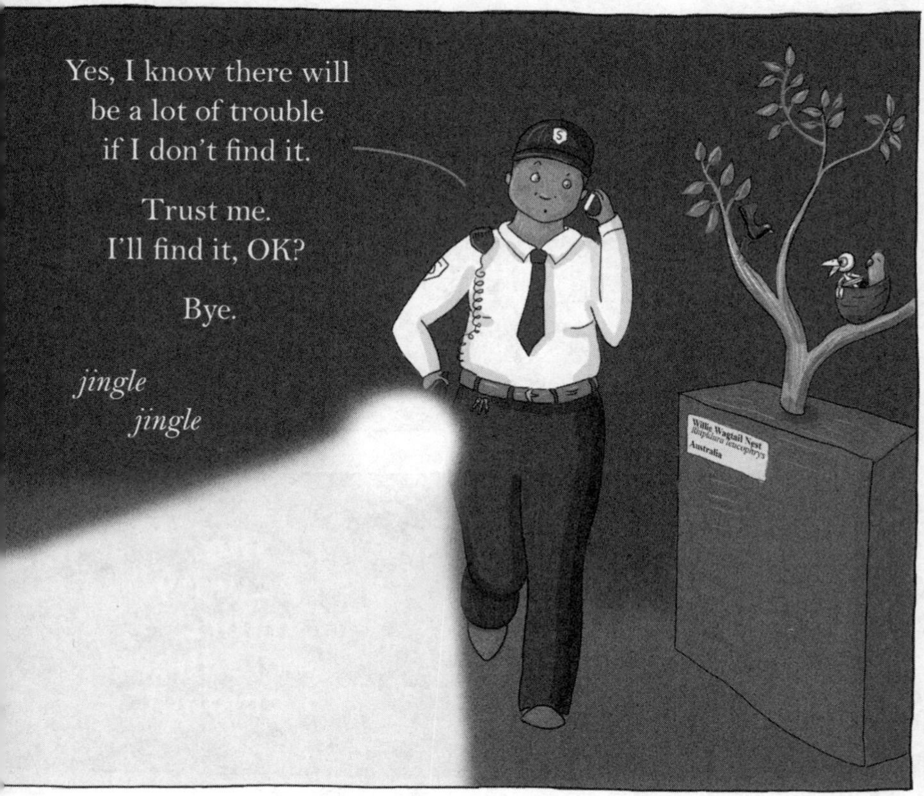
Yes, I know there will be a lot of trouble if I don't find it.
Trust me. I'll find it, OK?
Bye.
jingle
jingle
Willie Wagtail Nest
Rhipidura leucophrys
Australia

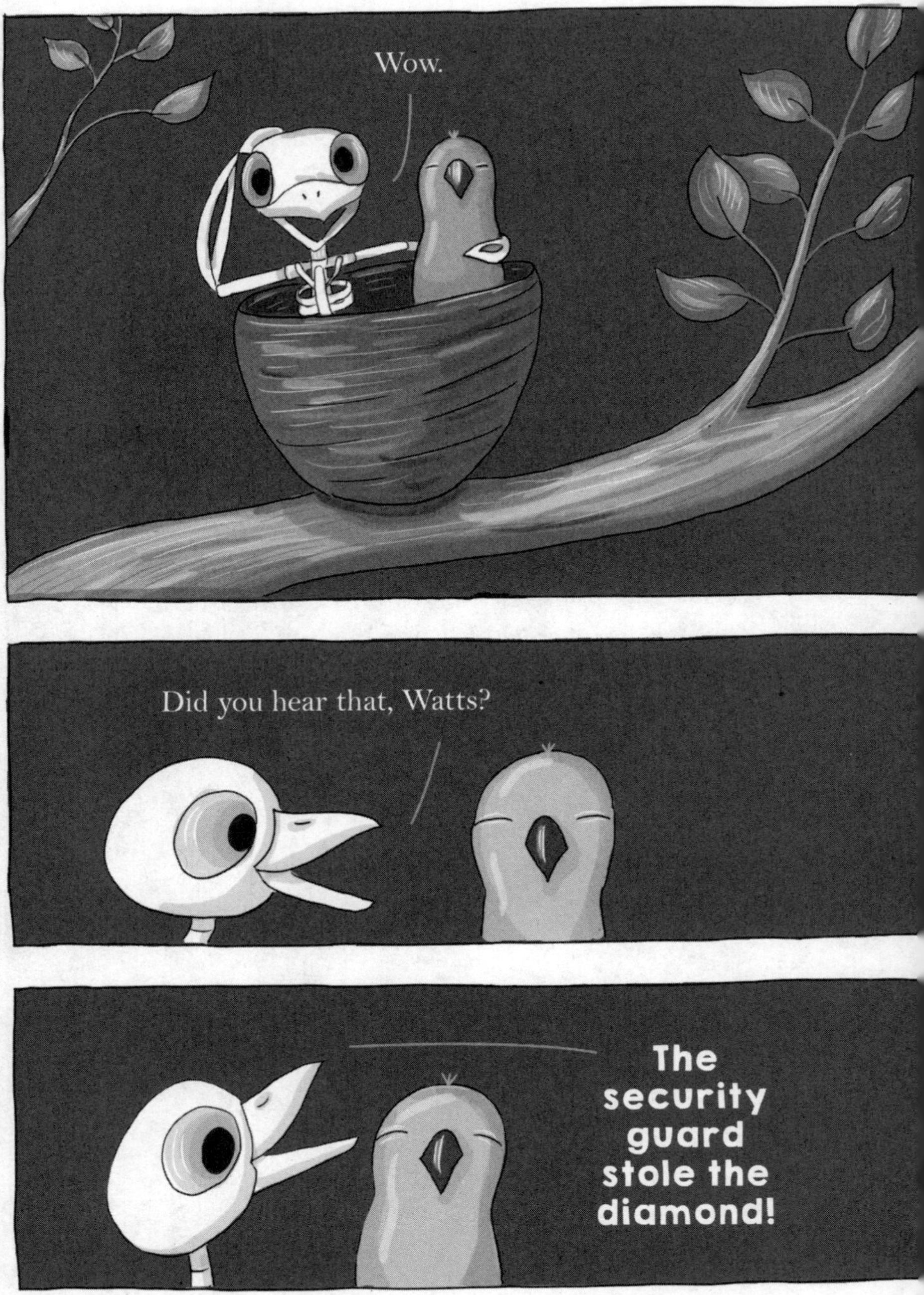
Wow.
Did you hear that, Watts?
The security guard stole the diamond!

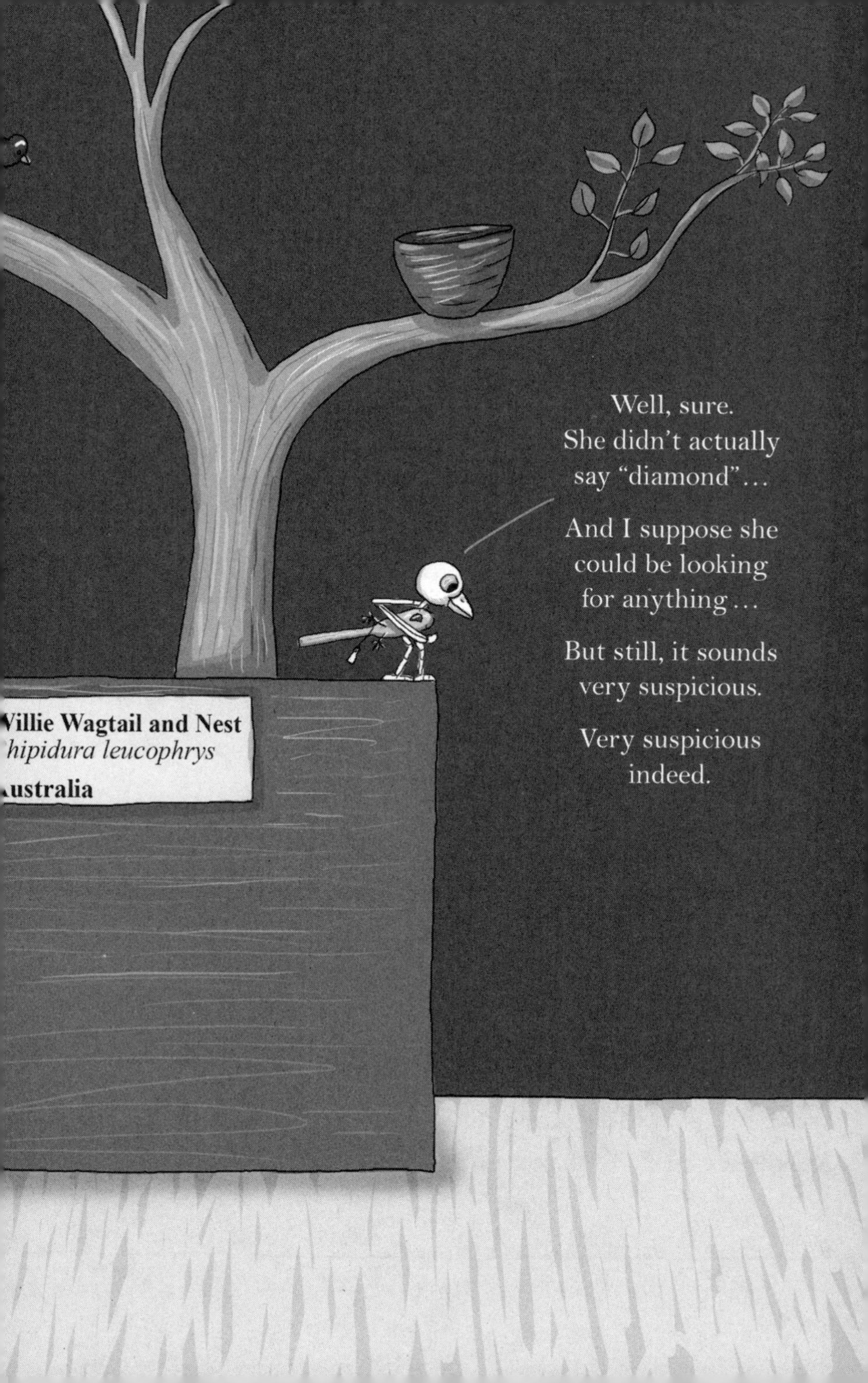
Villie Wagtail and Nest
hipidura leucophrys
ustralia

Well, sure.
She didn't actually
say "diamond"…

And I suppose she
could be looking
for anything…

But still, it sounds
very suspicious.

Very suspicious
indeed.

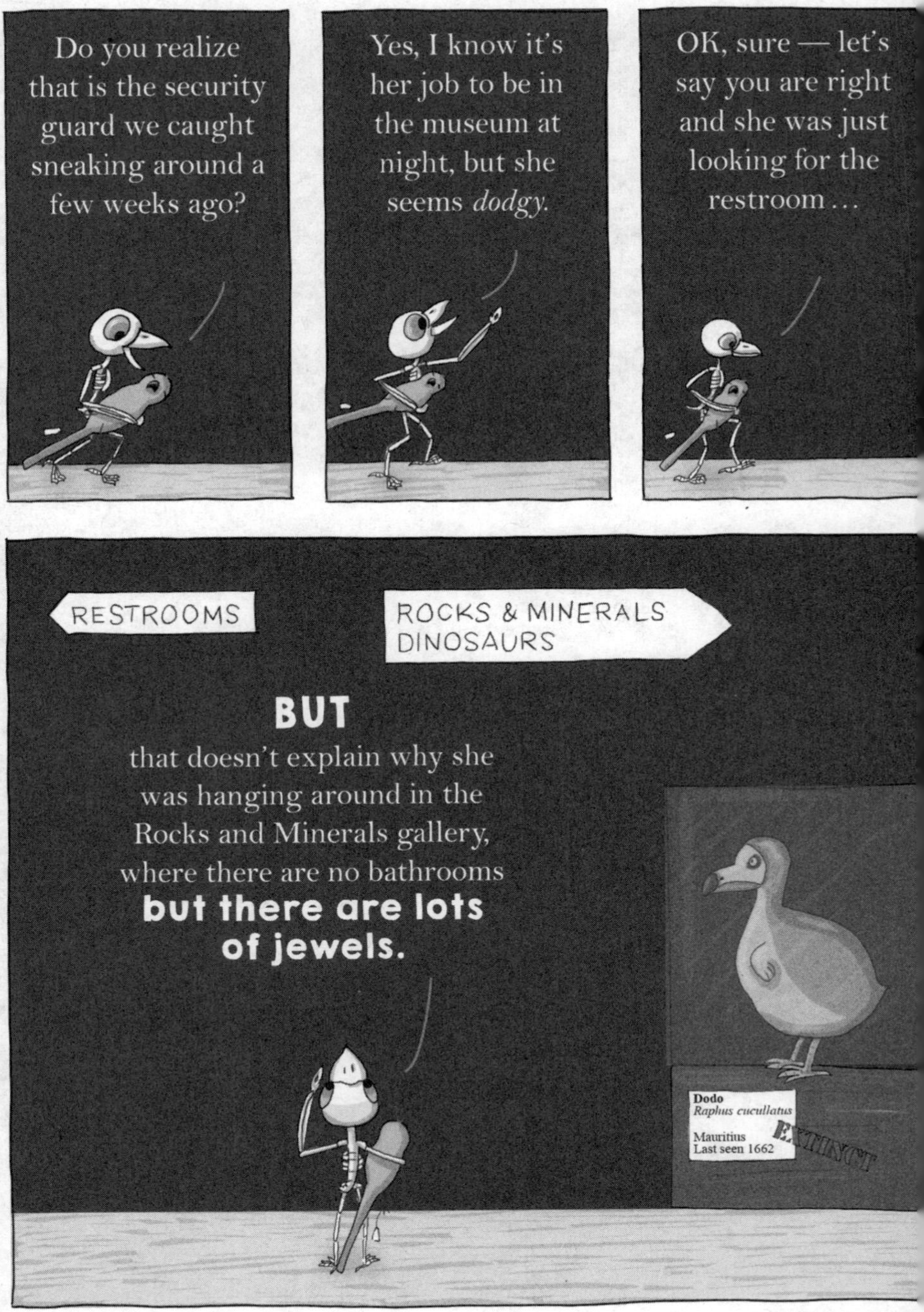
Do you realize that is the security guard we caught sneaking around a few weeks ago?
Yes, I know it's her job to be in the museum at night, but she seems *dodgy.*
OK, sure — let's say you are right and she was just looking for the restroom . . .
RESTROOMS
ROCKS & MINERALS
DINOSAURS
BUT
that doesn't explain why she was hanging around in the Rocks and Minerals gallery, where there are no bathrooms **but there are lots of jewels.**
Dodo
Raphus cucullatus
Mauritius
Last seen 1662
EXTINCT

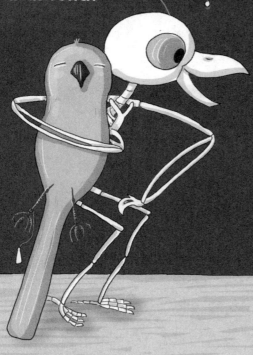

Do you remember the look on her face when she saw us? **Almost as priceless as the diamond!**

Dodo
Raphus cuc

Mauritius
Last seen 16

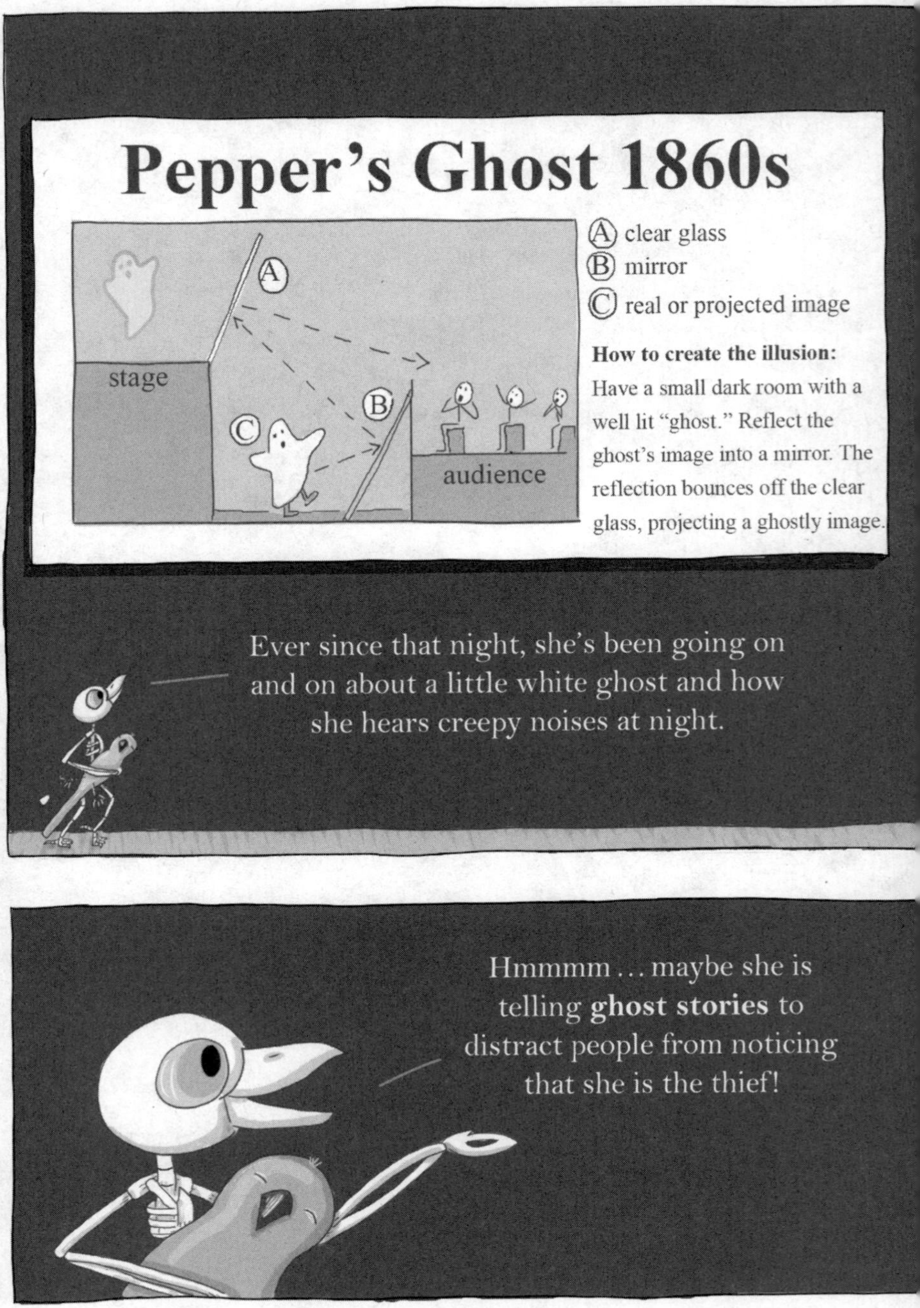
Pepper's Ghost 1860s
stage
A
B
C
audience
A clear glass
B mirror
C real or projected image
How to create the illusion:
Have a small dark room with a well lit "ghost." Reflect the ghost's image into a mirror. The reflection bounces off the clear glass, projecting a ghostly image.
Ever since that night, she's been going on and on about a little white ghost and how she hears creepy noises at night.
Hmmmm . . . maybe she is telling ghost stories to distract people from noticing that she is the thief!

People believe her. Even the police believe her.

But a GHOST-THIEF?

Seriously? They think that's
a good theory?

Let's just think about this
for a minute.

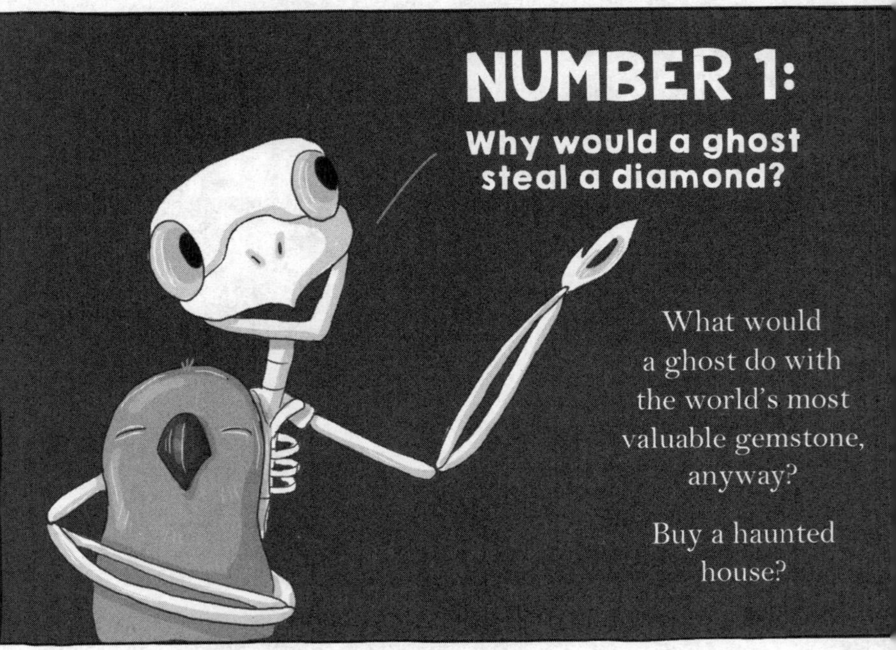
NUMBER 1:
Why would a ghost steal a diamond?
What would a ghost do with the world's most valuable gemstone, anyway?
Buy a haunted house?

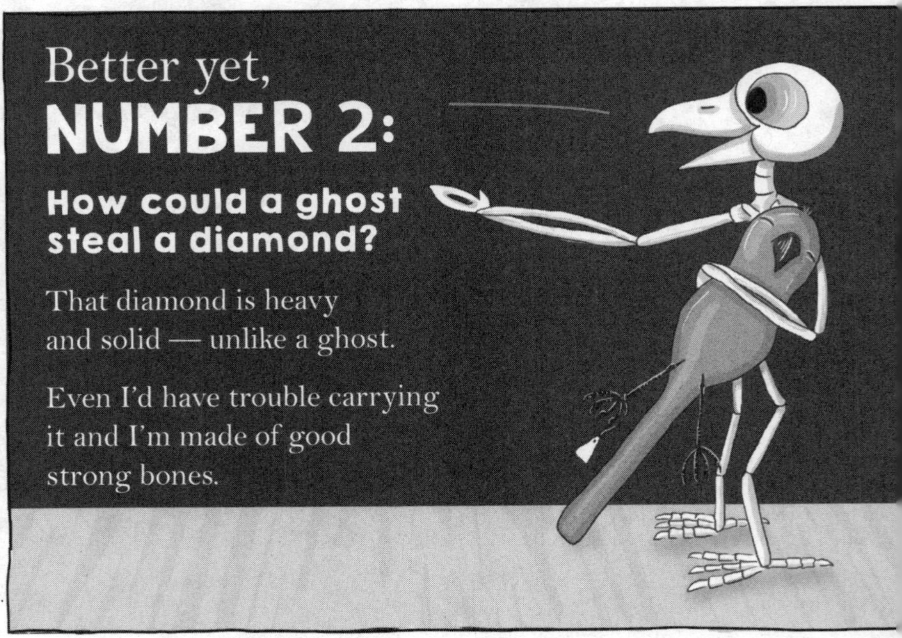
Better yet,
NUMBER 2:
How could a ghost steal a diamond?
That diamond is heavy and solid — unlike a ghost.
Even I'd have trouble carrying it and I'm made of good strong bones.

Ghost Stories from Around the World

Flying Dutchman
Mysterious ghost ship that legend says never made it to port and is forced to sail the oceans forever.

Horse and Carriage
Legends exist worldwide of old-style carriages pulled by ghost horses. Some claim they even leave footprints!

Haunted Hound
Monstrous beast of a spirit dog believed to be a guardian of the afterlife. Similar legends exist in Europe and the Americas.

Hmmm…Watts, what do you think ghosts are made of, anyway?

Air?

Mist?

Good point, Watts.
That would **TOTALLY** explain why the police are having trouble finding clues.

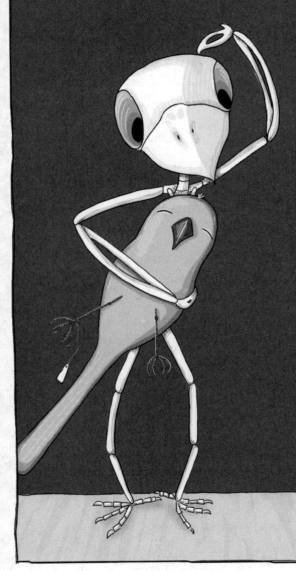

WAIT A MINUTE!

That's not helping!

**She thinks WE are the ghosts, remember?
And WE didn't steal the diamond!**

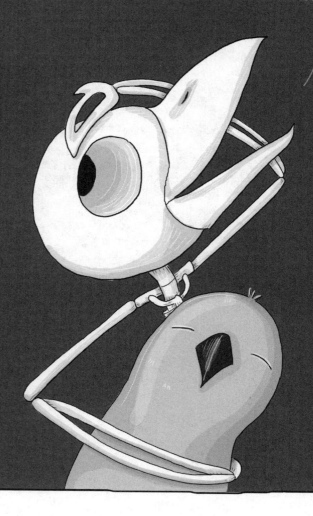

CHAPTER 4
Family Ties

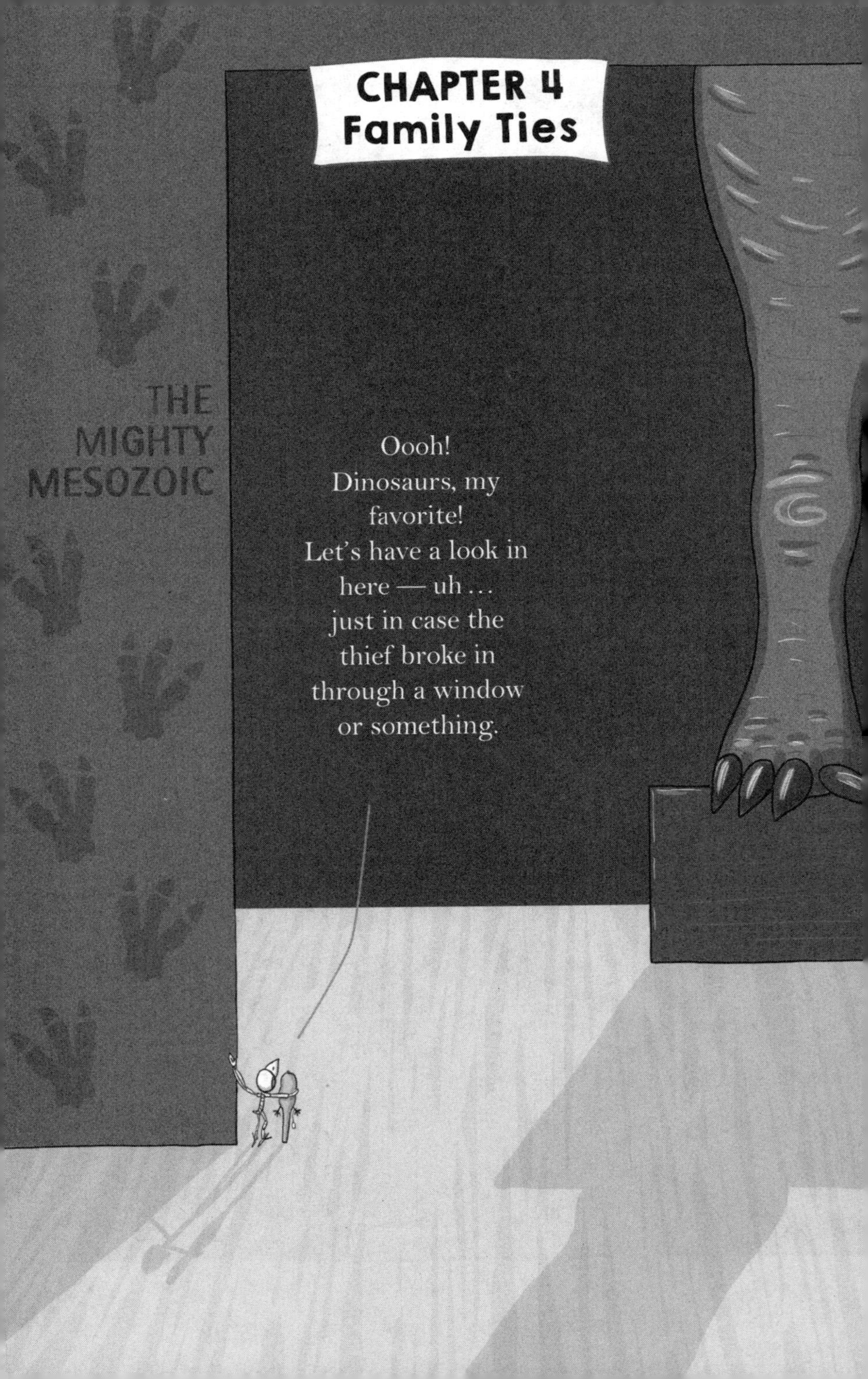
THE MIGHTY MESOZOIC
Oooh! Dinosaurs, my favorite! Let's have a look in here — uh . . . just in case the thief broke in through a window or something.

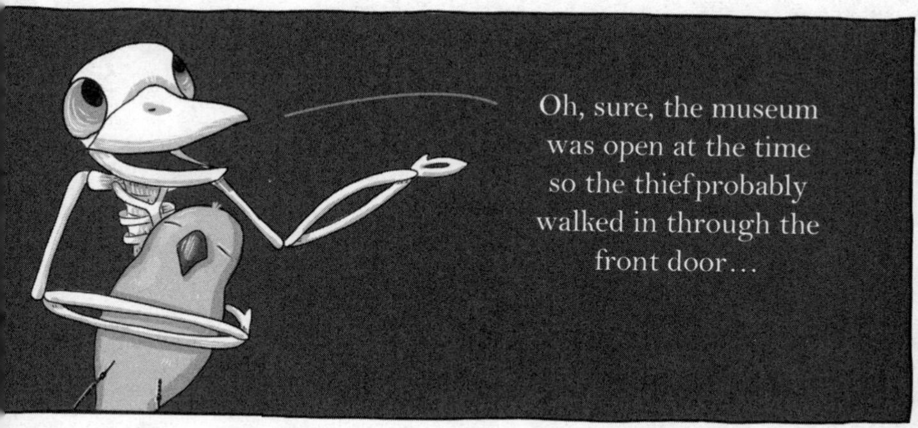
Oh, sure, the museum was open at the time so the thief probably walked in through the front door…

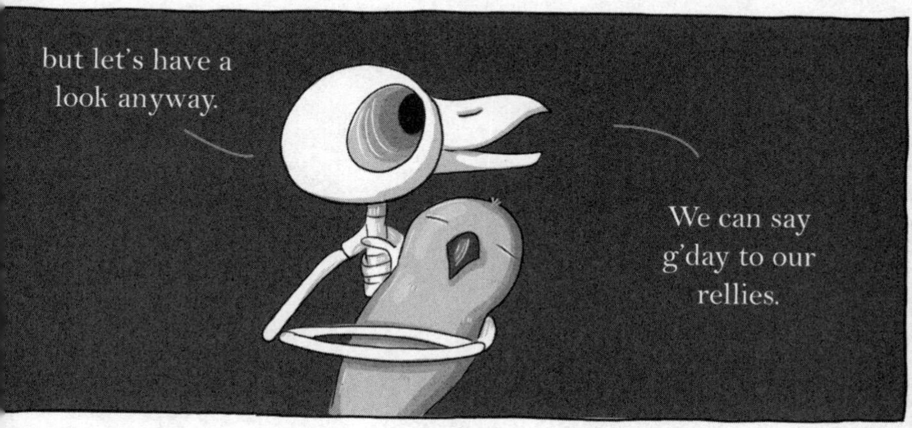
but let's have a look anyway.
We can say g'day to our rellies.

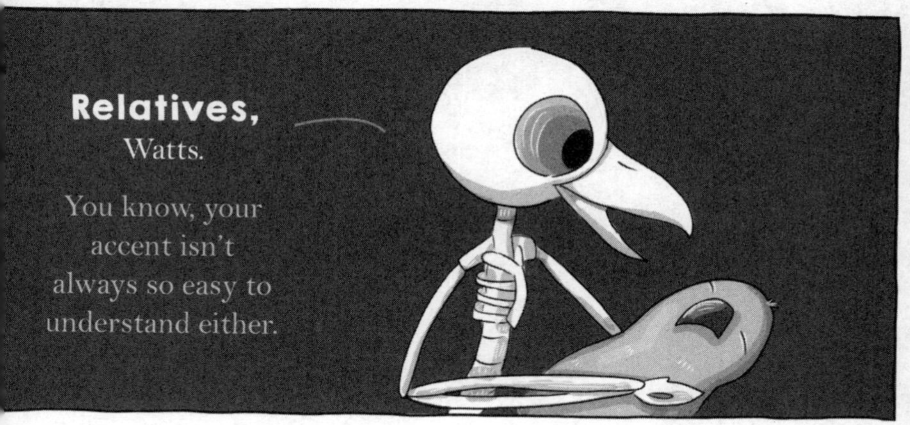
Relatives, Watts.
You know, your accent isn't always so easy to understand either.

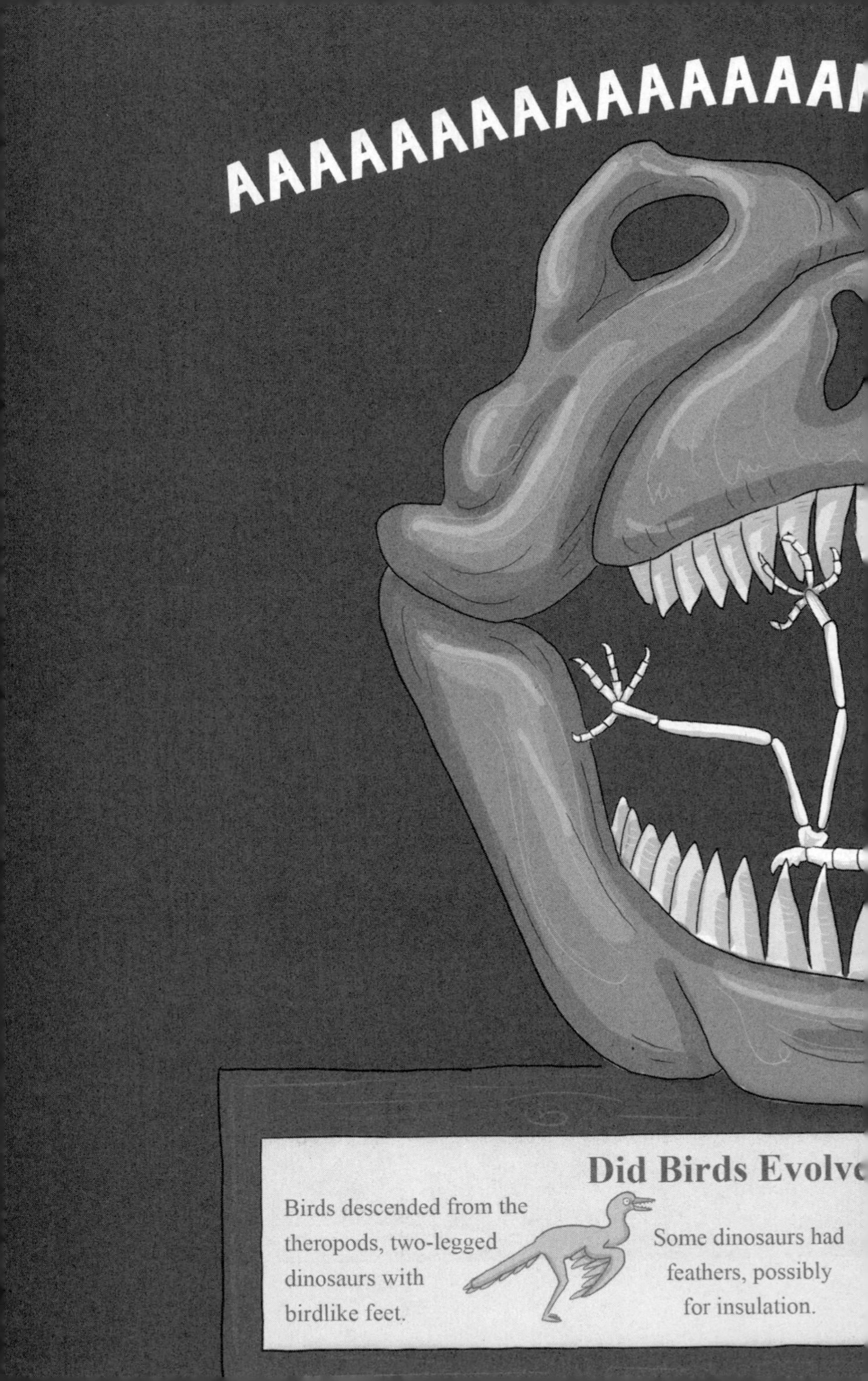
AAAAAAAAAAAAAAAAA
Did Birds Evolv
Birds descended from the theropods, two-legged dinosaurs with birdlike feet.
Some dinosaurs had feathers, possibly for insulation.

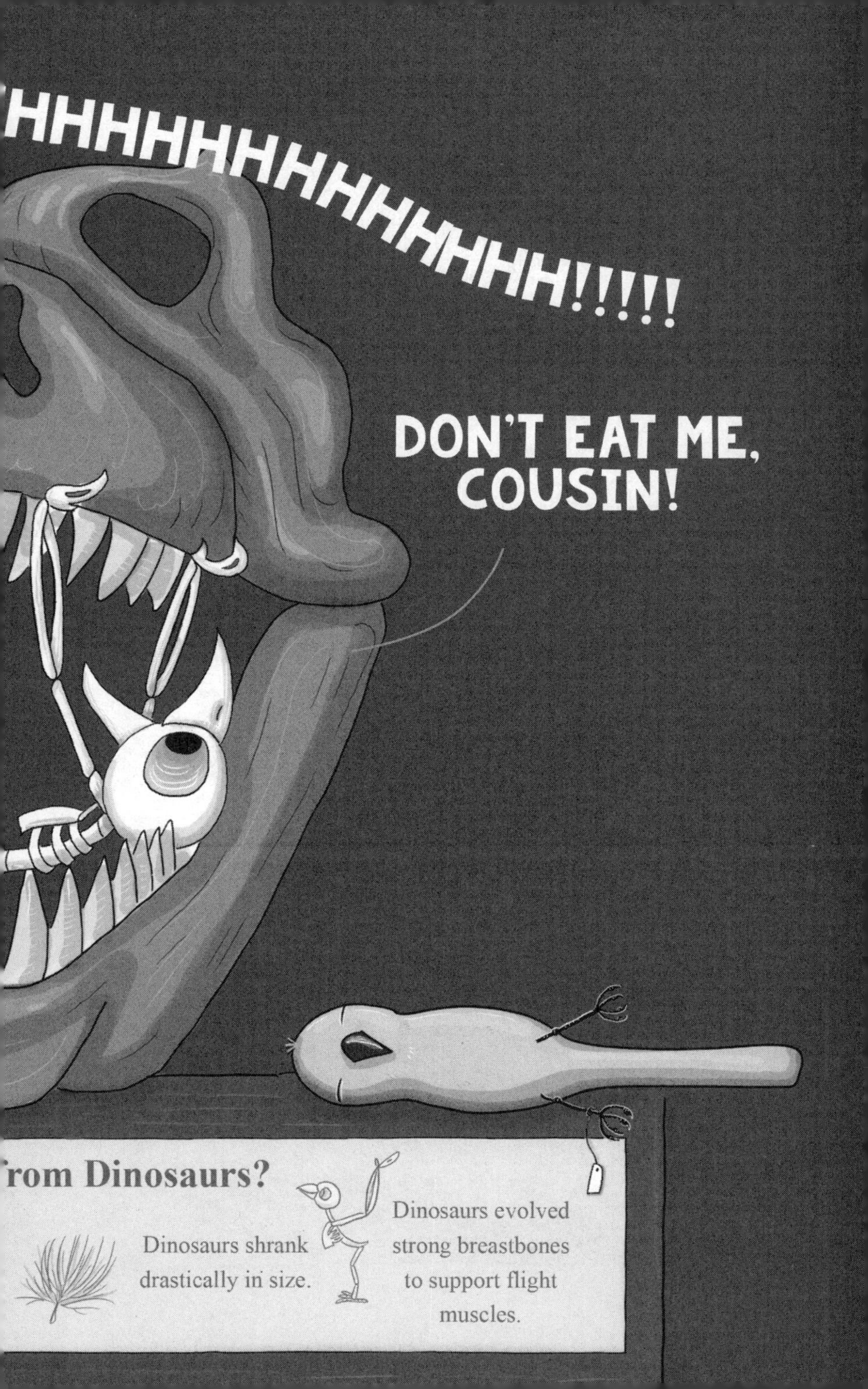
HHHHHHHHHHHHHHHHH!!!!!
DON'T EAT ME, COUSIN!
rom Dinosaurs?
Dinosaurs shrank drastically in size.
Dinosaurs evolved strong breastbones to support flight muscles.

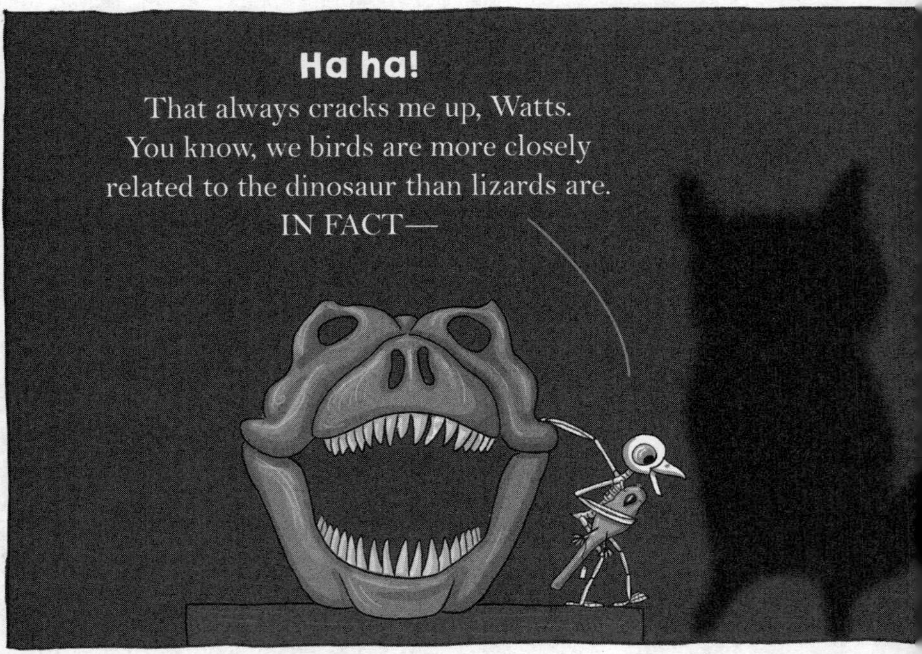
Ha ha!
That always cracks me up, Watts.
You know, we birds are more closely
related to the dinosaur than lizards are.
IN FACT—

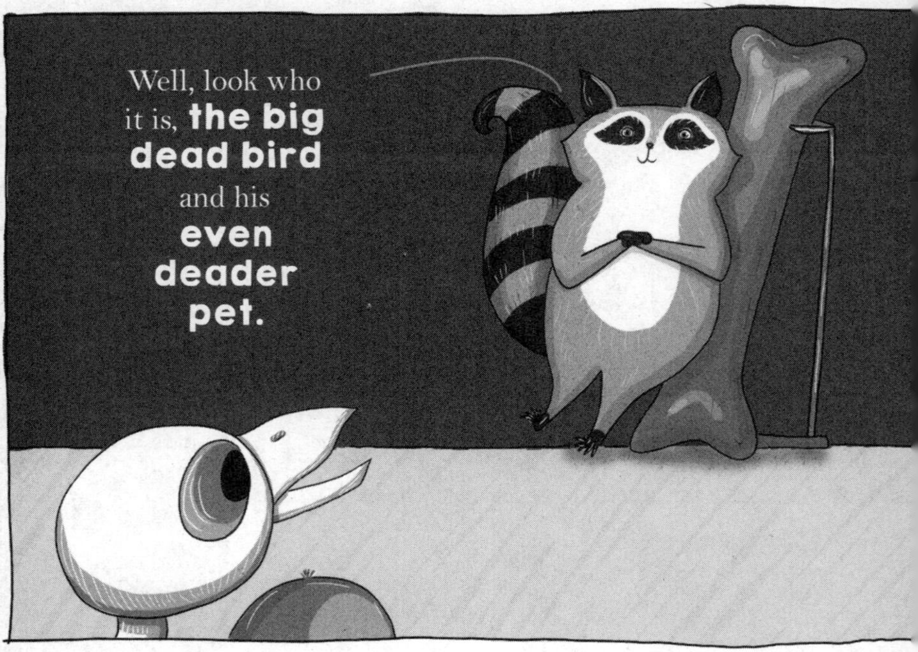
Well, look who
it is, the big
dead bird
and his
even
deader
pet.

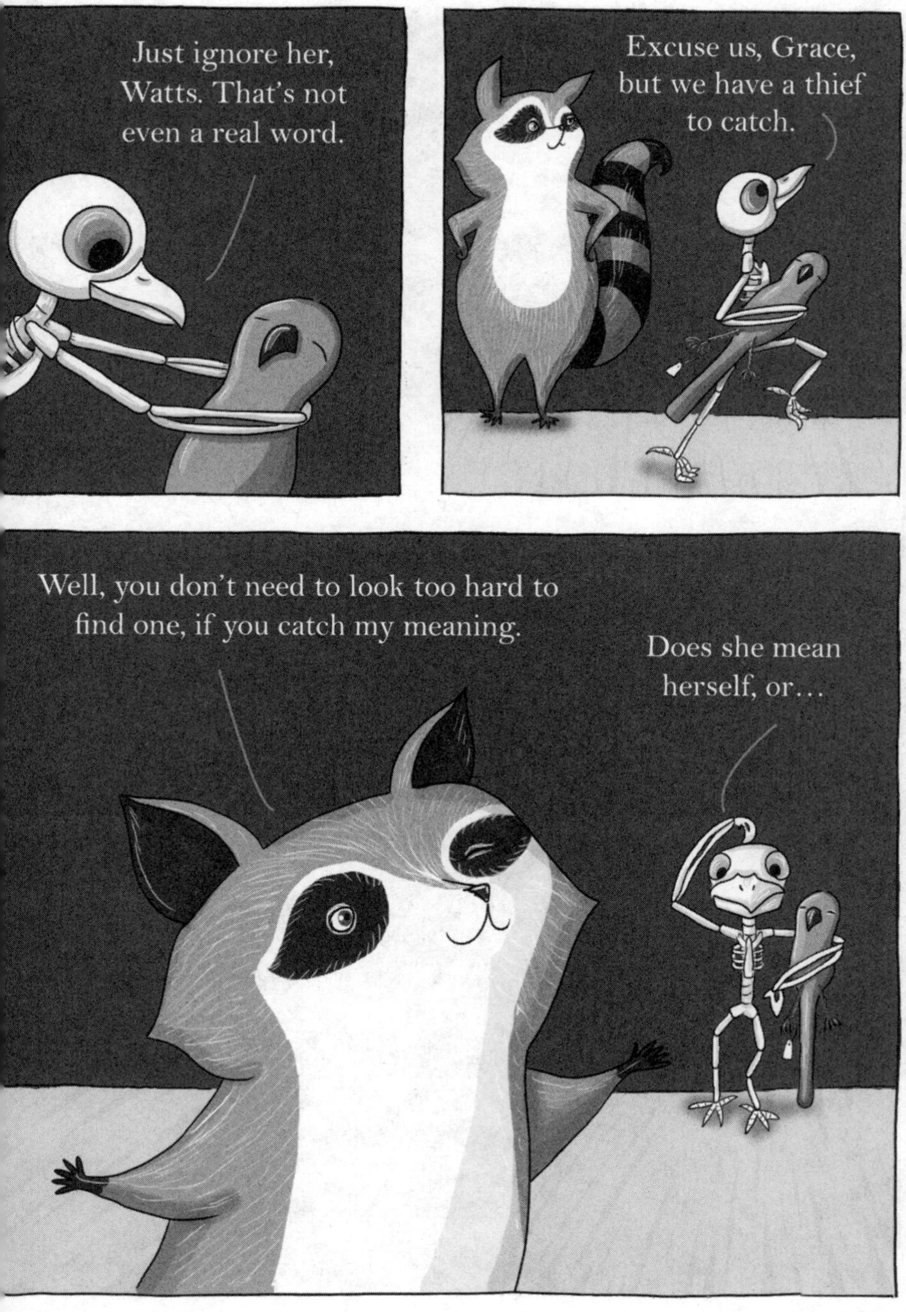
Just ignore her, Watts. That's not even a real word.
Excuse us, Grace, but we have a thief to catch.
Well, you don't need to look too hard to find one, if you catch my meaning.
Does she mean herself, or…

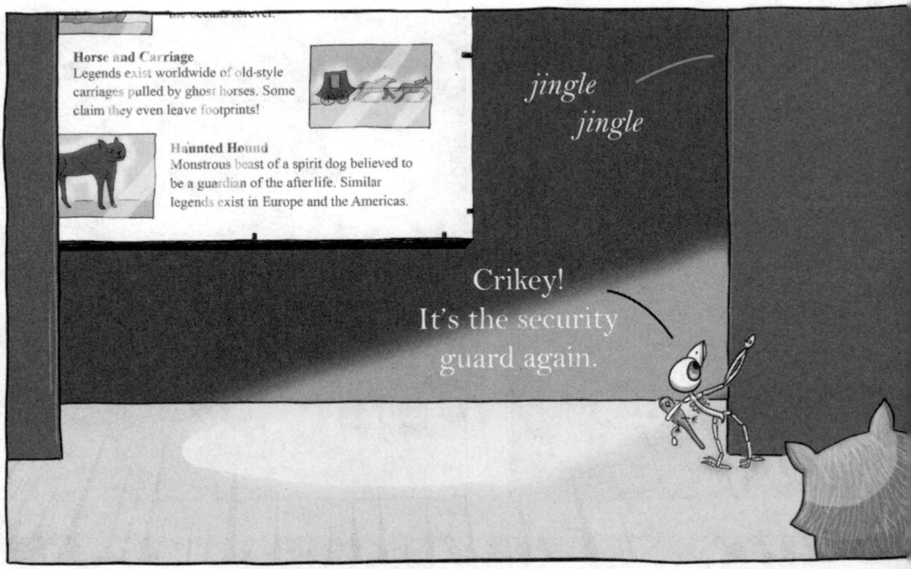
Horse and Carriage
Legends exist worldwide of old-style carriages pulled by ghost horses. Some claim they even leave footprints!
Haunted Hound
Monstrous beast of a spirit dog believed to be a guardian of the afterlife. Similar legends exist in Europe and the Americas.
jingle
jingle
Crikey! It's the security guard again.

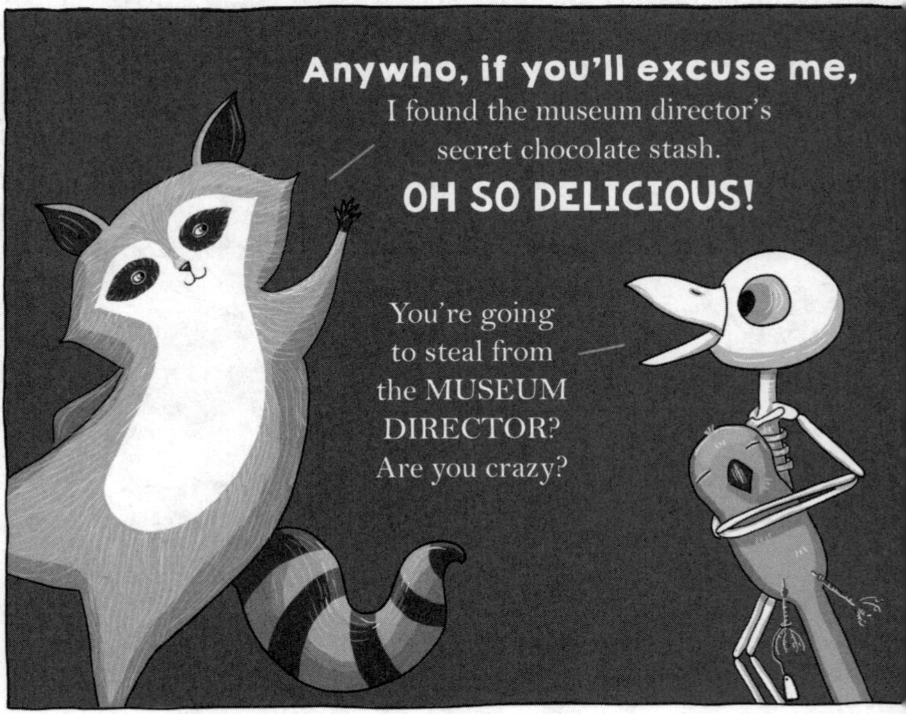
Anywho, if you'll excuse me, I found the museum director's secret chocolate stash. OH SO DELICIOUS!
You're going to steal from the MUSEUM DIRECTOR? Are you crazy?

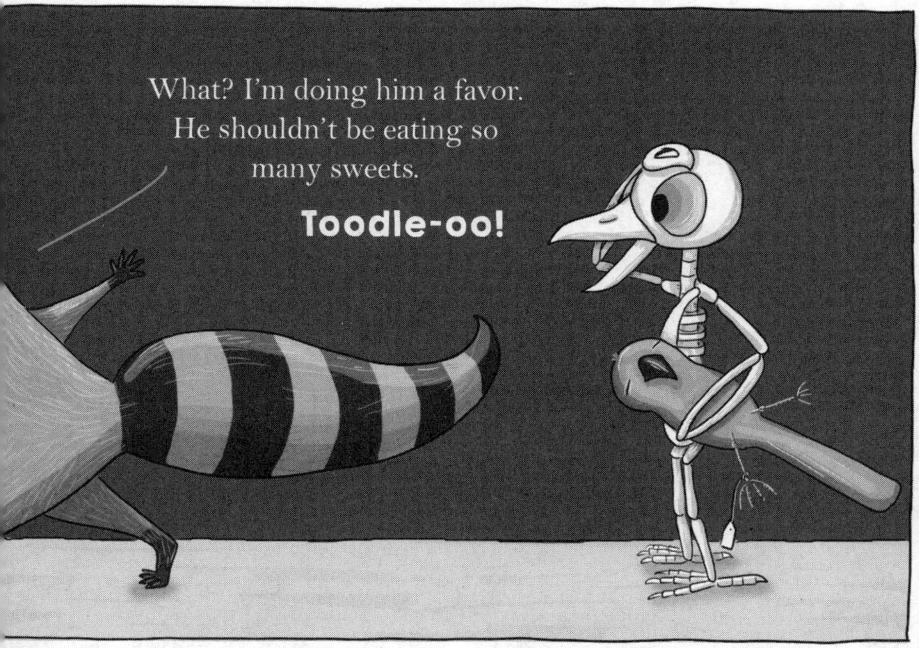
What? I'm doing him a favor. He shouldn't be eating so many sweets.
Toodle-oo!

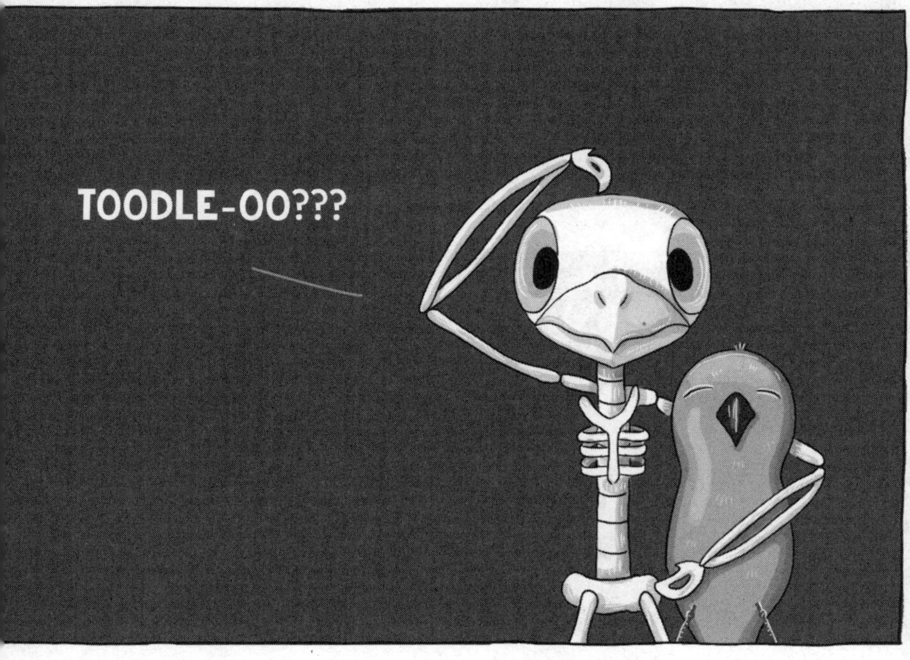
TOODLE-OO???

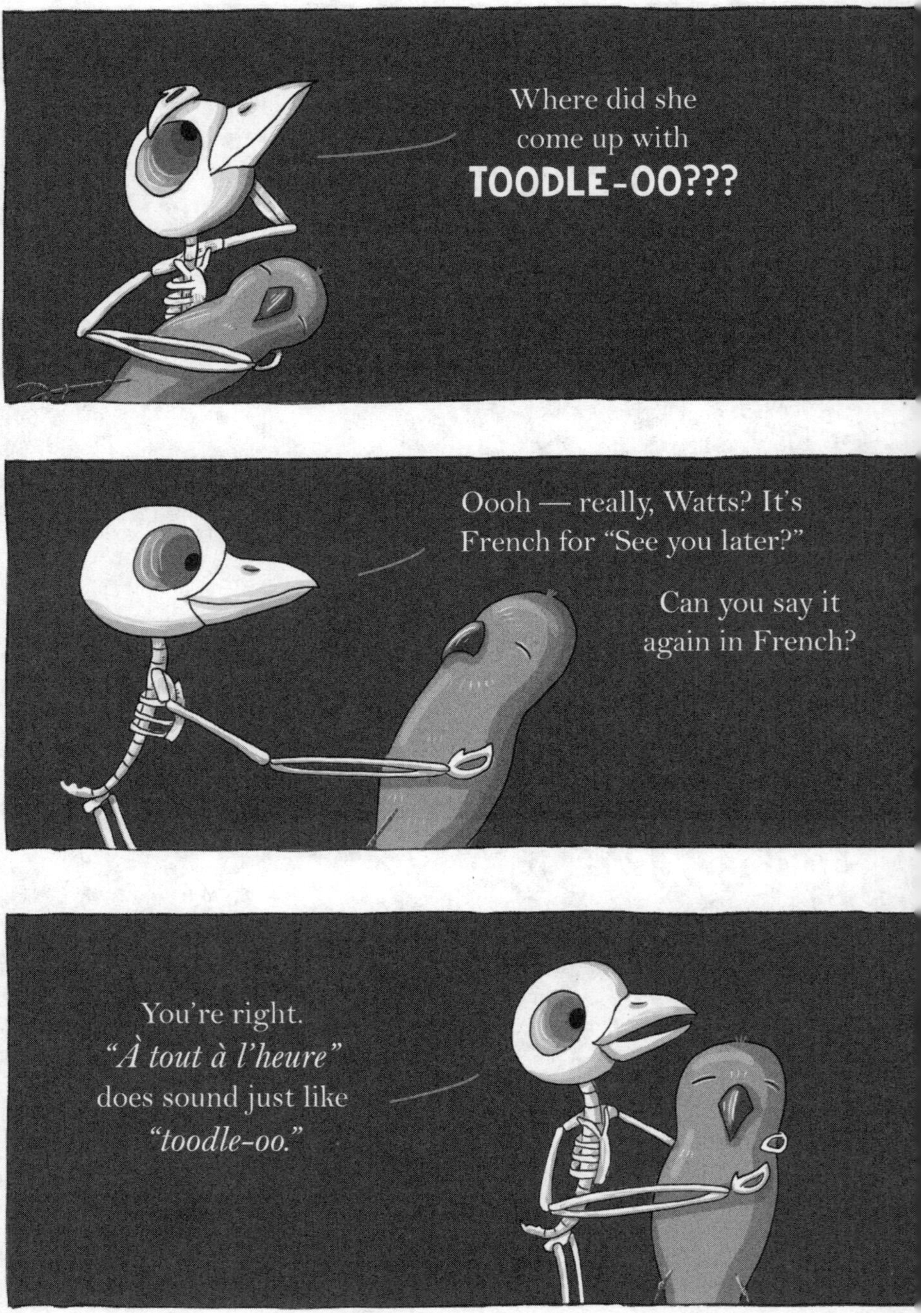
Where did she come up with **TOODLE-OO???**
Oooh — really, Watts? It's French for "See you later?"
Can you say it again in French?
You're right. *"À tout à l'heure"* does sound just like *"toodle-oo."*

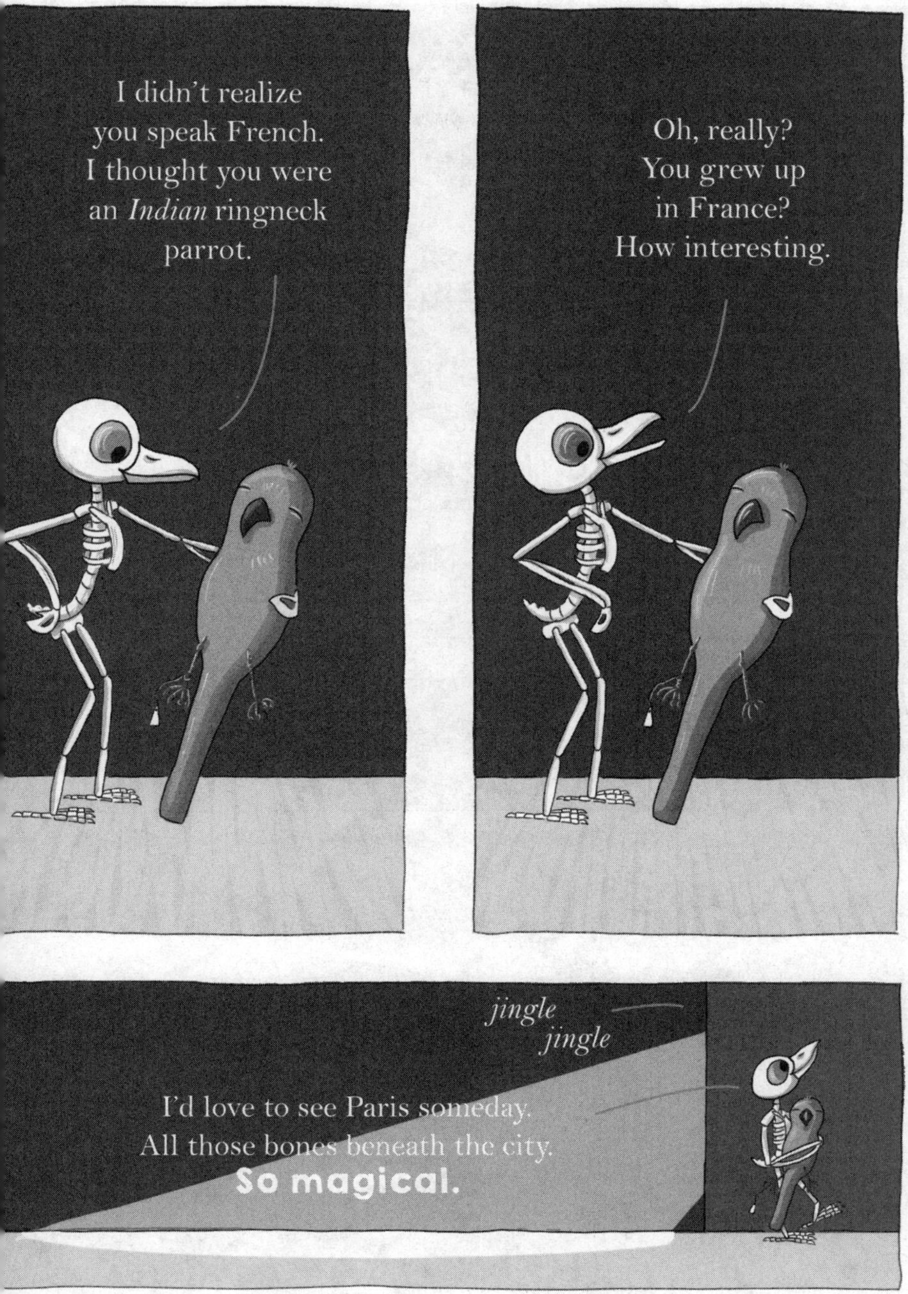
I didn't realize you speak French. I thought you were an *Indian* ringneck parrot.
Oh, really? You grew up in France? How interesting.
jingle jingle
I'd love to see Paris someday. All those bones beneath the city.
So magical.

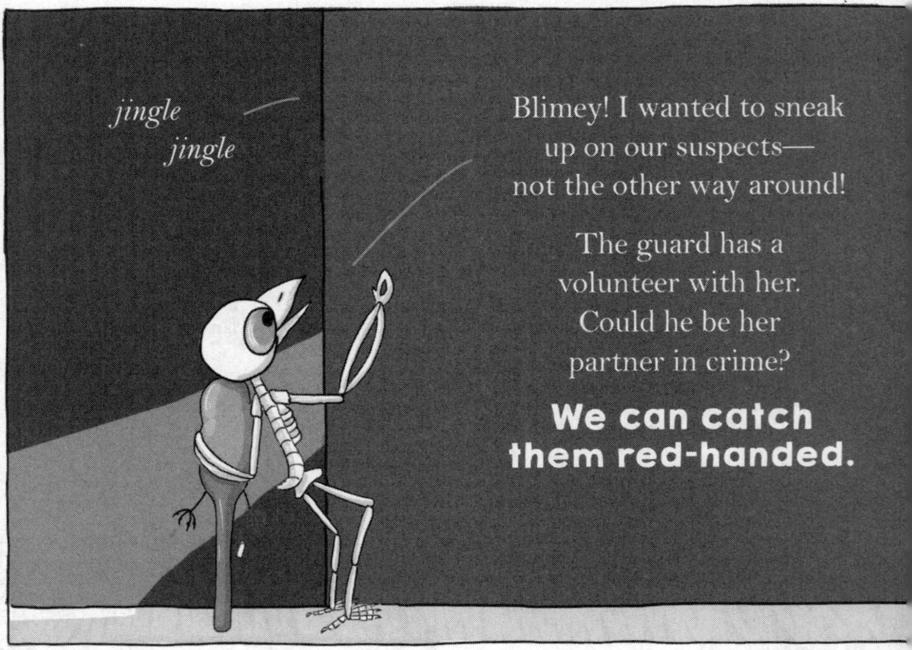
jingle
jingle
Blimey! I wanted to sneak up on our suspects— not the other way around!
The guard has a volunteer with her. Could he be her partner in crime?
We can catch them red-handed.

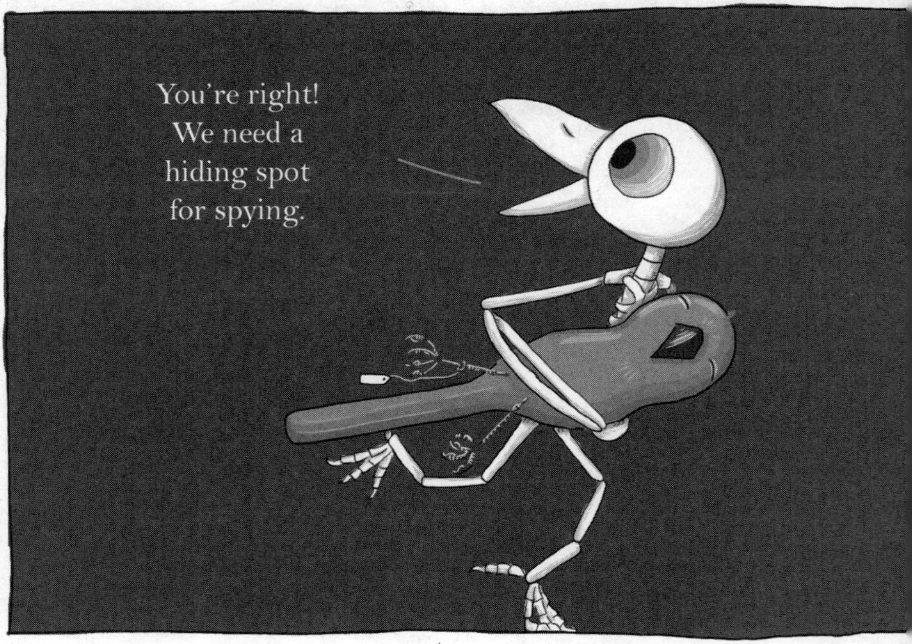
You're right! We need a hiding spot for spying.

Protoceratops andrewsi

Late Cretaceous
Sheep-sized Dinosaur
Discovered in Mongolia

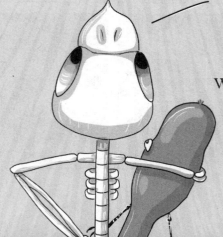

Good thinking, Watts.
We need a BIRD'S-eye view.

Or in this case, a
DINO'S-eye view
will work perfectly.

Wait here while I check it out.

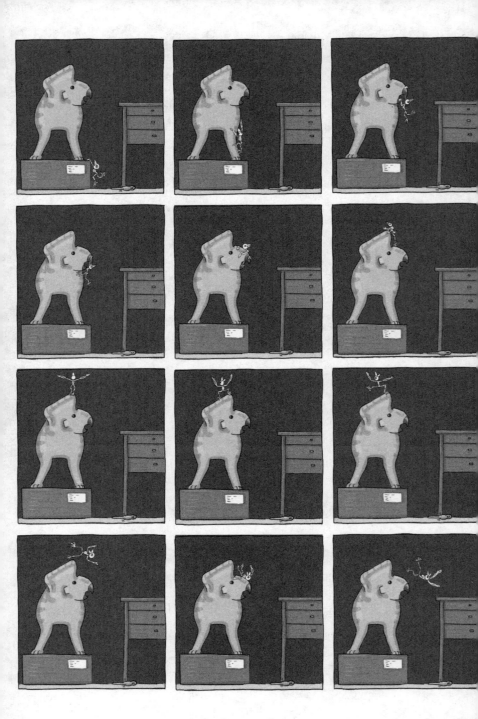

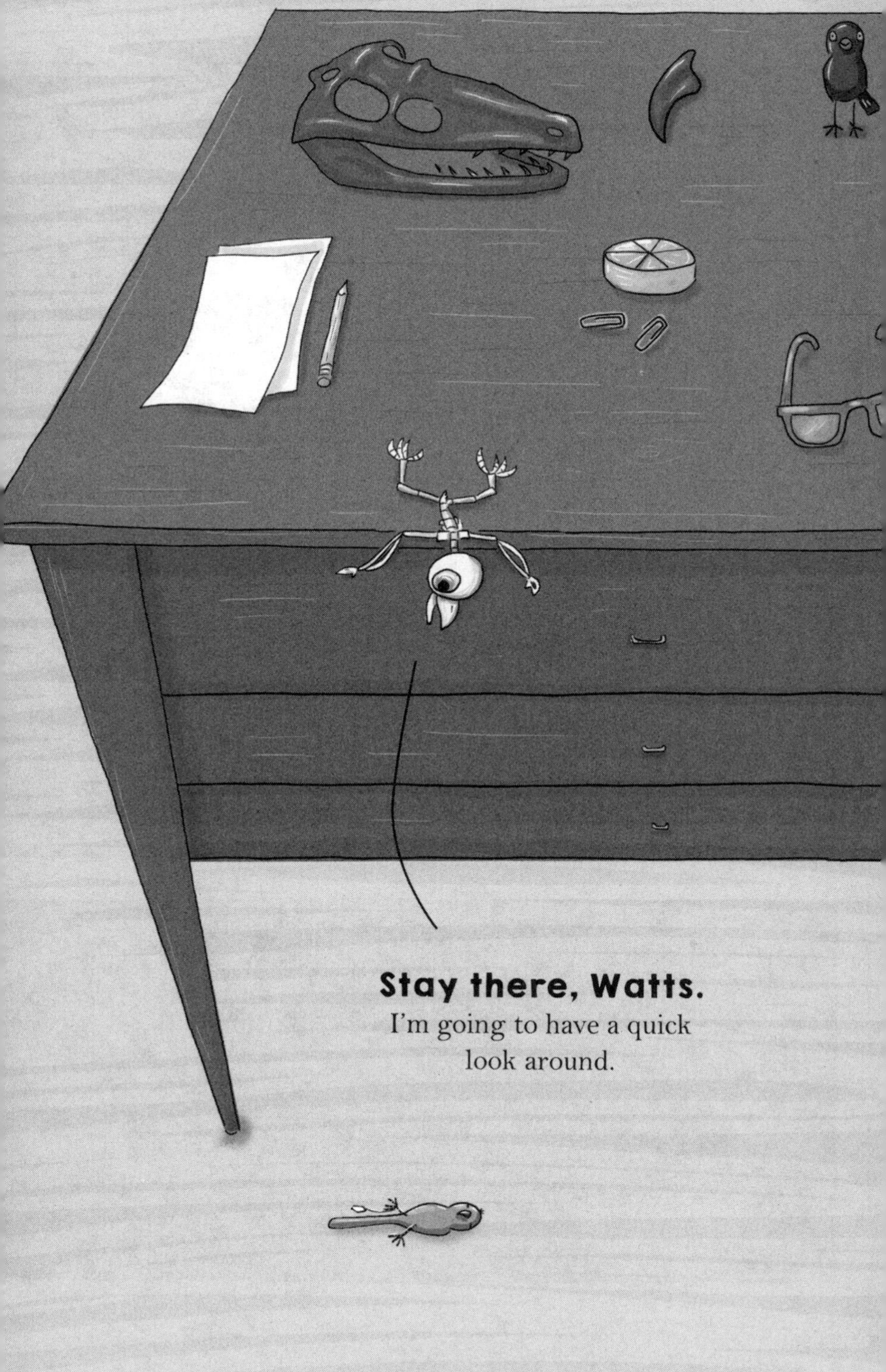

Stay there, Watts.
I'm going to have a quick look around.

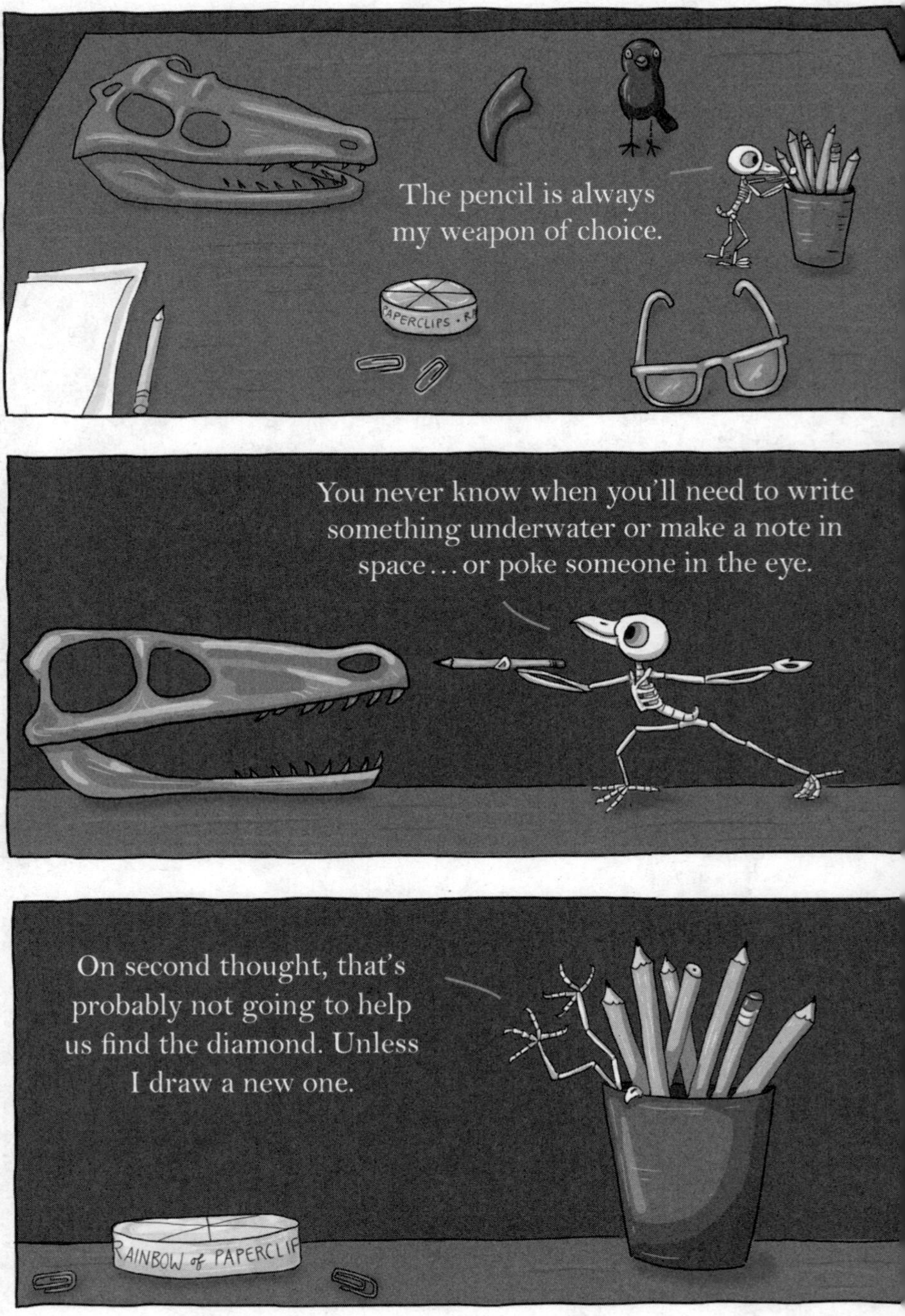
The pencil is always my weapon of choice.
PAPERCLIPS
You never know when you'll need to write something underwater or make a note in space... or poke someone in the eye.
On second thought, that's probably not going to help us find the diamond. Unless I draw a new one.
RAINBOW of PAPERCLIP

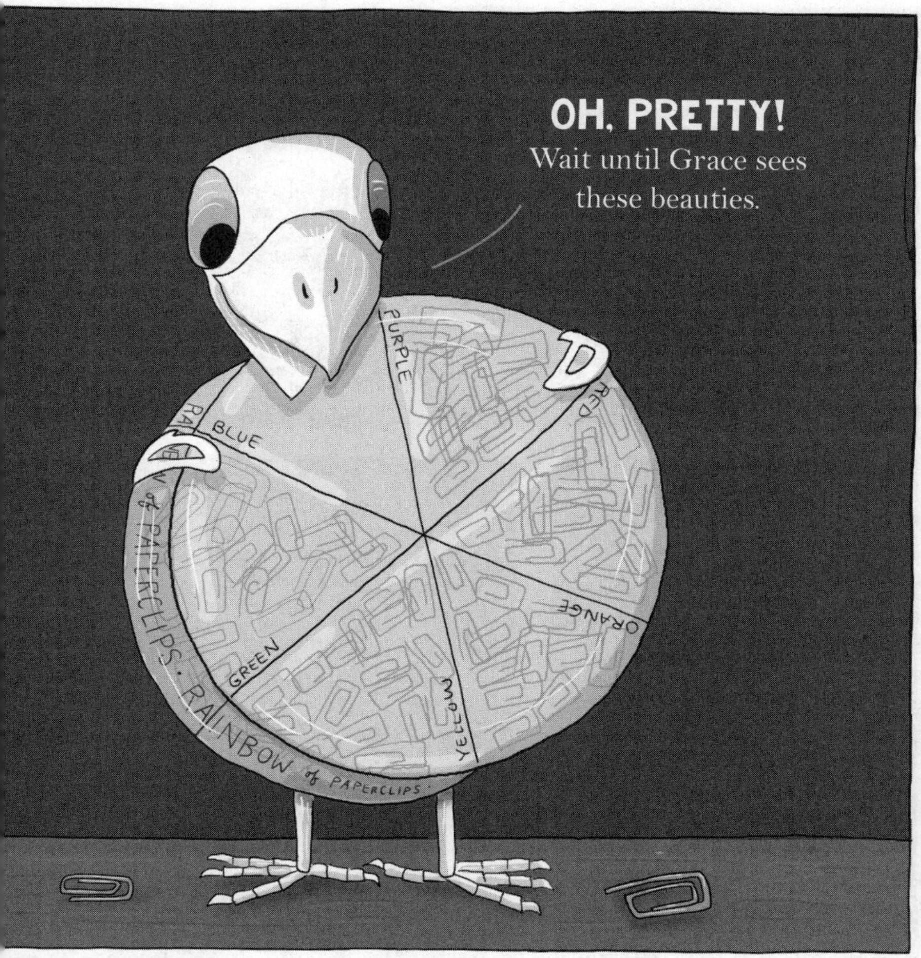
OH, PRETTY!
Wait until Grace sees these beauties.
PURPLE
RED
ORANGE
YELLOW
GREEN
BLUE
RAINBOW of PAPERCLIPS

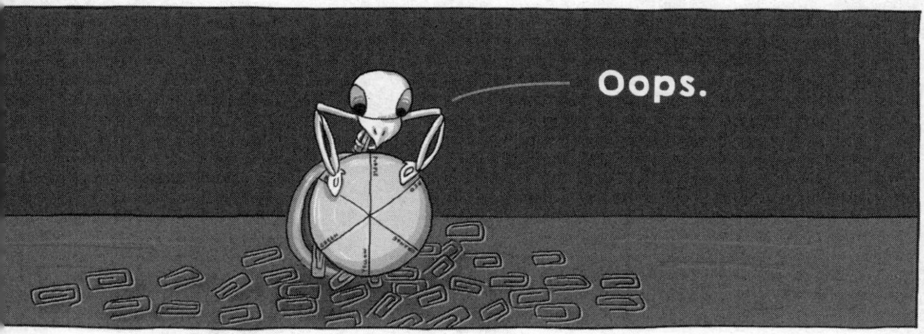
Oops.

Watts, did you know that the paperclip has remained pretty much unchanged since its invention over one hundred years ago?

Yes, I heard what you said about Grace.

I suppose you may be onto something.

She could have stolen the diamond...

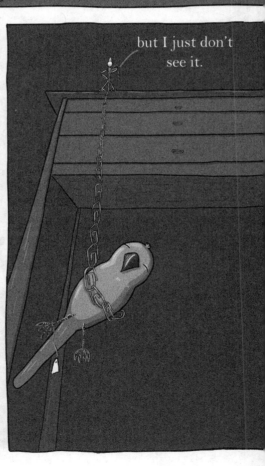

but I just don't see it.

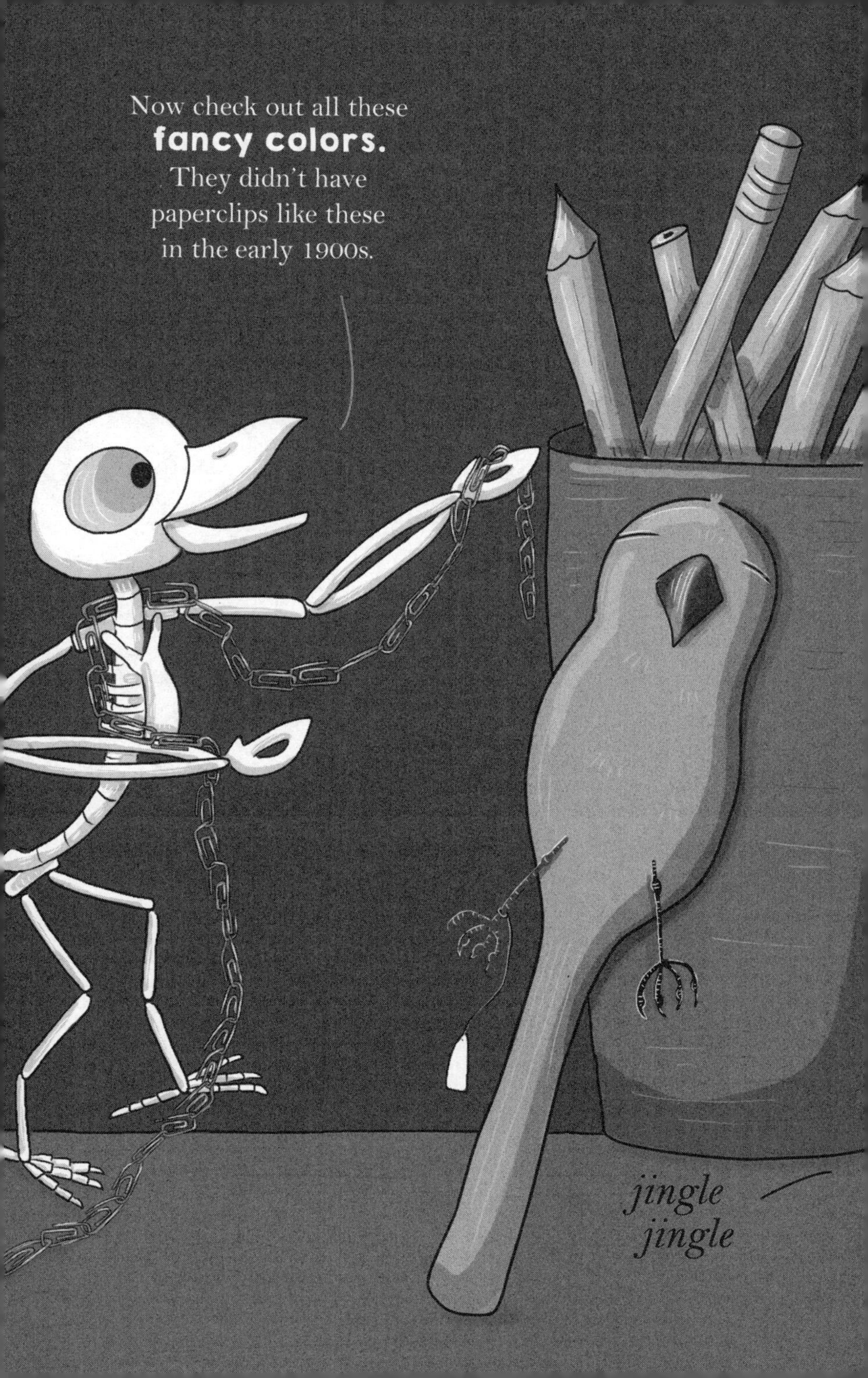
Now check out all these **fancy colors.** They didn't have paperclips like these in the early 1900s.
jingle
jingle

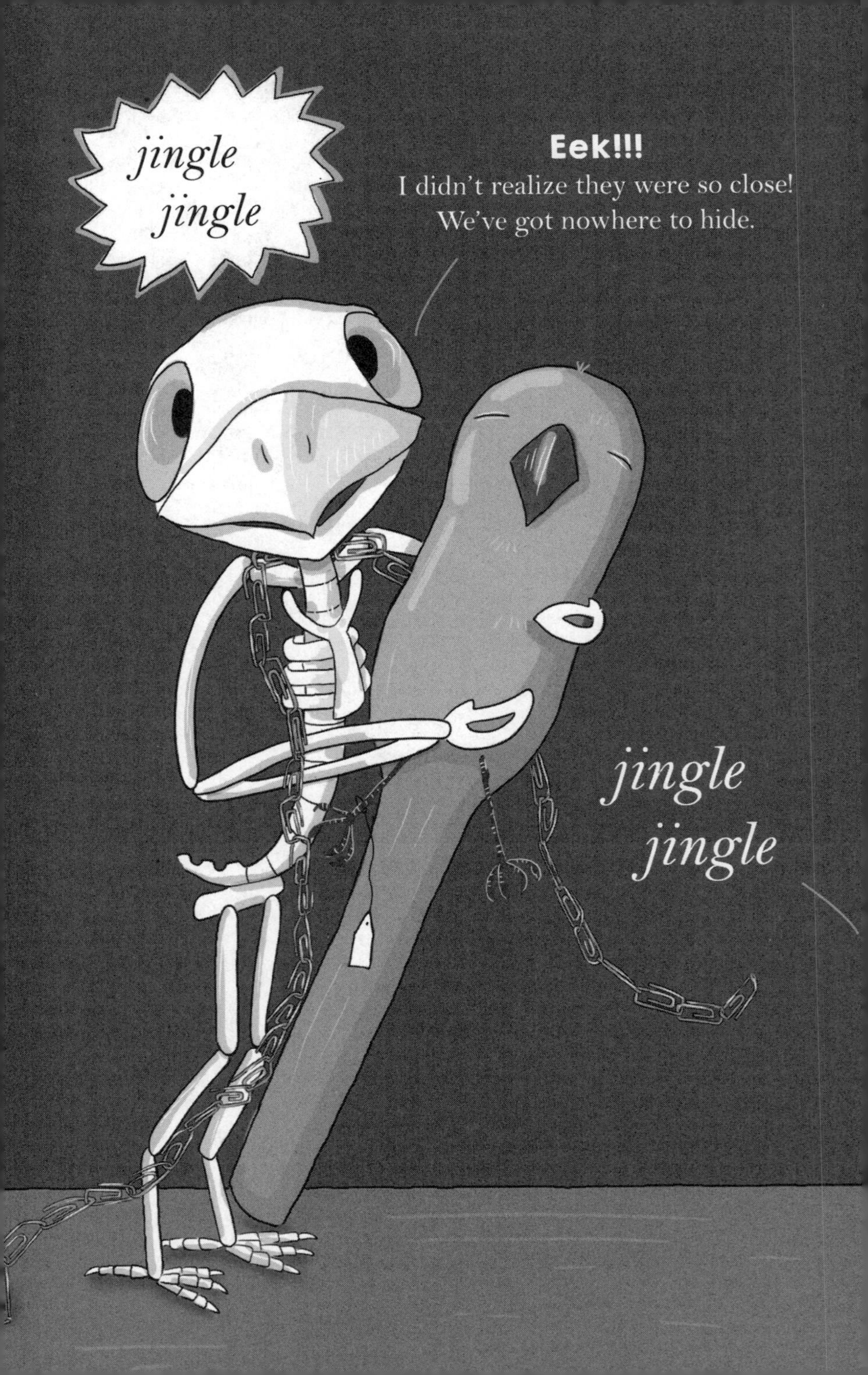
jingle
jingle
Eek!!!
I didn't realize they were so close!
We've got nowhere to hide.
jingle
jingle

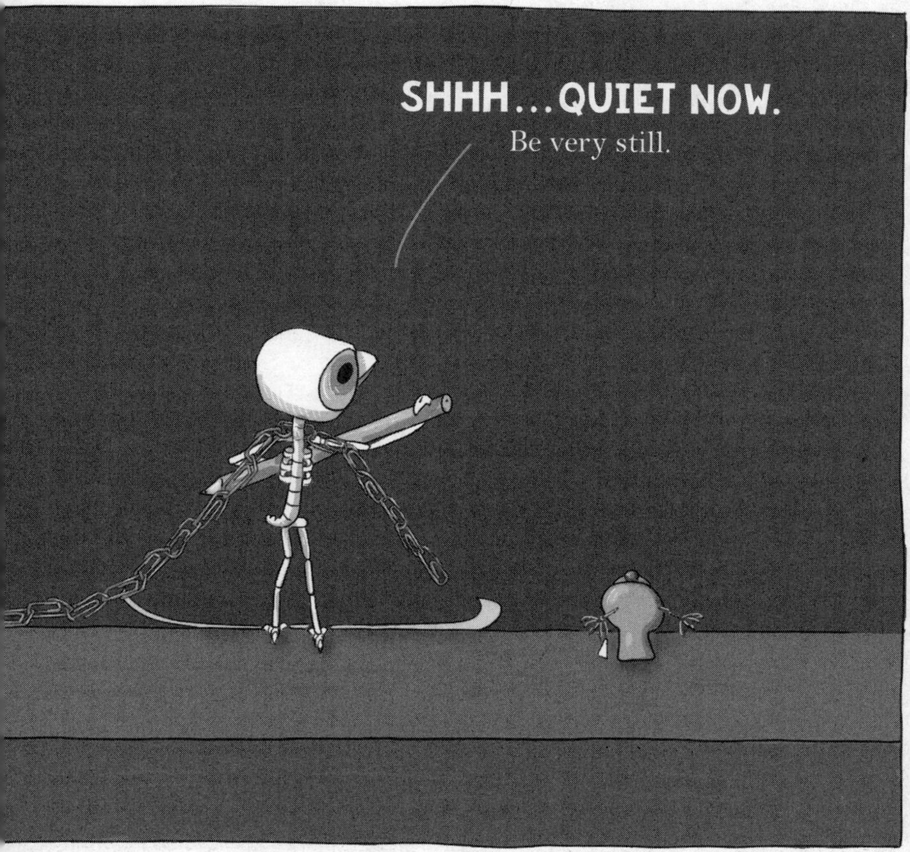
SHHH...QUIET NOW.
Be very still.

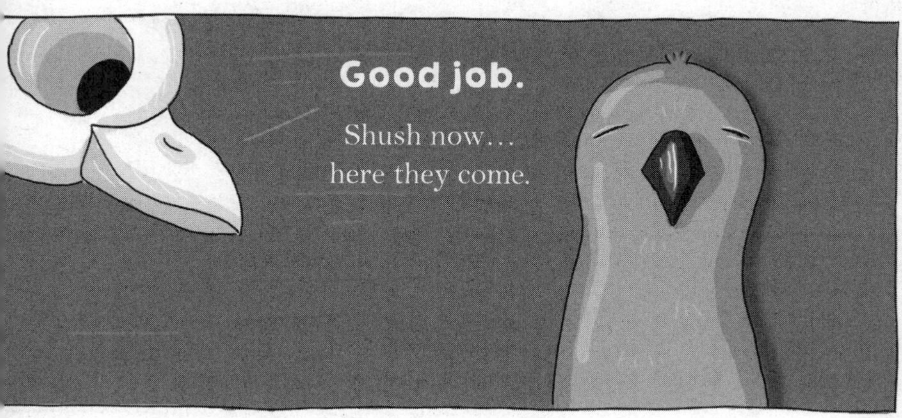
Good job.
Shush now...
here they come.

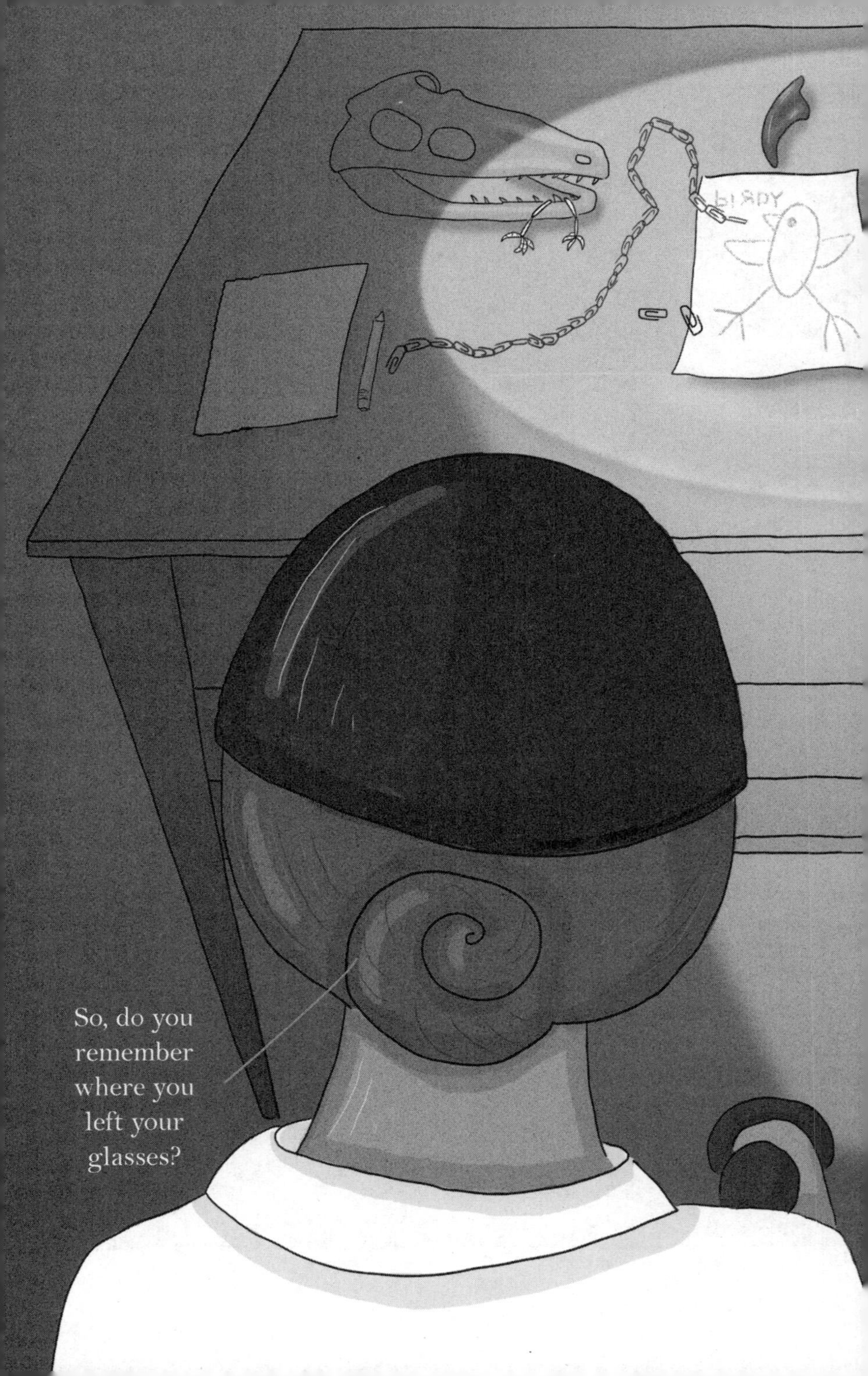
So, do you remember where you left your glasses?

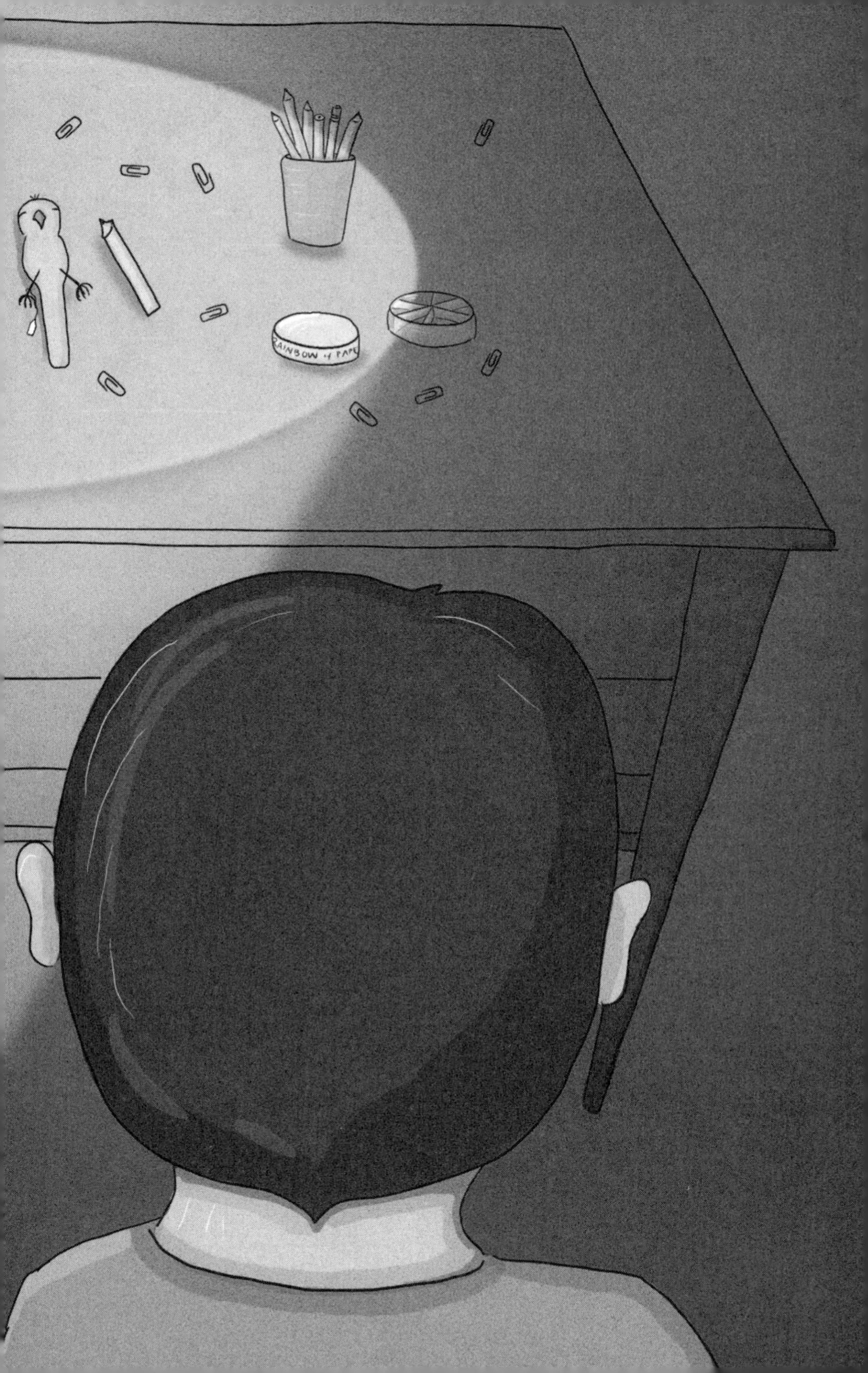
RAINBOW of PAPE

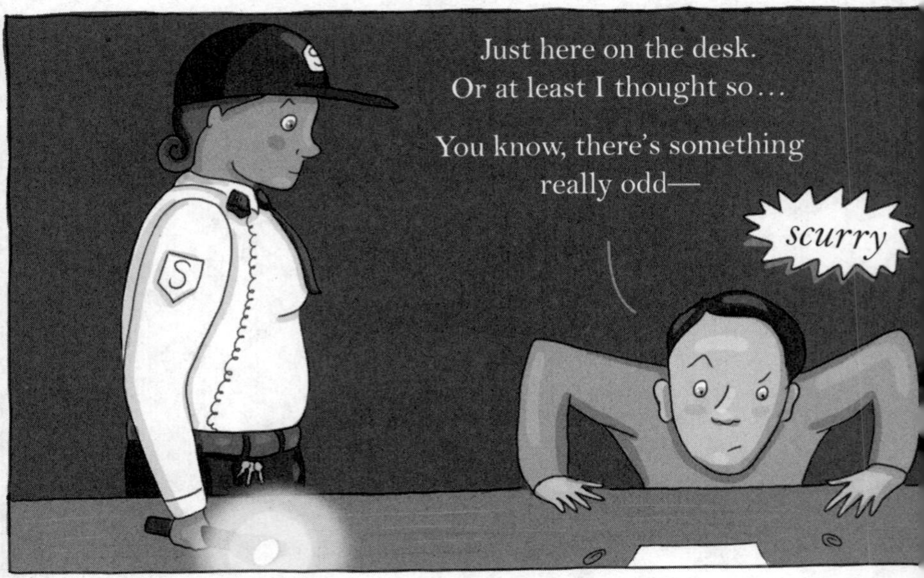
Just here on the desk.
Or at least I thought so...
You know, there's something really odd—
scurry

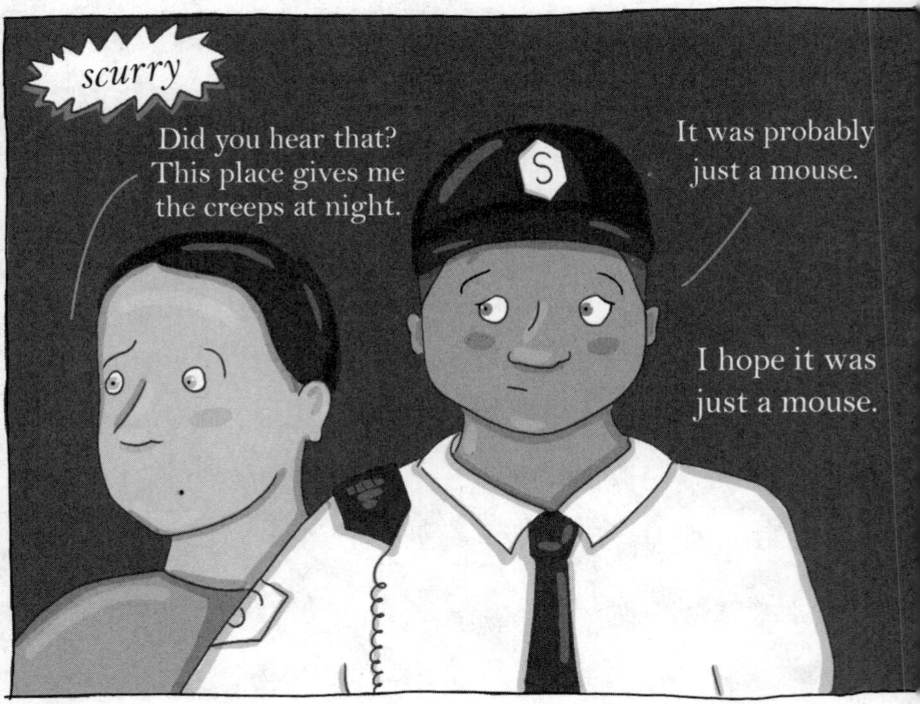
scurry
Did you hear that? This place gives me the creeps at night.
It was probably just a mouse.
I hope it was just a mouse.

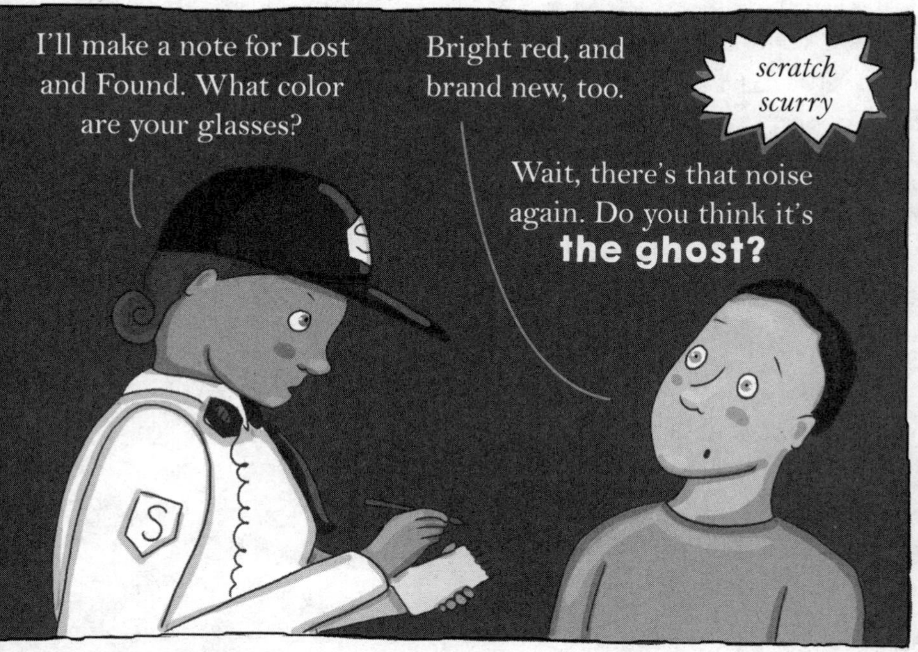
I'll make a note for Lost and Found. What color are your glasses?
Bright red, and brand new, too.
scratch scurry
Wait, there's that noise again. Do you think it's **the ghost?**

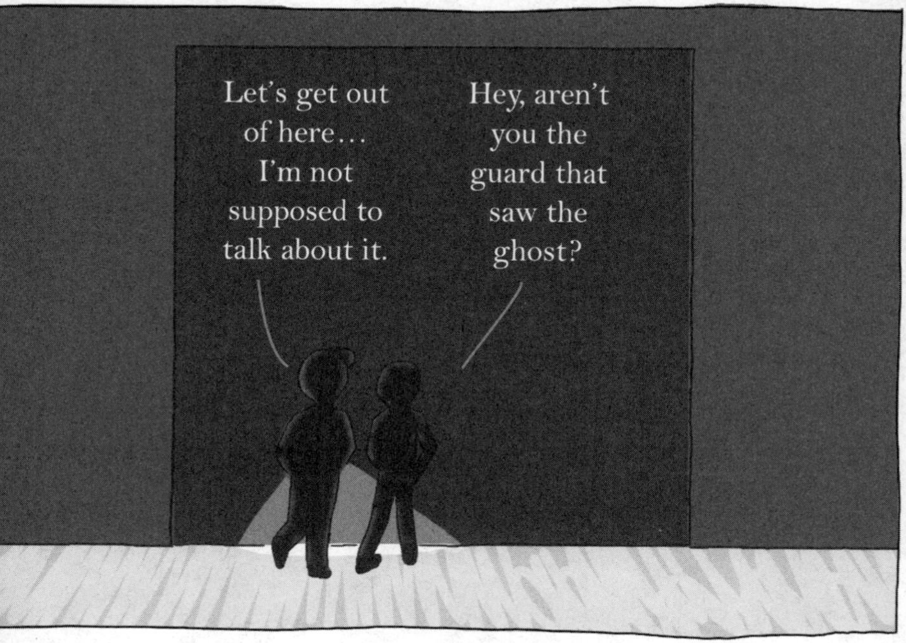
Hey, aren't you the guard that saw the ghost?
Let's get out of here… I'm not supposed to talk about it.

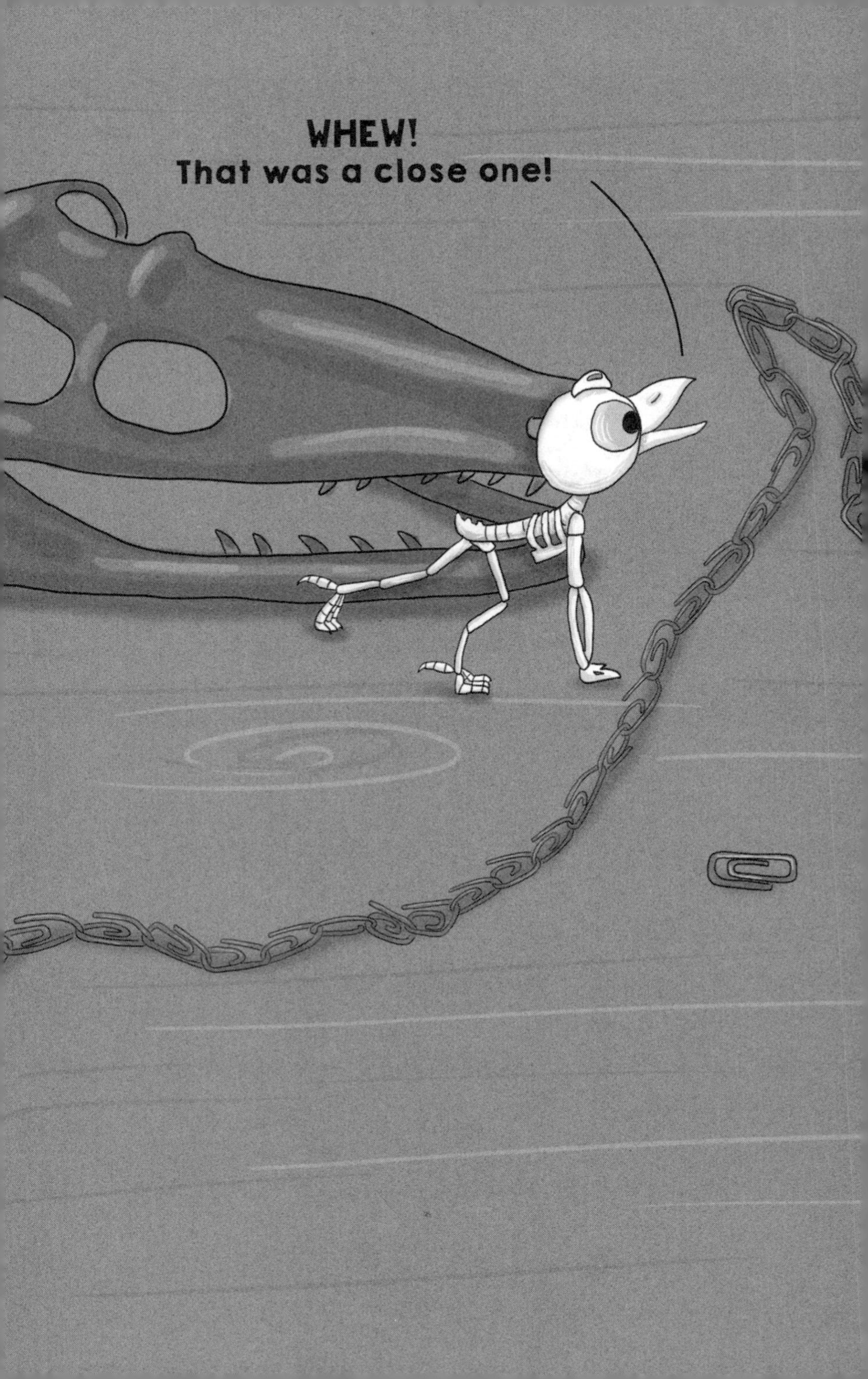
WHEW!
That was a close one!

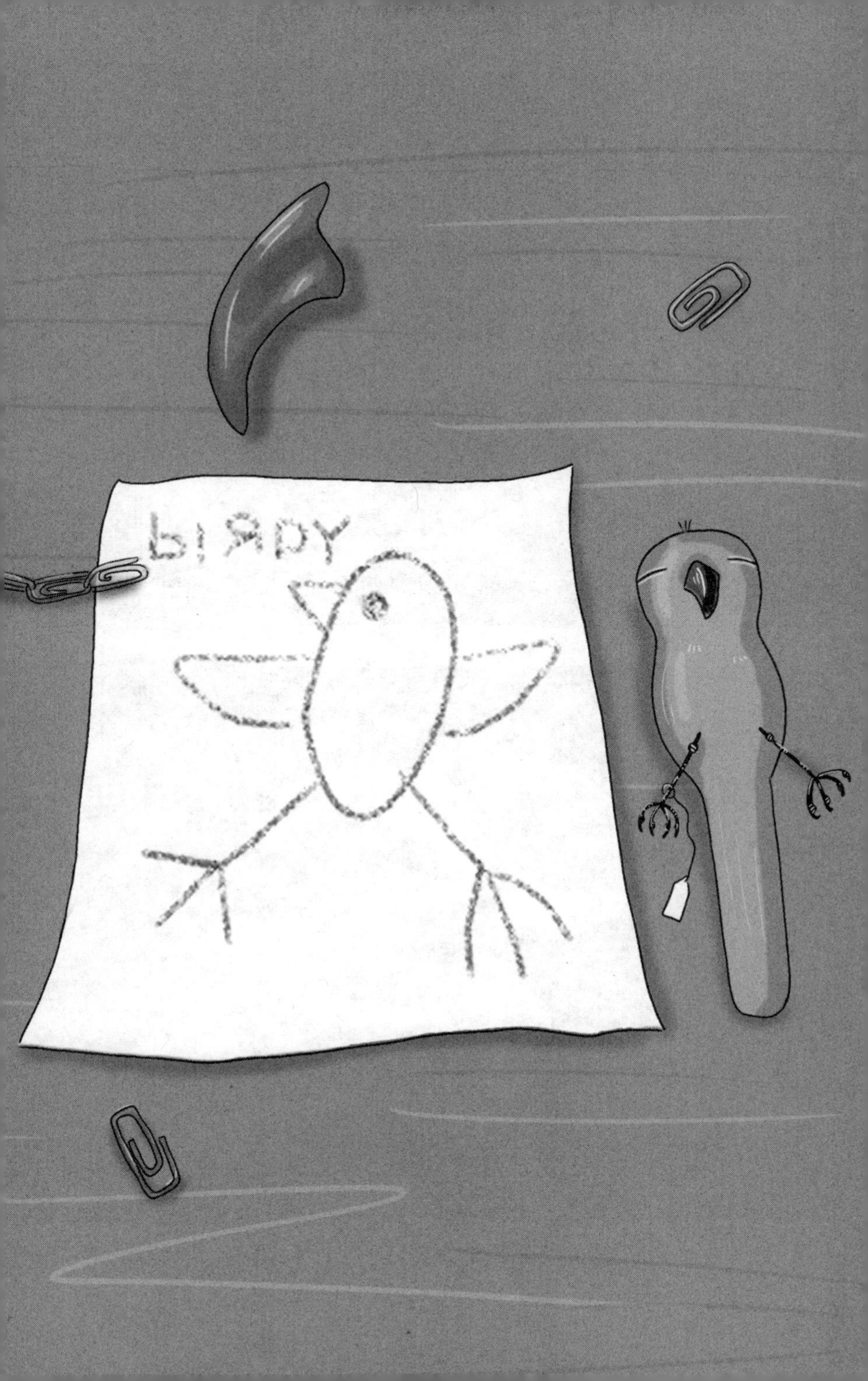
bIRDY

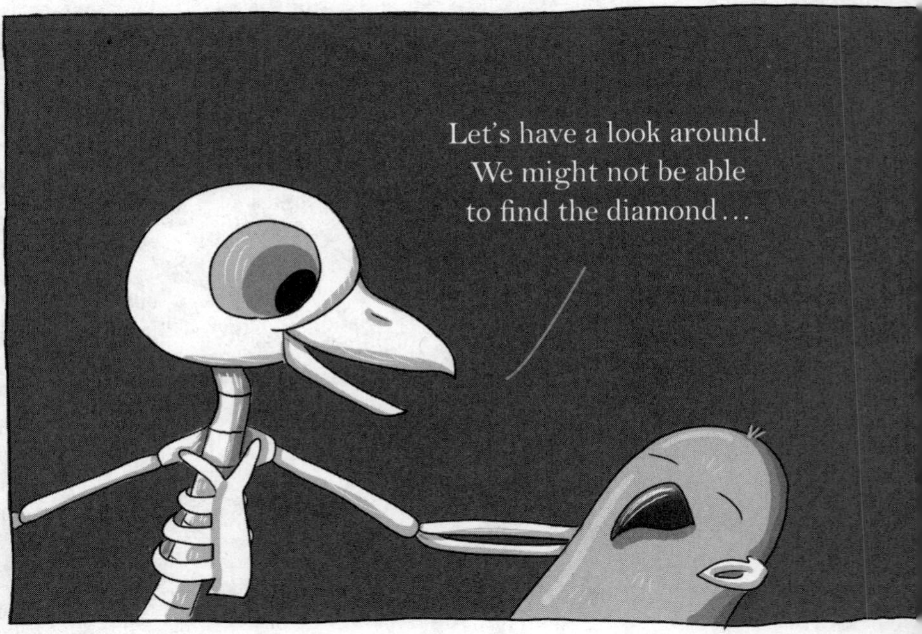
Let's have a look around. We might not be able to find the diamond...

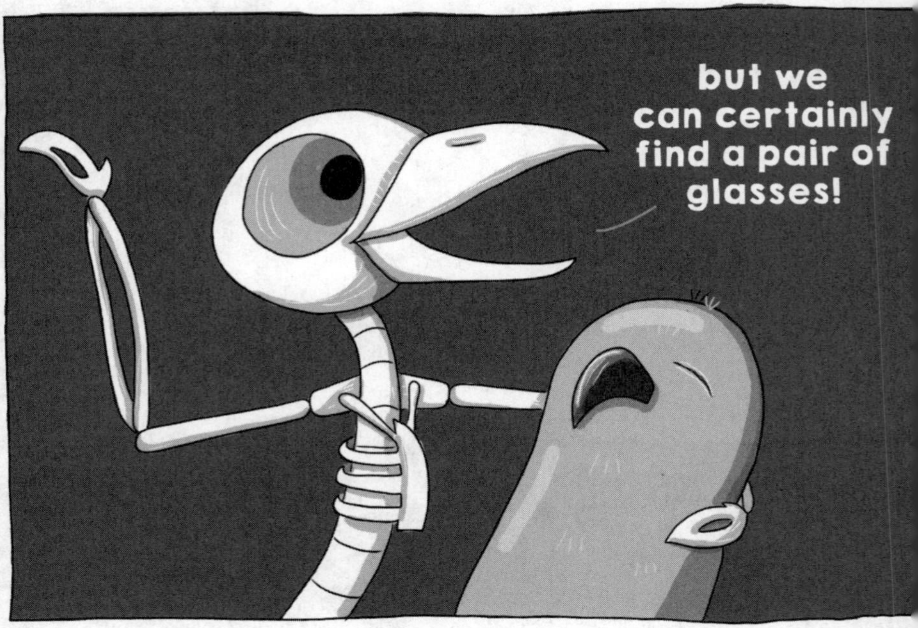
but we can certainly find a pair of glasses!

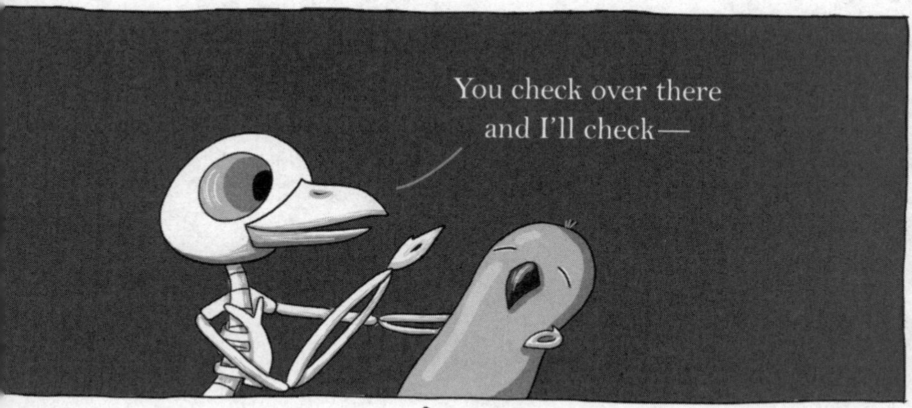
You check over there
and I'll check—

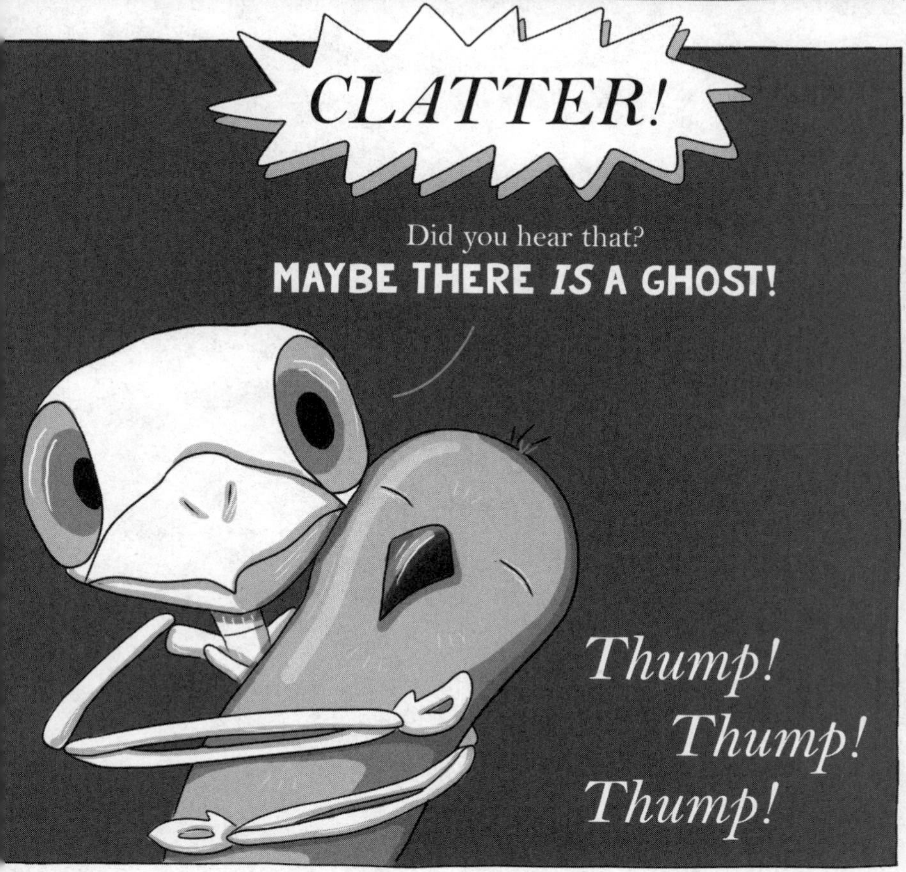
CLATTER!
Did you hear that?
MAYBE THERE *IS* A GHOST!
Thump!
Thump!
Thump!

CHAPTER 5
In the Spotlight

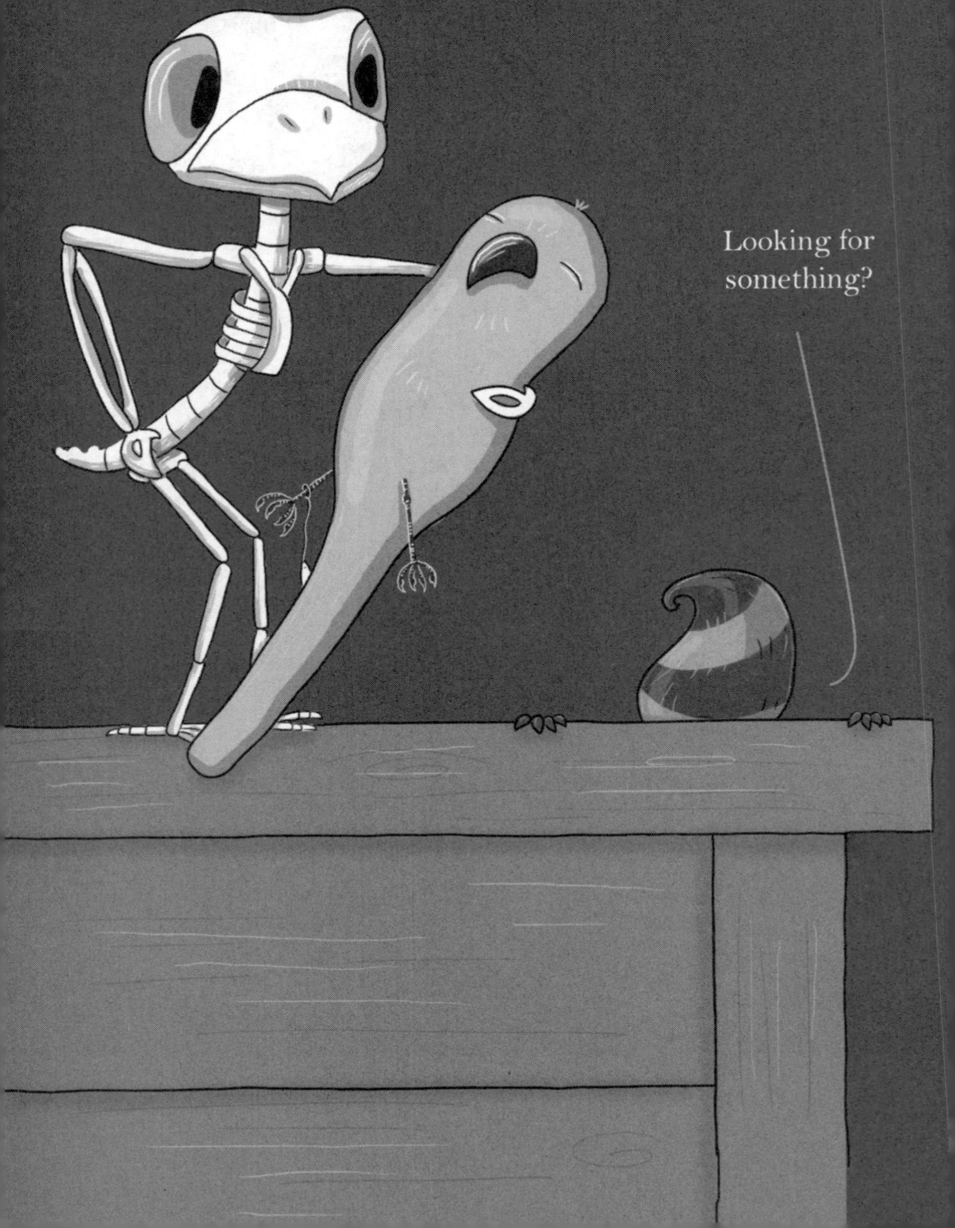
Looking for
something?

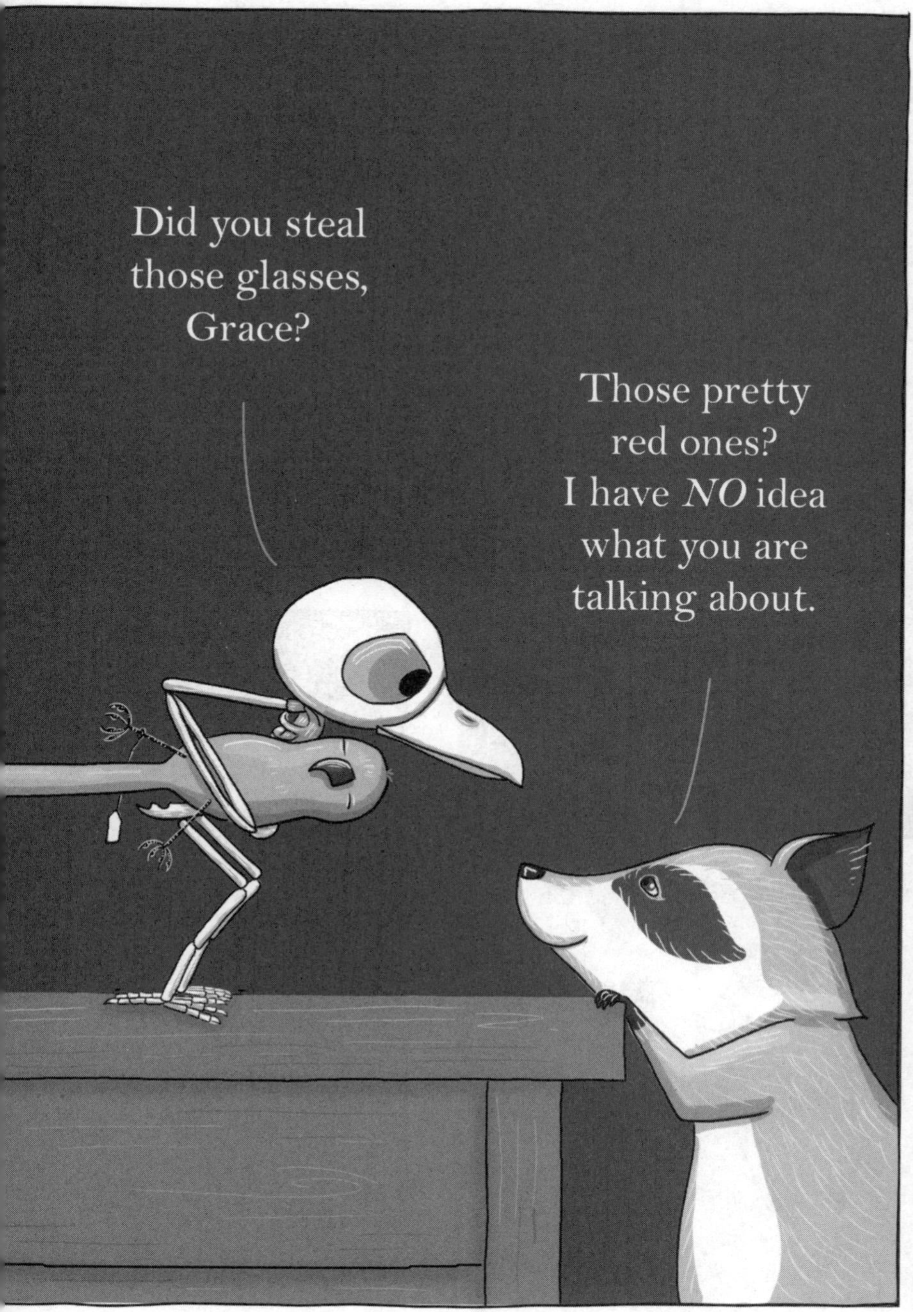
Did you steal those glasses, Grace?
Those pretty red ones? I have *NO* idea what you are talking about.

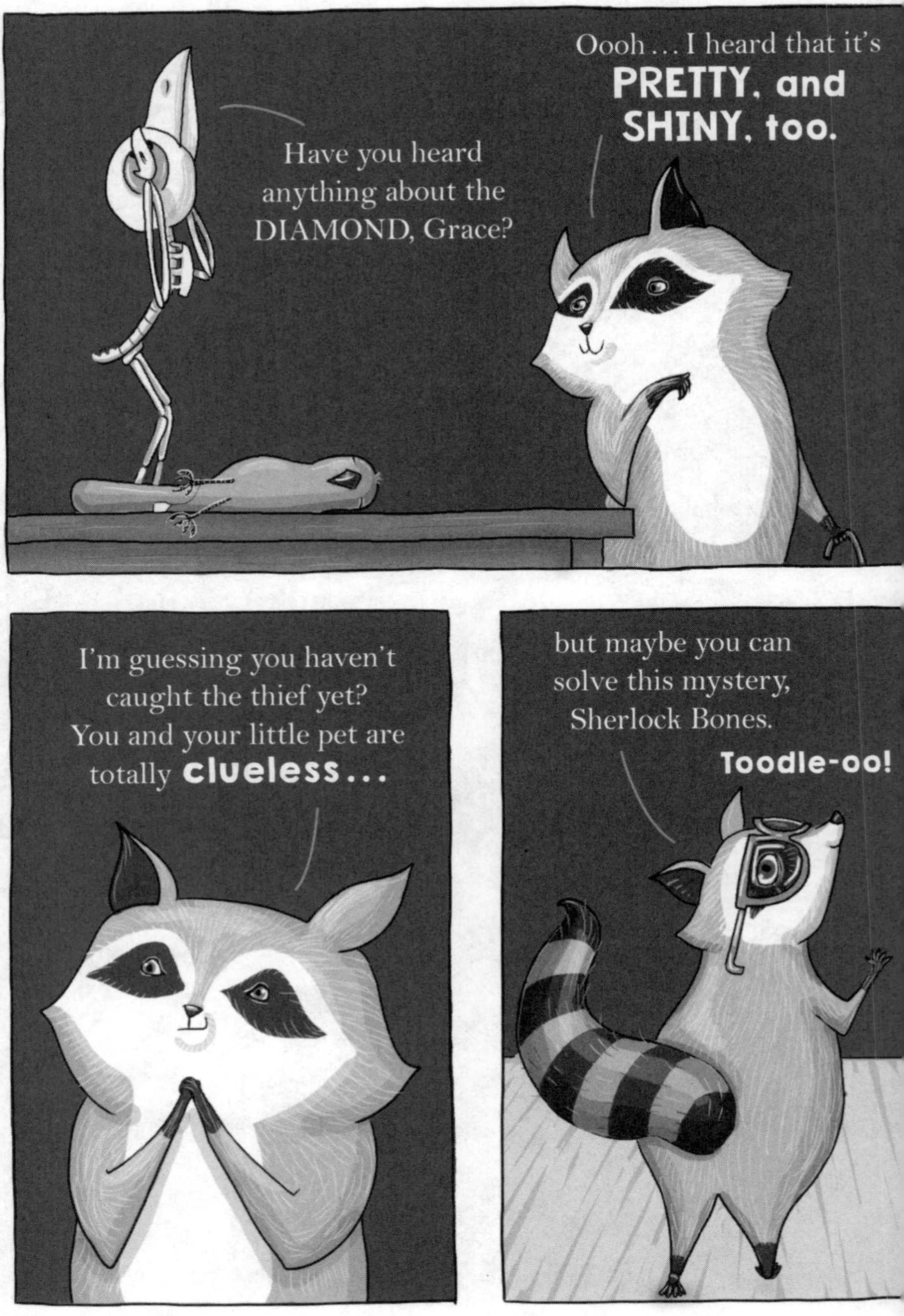
Have you heard anything about the DIAMOND, Grace?
Oooh . . . I heard that it's **PRETTY**, and **SHINY**, too.
I'm guessing you haven't caught the thief yet? You and your little pet are totally **clueless . . .**
but maybe you can solve this mystery, Sherlock Bones.
Toodle-oo!

Hey! I knew you stole the glasses all along!

Do you know what will happen
if the diamond isn't found?

You'll be out on the streets, Grace!

RUMMAGING THROUGH THE GARBAGE LIKE THE BIG STRIPEY NOT-EVEN-FRENCH RAT YOU ARE!

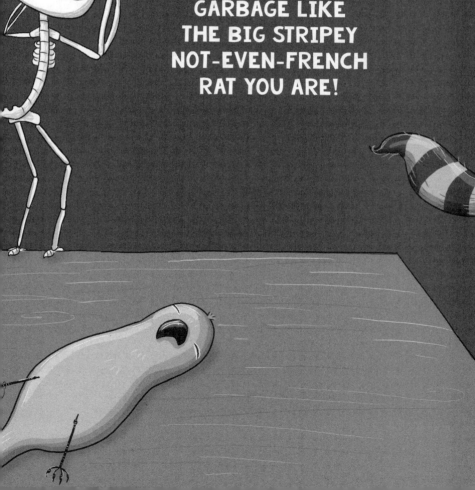

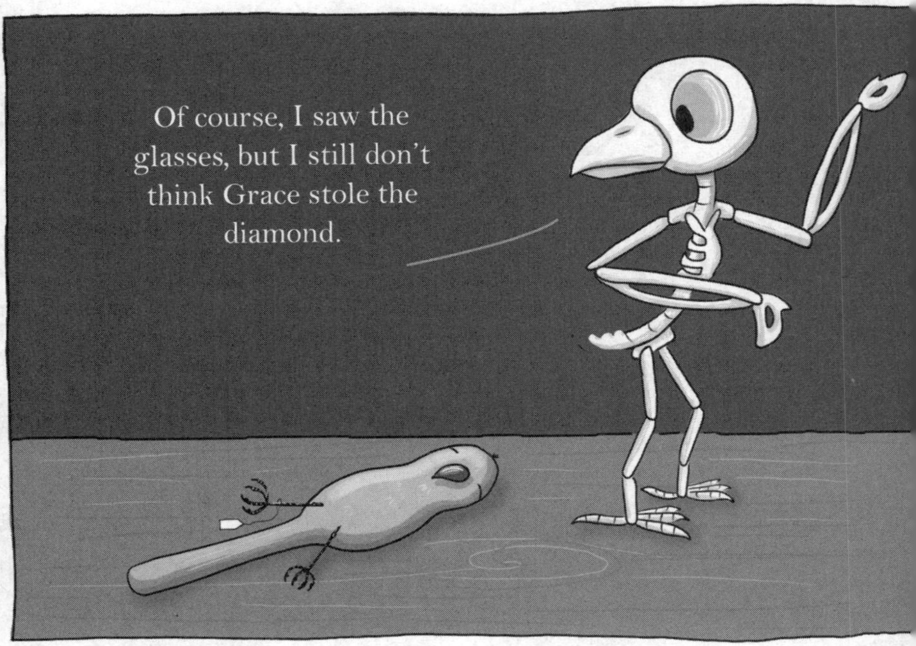
Of course, I saw the glasses, but I still don't think Grace stole the diamond.

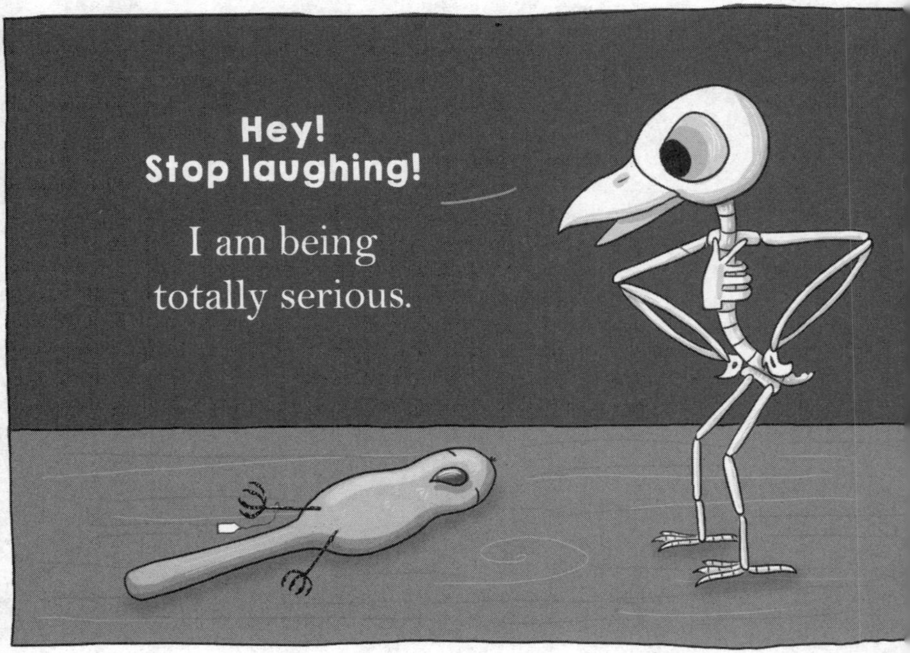
Hey!
Stop laughing!
I am being totally serious.

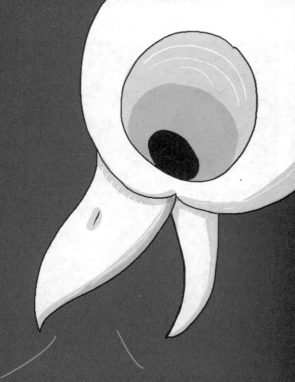

Do you really think Grace would be able to put the diamond down for **one teeny-tiny little second** if she already had it in her **sticky paws?**

My point exactly.
Grace doesn't have the diamond.
At least, not yet.

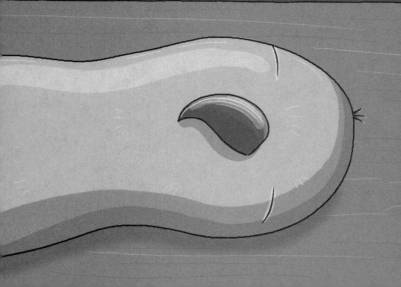

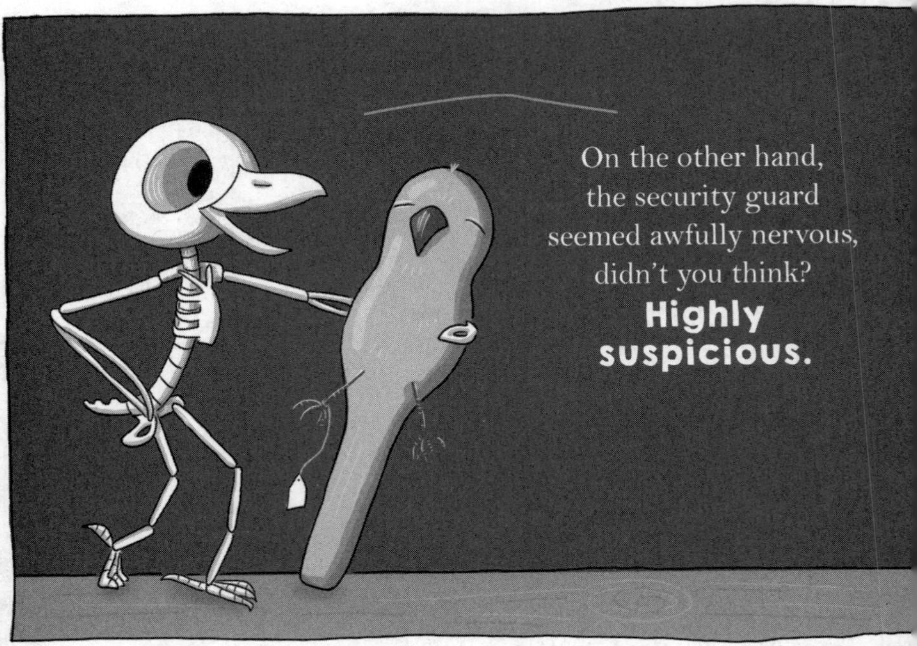
On the other hand, the security guard seemed awfully nervous, didn't you think?
Highly suspicious.

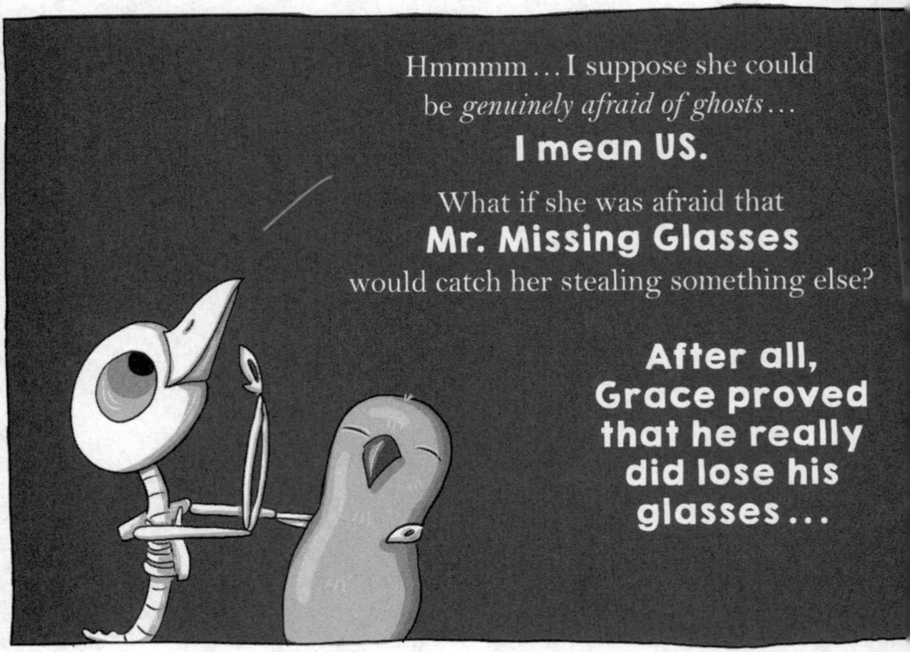
Hmmmm... I suppose she could be *genuinely afraid of ghosts*...
I mean US.
What if she was afraid that **Mr. Missing Glasses** would catch her stealing something else?
After all, Grace proved that he really did lose his glasses...

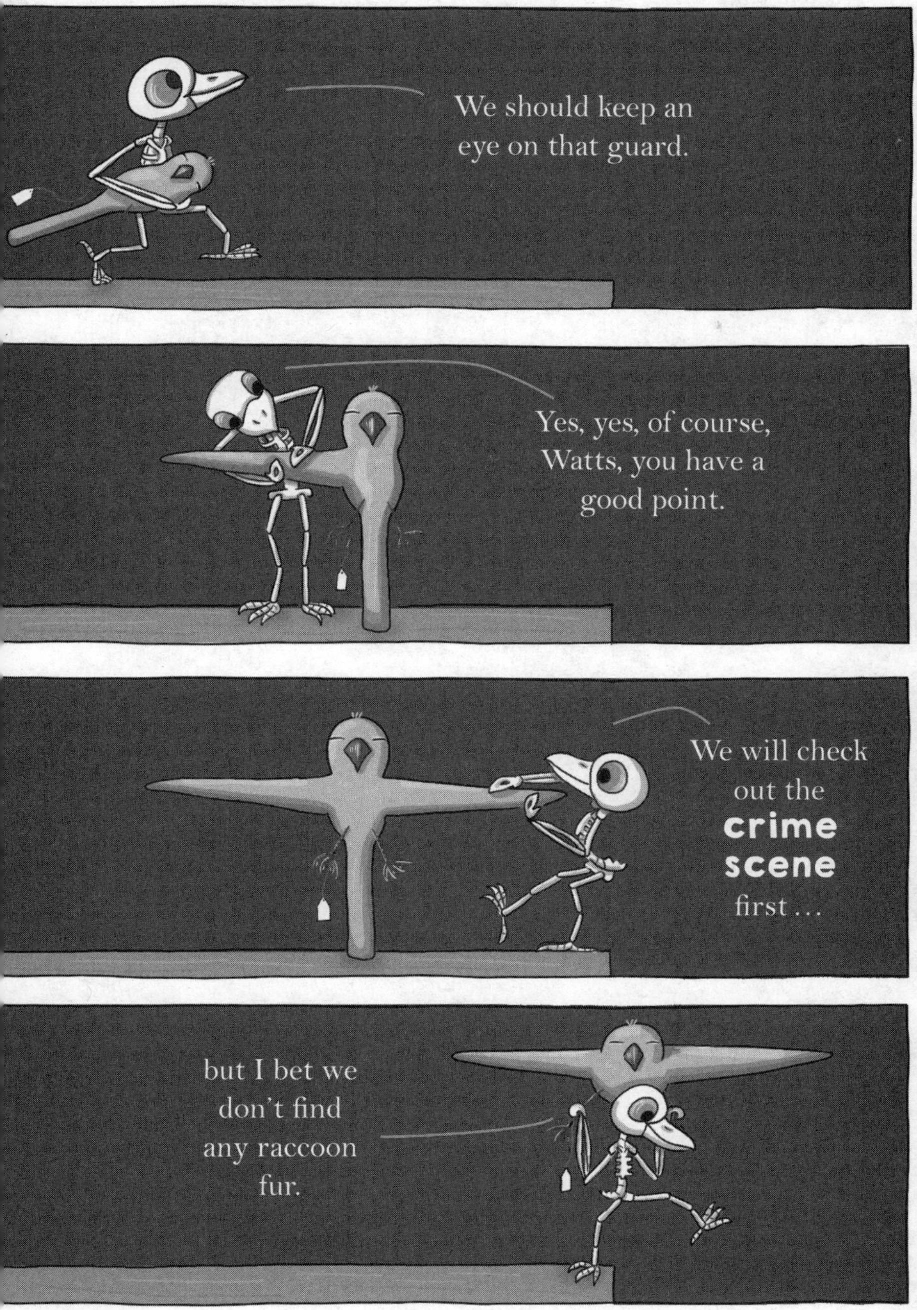
We should keep an eye on that guard.
Yes, yes, of course, Watts, you have a good point.
We will check out the **crime scene** first . . .
but I bet we don't find any raccoon fur.

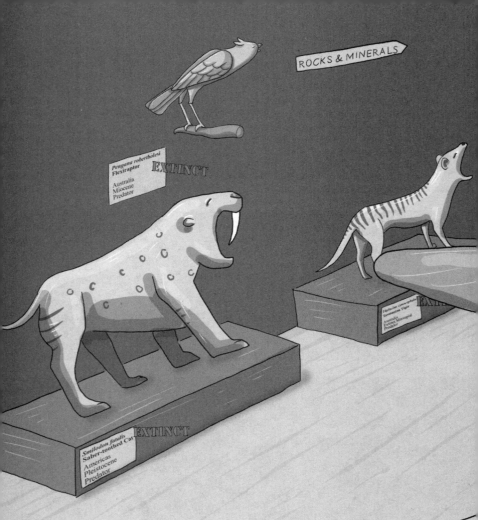

ROCKS & MINERALS

Pengana robertbolesi
Flexiraptor

Australia
Miocene
Predator

EXTINCT

Thylacinus cynocephalus
Tasmanian Tiger

Australia
Pleistocene Marsupial
Predator

EXTINCT

Smilodon fatalis
Saber-toothed Cat

Americas
Pleistocene
Predator

EXTINCT

NOW, THIS IS FLYING!

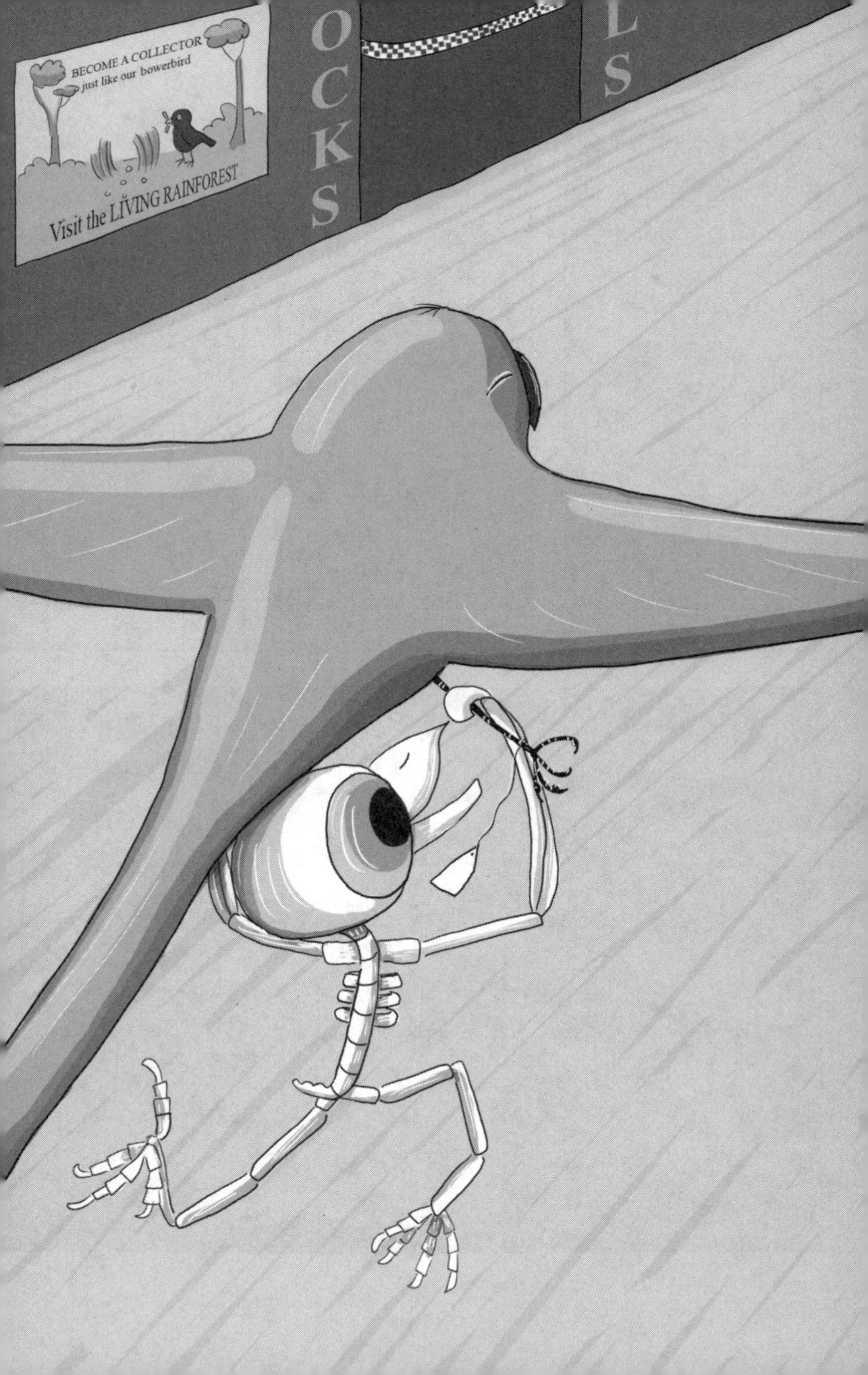
BECOME A COLLECTOR
just like our bowerbird
Visit the LIVING RAINFOREST
OCKS
LS

Like a little
police tape…

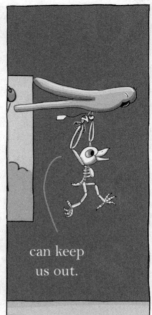

can keep
us out.

Uh-oh.

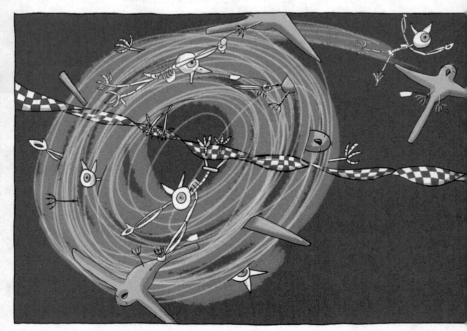

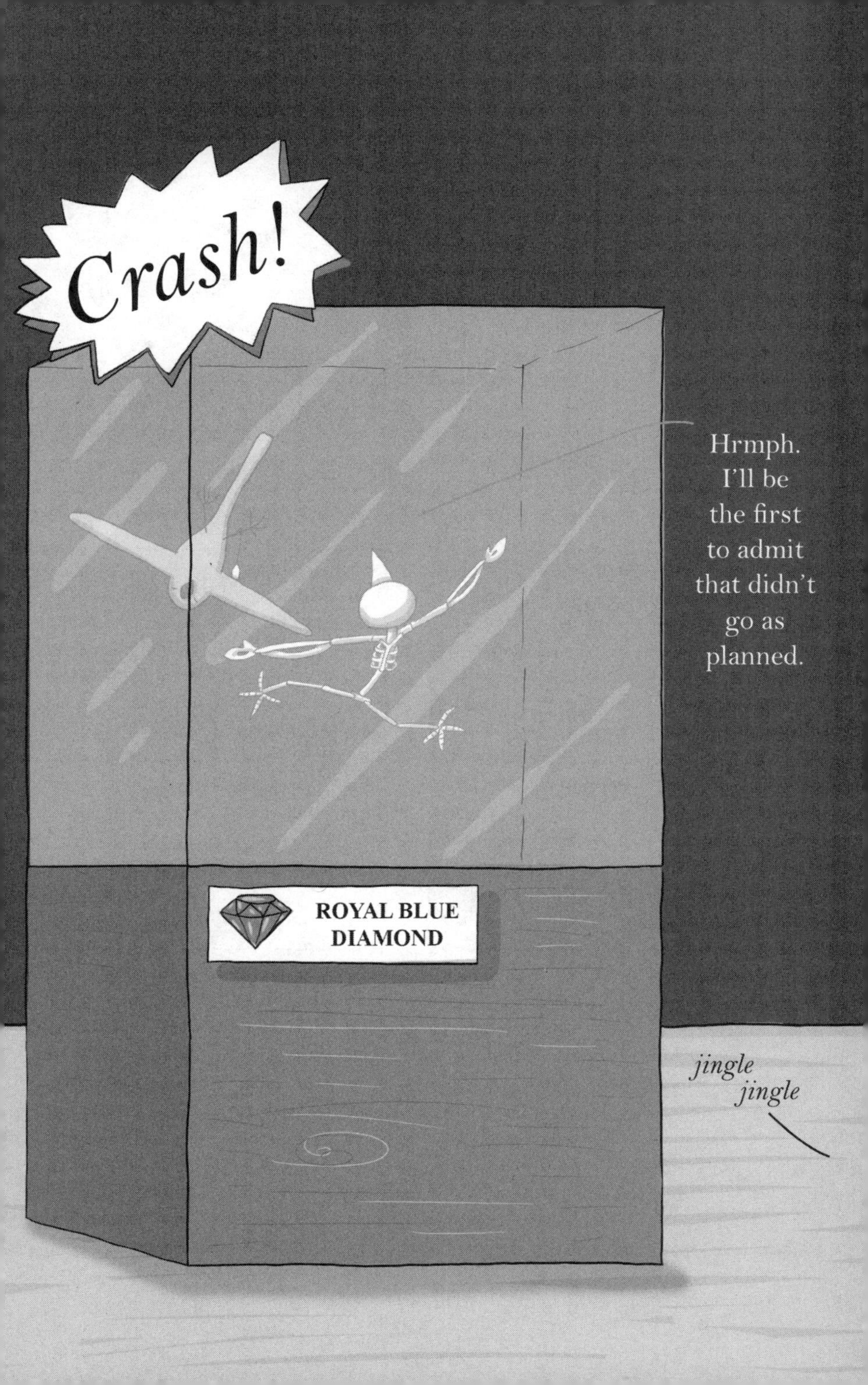
Crash!
Hrmph. I'll be the first to admit that didn't go as planned.
ROYAL BLUE DIAMOND
jingle jingle

jingle jingle

Wh-who's there?
H-h-hello?

Hey!
She's not supposed
to be in here.
This is a
**protected
crime scene.**

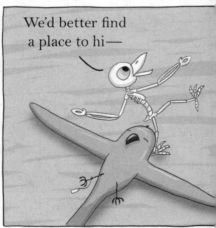

We'd better find
a place to hi—

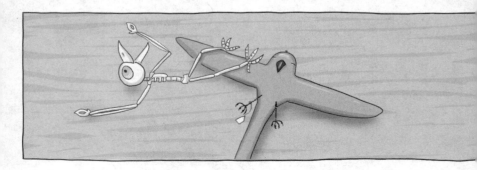

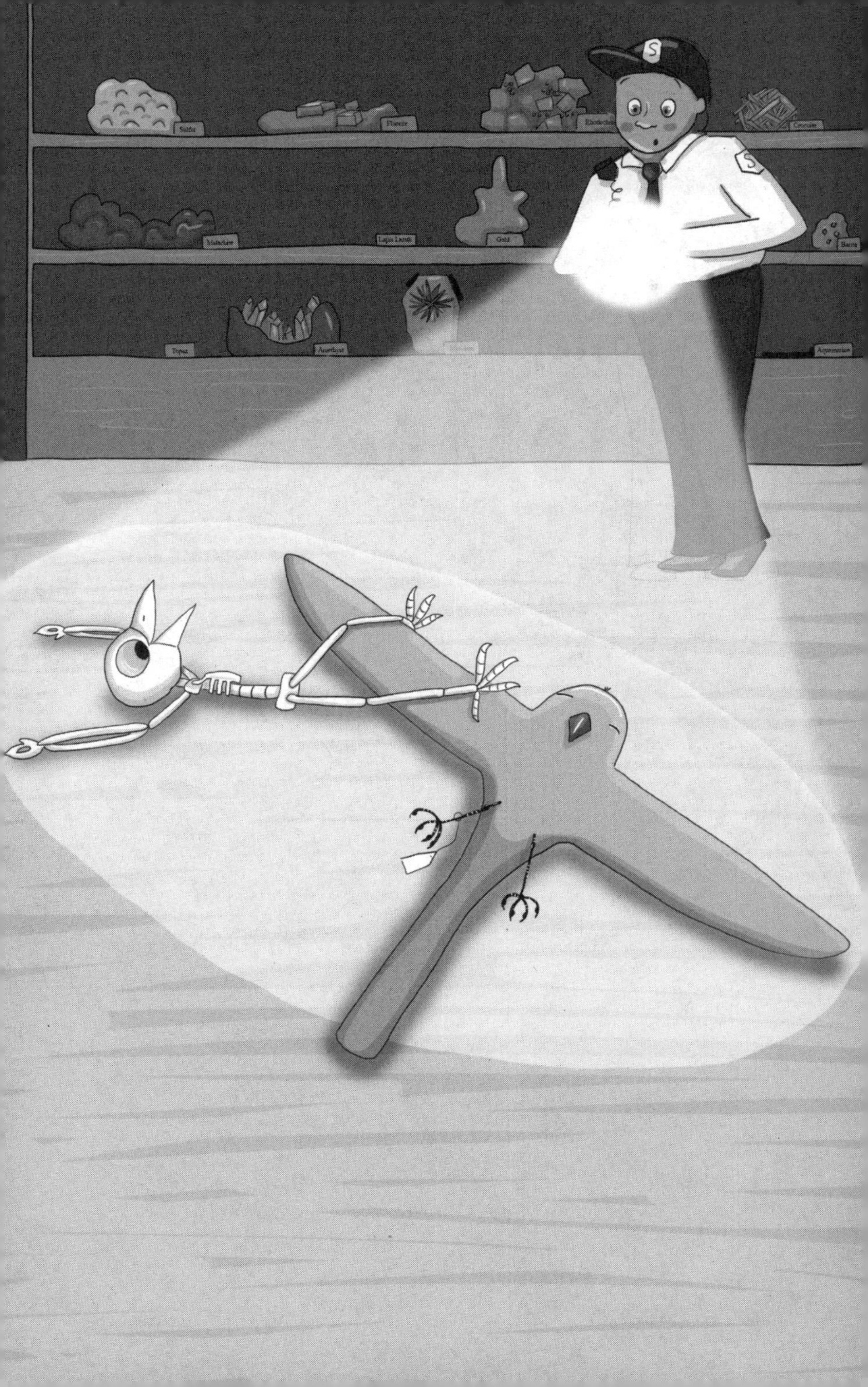
Malachite
Lapis Lazuli
Gold
Topaz
Amethyst

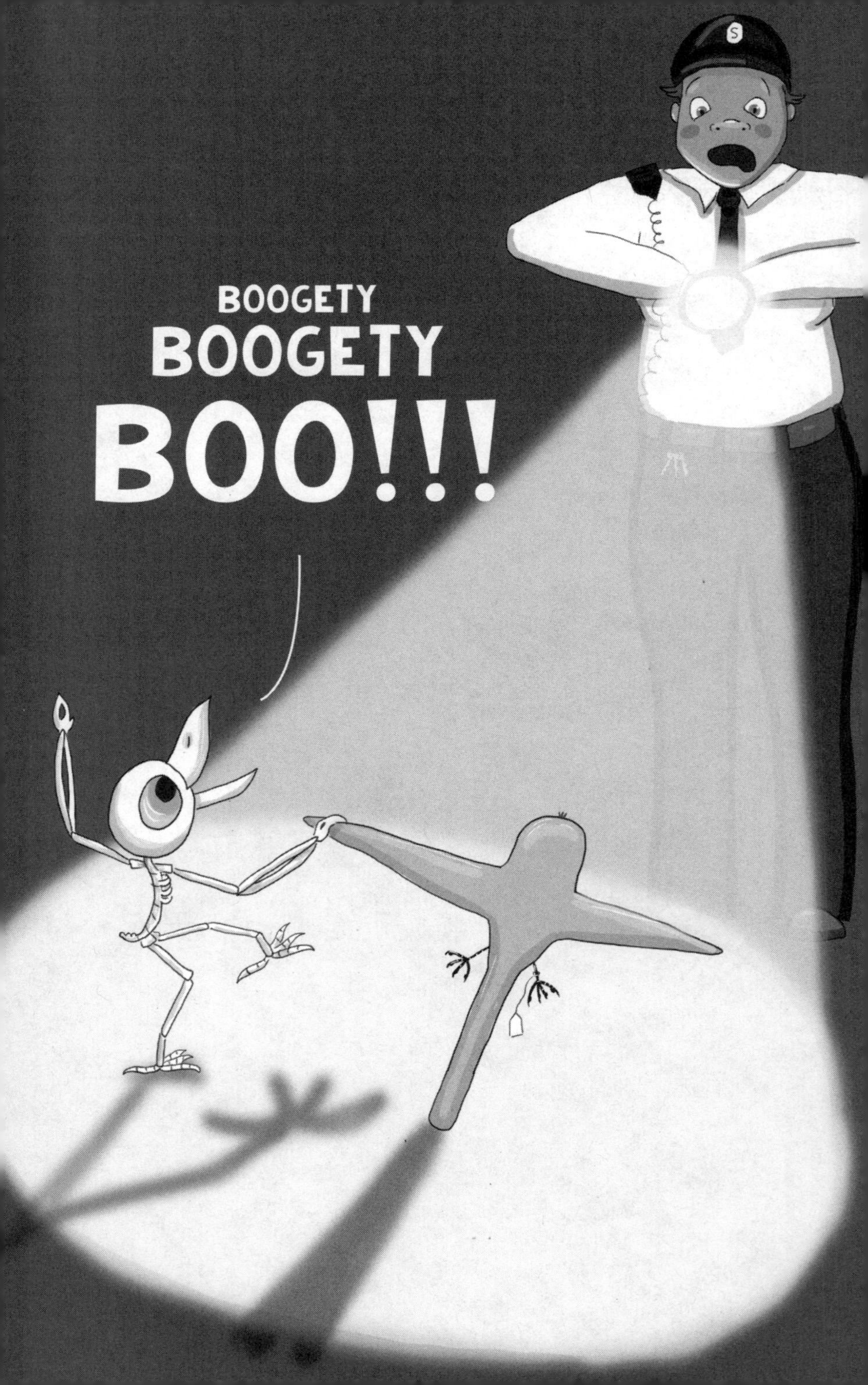
BOOGETY
BOOGETY
BOO!!!

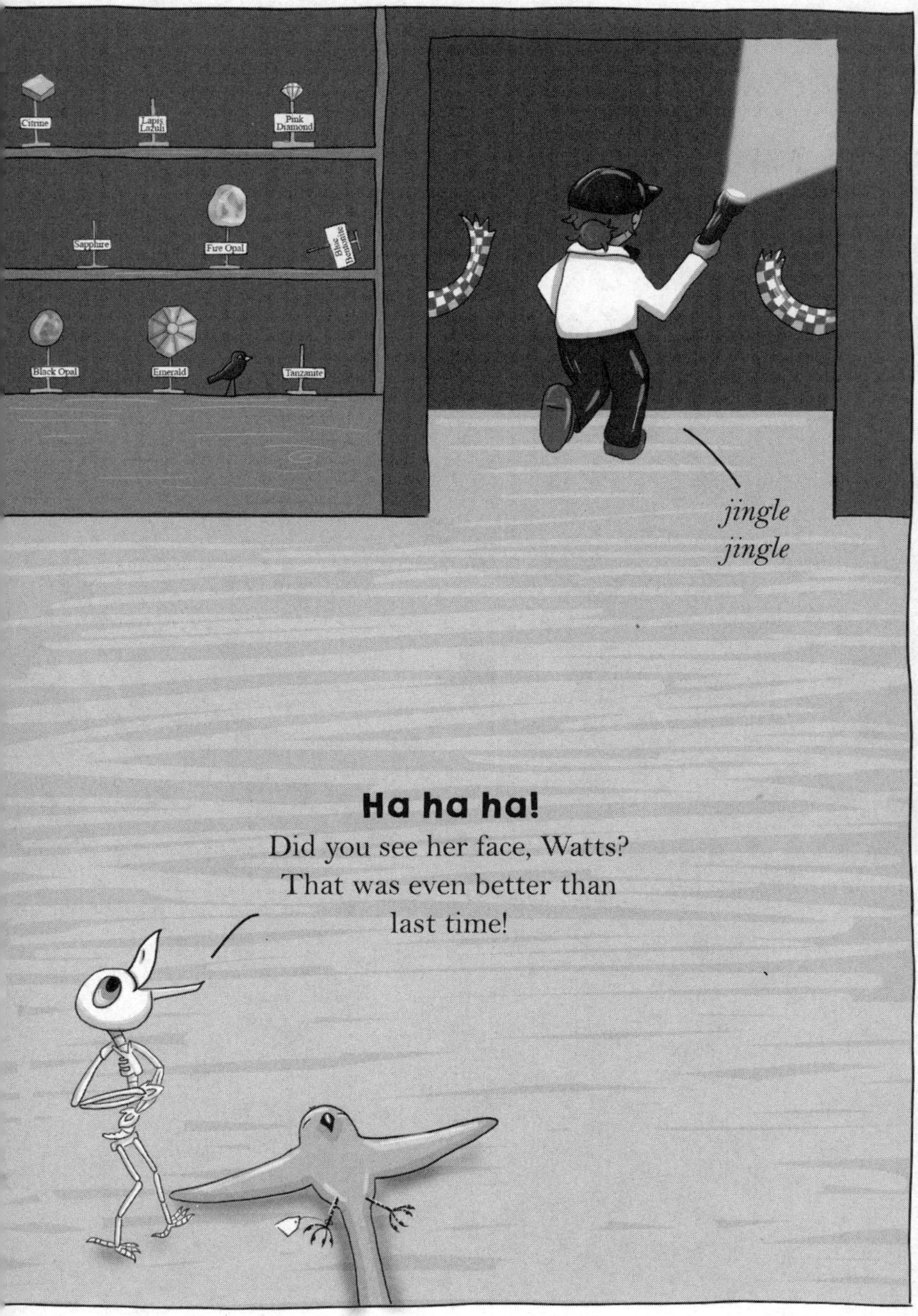
Citrine
Lapis Lazuli
Pink Diamond
Sapphire
Fire Opal
Blue Benitoite
Black Opal
Emerald
Tanzanite
jingle jingle
Ha ha ha!
Did you see her face, Watts? That was even better than last time!

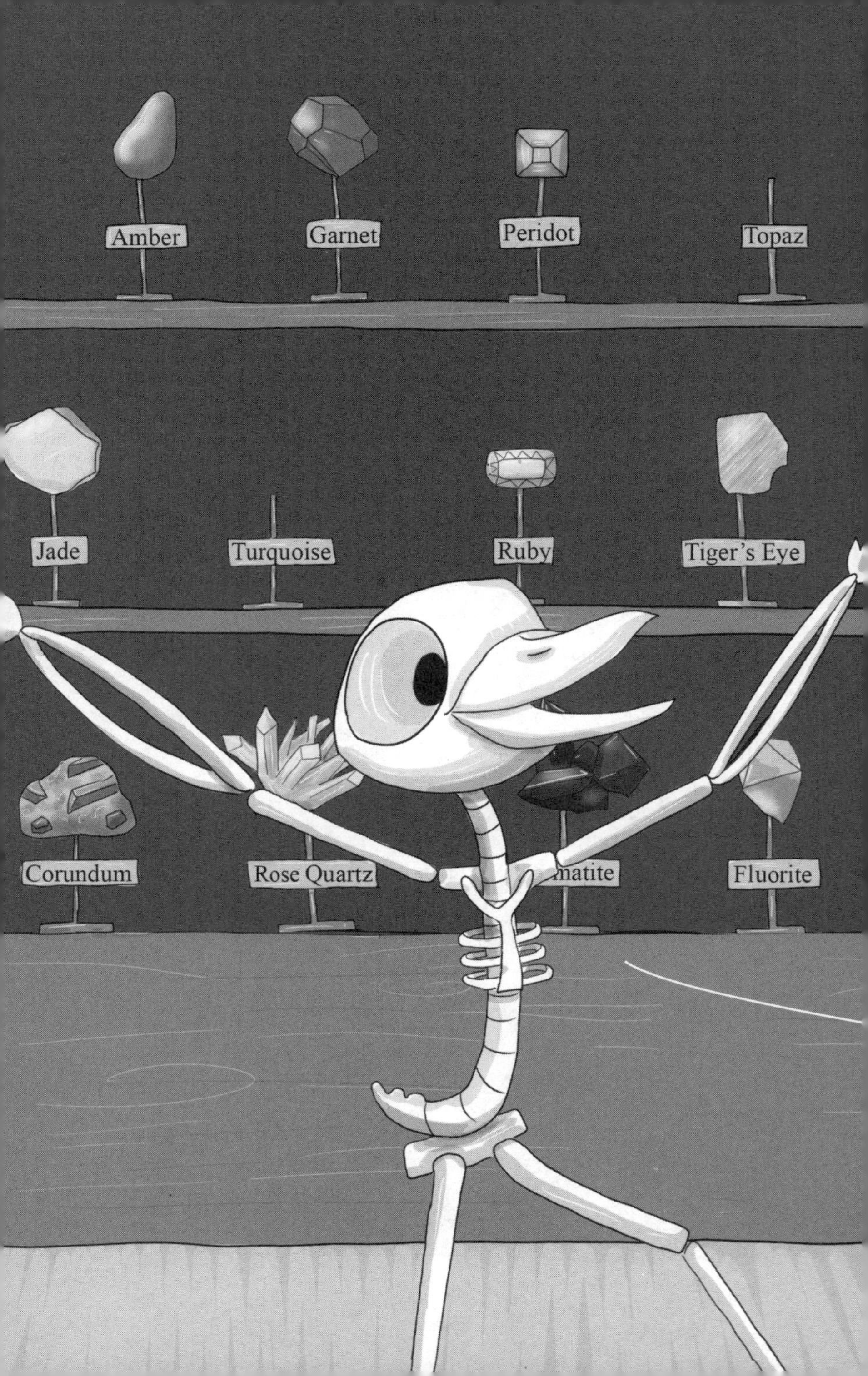
Amber
Garnet
Peridot
Topaz
Jade
Turquoise
Ruby
Tiger's Eye
Corundum
Rose Quartz
matite
Fluorite

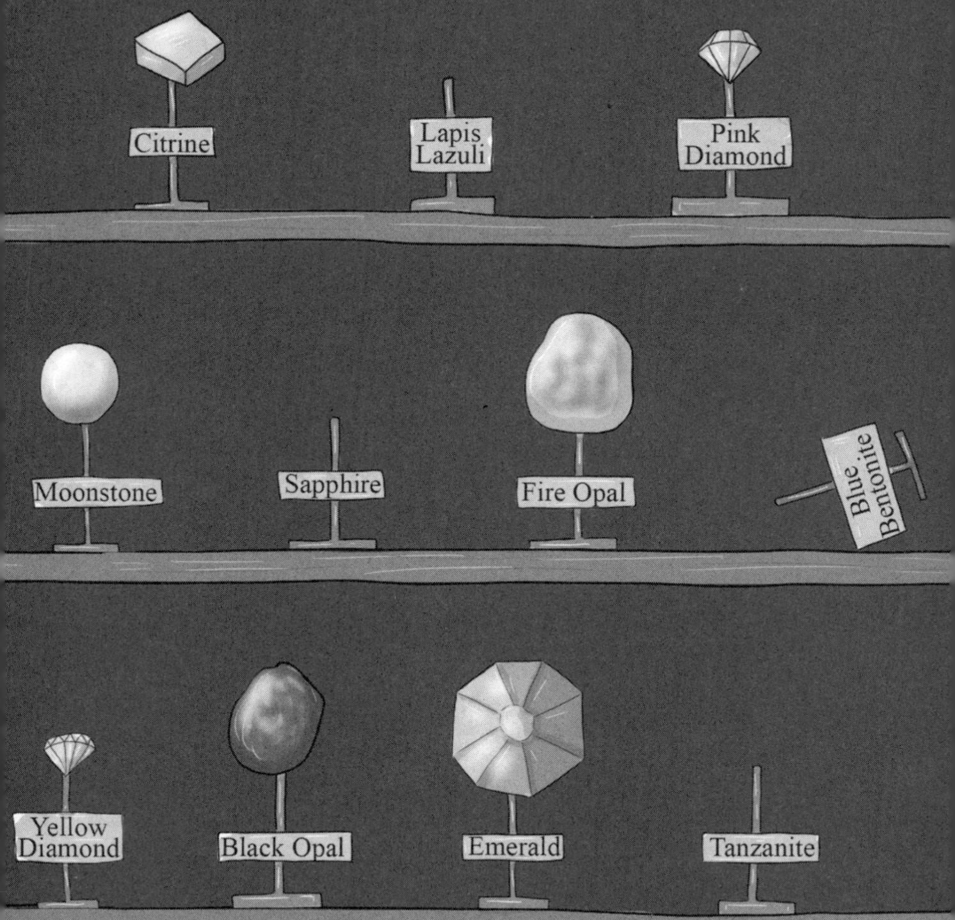
Citrine
Lapis Lazuli
Pink Diamond
Moonstone
Sapphire
Fire Opal
Blue Bentonite
Yellow Diamond
Black Opal
Emerald
Tanzanite

Anyway, here we are!

The scene of the crime.

The Rocks and Minerals gallery. Once home to the world's most valuable diamond!

CHAPTER 6
Sweet Tooth

You are probably right, Watts.

That wasn't the nicest way to handle the security guard . . . although you have to admit, it was pretty funny!

She's not supposed to be in here anyway.

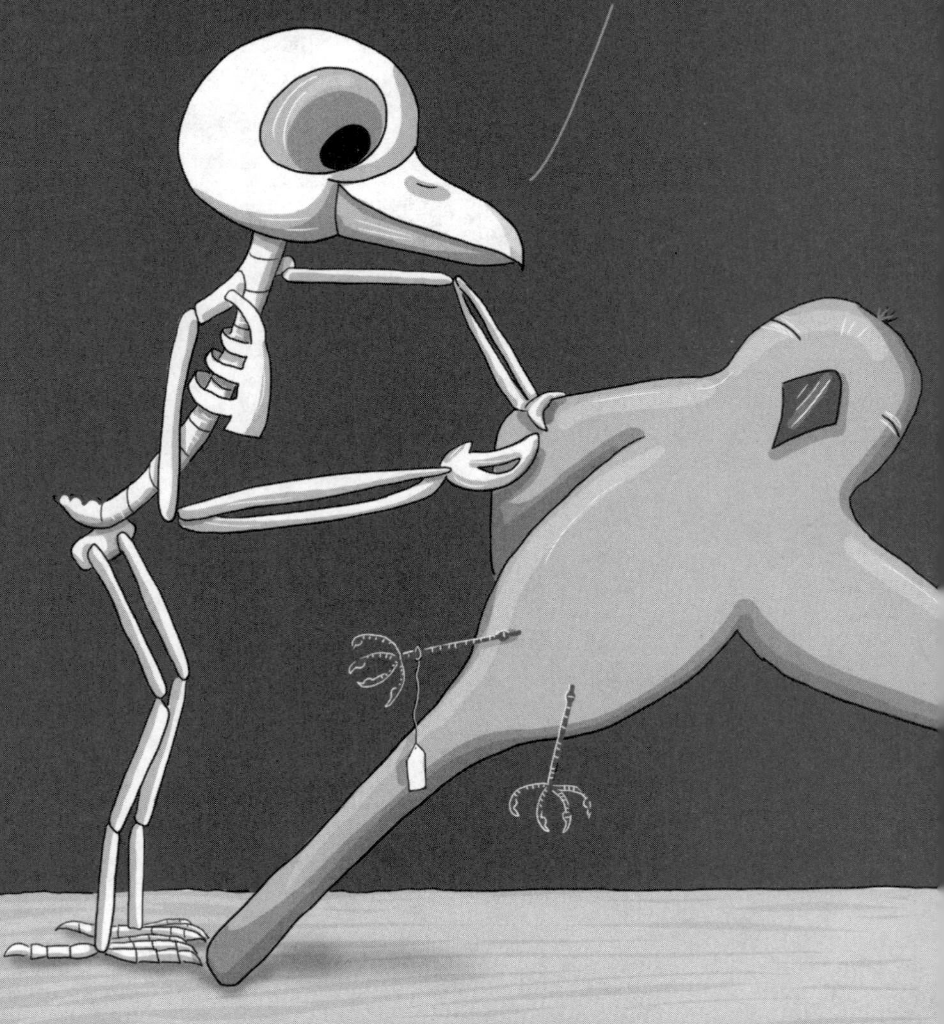

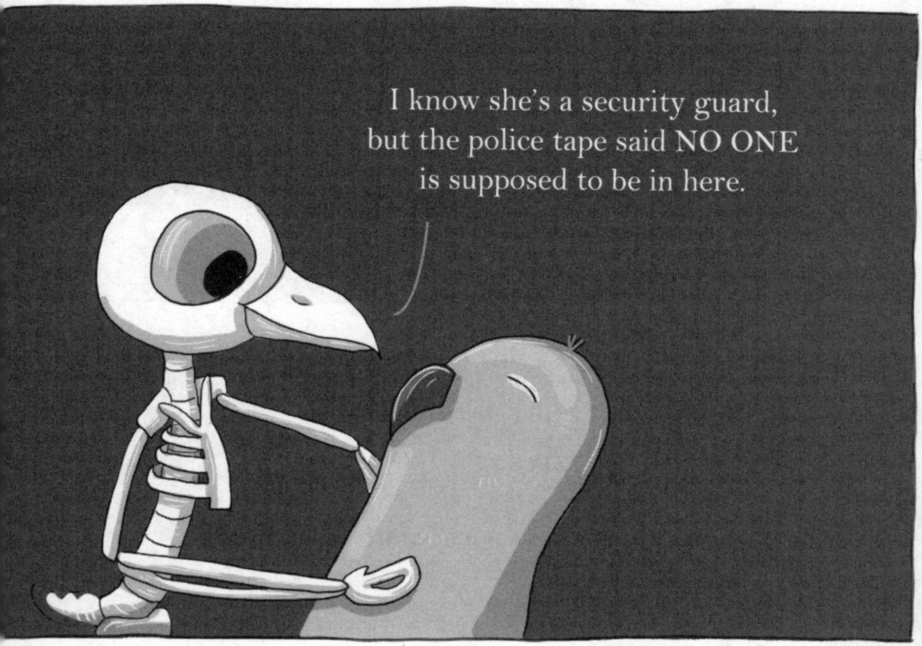
I know she's a security guard, but the police tape said NO ONE is supposed to be in here.

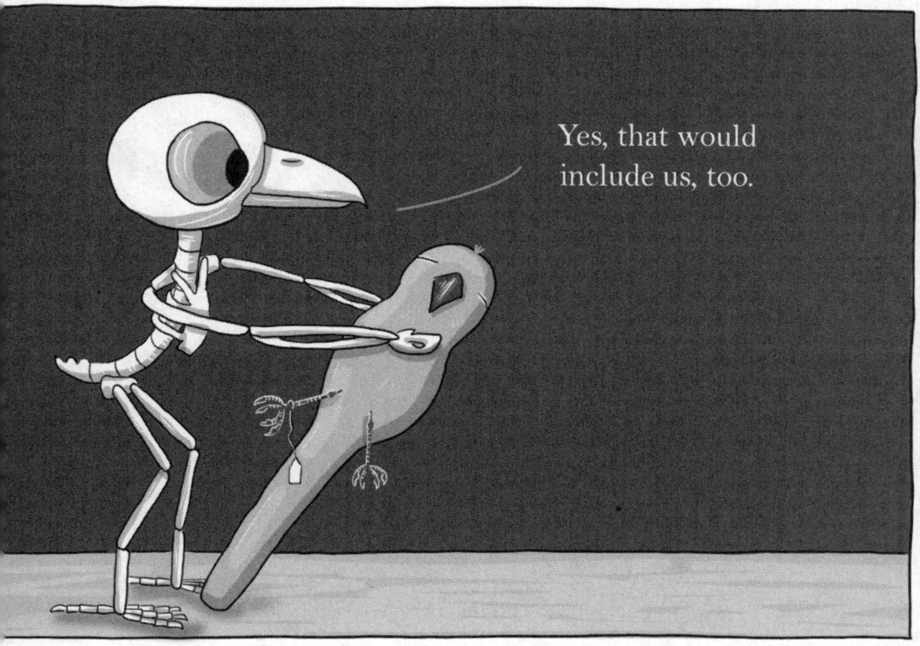
Yes, that would include us, too.

But we know we aren't suspects, so it's OK for us to be here.

That's a really good question. *I* think the security guard is up to something, and *you* think Grace is involved ...

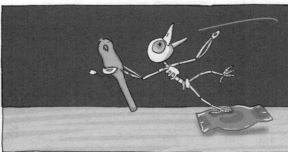

WHOA!

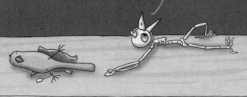

This job is more dangerous than I thought. Now, what was I saying?

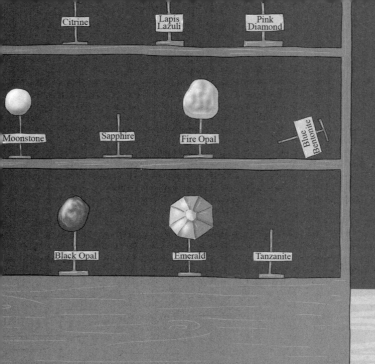

Citrine
Lapis Lazuli
Pink Diamond
Moonstone
Sapphire
Fire Opal
Blue Bentonite
Black Opal
Emerald
Tanzanite

That's right — we have
two highly suspicious suspects.

Let's find some clues.

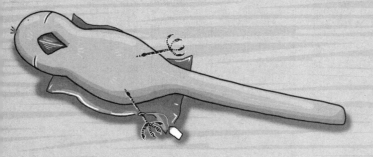

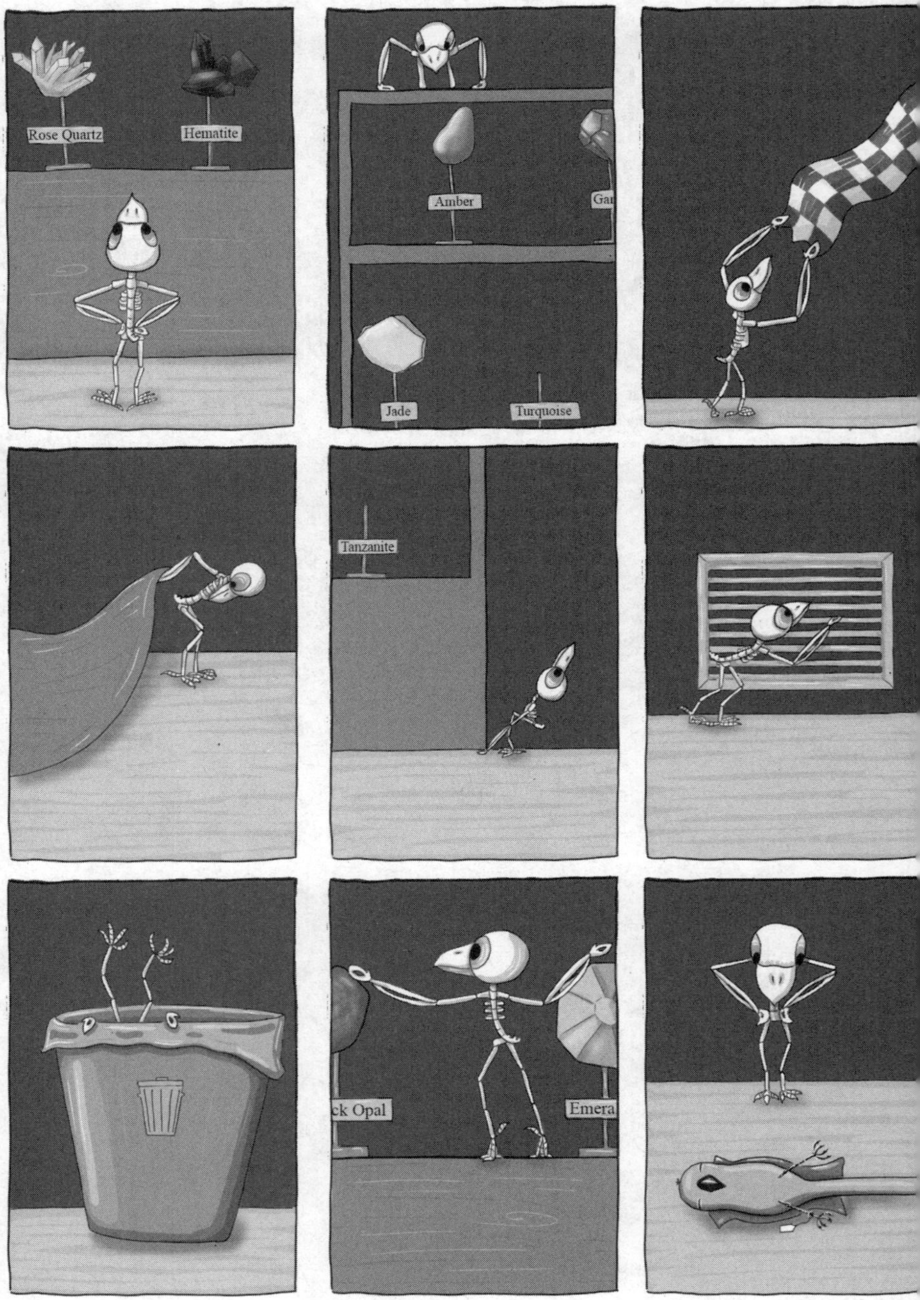
Rose Quartz
Hematite
Amber
Gar
Jade
Turquoise
Tanzanite
ck Opal
Emera

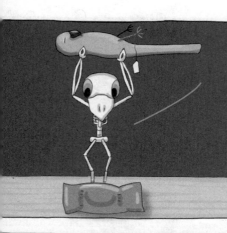

Watts! What kind of detective are you? **Are you eating chocolates at the scene of the crime?**

You've left quite a mess.

Yum. Chocolates. **The blue ones are my favorite too. MMM...DARK CHOCOLATE.**

The thief must have left these wrappers.

Great detecting, Watts!

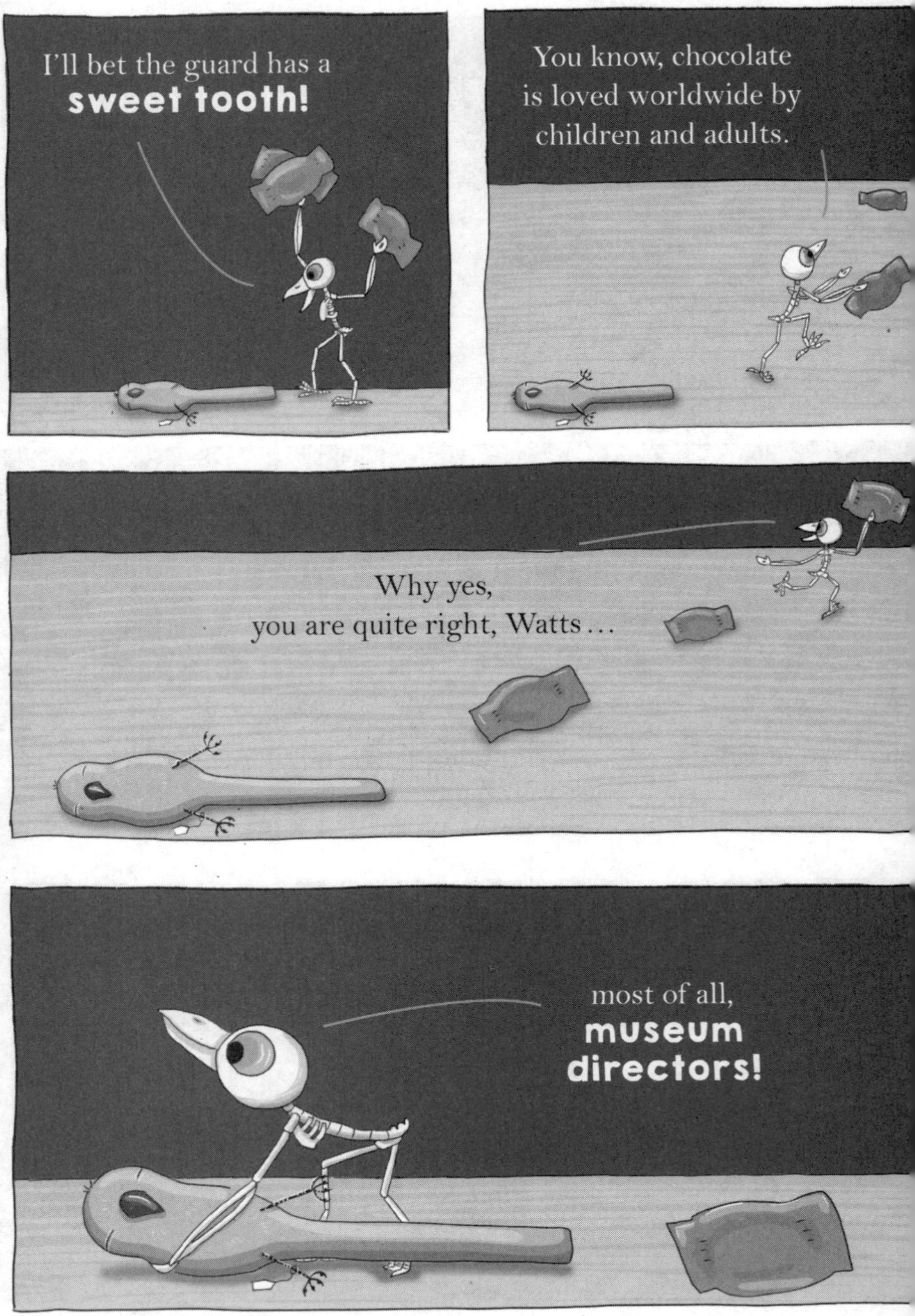
I'll bet the guard has a **sweet tooth!**
You know, chocolate is loved worldwide by children and adults.
Why yes, you are quite right, Watts...
most of all, **museum directors!**

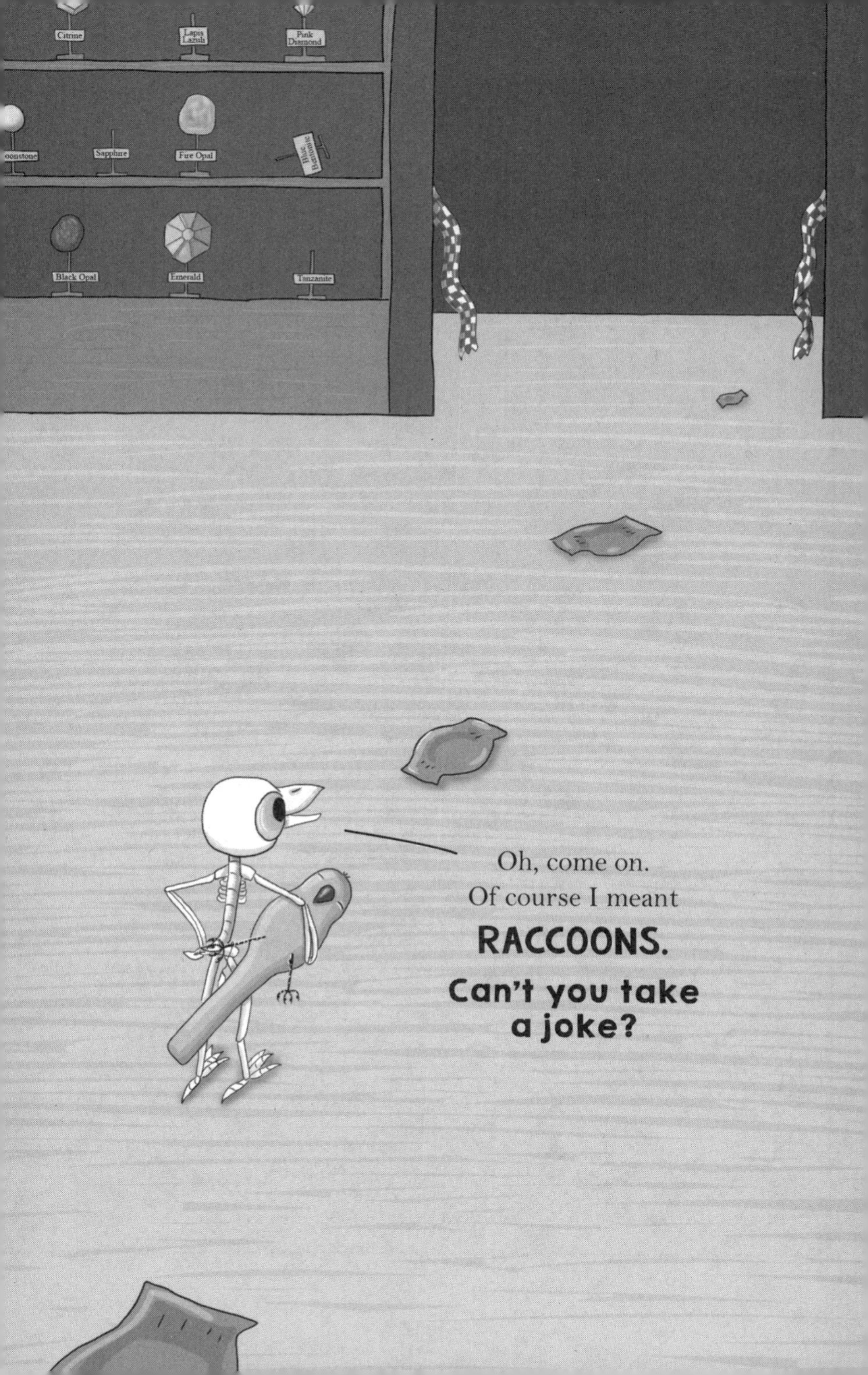
Citrine
Lapis Lazuli
Pink Diamond
Sapphire
Fire Opal
Blue Bentonite
Black Opal
Emerald
Tanzanite
Oh, come on.
Of course I meant
RACCOONS.
Can't you take a joke?

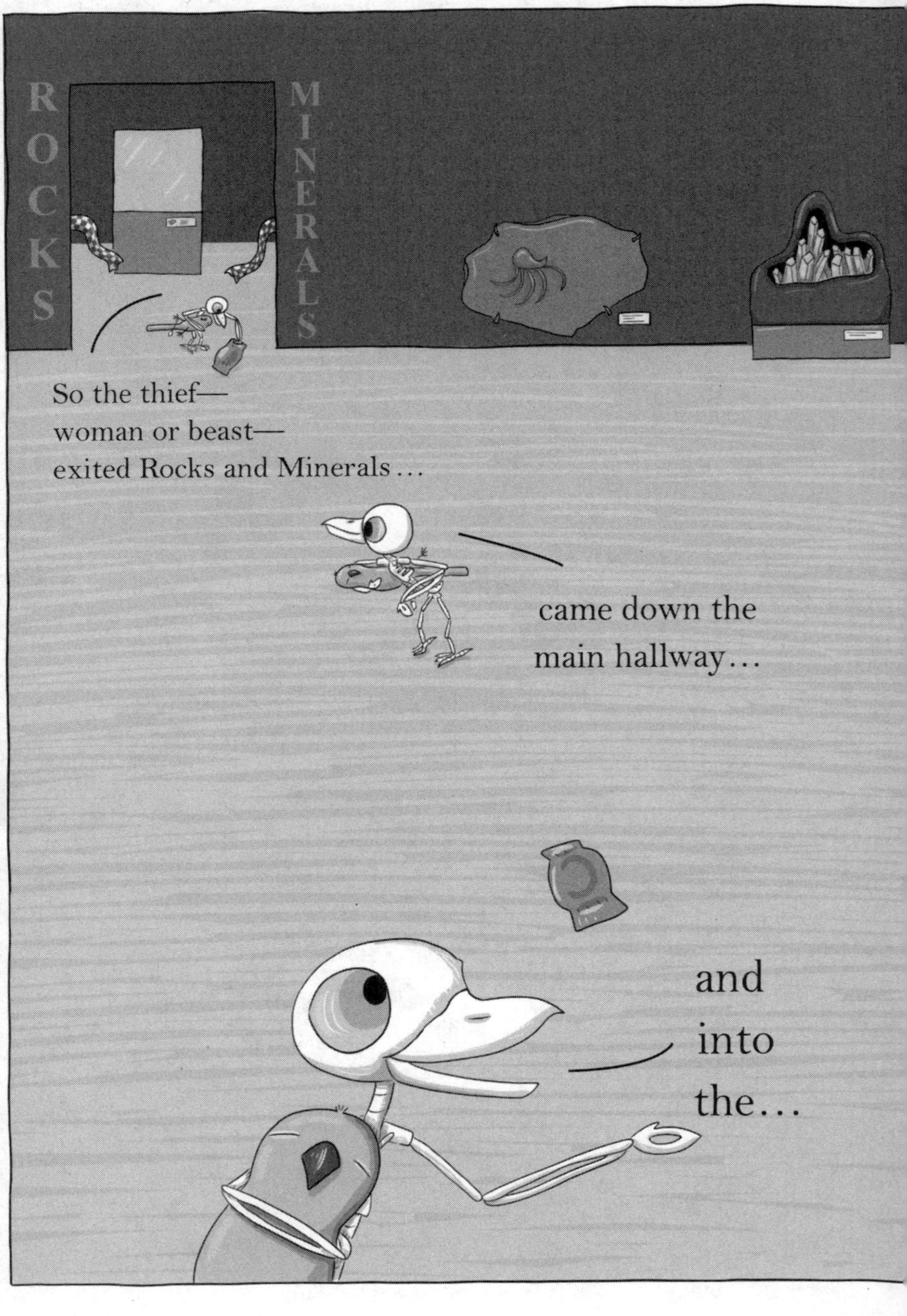
ROCKS
MINERALS
So the thief—
woman or beast—
exited Rocks and Minerals . . .
came down the
main hallway . . .
and
into
the . . .

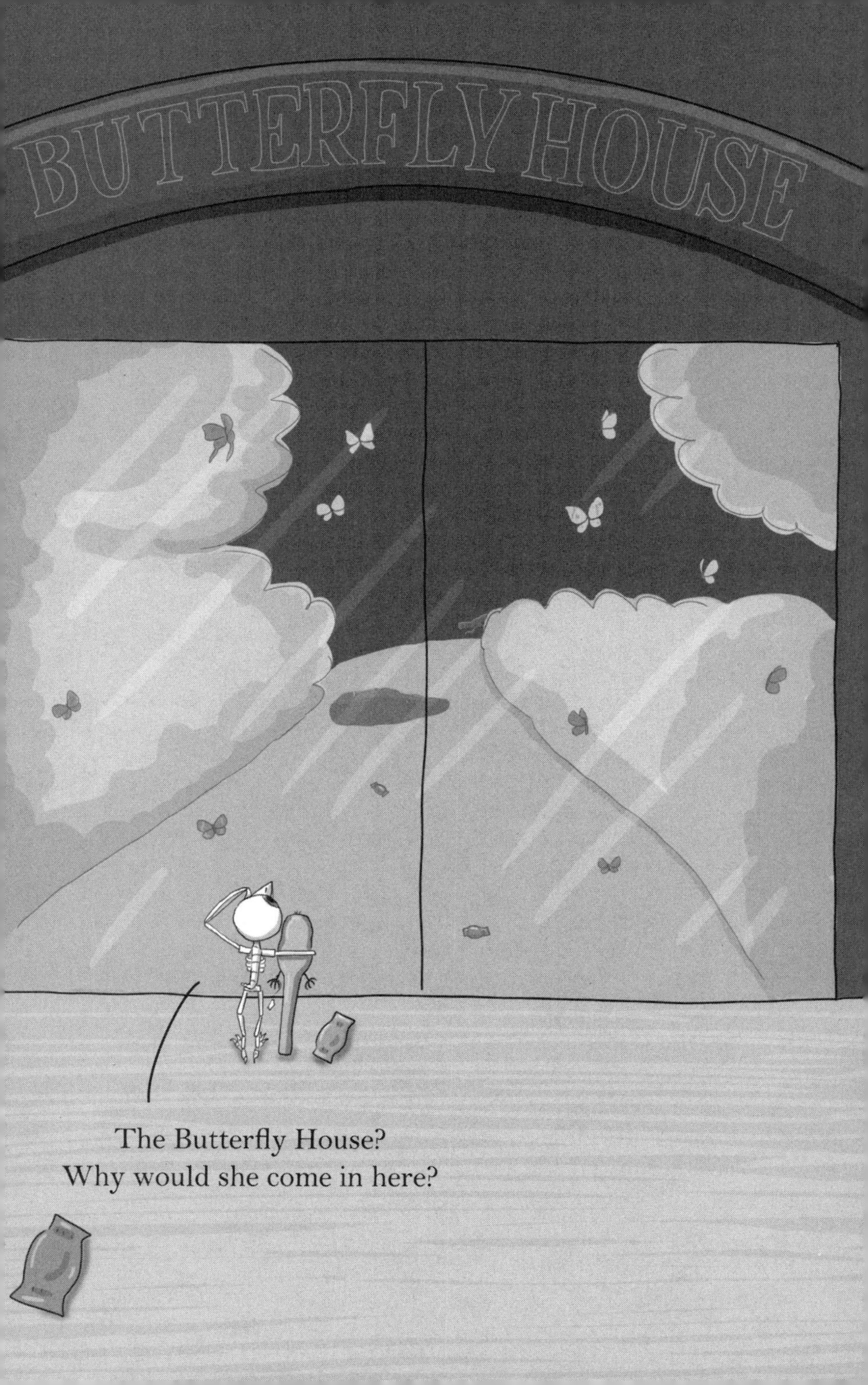
BUTTERFLY HOUSE
The Butterfly House?
Why would she come in here?

CHAPTER 7
Seeing Red

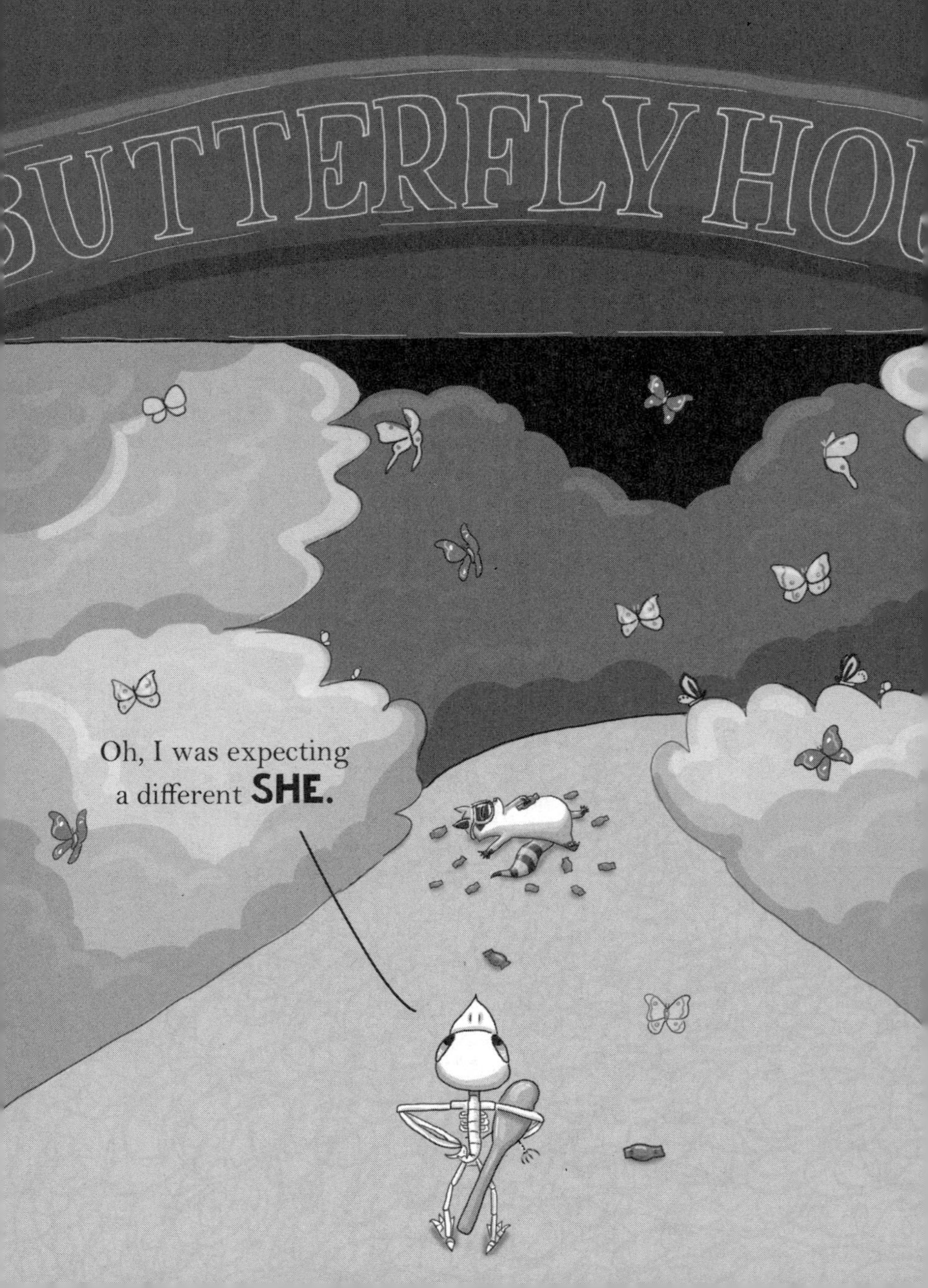
Oh, I was expecting a different **SHE.**

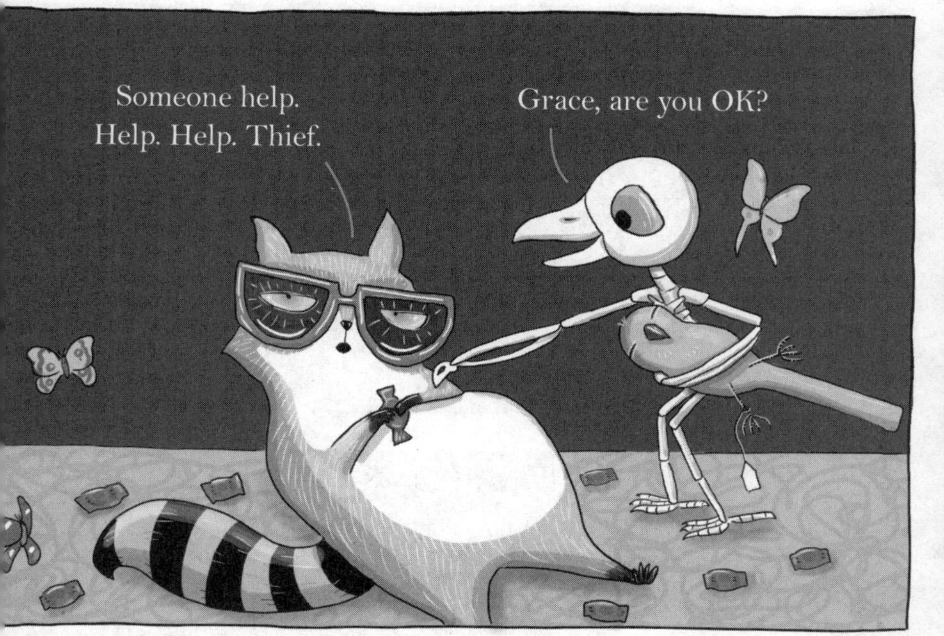
Someone help.
Help. Help. Thief.
Grace, are you OK?

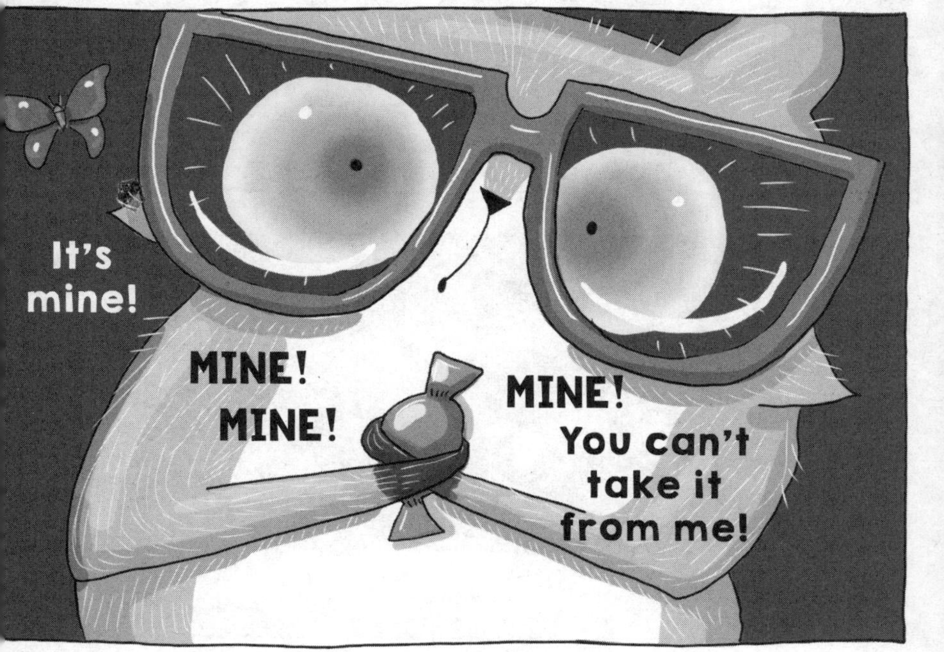
It's mine!
MINE!
MINE!
MINE!
You can't take it from me!

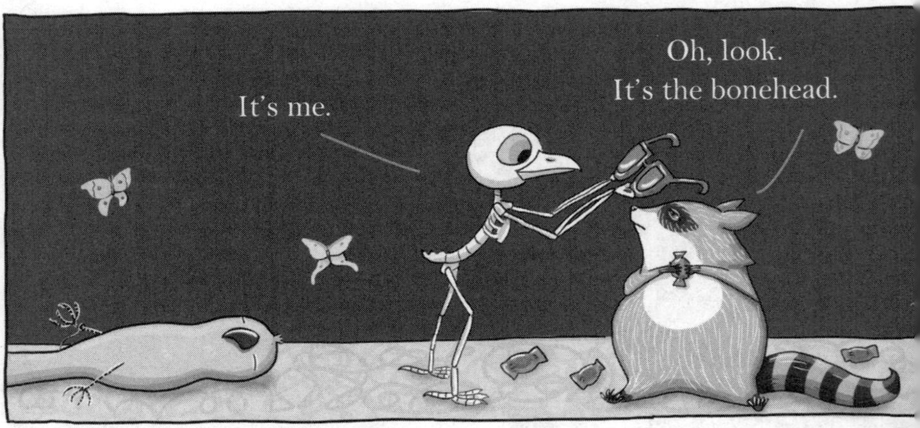
It's me.
Oh, look.
It's the bonehead.

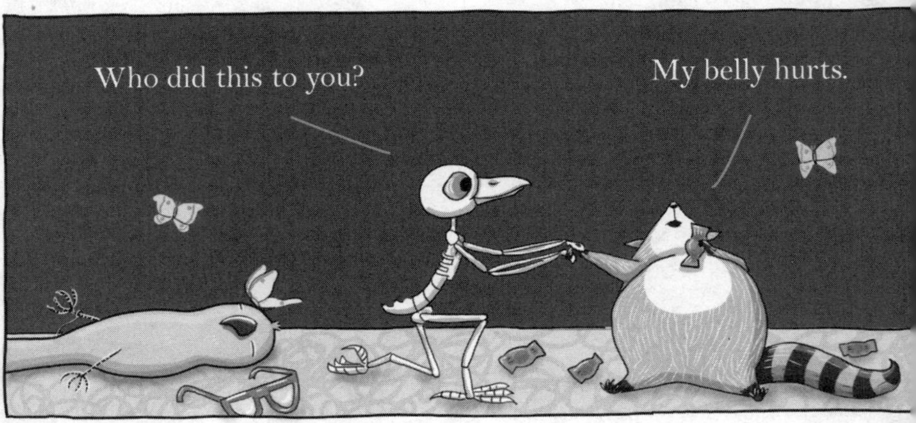
Who did this to you?
My belly hurts.

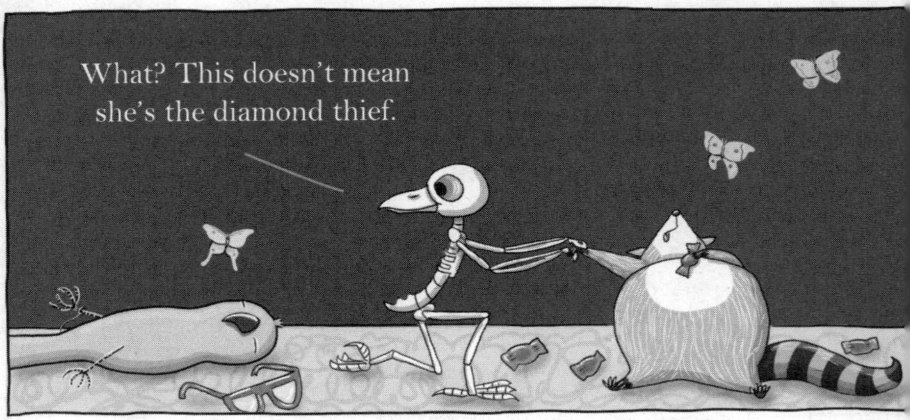
What? This doesn't mean
she's the diamond thief.

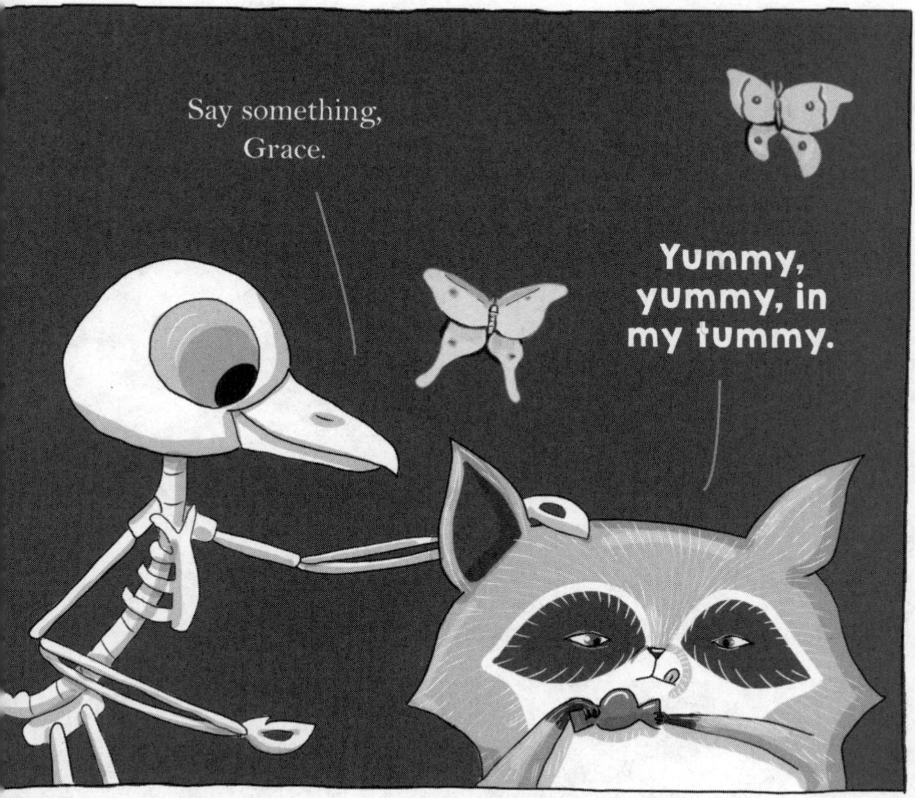
Say something, Grace.
Yummy, yummy, in my tummy.

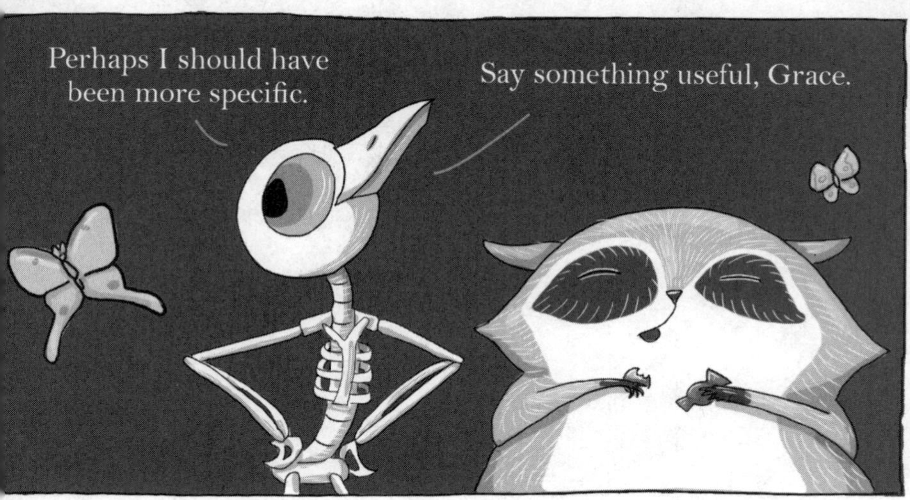
Perhaps I should have been more specific.
Say something useful, Grace.

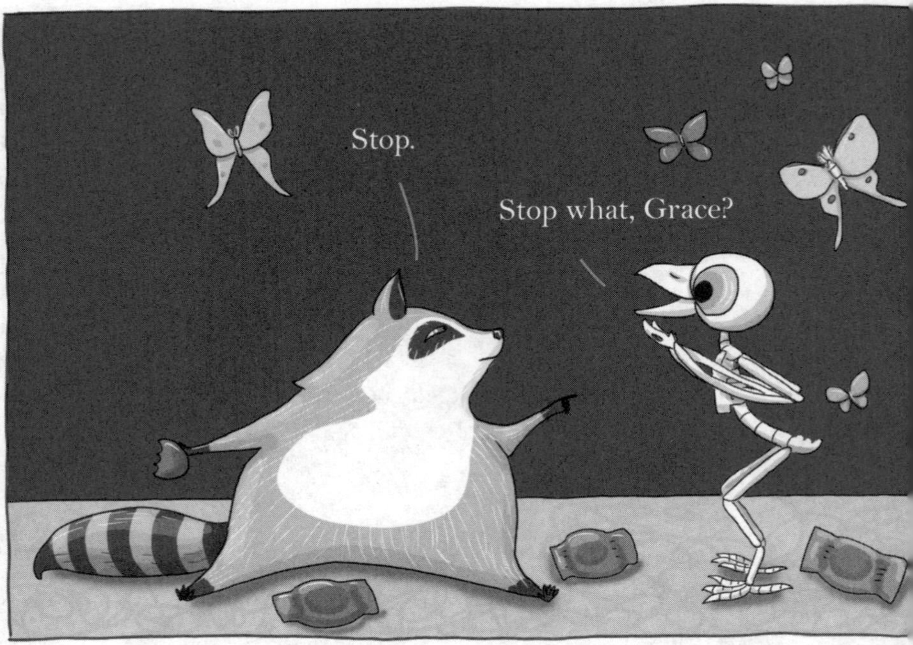
Stop.
Stop what, Grace?

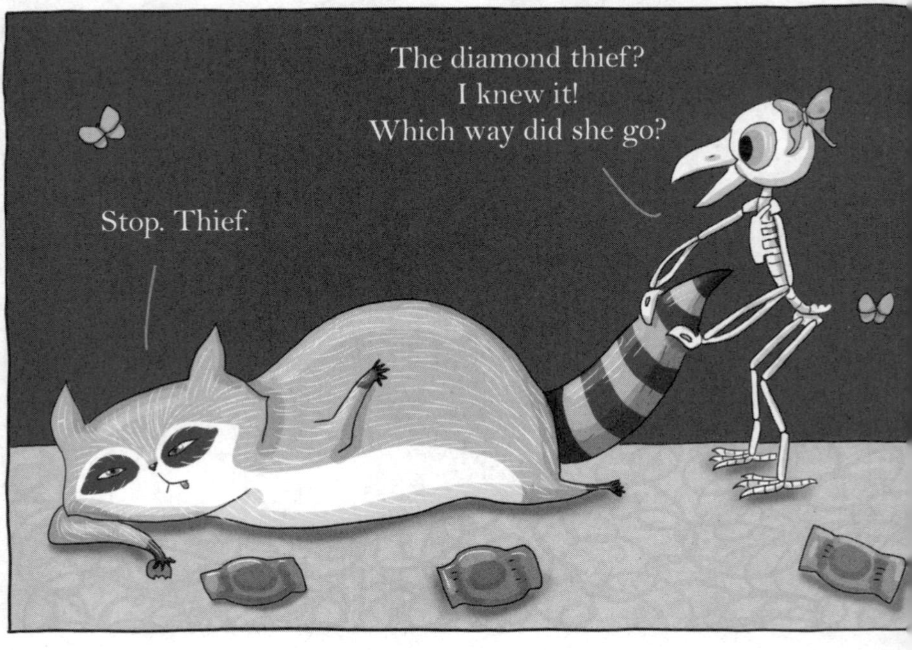
The diamond thief?
I knew it!
Which way did she go?
Stop. Thief.

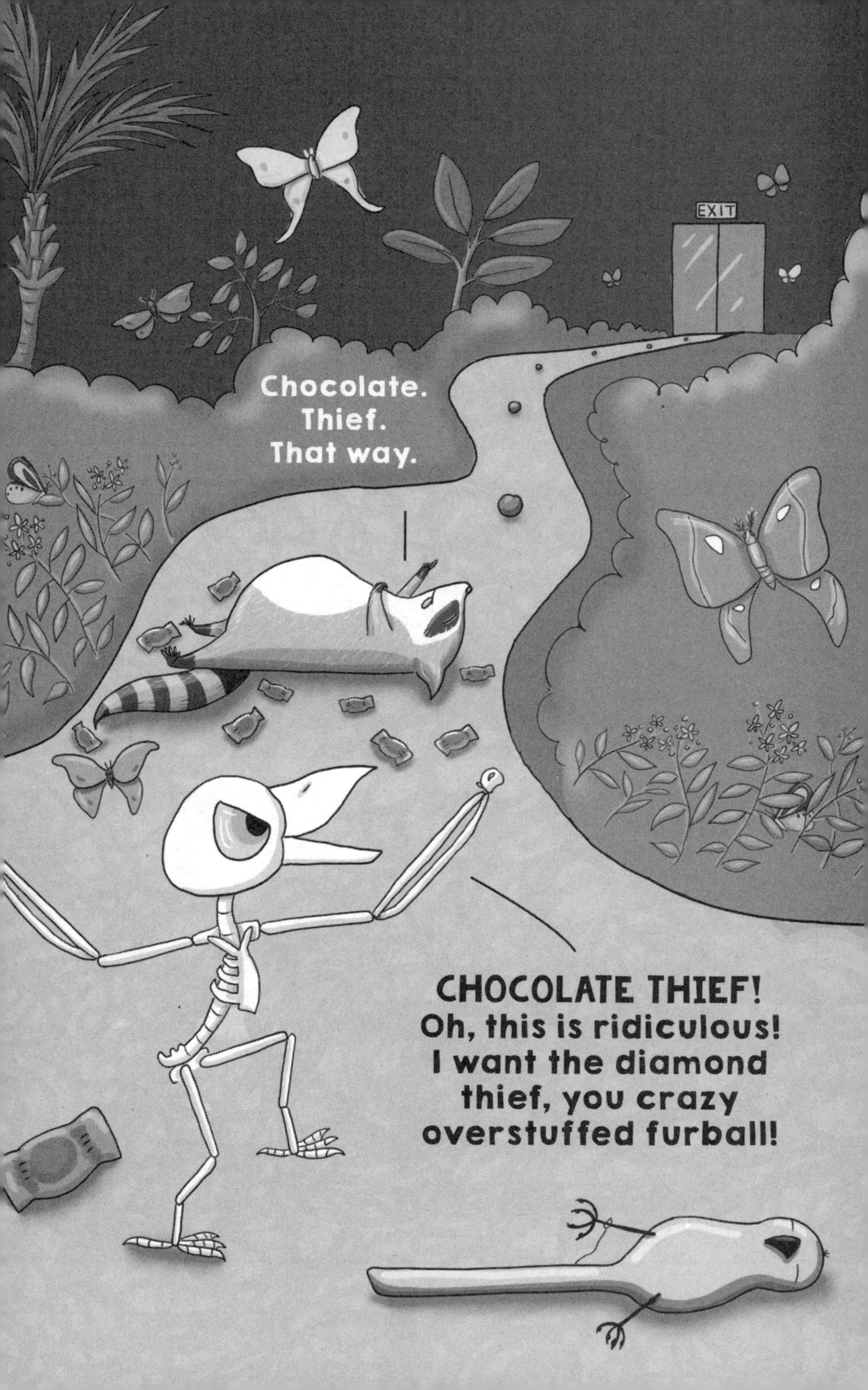
EXIT
Chocolate. Thief. That way.
CHOCOLATE THIEF! Oh, this is ridiculous! I want the diamond thief, you crazy overstuffed furball!

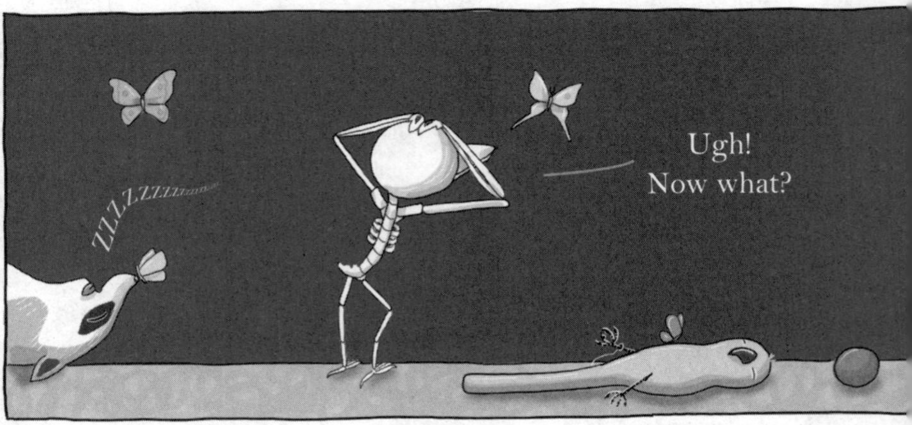
Ugh!
Now what?

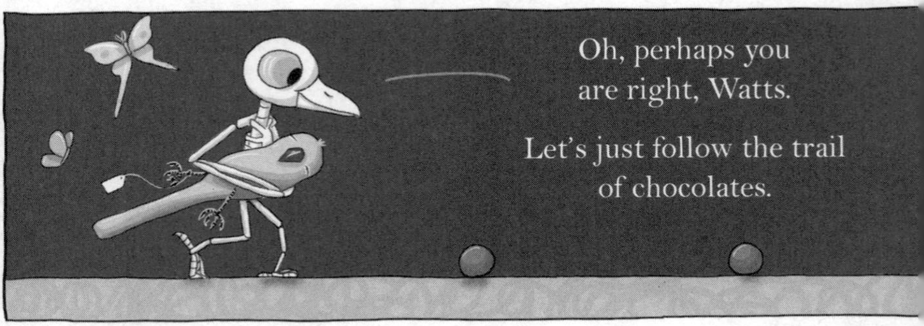
Oh, perhaps you are right, Watts.
Let's just follow the trail of chocolates.

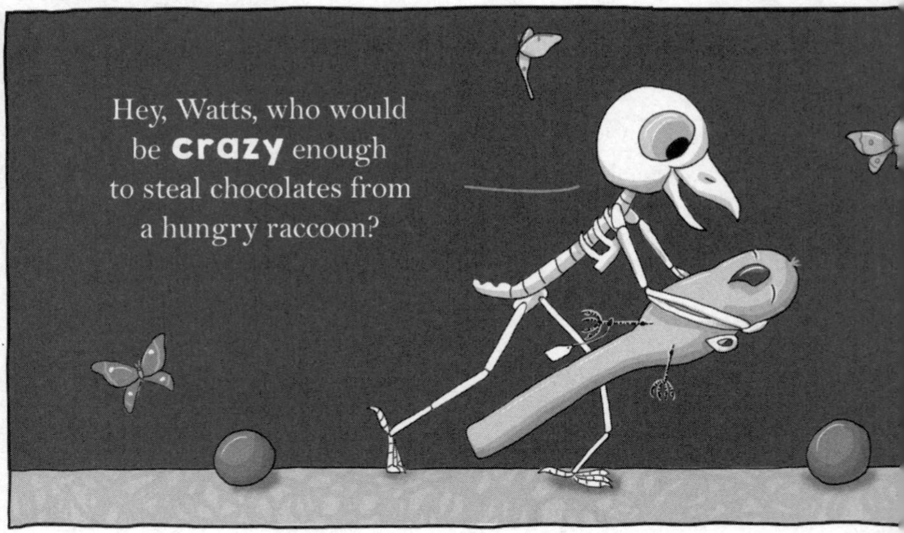
Hey, Watts, who would be **crazy** enough to steal chocolates from a hungry raccoon?

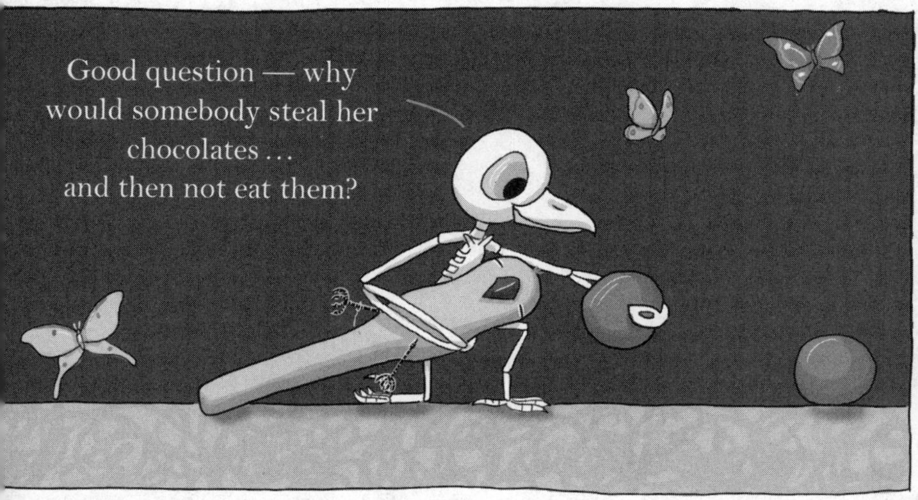
Good question — why would somebody steal her chocolates . . . and then not eat them?

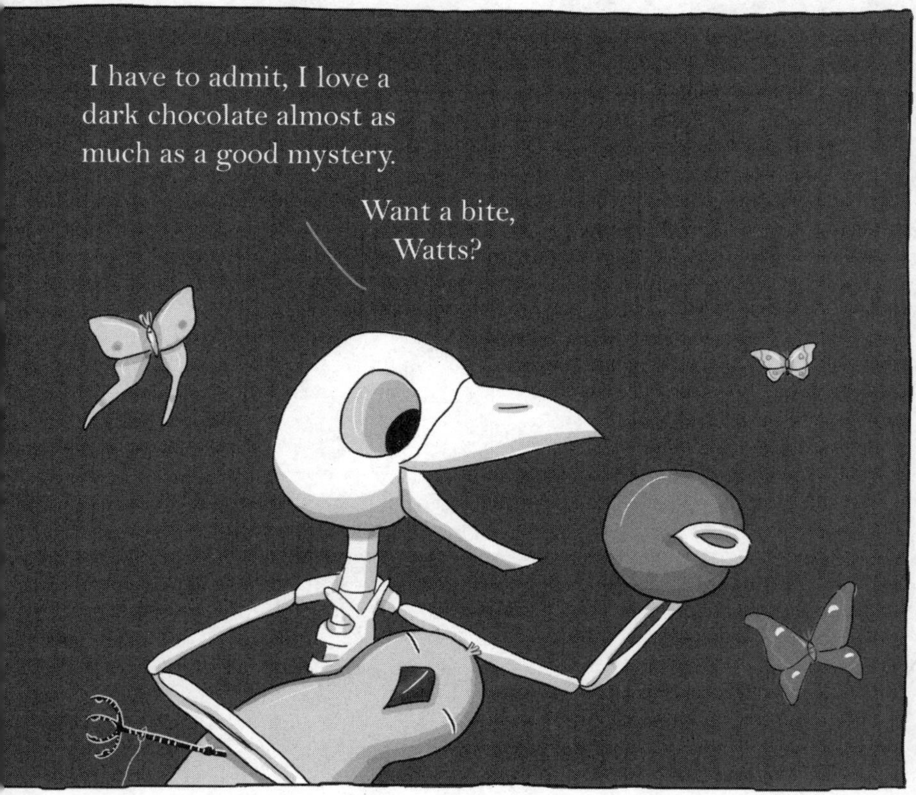
I have to admit, I love a dark chocolate almost as much as a good mystery.
Want a bite, Watts?

The Butterfly House is quite a magical place.
Although they really should call it

**The
BUTTERFLY and
MOTH House.**

BUTTERFLY or MOTH?

BUTTERFLY		MOTH
Club-shaped Antennae		**Feathery Antennae**
Resting Wings Up		**Resting Wings Open**
Mostly Diurnal		**Mostly Nocturnal**

Cassia Butterfly *Catopsilia pomona* Small Yellow	**Ulysses Butterfly** *Papilio ulysses* Large Blue and Black	**Cairns Birdwing** *Ornithoptera euphorion* Very Large Green, Yellow, and Black	**Atlas Moth** *Attacus wardi* Very Large Brown and White	**Luna Moth** *Actias luna* Large Pale Green	**Emperor Gum Moth** *Opodiphthera eucalypti* Large Light Brown

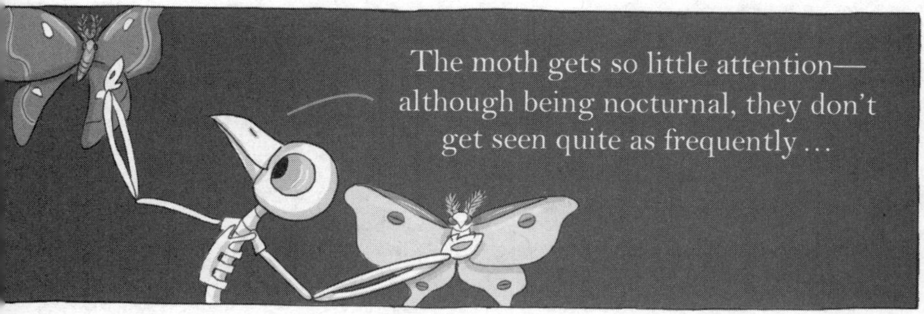
The moth gets so little attention—although being nocturnal, they don't get seen quite as frequently . . .

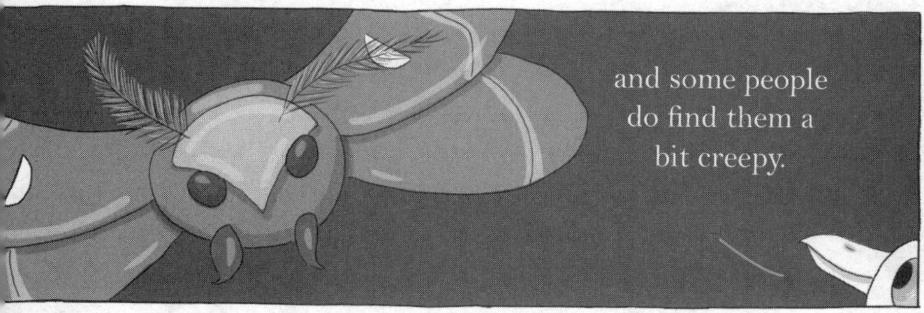
and some people do find them a bit creepy.

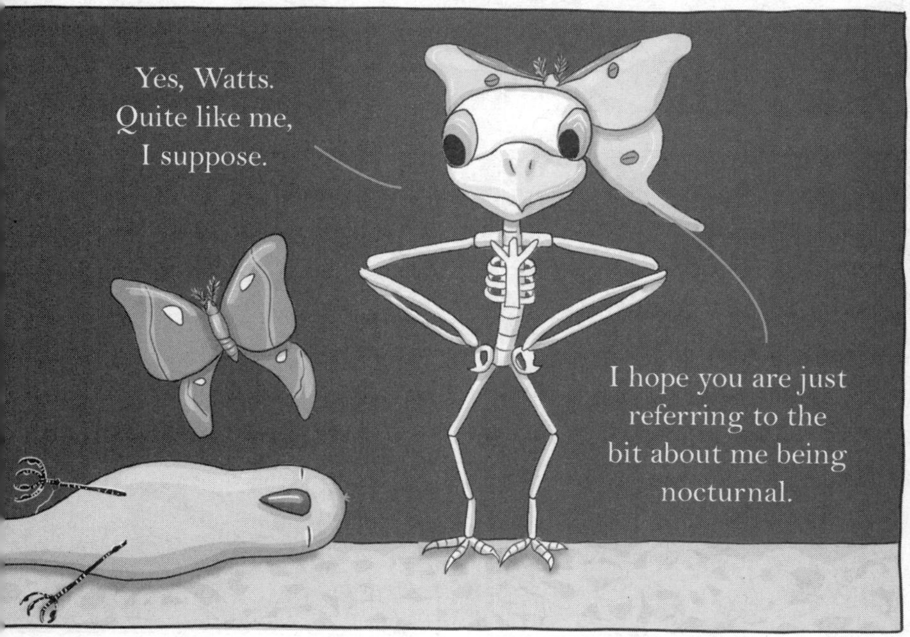
Yes, Watts. Quite like me, I suppose.
I hope you are just referring to the bit about me being nocturnal.

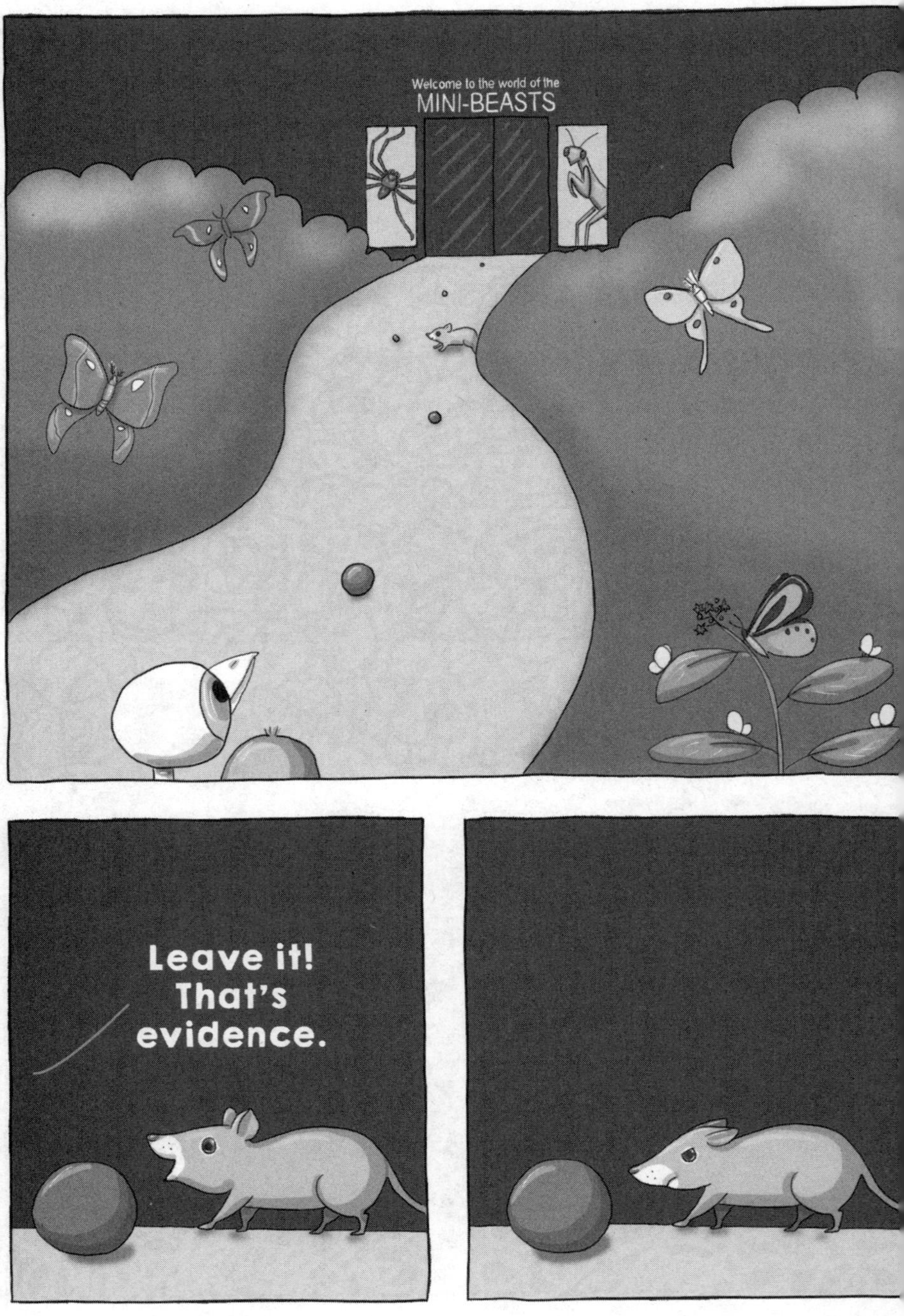
Welcome to the world of the
MINI-BEASTS
Leave it! That's evidence.

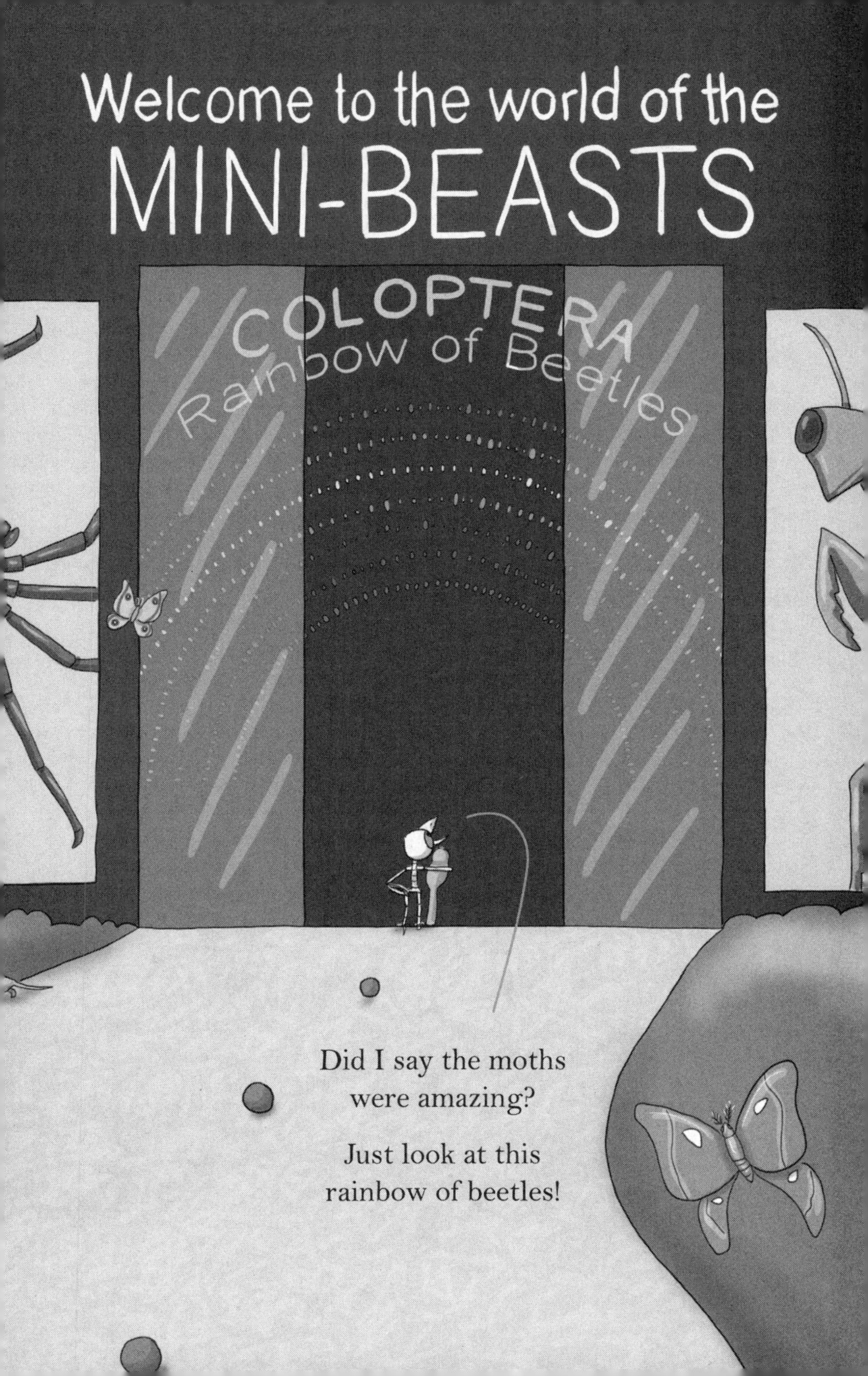
Welcome to the world of the
MINI-BEASTS
COLOPTERA
Rainbow of Beetles

Did I say the moths
were amazing?

Just look at this
rainbow of beetles!

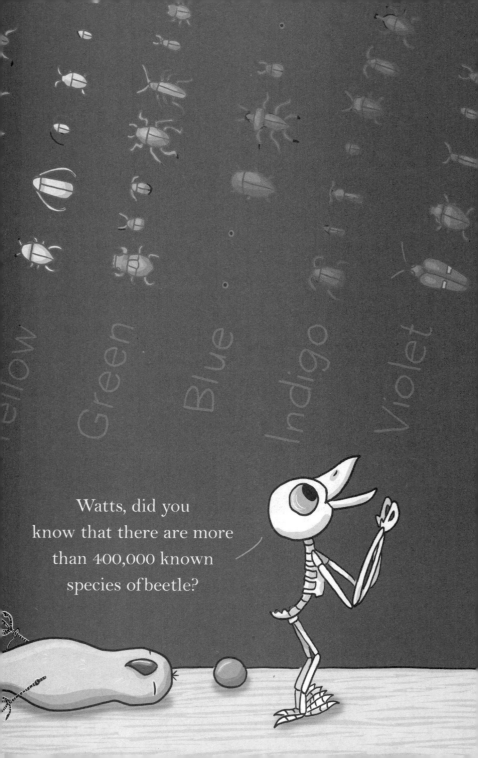

Yellow Green Blue Indigo Violet

Watts, did you
know that there are more
than 400,000 known
species of beetle?

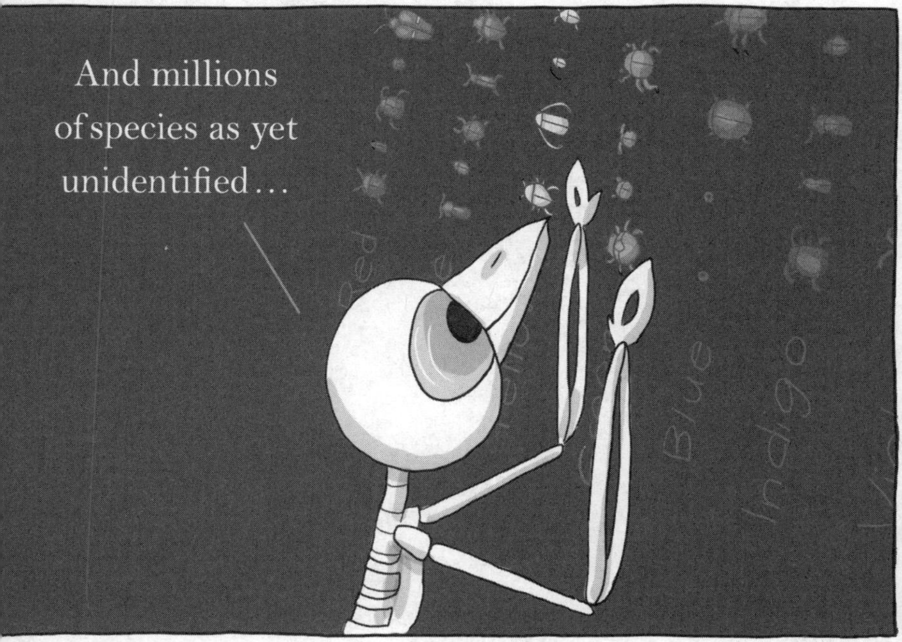
And millions of species as yet unidentified…
Red
Blue
Indigo

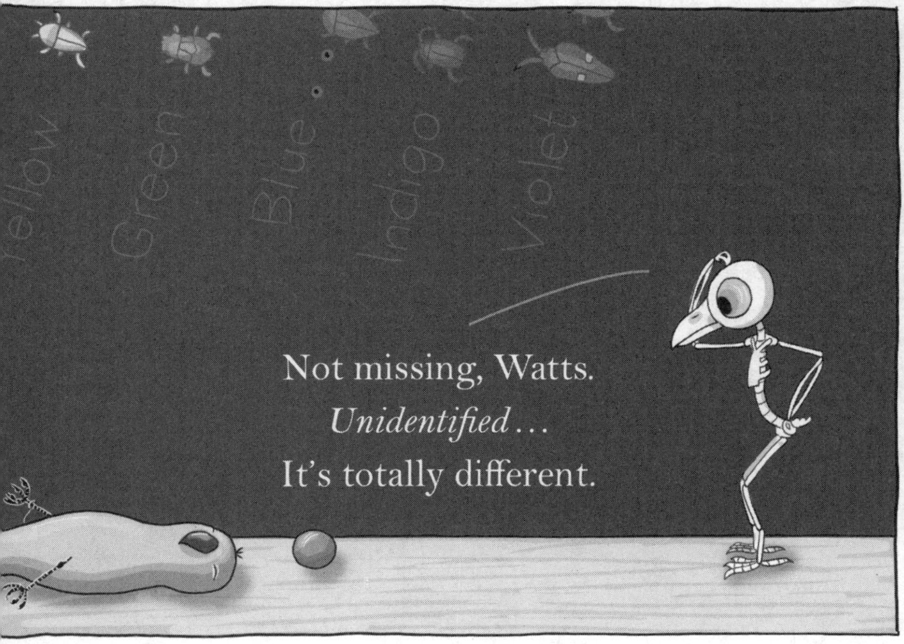
Green
Blue
Indigo
Violet
Not missing, Watts.
Unidentified…
It’s totally different.

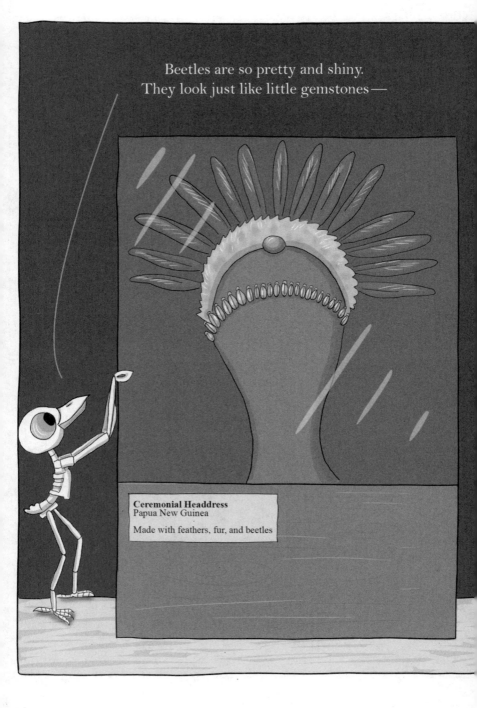

Beetles are so pretty and shiny.
They look just like little gemstones—

Ceremonial Headdress
Papua New Guinea

Made with feathers, fur, and beetles

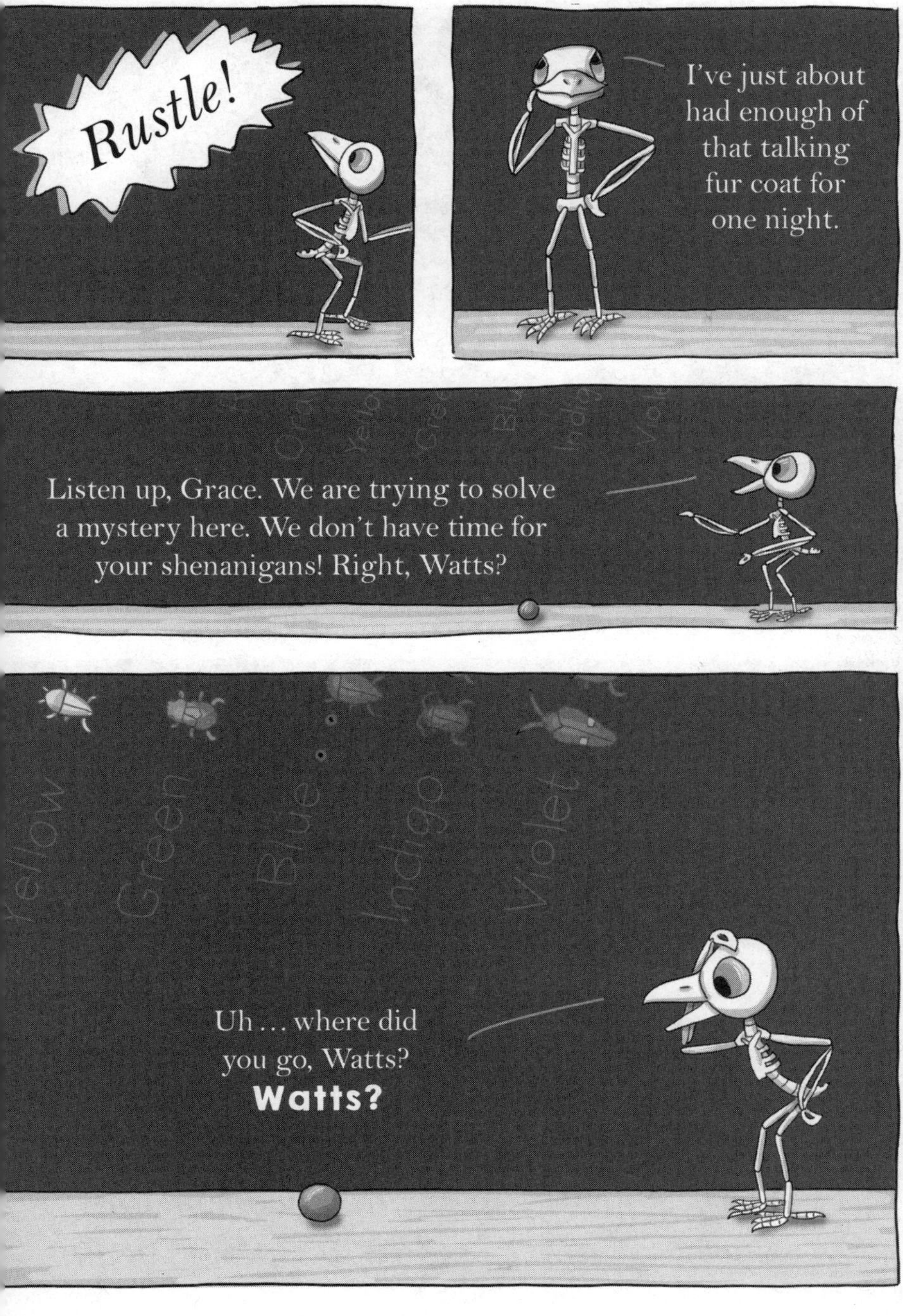
Rustle!
I've just about had enough of that talking fur coat for one night.
Listen up, Grace. We are trying to solve a mystery here. We don't have time for your shenanigans! Right, Watts?
Yellow
Green
Blue
Indigo
Violet
Uh ... where did you go, Watts?
Watts?

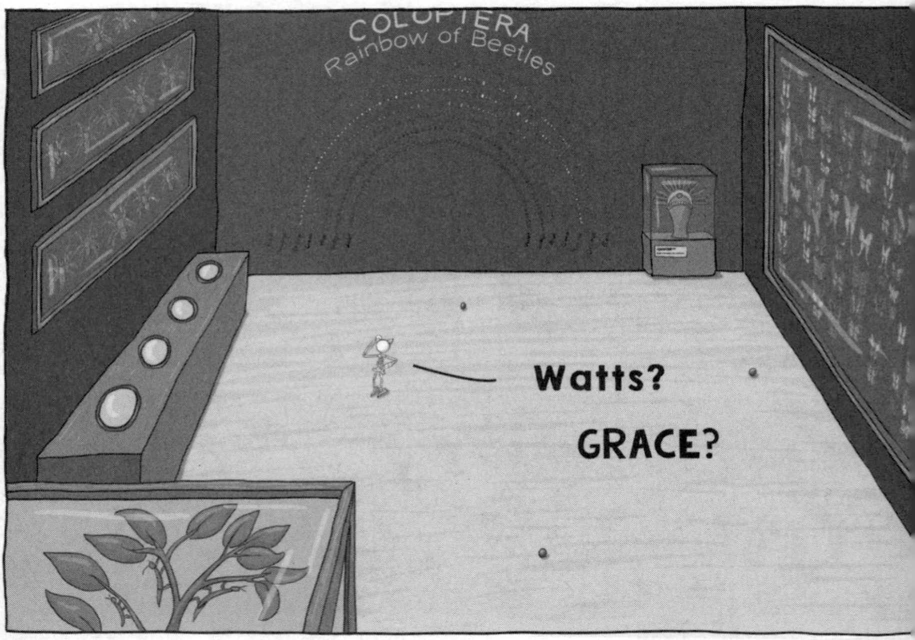
COLOPTERA
Rainbow of Beetles
Watts?
GRACE?

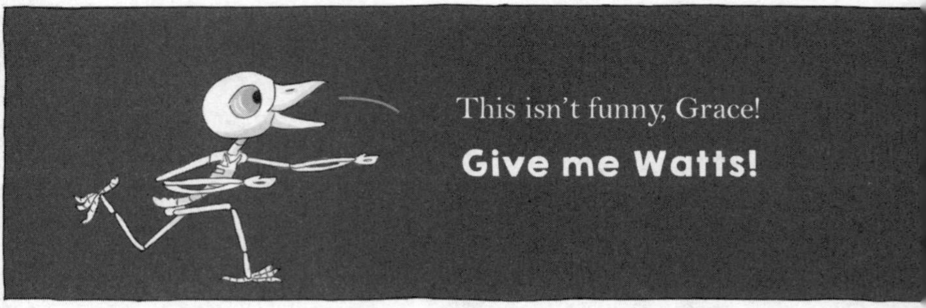
This isn't funny, Grace!
Give me Watts!

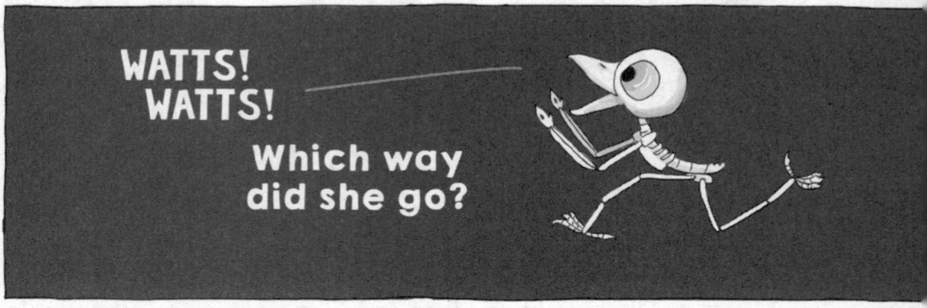
WATTS!
WATTS!
Which way
did she go?

GRACE!
GRACE!
I know it's you!

GRACE!

GRACE!

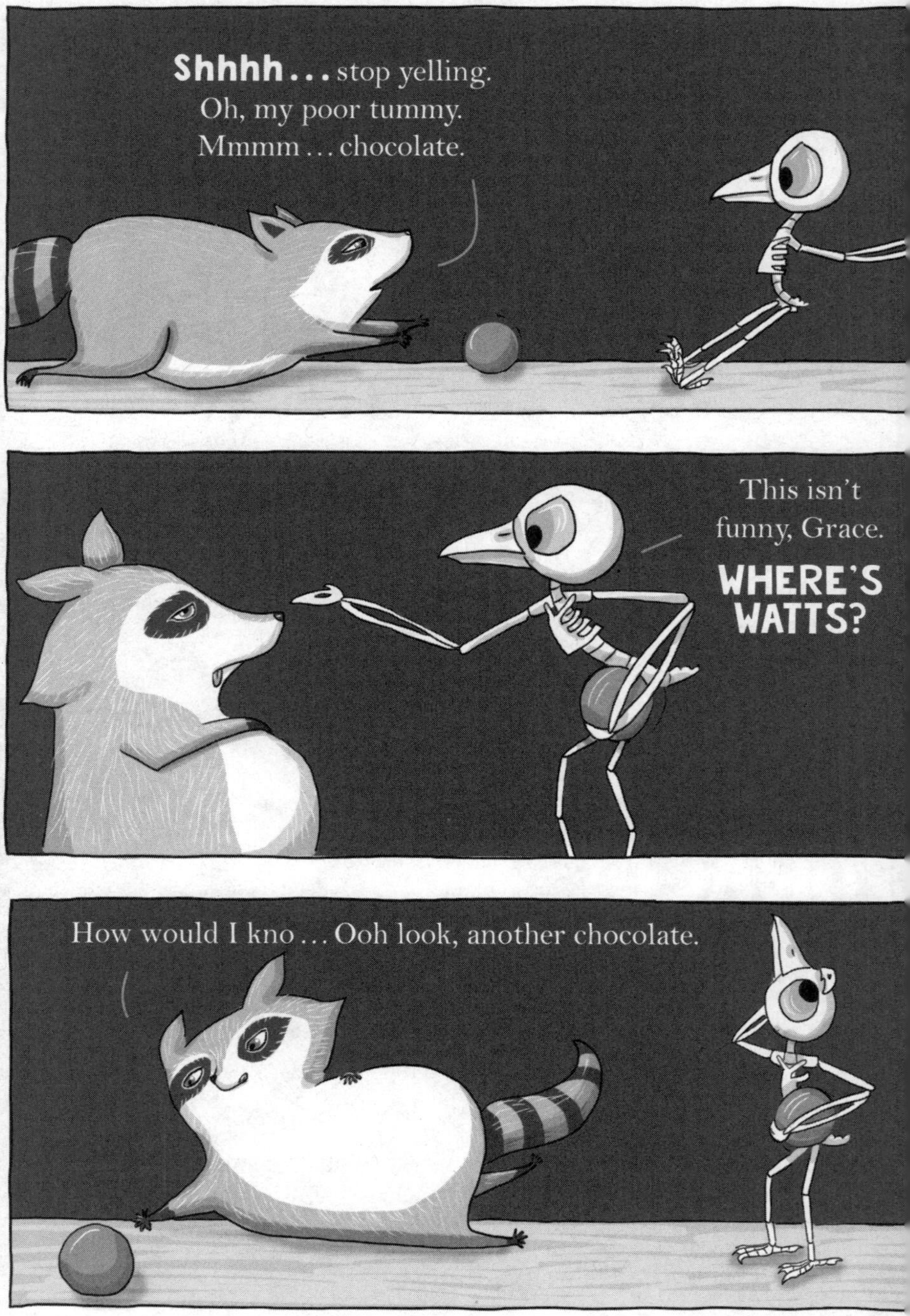
Shhhh... stop yelling.
Oh, my poor tummy.
Mmmm... chocolate.
This isn't funny, Grace.
WHERE'S WATTS?
How would I kno... Ooh look, another chocolate.

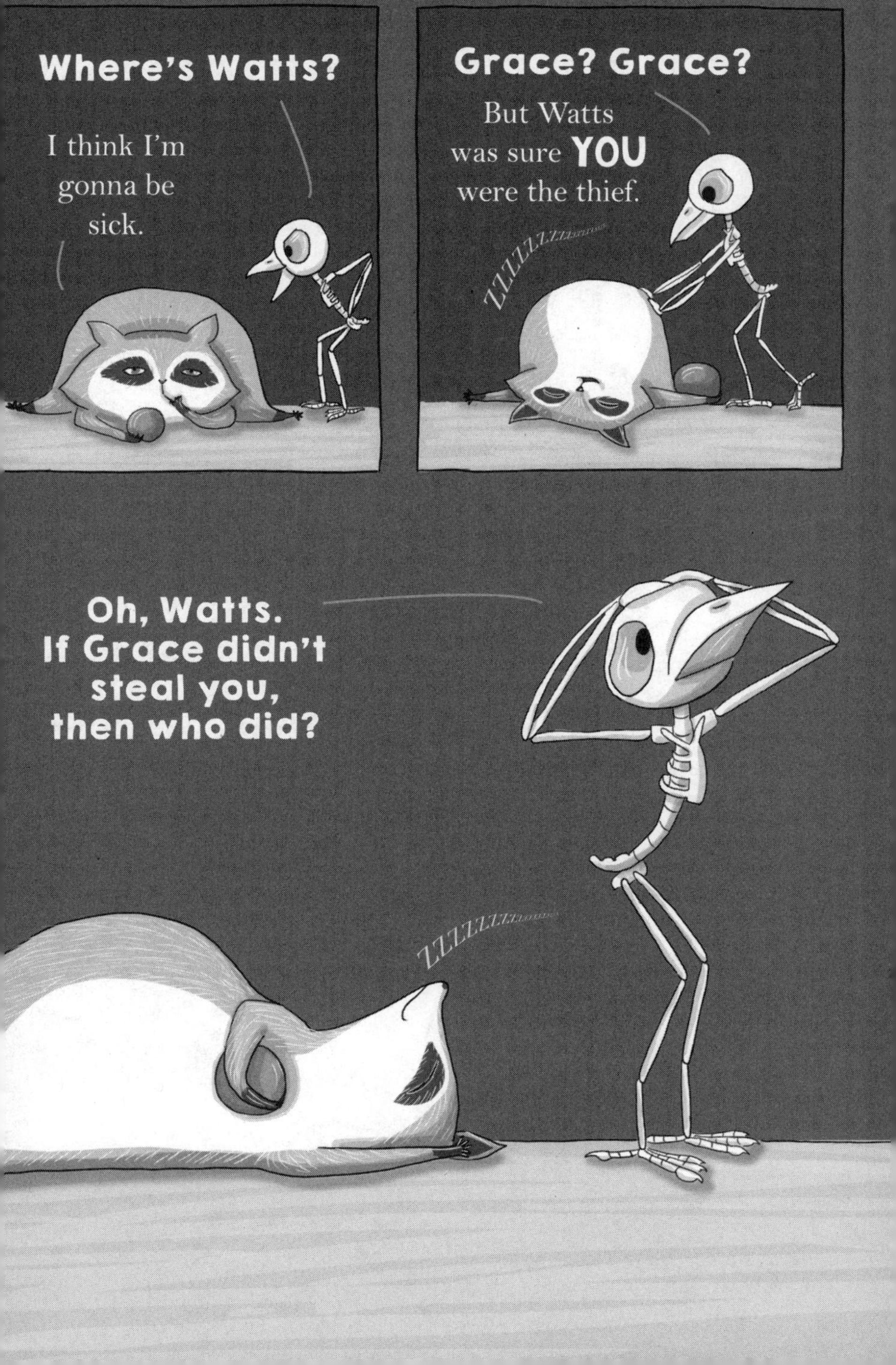
Where's Watts?
I think I'm gonna be sick.
Grace? Grace?
But Watts was sure YOU were the thief.
ZZZZZZZZzzzzz
Oh, Watts. If Grace didn't steal you, then who did?
ZZZZZZZZzzzzz

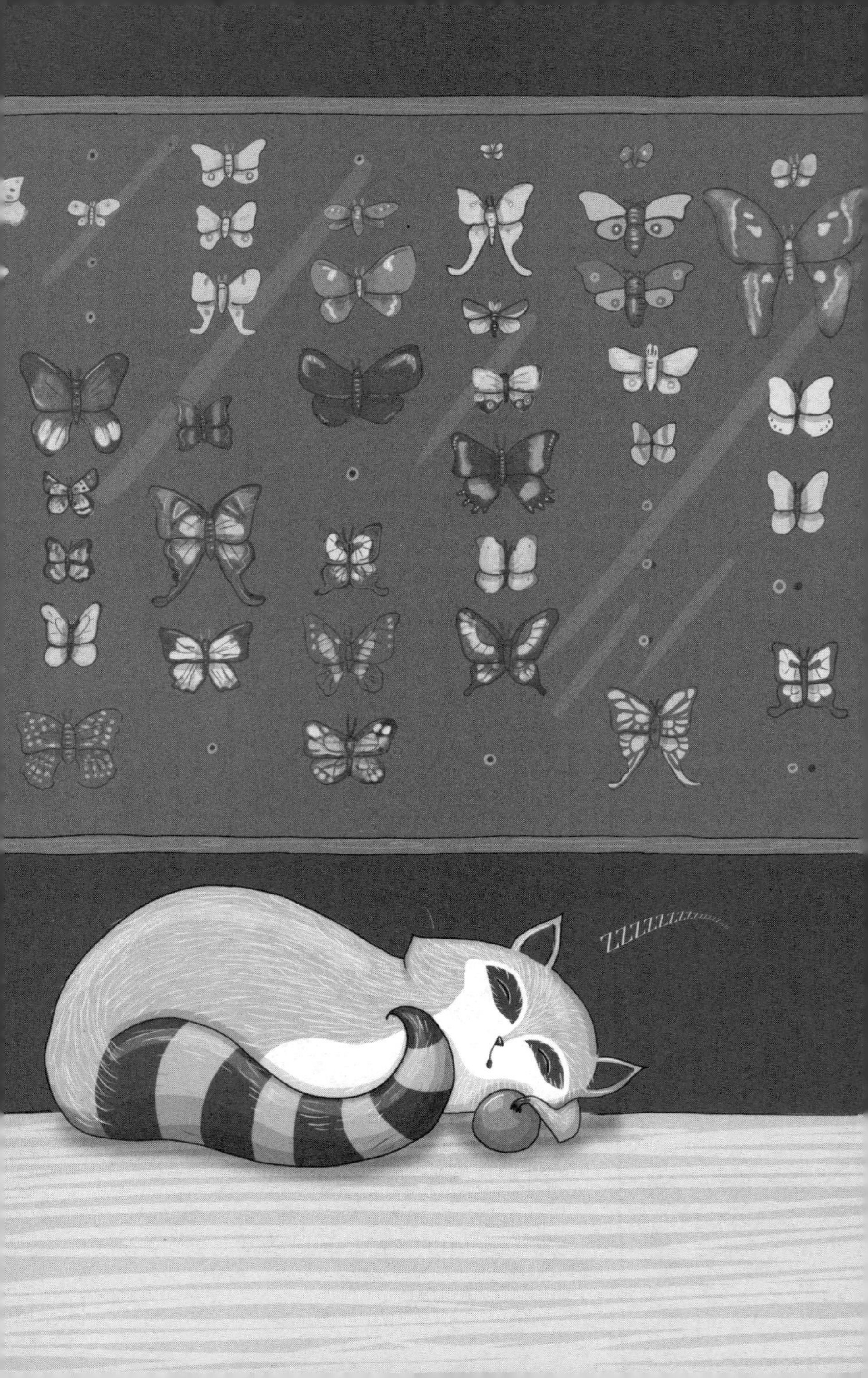

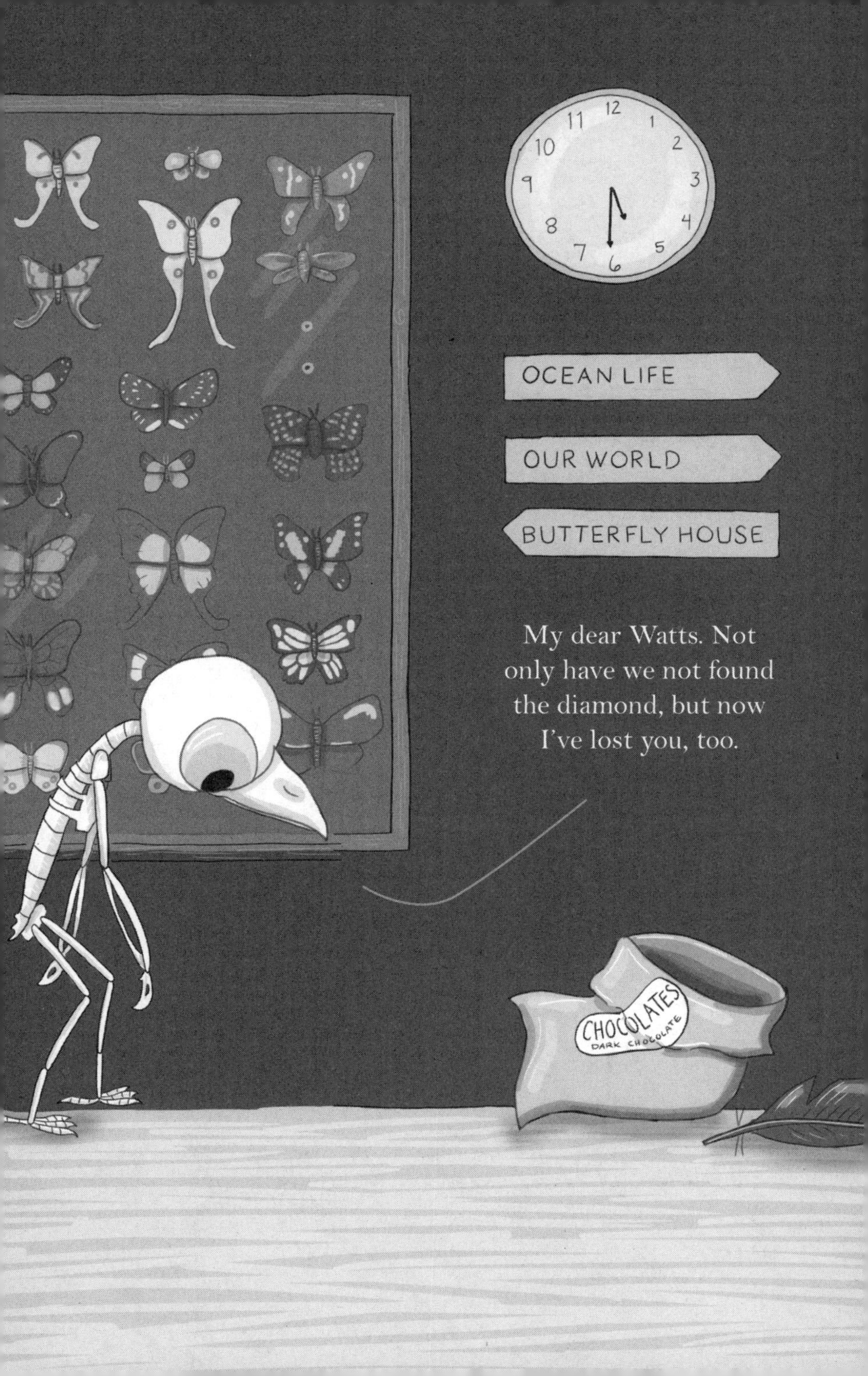

OCEAN LIFE
OUR WORLD
BUTTERFLY HOUSE
My dear Watts. Not only have we not found the diamond, but now I've lost you, too.
CHOCOLATES
DARK CHOCOLATE

CHAPTER 9
Bones Sings the Blues

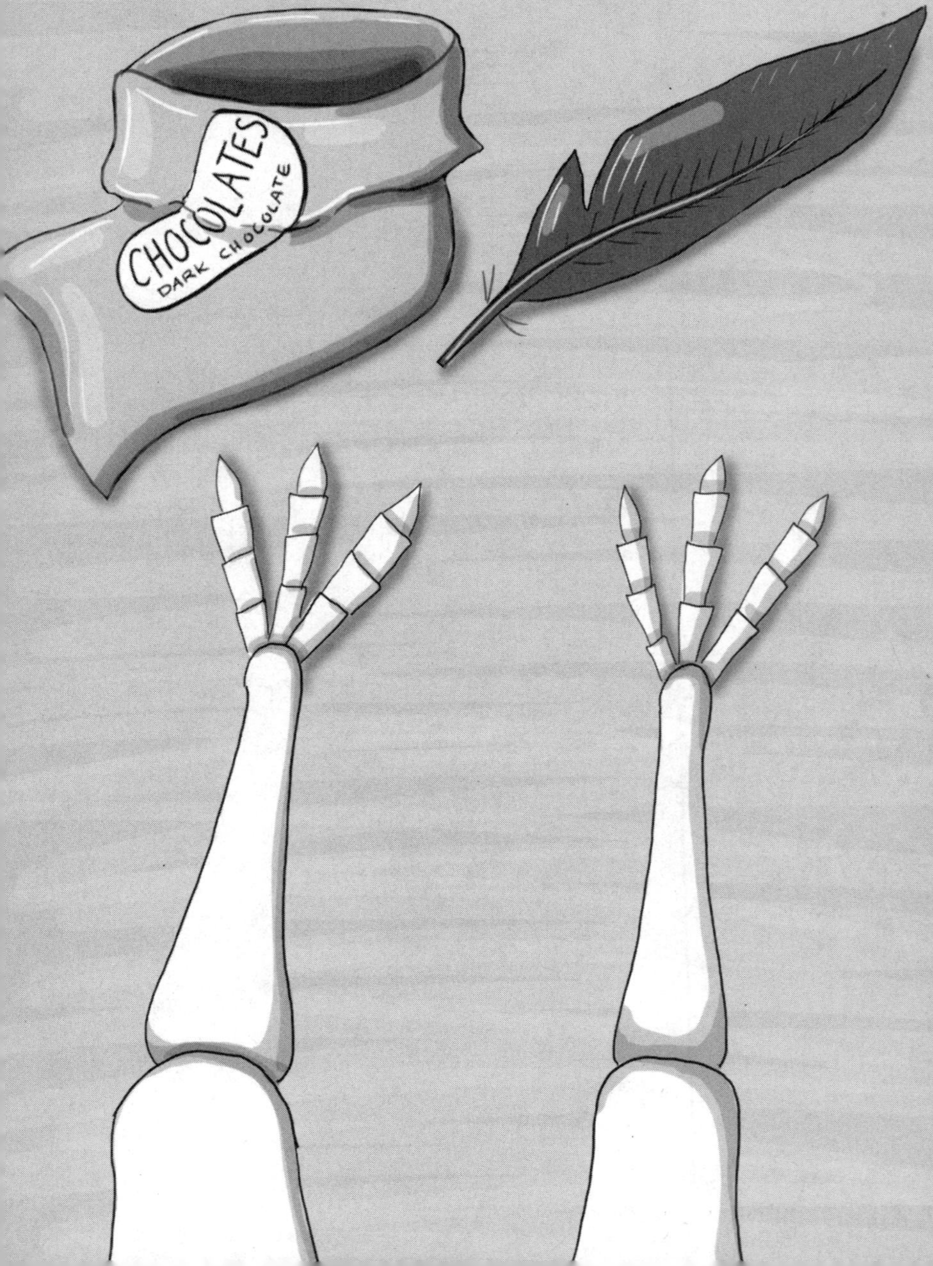
CHOCOLATES
DARK CHOCOLATE

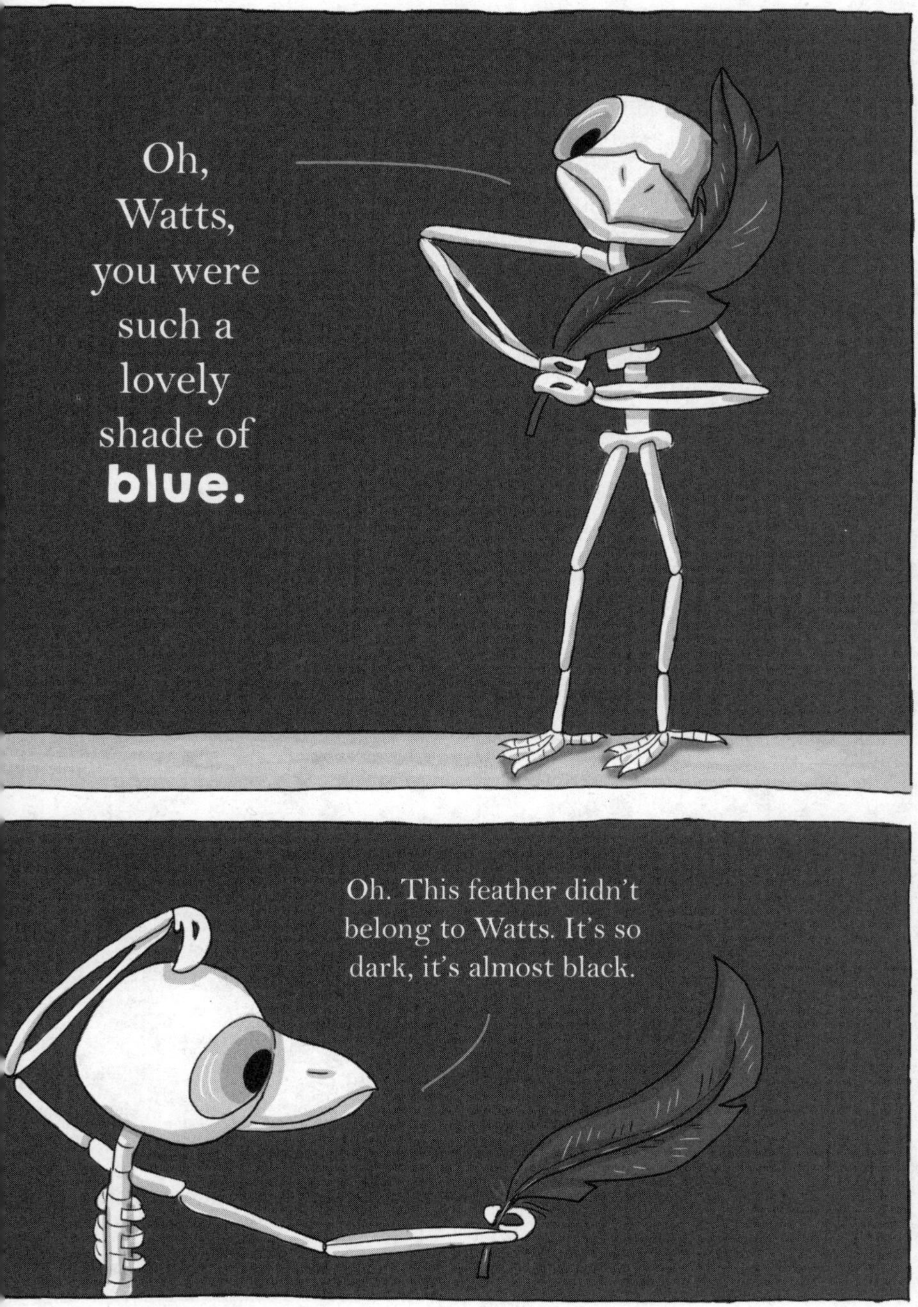
Oh, Watts, you were such a lovely shade of **blue.**
Oh. This feather didn't belong to Watts. It's so dark, it's almost black.

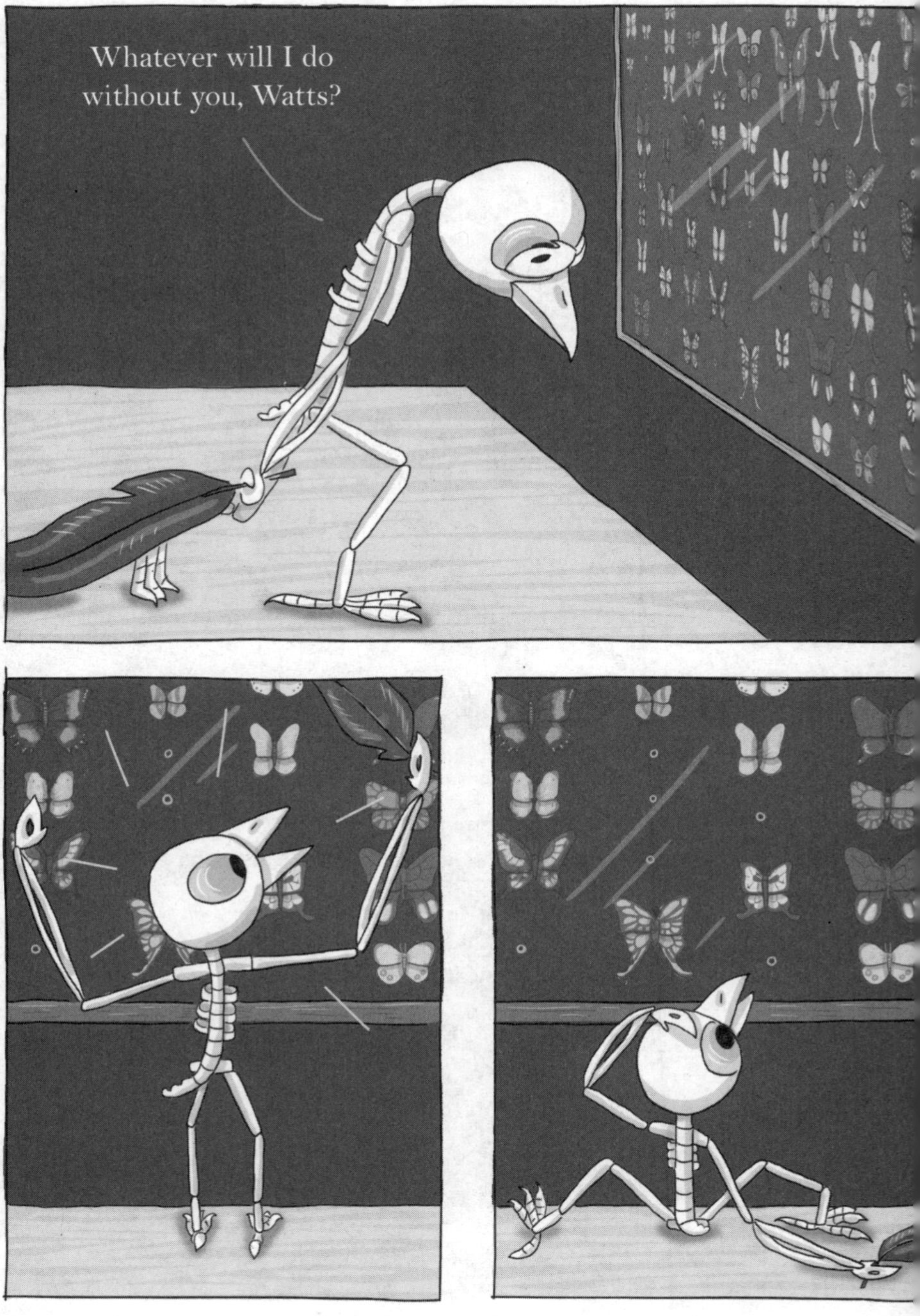
Whatever will I do without you, Watts?

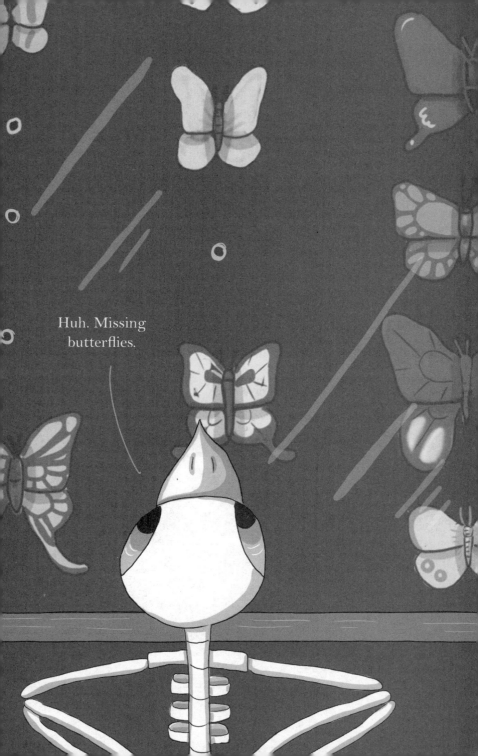

Huh. Missing butterflies.

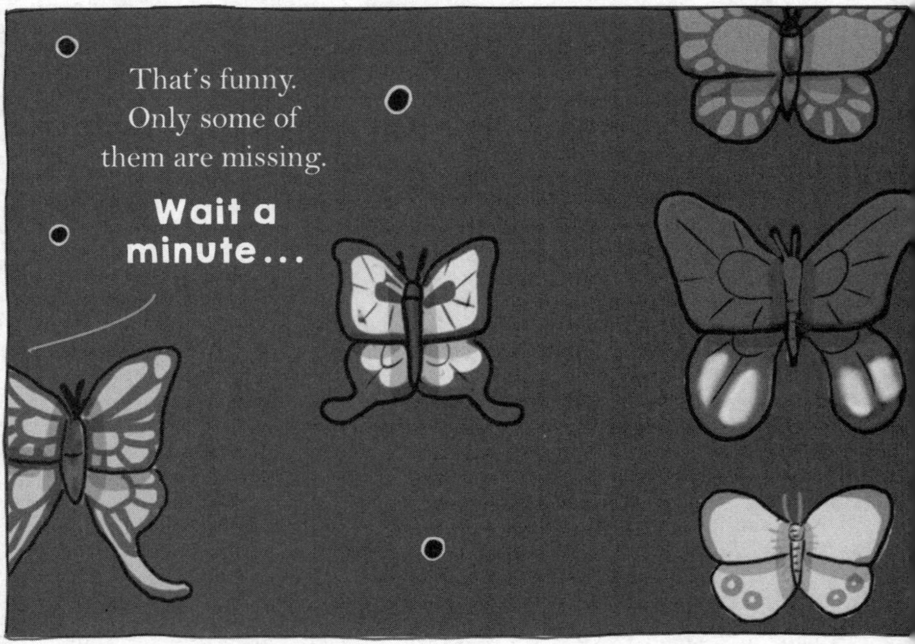
That's funny.
Only some of
them are missing.
Wait a
minute...

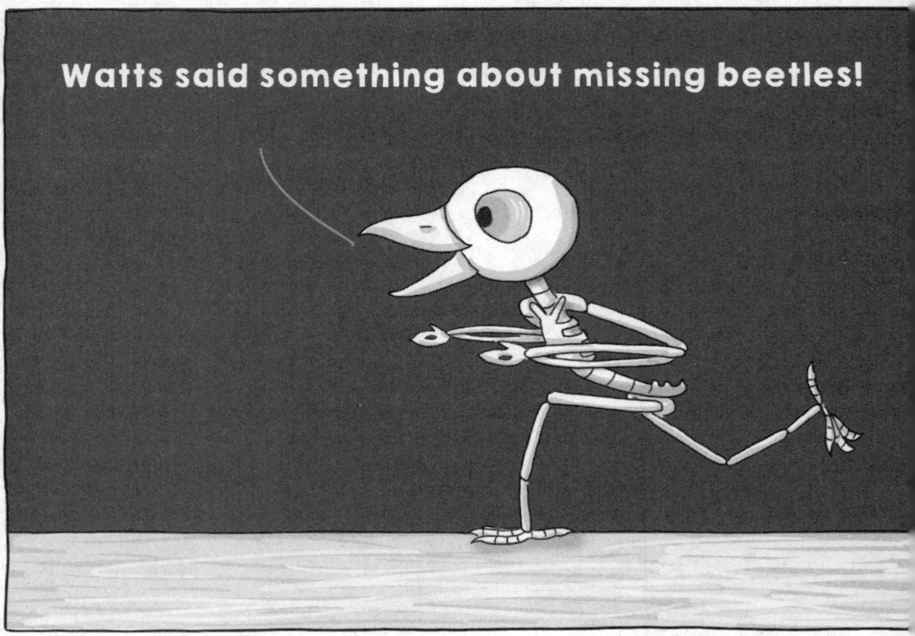
Watts said something about missing beetles!

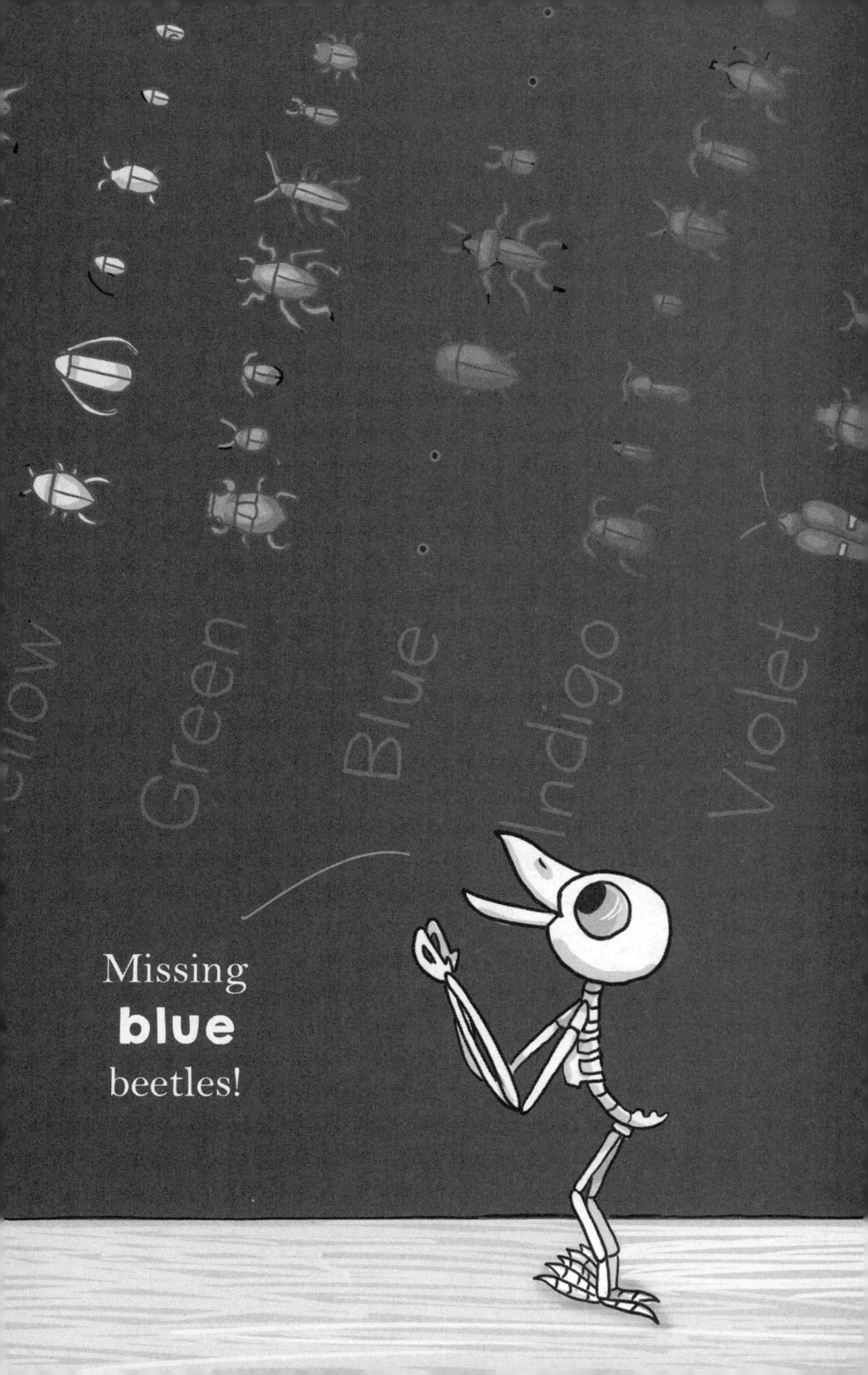
Green
Blue
Indigo
Violet
Missing **blue** beetles!

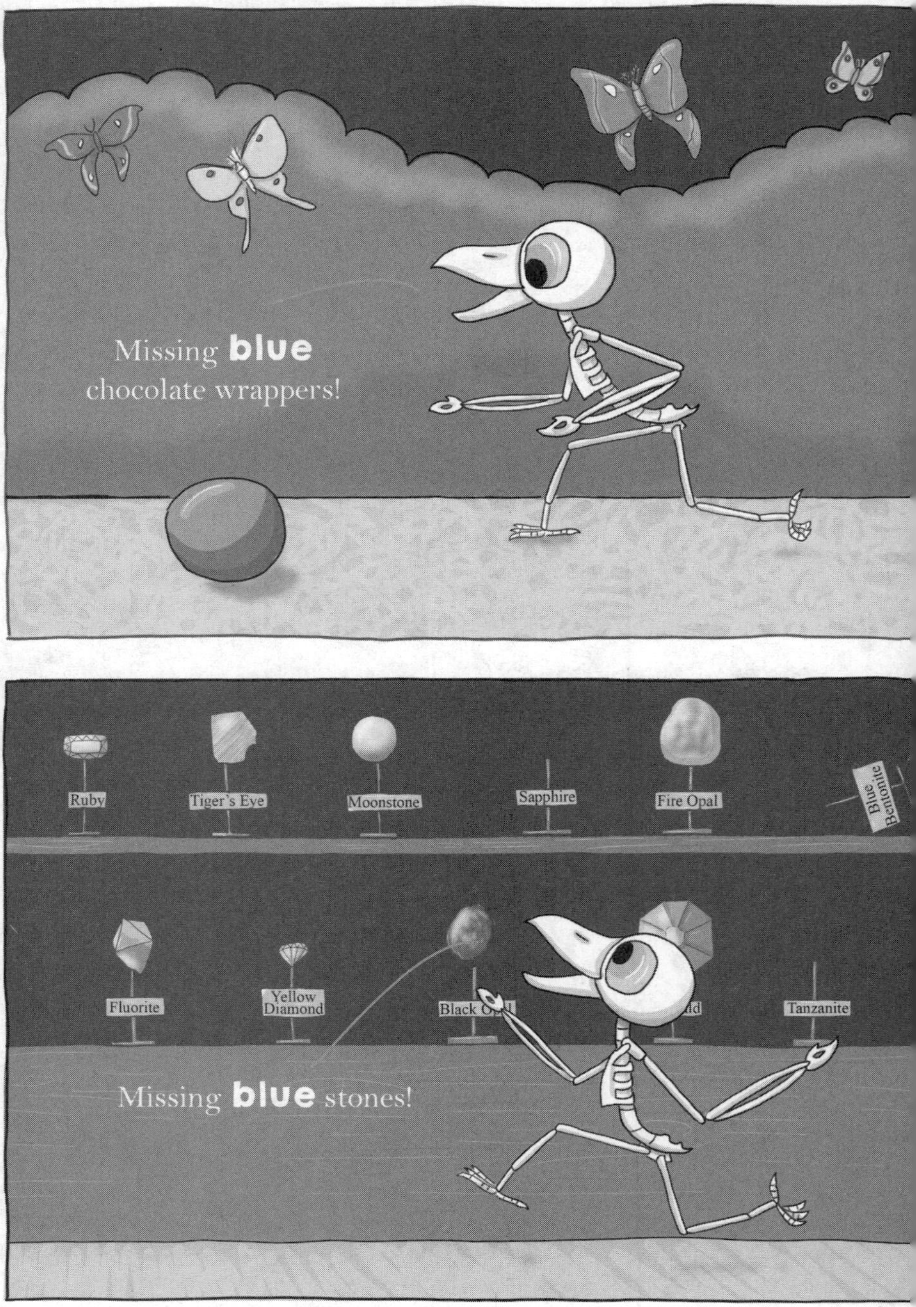
Missing **blue**
chocolate wrappers!
Ruby
Tiger's Eye
Moonstone
Sapphire
Fire Opal
Blue Bentonite
Fluorite
Yellow Diamond
Tanzanite
Missing **blue** stones!

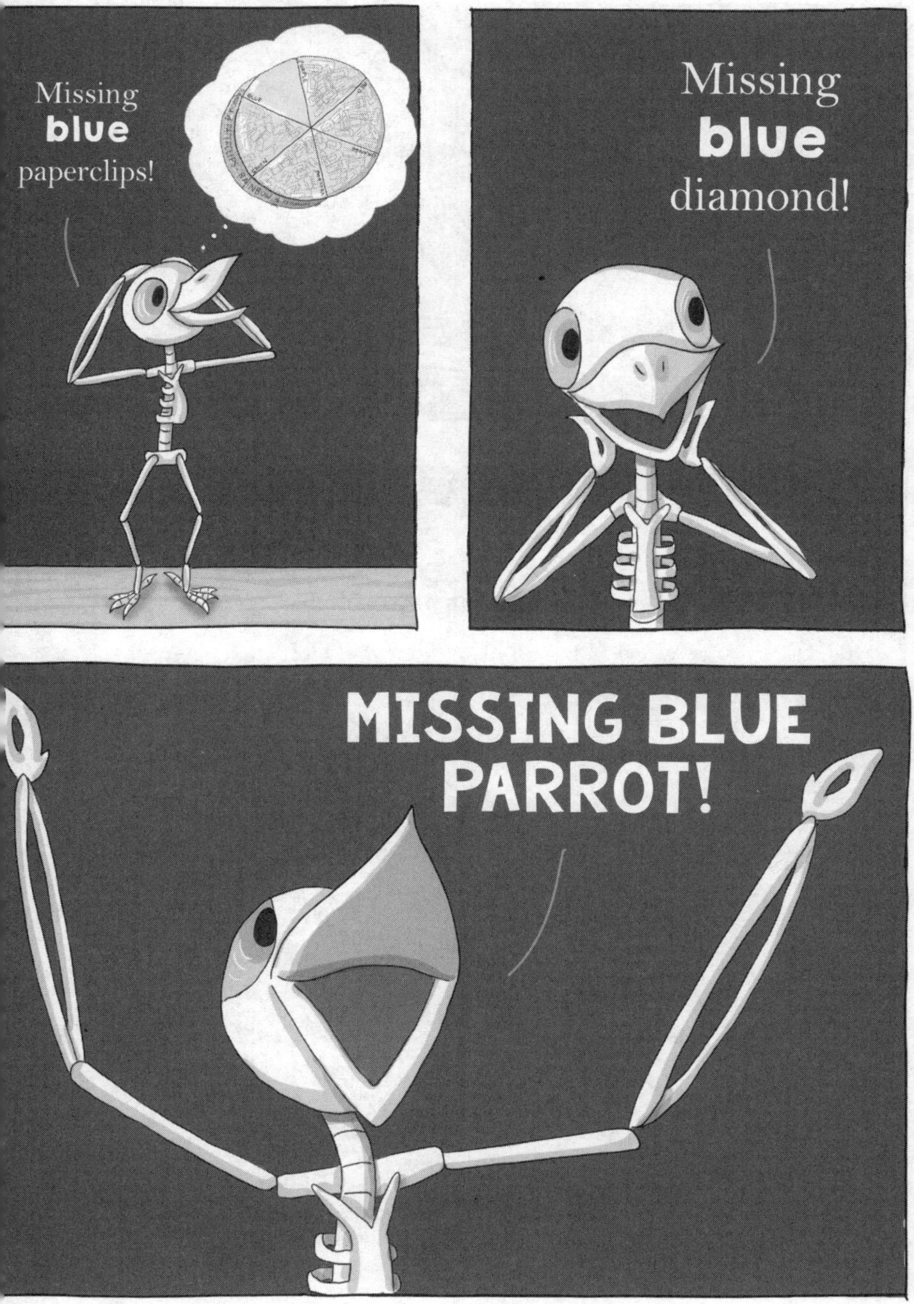
Missing **blue** paperclips!
Missing **blue** diamond!
MISSING BLUE PARROT!

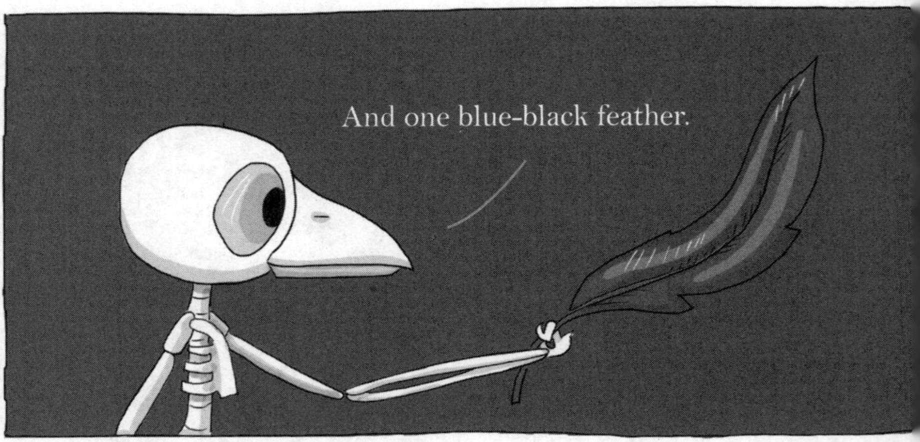
And one blue-black feather.

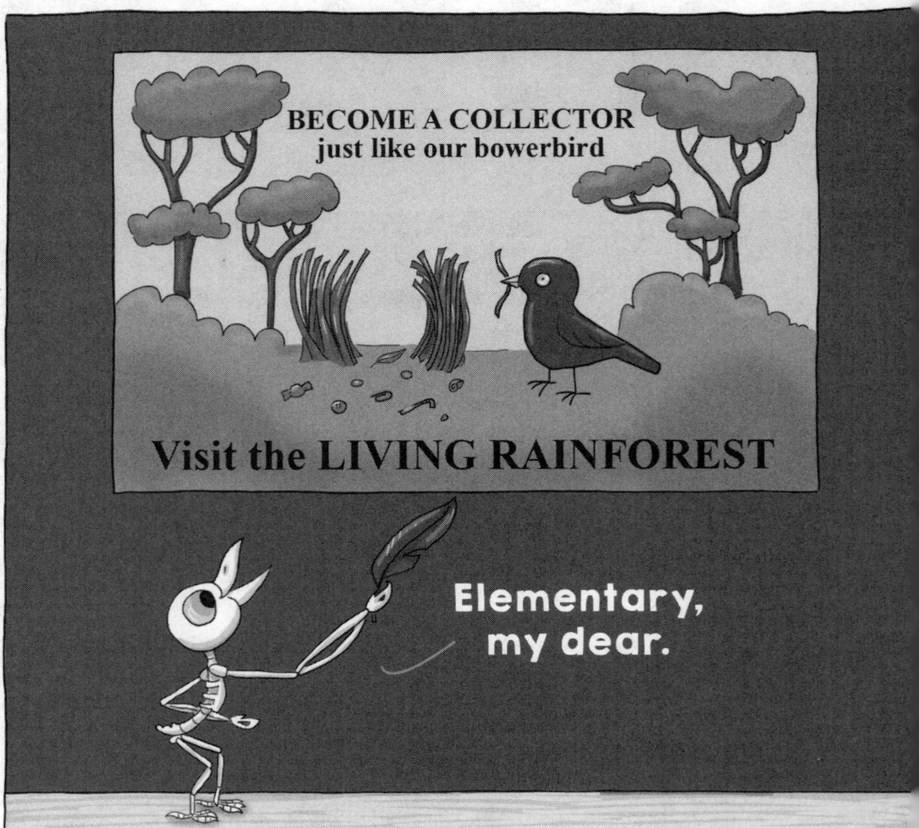
BECOME A COLLECTOR
just like our bowerbird
Visit the LIVING RAINFOREST
Elementary, my dear.

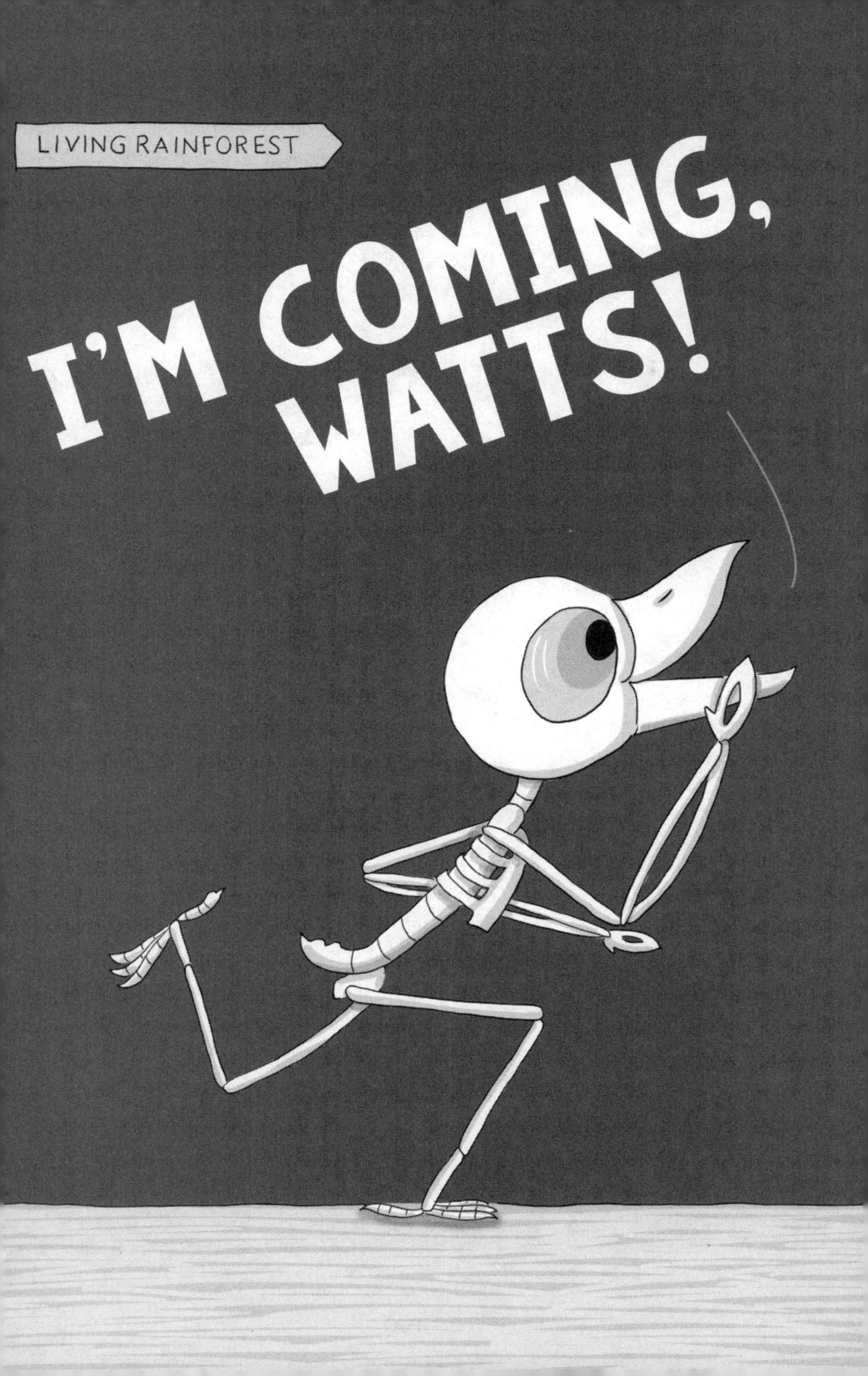
LIVING RAINFOREST
I'M COMING, WATTS!

I should have known it was a bowerbird. All those blue things. Poor guy, he's just trying to attract a lady.

PUSH TO OPEN

MAPS

Hey! Open up!

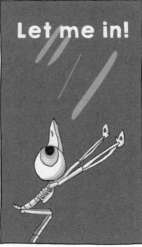

Let me in!

STUPID DOORS!

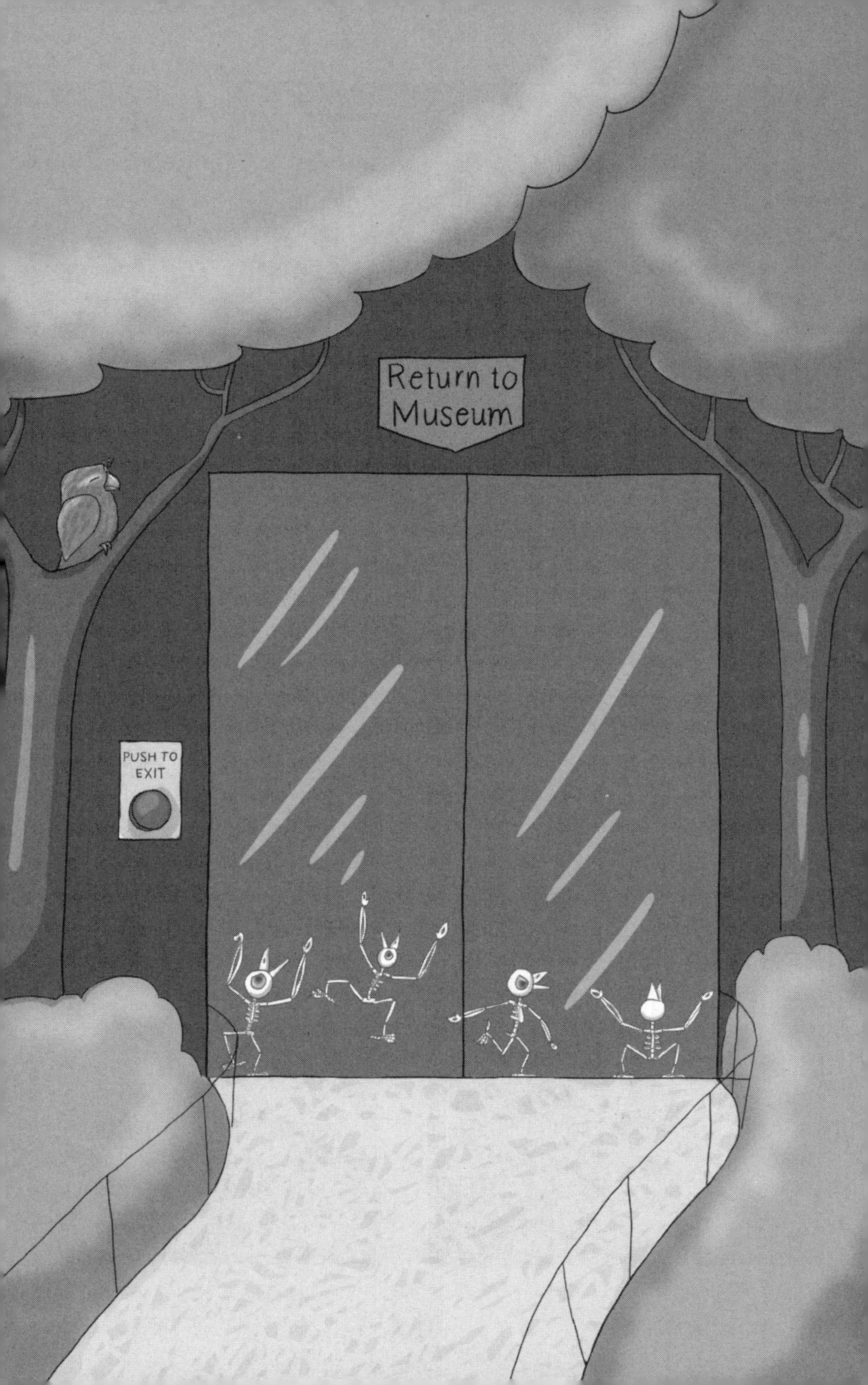
Return to
Museum
PUSH TO
EXIT

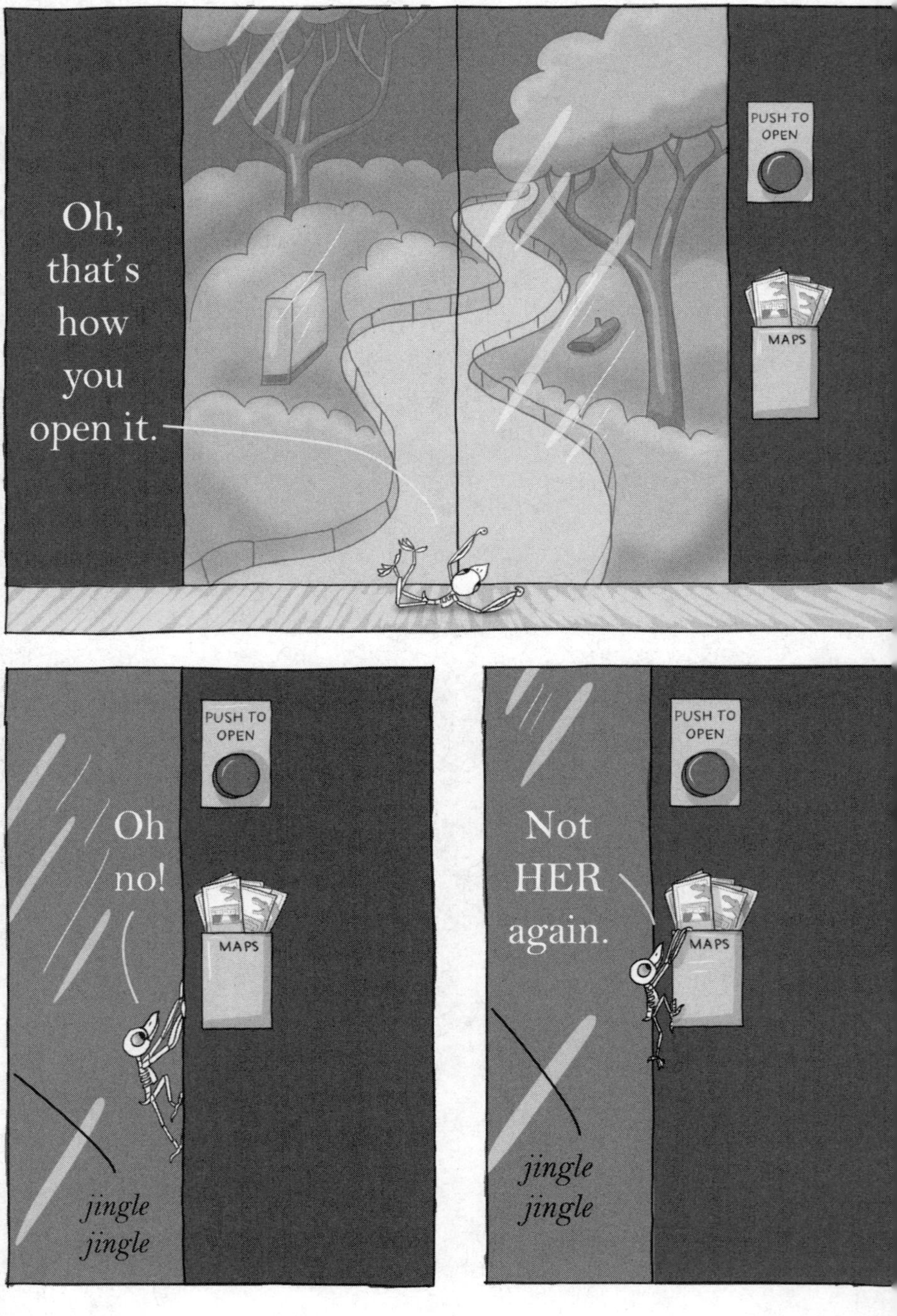
PUSH TO OPEN
MAPS
Oh, that's how you open it.
PUSH TO OPEN
MAPS
Oh no!
jingle jingle
PUSH TO OPEN
MAPS
Not HER again.
jingle jingle

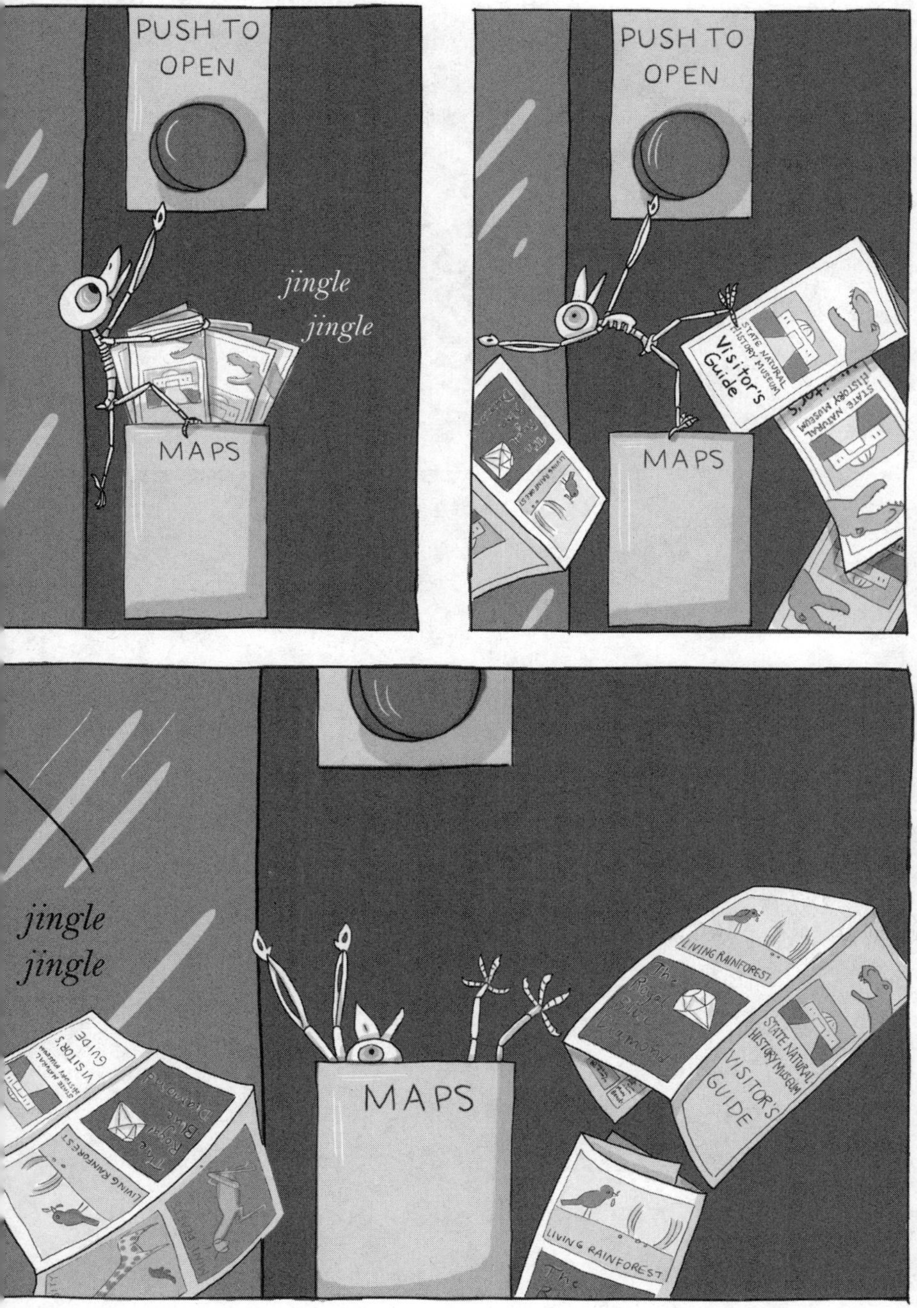
PUSH TO OPEN
jingle
jingle
MAPS
PUSH TO OPEN
STATE NATURAL HISTORY MUSEUM
Visitor's Guide
MAPS
jingle
jingle
MAPS
LIVING RAINFOREST
The Royal Blue Diamond
STATE NATURAL HISTORY MUSEUM
VISITOR'S GUIDE
LIVING RAINFOREST

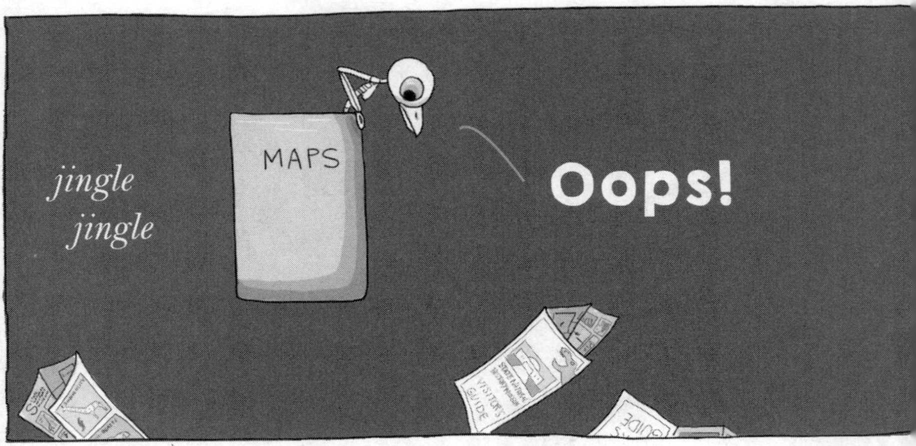
MAPS
jingle
jingle
Oops!
VISITOR'S GUIDE

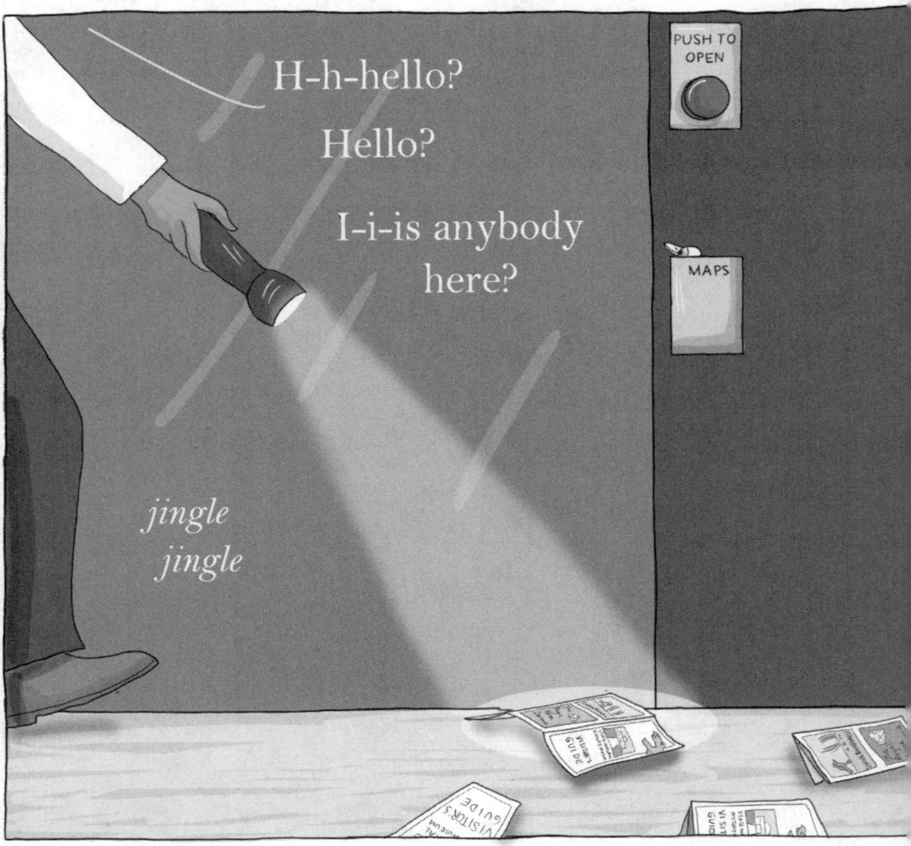
PUSH TO OPEN
H-h-hello?
Hello?
I-i-is anybody here?
MAPS
jingle
jingle
VISITOR'S GUIDE
VISITOR'S GUIDE

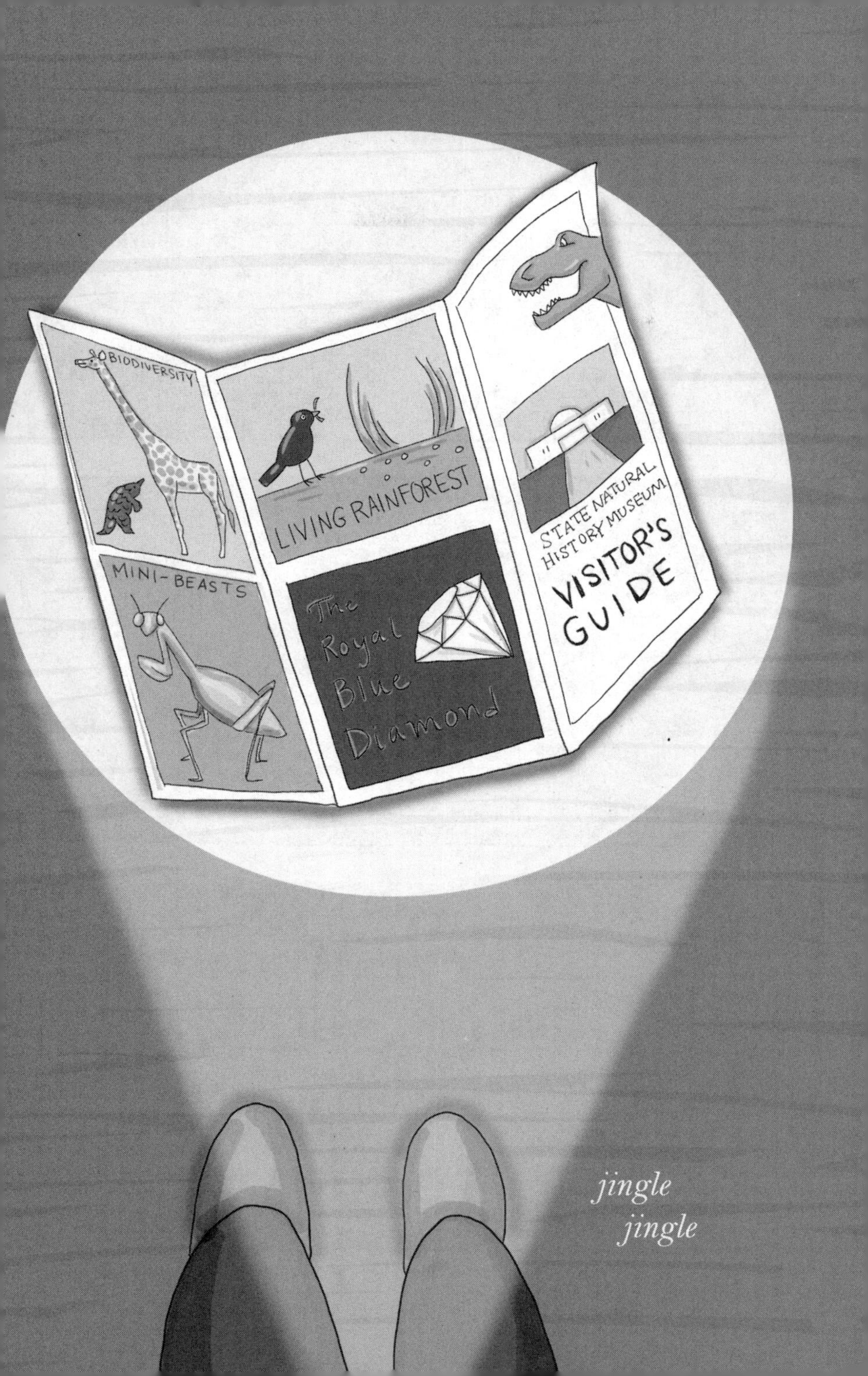
BIODIVERSITY
MINI-BEASTS
LIVING RAINFOREST
The Royal Blue Diamond
STATE NATURAL HISTORY MUSEUM
VISITOR'S GUIDE
jingle
jingle

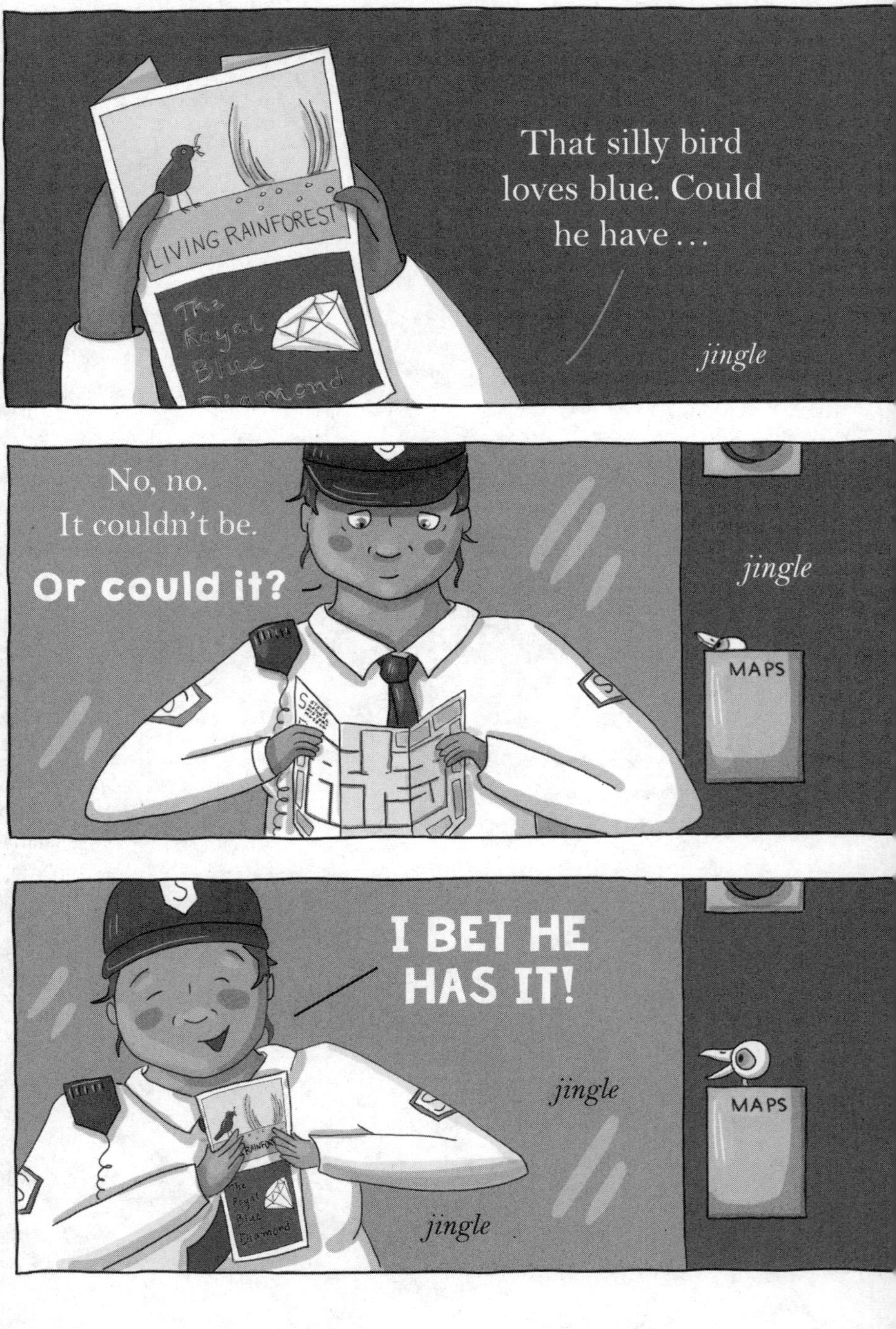

LIVING RAINFOREST
The Royal Blue
That silly bird loves blue. Could he have . . .
jingle
No, no. It couldn't be.
Or could it?
jingle
MAPS
I BET HE HAS IT!
jingle
jingle
MAPS

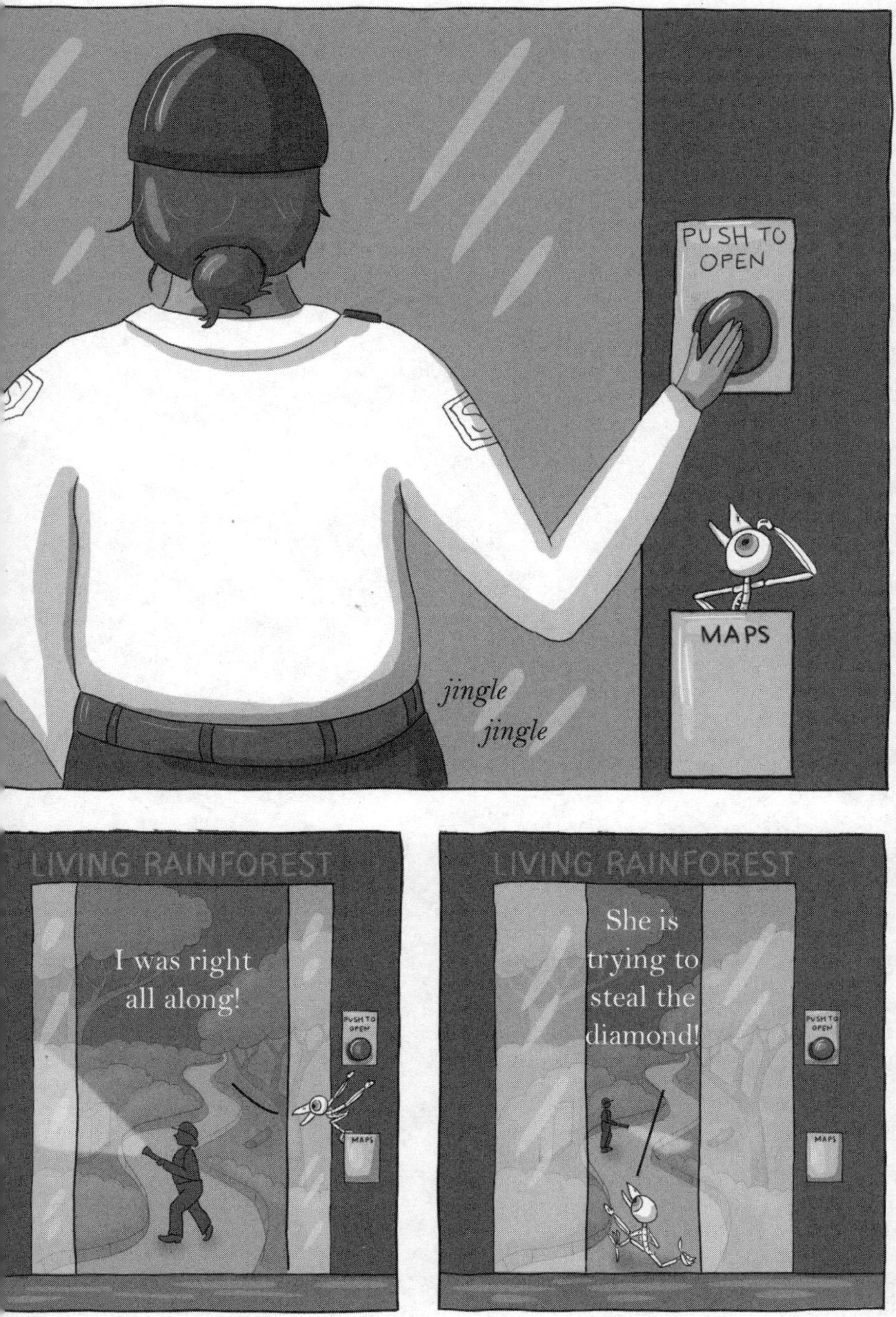
PUSH TO OPEN
MAPS
jingle
jingle
LIVING RAINFOREST
I was right all along!
PUSH TO OPEN
MAPS
LIVING RAINFOREST
She is trying to steal the diamond!
PUSH TO OPEN
MAPS

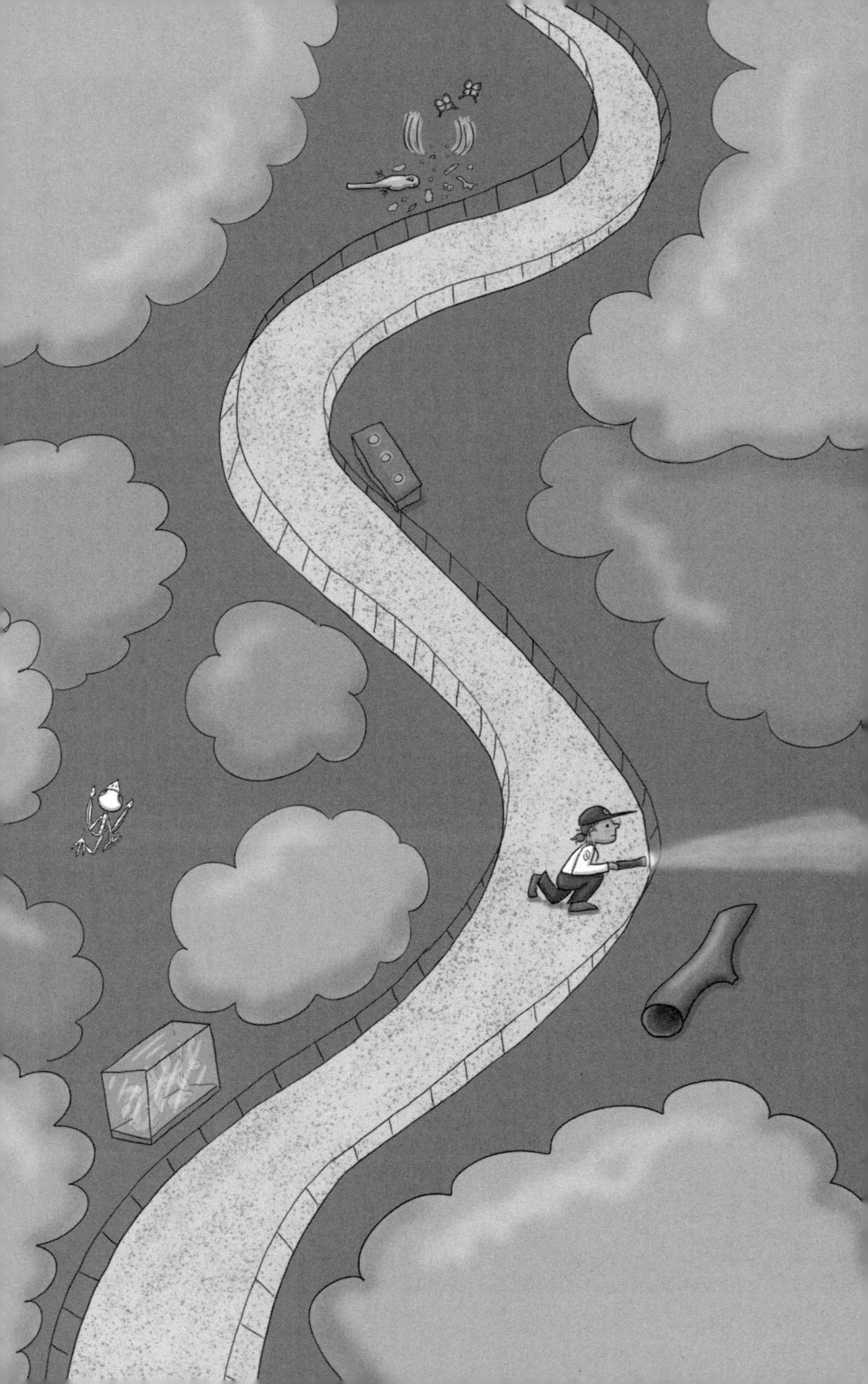

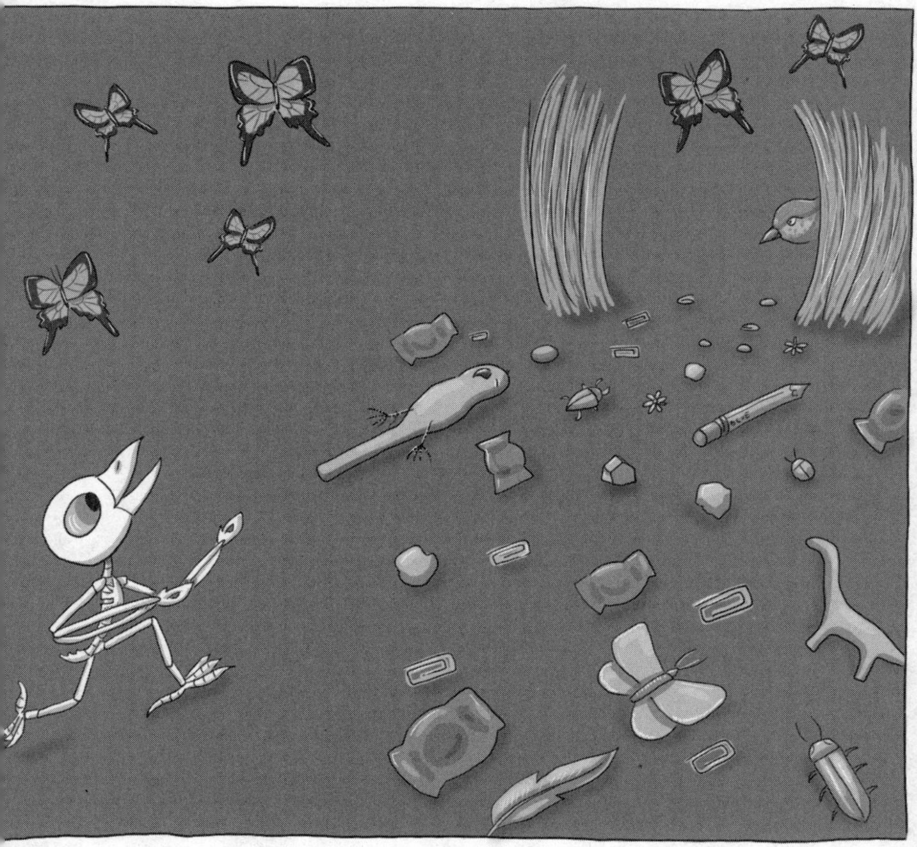

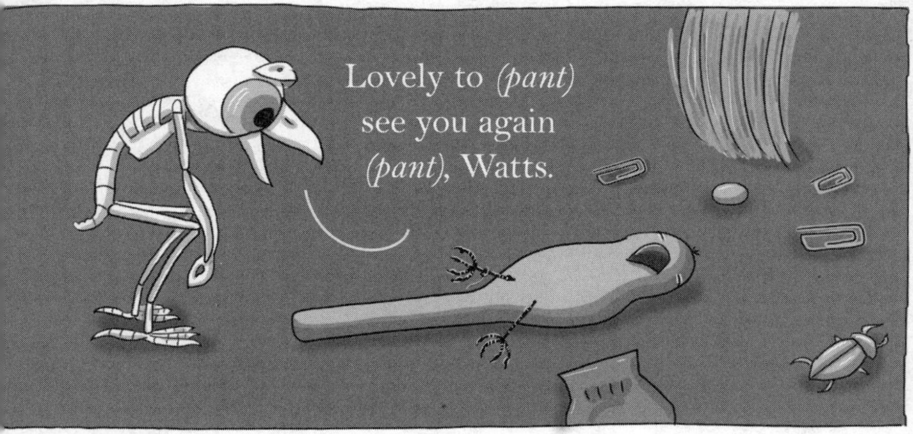
Lovely to (pant) see you again (pant), Watts.

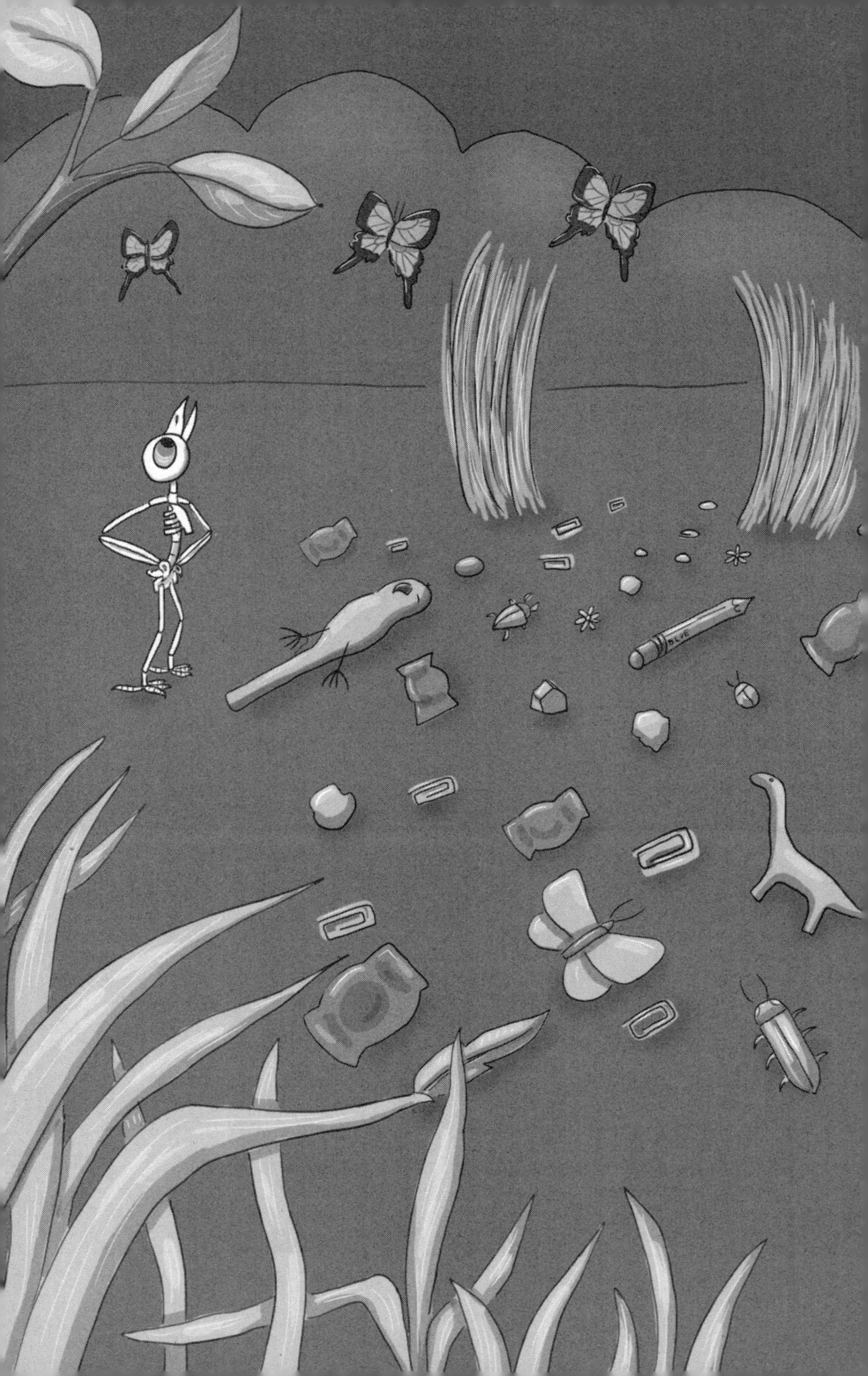

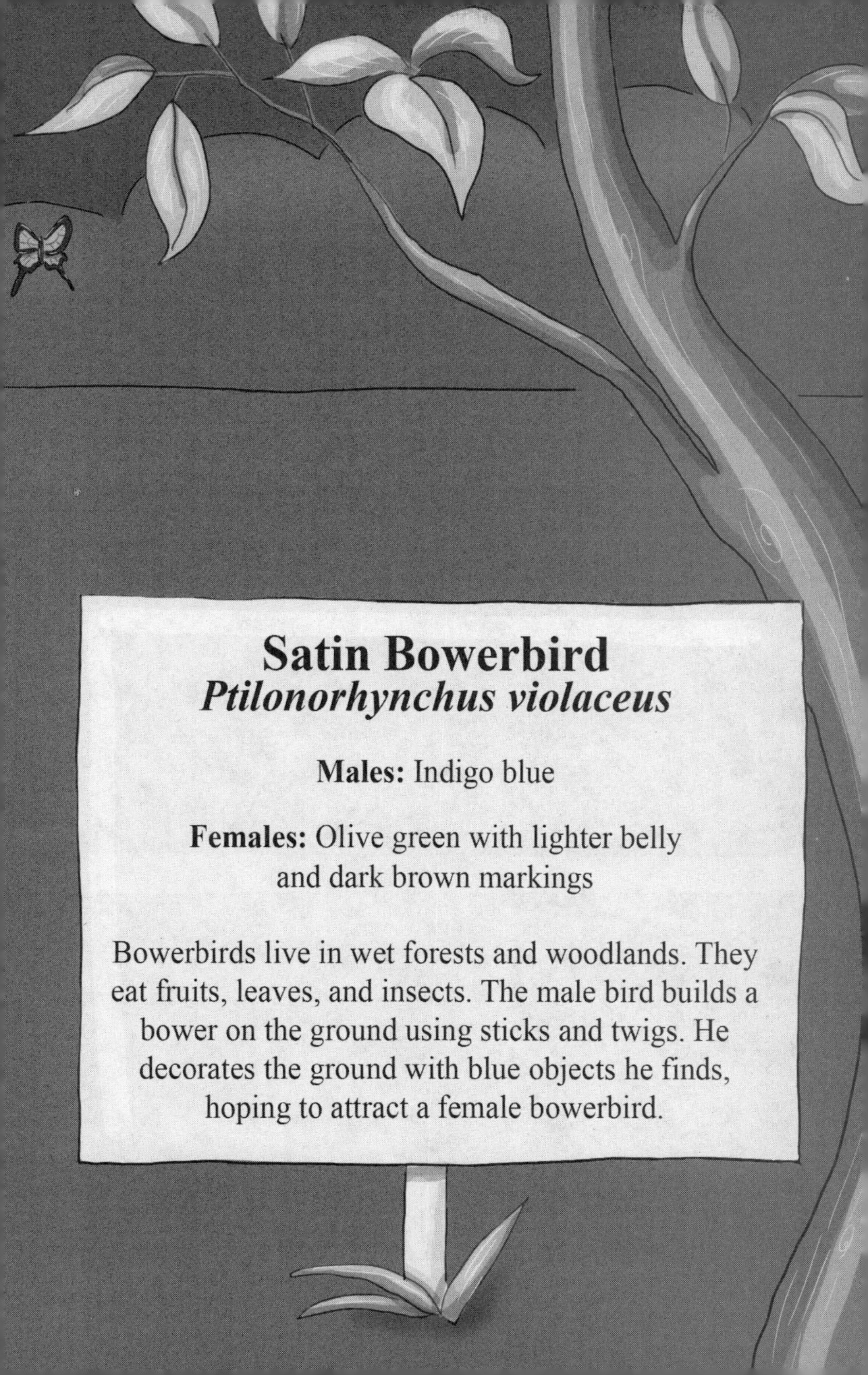
Satin Bowerbird
Ptilonorhynchus violaceus
Males: Indigo blue
Females: Olive green with lighter belly and dark brown markings
Bowerbirds live in wet forests and woodlands. They eat fruits, leaves, and insects. The male bird builds a bower on the ground using sticks and twigs. He decorates the ground with blue objects he finds, hoping to attract a female bowerbird.

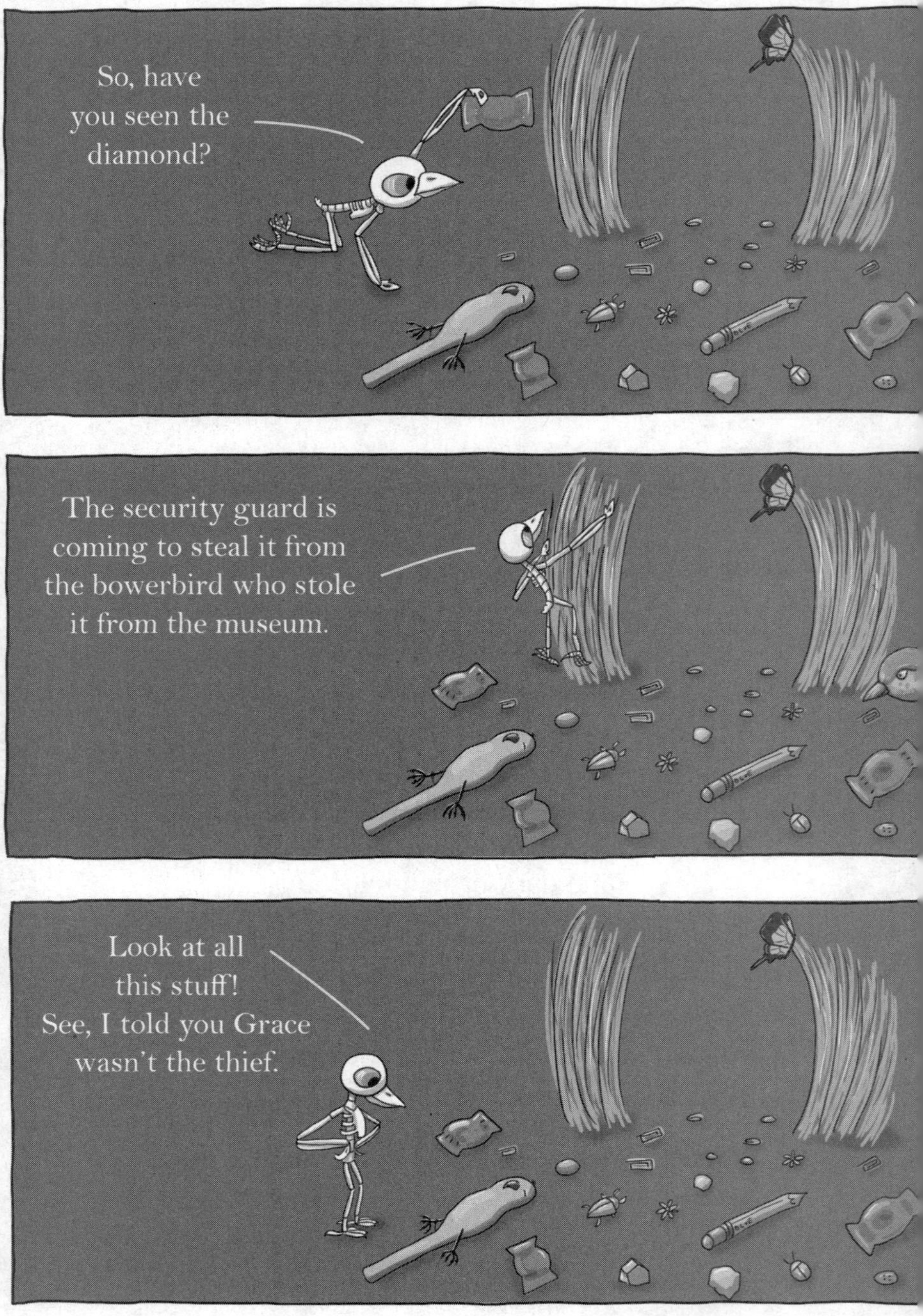
So, have you seen the diamond?
The security guard is coming to steal it from the bowerbird who stole it from the museum.
Look at all this stuff! See, I told you Grace wasn't the thief.

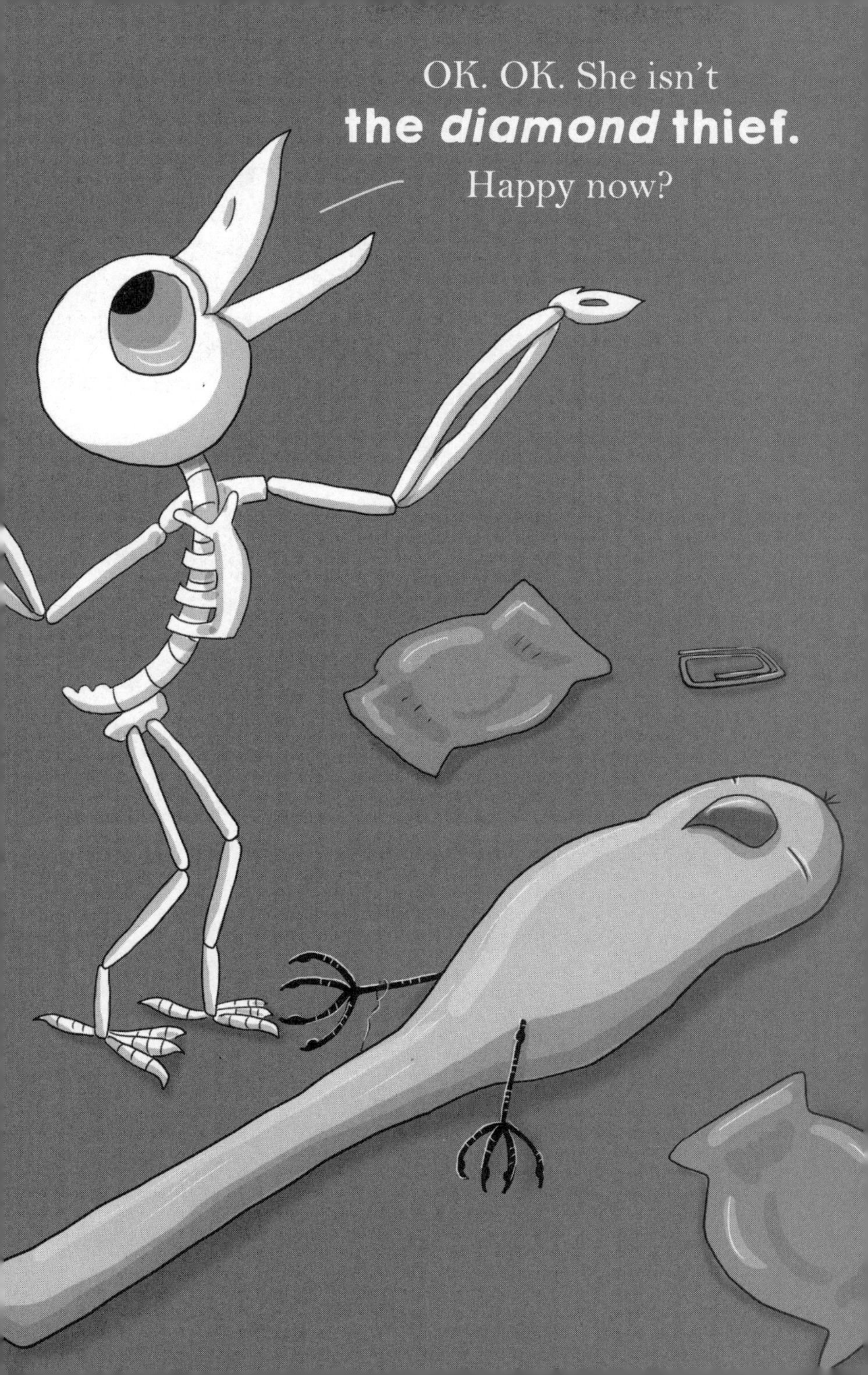
OK. OK. She isn't
the *diamond* thief.
Happy now?

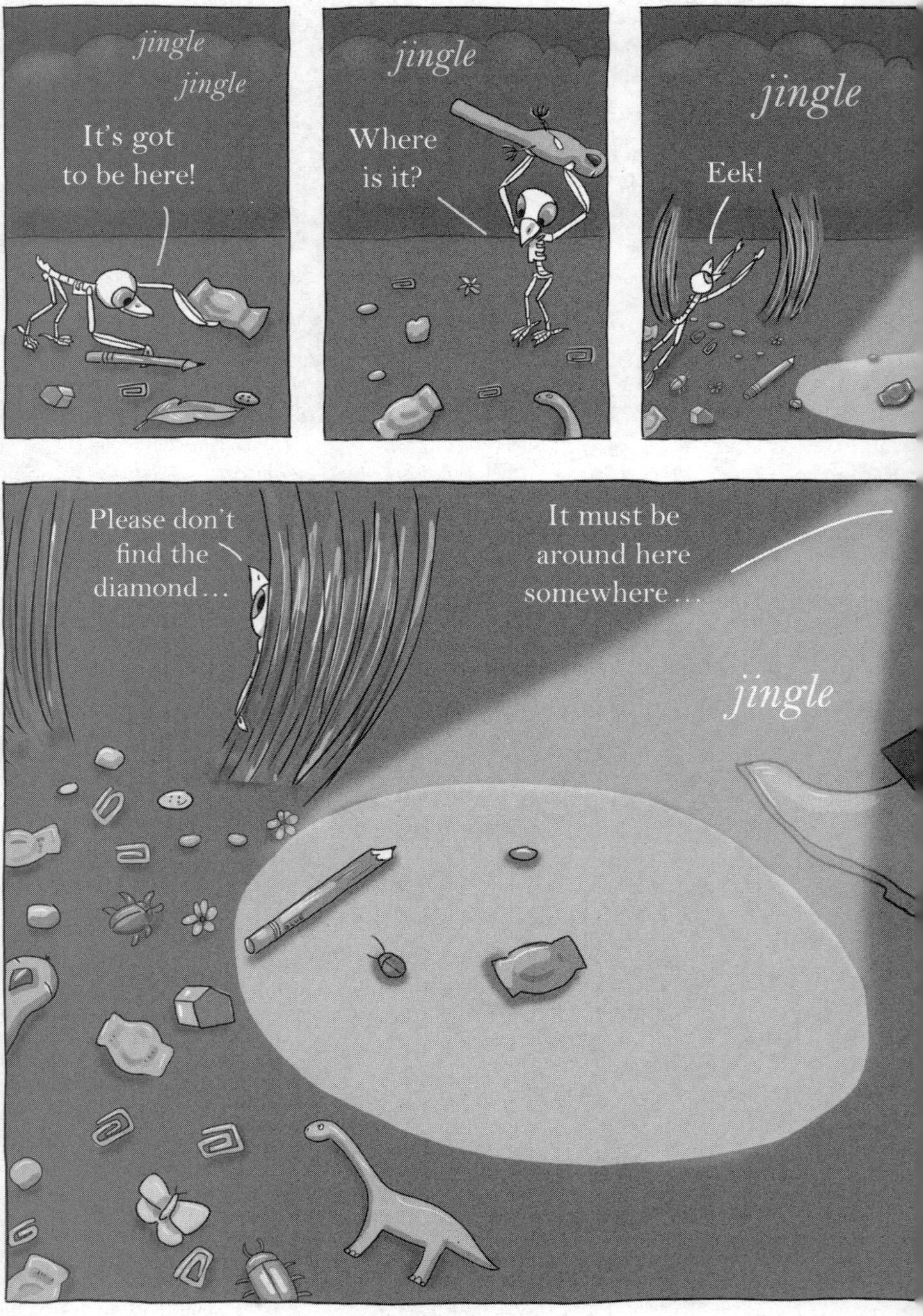
jingle
jingle
It's got to be here!
jingle
Where is it?
jingle
Eek!
Please don't find the diamond…
It must be around here somewhere…
jingle

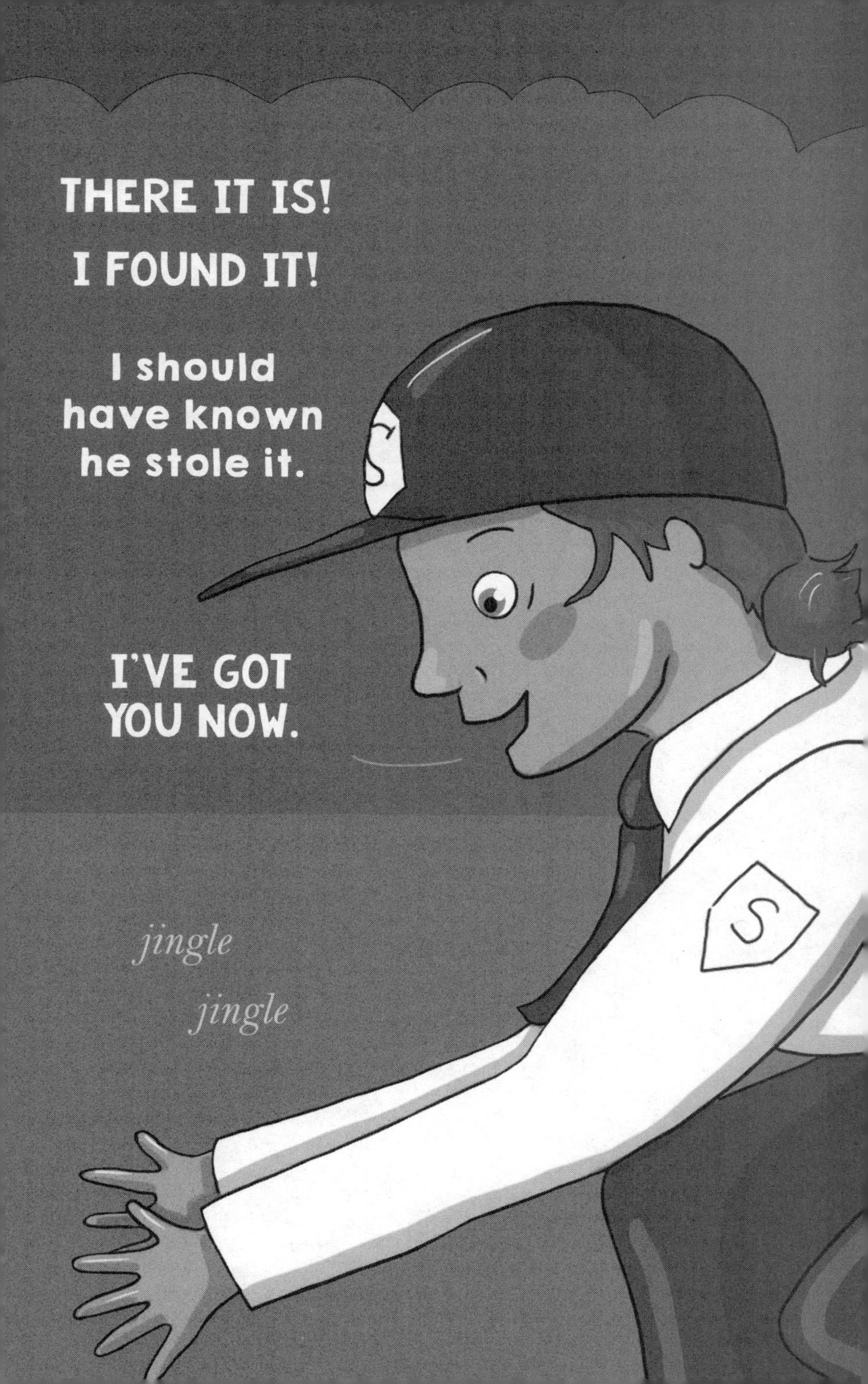
THERE IT IS!
I FOUND IT!
I should have known he stole it.
I'VE GOT YOU NOW.
jingle
jingle

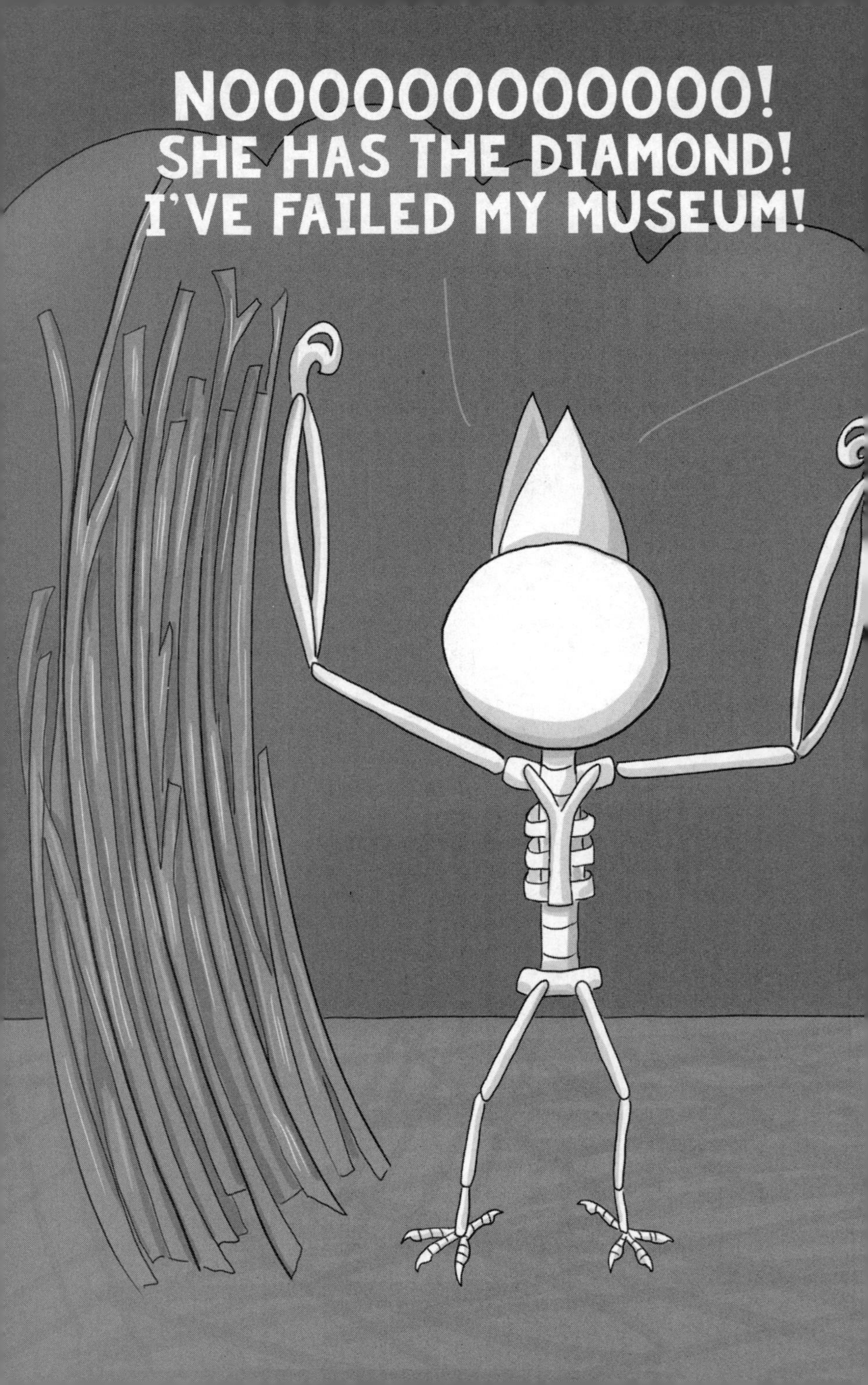
NOOOOOOOOOOOOO! SHE HAS THE DIAMOND! I'VE FAILED MY MUSEUM!

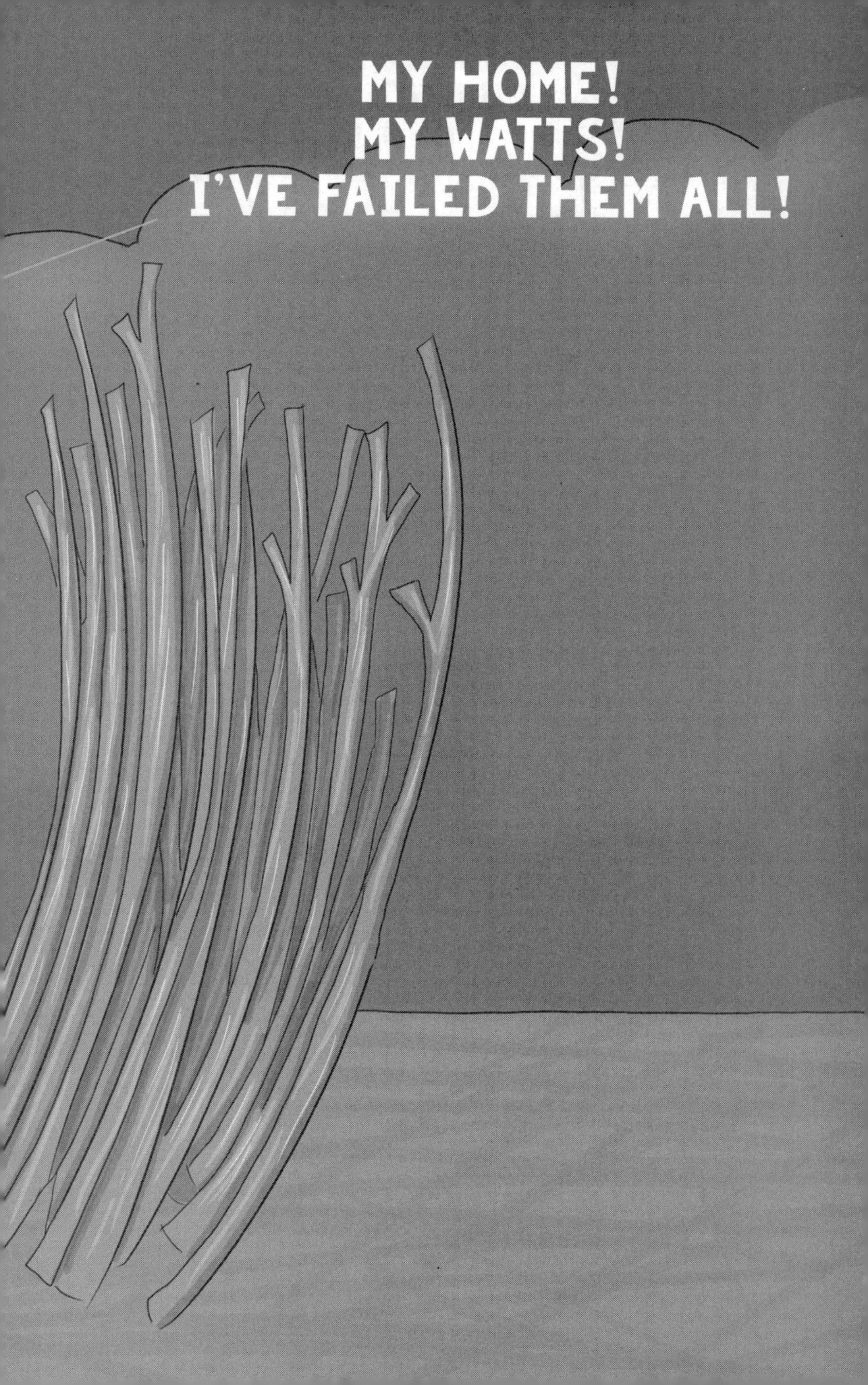
MY HOME!
MY WATTS!
I'VE FAILED THEM ALL!

CHAPTER 10
Birdbrain

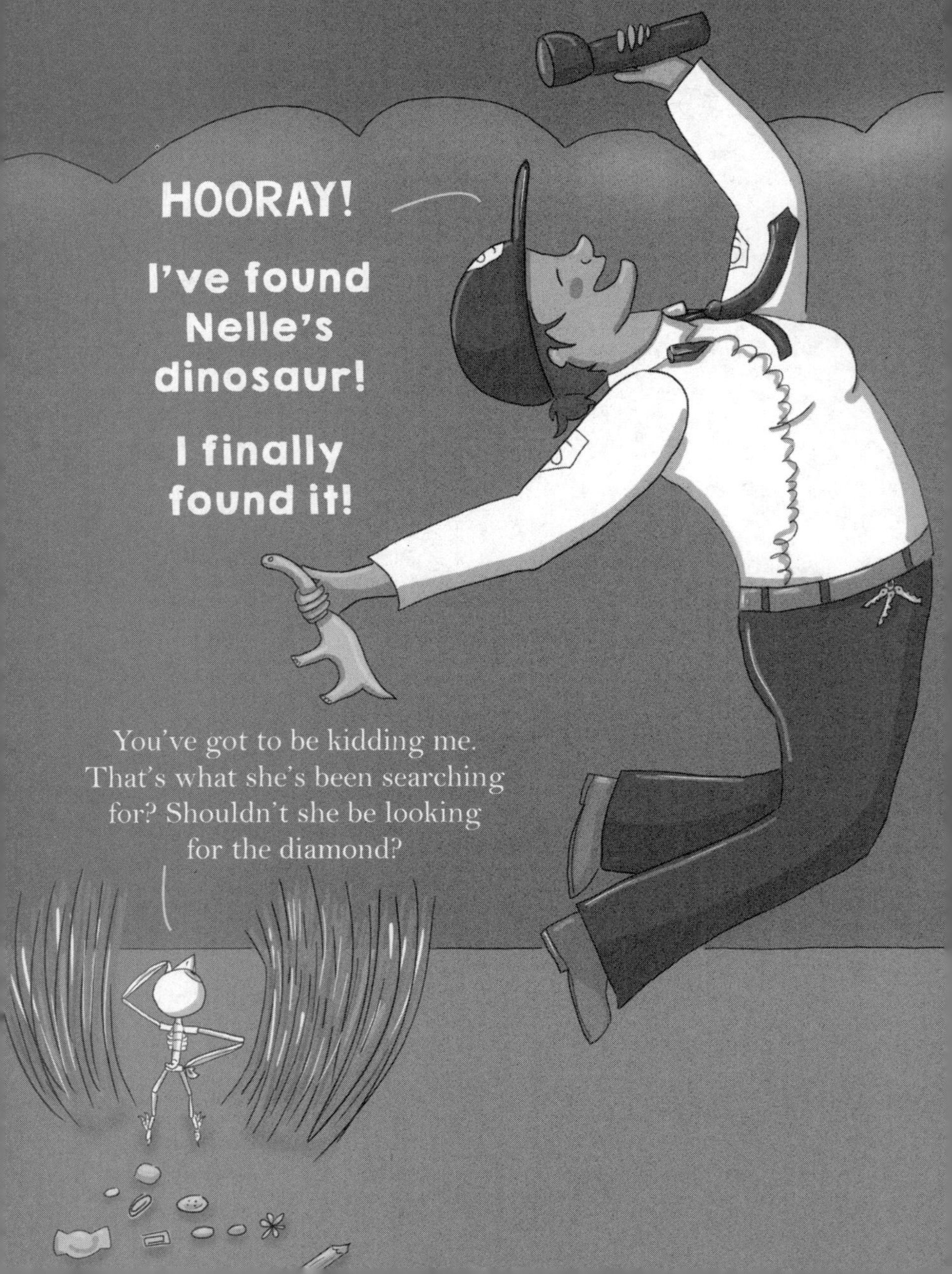

HOORAY!
I've found Nelle's dinosaur!
I finally found it!
You've got to be kidding me. That's what she's been searching for? Shouldn't she be looking for the diamond?

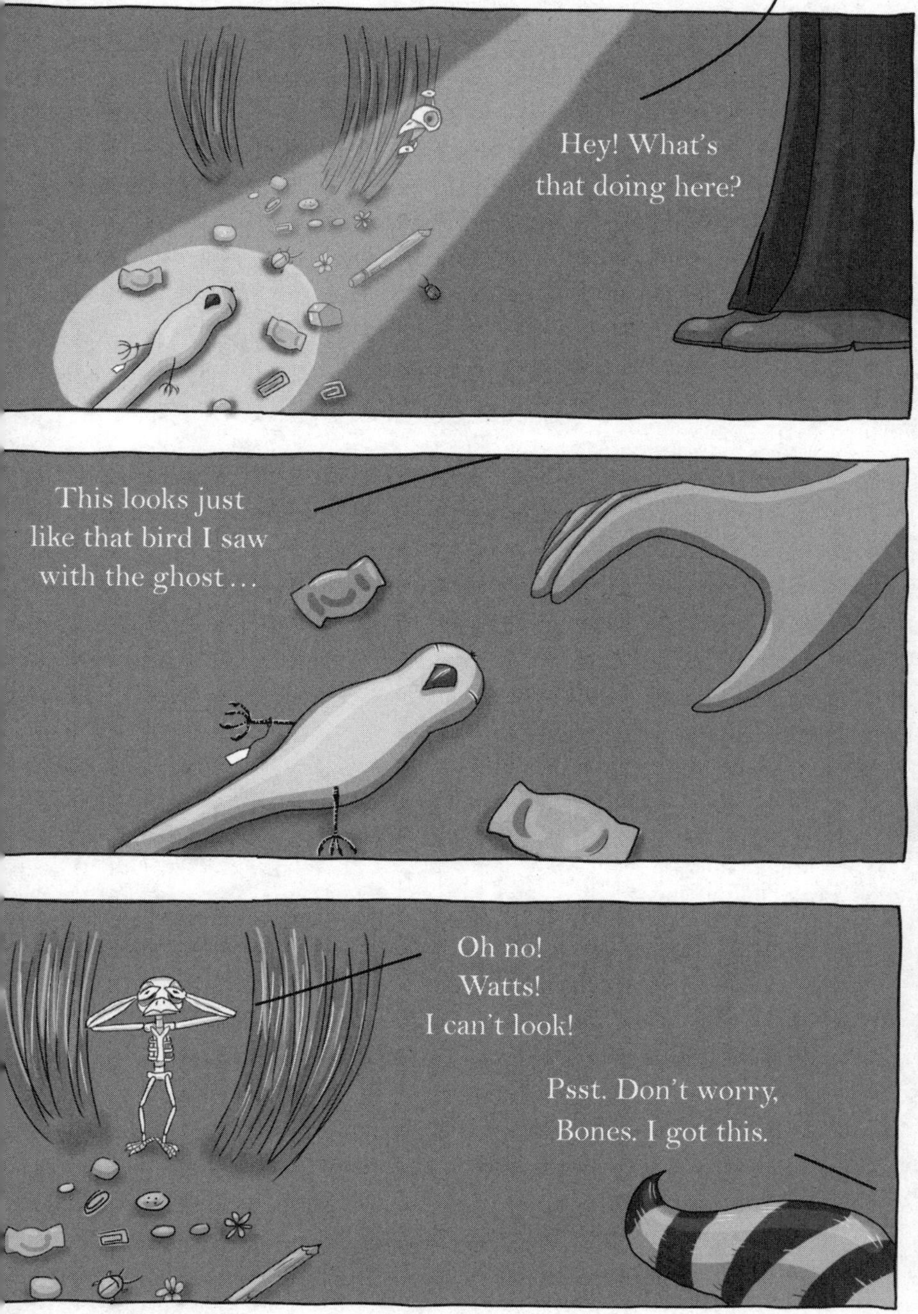
Hey! What's
that doing here?
This looks just
like that bird I saw
with the ghost…
Oh no!
Watts!
I can't look!
Psst. Don't worry,
Bones. I got this.

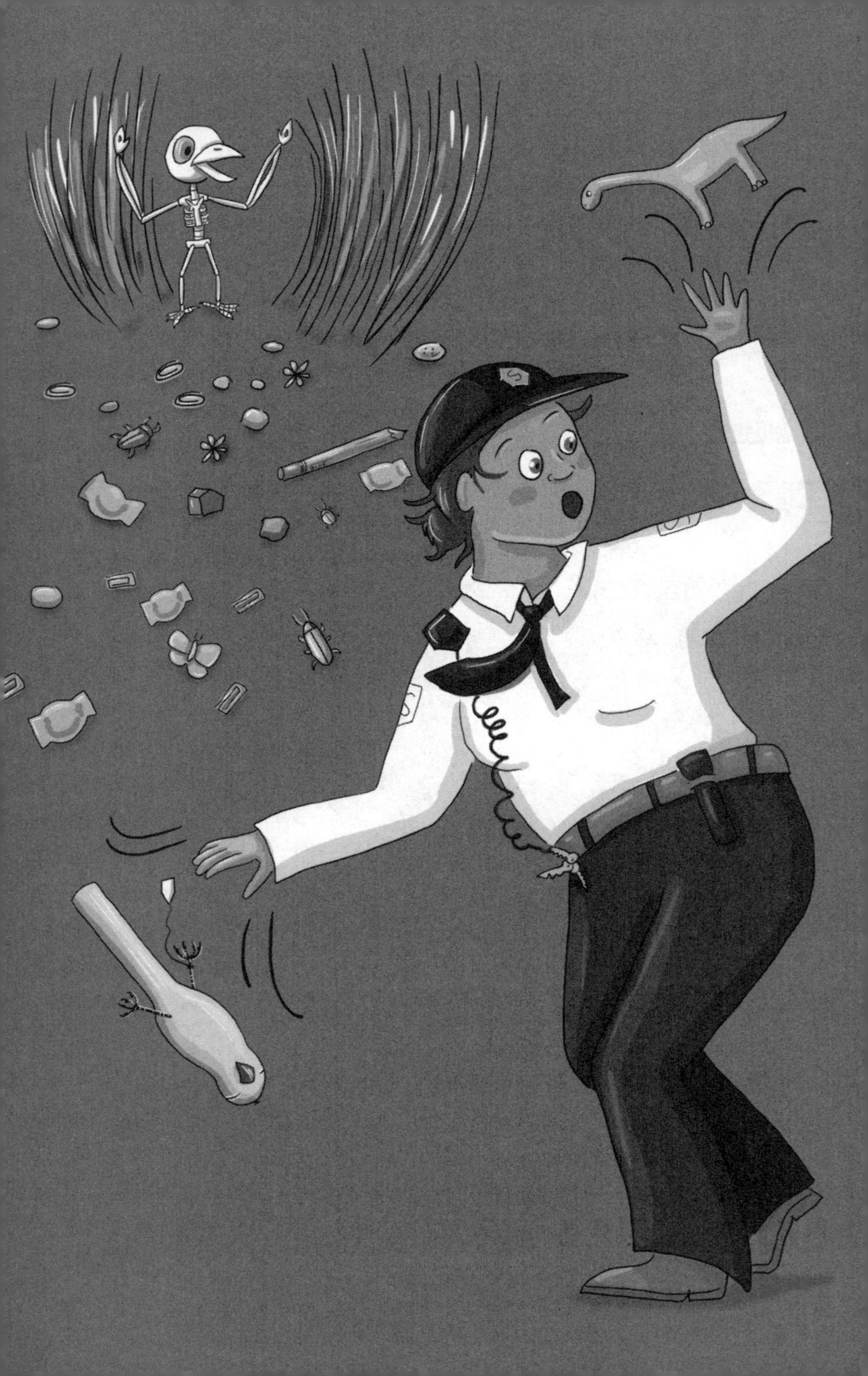

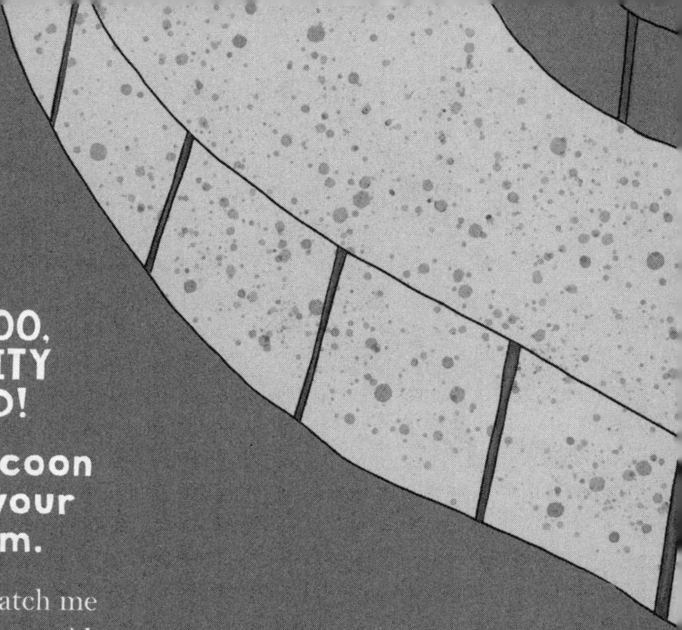

YOO-HOO, SECURITY GUARD!

It's a raccoon here in your museum.

Better try to catch me before I get into trouble.

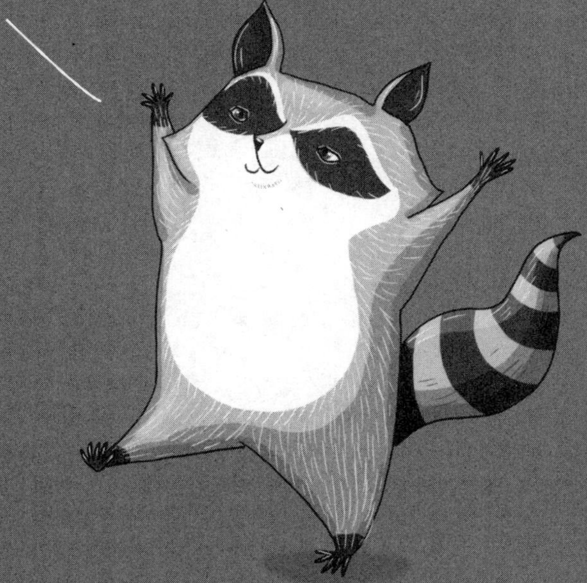

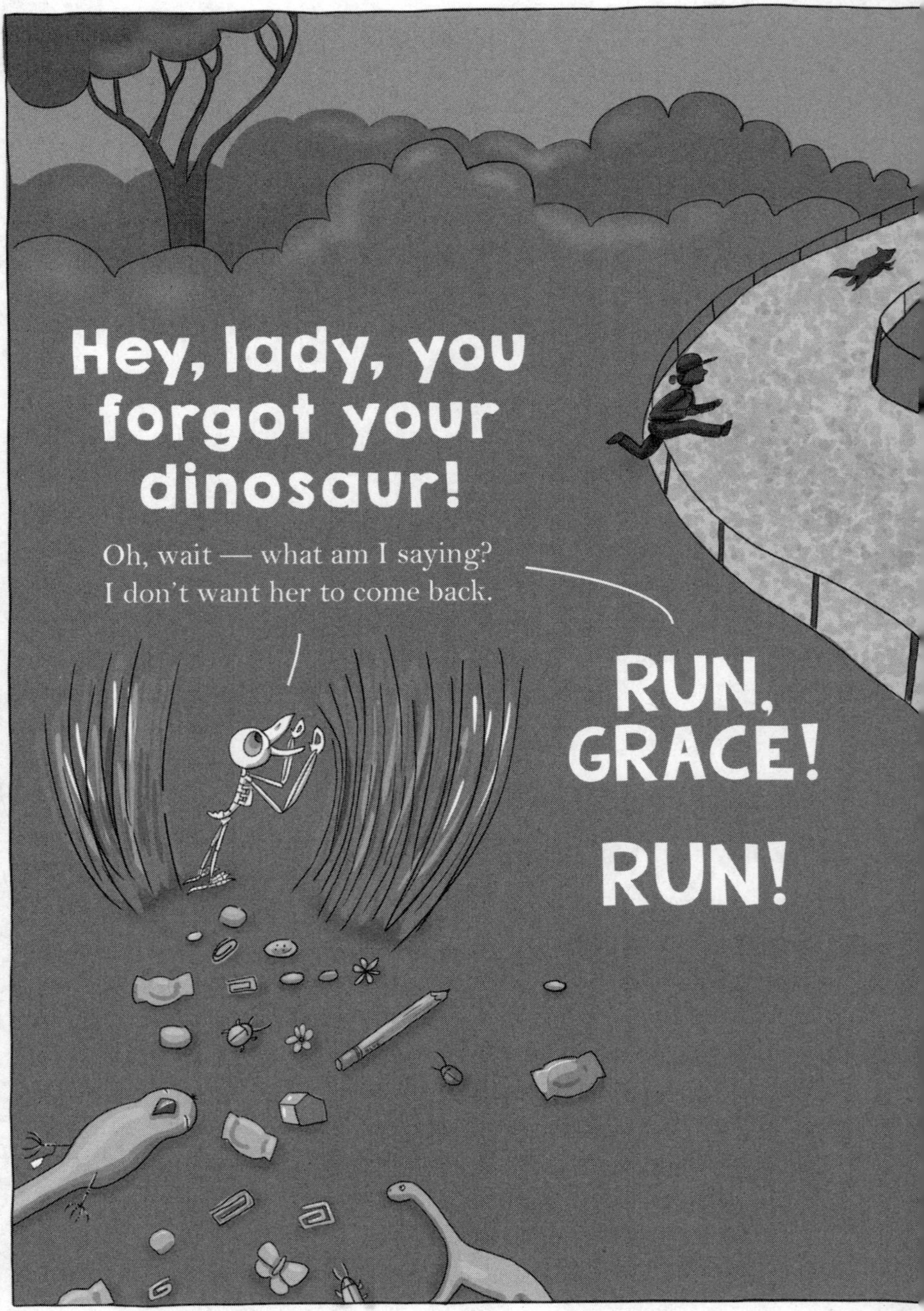
Hey, lady, you forgot your dinosaur!
Oh, wait — what am I saying? I don't want her to come back.
RUN, GRACE!
RUN!

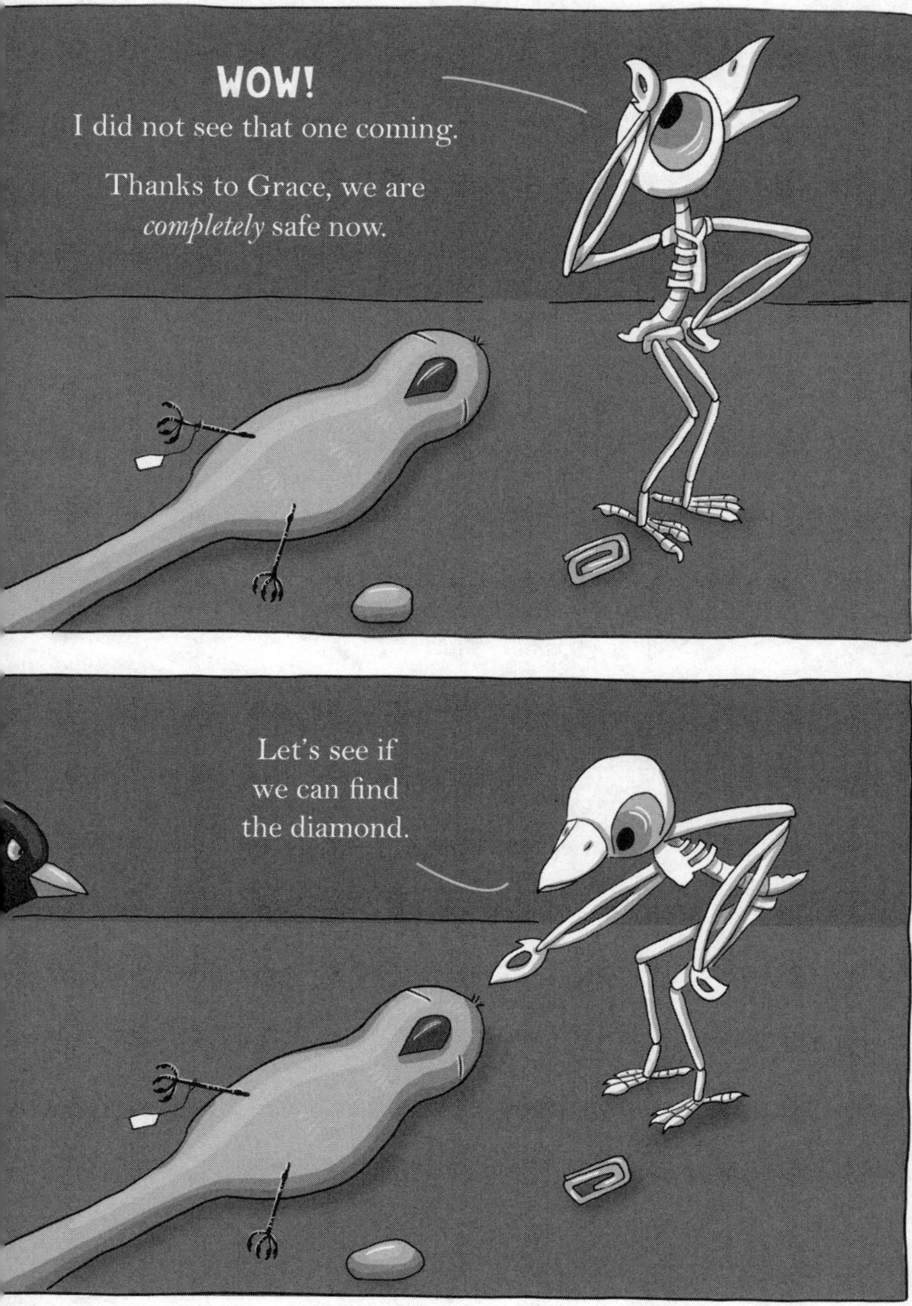
WOW!
I did not see that one coming.
Thanks to Grace, we are *completely* safe now.
Let's see if we can find the diamond.

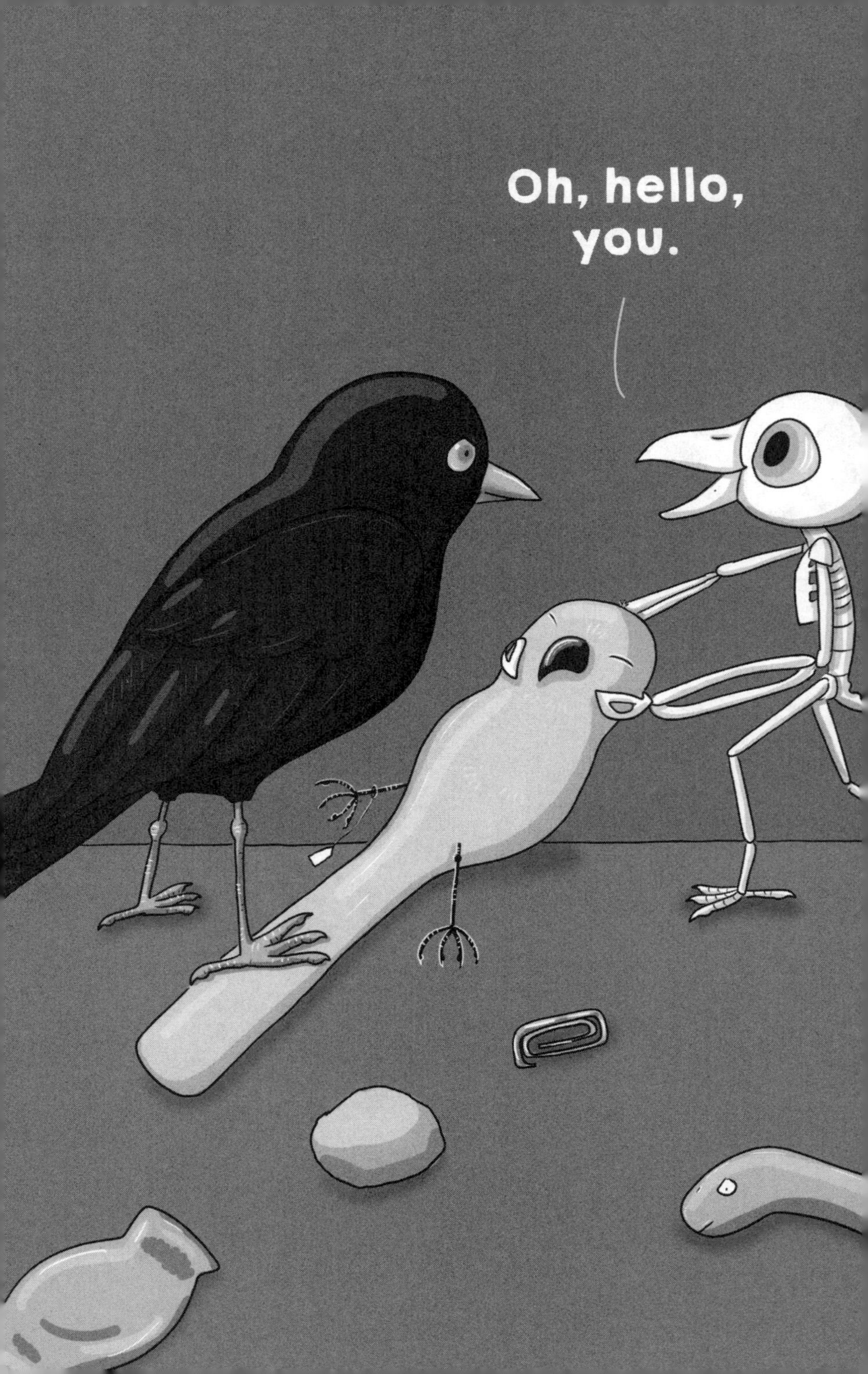
Oh, hello,
you.

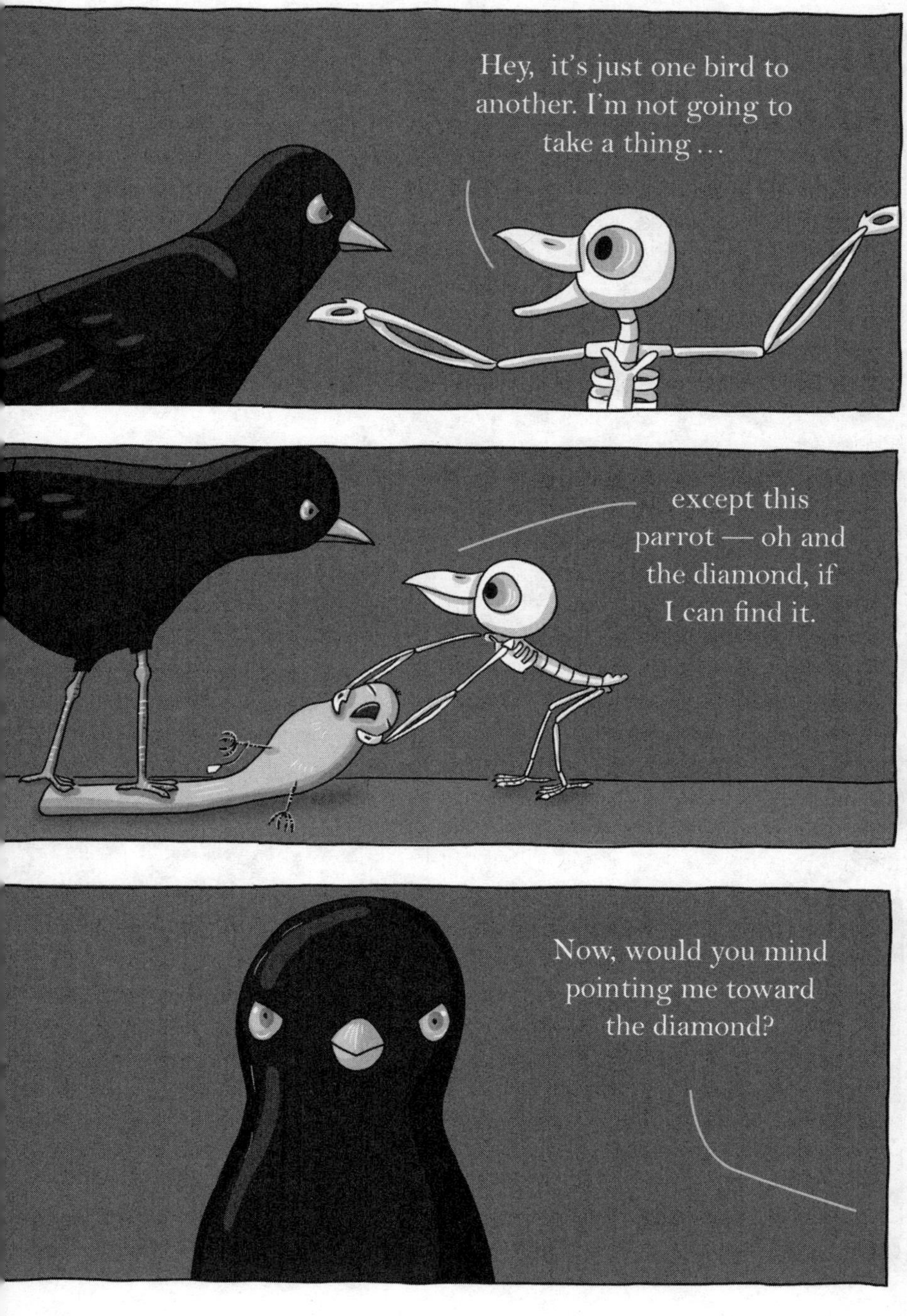
Hey, it's just one bird to another. I'm not going to take a thing . . .
except this parrot — oh and the diamond, if I can find it.
Now, would you mind pointing me toward the diamond?

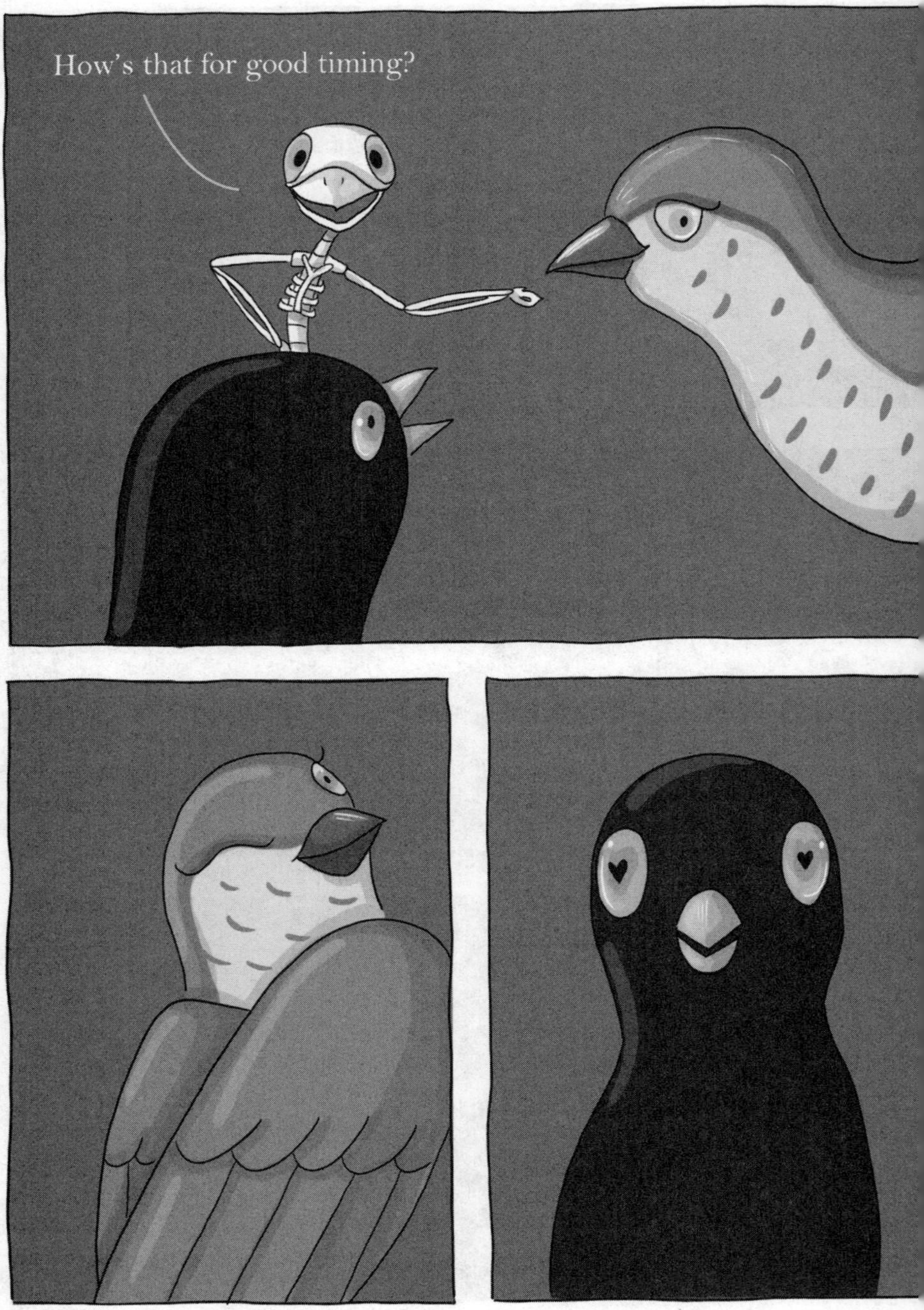
How's that for good timing?

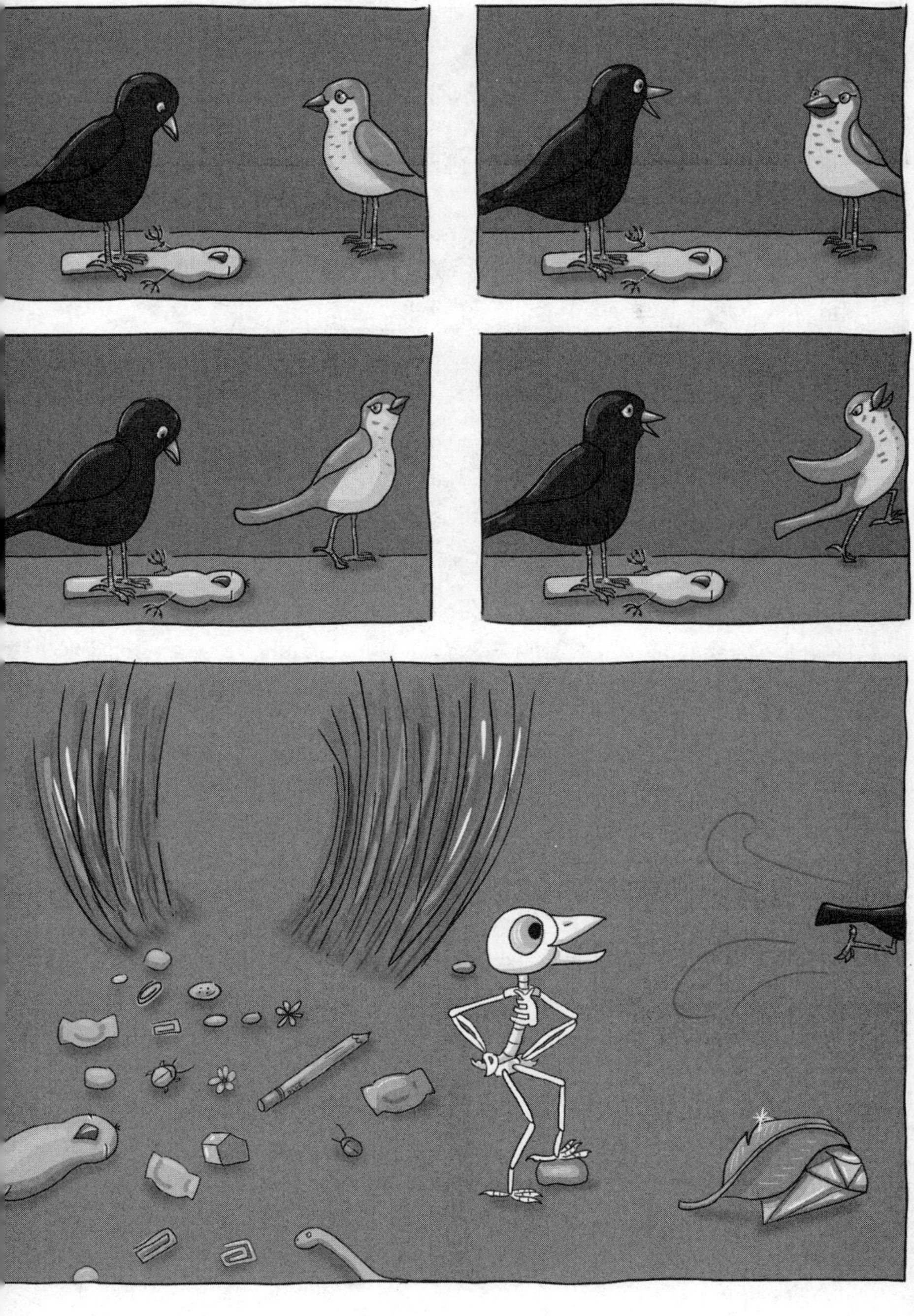

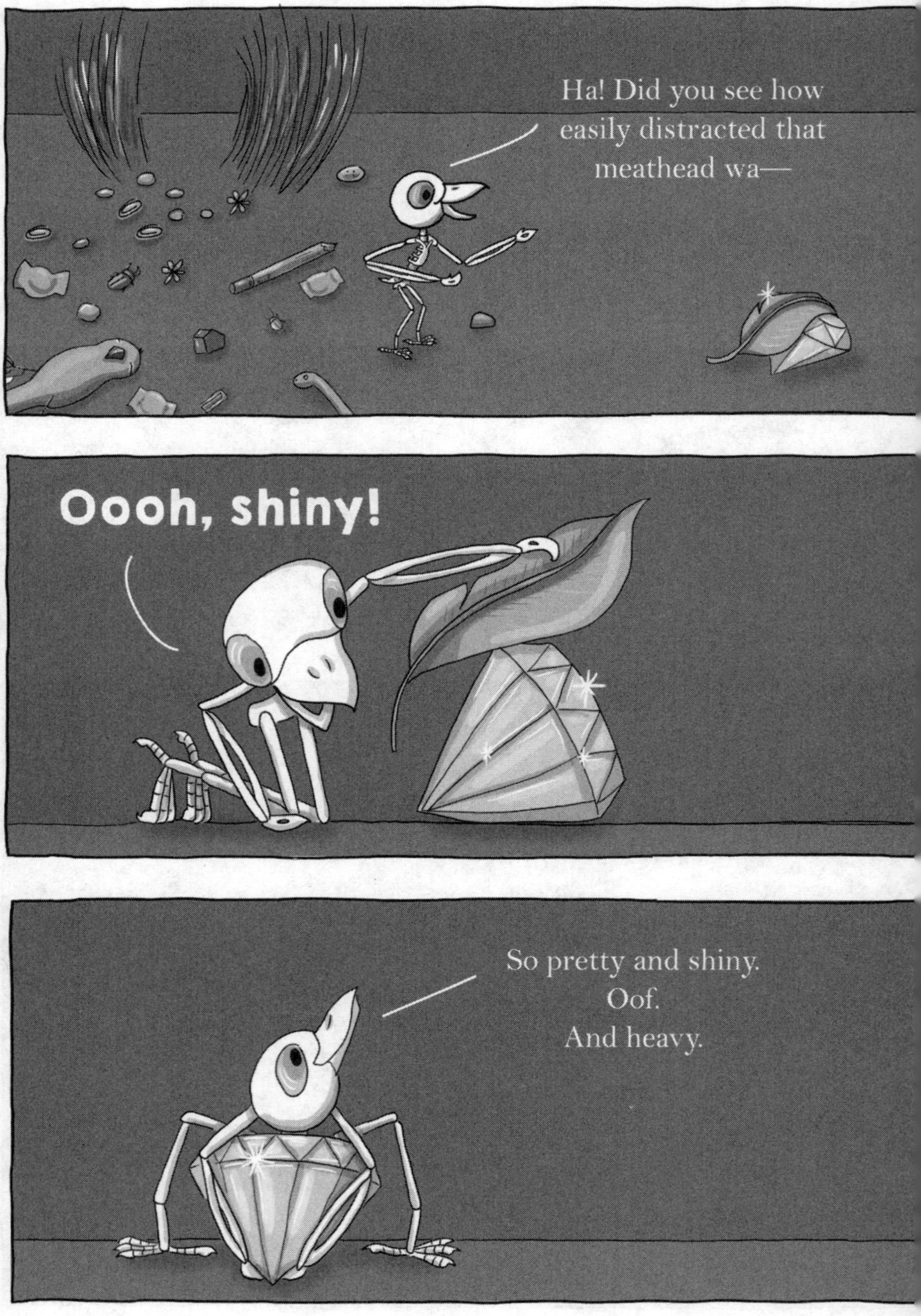
Ha! Did you see how easily distracted that meathead wa—
Oooh, shiny!
So pretty and shiny.
Oof.
And heavy.

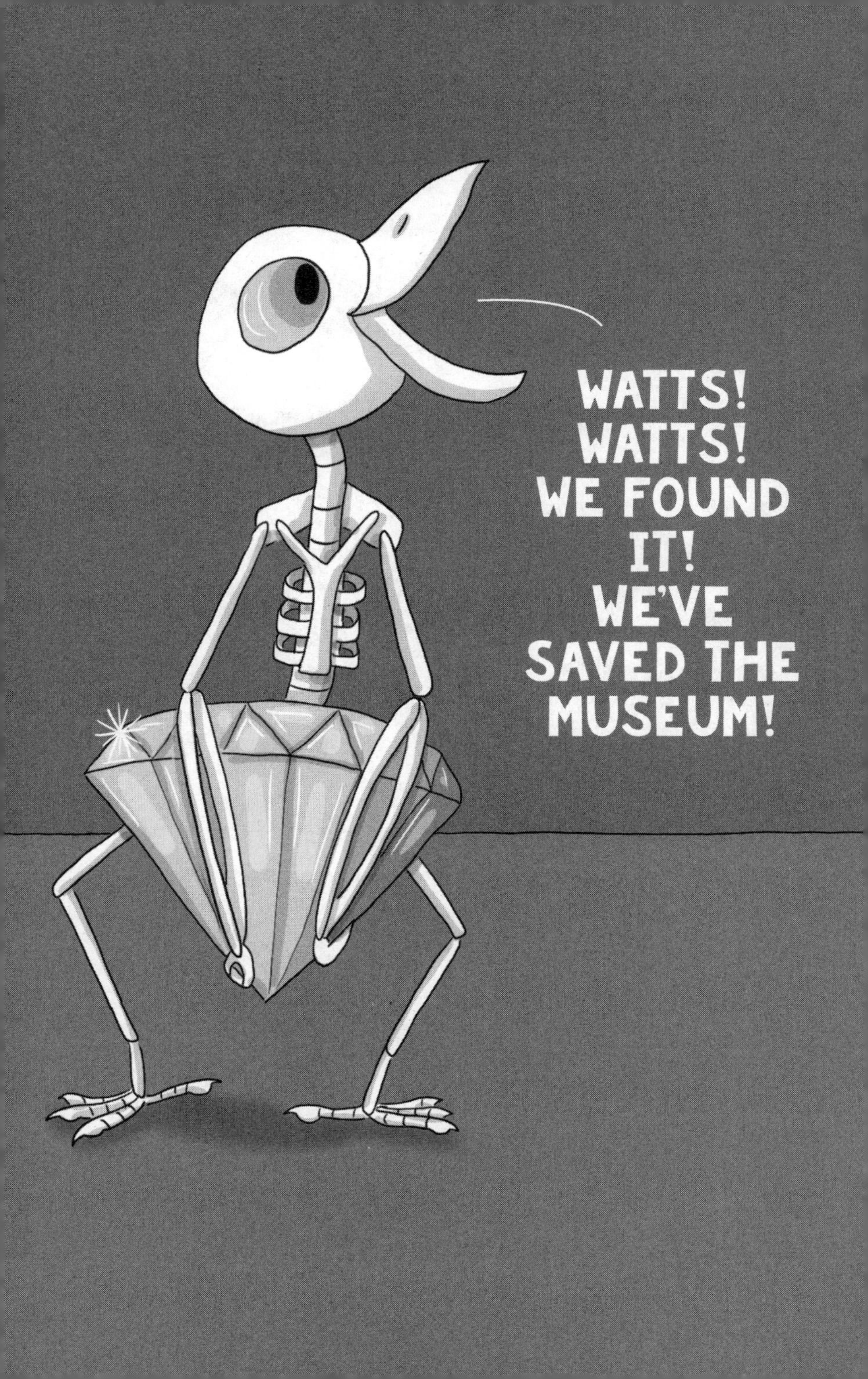
WATTS! WATTS! WE FOUND IT! WE'VE SAVED THE MUSEUM!

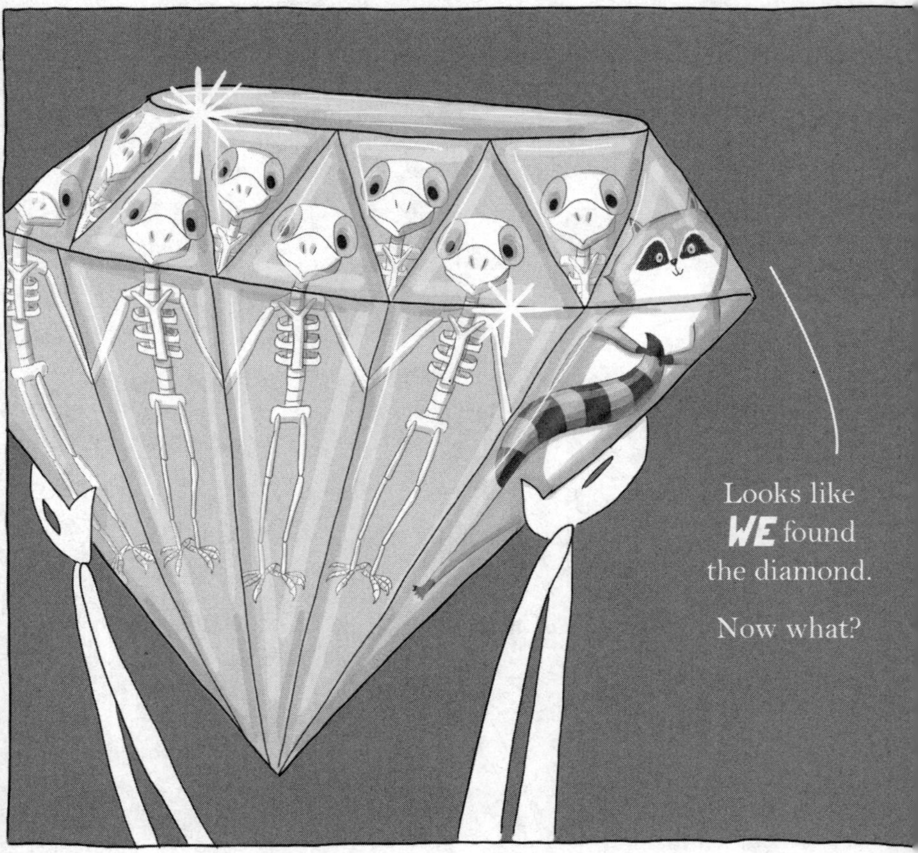
Looks like **WE** found the diamond.
Now what?

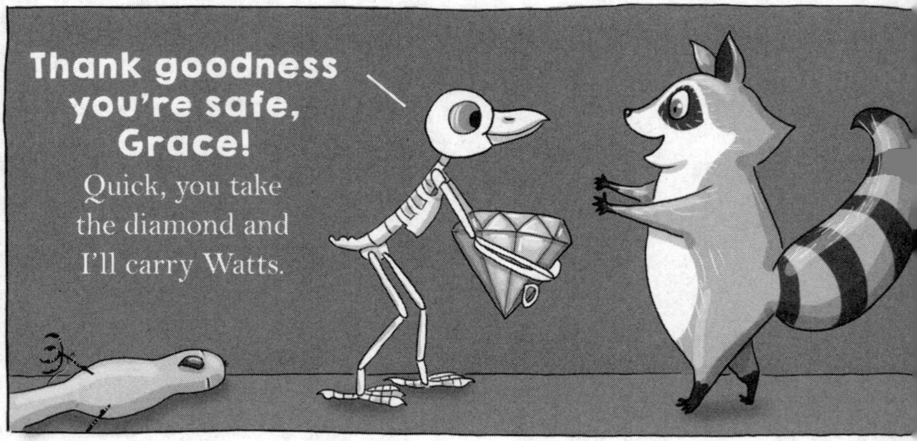
Thank goodness you're safe, Grace!
Quick, you take the diamond and I'll carry Watts.

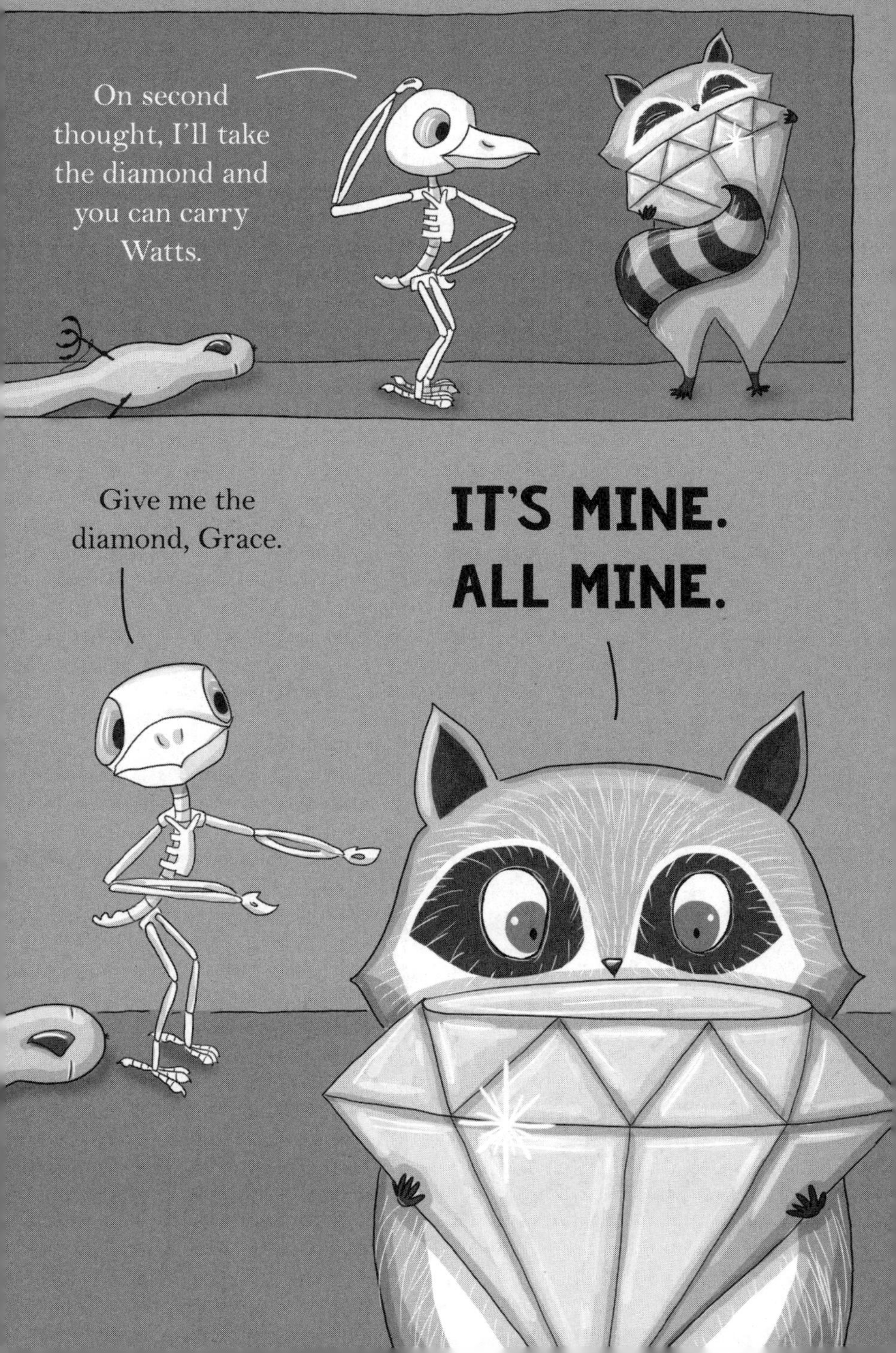
On second thought, I'll take the diamond and you can carry Watts.
Give me the diamond, Grace.
IT'S MINE. ALL MINE.

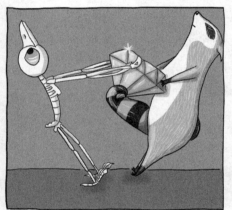

Shhhhhh...
Do you hear that?

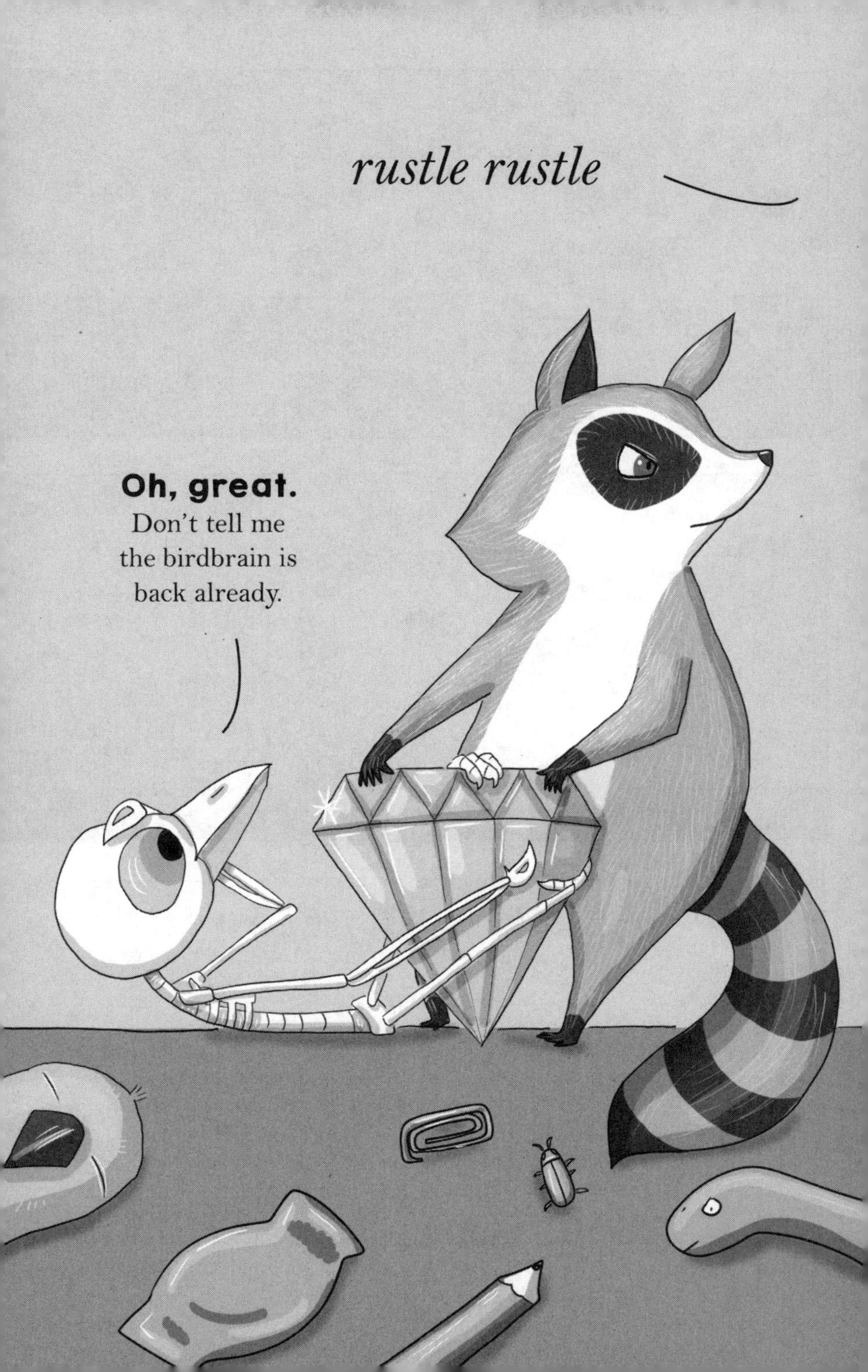
rustle rustle
Oh, great.
Don't tell me the birdbrain is back already.

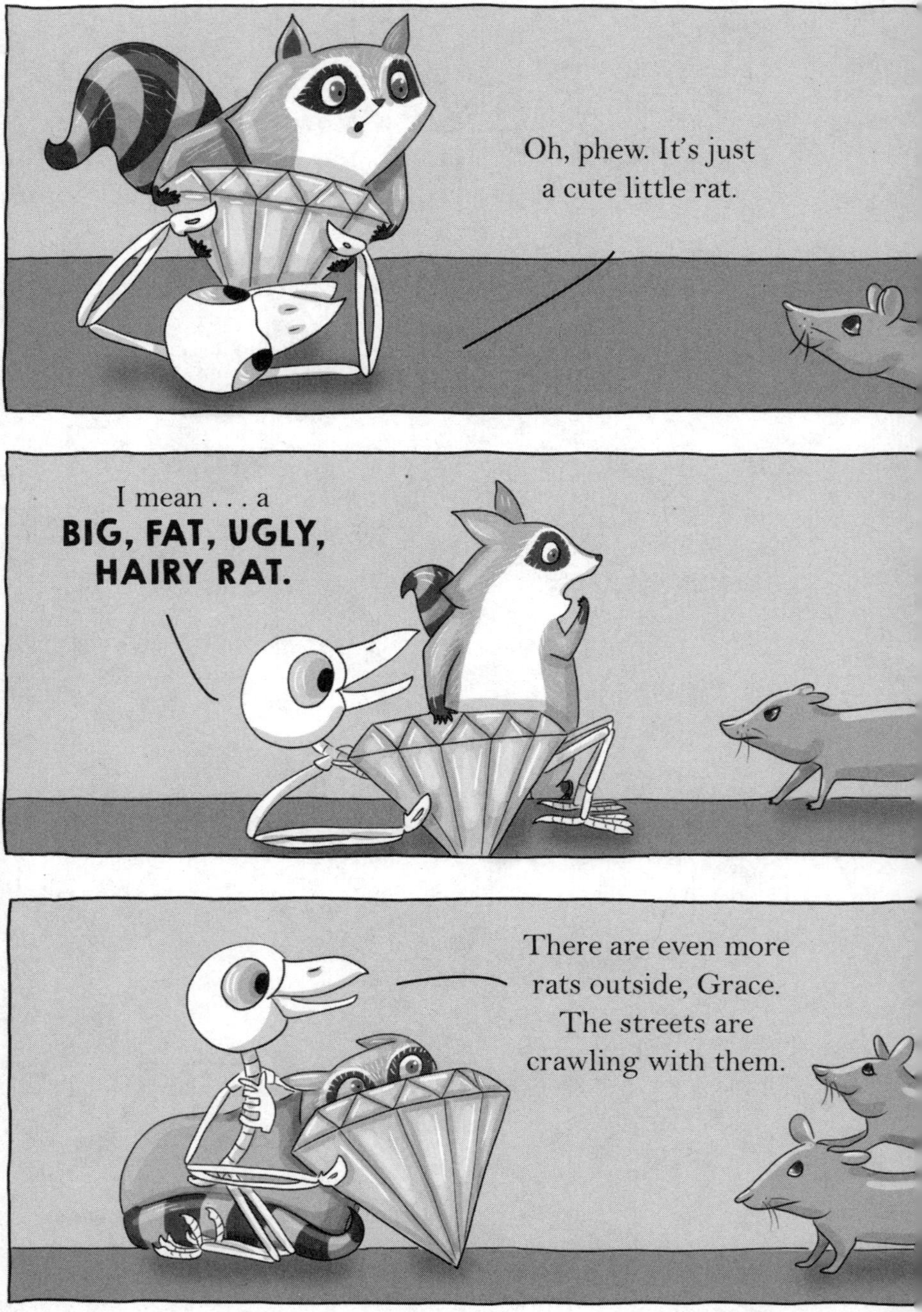
Oh, phew. It's just a cute little rat.
I mean . . . a **BIG, FAT, UGLY, HAIRY RAT.**
There are even more rats outside, Grace. The streets are crawling with them.

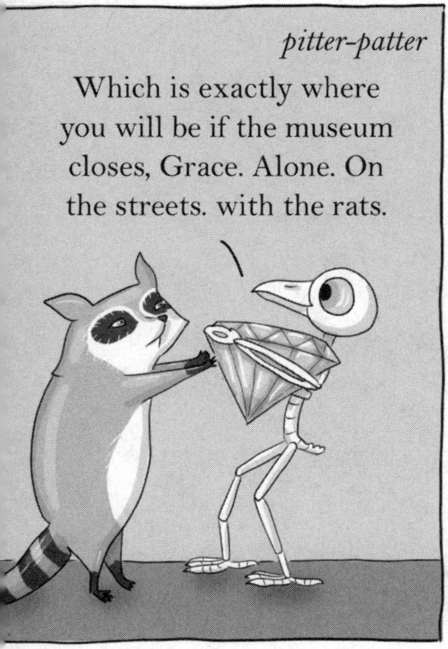
pitter-patter
Which is exactly where you will be if the museum closes, Grace. Alone. On the streets. with the rats.

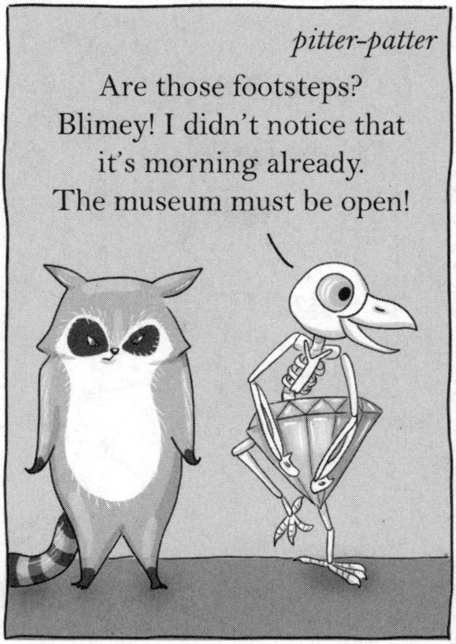
pitter-patter
Are those footsteps? Blimey! I didn't notice that it's morning already. The museum must be open!

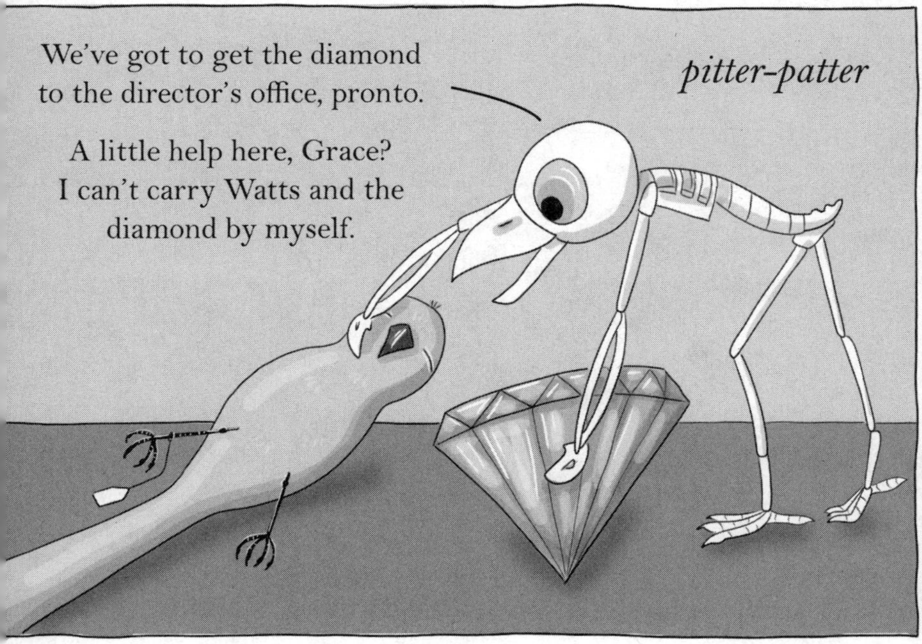
We've got to get the diamond to the director's office, pronto.
A little help here, Grace? I can't carry Watts and the diamond by myself.
pitter-patter

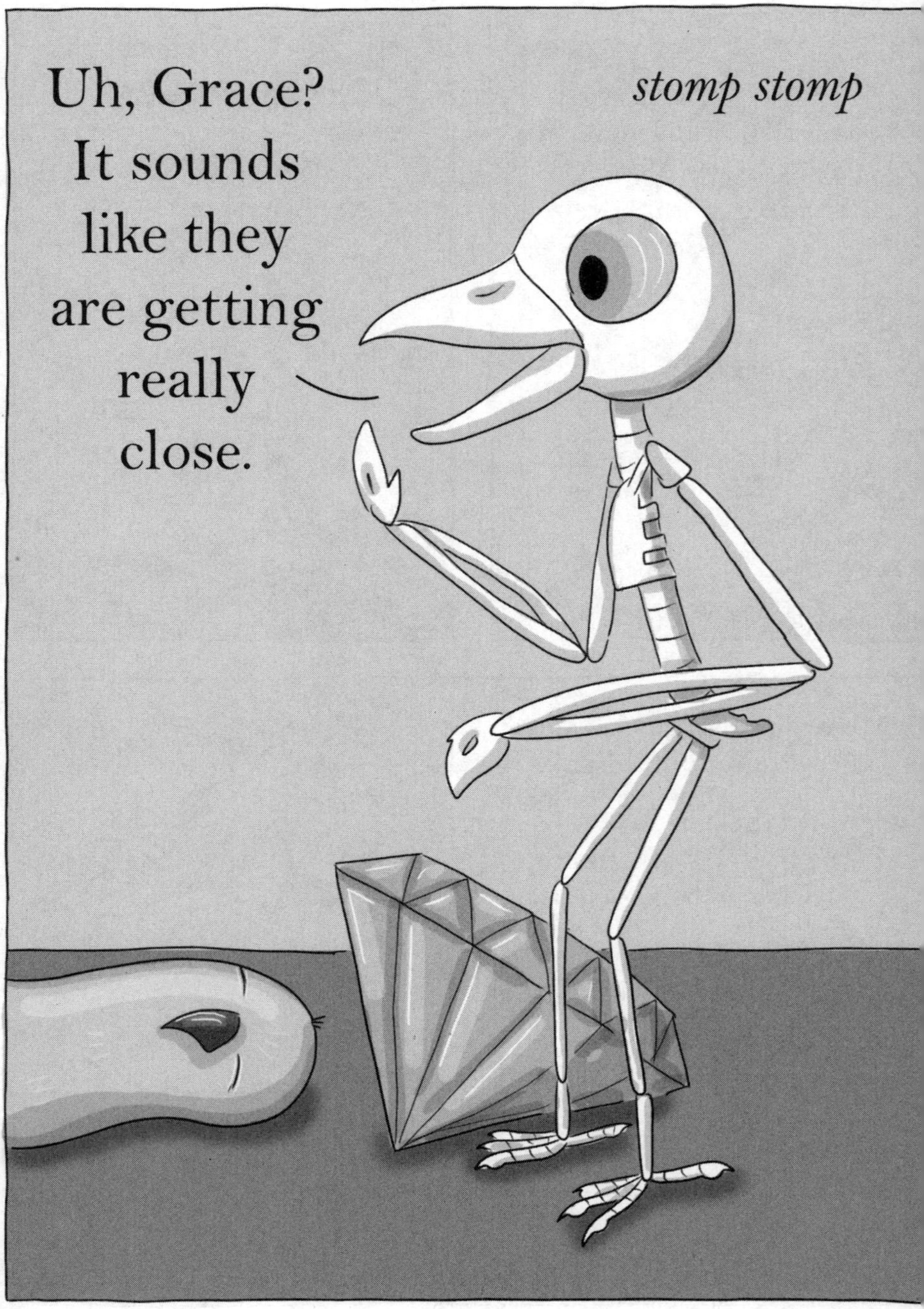
Uh, Grace? It sounds like they are getting really close.
stomp stomp

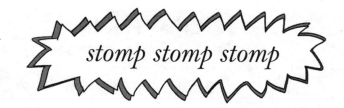

COULD THIS SITUATION GET ANY WORSE?

CHAPTER II
Yes, It Gets Worse

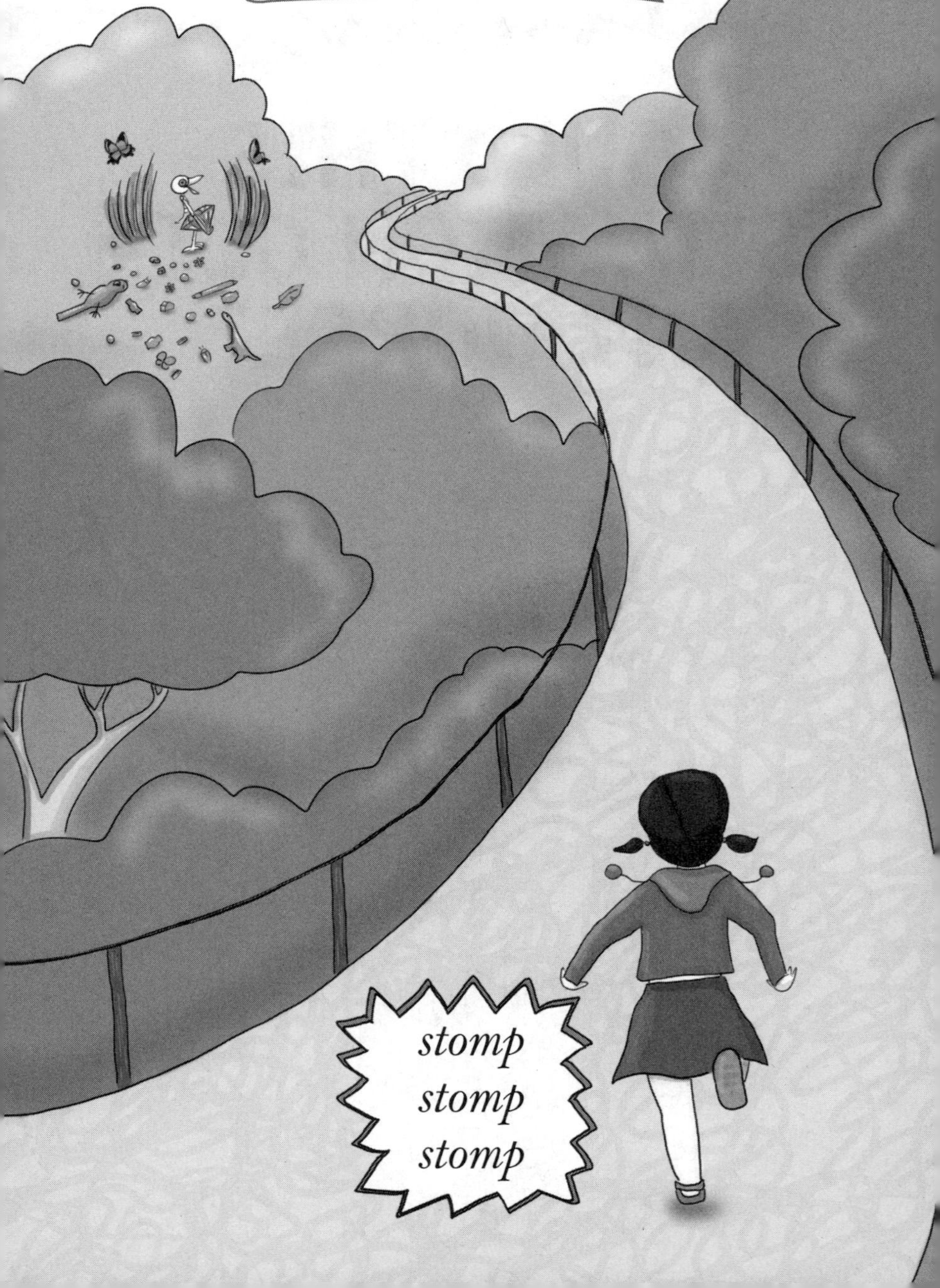
stomp
stomp
stomp

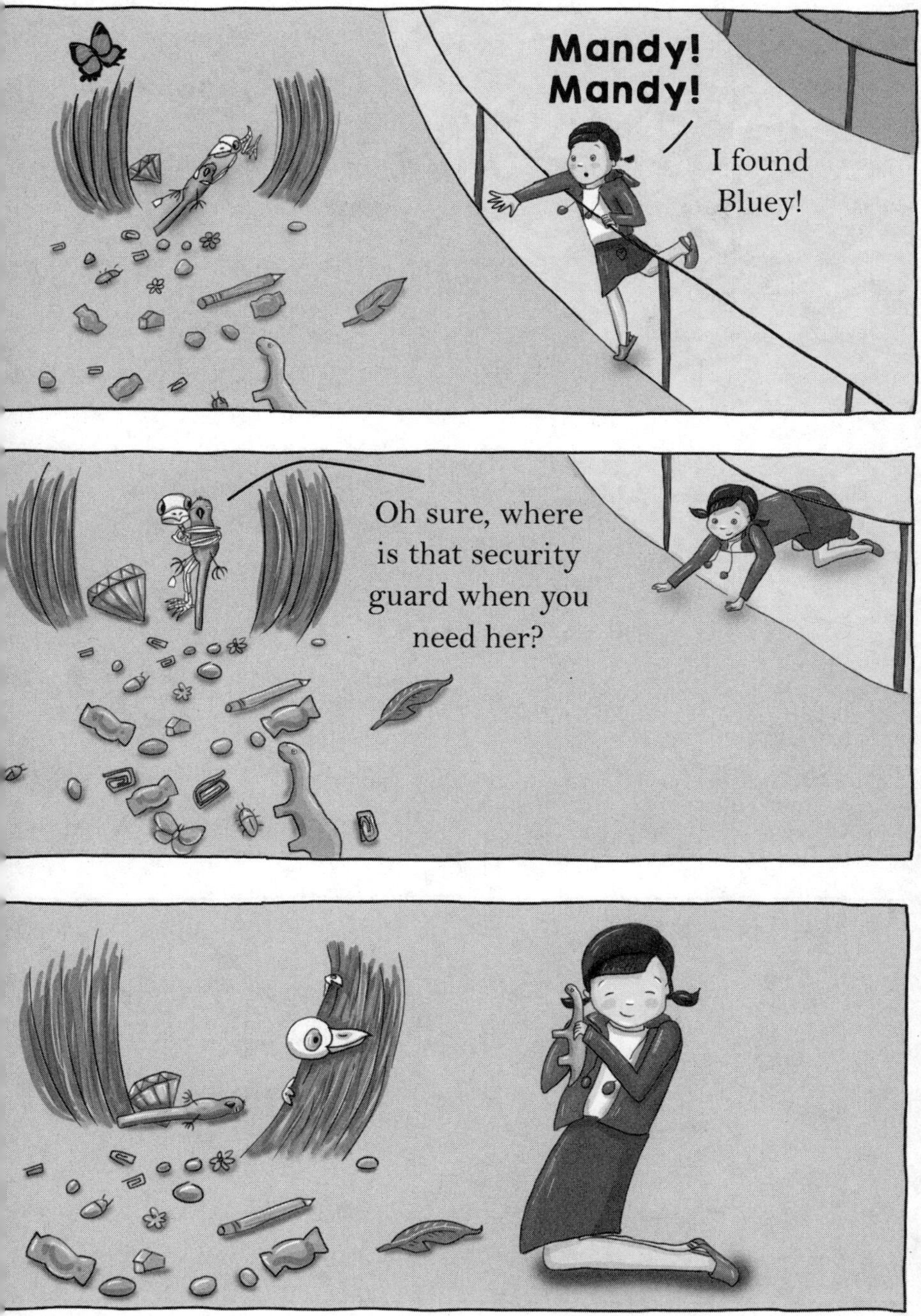
Mandy!
Mandy!
I found Bluey!
Oh sure, where is that security guard when you need her?

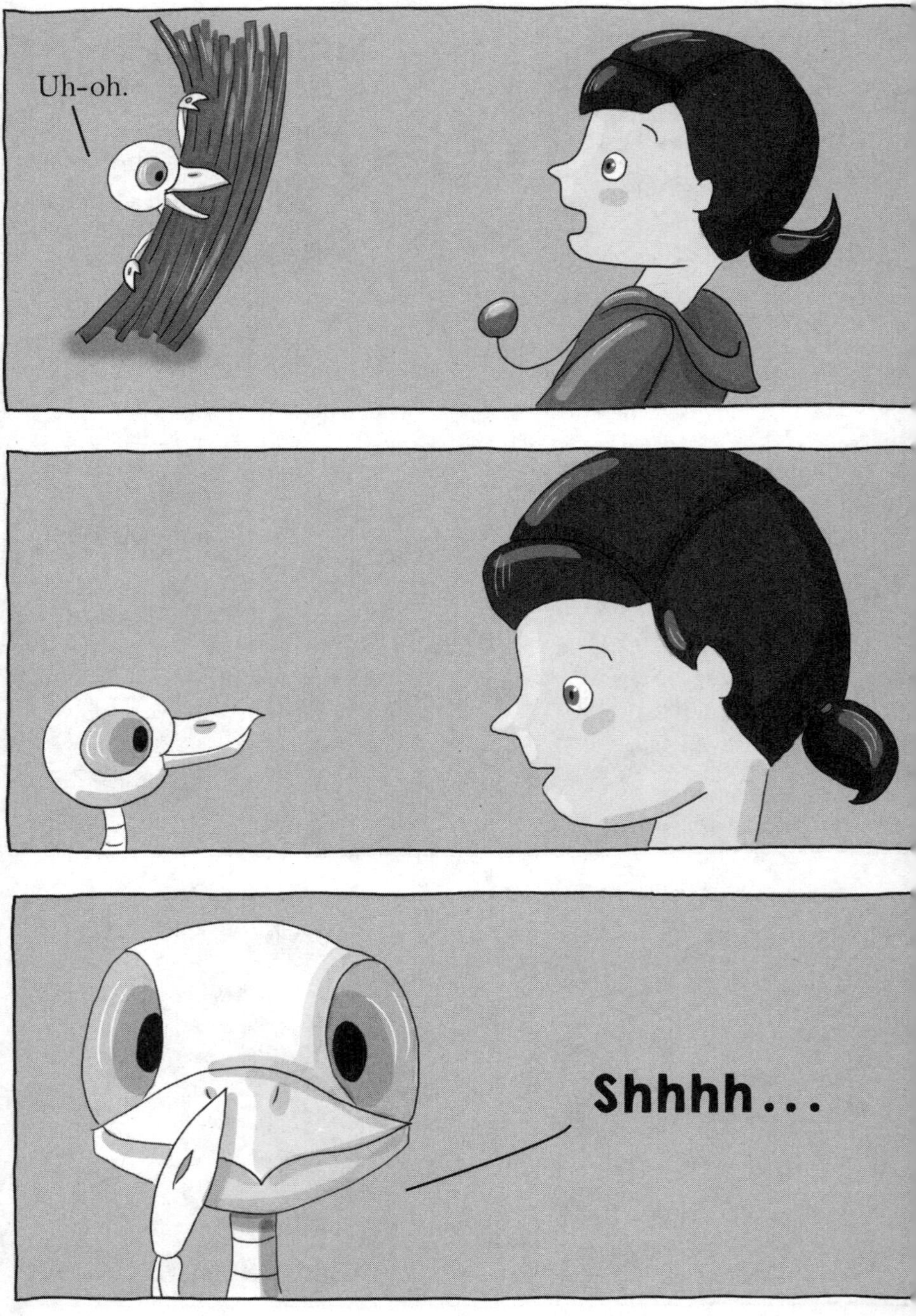
Uh-oh.
Shhhh...

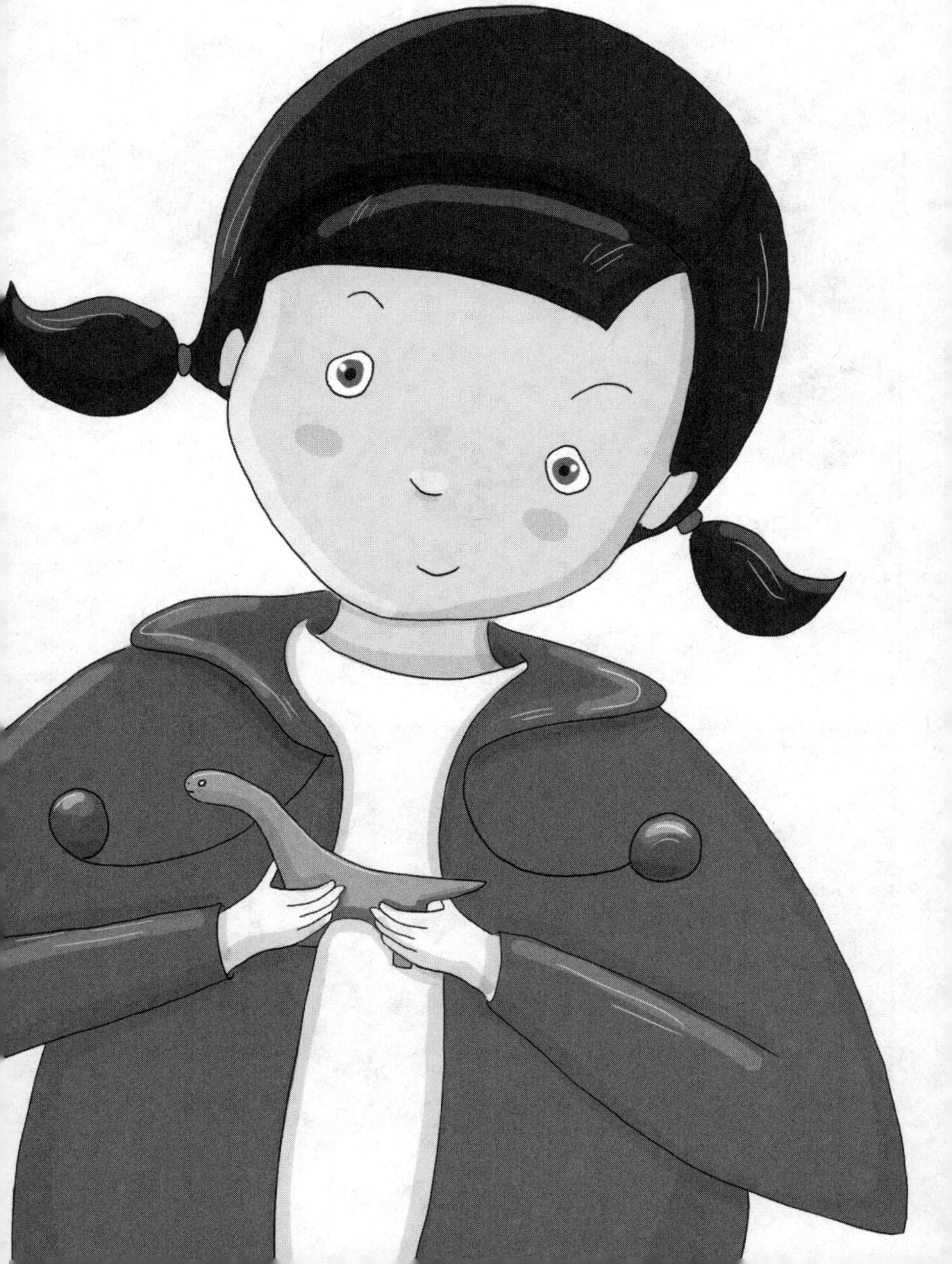

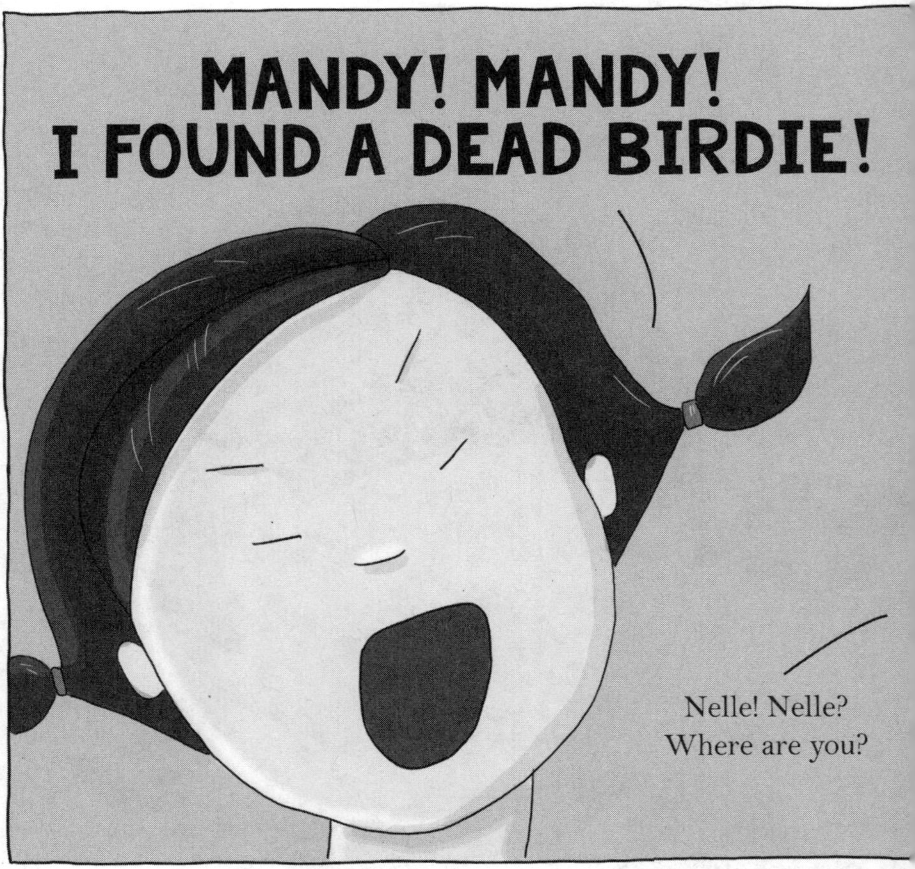
MANDY! MANDY!
I FOUND A DEAD BIRDIE!
Nelle! Nelle?
Where are you?

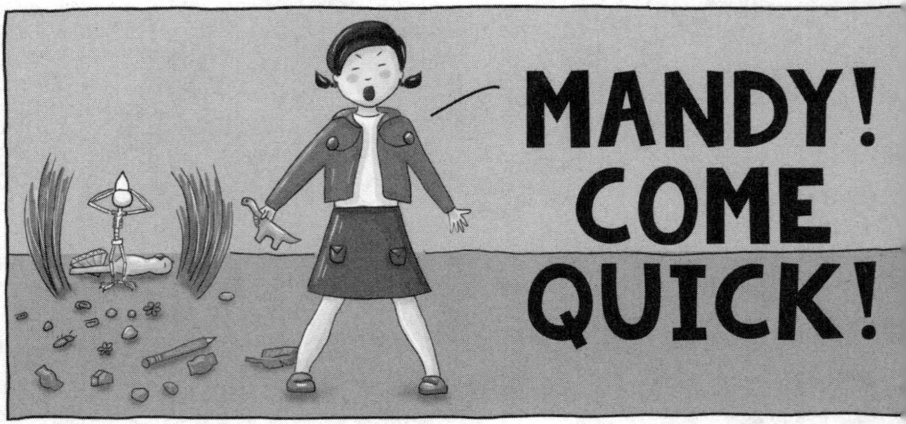
MANDY!
COME
QUICK!

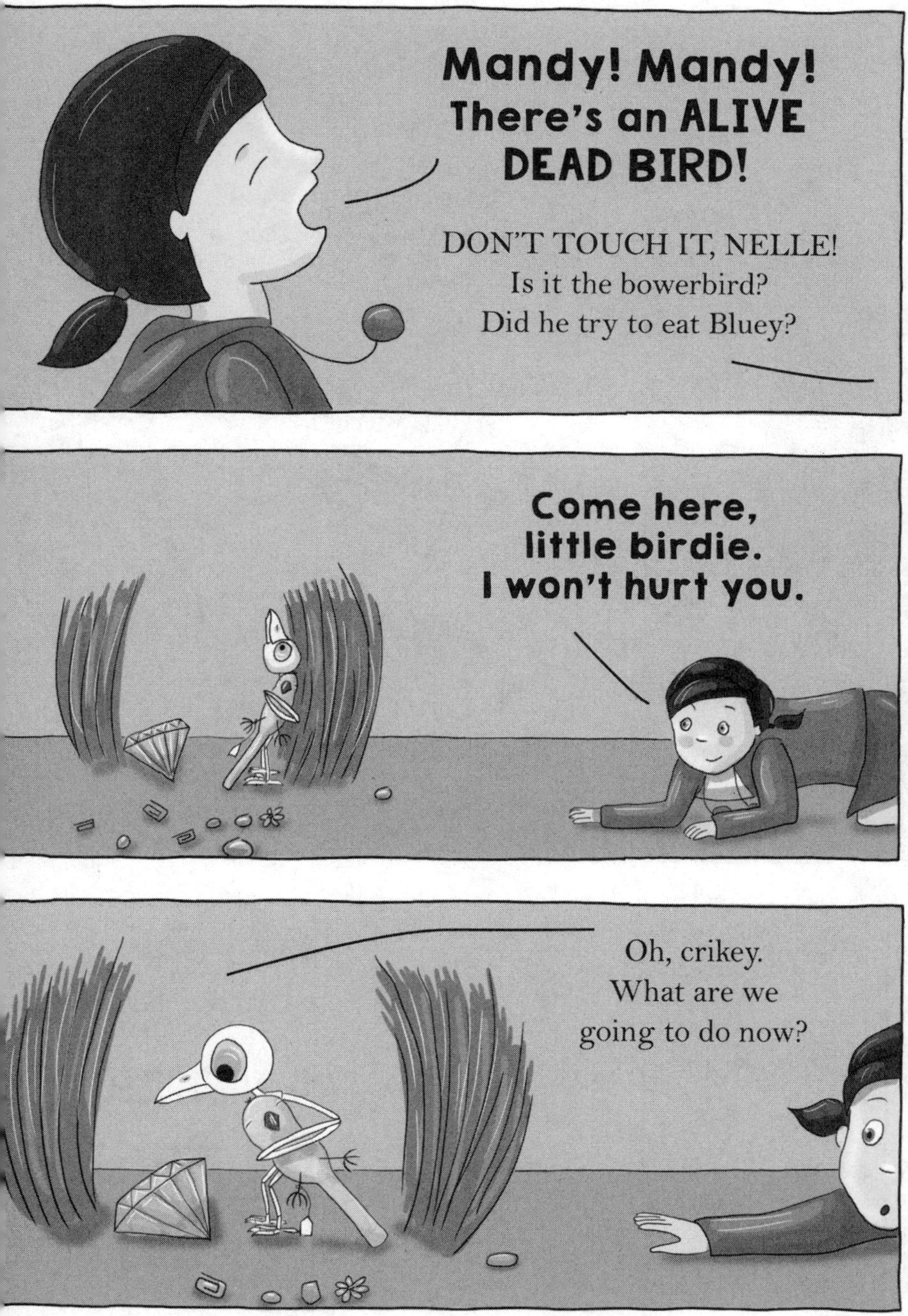
Mandy! Mandy! There's an ALIVE DEAD BIRD!
DON'T TOUCH IT, NELLE! Is it the bowerbird? Did he try to eat Bluey?
Come here, little birdie. I won't hurt you.
Oh, crikey. What are we going to do now?

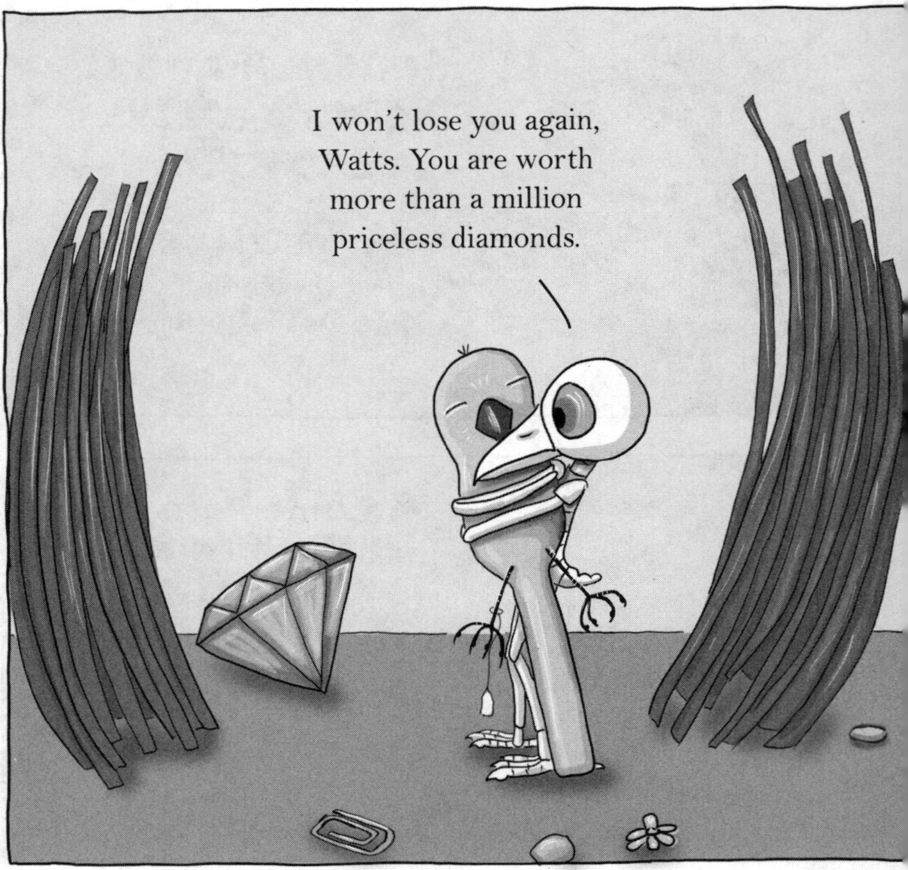
I won't lose you again, Watts. You are worth more than a million priceless diamonds.

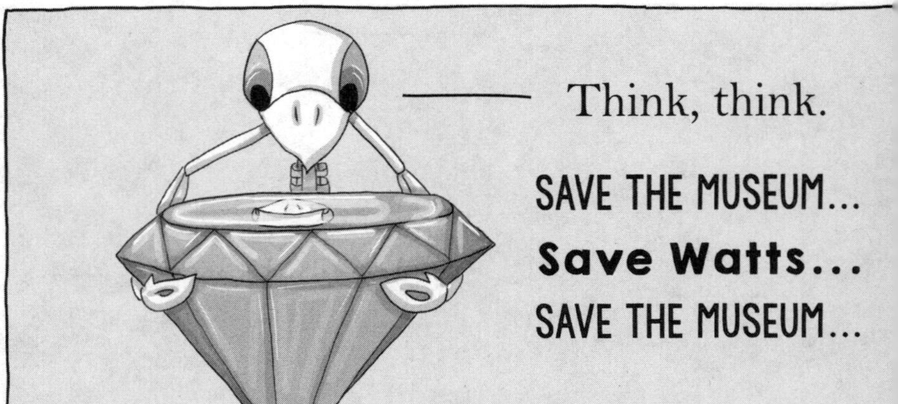
Think, think.
SAVE THE MUSEUM...
Save Watts...
SAVE THE MUSEUM...

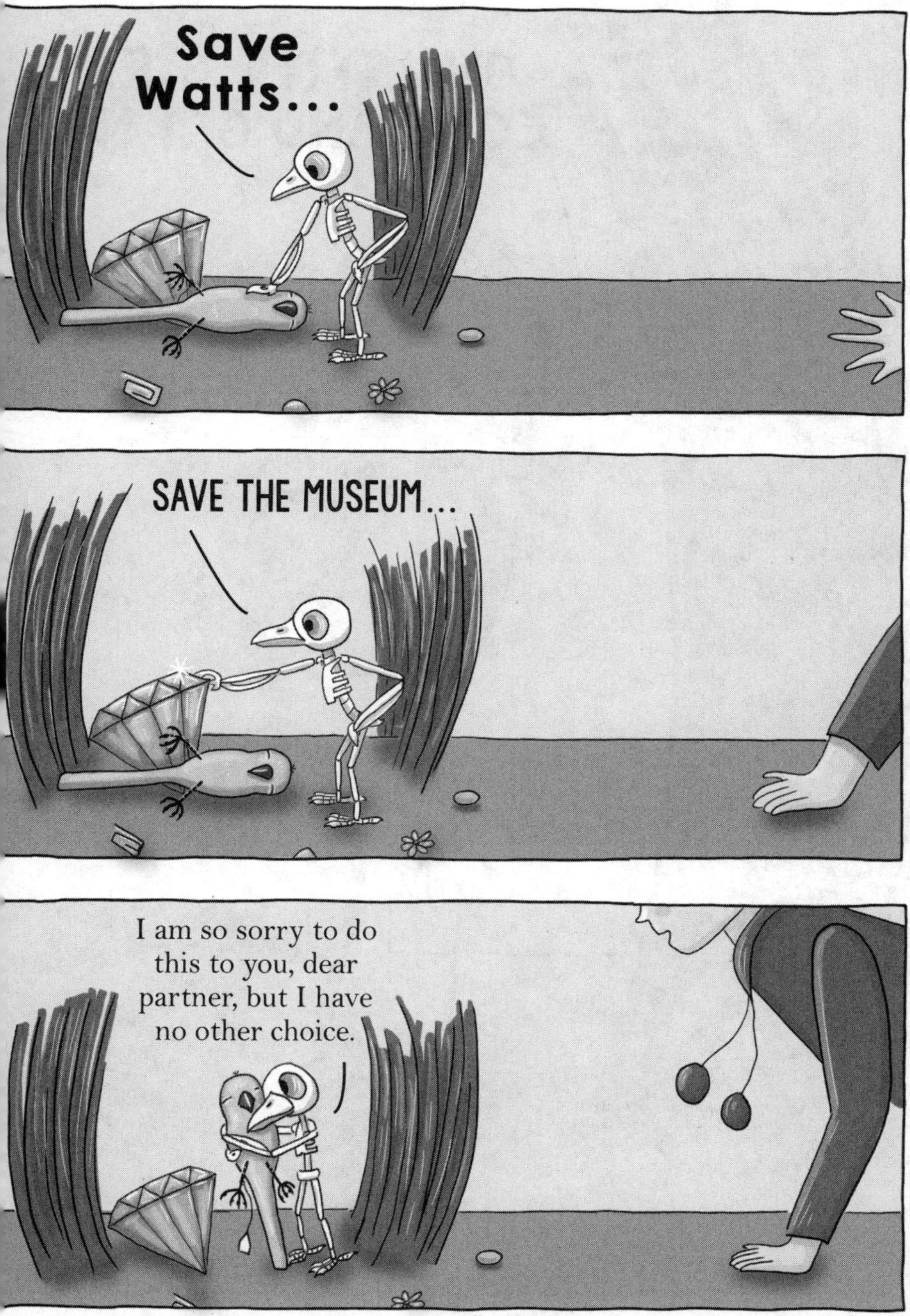
Save Watts...
SAVE THE MUSEUM...
I am so sorry to do this to you, dear partner, but I have no other choice.

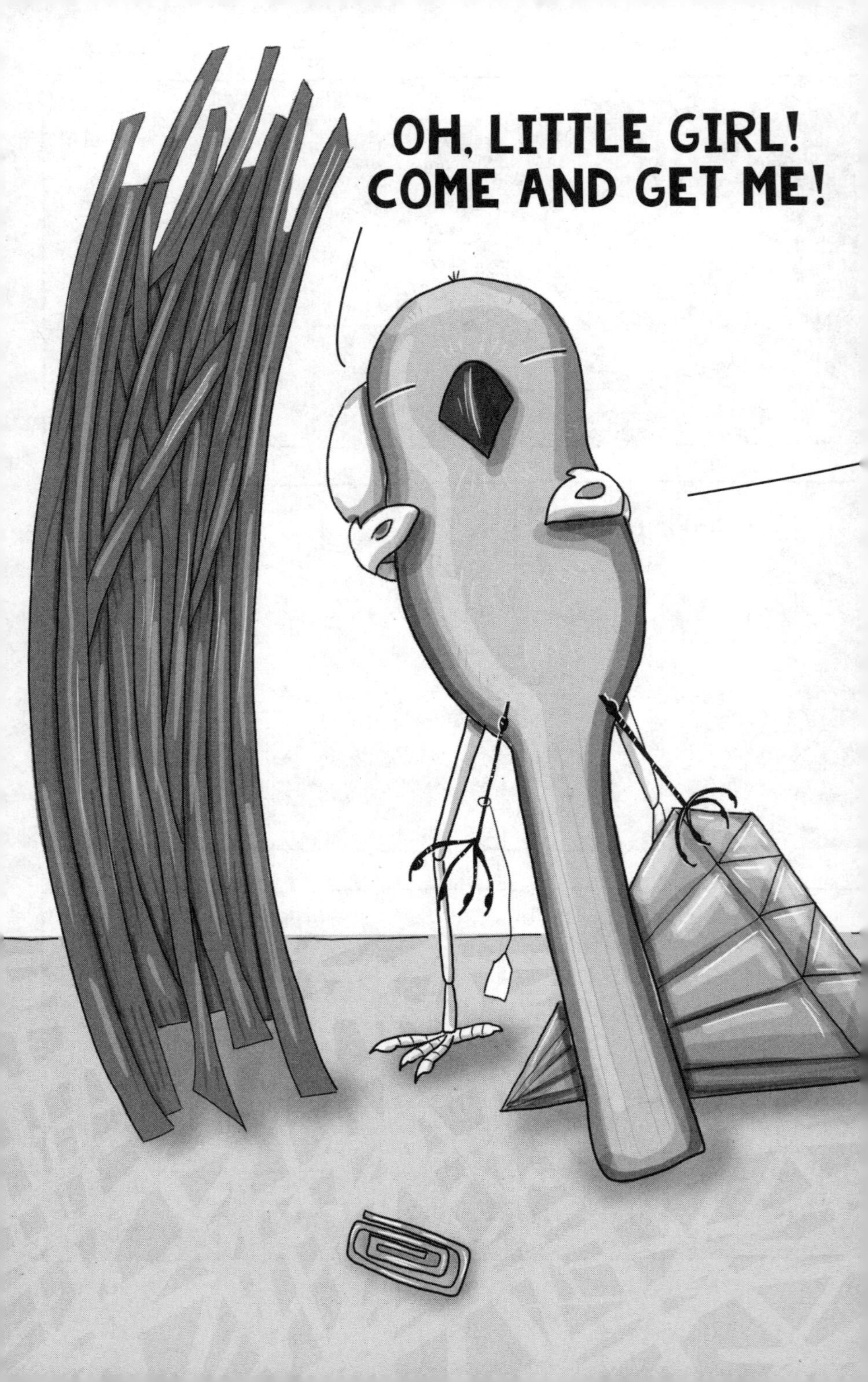
OH, LITTLE GIRL!
COME AND GET ME!

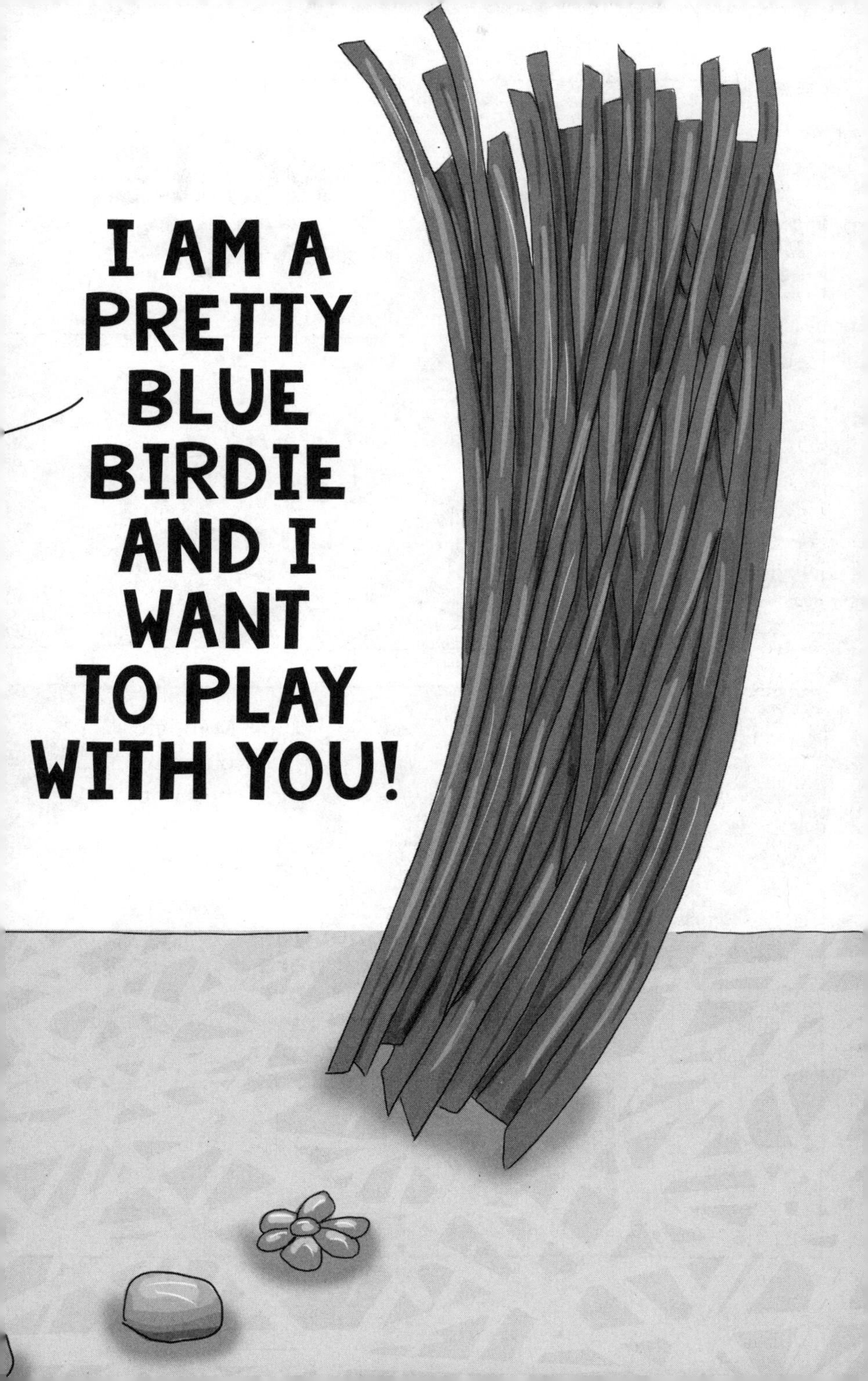
I AM A PRETTY BLUE BIRDIE AND I WANT TO PLAY WITH YOU!

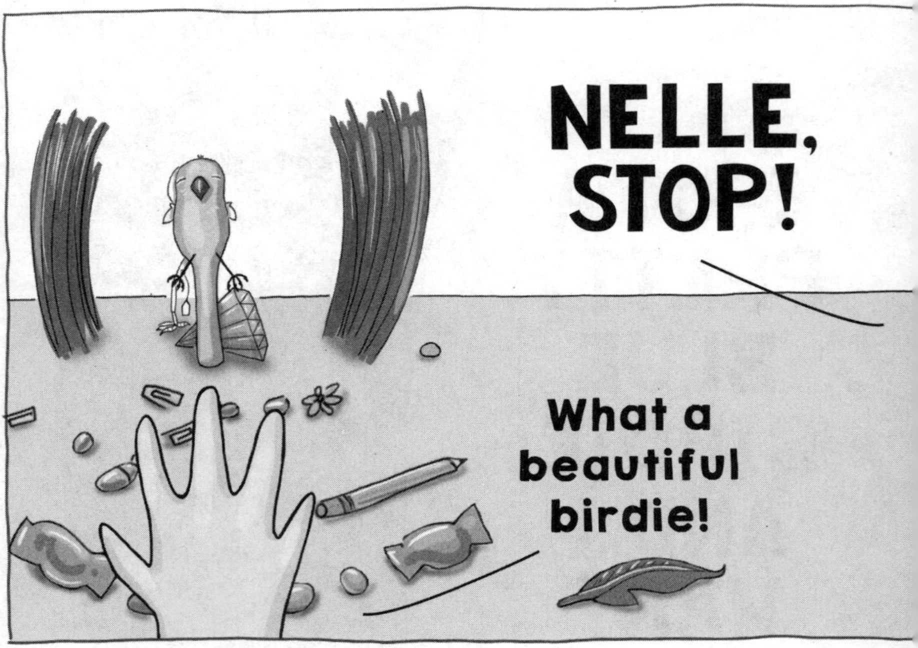
NELLE, STOP!
What a beautiful birdie!

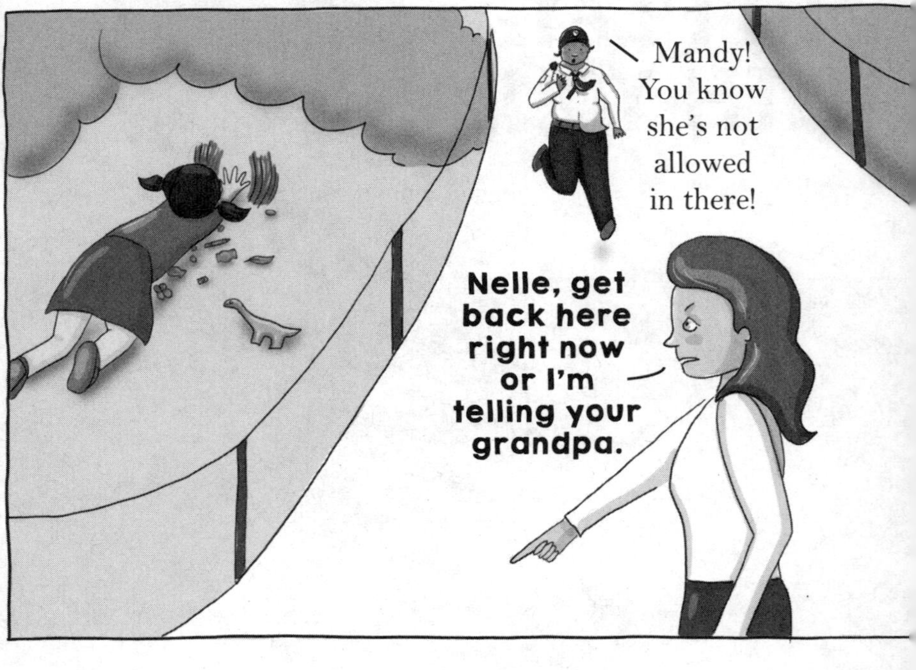
Mandy! You know she's not allowed in there!
Nelle, get back here right now or I'm telling your grandpa.

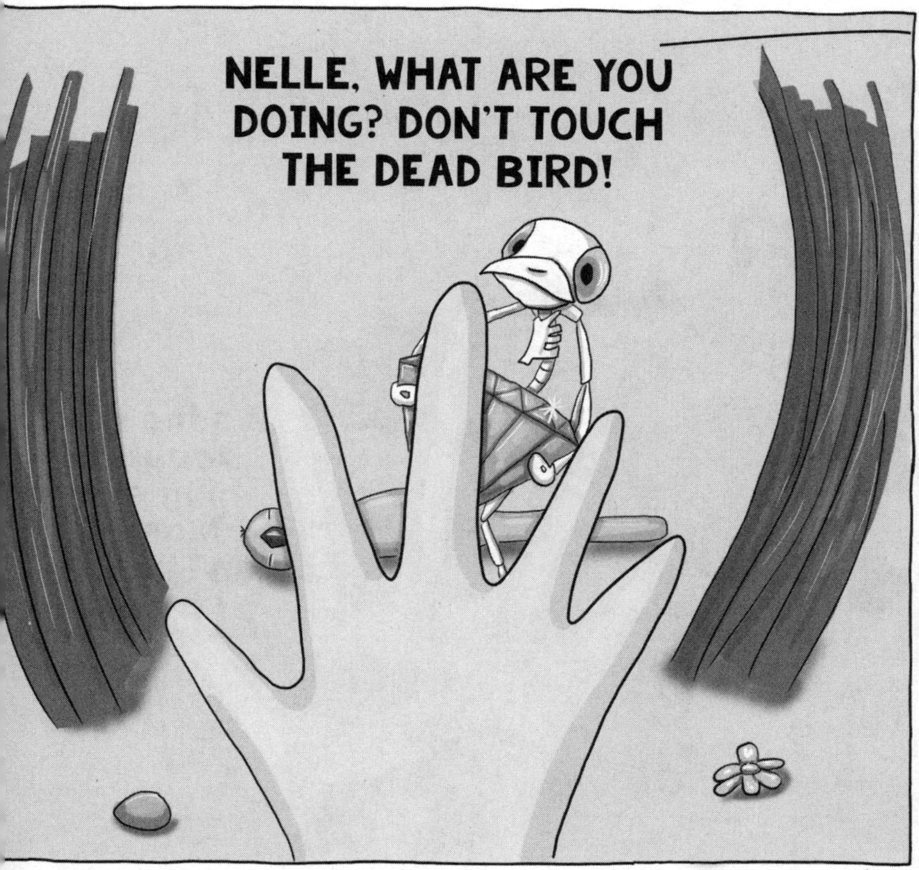
NELLE, WHAT ARE YOU DOING? DON'T TOUCH THE DEAD BIRD!

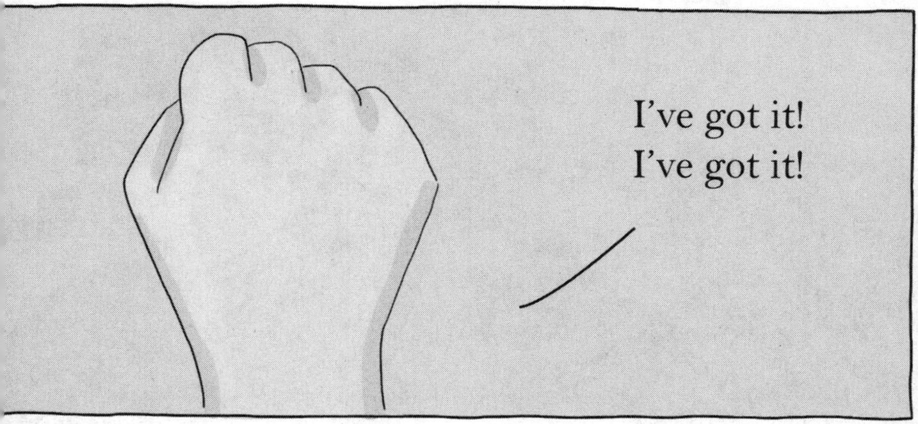
I've got it!
I've got it!

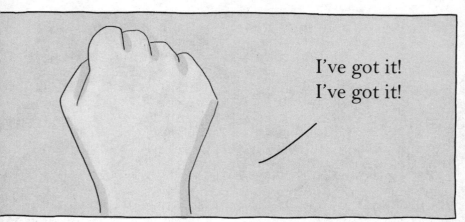

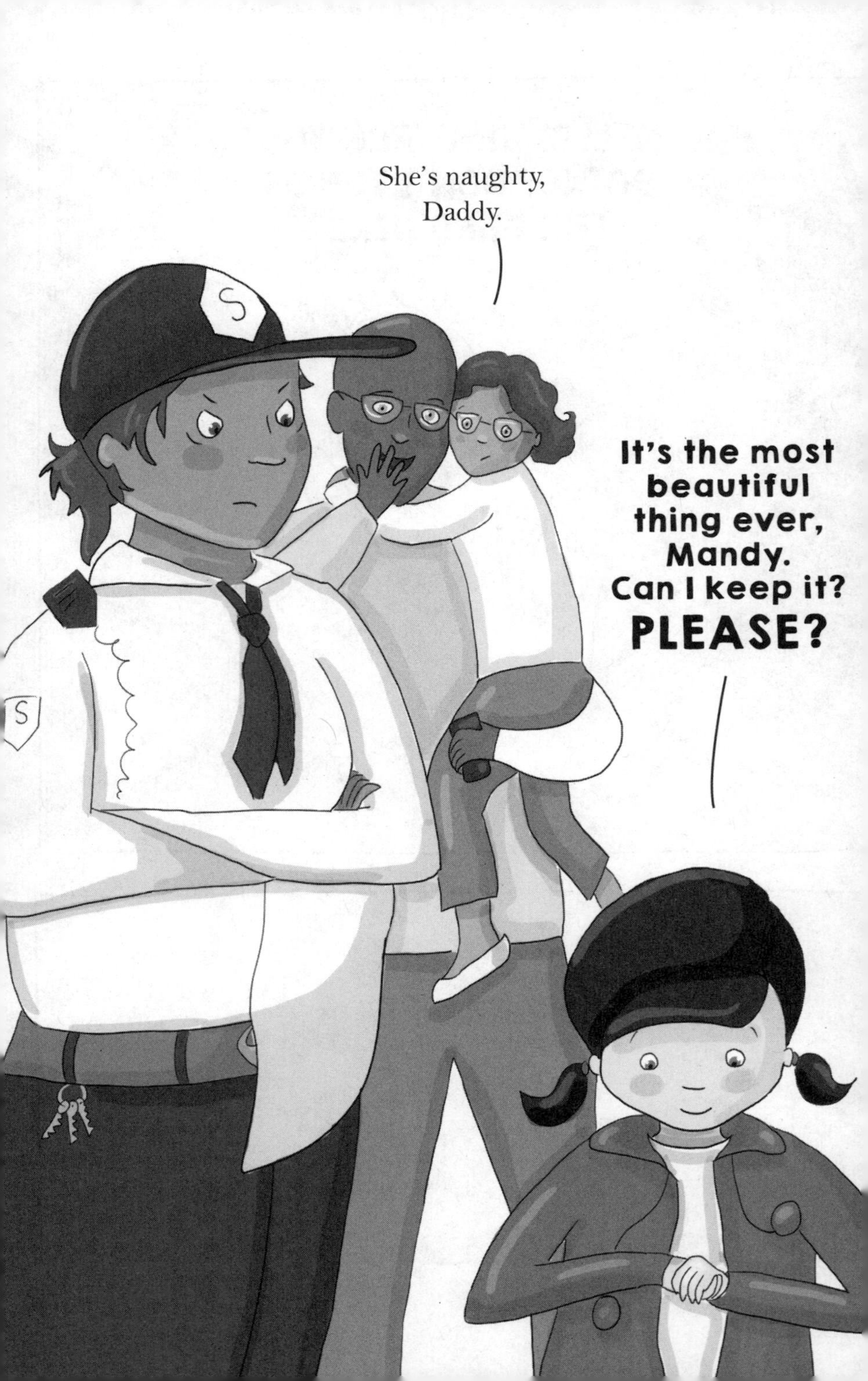
She's naughty, Daddy.
It's the most beautiful thing ever, Mandy. Can I keep it? PLEASE?

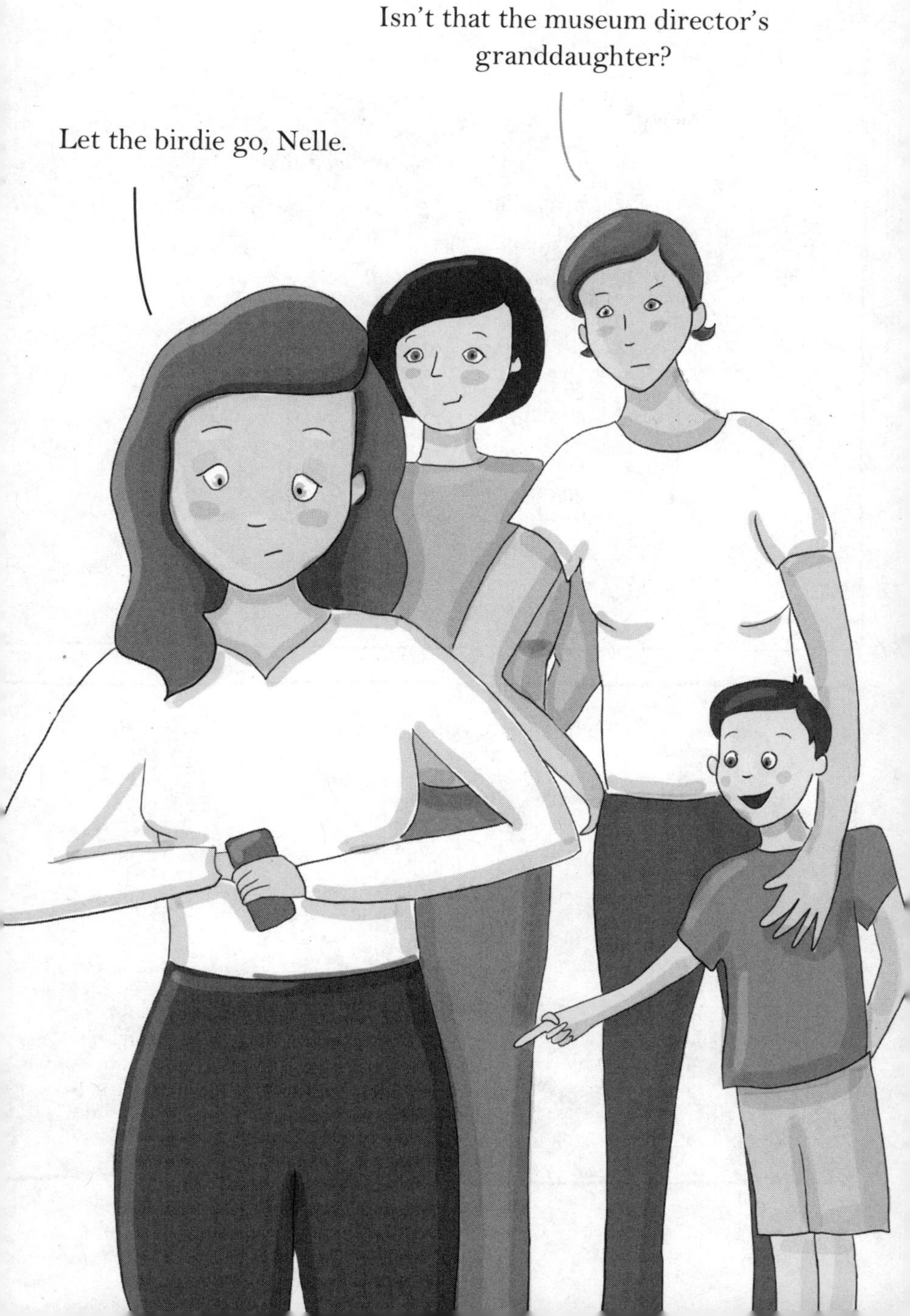
Let the birdie go, Nelle.
Isn't that the museum director's granddaughter?

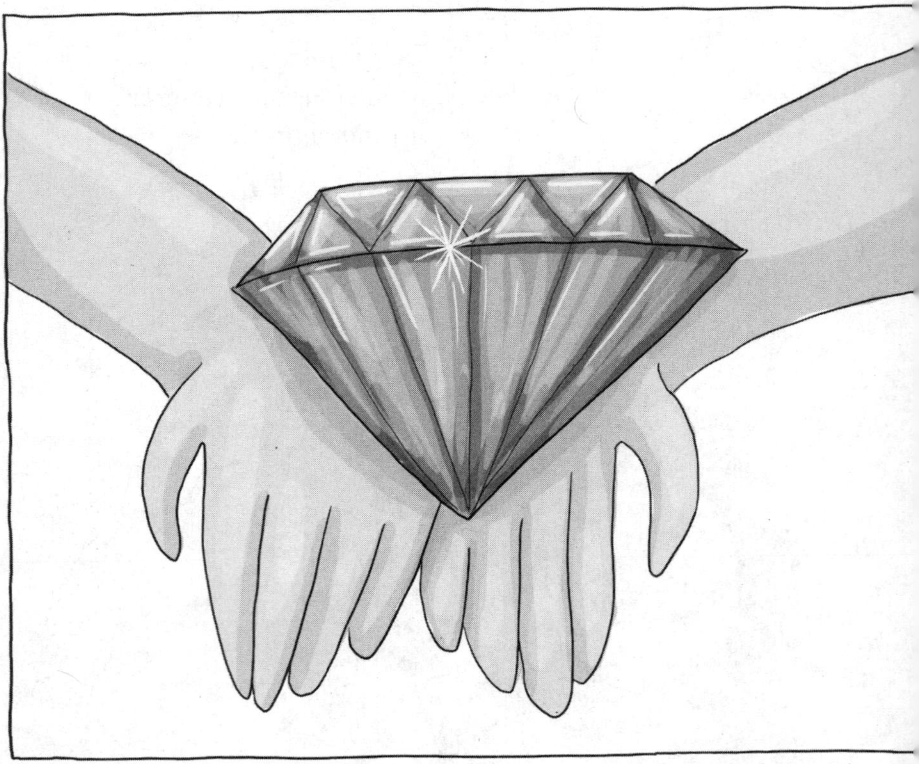

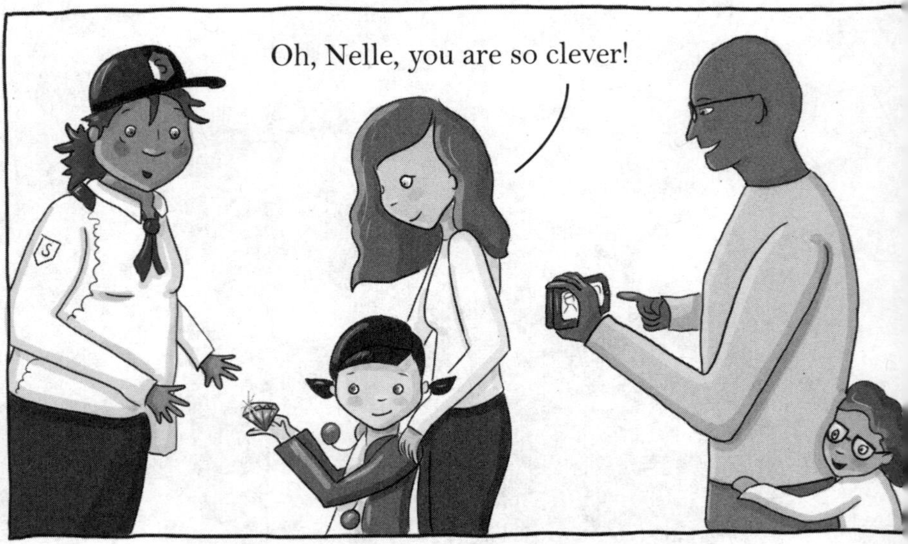
Oh, Nelle, you are so clever!

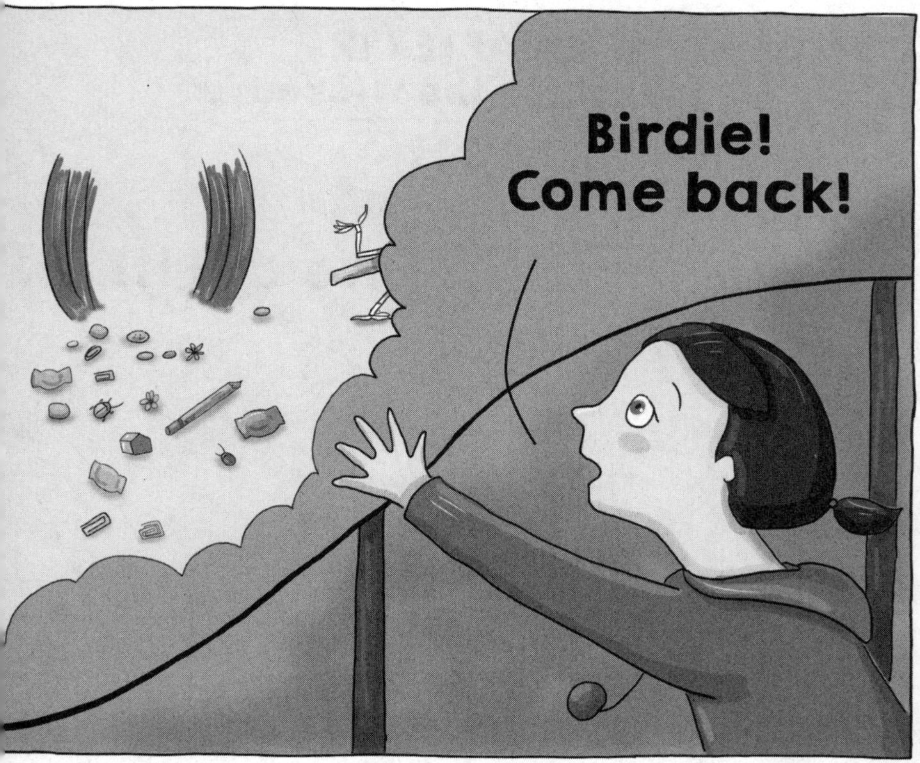
Birdie! Come back!

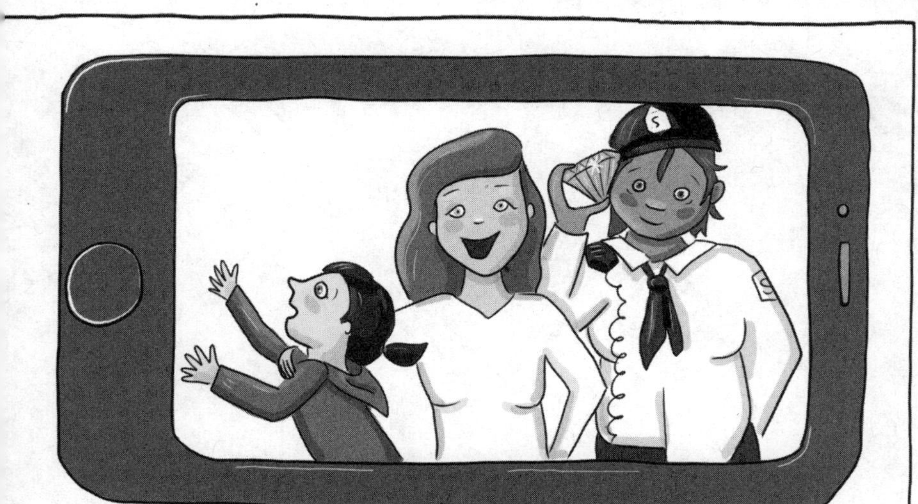

CHAPTER 12
Rest for the Wicked

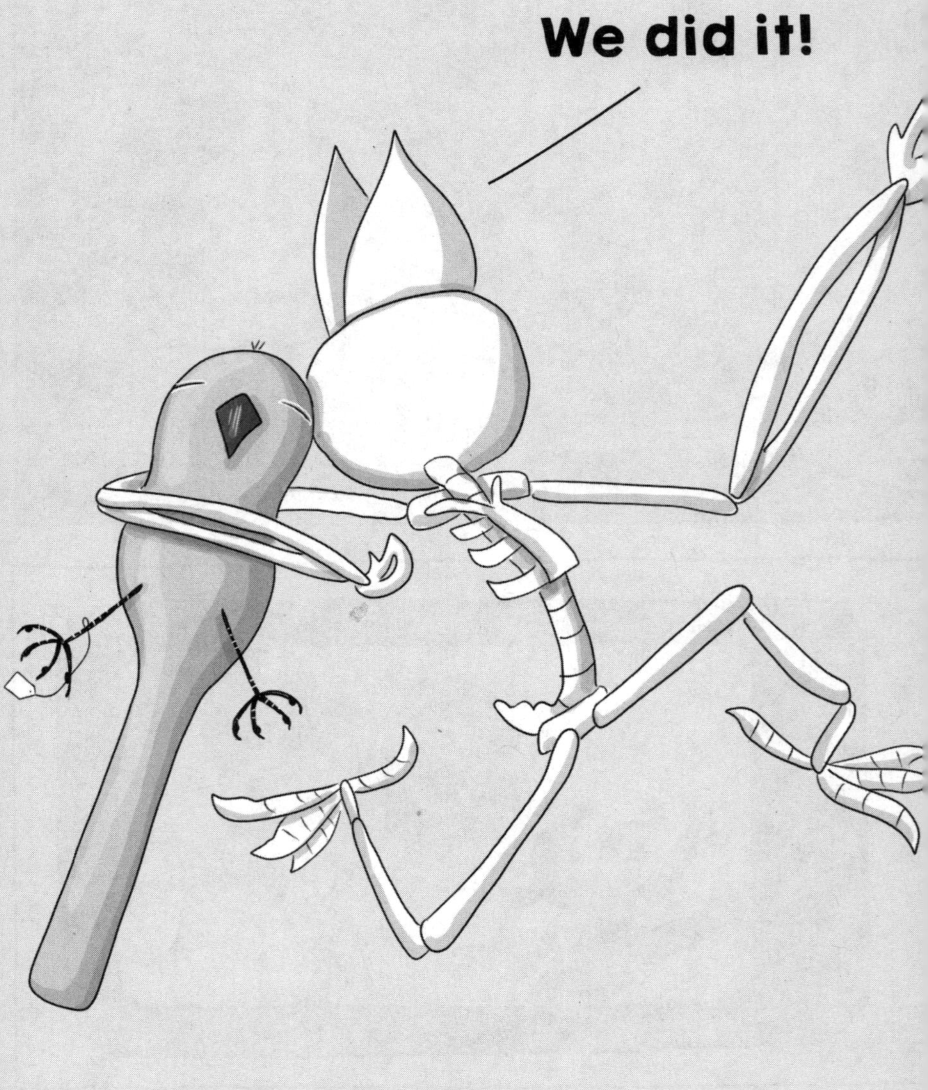
We did it!

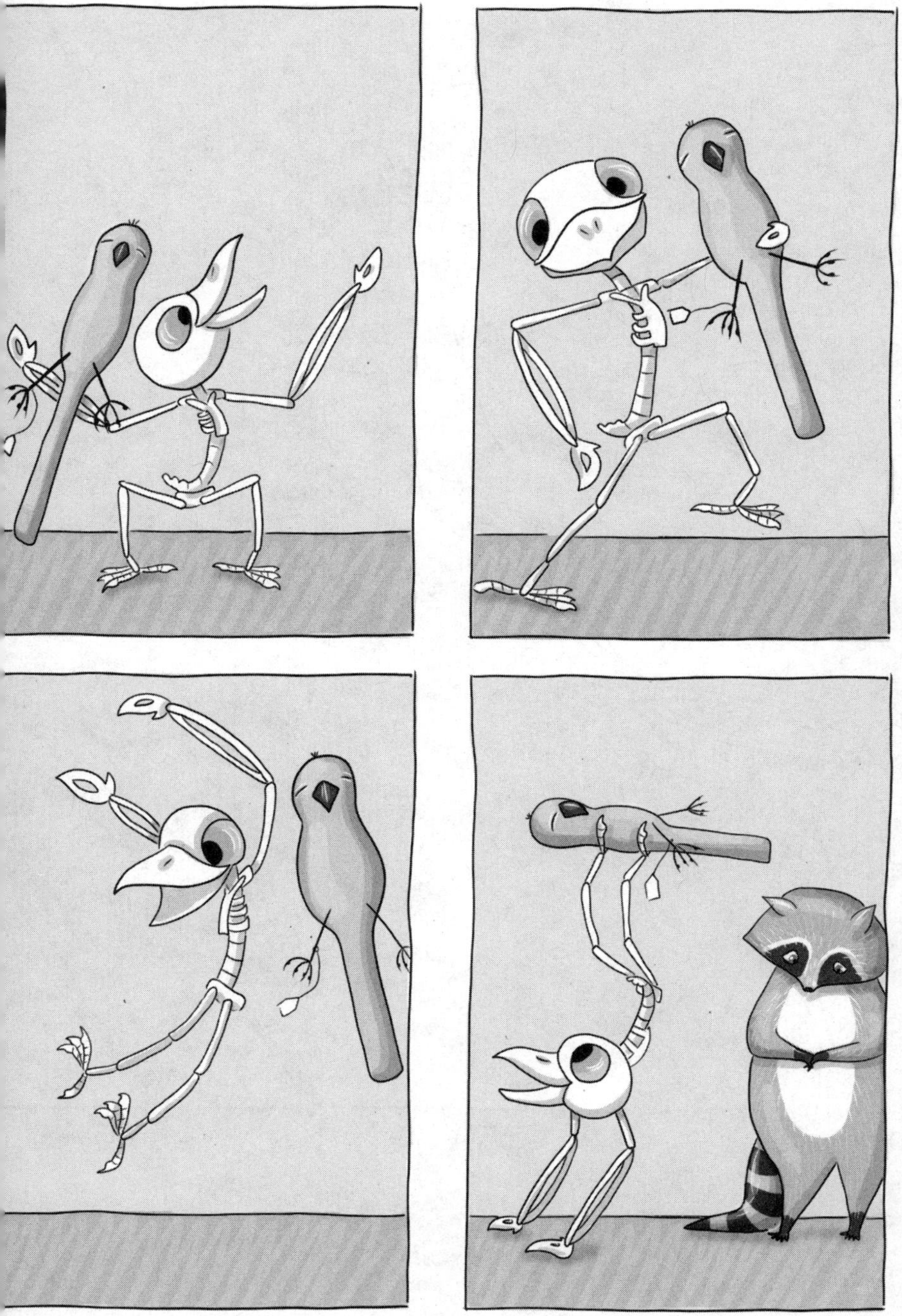

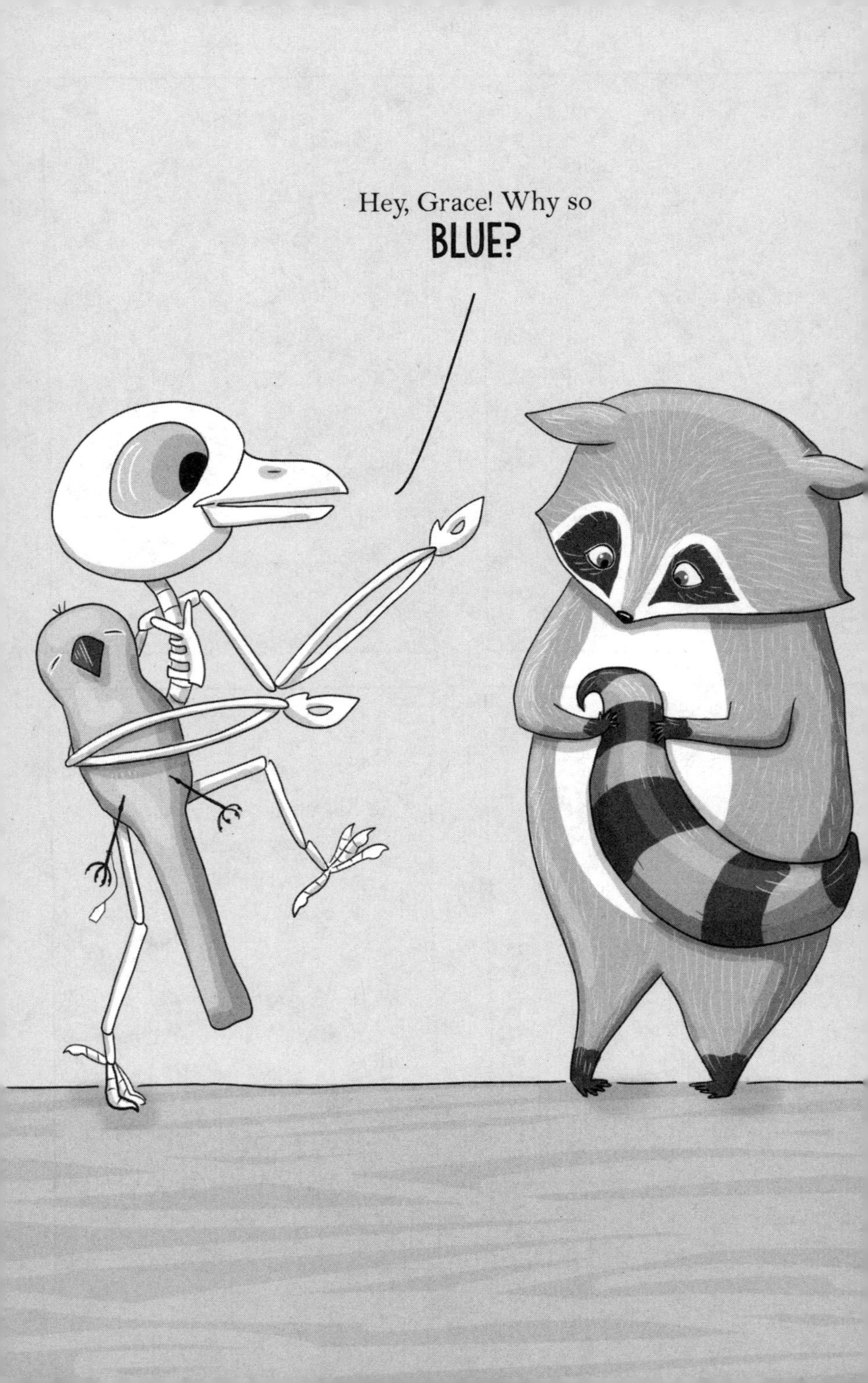
Hey, Grace! Why so
BLUE?

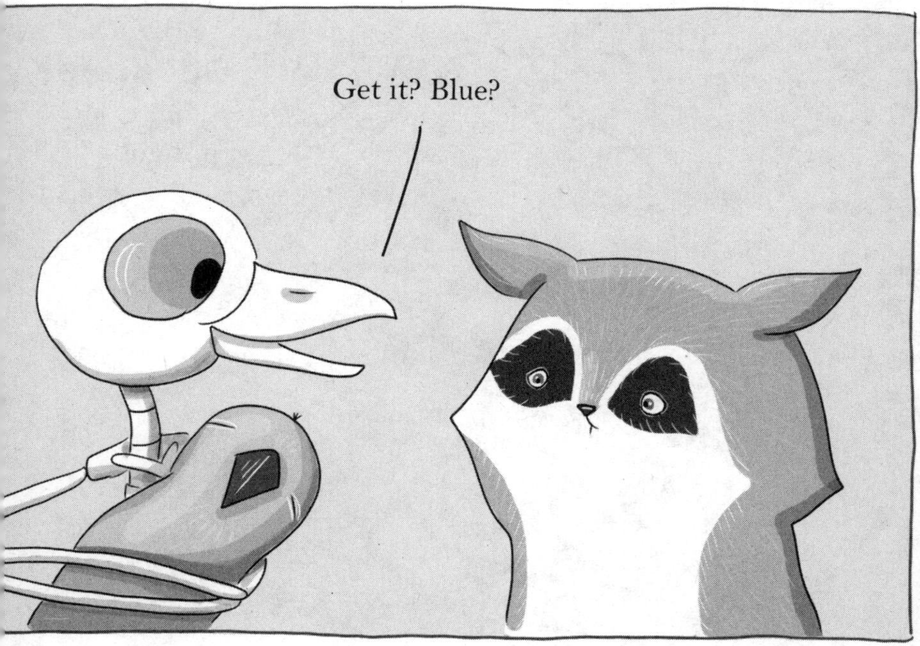
Get it? Blue?

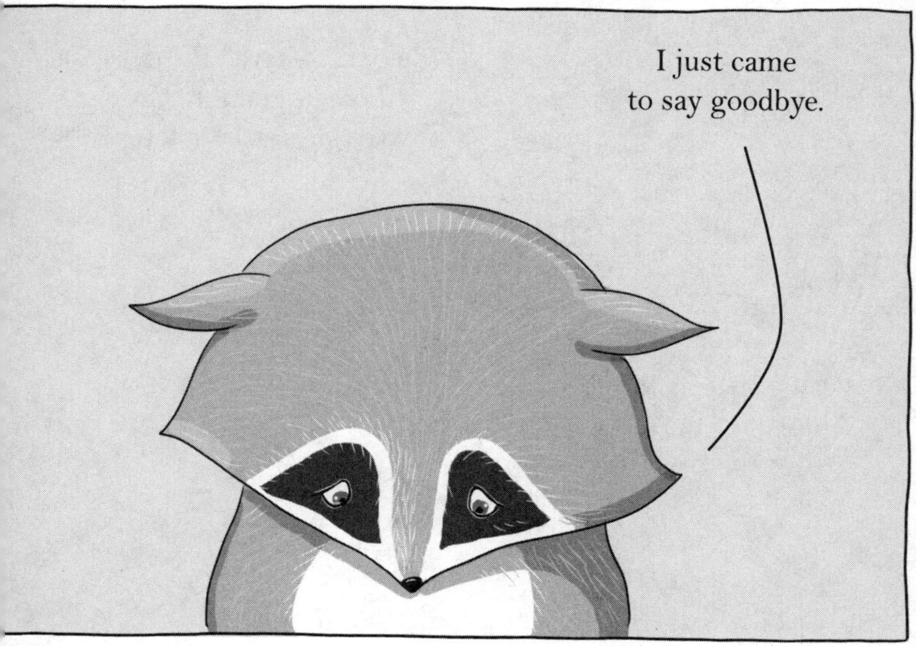
I just came to say goodbye.

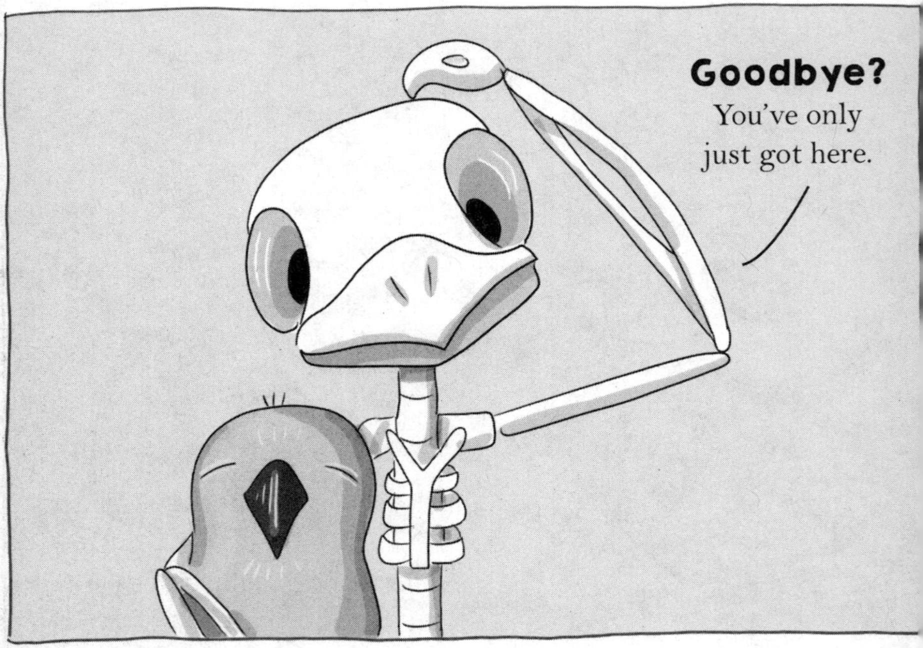
Goodbye?
You've only just got here.

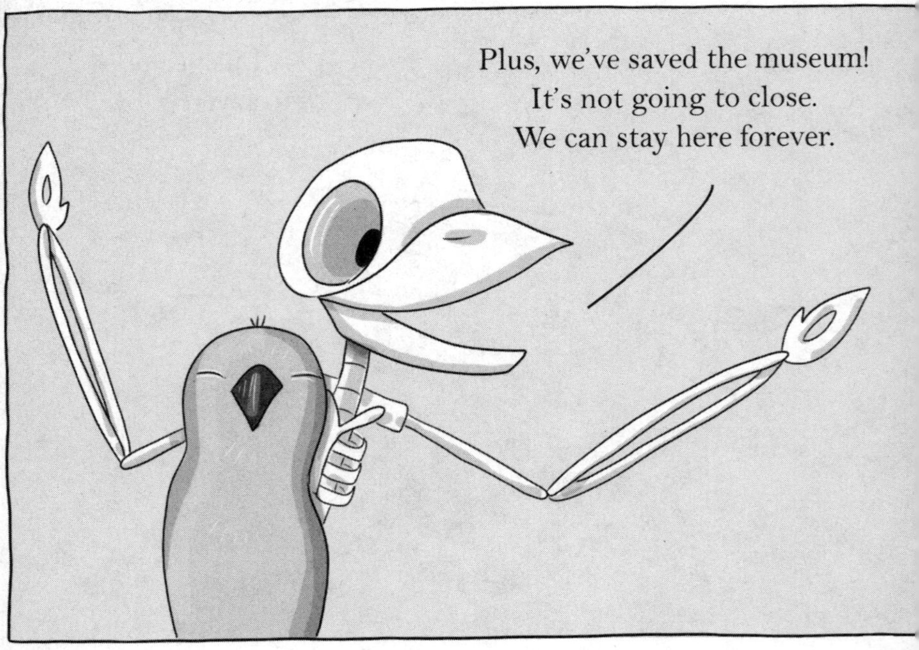
Plus, we've saved the museum! It's not going to close. We can stay here forever.

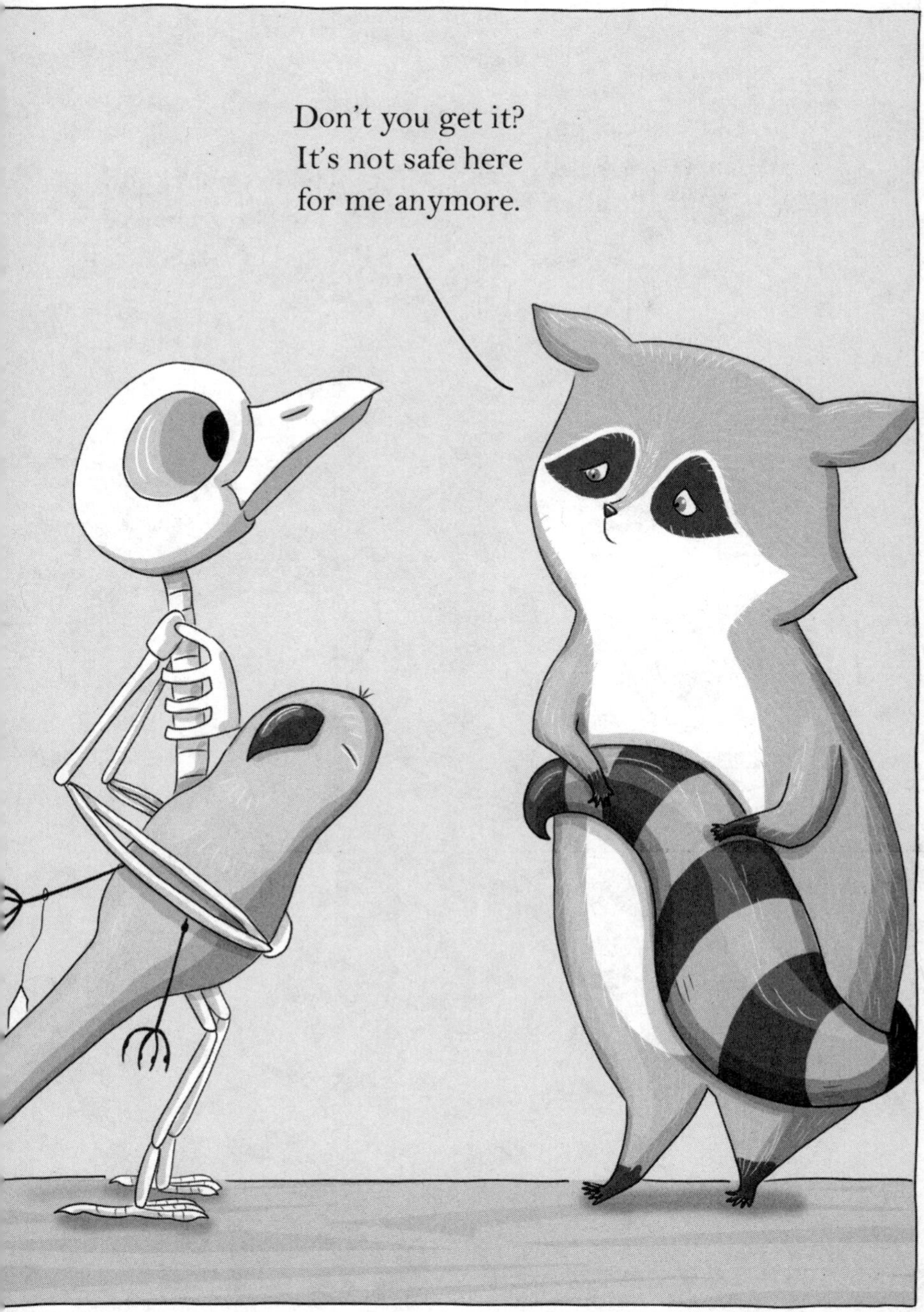
Don't you get it?
It's not safe here
for me anymore.

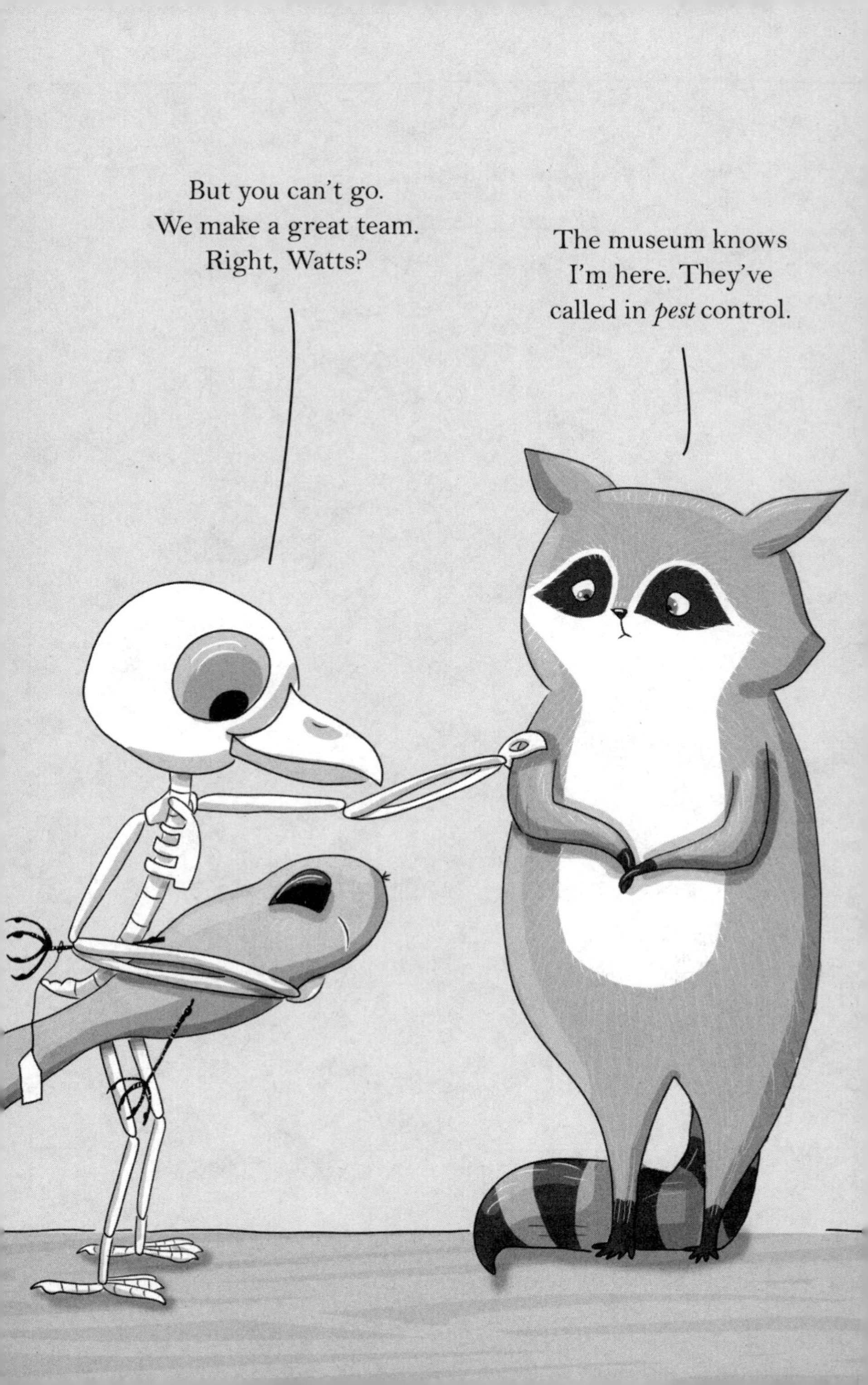
But you can't go. We make a great team. Right, Watts?
The museum knows I'm here. They've called in *pest* control.

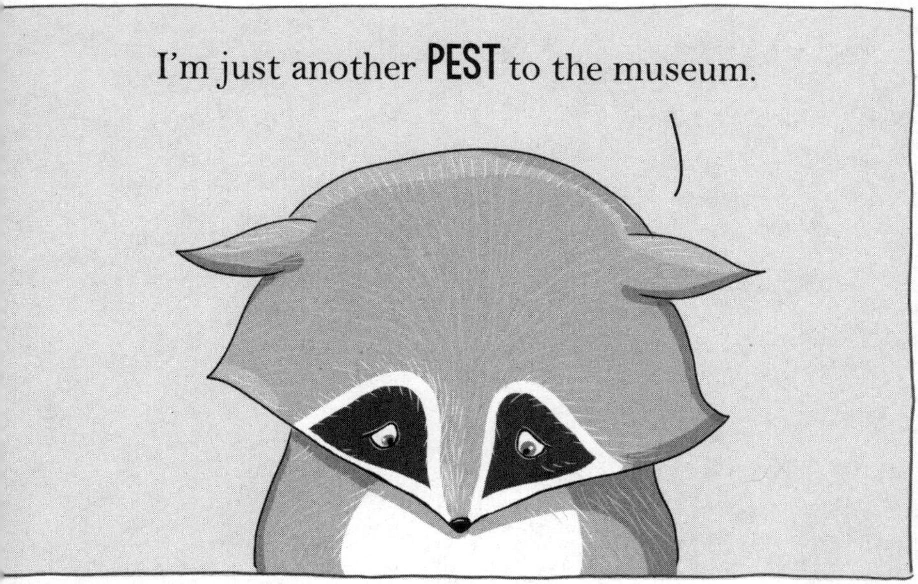
I'm just another PEST to the museum.

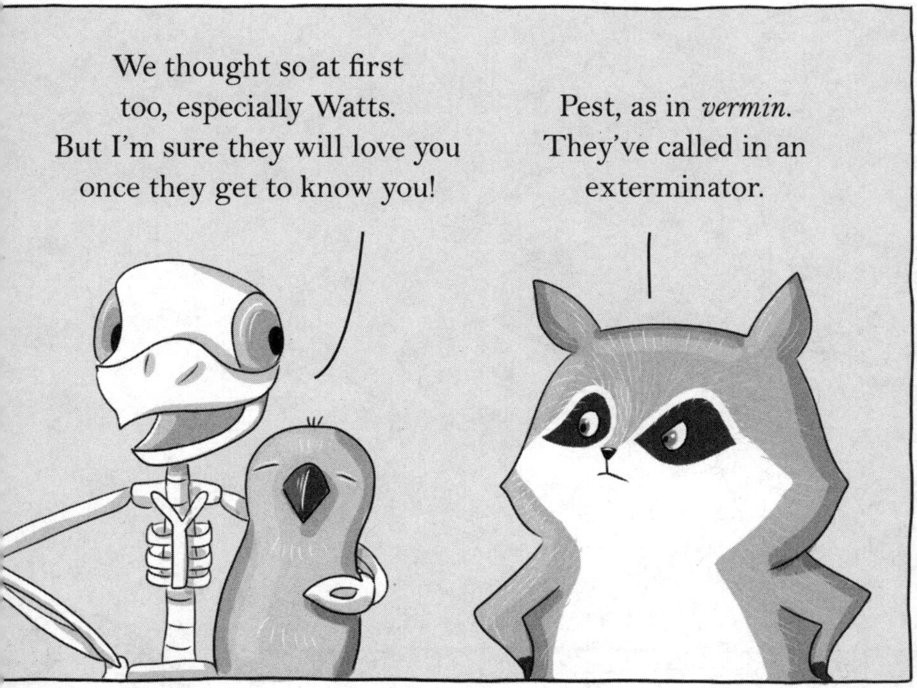
We thought so at first too, especially Watts. But I'm sure they will love you once they get to know you!
Pest, as in *vermin*. They've called in an exterminator.

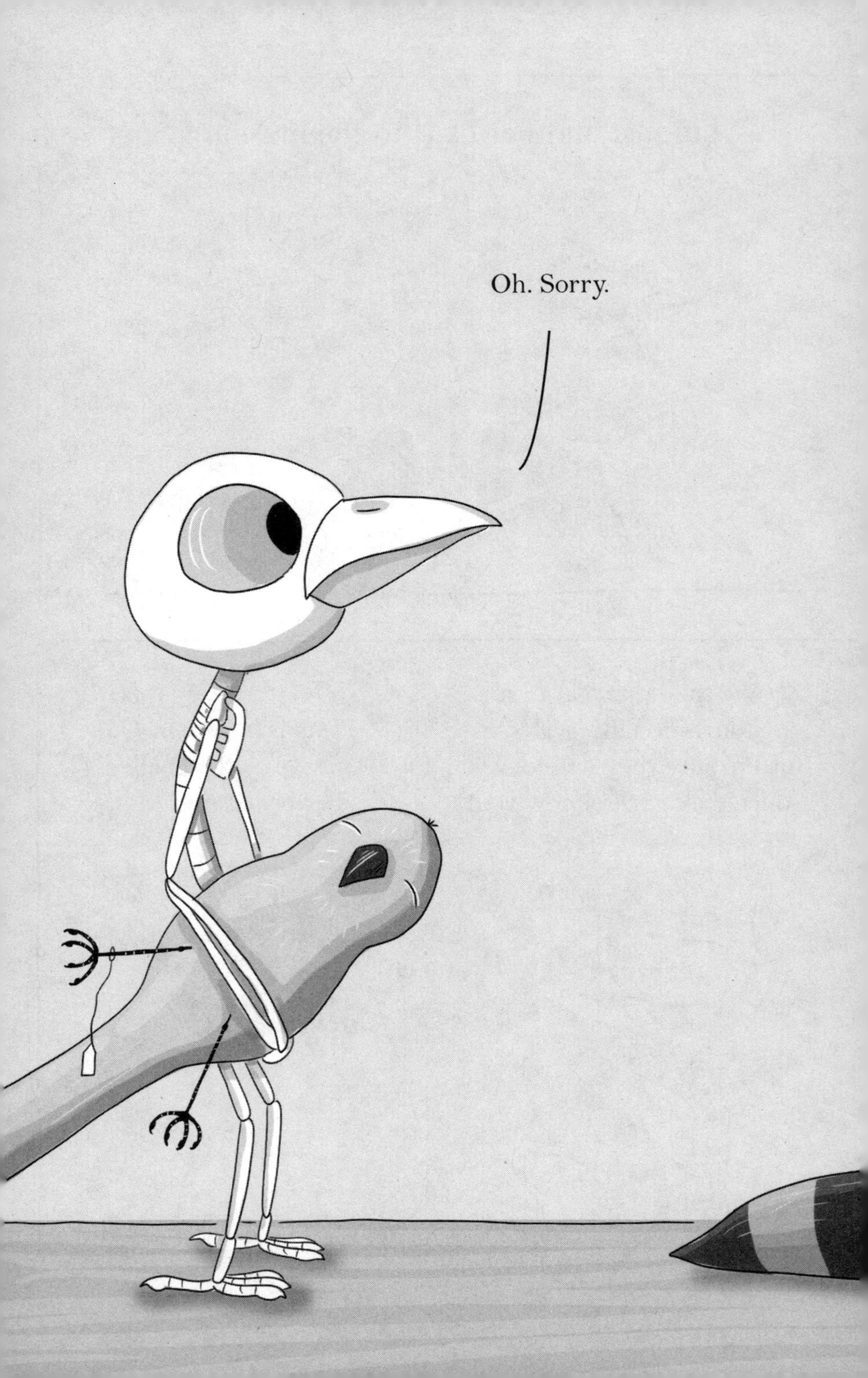
Oh. Sorry.

Don't worry.
I'll be fine.

Toodle-oo.

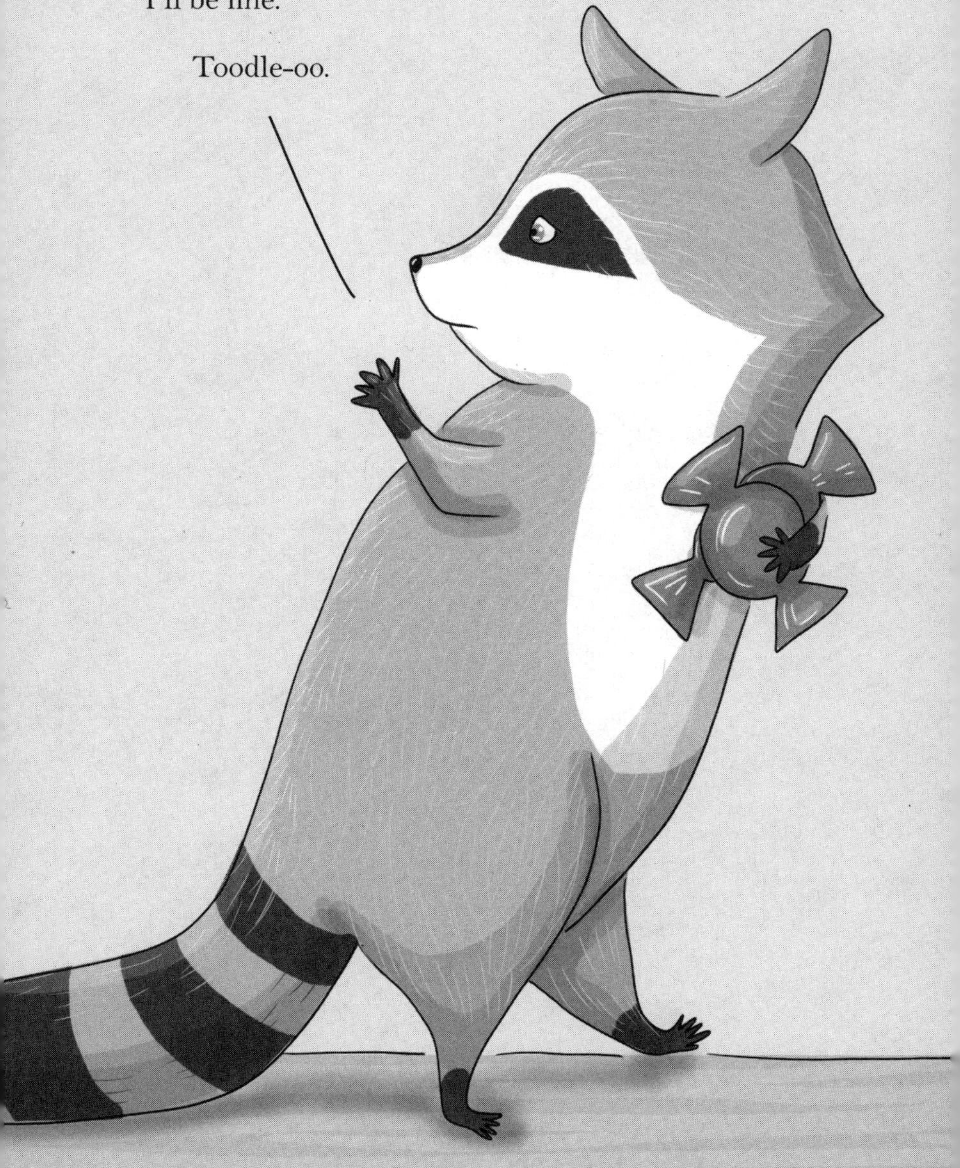

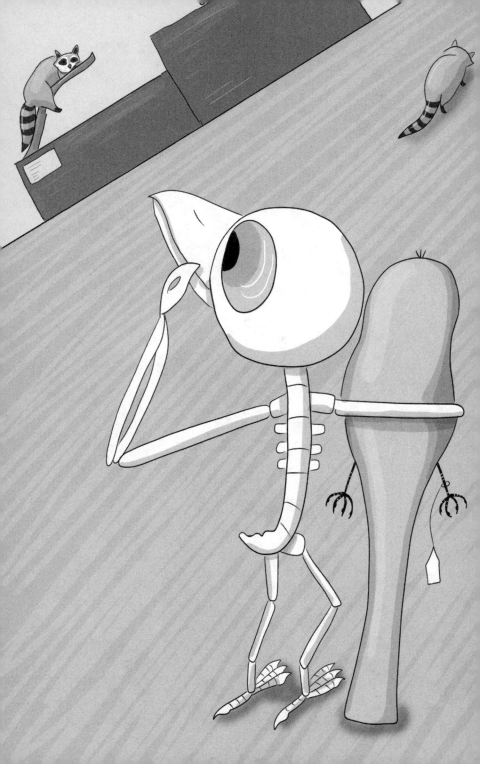

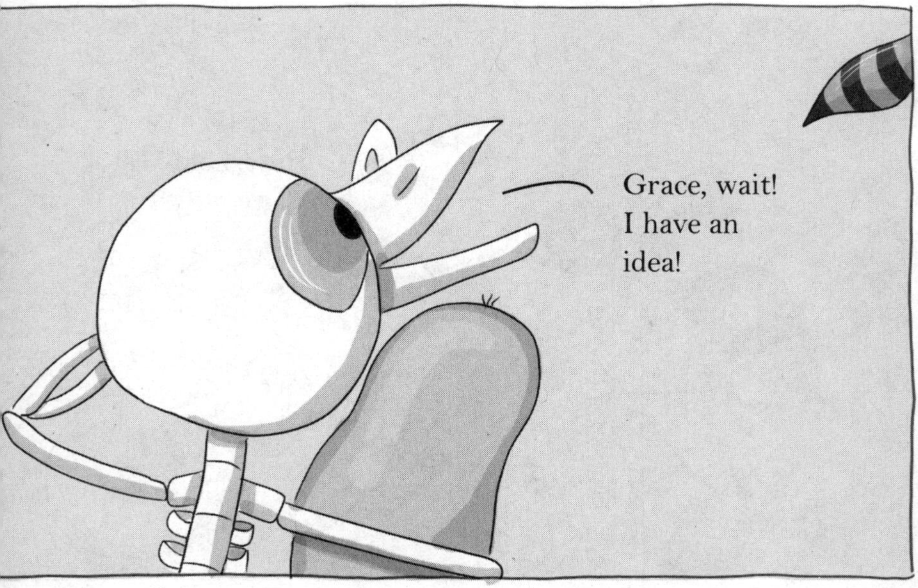
Grace, wait!
I have an
idea!

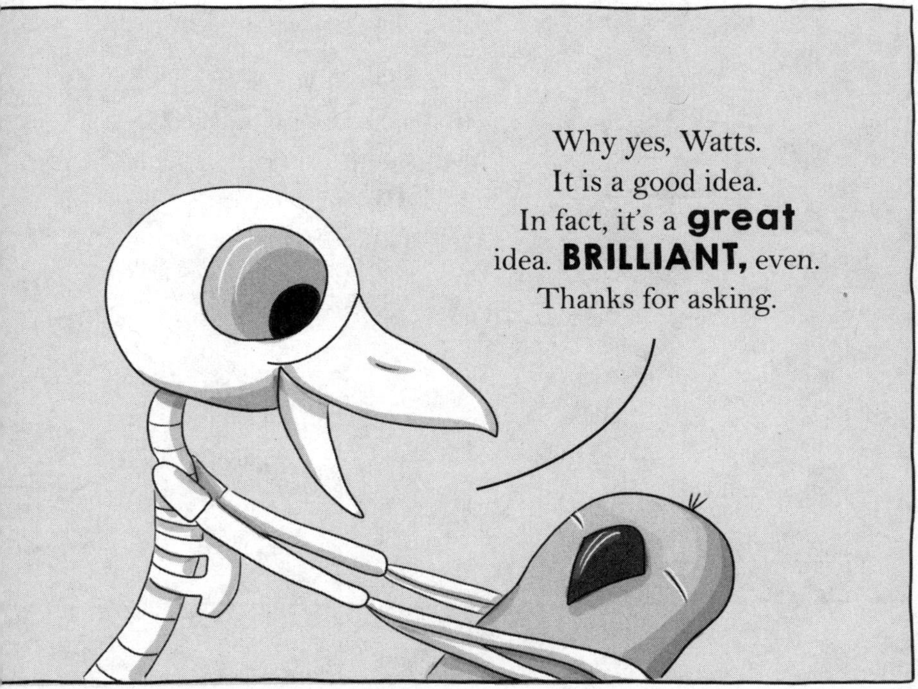
Why yes, Watts.
It is a good idea.
In fact, it's a **great**
idea. **BRILLIANT,** even.
Thanks for asking.

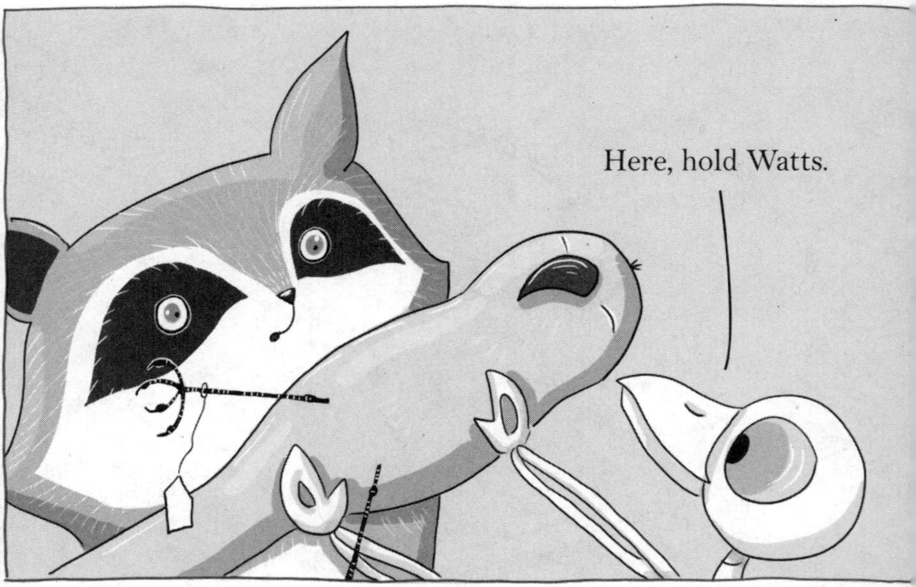
Here, hold Watts.

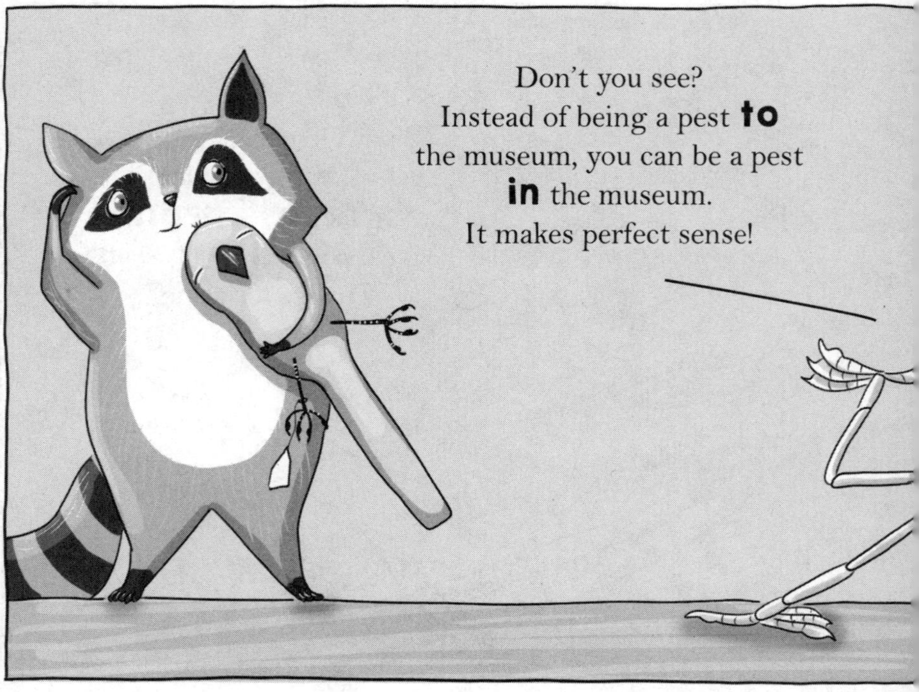
Don't you see?
Instead of being a pest **to** the museum, you can be a pest **in** the museum.
It makes perfect sense!

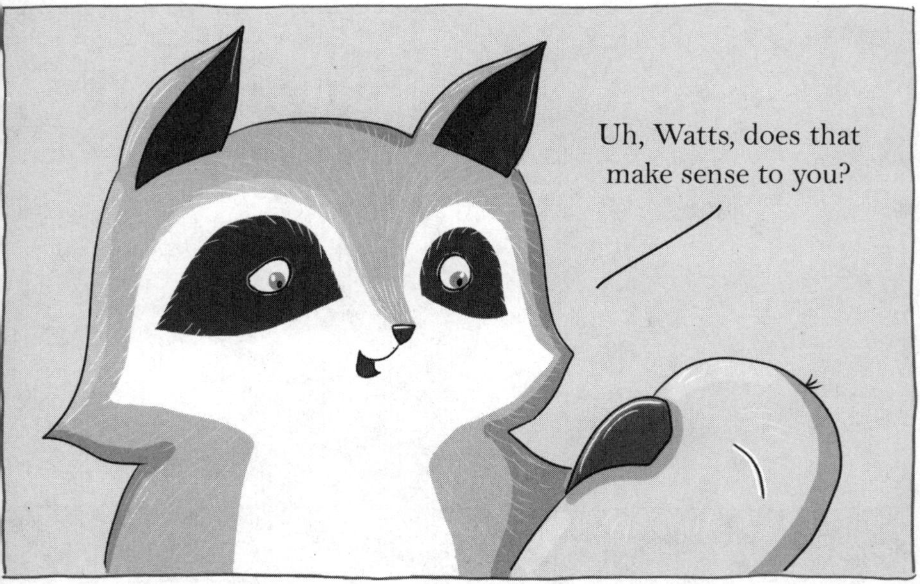
Uh, Watts, does that make sense to you?

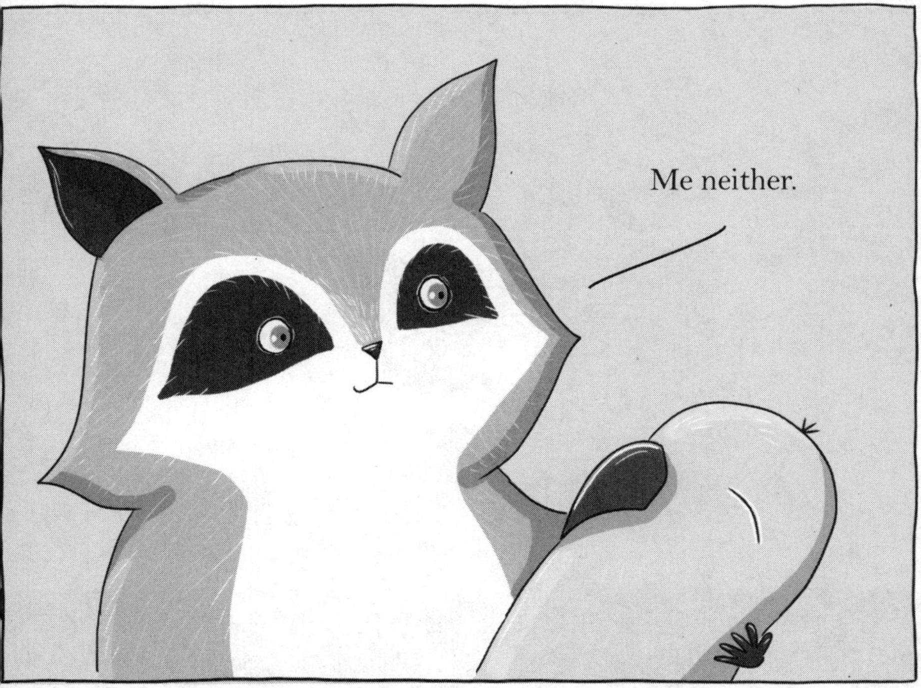
Me neither.

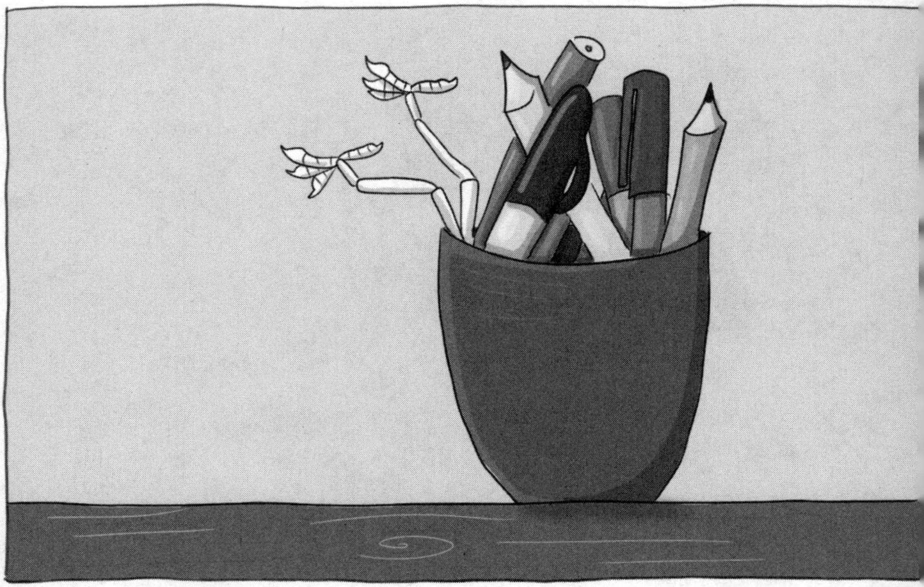

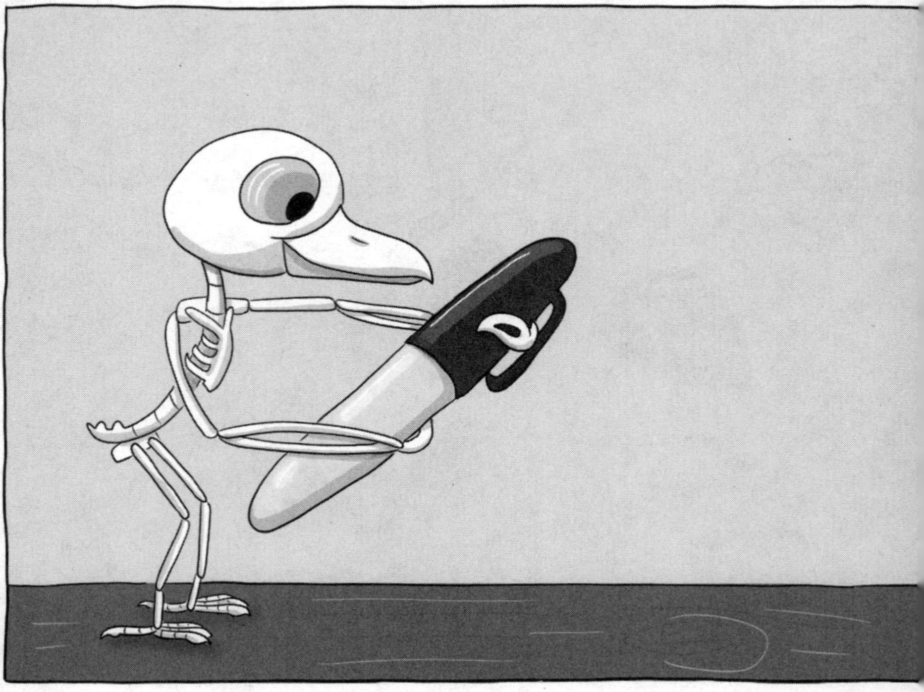

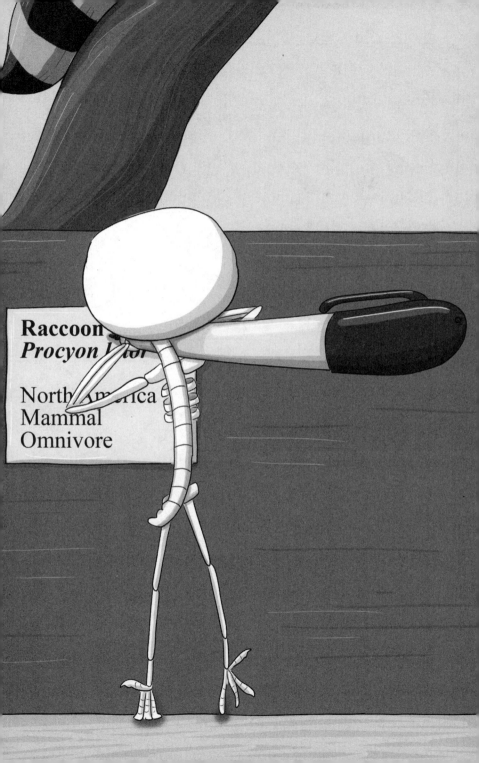

Raccoon
Procyon lotor

North America
Mammal
Omnivore

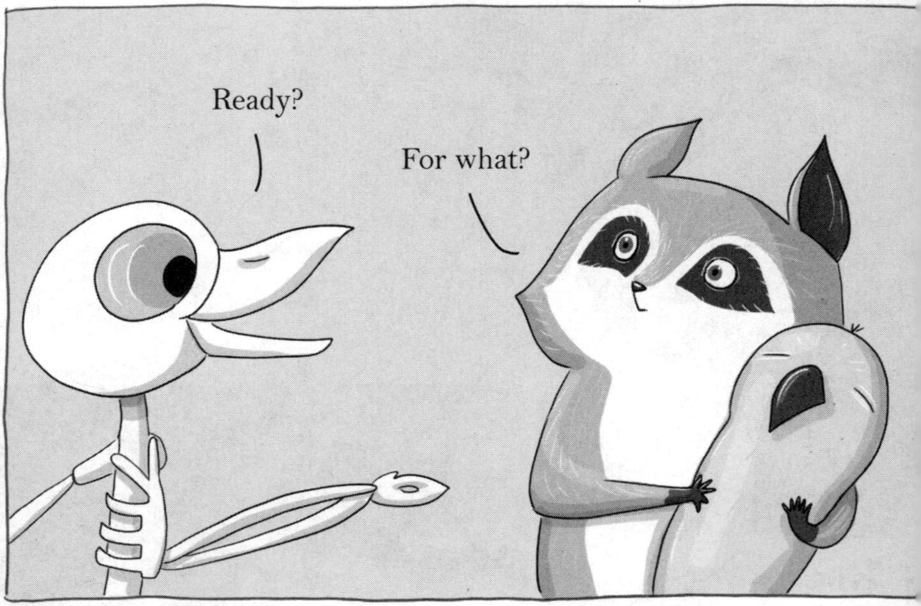
Ready?
For what?

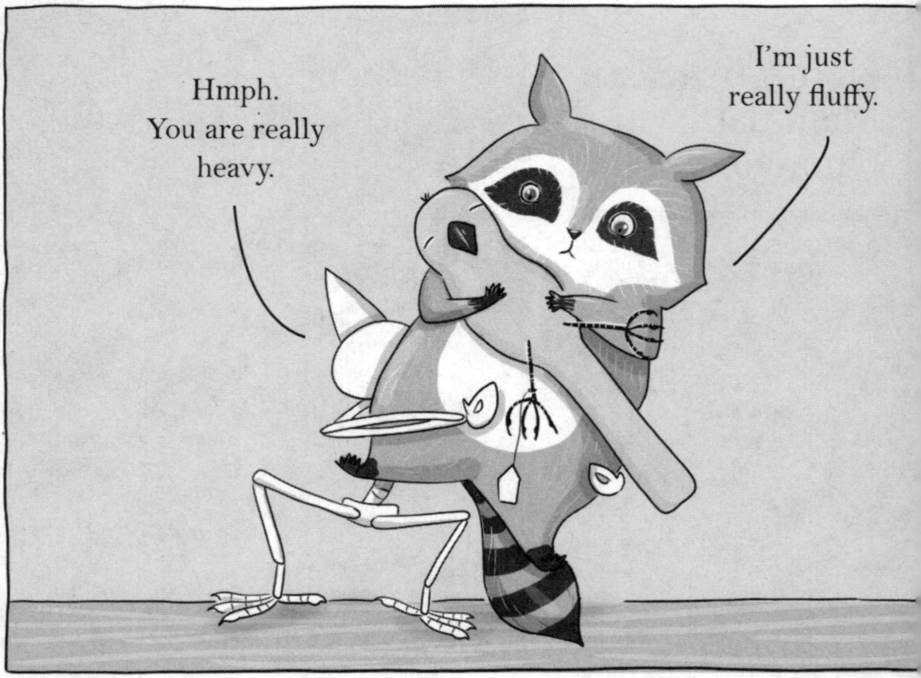
Hmph. You are really heavy.
I'm just really fluffy.

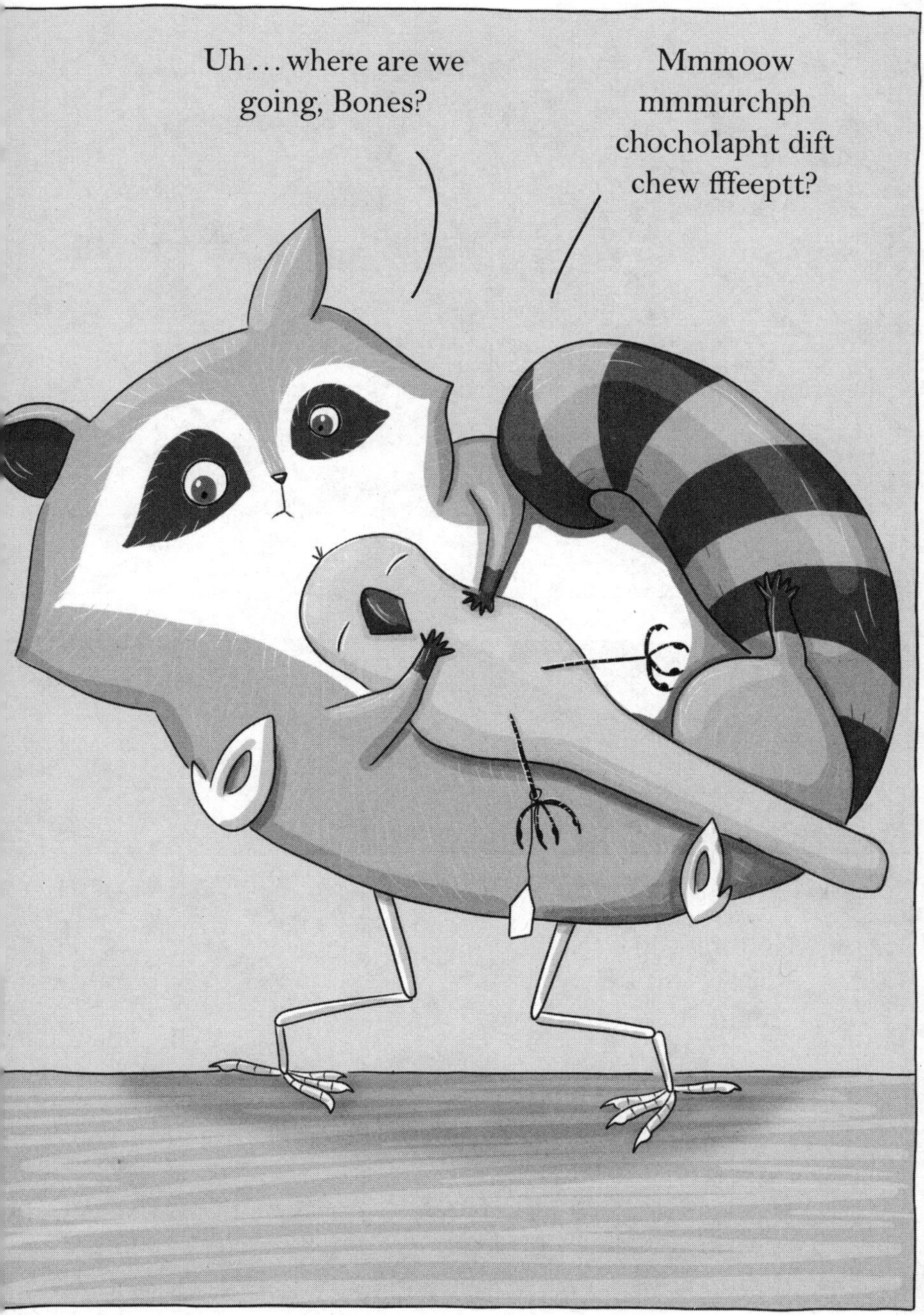
Uh … where are we going, Bones?
Mmmoow mmmurchph chocholapht dift chew fffeeptt?

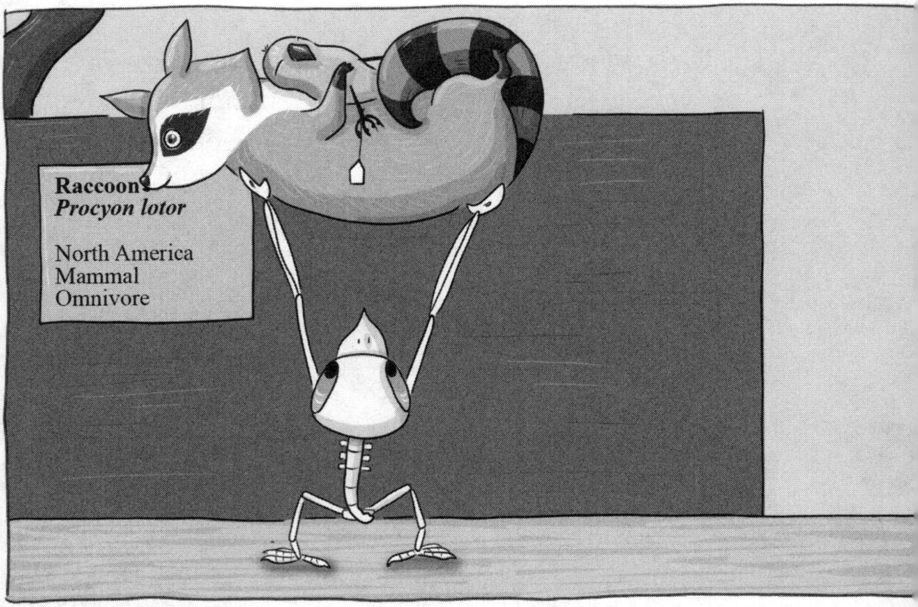
Raccoon
Procyon lotor
North America
Mammal
Omnivore

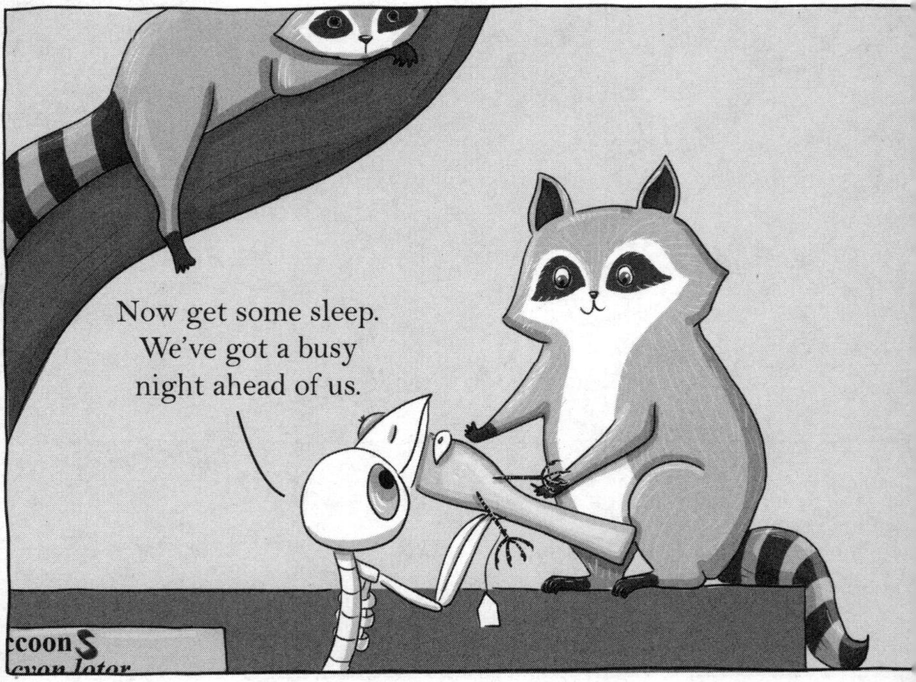
Now get some sleep. We've got a busy night ahead of us.
ccoon
cyon lotor

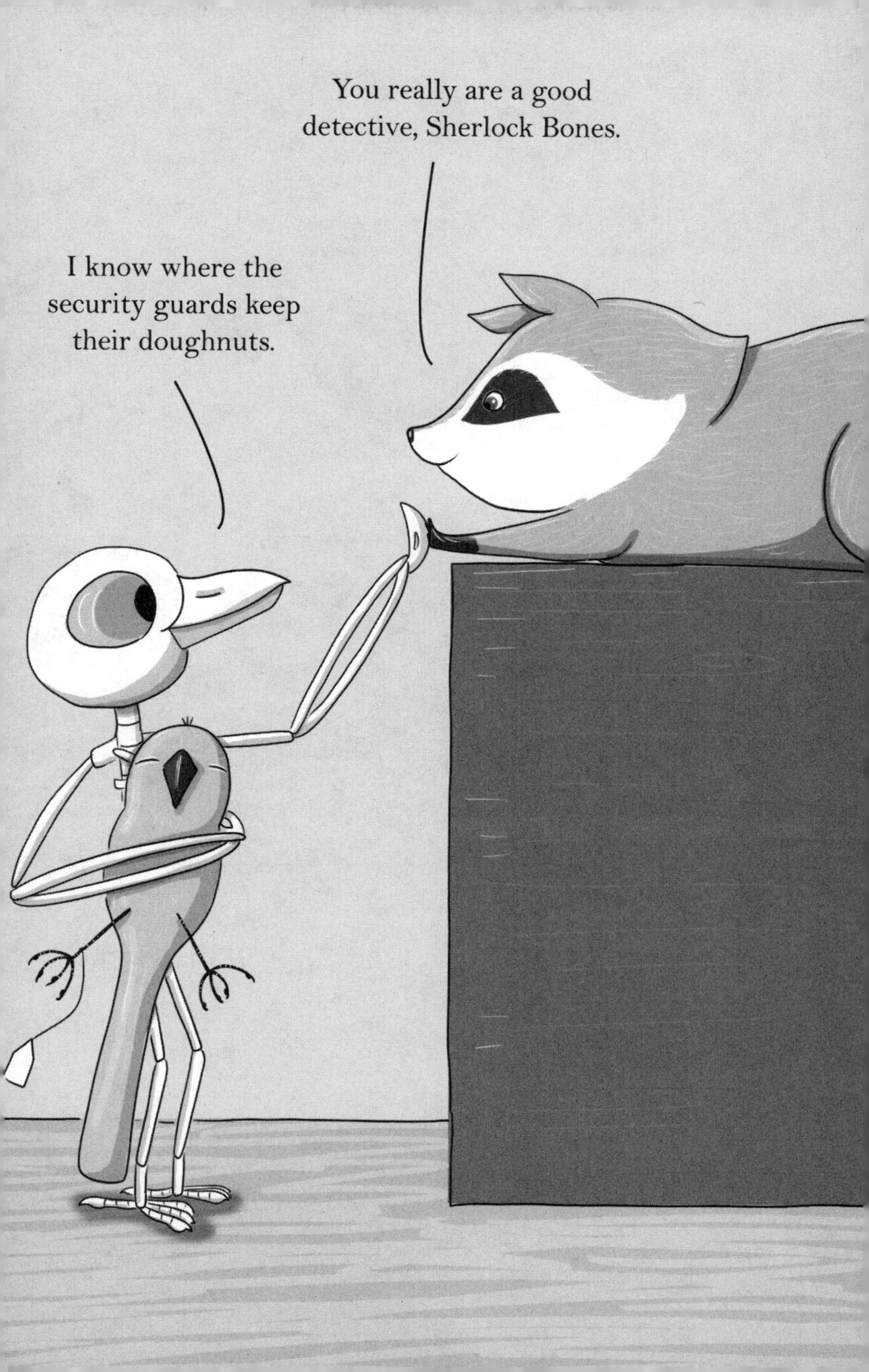
I know where the security guards keep their doughnuts.
You really are a good detective, Sherlock Bones.

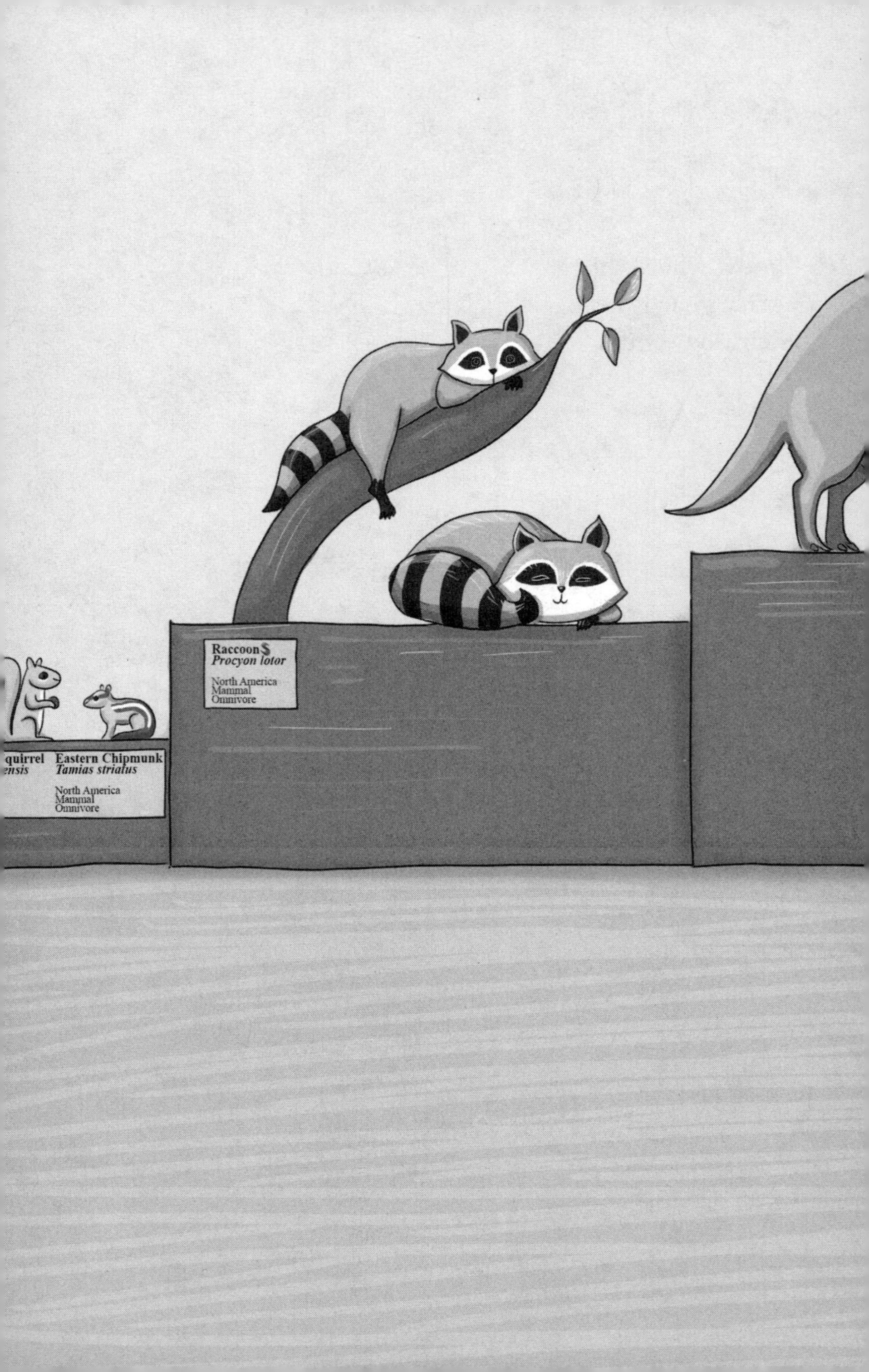

Raccoons
Procyon lotor
North America
Mammal
Omnivore
quirrel
ensis
Eastern Chipmunk
Tamias striatus
North America
Mammal
Omnivore

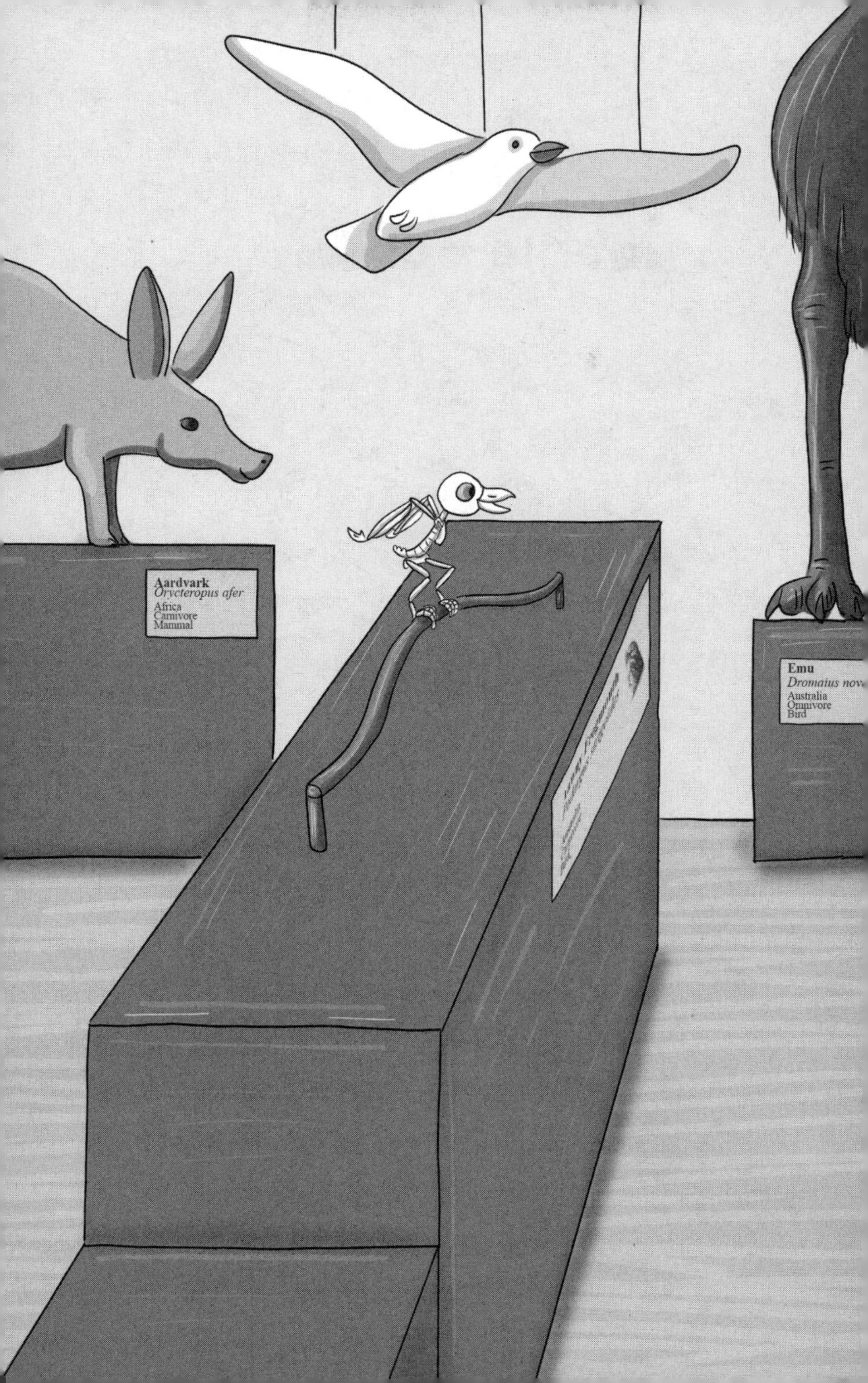
Aardvark
Orycteropus afer
Africa
Carnivore
Mammal
Emu
Dromaius
Australia
Omnivore
Bird

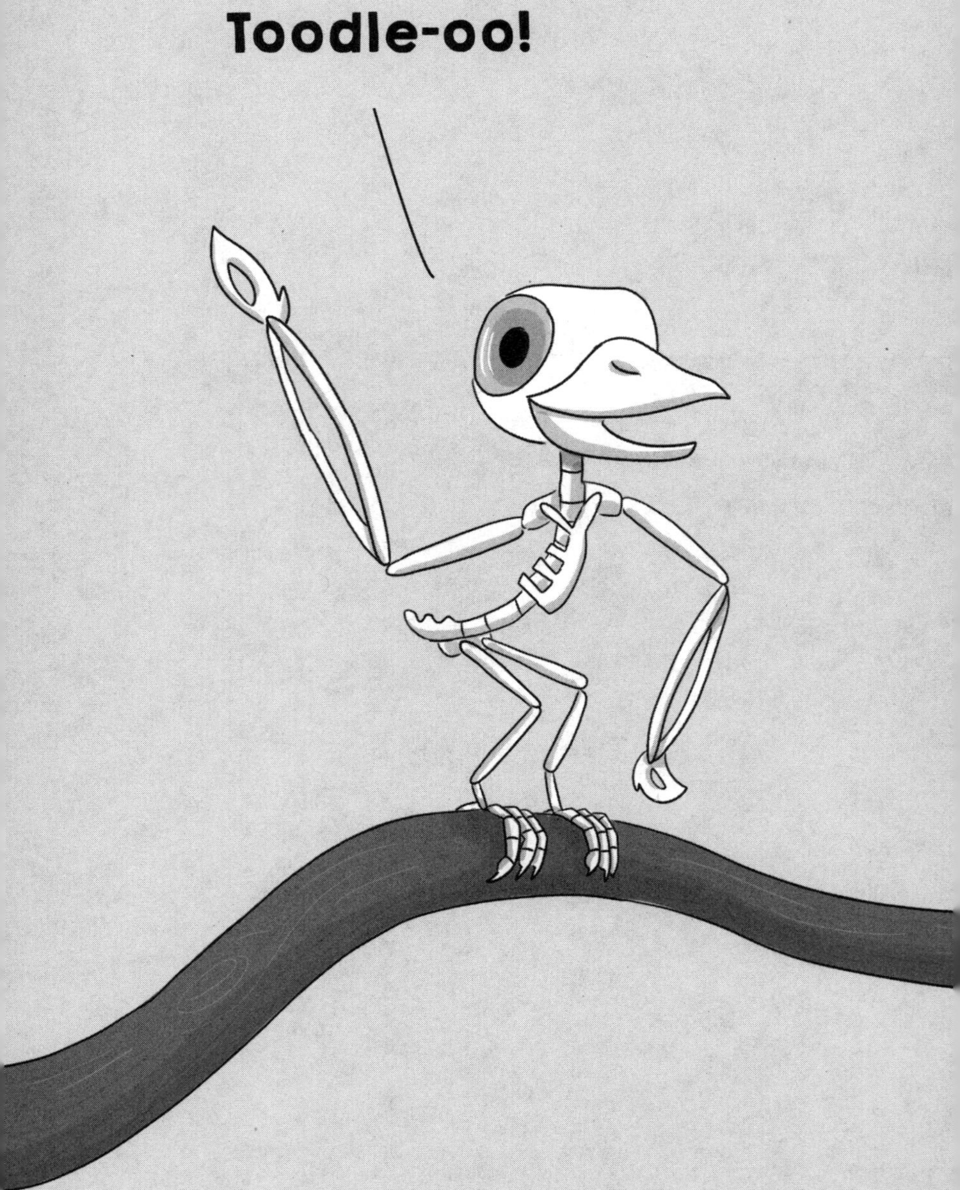
Toodle-oo!

Etch is an imprint of Houghton Mifflin Harcourt Publishing Company

First published by Allen & Unwin in 2019.

hmhbooks.com

The text was set in Bell MT.

The Library of Congress Cataloging-in-Publication data is on file.

ISBN: 978-0-358-31184-3 hardcover
ISBN: 978-0-358-31185-0 paperback

Manufactured in the United States of America
DOC 10 9 8 7 6 5 4 3 2 1
4500800033

ACKNOWLEDGMENTS

I am lucky to belong to the greatest writing group in the world and I owe them so many thanks for all their encouragement and support over the years ... and most importantly for never once complaining when I asked them to read *Sherlock Bones* again and again (and again). Thank you to Scott, Alison, Victoria, Vair, Lucinda, Adam, Caz, Chrissie, Hana, Cat, Michelle, and Robyn. A huge thank-you to Jude, who gave me excellent comments and suggestions early on, and to my former agent, Jill, for understanding that I just needed to write this book and not create other projects. I am so grateful for my editor, Susannah, who totally gets Bones and, along with the amazing team at Allen & Unwin, made this book come together (thank you!). Special thanks to my son, Calvin, and husband, Eric, who are mine and Sherlock Bones's biggest cheerleaders and supporters — I love you guys.